ARMADA

Robert Carter

MICHAEL JOSEPH
LONDON

MICHAEL JOSEPH LTD

Published by the Penguin Group
27 Wrights Lane, London W8 5TZ, England
Viking Penguin Inc., 40 West 23rd Street, New York, New York 10010, USA
Penguin Books Australia Ltd, Ringwood, Victoria, Australia
Penguin Books Canada Ltd, 2801 John Street, Markham, Ontario, Canada L3R 1B4
Penguin Books (NZ) Ltd, 182–190 Wairau Road, Auckland 10, New Zealand

Penguin Books Ltd. Registered Offices: Harmondsworth, Middlesex, England

First published in Great Britain 1988

Made and printed in Great Britain by
Butler & Tanner Ltd, Frome and London
Filmset in Monophoto Sabon by
Butler & Tanner Ltd, Frome and London

ARMADA

For Mike Gatting,
a captain courageous,
in whom the spirit of
Drake still lives

Book One

Chapter 1

Captain Amyas Poole died at the turn of the glass, four hours after midnight. Before first light his body had been stitched into a sailcloth shroud, bound with hemp and weighted with iron shot so that when it was consigned to the deeps of this unknown part of the Gulf of Mexico the corpse would sink and be devoured by crabs and bottom-dwelling fishes, as befitted a master mariner.

When the captains of the battered English flotilla came aboard, the weather began to worsen again, and the last of them to arrive, Richard Tavistock, stared down at the bloodied ensign as it whipped in the wind. Enclosed within was the body of the man who had taught him everything.

Christ Jesus! I'll get vengeance for your soul, Amyas! I swear it! he told himself, stiffening with anger. One day the Spaniards would pay, but first an urgent decision must be made for the sake of the four hundred Christian souls in their care. He thought again of his wife, Jane, and their young son back in Plymouth, and damned the tempest. Had it not come upon them, they would have been safe home, in sight of Rame Head, by now.

But this was the season of fierce tropical storms, the *furicanos*, when passage eastward was almost impossible. Still the sea spumed angrily from the wavetops and the deck of the seven-hundred-ton Queen's ship, *Jesus of Lübeck*, heaved in the swell under an overcast of pure white marble. The warm wind harped in the rigging of the three-master, making the shirts of the deeply tanned seamen who lined her upper works flutter like bunting.

In the ship's waist their Captain-General, John Hawkins, stood stern-faced, his cropped, black hair quivering in the wind as he greeted his West Country captains: Barrett and Hampton, Warren, Drake and Tavistock. Halberdiers in iron breastplates and morion helmets formed an honour guard. Beside them the drummer boy stood ready, his bare feet moving on the scrubbed deck as it rolled in the swell. The captains made a tight group around the body, keeping a minute's peace out of

3

respect, but it was not Amyas Poole's death that turned the silence bitter in their mouths, it was the way it had happened: he had been shot in the belly at close range by a Spanish arquebusier during their landing at Cartagena, and had festered in agony for seven weeks before giving up his life.

Tavistock regarded the proceedings grimly. Tall, blond-bearded and bare-headed under heaven, like the other captains he was wondering for the hundredth time if he had figured correctly where the storm had pushed them, for on that calculation they would, all of them, live or die.

In July they had left Cartagena at the muzzle of treacherous Spanish guns. As traders seeking profit they had not wanted their voyage to end like this. They had tried scrupulously to avoid conflict and to beat a way home, but a raging hurricane had caught them in the straits that lay between Cuba and the Florida coast and for three days their ships had clung desperately together. The force of the weather had almost sunk their rotting twenty-five-year-old flagship, then, overnight, the *William and John* had disappeared, and one after another they had fallen out of sight so that each thought the others lost. When, a week later, they had regrouped, they were back in the sea which the Spanish called *Golfo de Nueva España*. But where precisely in that great circular sea were they now? How many leagues west had they been blown? And where might a safe landfall be made? It was to answer these questions that Hawkins had signalled for them to come aboard. For that and to witness the sea burial of a brother mariner.

Those close to the body could smell the stink of corruption gusting from the canvas. Tavistock remembered carrying Captain Poole to the longboat. He had heeded the man's cries not to be left to die on land, and when Poole saw the purple mass of his own intestines, saw what they had done to him, he had begged Tavistock to finish him there and then, but Tavistock had not had the strength to do it and those cries still rang in his ears, haunting him like the growling pronouncement of Barber-Surgeon Grosse who said that a wound poisoned by gunpowder always rotted inside thirty days. So Tavistock had been given command of Poole's ship, the *Swallow*, and Poole had been taken aboard the *Jesus* to suffer seeing his belly turned to a stinking mire before his eyes. He had died in torment. Torment born of Spanish temper and Spanish treachery. And it wounded Tavistock doubly for he alone knew that this was to have been Amyas Poole's last voyage before retiring to keep an inn and watch his dozen grandchildren grow up.

He looked to the two Franciscan friars and the Spaniard, Villanueva, who they had taken on board two weeks ago from a lost and leaky pinnace that had crossed their path. They stood together mutely on the quarterdeck, but Tavistock hated them and wanted suddenly to bundle them over the side, get them off the ship where they could no longer pollute the air of a Protestant service. Lord God, he vowed as he tore his eyes off them and watched instead the far horizon, if ever we get home to England I'll pay the Spanish back ten thousand times over for your suffering, Amyas! I'll sail for the Indies with a good ship and a dozen brass cannon and I'll square things with the Governor of Cartagena, so help me Jesus!

'Man that is born of woman hath but a short time to live and is full of misery ...'

Francis Drake, stocky and barrel-chested, fox-eyed, with a rusty beard, read solemn verses from his prayer book over the corpse.

'... looking for the resurrection of the body when the sea shall give up her dead. Amen.'

Then, at Hawkins's nod, Browne and Gonson lifted up the rough board that had been lashed to the gunwale and Amyas Poole's remains slid away into three hundred fathoms.

As they held silence, Tavistock looked across the sapphire-blue sea to where his own weatherbeaten command, the *Swallow* rode, sails billowing. Beyond her lay the *Minion* and the *Angel*, and alone, ahead of them all, Drake's little fifty-tonner *Judith*. Together, they had penetrated deeper into the forbidden Spanish Main than any other Protestants, shattering the Papal decree that had created a Spanish monopoly of half the world. In three pioneering voyages, Hawkins's ships had driven a wedge into the golden heart of the Empire of the Americas, establishing a lucrative trade that suited all parties – except the jealous bureaucrats that represented the Spanish Crown. Tavistock had been with Hawkins on his first two voyages. Both trips had made a very handsome return, and the third had started off just as profitably.

At first, the settlers had been anxious to trade. They had been most willing to ignore the prohibitions imposed by King Philip against these unlicensed and therefore illegal merchants because the colonists needed hardy African slaves, manufactures and luxuries from the Old World, and had bought of them readily. Trading with the English avoided the crippling *alcabala*, or sales tax, that all Spanish supply ships were ordered to exact. But at Rio de la Hacha things had begun to change. There the Imperial authorities had forced Hawkins to land his cargoes under armed guard. There had been interference and double-dealing and so they had sailed on to Cartagena where they had discovered only unsheathed aggression. Hawkins had put to sea after a skirmish to think again, taking with him half a dozen wounded men and leaving behind two dead.

Yes, Tavistock thought with regret, the days of peaceful trading are over. If we are to sail again to the Americas we must sail in force. Our guns must show the Spanish that they may no longer exclude us from God's plenty. We must harry and disquiet them and one day we shall carve our own settlements here in places where the Spaniards are not yet come, make our own colonies and raise up our own Nova Albion!

Up on the forecastle, John, Richard Tavistock's younger brother, the one they called 'Gunner', set the firing match to the touchhole of his biggest culverin. It jerked back in salute, the long brass gun firing a blank charge of wadding, an admixture of mercuric powder staining the smoke crimson and scenting it like roses. The report boomed out over the sea, followed by another and another, a fourth and a fifth, in a regularly spaced broadside like echoes of thunder. Then it was done and the men were dismissed and Hawkins led the captains alone to conference on his high, narrow poop deck at the very aftmost part of the ship. Tavistock, last of the five to climb the gangway past the halberdier Barrett had posted for privacy, stooped down to see the chart that Hawkins was unfurling on the deck.

Laid out before them was the familiar five-foot parchment skin across which compass lines fanned out, and on which was drawn the coast of the New World. The diffuse shadows of spars and stays cast from an opal sky shifted back and forth over it as Hawkins circled a finger on the area of uncertainty. His voice, as ever when he took council, was soft and thoughtful.

'My best estimate has us here – at the bottom of the Gulf. Seventy leagues to our east is the barren Campeche coast, sixty or more to our west is Vera Cruz; our closest landfall is probably no more than three dozen leagues to our south.'

'And to the north?' Warren asked.

'To the north is certain death.' Hampton's phlegmatic eye measured their faces. 'Beating against the wind the *Minion* would founder before reaching the Atlantic current, and I judge that the *Jesus* is in no condition to face a crossing. We should make for Campeche, here, and head east. Then follow the peninsula round to the Caribbean Ocean.'

'I say we head south,' Drake said, shaking his head. 'We need nothing but to find a place to careen our hulls and take on water. The wind must turn again before long. We can reprovision at Cuba, or one of the other islands. Then we might meet our Spaniard friends with dry powder – and in strength!'

'Aye, and get taken as pirates,' Hampton growled.

'We're pirates already, in Spanish eyes! Or worse.'

'Worse?'

'Aye, John Hampton. *Enemies!*'

Hawkins moved between the two men. 'Captain Drake, we're not at war with Spain. We desire nothing so much as cordial relations with His Catholic Majesty's subjects.'

Drake's fuse burned brighter and he showed his teeth. 'How does it avail us to be at peace with Spain *when she is at war with us?*'

'The success of this and future missions depends on Spain remaining at peace with England, and upon our exemplary conduct. Even in the face of provocation.'

Hawkins turned to his most experienced captain. At forty-six years, Robert Barrett was ten years older than any other present except Warren.

He was also the most cautious among them.

'Master Barrett, what do you say?'

Barrett scratched at his grizzled chin. He was normally a man of few words, and did not enjoy being called upon to speak. 'I don't know – south there lie fever swamps, and the Spaniards' *portolamos* say the coast's no more'n a shallow shelf two fathoms all ways around to south and east so a man can stand chest deep a mile out to sea. If that is true, with the wind onshore, we'd run aground and stick fast for sure.'

'Master Warren, what think you?'

Tavistock considered as Warren crouched low and studied the map. He knew that like many older shipmasters both Barrett and Warren had a superstitious dislike for charts, but that the *portolamo* of which he had spoken was probably a reliable description of the coast. He had spent time in each of his three voyages to the Indies talking with Spanish pilots and assiduously recording what they told him. Barrett's beliefs appeared to tally but something disturbed Tavistock. Though he had waited his turn to voice his opinion, it was his belief that Hawkins had miscalculated their position badly.

Warren looked up challengingly. 'I say west.'

'West?' Drake hissed.

'Aye. Make for Vera Cruz.'

'That's suicide!'

Hawkins invited Warren to continue.

'If we try to fight the season by going north or east we'll have to tack a thousand leagues before we see Florida. It's not just *Jesus* and *Minion* that are in poor condition. And we're short of food.'

'We'd lose everything,' Drake said flatly.

'It's likely.' Warren glanced at Drake. 'And if we tried to fight the Spaniards with the small amount of ammunition we have on board, we'd be blown out of the water. Or hanged as pirates if we managed to reach England. King Henry bought the *Jesus of Lübeck* from the League of Hansa; she is a Queen's ship! To go privateering in her would be an act of war!'

Tavistock looked at their tanned, bearded faces: Drake was sunk in an angry silence; Hawkins was nodding; Hampton seemed to be in agreement. Each man knew that Queen Elizabeth's policy towards the Empire of Spain stopped short of open warfare. For the *Jesus* to attack Spanish settlements would implicate her directly in an act of aggression against Spain, leaving the way open for Philip to retaliate massively.

To Tavistock, the situation seemed fraught with dangers that extended far beyond the perils of their own position. For three quarters of a century under Papal protection the Spanish and Portuguese had drawn off huge riches from their overseas empires, growing vastly wealthy. The Spanish, under first their Emperor Charles, then later his fanatical son, Philip, had transformed that fountainhead of gold into the steel of military might, forging it into the shield and spearhead of the Catholic religion, using it against the burgeoning power of Islam and also as a white hammer against the heretical peoples of northern Europe.

Terrifyingly, to Philip's pious mind, the Lutheran and Calvinist creeds had been growing like unstoppable cancers in the Low Countries of Holland and Flanders. In the north-western parts of France, too, the Huguenots – French Protestants – struggled to maintain their faith against the persecutions wrought by a Catholic monarchy. Only in England's fortress isle was the Protestant cause free and unsuppressed, and King Philip knew that it was only by English aid that the Continental Protestants could survive. It had been Philip's personal dream, his life's dedicated mission, to stamp out the Lutheran heresy – to reunify Europe behind the Standard of the Five Wounds of Christ and beneath the cobalt-blue flag of Rome. He would be seeking an excuse to turn his savage legions loose on England.

Hawkins bent over the chart once more. 'Why Vera Cruz?'

Warren's leathery face creased and a blunt finger darted over the map. 'Because there is a sheltered, poorly defended anchorage near by at San Juan de Ulua, and because we're already heading for it. If we show ourselves in force, play the close hand, they might offer us all we require without need to threaten.'

'Vera Cruz is a mantrap,' Drake said scornfully. 'And the Spaniards have had all August to bait it.'

Hawkins seemed undecided. 'Richard?'

Tavistock's thoughts solidified suddenly and he stirred. 'I don't like Vera Cruz, it's too dangerous. But we must lay up and reprovision. That's unavoidable. And wherever we go we'll lack for a welcome. It's my belief that running before the wind we shall be in Vera Cruz before sundown.'

'Today?' Hawkins asked. 'Sixty leagues?'

Each league was about three miles. If the wind kept up, the squadron might average six knots. By midnight, in sixteen hours' time, they could hope to cover only a hundred miles, or half the distance.

Tavistock shook his head. 'No, Captain-General. I believe our true position is here.' He stabbed a finger at the chart. 'I calculate that the wind has carried us much further west –'

There was a commotion at the main masthead, then the boatswain's voice replied to the lookout. When the lad shouted down again, his message stunned them.

The boatswain shouted up from the quarterdeck, saluting smartly to Barrett. 'Begging your pardon, sir. Lookout says there's land off the starboard bow. Three leagues, west nor' west.'

'Thankee, Bowen.'

Hawkins stood up, his grey eyes searching the horizon.

'Gentlemen, it seems that my decision has been made for me. We must give thanks to God and trust to His mercy. Then I suggest we get about our business.'

Gunner Tavistock had heard the cry of 'Land ho!' from the masthead that brought the crew crowding the deck of the *Jesus*, and he had climbed the ratlines of the foremast, searching out the pale-limned irregularities that the lookout had distinguished from imagination. As the morning wore on a flat coastline of murky reddish-browns and greens backed by a range of hills grew ever more real. Three tiny islands speckled the shore, two low banks of sea stones little more than reefs that flared white under the power of the breakers, and a third, larger, with buildings and cannon and a dozen Spanish ships tied up. This was the port Señor Villanueva had spoken of when they had questioned him yesterday. But the little dog-leg island was nowhere more than six feet above the sea, on the weather side rollers that had fetched across five hundred leagues crashed continually into its rock-rubble. On the lee side the water was calm and the Spanish had mounted a series of great iron ringbolts along the quay where ships might be secured.

Bowen, the *Jesus*'s boatswain, stood with the Spaniard beside him. He was a stocky, muscular man, shag-bearded with brows and high cheeks that made slits of his eyes.

'Shift yourself, Ingram, you whore's son. Before I snap my cane over that neck of yours,' he told the big able hand who barred his way.

Ingram looked down at him with a puckered face, hiding his sullen disrespect poorly, and loped off.

'He's a lazy bastard, and ugly-minded with it.'

The wind tossed dark curls about Tavistock's ears. Half a head taller than Bowen and leaner, he smoothed his moustaches out between finger and thumb and blew on the match, a smouldering stub of impregnated rope that glowed and sparked ready to be put to the gun's firing. He looked away from the crowded forecastle two bowshots distant of the *Jesus*'s starboard beam where his brother was striding restlessly round the poop deck of his barque *Swallow*. Like a tiger dressed in a red leather jerkin, shouting orders under a bursting lateen sail, he thought proudly. Their five ships made an impressive squadron, bearing down on the Spanish port, but the Gunner remained uneasy. What if the Governor of Vera Cruz had received the same instructions as the authorities at Cartagena and gave them the same fiery welcome? He looked over the gleaming brass culverins that were his special care and compared them with the big, clumsy shore battery. If they speak to us in anger, my beauties, he said silently, slapping the breech of the nearest, we'll have a surprising sharp answer for them this time.

'Is that San Juan de Ulua?' Bowen asked scornfully. ''Tain't hardly much to keep the wind off us.'

'The Captain-General says this island's the only anchorage on the entire Godforsaken coast.'

The Spaniard listened suspiciously as Tavistock spoke, his eyes downcast, a weaselly half-smile on his face.

'It's deep enough for ocean-going ships, and port to the city of Vera Cruz which lies on the mainland beyond,' Tavistock went on. 'This is where the gold trains from all over Mexico end up – mules laden with bullion. Mountains of silver! Gold like you've never seen, and emeralds the size of duck eggs arrive here. Is that not so, *señor*?'

Villanueva inclined his head, giving nothing away. '*Señor*, I have never been to Vera Cruz.'

'Do not the Spaniards say there are pearls as big as ... as *avellanas, señor*? Filibert nuts, Bowen. Think of that!'

'You speak Spanish?' Villanueva said guardedly.

'Not right well as yet, *señor*. All I have of your tongue I learned on our trip, but they say I have a talent that way. And next voyage I mean to sharpen it keenly.'

'Gunner Tavistock has the looks of your countrymen, does he not?' the boatswain asked, planting his feet and knitting his muscular arms together. 'The lively boys of our crew do call him a Portugall in jest, but he mislikes it, counting it a charge of bastard since his brother is so fair of hair.'

'Better a bastard than a Spaniard!' the Gunner joked, but Villanueva merely looked away. To Tavistock he seemed watchful and tightly drawn under his surface calm, as if he was hiding something.

Augustin de Villanueva had come aboard with two Dominican friars when the *Jesus* had spotted their sails yesterday. A gentleman by his dress, and used with courtesy by the captain, but for all that, his reasons for taking ship for Santo Domingo were only half-reasons, and Tavistock had been wary of him. Overnight, the Gunner had listened openly to his whispered conversations with the taller monk, picking up oaths and small details here and there until he had learned enough.

Hawkins came up behind them and Villanueva turned to him. 'Is it not as I told you a most suitable harbour, *patron*?'

The Captain-General eyed the roadstead glassily. He was a wiry man in his prime, dark-haired, thin-faced, and with hood-lidded eyes that gave him a look of remoteness that went with his commanding rank. The salt sea ran pure in his veins. He had put on his steel war gear.

'Easy as she goes at the head, boatswain.'

Bowen stared with his customary bluff expression at the hulks that rotted on the beach. He said, 'In this norther a ship that can't tie up in the lee of yonder island'll be smartly driven ashore, General.'

'Aye, they will. What are those hulks, *señor*?'

The Spaniard shrugged and tossed a hand at the shore. 'You must know, *patron*, that the *flota* of King Philip comes here every year to carry gold to Seville. Maybe some old ships have been broken up. Believe me, San Juan is very safe.'

'I hope you're right, *señor*.'

As they closed with the port, the flotilla swung south-east, turning parallel with the coast, and passing along a roadstead just two bowshots wide between the island and the low, white buildings of Vera Cruz where a stone mole jutted into the surf and intermittently threw up great fans of white spray. The channel was narrow enough to discourage any manoeuvre of warlike intent.

A cannon was discharged from the shore battery, then a moment later, a second. They watched the white smoke billow quickly up from the muzzles and disperse.

Hawkins's order was sharp. 'Signal our intentions to shore, Gunner. Let them know we mean them no harm.'

'Stand clear of the ordnance!'

The demi-culverin, a brass cannon ten feet long, was already chocked up. Tavistock put the stub of smouldering hemp to the powder and the gun jerked back powerfully, roaring a salute against the violence of the wind.

Presently, the boatswain shouted, 'Mean us no harm?' He began to point and roar with laughter as an unlikely conveyance put out from shore. 'Look at the state of it, will you now!'

Tavistock saw the boat, driven by four oars each side, with a gilded prow and absurdly canopied in the manner of a Venetian state barge. It was stroking towards the *Jesus* like a bucking horse. Hawkins watched the boat approach for several minutes then he went down to the main deck to welcome the disarrayed Spaniard aboard, taking Villanueva with him.

'Come down too, Gunner. I have need of your Spanish.'

The visitor was a fleshy man weighed down with rich red ceremonial velvet. A long feather whipped from his hat, and his gold and enamel chain of office chinked as he came on deck. He was handed up the side of the ship by two soldiers in steel breastplates and crested morion helmets, and followed on board by a pair of notaries. At Hawkins's order, the visitors were addressed by Villanueva as soon as they climbed over the gunwale. Tavistock saw how they were seized by a sudden loss of dignity when they realised that the ship they had boarded was not Spanish.

Hawkins swept off his own helmet and bowed in a courtly fashion.

'I am Captain-General John Hawkins, and this is my fleet. We are traders sailing under the flag of Her Majesty Queen Elizabeth of England. I humbly request berths for my five ships and facilities to repair them. Be assured it is our desire to return home as soon as possible and that we intend fair payment for all victuals we take aboard. Translate, *señor*.'

As Villanueva conveyed the greeting, the visitor blanched, his eyes flickering from the translator to Hawkins and back. He shook his head strenuously and produced a rapid stream of words that Tavistock struggled to comprehend.

'His name is Don Luis Zegri, Mayor of Vera Cruz. He says you cannot come here, *patron*.'

Tavistock added, 'He also calls it piracy to go without colours at our masthead to deceive honest men.'

Hawkins's face hardened. 'Tell him we are not pirates. The ensigns we carry are bleached by a year's sun and salt spray. Our ships are in need of repair. We do not have enough food to return to England. We *must* come here. Tell him!'

There followed a lengthy exchange during which the official looked imploringly to Hawkins. At last, Villanueva spoke. 'Don Luis is sorry, but that is out of the question. You must go. *Now*. There can be no berth for your ships here.'

Hawkins asked Tavistock, 'Does he report the man truthfully?'

'He does, Captain-General.'

Hawkins turned to Don Luis once more, his hands resting on the hilt of his sword and the pistol butt that jutted from his broad belt. 'Ask the Mayor why he would refuse us. There are no more than twelve ships at his quay, and an equal number of empty berths.'

The Mayor spoke through Villanueva again. 'He says that soon there will be many more Spanish ships here. Great ships. King Philip's war galleons, with many thousands of soldiers for New Andalusia and New Spain, and many heavy cannon, commanded by the respected veteran, Admiral Luzon. His biggest galleons are twice the size of this fine ship on whose decks we now stand, Captain-General.'

Tavistock frowned at the Mayor's blustering words. He said in a low voice to Hawkins, 'The *flota de oro* – the gold fleet is due, Captain-General. I heard the Spaniard say that last night.'

Villanueva flashed him an ugly expression that was quickly gone.

'Is this true?' Hawkins pierced the Mayor with a penetrating stare. 'Is this fleet of which you speak the *flota de oro*?'

The Mayor swallowed fearfully at the Spanish phrase. He was sweating. That's why he's dressed in his Imperial finery, Tavistock realised suddenly with mounting wonderment. They've mistaken us for the *flota*. He's come aboard with his speech of welcome scrolled in his hand! Look! He's terrified of our guns. Doubly so now we know the fleet's due. Christ alive! Vera Cruz must be packed to the rafters with gold awaiting transhipment to Spain!

'Answer me.'

'*Si, patron*. He says he looks for the warships of the Indies Guard daily. He adds that they will be most disappointed to find an English – trader – here in their place.'

Hawkins slid out his sword and touched its point to the Mayor's dimpled chin. 'Then your *flota* will be disappointed, *señor*, and maybe a little surprised, eh?'

Don Luis nodded carefully.

'He regrets that he cannot vouch for your safety, *patron*.'

'My safety is my own concern.'

'He says you are either a very brave man, or you are *loco rematado.*'

'Tell him that my requirement is for five berths.'

At Hawkins's order, a letter was drafted to the Presidents and Council in Mexico City, explaining their presence in innocuous terms, then Don Luis and his officers were dismissed and sent to the island comforted by an armed English 'honour guard'. They remained under escort until John Tavistock oversaw the remanning of San Juan's ordnance by his own gun crews. Then the ships were warped in close, side by side, so the bowsprits overhung the quay, and all were securely made fast.

On the island there was a small chapel made from the bodies of wrecked ships and at each extremity a low breastwork on which he stationed two gun crews of five men each to cover both approaches. Men without duties were free to buy rough liquor at any of the island's three trugging houses and fight for the attentions of the fiery whores who regularly serviced the men from the coasters, and who had collected here from all over the heel of Mexico, anxious for the arrival of the *flota*. The cries of the pimps could be heard all night. Screams and moans and table-banging songs rose up continuously, making John desire the freedom his men were enjoying. But there was work to do.

Thomas Fleming, the big sandy-haired Scot from the *Minion*, came down the quay to him with a big breasted mulatto on his arm as the Gunner secured the last of his batteries.

'They've got wenches of every colour and size down there, Gunner,' he shouted up with a greasy smile. 'It's damned near heaven's gate to men who've not tasted the pleasures of a dell's crack in two months. I'm coming up for number four myself. You want to get down there afore the best of 'em're trugged out.'

The doxy waved up at him then hoisted her skirts revealing her wares.

'Not for a day or two yet by the looks of her, Tommy-lad!'

'Please yourself!'

'I wish I could.'

As commander of the shore batteries he was to dine with Hawkins and the other captains tonight. Since Amyas Poole's shooting and Richard's promotion to the *Swallow*, the brothers had seen little of each other. He missed that, enjoying those calm nights whittling or playing chess under the taffrail lanterns; watching flying fish or the mysterious luminescent patches of the tropical ocean, pulsing and patterning under these strange southern stars. There was a whole world of new things to see, new experiences never dreamed of at home. But also perils that he could not have imagined.

When the flotilla had been scattered by the storm off Florida he had wondered if he would see Richard again. He never doubted his brother's superb seamanship or his ability to take *Swallow* home. This was Richard's third voyage for Hawkins and he knew how to handle the trim of a ship better than almost any Englishman alive. He had been in love with the sea since being apprenticed at the age of twelve. John had laid a wager of thirteen golden pesos to five of the boatswain's that when the ships hove in sight of each other again it would be *Swallow* that found the flagship first. Bowen was still mourning the loss of his forty-five shillings.

That night, by custom, the officers ate meat and drank brandy at the Captain-General's table aboard the *Jesus of Lübeck*. Don Luis had stiffly declined the invitation and was conveyed to his residency on the mainland to pray for his soul and beg God for the speedy arrival of Amiralte Luzon's fleet. The northerly gale, showing no sign of abating, continued to shudder the timbers of the ship. The sea slapped implacably in the spaces between the hulls. Occasional flashes of dry sheet lightning lit the eastern sky soundlessly. Inside Hawkins's cabin the light flickered from a dozen wax candles and the draughts that filtered through the spaces between the planks were sickly humid and charged with rain. The air was as thick as broth.

For a reason John Tavistock could not at first identify the atmosphere at table was equally tense. Captain Drake said grace movingly, thanking God for giving them safe haven, but after they broke bread the Gunner found the conversation became strained and subdued. Sam, the Captain-General's young Negro page, refilled their cups twice but still no one relaxed. We've been afleet eleven months, Tavistock reminded himself, the worst time for morale, and there are other reasons too. After the storm the *William and John* did not reappear, she's surely lost, or safe at home in Plymouth now. Either way it was a sore subject for a man to dwell on, but those doubts could not account for the hostility he felt simmering around the supper board.

For John Tavistock it had been an exhilarating first voyage. His 'rank' of gunner was a nominal one; he had won his place aboard the *Jesus* at Richard's recommendation and out of necessity: his skills had been developed in the cannon foundries of Thomas Stanton on the Sussex Weald, under whose eye he had learned to cast the deadliest naval guns in the world. 'My investment in your voyage shall be in kind,' Stanton had told Hawkins. 'Guns for the *Jesus of Lübeck* at two-thirds their real price providing that John Tavistock, whose art has been in making and testing our ordnance these past eight years, may go with them.' Hawkins had readily agreed. Stanton's older guns were mostly of iron: cannon, demi-cannon and culverins, but the newest and the best were of brass, and their power and accuracy at extreme range was improving year by year. Only by going with them and handling them in real actions could the practical difficulties of protecting a trading fleet so far from home be understood and solved.

Tavistock drained his cup and looked from his brother to the Captain-General. Hawkins had treated him well, and in return he had worked hard to train the powder makers and gun crews of the *Minion* and the *Jesus*, at the same time experimenting with novel proportions of charcoal, nitre and sulphur in the black powder that better suited the long-barrelled weapon. By now he had brought the ships' gunnery to the point where they could trade shot for shot with any ship on the seas at long range.

As he carved into the breast of their supper fowl, Tavistock saw from his brother's demeanour that the weighty matter that lay heavy upon him was about to be cast off.

'So, what's it to be, General?'

Barrett's question brought the matter to a head.

'What's it to be?' Hawkins smiled and sat back in his chair, studying their faces. In each he saw dangerous thoughts; at their last meeting there had been a preoccupation with survival, with the cost of restoring the flotilla to seaworthiness and computations of their chances of making a straight run home with their shares intact. This time it was different: a brooding sense of expectation, something no one was willing to voice first. Hawkins had seen it before, and he recognised it now. It was the most destructive form of greed Satan could place in a man's heart: the lust for gold.

All their eyes were upon him. Dare I lay the alternatives before them openly, he asked himself. Or shall I command them so they see little of what passes in my mind? Take care, John Hawkins! You chose as your captains men who can read other men's intents. Perhaps they can read yours. A year at sea is long enough for that. Can you – should you deceive them? *Or can you trust them?* Already the rumours have started. The Spaniards in Vera Cruz are skulking about like frightened rabbits. The ships tied up alongside *Swallow* have two hundred thousand pounds in gold and silver in their bellies. Divided among four hundred Englishmen, that's five hundred pounds each – *twelve years'* pay for an able hand! Men have murdered their Captains for much less. And Captains their General.

Hawkins said very deliberately, 'There's a store of treasure in Vera Cruz to rival that of King Midas.'

He saw Drake's eyes flare up like Huguenot brandy, and Hawkins looked away from him. The Queen's Privy Council – the most powerful group of men in England – had personally invested in the venture. Sir William Cecil, the Queen's most intimate confidant, had staked a sizeable fortune, and much more. For ten years Cecil had recognised the need for England to challenge the seventy-five-year-old Papal decree that was looting the entire world beyond Christendom, but it needed more than fine words carried between London and Madrid to end the monopoly; it required men prepared to die or else win their fortunes by testing Spanish mettle, and such men were hard to dissuade from a course once they were determined upon it.

At length Warren's cold blood stirred in his veins, prompting him to speak. 'We've gambled in the past and won. Why not now? Are we to shrink from the prize when by God's grace we have fallen upon it so nicely? God gave us free wills, and the strength to choose. Must we always scorn temptation?'

Drake jumped in hotly. 'I say we take Vera Cruz apart!'

Hawkins's shoulders braced. 'If the weight of a single groat of the King of Spain's wealth is touched we will stand accused before Her Majesty as pirates and common thieves. And rightly. I remind you all that *Jesus* and *Minion* are both Queen's ships. Are you ready to steal them away from her? For I will not countenance that.'

'The Spaniards owe us more than a groat, Captain-General,' Hampton said darkly.

'Amyas was a fine seaman and a lifelong friend to me,' Barrett muttered. 'Spanish gold would ease the hurt to his widow and seven young sons.'

'Aye! And we should take compensation for injuries to our trade,' Warren added.

Hawkins's drinking cup froze in midair. His free palm moved minutely towards the jewelled pommel of his dress-dagger. 'Then tell me. Who do I sup with? With gentlemen? *Or with thieves?*'

'Cannot a man be both?' Drake whispered, touching the hilt of his own knife.

'No, he cannot!'

'*I say he can!*'

'Thou shalt not steal!'

'Thou shalt not kill!'

The silence pounded in the veins of Hawkins's head, brittle and loaded with pain. Beneath the table the feet of both men moved back on each side of their chairs. If either man snapped, the other would be forced to draw steel.

'*It means war, Francis.*'

Richard Tavistock's voice was clear, reasonable, vastly calming.

Drake flashed a glance at him; he bared his teeth and hammered a fist into the table. 'God's death! We're damned near at war now!'

'But we are *not* at war.' Hawkins put his pewter jug down with conspicuous care. 'When is the Spanish fleet due here, Gunner?'

John Tavistock answered smartly, 'Señor Villanueva spoke of it as being two days late already, General.'

Drake, his shoulders broad as the table, grasped a handful of air. 'Whenever they arrive, we should wait and take them!'

'The opportunity is heaven sent, General,' Warren said persuasively.

Hawkins judged it right to reason. One false step and England may be plunged in war, he told himself, controlling his anger with Warren. 'In this foul weather the *flota* might not appear at all.'

Drake appealed to them, imploring, 'In that case we have time to repair, to reprovision – and take honest damages away with us from the treasury of Vera Cruz!'

'Honest damages? I think not, Master Drake! The Queen's law –'

'The Queen's writ does not run here, General. She sits in London, sixteen hundred leagues away!'

'Still close enough to have your head on a spike.'

'All our heads.'

Hampton said, 'The General gave his promise to the Mayor that we would pay in full and leave peaceably. Would you sully his honour as well by breaking his word?'

'Bugger the promise!'

'That's enough!'

Their eyes turned to Hawkins and he held their stares. I've drawn them, he thought. Now I must impose my will. He leaned toward Drake threateningly. 'Understand me plainly, sir. I will not have this treasonous talk on my ship. From you or from anyone!'

His eyes locked on Drake's and they struggled. The older man finally faced the younger down. In a more composed voice Hawkins said, 'The Spanish King has tightened his domain against us, but it will not always be so. The Indies colonists have shown they are anxious to trade with us. Profits are good, so we must be patient until relations between the Courts of England and Spain wax friendlier again, which they must eventually do. Then will come the likelihood of our securing a regular concession in the Indies. Never forget, we are traders, and it is our aim to win for ourselves a constant, acknowledged portion of the New World market.'

'I agree with the General,' Hampton said. 'If the Spaniard has wronged us, the Spaniard must be made to pay. But he shall pay dearest in the long run. We've turned a goodly profit on this trip. Let us sail for home and leave the goose a-laying for tomorrow.'

Hawkins watched Drake sit back sourly, but he nodded his assent. Perhaps now, he thought, they will remember who is in charge.

Hawkins's own mind probed the bigger question delicately. The Queen's parsimony is well known, he thought broodingly. Those at Court say she may be easily flattered by diamonds. What *would* the Privy Council do if a fleet were to appear in the Tamar three months hence with a sea chest full of jewels, and gold enough to finance all England for five years? Such a question! But the Queen must avoid war. That, above everything. Her government's aim is to enrich the land after the excesses of King Hal and the tyrant Mary. Elizabeth understands well that warfare is the costliest of pastimes. A war with her mighty brother-in-law, Philip, might easily cost her her throne. How Elizabeth would grovel to avoid that! No, even if we were to sack ten Vera Cruzes, the gold and silver would be returned with apologies and our heads would decorate the spikes of Tower Bridge the moment we landed.

Before the supper ended, Hawkins called for quill and ink.

'It is agreed. Post this to your crews and inform them thus: No man shall approach within ten paces of any Spanish ship moored here except those boats conveying to our own vessels; no man shall seek to go ashore to the mainland except at strict order of the victuallers; no man shall speak of gold, or silver, or of any Spanish treasure, *under pain of death*. This is my order, signed by me this Thursday, being the sixteenth day of September, year of Grace fifteen hundred and sixty-eight. Let no one break it.'

Richard Tavistock returned to the *Swallow* and stood his men to, ordering three sergeants-at-arms to scour the whorehouses and have those insensibly drunk sluiced down with brine. Then he acquainted his complement of thirty-three with the order. It made sense. Though it was unenforceable it made Hawkins's wishes quite clear, but it also lit a fuse attached to a massive powder keg. The longer they remained tied up at San Juan de Ulua, the closer the fuse would burn, until some wretch would have to have his neck stretched at the sailyard as an example. It would need at least seven days for the *Jesus* to take on sufficient water and provisions, and in that time Tavistock knew he must keep the men under his command too busy to think. During daylight hours that would be hard enough, after nightfall it would be near impossible.

In the early evening, under the light of a rising full moon, he mounted the steps to his customary and now familiar place of command. He felt an ache in his stomach – the mulligrubs from unripe fruit he had eaten at supper – and broke wind. His crew were mostly aboard and sleeping, just one man of the watch walking the deck slowly, back and forth, aware of his Captain's presence.

God, I don't like this place, he thought. I wish we were under full sail and speeding from it. Now. Tonight. Another month gone and we're further from home than ever. I wonder what time is it in Plymouth? Is Jane asleep? Is she feeding Harry at her breast? Is he weaned yet? Yes. Christ! He's almost two years old now. And this trip's spanned almost half his life. She's twenty now, long fair hair, and slim as a willow sapling. How easy it is to forget. What a pity there's no magic to transport a man home on Sundays, just one day in seven to check on things and see that everything's all right. That's a provision the Good Lord overlooked when he created mariners to sail his seas, right enough. How much easier it would be for my peace of mind, how much it would comfort Jane. She's delicate but she's strong-minded and she knows what being a sailor boy's wife means, and a long homecoming has a special sweetness all its own.

In the east, the moon's bloated disc struggled up through rags of cloud that threatened storm. He shrugged the tiredness from his muscles, took a final stroll around the deck, and turned in.

In his cabin, he passed a restless night. A pair of howler monkeys caged in the bows screamed each time the watchman stirred on deck, and rumbles of thunder rolled in on the wind. All night demonic visions plagued him. Out of the swaying, creaking darkness he found so comforting at sea he conjured only vile images: the living skeletons of the *danse macabre* seen in his mind's eye. Time and again he thought he saw the fires of Smithfield burning in the night sky, and the rotting head of Francis Drake, with raucous black crows picking the eye sockets hollow on the traitor's stave above the Thames.

When at last dawn came bloody red through his deadlights, he got up and pulled on his boots. The wind had slackened. Rain fell in huge, heavy drops refreshing him as he walked the main deck, testing the lashings that secured the ship's boats. The decaying smell of jungle trees was on the wind, and the deck was spotted with gorgeous green moths that had been drawn by the riding lights and downed by the cloudburst. He saw the damp copy of the Captain-General's order he had had nailed to the forward bulkhead. It was untouched by the men. Though none of the mariners could read, it served as a powerful reminder for they feared written laws, and it helped him as Master to gauge his crew's attitude.

'Captain! Captain!'

He whirled round, then looked up, shielding his eyes against the brightness. The boy, Momfrey, was leaning down from the maintop, gesticulating like a mad thing.

'What is it, lad?'

'Ships, Captain! Ships! A hunnerd of 'em, bearing down from the north, a league distant!'

Tavistock was instantly alert. 'How many?'

'I can't figure it, sir.'

And I can't see from here, he thought, cursing. But the boy can't count. Is he seeing things or panicking over a convoy of coasters?

As he swung up onto the ratlines and scrambled up, the ropes felt clumsy under his boots; this was a barefoot task. When he reached the round wooden platform halfway up *Swallow*'s mainmast he twisted and saw a vista that sent his mouth dry.

There, streaming in under a press of sail, was a tall, four-masted galleon, another half a mile behind, and another, and another. There were smaller vessels also, but he counted thirteen great ships in all, too distant to discern their pennants.

It's the *flota*! And here at the worst possible moment with lading hardly started and our vessels in disarray. They might be upon us within the hour!

'You there, Ingram! Twide! And you, Fleming! Get the word to the other ships that the Spanish fleet's coming!'

Alarm trumpets sounded through the English ships, the boatswains' whistles shrilled, sending men onto the gangplanks and swarming up aloft. The gun crews raced to their stations on the island, and began to reinforce their defences with six fourteen-pounders hauled from a Spanish carrack. Hawkins dispatched Tavistock under a truce flag to inform the Admiral.

'Tell him I control the shore batteries and that I must have an accord agreed before I can admit him. I trust you'll dress up my meaning in polite terms.'

'However that's said, he won't like it.'

'He'll like it less if we keep him out for lack of a treaty.'

'Can we?'

'With God's help, and your brother's good aim.'

'But if we deny him entry to his own port his heavy-laden merchantmen will certainly founder as soon as the wind blows up again!' Tavistock objected.

'Then he'll have to treat with us on our terms.'

'Hidalgo pride will never –'

Hawkins's temper broke. 'Hidalgo pride don't enter into it! Their Admiral's responsible for two million pounds' worth of shipping. He won't risk losing that. Now get under way!'

Tavistock left with that fabulous sum running unstoppably through his mind. Two million pounds was more than the English Crown raised in tax revenues *in ten years* ...

His pinnace returned within the hour, bringing to a parley on the island a straight-backed messenger in fine Spanish attire of claret and gold, a captain with rapier and white lace ruff who spoke English fluently.

'I am Vice-Admiral Hector de Ortega, representing Admiral Don Francisco de Luzon and His Excellency Don Emilio Martinez, Viceroy-designate of New Spain. I bring his Excellency's greetings. He asks what business you imagine you have here, and invites you to vacate his port immediately.'

Hawkins's stomach had clenched convulsively at mention of the Viceroy. If he was aboard, then King Philip's own instrument of government in the New World was here. *In person.* He looked at the haughty bearing of Ortega and knew that by a cruel twist of fortune he had been brought suddenly to the very edge of disaster.

'Then you agree our terms?'

Ortega stepped forward stiff and formal, his mouth betraying disdain. 'I regret to say, *Capitán*, that your demands are utterly refused. Your ships will leave our port within the hour.'

The next step was unavoidable. Hawkins shook his head.

'That I cannot do, sir. Please inform His Excellency that his ships are at this moment in no position to dictate to me. I must have my terms met.'

Ortega hid his outrage manfully. 'That is your final answer, *Capitán*?'

'It is.'

'Then, I will convey it faithfully to His Excellency.'

Ortega turned arrogantly on his heel and took his leave. Tavistock watched him weighing the strength of the island's defences as he went. Despite himself he had been impressed by the Spaniard's easy assumption of superiority.

Drake kept his voice low, hating the aristocrat on sight. 'They're a pack of treacherous dogs. We'll have to sink them to save ourselves. Let's take them, John. I beg you! We'll never have a better chance.'

Hawkins's stare was like a dagger. 'They'll be back. This time on our terms.'

Drake hissed, 'You're going to let them in? They'll cut our cables and have us wrecked ashore as soon as piss!'

'If they agree to bind over a dozen of their gentlemen as hostages, and suffer our keeping control of the island's guns, I will admit them.'

'You can't trust them, Captain.'

'I hope you're wrong.'

Tavistock went again to Ortega later that day, and carried back with him the Viceroy's answer. This time the message was honeyed with fair words and agreed to all of Hawkins's conditions. Twelve hostages were exchanged and, as Monday night fell, the *flota* began to come in.

From the highest deck of the Admiral's flagship, *San Felipe*, Don Emilio Martinez, a tall, darkly handsome figure with steel-grey beard, looked at the preparations with satisfaction. The wind had begun to blow again, and the sky which an hour before had been scoured of cloud was darkening once more. Below him the last of the passengers were climbing down into shore boats. They included Dominicans and Jesuits, the secretaries and staff of the *Casa Contratación* and, of course, the women.

Climbing delicately into the boat now was the delightful Maria de Escovedo.

She had been his wife's travelling companion, the only woman besides Doña Isabella herself aboard the *San Felipe*, and what a torture she had proved for every man aboard. Even Luzon's rough-handed mariners had risked the lash willingly, loitering at the gunwales whenever she had appeared on the open promenade that straddled the galleon's stern. Now, along with the other ladies and non-combatants who had voyaged to the Indies in the *flota*, she was being taken into Vera Cruz where she would be safe. She needs to be, he thought, relishing the prospect. I have chosen noon as the time to cover myself in glory.

It had taken a couple of days to draw all their ships up in the vastly overcrowded anchorage, but by Thursday morning all was done and the English ships were sectioned off together like fish in a net. The *piratas* had lost almost three days' lading time, but were now trying to make it up as rapidly as possible, understandably most anxious to take their leave.

'Who are these Englishmen who presume so much?' he had demanded of Luzon.

'Slavers, Excellency,' the Admiral had replied, disgust rippling his falcon-like face. He had looked down his sharp nose, using his five years' advantage and the fact of his position as absolute master of the *flota* to intimidate even the Viceroy. 'They are well known here and come into our waters every other year.'

'Then they have been granted an *asiento* to trade here?' he had asked doubtfully. 'Are they licensed like some of the Portuguese traders?'

Luzon had laughed. 'No, Don Emilio. Hawkins has tried many times to wheedle his way into the Indies with official blessing. He has given bribes, devised all kinds of clever schemes. He has even offered to put his ships at the disposal of His Majesty, to help Spain against the Turks and the French.'

'God punish their impudence!'

'They come here with slaves stolen from Portuguese Guinea.'

'Which our colonists flock to buy illicitly wherever they can?'

'Only under duress, Excellency.'

'And to avoid the *alcabala*, eh, Don Francisco?'

Luzon had smiled. 'The Indies is a pestilential place, Excellency, full of dangers and offering few pleasures to a civilised person. No man comes to the Indies without thoughts of enriching himself – unless he has to.'

Don Emilio had flamed inside at that remark. During the voyage he had pledged a hundred times to knock some of the arrogance out of Luzon once the *flota* reached Vera Cruz and passed into his jurisdiction.

It was entering the tenth hour of the day when Don Emilio watched the last of the ladies raise her skirts and step down into the boat. He thought irritably of the inconvenience that the English had caused him. I could be entrained for Mexico City now, enjoying the company of fine ladies, were it not for these damnable pirates. They're heretics with no respect for the law. But here I am the law! With God's help, I will see the Englishmen dangling with meathooks through their jaws before sundown. They give me just the excuse I've been waiting for to make Luzon jump to my command. And it will be the Admiral's ships that will have won me my victory!

Preparations were almost complete. The previous evening he had received the murderer Villanueva and promised him clemency for his crimes in return for a favour. Three swimmers had drowned carrying a secret letter to Don Luis Zegri, who was at this moment quietly mustering a thousand soldiers of the Indies garrison and smuggling them aboard the caravel hulk anchored in the strait. Guns were being inched into place aboard a great ship of nine hundred tons, ports cut in her timbers so that at Ortega's signal they could be trained on the enemy. Even now she was being warped next to the English slaver *Minion* with three hundred armed men hidden aboard.

Ortega appeared at his side with one of the pirates.

'The English Captain-General has sent this man to crave your indulgence once more, Excellency,' he announced formally.

'Indeed?'

The man was strikingly dark of colouring for an Englishman. The

Viceroy had noticed him several times, working on the shore batteries that the English guarded so jealously. He had even asked Ortega to discover if the man was a deserter and therefore of some use – as Villanueva had been.

'What is it?'

'If it please you, Excellency, my General counts too many men passing to and fro on the island, more than your agreement stipulates. He asks if you would be good enough to order them back aboard ship.'

Don Enrique felt a flush of indignation at so insubordinate a question delivered in such appallingly poor Spanish. Certainly an insult, since this man was clearly not a gentleman.

'These labourers – they are merely my Admiral's work parties. They are necessary to the proper order of his fleet.'

'Then, may I tell my General you will order them back, sir?'

The Viceroy's eyes blazed with anger. 'This is a Spanish port. I have authority here.'

The English had already accepted Don Enrique's assurances that the activity they saw was no threat to them, and he had salved their suspicions twice with carefully worded explanations. Their insistence was becoming tedious but he knew he must control his anger a little longer.

'But the agreement specifies –'

'Yes, yes! Tell your General what he asks will be done.'

The Englishman remained at Ortega's side.

'Well?'

'I beg your pardon, sir?'

'What is it? There's more you wish to say?'

'I apologise for my poor Spanish, sir, but my General also questions the purpose of the merchantman now being brought alongside our second vessel.'

Ortega started forward, his eyes flashing anxiously, but the Viceroy motioned him to be still. Nevertheless his hand tightened on his pistol grip as Don Emilio said with an artificial lightness in his voice, 'As you see, the anchorage is crowded. The ship to which you refer is simply coming alongside to discharge cargo. There is nowhere else.'

As soon as the Englishman bowed and withdrew, Ortega said, 'They are too suspicious. You should have chained him below decks, Excellency.'

'Patience, Ortega.'

'But, Excellency –'

'At this moment the English pirate chief is preparing to lunch with Señor Villanueva. I trust God will preserve our purpose two hours more.'

Ortega was trembling with anger. He had read the signs and judged the Viceroy's plan too complex to work once the English were alerted.

When Don Emilio moved away he balled his hand and struck the stay of the bonaventure mast in frustration, then made for the soldier-packed merchantman before Don Emilio's plan fell completely into chaos.

The table in the *Jesus*'s great cabin was set with silver plate and the finest delicacies to be got in the port. Barrett and Hampton were there beside Richard Tavistock. So too were Señor Villanueva and his priestly companions. He had asked to be allowed to say his farewells to Hawkins with due ceremony, and Hawkins had agreed. It had seemed to Tavistock an unlikely, if appropriate, gesture. Today they had finally begun loading the barrels and sacks that had been purchased and stock-piled on the island, and by tomorrow night they could set sail for England.

As Hawkins sat down at the head of a table of six guests, Chamberlain, his steward, poured a cup of Madeira wine provided by Villanueva. Silently, Tavistock congratulated his General, feeling that he had somehow traversed a difficult sea by diplomacy and firm dealing. His ships were in good sailing condition, he had secured, albeit at a high price, the stores he required, and above all he had convinced a Spanish nobleman of ancient lineage, the Viceroy of all Mexico, that an orderly withdrawal was the best course for them both. Don Emilio's word was in black and white, and all without a single shot being fired. Then why, Tavistock wondered, were the muscles in his chest and neck as tight as the braces on a storm topsail?

Augustin de Villanueva's goblet was raised in salute.

'To our English hosts and their gracious Queen!'

'To our friends in the Indies, and the King of Spain!'

Tavistock muttered the words and sipped. As pretty a party as you could hope for, the mocking part of him said. What's wrong? Can't Spaniard and Englishman compliment one another in friendship? Do you hate them that much? Wasn't it Spanish trade that bought you your house in Plymouth? Isn't it Spanish gold that'll buy you your own ship when you get back? Go along with it. Smile. Treat the General's guests civilly.

'To John Hawkins of Plymouth: a Captain-General among men!'

'And to you, Señor Villanueva: an honest interpreter.'

Tavistock raised his pot but this time he could not touch it to his lips. It was a Spaniard that gave you your first command, too, the other, suspicious part screamed back, Spanish iron that blew Amyas Poole's guts out, and Spanish treachery that will sink the whole fleet! Look at it! Stop ignoring it! Stop fooling yourself! They've already broken the treaty. They're shifting shipping all over the channel. Spaniards are swarming all over the island. Big well-fed men who don't ever look you in the eye, all doing the work of slaves. It doesn't add up.

'To your fine captains: may they never lose their ships in a storm.'

'To the holy fathers, the Black Friars. Would that they could understand English.'

They're soldiers! Soldiers! They're waiting to fall on us! At the moment the goblets clashed, Tavistock's eye caught a flash of steel. Villanueva's frilled right sleeve was hidden under the table and with a deft flick of his forearm he slid from it a glittering poniard nine inches long.

Hawkins leaned forward, unaware of the dagger poised in the Spaniard's hand. Desperately Tavistock realised that Villanueva was about to strike. Villanueva was too far across the table for Tavistock to stop him, too distant to reach directly, and if he gave warning the man would snap like a steel spring. There was no time to think, no time to consider. No time to save the life of a man who had been like a father to him . . .

Tavistock's instincts shut out his helpless brain. He acted blindly, instantly. Without warning, he sent his fist crashing into Hawkins's jaw and threw him sprawling backwards over his chair. The General's wine swilled red across the table as the poniard darted from view, then Tavistock leapt at Villanueva's throat, scattering the amazed guests in confusion.

'He's got a knife!' Hawkins's young steward shouted. Hampton lunged for Tavistock's arm.

'He's gone mad!' Barrett cried as the monks jumped to their feet.

When Villanueva's hand came up it was in a deadly arc. The dagger sliced through the air and deeply into Tavistock's tunic but he twisted away from the strike with incredible agility, shrugging Hampton off him as he did so. Then the Spaniard's arm jerked wide, caught now in Tavistock's iron grip. Hawkins had recovered his feet and flung himself across the table, pinning the man's wrist back so that the dagger fell to the table. Immediately, the steward grabbed it up and held it to the assassin's throat, stopping the monks in their tracks.

The door burst open and Bowen spilled into the cabin with two burly carpenter's mates who instinctively seized the Dominicans. Hawkins forced Villanueva to face the murderous redness in his eye. He pounded the Spaniard's head against the ship's timbers.

'Lying Spanish filth!'

Villanueva breathed hard, sweating, enraged at his failure. '*Inglés inmundicia!*' he replied through gritted teeth, then spat. Hawkins stepped back and swung. Villanueva's head catapulted. His eyes rolled up in pain and he fell limp.

'Bowen! Lock him up before I kill him! Lock them all up!' He threw off his wine-sodden velvet jacket and pushed his way out on deck tearing his primed crossbow off the wall as he went.

Tavistock searched the chest of his jerkin inside the tear where the knife-point had opened his shirt. It had barely scratched him. He shouted for the armourer.

'Break out the guns and beat to arms! Bowen! Find the trumpeter and rally the men aboard!'

He followed Hawkins out and sprang after him down on to the deck

of the *Minion*. On the far side the big Spanish merchant ship had sent
a thick hawser looped from her beakhead to one of the ringbolts. Five
men heaved on it desperately, one was Ortega.

'Devils take you, Spaniard!' Hawkins shouted and loosed a bolt at
him. Ortega staggered back as one of *Minion*'s arquebusiers blew open
the chest of the man beside him, spattering the Vice-Admiral with gore.

'Santiago!' Ortega shouted back defiantly. The Spanish war cry
echoed across the fleet and hundreds of the Viceroy's men swarmed to
the call. Trumpets blared and English seamen appeared from below
decks, some in breastplates, others strapping helms to their heads, all
with weapons to hand.

The merchantman had closed with grapnels. Spanish troops swung
in on ropes secured to the yards hacking the defenders back with swords
and spears. Primed muskets fired and raked the deck, slaughtering the
Minion's crew. They retreated before the brunt, Hawkins falling back
with a dozen men to call up support from the *Jesus*.

Tavistock was isolated. Trapped against the bulkhead he fought back
desperately with wild swings of his boarding axe until in the counter
the Spanish were driven away under a hail of fire from the *Jesus*'s high
stern. English seamen were now pouring into the mêlée but their own
attack had caught them in a trap. The first group found themselves
pinned in the *Jesus*'s waist, under a withering crossfire from forecastle
and quarterdeck, and already the Spanish were mounting a second wave,
attacking from all quarters.

My own command? Tavistock thought desperately. No time to think
of *Swallow*. Trust your crew to keep their heads. We must get *Minion*
away. Stop them getting aboard. Stop them coming across her decks again.

A crossbow bolt flashed past his head and struck off the ship's bell.
He flung a heavy boarding axe to the nearest man, a huge Guinea
Negro named Boaz.

'Loose the headfasts!'

Boaz bounded forward. The axe flew twice and parted the thick
hempen line that secured the bows. There was no time to think about
setting sail, and no chance of manoeuvring her, but mooring lines were
stretched to anchors from hawseholes on the after gun deck. Tavistock
sent men there to pull on *Minion*'s sternfasts, to try to ease the three
hundred tonner out.

The cannon on the low island thundered. Looking ashore he saw
Luzon's men levering round the gun carriages to bear on the English
ships.

John! Where's John! he thought as he saw Roger Briscoe, the *Jesus*'s
chief armourer, and able hand David Jordan both cut down by flying
iron. All across the island Spanish soldiers had fallen on the English;
the shore was littered with bodies. A hundred or more had been cut
down at the water's edge so that the sea ran red with their blood. There
would soon be no chance for John to get aboard. Already the *Minion*

was pulling away from the *Jesus*, whose own decks were swarming with Spanish troops.

A heavy bombardment began. Chain shot whipped from the shore battery taking down the *Jesus*'s yards and cutting her rigging, but both *Minion* and *Jesus* were loose two ship's lengths, drifting slowly as the wind caught hold of them.

Shaking with a terrible fury, Tavistock climbed into the flagship. He swept up a thick-bladed cutlass and charged screaming into three armoured men who turned on him with halberds. His steel took the head off one spear and on the upswing struck sparks from the second's morion, but a blow from the third's broken haft knocked him sideways and he was forced hard up against the gunwale by their massive sergeant.

He saw the rapier levelled at him, saw the white teeth of the Spaniard in gleaming breastplate and crested iron helmet, and felt his shoulder absorb the blade as it bowed with the force of the thrust and stuck deep in the bulkhead beyond.

I'm a dead man now, he thought, *pinned to the timbers of our own flagship.*

Tavistock gripped the sword blade until the edge cut into his hands but it would not move. His adversary cast about for a weapon but as the shore fire raked them again the big Spaniard was carried off balance. More tackle rained down over the decks around him, but he recovered, towering now over young Martin Preston. The boy tried valiantly to fight back with a boathook but was hacked down almost at once. Lord Jesus! Tavistock mouthed as he watched the slaughter. He's almost cut him in two. But I'm not dead yet. I must work the steel loose and endure the pain.

The seconds seemed like agonising minutes as the sergeant's rapier ground sickeningly inside his shoulder just above the scratch Villanueva had given him. Though he hung his full weight on it the Toledo blade would not snap. Tavistock's leather jerkin was now sodden with his heart's blood, and the tattered shirt beneath soaked deep red. The Spaniard turned again.

Tavistock gathered himself for a last furious heave and forced his body away from the bulkhead along the entire length of the sword. A surge of pain flooded him as he reached the hilt and the blade came free. He could not wrench the rapier out of his flesh, but at least he could defend himself.

The sergeant hacked at him. He dodged the cutlass badly and its point caught the rapier's handguard, spinning him round. With an immense effort he drove his assailant back and thrust his own cutlass into the Spaniard's bull neck directly above the centre crease of his breastplate.

The man staggered. Then he hugged Tavistock to him and crashed to the deck on top of him. He felt the blade spring under his back and the sudden crack as it snapped off against the *Jesus*'s deck.

I must get help, he told himself. Must pull out the steel and stop the bleeding, find someone to plug the wound. He felt his strength and rage ebbing as the shocking wound fuddled his brain. I must get out, he told himself. I must not faint away, or I'll never wake. I must get back to my ship, get revenge for my brother ...

Then the weight of the dead Spaniard crushed the wind from his lungs and darkness closed over him.

'Don't shoot! It's the Portugall down there!'

'Jesus be praised! It's the Gunner!'

John Tavistock touched the timbers of the *Minion* and allowed himself to be heaved from the water. As he lay gasping for breath on the bloodied decks he saw bodies being thrown over the side. Of his gun crew he was the only one alive; on the island out of a hundred and fifty men only three had got off alive. He watched Hawkins, now strapped up in his fighting gear and giving orders.

You stubborn bastard, he thought savagely. If you'd listened to my report we would have been prepared. But you wouldn't. You thought you'd got away with it, that the Spaniards were impressed by your firm dealing. Richard told you that you should have been more vigilant. He tried to warn you the Viceroy was planning treachery. Now two hundred men have paid for your stubbornness with their lives.

'Where's my brother?'

Hawkins whirled. An ugly bruise swelled his cheek. 'Gunner!'

'Where's Richard?'

'His ship's taken. Maybe him too.'

'Dead?' John felt the force of the word in the pit of his stomach.

'Like us all if you don't get those guns working.'

Bowen shouted, 'I saw your brother board the *Jesus* in a blood-spitting temper just before we parted. He was aiming to drive the Spaniards off her.'

The flagship was drifting close by, her masts and rigging in ruin. There was no sign of Richard, nor anyone moving on deck.

Despite intense shore fire the *Minion* was coming to battle order. She had been wound out two ship's lengths, her cables cut and setting canvas. Both Queen's ships were now beyond boarding range, but they were being cut to pieces each time the island's guns fired. To protect *Minion* Hawkins worked her close to the *Jesus*, and seeing this the Spanish Admiral ordered his ships to cut loose and come behind to bring their guns to bear.

John Tavistock got his gunners to work quickly, sending powder boys below to bring up dry kegs and bags of grapeshot. In the fury of the battle he looked inward for the nexus of calm that would sustain him but found only furious questions. He knew that Richard would not have waited to throw himself into the assault. He had always said that in battle the man who acted on instinct, abandoning himself to God and to his fate, was safer than the man who cowered from the bullets. It was especially true when the instinct had been ingrained by long training. John remembered that and found refuge in his own skills. He narrowed his mind to the task in hand and gathered his men, pressing others to stand in for the men who had died ashore. Methodically, they reamed the barrels of his five big guns, charging them with powder wadding and shot, packing the whole tight, fusing them, setting azimuth and elevation on the massive oaken carriages.

He shouted to the quarterdeck where the sailing master signalled his readiness to accept the gunner's aiming directions. He hand-signalled back 'more to larboard'.

Hacking orders and the sharp whistles of the *Minion*'s boatswains had driven the hands aloft. Already they had broken the main and fore-courses out, then the spritsail blossomed and as it filled her head came around swinging the line of Spanish shipping past his waiting muzzles.

'Fire all guns!'

'Firing, zor!'

An infinitesimal gap of time as simultaneously five matches touched home, then *Minion*'s timbers were hammered by a closely-timed concussion that filled the waist of the ship with acrid powder smoke.

The first broadside was wide, the balls skipping off the waves in a long series of white dashes. Immediately the crews set about reloading and the second broadside was brilliantly on target.

The Spanish Admiral's ship was hit just above the waterline; a lucky shot penetrated the magazine, and the bows of the vessel were ripped apart by a concussion that shook the whole roadstead. Men were blasted high by a searing orange explosion that littered the entire channel with burning wreckage.

Tavistock tore his eyes from the devastation. The *Minion*'s crew were cheering wildly and cheered again minutes later when her guns set the Spanish Vice-Admiral afire. One after another the broadsides pummelled the great ships, a merchantman, then the Viceroy's own flagship which began to sink but settled in shallows.

'She burns with Don Emilio aboard!' someone shouted. The stink of powder filled Tavistock's nostrils and the roaring guns deafened him. He saw the sails fill on Drake's barque *Judith* as she stood off.

You've got your wish, he blamed Hawkins silently, filled with the spirit of vengeance. The Spanish have paid the price, but our fleet is doomed: the *Angel* is sinking, *Swallow* taken and the Portuguese caravel recaptured. The *Jesus* is abandoned and useless. Only *Minion* and *Judith* remain. God damn your eyes for Richard's death!

Across the bay Don Francisco de Luzon listened to the soldier with alarm. The sergeant had left the burning flagship in a small boat to tell him that the Viceroy would not come ashore.

The man's expression was imploring through the streaked dirt of his face.

'His Excellency's anger is beyond all reason! He will not listen.'

Cursing, Luzon told the sergeant to find seven men and an equal number of leather buckets, and went after his Vice-Admiral. If anything will blast Don Emilio out of his fury, he thought sanguinely, the sight of Ortega will. Together they rowed out, and he found the Viceroy white-faced, stiff-limbed with rage, still brandishing sword and pistol at the English, but utterly powerless.

Luzon sent his men away to douse the fires as best they could.

'Excellency!'

Immediately the Viceroy saw Ortega his face began to suffuse with blood.

'Santiago! Get off my ship, you coward! You traitorous *bastardo*!'

Ortega paled under the attack, but stood his ground.

'I had no choice, Excellency. We were discovered. I myself was almost killed by a crossbow bolt at the hands of the English Captain-General. My boatswain was shot down at my side. I had to give the signal.'

Luzon watched Ortega kneeling in supplication. That's right, he told his Captain silently, humble yourself. You know you gave the signal to attack an hour too soon. We were not prepared. If we had been ready the English and their ships would have been obliterated just as surely as those who were slaughtered on shore. Instead we have lost three capital ships, and still the English live.

Don Emilio's eyes opened wide in disbelief. 'The English corsair lives? You lie! Did Villanueva not have my orders to kill him? You raised the signal to save your own miserable skin!'

'Not so, Excellency. The plan was known to them. We were betrayed. I swear it!'

Don Emilio hesitated, and in that moment Luzon stepped forward.

'My men have taken the shore batteries. Look, Excellency! They are crushing the English ship.'

The Viceroy turned to stare at the pirates. 'What are they doing? They are allowing them to get away!'

'Excellency, they are crippled. They have nowhere to go.'

'Prepare a fireship!'

'But Excellency, the wind –'

Don Emilio's eyes burned like the coals of hell. 'You *dare* to question my orders?'

'Certainly not, Excellency.' Luzon took hold of Ortega angrily. The man was still on his knees. 'Did you not hear the Viceroy-designate's orders? Prepare a fireship immediately.'

Ortega looked helplessly back, but got to his feet and left to do his Admiral's bidding.

Across the harbour the culverins and heavy shore cannon were getting the range of the English. Luzon's own men in the forecastle were bringing the fire under control so that the need to evacuate the Viceroy forcibly from his ship had subsided. Despite the freshening north westerly, the air tasted sickeningly of powder but through the ragged smoke Luzon could see that both English ships had managed, through a feat of extraordinary seamanship, to stand off a cable's length – about two hundred paces. Undoubtedly, the corsair's flagship was stricken, her mainmast shot through, and, even as he watched, a cheer went up from the soldiers on shore as her foremast was carried away by chain shot.

She is old and rotted; her hull is splintering, Luzon thought with satisfaction. Soon she will sink. Soon we will have these Englishmen in irons. Then Don Emilio will have his revenge. Christ Jesus and the Holy Virgin! The Viceroy has no understanding of sea war. I hope he takes them and burns them all for the heretic pirates they are, but a fireship is madness!

The Viceroy's hands remained tight on his pistols, but as the truth of the enemy's plight grew clearer he began to calm. I am Don Emilio Martinez, Captain-General of New Spain, Viceroy of Mexico, Admiral of Castile, and trusted representative of His Most Catholic Majesty Philip, he told himself proudly. I know how to deal with godless Protestants, and soon they will be mine.

'When will the fireship will be ready?'

'Excellency, I must prevail upon you to reconsider. If –'

'*When will it be ready?*'

Luzon stifled his insubordination. 'As soon as Ortega can execute your order.'

'Good. None of them must escape.'

For the next hour Don Emilio paced the deck restlessly, his burnished armour hot and heavy on his sweat-drenched body. He was bleeding inside at the loss of his Admiral's finest ships.

How had they done it? How had the tiny English vessels inflicted such disproportionate damage? How was he to know that the insects had the sting of scorpions? How would he explain the situation to the King?

It would be useless to count on the Admiral. He had detected overt reproof in Luzon's manner, and hadn't he heard him say 'Viceroy designate' to Ortega – it was the truth, but it was also a slight. An unconscious slip? Perhaps. In which case Don Francisco would have to be taught a lesson.

Calmer now, Don Emilio watched as the helpless English ship was lacerated by a fresh hail of iron. A grim smile curved his long face, making his black moustaches lift like raven's wings.

He turned to Luzon. 'Have the English corpses be heaped like logs on the spit below the batteries as a taunt.'

Luzon passed on the order emotionlessly.

'It will be a long time before the slavers come to Vera Cruz again, eh, Don Francisco?'

The Admiral seemed about to betray himself, then said only, 'Perhaps.'

'Are they not utterly destroyed?'

'The English are a stubborn people, Don Emilio. They did not stop coming to the Indies when the Pope ordained it, they did not desist at King Philip's command, and I doubt if they will heed you.'

'Then you would have treated them differently?'

'It is not my place to criticise your actions, Excellency.'

'Who can say I acted incorrectly? If the English were too stupid or too cowardly to believe I would try to destroy them, is that not their failing?'

The Admiral fixed his eyes stiffly on the English flagship and made no reply, infuriating Don Emilio.

'What binds the word of a gentleman when given to a heretic and a blackmailer? Nothing!'

'Who can say what binds the word of a gentleman?'

Don Emilio stared at his Admiral.

'Damn you to Hell, Luzon! Have not the Americas been made the possession of Spain by Christ's Vicar on Earth himself? Pope Alexander has made everything west of the Azores Spanish, except Brazil. Is it not God's will that the Empire be protected against these marauders?'

Luzon made no reply, but his stare hardened, forcing the Viceroy to a greater pitch of anger.

'Now I am Viceroy there will be a new regime. I carry the King's personal brief to make Mexico secure and by God's blood I shall do so!'

Don Francisco de Luzon's family was not of great rank. His lineage was ancient, but his hawkish face betrayed more than a hint of Moorish blood. The Viceroy had seen too many like him not to be wary of them. Such men must be watched carefully, their ambitions stifled before they grew too dangerous. More than once on the crossing from Seville the Admiral had showed himself to be overly self-important. He would not be content until he had risen high up the golden stair of power, and he was foolish enough to believe that he could do it through tireless service and loyalty in ferrying the King's gold across the seas. But this is where your loyalty has been tested, Admiral of the Ocean Seas! You are flawed by disobedience, and I will see you brought down for it, ferryman!

He began to sketch the opening of his first dispatch to his King. He would begin by revealing how the fool Ortega had been responsible for confounding his excellent plan by giving the battle signal too soon. He would make sure Ortega was put to death and then he would deal with Luzon's disobedience.

Then the smile on the Viceroy's lips faded. He saw that the smaller English vessel had managed to work back towards the flagship. It was then that the impossible began to happen.

In the *Minion's* waist, John Tavistock listened intently to his Captain-

General. John Hawkins's face was alight as he exhorted his crew to greater efforts. He had seen that if only the *Minion* could be brought under cover of the *Jesus*'s much bigger hull she would be shielded from the deadly fire of the shore batteries. They could also take on board the precious provisions that were already stowed in the flagship's hold, and give themselves some slim chance of survival.

The shore fire faltered as *Minion* turned. It was as if the Spanish gunners could not believe the ship was coming towards them instead of running for the open sea. They had covered the channel, anticipating retreat, and it took them some minutes to re-aim their muzzles on the crippled English flag.

As the hulls of the two English vessels touched, Hawkins's orders to his officers were explicit:

'Take twenty men each aboard the *Jesus*. Put them to work in gangs of four, transferring provisions. Water and victuals – nothing else. Now go to it!' Hawkins turned to Hampton. 'Come with me. And you, John Sanders – get your belly shifting or lose it to those dung-shovelling cannonades! Help get our wounded below. We'll get *Minion* home if we have to row her all the way!'

The crew scattered as a tangled mass of blocks and sheets was ripped from the *Jesus*'s crosstrees and was flung down among them. A man who moved too slowly was axed down by the debris. Two of his crewmates moved to help him.

'You heard the General!' the Gunner heard himself shout. His heart hammered at his ribs, but his head was clear and cool as he considered Hawkins's orders. Inside the *Jesus*'s strongroom was the profit of their entire expedition. But the keys were lost, and this was no time to worry about money: no man could eat gold. Still, the irony of it gnawed at him.

As young Twide, John Browne and John Hooper made *Minion* fast alongside the *Jesus* by the forecastle, Hortop, the powder maker, pulled on the grapnel aft, binding her tight. Planks were lashed across the gunwales and they began the hazardous operation.

The *Jesus* was listing twenty degrees. She was a shambles. Many men had been killed aboard her; Spanish and English bodies were strewn across her decks, some whole, some torn into slaughterhouse meat by the bombardment. Tavistock fought down his revulsion and the urge to turn them over in case one had the face of his brother. All around him, his men were like monkeys, fast, alert for the shots that still crashed into the *Jesus* showering them with fractured timber. Hawkins himself had gone aboard and appeared with Hampton at intervals carrying scrolled charts and navigation instruments, the ship's log and her Bible.

For half an hour, the Englishmen laboured under withering fire. Tavistock's men brought out twenty empty water butts, each one of a hundred and twenty-six gallons' capacity, manhandled from the hold and hoisted across from ropes rigged to *Minion*'s main yard. They brought out fifty full kegs of powder, salt pork, beer puncheons and a store of beans and mustard seed. He helped carry sacks of oatmeal across, followed by fifteen crates of dried fish which Master Barrett had bought at Santa Marta, and all the while they worked knee-deep in foul water in the murky darkness of the hold.

Spanish gunnery had holed the flagship and reduced the orlop deck to a wasteland of splintered wood. Her landward side was smashed in and all Tavistock's magnificent brass guns were thrown back from their ports in disarray. Coldly, he began to search for ways to make the Spanish pay for what they had done, and he hit upon a plan.

'Sir, she's fair cleaned out for'ard,' Cornelius the Irishman reported, his eyes straying towards the safety of the *Minion*.

Hawkins and Sanders had already left with his detail. Tavistock watched the Negro Boaz who leapt down into the arms of his crewmates from the *Swallow*. They were the last aboard and orders were being shouted in the *Minion*, hands hastily casting off forward.

Tavistock seized a huge arquebus, almost as big as one of the falconets that they mounted on swivels in the bow. He double-primed it and faced the Irishman. 'Do you want to go home a pauper or a rich man, Cornelius?'

'And leave our wages here? Not I!'

'Then you six get aft! While we're afloat we'll not leave a brass button for the Spanish.'

Pollard protested, 'The Captain-General said victuals only.'

'Then eat dirt in England! You're under no compulsion. Do I see five rich men? Then follow me!'

The last hands aboard swarmed belowdecks after him, and as John Tavistock swung down through the hatch, he saw piercing bright turquoise through the shattered side of the ship. Seawater swilled underfoot, and a body lolled grotesquely in the gaping hole at the waterline, its head smashed into a ruddy cloud surrounded by a halo of tiny fish. He stepped over it and jammed the dangerously overloaded arquebus against the deck support. There was a bright flash, a tremendous explosion which carried away the side of the door, wrecking the hinges, then he ducked into the strongroom and as his eyes grew accustomed to the blackness within he saw the glint of silver bullion piled in shining cast bricks that had been scattered across the deck. In addition, there were three huge locked chests of pearls and gold plate, and ten thousand pesos' worth of precious stones.

'The chests – damn you, Ingram!'

'They've stopped firing.' Ingram, insubordinate and broody, wild hair like a horse's mane, flashed anger.

Rively and the boy Momfrey pushed towards the jagged hole in the *Jesus*'s timbers. Momfrey's round eyes were on the swarm of feeding fish; Rively's were on the towering mass of flame across the bay.

'God preserve us!'

'What is it, man?'

Rively, a ragged, pock-faced man, shook his head in disbelief. 'We've got to get out of here! She's upon us! A fireship!'

'The wind's backed westerly!' John Moon, the carpenter's mate shouted. 'She's coming down on us!'

His cries panicked them. Tavistock fought to gain control, then put his own head to the gap. The Spanish had ignited one of their two hundred tonners and the sight of its decks packed with Trinidad pitch, alight from stem to stern, was enough to drive fear into the minds of any seaman. For Tavistock it was the purest liquor of dread. His earliest memory, one that had wiped out all that had gone before, was of the fires in Smithfield, when as a four-year-old boy he had looked upon the stakes of Bloody Mary's executioners when twenty Protestant diehards were immolated for their faith. He forced his terrors deep down inside him. If the doused sails of the fireship caught quickly there might still be enough time. Or if they were very lucky the lashings that fixed the rudder would burn through and she would veer away.

'Bring the chests aloft, I said.'

Rively was first to snap. 'She burns like the fires of Satan, Gunner! *Minion* will cast off and we'll roast alive!'

'Or drown!'

'I can't swim!' Moon shouted helplessly.

'Nor I,' the Irishman replied.

'You're wasting time.' Tavistock stood foursquare in the exit. He slapped Ingram down into the sluicing, bloodied water when he tried to pass, but Ingram leapt up and braced himself as if to spring. Only Tavistock's strength of will stopped him.

'Ignore my orders, you son of a whore? Take that chest, Ingram, or we'll all burn together!' Tavistock held his stare. Five pairs of eyes nailed him, darted past him to judge a rush to freedom. But no one dared enough to try. When you give an order, make it stick. Never, never go back on it, he remembered – that was the second rule of command, a lesson his brother had drummed into him. The first rule was never to make orders you needed to countermand.

In the sudden silence the ocean lapping at the hull grew loud. Then the roaring sound of flame came to them on the wind. Momfrey was shaking. His pathetic whimpering almost unnerved Tavistock. He grabbed the ten-year-old boy and heaved him toward the hatch. 'Get aboard *Minion*, lad. This is men's work.'

The moment passed. Cornelius the Irishman began heaving on the chest. It was iron bound and big enough to contain two men; it weighed three or four hundredweight. Tavistock prayed that the sailmaker had picked the most valuable of the three. Then there were five pairs of hands dragging the first chest out of the strongroom.

In the time it took to hoist the chest on deck, the fireship had come on fully a bowshot – a hundred yards. Her masts were fully alight, blazing up in a mantle of flame. She had held her course and was closing.

Hand over hand they hauled on the severed mainsail tack, swinging the chest clear of the gunwales and into *Minion*'s belly where it crashed down into the deck.

Tavistock froze as he stood on the quarterdeck, his terror now too much to conceal. Hortop had cast off. The turquoise gap between the hulls widened. He could feel the flames of the fireship as its bowsprit lanced the air above his head and then he was knocked down by the impact. Choking black smoke gusted over him, filling his head with the acrid smell of powder and charring wood. He sprawled across the planking and then he saw a flash of red beside him. An arm clad in crimson leather. A hand with a gold ring on the last finger, a ring bearing a jet black stone.

'Jump, Gunner!'

'Richard!'

The face was waxen, the colour of ashes.

In horror he rolled the massive Spanish body off his brother's chest, and as he did so dark blood welled from around the hilt of a rapier that emerged from a ragged gash in Richard's shoulder. The ornate iron cage of a handguard was impaled on his upper chest.

God in heaven, he's alive!

Tarry rope crackled overhead in the intense heat.

Shouts rang out.

'Jump! For Christ's sake!'

'Save yourself!'

He slipped his fingers through the rapier's hilt and knelt on his brother's outstretched arm ready to drag the weapon out. Then he realised that only the steel was plugging the wound, stopping the bleeding. With a maniac's strength he heaved Richard's body over his shoulder. Ten feet, twelve, fifteen feet now lay between the two ships. Too much to jump now – even to save himself.

Fire blazed all around him, incinerating everything it touched.

Staring round in desperation through the rippling air, he saw a coil of rope attached to a grapnel snaking slowly over the side – one of the hoists they had been using to move the stores. It was secured to *Minion*'s main yard, and as she pulled away the rope followed, dragging its hook across the deck. He dived for the steel hook and rammed it under Richard's belt. The line tautened so that his brother's body jerked up like a dead thing come suddenly to life. Blood ran down his arm and dripped from his fingers as he was lifted clear and hung grotesquely over the sea.

Hawkins's men pulled the stricken captain inboard and watched helplessly in horror as powder kegs on the fireship detonated, spreading burning pitch all across the *Jesus*'s quarterdeck.

When the black smoke cleared the Gunner was gone from sight.

Chapter 2

Overnight the *Minion* hugged the lee of one of the two other small islands, the one ominously called by the Spaniards *Isla de Sacrifiço*. Drake's ship, the *Judith*, had vanished; the *Swallow* was captured and the *Angel* sunk. Hawkins was forced to put out his two remaining sea anchors, but the sea bed was sandy and as the winds got up again *Minion*'s position continued to slip, threatening at each turn of the hourglass to wreck them on the shore.

'What will you do, John?' Hampton asked when they were alone at the taffrail.

Hawkins looked at his sweating, dirt-streaked face. Hampton was a quiet man, lean and secretive about his feelings. As a captain he was cold and distant from his men. He commanded his ship efficiently, but he could be ruthless. Hawkins had first employed him ten years ago, and in all that time had found him utterly loyal.

'First, we must find water.'

Hampton's creased cheeks moved mournfully. 'On tight rations full butts will see us to the Bahamas channel, no further. Then we'll need rain. But by then I deem water will be our lesser problem.'

'And our greater?'

Hampton kept his voice low. 'Provender, John. With two hundred mouths aboard we've enough for just five days. On quarter rations, twenty.'

Hawkins knew that even with fair weather the crossing must take at least seventy-five days, probably nearer a hundred. Many of the wounded would die, after a month on a starvation diet many more would fall sick, and those left would be scurvied skeletons too weak to climb aloft. I have no choice, he thought. If two hundred men set sail for England no one will reach home, save cannibals.

'Put everyone on a strict quarter ration of oatmeal. Save the beans and salt meat and anything you deem will keep. Give spirits to the wounded, but none to the able men. And dispatch the dead smartly.'

'Then?'

'Then, I must take up my sword.'

Hampton nodded, understanding.

Hawkins went aft and closed the door on his troubled ship. Before God alone, he took from the drawer his General's sword and drew it from its scabbard, planting its point in the deck so that its hilt formed a golden crucifix. He sank to his knees, kissed the blade and prayed silently, fervently, seeking an answer, a sign from the Almighty that would strengthen him in his difficult task and help him decide what to do. Then he rose up and stepped through into the tiny space where the mizzen mast thrust up through the deck. It was the sailing master's cabin, and was hung about with cross-staff and astrolabe, a brass quadrant and dividers, but also the iron cage of a rapier handguard, its blade snapped off six inches from the hilt.

Peter Grosse stood with his red face brooding down and his black barber-surgeon's skullcap pulled tight on his head. Sweat beaded his stubble and dripped from his chin onto where Richard Tavistock lay, his body close to death and his spirit drawn deep inside him, as if doing battle with great evil.

'He has uncommon strength of will, but I fear the morbidity must overcome him,' Grosse said gruffly, wiping his hands on a filthy rag. His butcher's apron was caked with gore from his night's labours; his side whiskers and pig's eyes made the mariners fear him, few could forget that he carved men's limbs from their bodies as easily as the carpenter cleaved a ship's spar. 'I shall bleed him again.'

'No. He's lost enough blood already.'

'His injury has turned it bad. Bad blood kills a man. There's no remedy but to let it out.'

'Let him be, I told you!'

Grosse straightened. 'The wound will grow noisome and he will die.'

'He is in God's hands now. Who sent you here?'

'Captain Hampton.'

'Go about your business below. Or sleep if you can.'

As the surgeon left, Hawkins looked at the cotton compress that his steward, Chamberlain, had strapped across Tavistock's chest. He had been swabbed with seawater and the air had been sweetened about his head with a pomander of cloves to ease his laboured breathing. I might have been lying here, he thought, with him standing over me instead. He fingered his cheekbone tenderly where he had been punched, and probed the place where his tooth was now loosened. When he had been struck Hawkins had reeled back in amazement. For a split second he had been unable to understand and the suspicion that it was treachery had flashed through his mind. He regretted that unworthy thought now, leaning closer. Your blood is mixed with that of my own wife's family, Richard. That's why I took you and trained you up from a boy. And now you've saved my life. Aye, you're a brave man and a clever one. Jane's lucky to have a husband, and Harry a father, such as you. She deserves better than that you perish here.

He got up as Bowen appeared at the door with his report. He seemed unsure of Hawkins's humour and unusually subdued.

'General, if it please you, sir, I sent down divers. They say our hull is sound below the waterline. The water in the bilges may be got out by tonight if the pumps can be repaired. Our masts are sturdy enough. Though we lost the forecourse and main top yard in the action we may have them both somewhat restored by the morrow. Wind's slackening, veering easterly with the dawn and the Master's roaring for a new heading.'

'I'll speak to him, Bowen. Keep the men busy baling out, and rig sunshades fore and aft so that the wounded may be brought up until night.'

'Yes, sir.'

'And, Bowen?'

'Sir?'

Hawkins eyed his boatswain carefully. 'Do you think me too severe to the men, tonight?'

Bowen shuffled with embarrassment. 'I . . . I can't say I thinks about that, General.'

'See they're kept busy and the work apportioned fairly.'

'Yes, sir.'

Hawkins's eyes followed him from the cabin. A pity there aren't more like you, he thought. Never a complaint in five years' service. I'm only sorry I probably won't live to promote you further. And by God, your own tasks will grow tricky enough before long.

Hawkins set a course nor' nor'east, following the coast. In sight of land the men would be more hopeful and more easily persuaded when the time came to deal toughly with them. Alone, Hawkins turned his mind to the ruin of his enterprise. We've lost everything we ever hoped to gain, he thought as he slumped into his chair. Nothing is left to show for our year of labour but two chests of yellow metal and a casket of jewels. Ten thousand, maybe fifteen thousand pounds in all. Two ships lost, and one loaned by Her Majesty. All is ruin! Ruin! And they'll say it's my fault.

The loss of the *Jesus of Lübeck* was Hawkins's heaviest single burden. The royal loan had been made on the understanding that any damage sustained by her on the voyage would be made good at the Hawkins brothers' expense, but if she was destroyed completely then the Queen would bear the loss. Had the *Jesus* been sunk by an Atlantic storm, or wrecked on an Indies shoal he could have fairly claimed an excuse. He felt his heart falter as he imagined the interview at which he explained to his sovereign's death-white face that he had lost her ship to Spanish gunfire.

At worst, he thought, my brother William might suffer the same ultimate penalty. None of us can expect quarter.

Elizabeth was a supremely capable Queen. She had ruled England with a semblance of her father's iron authority, but with her own special political genius, for the last decade. Feared at her own Court, respected by the people of England, reviled across Catholic Christendom, nowhere was she ignored. Her single purpose had been to maintain England as a Protestant land, but to do so and to remain Queen she had had to rewrite the rules of diplomacy. If the world worked to a system that disadvantaged Elizabeth, then Elizabeth must change the world. Which, in part, was why she had become Hawkins's sponsor. Other key investors were Sir William Cecil, the Queen's closest and most trusted servant; Sir Nicholas Bacon, the Lord Keeper of the Tower; the Earl of Leicester, the Queen's favourite. And there were other powerful men, all members of the Privy Council. Hawkins imagined their pique when he told them that the thousands he had promised to multiply for them were lost – and yet *he* had returned alive to tell them so.

Shares in his expedition had been sold on a strictly speculative basis, all loss and all gain to be borne according to the size of the original stake. But these men were not common merchants, and his venture no simple trading mission. Not one of them, he was certain, would stand their loss like common merchants. Each would reassure him, then seek to squeeze a return by taxing their influence higher, by extortion over trade permits and licences or simply by pricing high the grace of their favour. Because they stood between Hawkins and the Queen's person there were a thousand small ways they could arrange the settling of their losses against his future.

He had undertaken a volatile mix of commerce and politics that magnified the rewards – *but also the risks.*

If this was but a matter of lost ships, he mused bitterly, I could sell my London house and liquidate all assets. The Hawkins brothers can muster perhaps twenty thousand pounds. That would easily be sufficient to cover the debt to the Queen and to appease her courtiers, but this is not so simple a misfortune, and I can see no escape from the coils of this serpent.

He got up and began to pace about, thinking feverishly of the political ramifications of what had happened, and as he thought the prospect grew ever more bleak. Now that the cannons were silent and he was at sea he could meditate upon it. There was a vastly bigger picture to consider. One more dangerous still, where the stakes were the very future of Christendom.

Undoubtedly, one of the Viceroy's *avisos*, fast dispatch boats, was even now preparing to sail for Seville with the Spanish account of the incident. If King Philip was goaded to anger, war might easily be the outcome. And it was not a war little England could possibly win against the mighty Empire of Spain. We are a poor country, he reminded himself, an island nation of three million people, a mere splinter of land on the fringes of Europe, surrounded by Catholic enemies in Scotland, barbarous Ireland and France. We fish our coastal waters and tend our pastures, fattening sheep for our tables and spinning their wool to sell in Antwerp, and we survive. But Spain – mighty Spain! Ten million Catholics under a King who thinks himself God's commander on earth, whose tough mercenary troops are raised in every village and hamlet in the Empire. They've never lost a battle in a hundred years. Those invincible battalions even now scourge the Low Countries, driven by a maniac King whose veins run with American silver and whose pious convictions go utterly unquestioned by prince or Pope. A single ship of their treasure fleet carries more wealth in her guts than the entire city of London! The exchequer of Seville exceeds that of the whole of England! Once Philip decides to crush our Protestant land, he will do so with no more difficulty than stepping on a cockroach. And with as little compunction.

How fiercely would the Queen fight to avoid war? How artfully would she seek to knit the wound and heal the scar with Philip? In order to steer a course away from a war with Spain, she would fight like a wildcat. Nothing was beyond her. She would offer marriages, make gifts of restitution, appease Philip's haughty ambassadors and order executions. To save her realm she'll shovel me and mine into the furnace of Philip's wrath until all is consumed.

The prospect weighed heavily upon Hawkins. He called for Sam and ordered him to bring a flagon of wine. The creaking of the *Minion*'s timbers and the sound of his carpenters hammering on deck reminded him with each blow that she was a Queen's ship. He took the wine and dismissed the lad curtly before drinking a deep draught. It would be better if the *Minion* were to sink now, and put an end to it all, he thought sourly. The suffering ahead will be terrible! The one vision capable of sustaining such hardship is the desire to see those chalk-white cliffs of England rising up from the horizon again. But not now. Not when that sight means impeachment, the block, a pauper's grave. It's hopeless. Should I take a lighted taper to the powder room now? Should I blow *Minion* to hell and save a deal of suffering? But there was Kate. And his eight-year-old son Richard. He pursed his thin lips, wiping them on his sleeve, and knew that he could do no other than try to bring the ship home, whatever the cost, whatever the consequences. Loyalty to the Queen, loyalty to his family and loyalty to his men all demanded it. It was the only decision a Captain-General could make.

All that night the ship groaned in complaint at each sea. It was as if every plank had been loosened against every other. They sighted no sail, and if pursuit had been attempted it had failed. By noon the next day fourteen of the most severely wounded had died and been dispatched over the side with little ceremony. Thirst turned the men's voices to dry croaks as they shouted their orders and hunger began to gnaw at their stomachs, but they had good winds and fair skies and made reasonable way.

In the sailing master's cabin Hawkins studied the charts. He had been hoping for clouds to hide the merciless sun and rain to fill their water casks, but none came. They must try for fresh water at the mouth of the Panuco River, he had decided. Eighty leagues – a week's sailing at this rate. He laid down his dividers and was about to go back on deck when a groan made him turn.

Tavistock's mouth was open, his eyes dully half-lidded, and his limbs were stirring like a man emerging from a nightmare.

'Easy,' Hawkins said, and shouted for Chamberlain to bring broth and a cup of warm water sweetened with honey.

The Captain was still deathly pale and his lips puckered with dry skin, but he was conscious. Hawkins eased him up, cradling his head.

'We're at sea?' Tavistock said weakly.

'Aye, we're safe and sailing home, Richard. Jesus be praised you're with us.'

'Jesus? We're aboard *Jesus*?'

Tavistock tried to sit up but the effort creased his face and he collapsed back, breathing heavily.

'We're aboard *Minion*. Heading north for water, and all our company with her.'

'*Swallow* – who's at the helm? Is she damaged?'

'Calm yourself. We're making good time. Soon we'll be standing on Plymouth Hoe, and wishing ourselves at sea again.'

'How long have I been – ' Tavistock tried to raise himself again but a jag of pain exploded across his chest.

What's the matter with me, he wondered groggily. Why can't I sit up? I feel sicker than a dung-eating lubber. He felt the burning skin of his chest. There was soreness round his neck and he ached all down his left side.

'You're too slow, Richard. You were hog-spiked by a Spaniard and damned near done to death.'

Tavistock groaned again. He looked hazily at his chest and the bandages. As he pulled them back he saw a ragged purple puncture, the size of a shilling, four inches above his nipple. All around it he was bruised black.

It's nothing, he thought. Nothing at all. I've seen a man fight on with half his arm missing.

'This laid me low?' he croaked.

'They say the men of the Indies garrison often poison their steel with venom got from the savages.'

'So – a serpent bit me?'

'You're lucky it missed out your vitals.'

'Who's commanding *Swallow*? Is John aboard her?'

His head was spinning, but his memory of the battle was beginning to come back. The small arched port above his head was open and light dappling from the sea moved in dancing patterns on the timbers. A cooling breeze washed him.

He could remember the Spaniard who had run him through. A bull of a man, with striped sleeves and burnished armour. I killed him. Sent him to Hell for his treachery, like I promised Amyas Poole. And what treachery! They set on us like rats from a stinking dunghill, after their commander's bonden word was given.

'We gave as good as we got. *Swallow*'s captured, Richard.'

His mouth puckered with pain at the news. 'How many were killed?'

'Two hundred.'

'Half our men – and my brother John?'

Hawkins's face was grave, his eyes hooded. 'Left behind.'

Hawkins told him of the fireship, of the way the *Minion* had been forced to cut loose, and how he had been hoisted aboard.

'Then, he may be alive!'

'He perished on *Jesus*'s deck.'

'Is that sure?'

'Yes. If he was taken by the Spanish – they showed little mercy on the island.'

'But no man saw his death?'

'That I can't say.'

Tavistock felt the anguish surge up within him. I'm to blame, he told himself. It's my fault. I've broken the solemn promise to my mother that I would be his protector. It was I who fixed him a place on this trip, I who got cut up in the first bit of trouble, I who caused him to tarry too long on the *Jesus*!

He closed his eyes and panted for breath. Hawkins was called urgently on deck, and Chamberlain came in with bowl and cannikin. The steward gave him sup to clear his throat and fed him with a spoon then laid him back gently. But he would not be still. A hundred questions boiled in his brain. Was *Minion* alone? Who else had got away? Two hundred men aboard *Minion* was impossible. What of Drake and Hampton and Robert Barrett? Had anyone actually seen John die?

When Chamberlain turned his back Tavistock struggled to get up. He swung his naked legs out of the cot and stood swaying, grasping the chair, but collapsed into the steward's arms.

'You're still very weak, Captain. Try to rest.'

Tavistock's eyes clouded but he was fighting to keep them open. Chamberlain spoke softly to him, mesmerically, soothingly.

'We're sailing home. Sailing back to Plymouth and our loved ones, Captain. You'll be seeing your wife and son, and I'll be seeing my sweetheart again soon. With my share of the prize I'm going to marry. I'll buy land and settle down. She's a sweet one, my girl. Amy's her name, sweet and gentle with cheeks like apples in high summer and hair the colour of a chestnut mare. I'm a lucky man to have her, Captain.

We'll have six sons, and six daughters too, and they'll help me fetch and carry, just like I did for my father when I was a youngster. And all because of this voyage and good General Hawkins and your good brother's tidy work. I saw the *Jesus*'s chests come aboard, Captain. There's a heap of money there. Gold and silver by the pound. Some for the Queen and some for the General, and some for us poor lads who he lets work his ships ...

'Sleep now, Captain. That's it. Sleep's the best remedy. And when you dream, dream of home.'

As Tavistock's eyes closed Chamberlain swabbed his face gently.

Aye, and you're a lucky one, Chamberlain thought. God's got his finger on you, Master Richard, and it lights you up like a beacon, so it does. By rights you should be burned to a cinder, just like your brother was. I saw the *Jesus* charred to the waterline. It was a sight to see. And a tale to tell my grandchildren. Her timbers roaring from stem to stern, her masts flaming like three holy crucifixes on Calvary hill. She's gone now, just like the Gunner who I saw burn with her. Saw it with my own eyes.

Five days had passed. With new yards rigged, *Minion* had come on fifty leagues but there had been no rain and their water was down to the last cask.

Tavistock had been on his feet two days now, his arm strapped up across his chest in a sling and most of the ugly bruising gone. He had refused extra food and water once he knew the situation, and spent most of his time standing alone on the poop deck staring at the wake or regarding Hampton's set of sail without comment.

Once a man tastes command it's hard to go back to having his decisions made for him, Hawkins thought. Especially when he has to carry the burden of his ship's loss. He's a good officer, best navigator in the company after Drake, and, like Drake, hungry for command.

He stood propped up alone now, in his customary place, remote and in sorrow for his brother, and Hawkins chose to give him the privacy of his thoughts.

Tavistock's empty belly ached. His wound was healing slowly. The poison had not left him and he was still weak. I need water to flush it from me, to let the air at it, he told himself. Better than stewing abed. Stand up, walk the deck, anything but lie here in sickness.

He had forced his mind away from the tragedy, and in the long empty hours had begun calmly, quietly, hatching a plan. He watched Sam climbing aloft again. The boy's determination to take another of the brightly coloured fowls pleased him. Then he heard the shout.

The page began to wave madly.

'What's he say?'

'The river,' Boaz said.

'He's spotted the lagoons!'

Orders rang out. Hands hurried for the ratlines and braces.

'He's right, by God!'

Tavistock stirred. 'There's a danger the Spaniards call the Galleguilla Reefs to the north.'

Hampton acknowledged the information with a nod, and began to bring the *Minion* about. They worked shoreward for an hour, then slackened their headway. A man was sent forward with a seven-pound shoal-water lead and fifty-fathom line coiled on the weather side. He swung it in a circle and repeatedly cast it out a long way ahead into the clear water. It was marked off with knots at fathom intervals and he shouted the depth each time the ship came alongside. Hampton recorded the depths in a notebook. Then sea anchors were readied.

As *Minion* hove to, Tavistock joined Hawkins at the taffrail. 'I'd like to put this to you, General,' he said slowly, formally. 'We're on the Devil's fork, but I think I know a way we can get out of it.'

Hawkins turned to face him, his thin lips unsmiling. 'Go on.'

'This whole coast is plied by Spanish coasters fetching and carrying between their settlements. They're small ships, I know, but if we create a supply base then lie in wait we can run any number of them down, take their cargoes and arms –'

Hawkins cut him short. 'You're advocating piracy, Captain.'

Tavistock hesitated. 'You can call it that, but the way I see it –'

'I do call it that!' Anger flashed suddenly across Hawkins's face. 'I won't have you speak of this here. *Minion* is a ship of Her Majesty's fleet. My duty is to bring her home.'

'General, after what happened we have a right to –'

Hawkins eyes pinned him. 'Don't provoke me, Captain. You forget yourself. I raised you up, but I can sooner break you down. I'm taking *Minion* home, or I'll die trying.'

Tavistock watched Hawkins's face trembling. That's right, he thought, his belly tightening, you will die trying, and you'll kill us all. When it's the Spaniards who should die!

'Please take my view, General,' he said levelly. 'The *William and John* may not have gone down. Francis, too, might somehow struggle home again. We're out of touch. A year away from the gossipings of the Court, can you be sure of anything? Francis was right, in that time war might have been declared, legitimising everything. Elizabeth may have fallen dead of a poisoned dart, or the Catholic Queen of Scotland taken her throne!'

Hawkins's hand came up and struck him across the face. It was a slap that on land would have brought a woman to her senses, or goaded a gentleman to duel, but it was so sudden it went unnoticed by anyone else.

'You speak treason!'

Tavistock's frozen stare melted. Inside he seethed with anger, and he controlled it only by the memory of the blow he had dealt Hawkins before the battle. He breathed tremulously and forced his eyes away from Hawkins's own.

'I apologise,' he said, finding discipline at last. 'And I thank you.'

'Do you, now?'

'I shouldn't have said that.'

Hawkins waited for him to continue but he stayed silent.

'Then, I accept your apology. And we'll consider it unsaid.'

As he watched Hawkins go down onto the quarterdeck his whole body shook with anger. You bloody fool, he told himself. You know how to persuade John Hawkins. You should have known he would react that way. What were you thinking of? What devil made you say it? You spent days working that plan out, couldn't you have chosen a better time than this? Spewing it out on the moment like vomit? Now it's dead. Dead. And two hundred lives were riding on it.

He wiped the sweat from his numb face and looked out at the beach. Its white sand was no more than a bowshot distant and he could hear the surf breaking against it. To the north the Panuco River discharged into the sea, dyeing it red-brown.

You're getting old, John Hawkins, Tavistock thought. We could survive on this coast indefinitely with a handy ship of twelve cannon to prey on the Spanish. There's timber here aplenty. Fresh water and fertile ground to plant. With half our men ashore in a hidden stockade and the rest patrolling on *Minion* we could menace anything and everything that came by. We could paralyse the entire gulf, and when we'd had our fill take one of their big galleons and sail her home in triumph with a bucket full of pearls for the Queen! And if we hang as pirates then so be it!

The trumpeter blew the company to attention. Hawkins stood at the centre of the quarterdeck rail and planted his sword in the deck caulking. His voice was raised, strong and firm. He read out a prepared list, commanding the thirty-six named to stand together on the starboard side of the ship.

'I have walked daily among you and I hear much dissent. Some of you look to salvation at the hands of the Spaniards, others would cast themselves upon the mercy of savages and infidels. Hear, then, my decision: with this sword I shall split the ship's company in two equal halves. The men I have named and who stand to starboard of the sword will brave starvation and storm and try for England. Any who so desire may join them. The rest will stand to larboard of the sword. They will land ashore and take their chance as they will, to shift for themselves with the Indians, or with the Spanish as they choose. If you find no agreement you shall draw lots.'

The crew shuffled uncertainly now, staring up at the quarterdeck and into the sun, then they began to look to one another anxiously. All those essential for the ship's working and maintenance had been named. Sixty more were to go.

Tavistock spoke up. 'If it please you, Captain-General, I would go ashore.'

A hush descended. Then a chorus of voices began to beg for Tavistock's place.

Hawkins silenced them. 'Master Tavistock was named. He must remain aboard.'

Tavistock's voice came back at him. 'The men to be landed are leaderless. There must be a commander or they will surely perish.'

Again, dissent blazed from the crew.

Hawkins motioned down to where an iron-bound chest stood on the deck. Hampton threw open the lid and dug his hands into the golden pesos that glittered there, letting them spill through his fingers so that all present saw.

'I have not forgotten your pledges. No man has broken his oath to me. Indeed, many have far exceeded my expectation, and no man shall see me break faith with him. All who go ashore are due their share. Each will therefore have money – pay, bonus and prize share together are ready, or if he sees fit it will be given to his family should *Minion* escape disaster and reach England. I further pledge to you now that I will return here next year, if God allows it, to fetch you home, giving pay for the interval.'

The lid of the chest stayed open, the sun played over the thick gold coins as Hawkins told them to choose.

Fuller stepped forward. 'I have a wife and three children, sir. Take them my share.'

A second man made his decision. 'And I.'

'So be it.'

Three more came forward and were handed their share. Then another and another.

Tavistock looked on. Across the deck men began to argue, others to cross themselves and pray for guidance.

It's fifty miles of wilderness to the first Spanish settlement from here, he thought. Fever swamp and forest thick with savages, and no guarantee that the Spanish won't spill your guts the moment they see you. But I have a reason to stay. I must know if my brother is still alive. Maybe that was what warped my tongue earlier? Maybe.

Thirty men had come forward and no more. Hawkins recorded their names and when the rest begged for a proper space of time to consider he adjourned the proceedings. The small boat was lowered and those that had chosen to depart were rowed to the shore without delay.

The task of filling the water casks began and was carried on throughout the afternoon. During it, Tavistock busied himself with transferring depths and sketches of the anchorage into his own navigator's log. He said nothing more to Hawkins until late in the day. Hampton told him that those appointed to return home had been ordered to remain on board but he went to Hawkins to ask permission to accompany the boat to the estuary.

'If I can find fruit trees it will help us bear the voyage better.'

Hawkins looked at him closely, then said, 'Take Chamberlain and two others from the watering party.'

'Thank you, General.'

As they rowed half a league northwards, parallel to the shore to gain the river mouth, the sun began to sink towards the flat western horizon. It was to be the last trip to the river and the oarsmen stroked slowly, their arms aching from a long day's work. Tavistock took the tiller and eyed the darkening eastern sky with caution. All around the boat the sea was chopping up, and a fresh breeze was blowing up stronger by the minute.

A night storm coming, he decided as he watched pregnant rain clouds rolling down from the north. It's a bad omen. The season of hurricanes has trapped us here far too long for comfort. It should have blown itself out by now. Our ships just aren't built to work to windward. We need a foremast with topsails and some way of bracing the main course so we can stay closer to the wind. With a high forecastle and poop deck too much of the wind bears on a ship's sides, making her heel and spill her sailpower. To work the Indies we must have ships with a deeper keel, a hull that sits lower in the water presenting as little a target as possible to the wind, or to Spanish cannon.

They landed on a muddy spit that flanked the estuary and while the barrels were being filled he led his detail along the shore. They found guavas and took a few score in a canvas bag. Chamberlain returned laden with what looked like small cucumbers. 'The Indians call the fruit *nochole*. I brought all I could carry.'

'Are there more?'

'Many, Captain.'

Tavistock adjusted the strapping on his sling and looked at the twilight sky. It gets dark fast at these latitudes, he thought. There was no moon and no stars would shine through the overcast tonight. In the bay *Minion* was showing riding lights. He checked how long the water barrels would take to fill, and picked up the last canvas sack.

'There's time. Show me where.'

They reached the clearing quickly and began to pick the fruit. Overhead, large bats whirled in spectacular loops and all around in the forest night insects and frogs began their chirruping calls.

'I've been thinking, Captain. Maybe I should volunteer to stay.'

Tavistock looked at the steward with surprise. He liked the man's gentle nature, one he kept well, and with dignity, among the coarseness of shipboard life.

'I thought you planned to marry, Chamberlain.'

'So I do, Captain, but I have debts. Amy and me would benefit from the pay over a year's marooning. It'd be like making another voyage.

She'll wait for me.'

'If you take my advice, Chamberlain, you'll take your chances in the lottery with the others and put thoughts of volunteering out of your head. Leave such decisions to Almighty God.'

'But you volunteered to stay, Captain.'

Tavistock cleared his throat. 'Aye – but that's different.'

Chamberlain fell silent and Tavistock moved away, regretting his words. It had set him thinking about home again, and had opened for inspection the raw complications of his lot. He had a wife and son at home, and a debt of duty to them. But there was more than one kind of duty. How could a man ponder the debts of his own life, especially when that life was owed to his own brother? A brother who was probably dead, but who might even now be chained in some stinking Spanish torture hole, looking vainly for rescue? How could he begin to set a value on such a thing, when it was in terms of his own family? Then there was the duty he owed John Hawkins, a debt sharpened by the loss of the *Swallow* and by his unpardonable insubordination. Finally, there was the duty he had to the men – all of them. Many he had known for all the years of his life, all now faced marooning or starvation. It was too much for an honest man to properly comprehend.

He reached up for another wild fruit and felt something whistle past his head. He heard it thud into the trunk of a tree and realised instantly what it was.

'Jesus God, Chamberlain! Run for the boat!' he shouted, dropping his bag of fruit and pulling a primed pistol with his good hand. Another arrow speared the ground by his foot. In the semi-darkness he could not see how many there were, but he knew that Indians who lived by their bows did not generally miss a target twice.

They ran back toward the beach, Tavistock trailing, trying desperately to cock the mechanism of his gun. When it clicked home he steadied it and attempted to discharge it into the foliage at his back. An agonising quarter second passed as the flint sparked and fizzed then there was a bright flash and a loud report.

He heard a yell and caught a movement in the brush, but did not wait to see what emerged. He and Chamberlain gained the beach together, scrambling breathlessly toward the boat. More arrow shafts whistled through the air and stuck in the mud ahead of them. The gunshot had alerted the men who were waiting in the boat and they acted, some heaving it into the surf, others coming forward to cover their retreat with pistol fire.

Only when all five were inboard and the prow was bursting through the waves did a dozen long-haired figures break from the treeline and run down to the beach, yelling and waving their arms.

The oars carried the Englishmen away from the shore quickly and into the river current.

Tavistock counted heads. Two of the shore party were missing. It's too late, he thought. Nothing for it but to pull for the ship. The wind favoured them and as they came alongside Hampton questioned him about the missing men.

Tavistock explained.

'Savages?' he grunted. 'Better say nothing to afright those bound for the shore. Their lots have been cast already.'

As soon as they had hoisted the water barrels from the boat, Hampton ordered it filled with the luckless. In their absence, Chamberlain and four of the watering party had been appointed to go ashore.

'Then, my decision is made,' he said to Tavistock. His eyes were full of fear now. The attack had badly shaken him.

'God go with you, John Chamberlain.'

'And you, Captain.'

They clasped hands.

'Tell your shipmates it'll be best to try for Panuco. Fifty miles up-river. You'll find Spaniards there.'

Tavistock twisted off his ring. It was of gold and bore a large black stone on which was carved a phoenix in flames; it was the first time he had taken it off in seven years.

'Take this.'

'Oh, no, Captain —' Chamberlain tried to protest, but was quieted.

'I'll see your Amy receives her gold. If you find my brother John alive, give him this ring as a pledge that I will come back for him — and for you all.'

The steward slipped the ring inside his shirt and climbed over the gunwale into the bucking boat. As it drew away from the side a dousing rain began to whip the sea. The crew lined *Minion*'s side, waving and shouting words of hopeful parting.

Chamberlain watched the ship grow small. After landing he stood on the beach a little way apart from the hundred others who huddled together for comfort. He drew the ring from its secret pocket and slipped it on, but it was too big for his fingers. Although the rain drove into his eyes, he continued to watch, staring blindly at the points of light that were all that could be seen of the old, familiar world, until they at last were extinguished and he knew with finality that he would never see England or his Amy again.

Chapter 3

The two women sat together, alone at the rear of Don Luis Zegri's house, in the cool shade of an open veranda amid a riot of heavy-scented blooms. But their peace had been shattered by the new prisoner. The sight of the newly captured Englishman filled the younger woman with wonder and excitement. She was Maria de Escovedo, daughter of Don Bernardino de Escovedo, Knight of Castile and owner of one of the big *haciendas* – estates, near Mexico City. At the request of her father she had left Madrid to join her family, to attend at her mother's sickbed. That was the official reason Don Bernardino had put in his letter to the King; he had, of course, said nothing about the rape, nor the delicate matter of the *Infante*.

Beside her sat the regal Doña Isabella, meticulously embroidering a cloth with tiny stitches. In her early forties, devout, upright, and of the generation that had flowered in the glorious days of the Emperor Charles, she had been brought to Mexico by her husband, the Viceroy. But she had suffered constant sickness on the voyage. She hated the ship, she hated Mexico, she even appeared to hate Don Emilio. And she hated with such vehemence that, by the end of the passage, Maria thought she must hate life itself.

The new prisoner, Maria saw, wore nothing but ragged breeches and caked filth. He was shackled at wrist and ankle. Each of the three soldiers who led him held a long rope attached to his iron collar like those used to subdue valuable slaves without damaging them. Mud matted his hair and beard, but he looked around him with unbounded interest, and there was something else about him, a certain pride of bearing that gave him dignity.

It's two weeks since the great battle, she thought. During that time he must have been hiding in the mangrove swamps or in some secret lair in the five-hundred-*fanega* plantations that lay beyond the fringes of the town. Had the soldiers captured him? Had he given himself up? Or was he perhaps scented by one of Pedro Gomara's lurchers while searching for food?

The noise from the prison increased. At the sound of his shipmates, she saw him put his fingers to his lips and heard him blow a distinctive piercing whistle that brought a clamour of approval from the captives. When he passed the veranda he was fifteen paces from them. What happened next brought a rush of blood to her cheeks because he looked directly at her, stopped, and, before the guards could react, affected a courtly bow. He was swiftly kicked down for his insolence, but he fought back even though he was weak and the chains that bound him were heavy.

With deft jerks on the ropes the soldiers strangled him into the dust, and began dragging him along like a dog. But he was not a dog, he was a man. And he had showed them that he had spirit.

'They should all be killed,' the older woman snapped. 'They are not Christian men, they are no better than the painted savages who live in the jungle!'

'Oh! How can you say that, Doña Isabella? Their souls belong to God for all their evilness.'

Despite herself Maria's eyes continually strayed towards the gaol. She found herself fanning the blood from her cheeks under Doña Isabella's questioning eye.

'They are even worse than savages. They stink! Can't you smell them, Maria?'

'No man smells sweet in a prison cell.'

'But Maria, you misunderstand me. Theirs is a reek no water can wash away. These English smell of heresy. The only remedy for a stink like that is burning.'

Doña Isabella regarded the younger woman silently. She had seen the way the officers of the guard looked at her with the kind of half-concealed longing men reserve for the beautiful and the impossibly out of reach. Maria's skin was blemishless, honeyed-gold and her eyes dark and moist under fine black brows that sometimes arched with annoyance.

I can see you secretly glancing at the prison, Maria de Escovedo, she thought. How delighted you were in your foolish pride when that heretic bowed just then. Are you still a virgin? Or have you let some Madrid courtier spoil your prospects? We've been together nearly three months now but you've told me almost nothing. Have you been disgraced at Court like your sister was? Are you secretly with child? Is that really why you've come to this hell on earth? Well, pregnant or not, your good looks won't last long here, my dear. Mexico is the uttermost end of the earth. I hate it. And I rue the day my husband's honour forced him to involve himself with the King's personal intrigues.

She scratched through the thick material of her sleeve at the bites that itched and itched. You gave no thought to my comfort, Emilio. You should have listened to me. Why couldn't you see that it would all end in misery? Can it be that you still imagine that the King has honoured you by sending you here? Perhaps you were infected by Don Carlos's devils. This is exile! You should have known better than to have anything to do with the *Infante*.

She shifted to ease the pain in her back.

Maria said, 'Don Luis tells me that Vera Cruz is the oldest city in Mexico, that Hernan Cortés came here fifty years ago to found it.'

Doña Isabella grunted. 'Did he also tell you that Cortés burned all his ships here to prevent his *conquistadors* deserting him?'

'He says that this very porch is made from the wood of Cortés's flagship.'

The drone of voices filtered from inside the house. The Viceroy's anger punctuated the proceedings at intervals as the enquiry into the battle continued. Maria strained her hearing, following the testimony, knowing already what the outcome must be.

'Are you listening to me, Maria?'

'Yes, Doña Isabella. Of course. You know I am.'

Maria touched the bleached, cracked wood of the veranda's rail. Close by, a trail of minute red ants followed a sinuous path up the whitewashed wall, carrying tiny offerings of tribute to their ant king. Yes, she thought, I listen to you far more than you imagine. I'm listening to you now, I listened to you on the ship and I listened to your sleeping secrets. I understand what is going on in your husband's inquiry, and I know that it's little to do with the truth.

Don Emilio was trying to insulate himself against blame for the loss of the King's ships, but the Admiral was too experienced, too wily to be entrapped. His Vice-Admiral, however, was much younger, full of courage and enterprise, the sort of man who considers only the problem in hand and pays little regard to consequences. Captain Ortega would be easy prey, the perfect choice for a scapegoat. How I despise you for what you are doing to him, Don Emilio. I know what kind of man you are. You have no honour – in battle or out of it.

She remembered standing at her high balcony that terrible morning two weeks ago. She had just come ashore and had marvelled at the size of the room she had been given in Don Luis Zegri's house. After so long at sea every odour here was piquant: horses, the scent of jasmine, the warm, yeasty smell of new-baked bread. After long weeks confined to the tiny cabin and cramped walkway that overhung the stern of the *Trinidad*, this was like paradise. A New World indeed, but, oh, how the floor seems to shift and sway with every step! Will I ever get used to dry land again?

It was an imposing house, the grandest in Vera Cruz, as befitted the *Alcalde* – mayor – and her room was clean and white with a tall ceiling and a balcony surrounded by a worked iron rail wound with creepers that showered the street with vermilion petals each time the wind blew.

She had been honoured by the doting Mayor because of her father's standing, and her window had a magnificent view of the harbour. She had thrown open the shutters that morning, filling the room with sunlight. The turquoise bay had glittered like a thousand gemstones, and the ships of Don Francisco's fleet had seemed like so many small toys. And below, in the street, Gonzalo had ridden by on his bay horse, followed by three servants who had walked all the way from Mexico City, and she had not recognised him in his smart uniform.

There had been heavy linen meshes rolled and taped back over the bed; her new maid, Clara, promised that every night she would check carefully that there were no gaps to let in the bloodsucking *tequani*. She had sent the girl to bring fresh flowers, and had been turning down the sheets of the big bed and testing the softness of the feather mattress when it had happened.

At first she had thought it a ceremonial salute, but as the cannonades had begun to fill the wind with sharp cracks, the balconies had become crowded with excited watchers and she had run to her own. There were shouts of encouragement and the sight of running men in the street below. Out in the harbour ships had begun to move, then she had watched in disbelief as the biggest of them, a great beflagged galleon of a thousand tons, had blossomed into an enormous ball of fire. Seconds later she had felt the shock as the sound of the explosion carried to her; she had felt it across her chest and stomach like a physical blow.

And she could still feel it now.

'No doubt my husband will deal with them very soon,' Doña Isabella said. 'I can't imagine why he hasn't hanged them already. That way they could have been burned with the dead bodies. Ugh! How they make my flesh creep to watch them. They are base and filthy and they gabble away in their vile tongue, saying I don't know what terrible things.'

Maria fluttered her fan and watched Doña Isabella's brass thimble dance across the circle of linen. 'Their countrymen have caused your husband so much trouble, but aren't these gentlemen the hostages that were exchanged before we were permitted to enter harbour?'

'You cannot call them gentlemen, Maria. You cannot call any heathen Englishman that.'

'I suppose your husband is right to call them pirates.'

'Did you see the gesture that one just made to me? Such indecency! Such lewdness.'

'He only bowed to us, Doña Isabella.'

Doña Isabella's needle paused. Mildly, she reproached her companion. 'How dare you defend him, you good for nothing? Let me tell you, Maria, I know their English manners very well indeed. Fourteen years ago, when I was little older than you are now, I was taken to their despicable little island in the retinue of our good King Philip. He was a prince then, twenty-six years old, and the woman he was to marry was thirty-seven. She was Queen Mary of England. Of course, she was half Spanish – her mother was from Aragon – but her other half was purest English filth spawned by that fat, godless swine King Henry. Although

Mary was a Catholic, there is no doubt that the curse of her father's heresy passed to all his offspring.'

Doña Isabella crossed herself.

'Oh, yes, it's true that there is no life outside Spain. No *civilización*.'

'Not even here, in the Empire, Doña Isabella?'

'Especially not here.'

Maria snapped her fan shut. You talk as if Spain was paradise, she thought. But it's not. And for years the Court in Madrid has been a terrifying hell. King Philip had married once before. In his teens he had wed Mary of Portugal who had borne him a lunatic son, Don Carlos. The thought of that cackling, misshapen monster haunted her still. Insanity had run in his mother's family for generations. The *Infante* had been born mad and as the years passed and his father absented himself more frequently from his capital, Don Carlos's vindictive rages had steeped the Imperial Court in fear and loathing.

Maria's stomach tightened as she recalled the royal maniac who had terrorised her sister and made her time in Madrid a living hell. Oh, yes, I remember you, Don Carlos. They had to cut a hole in your head to let out the spirits that tortured your soul. The same hell-demons drove you to torment anyone that came near you. You who in high summer slept naked on a bed of Pyrenean ice. You who roasted dogs and rabbits alive in your apartments. You who flayed horses to death to glory in their agony. And you who whipped my sister half to death before you raped her. And nothing could be done because you were the King's son. You're dead now but your immortal soul will never rest.

Maria forced the evil thoughts away. Very soon now she would meet her mother and father again. It was almost ten years since they had been together as a family. Ten years! When a young girl she had been sent to Spain with her sister to live with her aunt, a lady-in-waiting at the King's Court, and learn refined manners. Very soon, she thought, and breathed the air of a New World that meant freedom to her.

Maria fingered the worn figure of Christ on her big pendant crucifix and recalled the stories she had heard about England and its tragic Queen. The burnings and the bloodshed and the imagined pregnancies. How Mary must have prayed to God for a son to settle the succession, but her womb had been barren, and though her monthly bleeding had stopped it was not through being with child. The next year, 1555, her father-in-law, the Emperor Charles, grown weary beyond endurance, had retired to the monastery of Juste and abdicated all worldly matters, leaving the Holy Roman Empire to his brother Ferdinand and Spain to Philip. There had been a tearful farewell between Philip and Mary at Greenwich when he had left England, but many said that he was thoroughly glad to be gone from its dank shores and his lard-faced wife.

In her consuming desire to bring the English to Catholicism, and perhaps to bring her husband back to her once more, she had rounded up the chiefest and loudest among the Protestants and sent them to the stake. Hundreds were burned alive, denied the luxury of a last-minute recantation that would have meant strangulation before the faggots were blazed. But Philip had been embroiled in complex intrigues against the French and the French-sponsored Pope, the consequences of which were far too important to jeopardise for the company of an ageing, dropsical Englishwoman.

Only after three years, when the campaign turned on the English-held port of Calais, did he return to her side, and then for just four months. Again the phantom pregnancy came, again Philip left her. Calais fell and Mary was sucked down into a deepening melancholy. Her own people, whose salvation she had so strenuously sought, hated her and blamed her for losing the last English foothold on the Continent. That autumn, the Emperor Charles had died along with his sister, Mary of Hungary. Even Mary Tudor's staunch friend, the Archbishop, Cardinal Pole, was dying in his palace at Lambeth. With them died the vision that Mary had dreamed with Philip of a Europe once more united in the blood of Christ.

Her life must have seemed so futile, Maria thought. Her husband estranged from her, alone and denied love. With nothing more to live for she had died, childless and despised, leaving her realm and her crown to her half-sister.

'. . . and that hellcat, the bastard Elizabeth, usurped her throne.'

'I'm sorry, Doña Isabella, what did you say?'

'That mistress of heretics who sits on the throne of England – she stole the Crown, no?'

'Oh, yes.'

A *mestizo* servant brought them lemon juice in a cool, earthen pitcher from the stone cellars under the house. It tasted tart and sharp on her lips. Maria looked again at the prison. After a while, she said, 'What do you think Don Emilio will do with the hostages?'

Doña Isabella laid aside her needlepoint. She frowned, glancing up at the prison once more. 'Let us go indoors, Maria. I can see the heat is affecting you.'

As they reached the large airy staircase and began to climb Maria heard the sound of halberd butts crashing to the flagging as the viceregal guard presented arms. It was the Admiral, come with impeccable timing, to plead, no doubt, for the life of his second-in-command.

'Was it not Spanish enterprise that discovered the New World and the force of Spanish arms that subdued it? Then, by God it will be unto Spain that its tribute runs!'

Luzon heard the Viceroy's words blustering from the chamber. His gaunt notary, Lazaro, was seated patiently at his side and around the huge table were numbers of priests and lieutenants, aldermen and councillors.

The walls of the council chamber were thick and pierced with arched portals that had been barred with ornate wrought-iron grilles. Behind them, at a small table, the Admiral stopped, pulled off his gorgeously worked helmet and dabbed at his forehead where the headband had impressed a red mark. Above it his hair was cropped short, an even mix of grey and black. His shoulders were plated like a lobster's tail and his forearms and elbows encased in plate gorgeously scrolled with crosses and roses. He wore a white lace ruff-collar under his beard and a cobalt-blue silken sash drawn diagonally across his breastplate.

Even thin ceremonial armour cooks the body like an oven out here, he thought as he felt the sweat trickle down his back. How a gentleman suffers for his position in this world. Oh, to be serving in the Netherlands now, under the Duke of Alva. Oh, to be a man of action once more!

He stuffed his gloves inside his morion and put it under his arm. He had spent a difficult morning on the island of San Juan, watching the priests reconsecrating the chapel there after the traumas. For two weeks the stench of death had blown into Vera Cruz from the bloated washed-up corpses of the English that the Viceroy had ordered left there as a reminder.

'A reminder to whom?' he had asked, astounded. 'To my sailors? To the townspeople? To their slaves? To Captain Ortega? We are here to proclaim God's mercy to the savages, to serve God and His Majesty. Let me fire the bodies, Don Emilio, before they corrupt the air and the whole of Vera Cruz comes down with the plague.'

Three days later, reluctantly, the Viceroy had permitted it.

He went in, heralded by a sharp clash of halberds.

Don Emilio acknowledged him curtly and motioned him to a seat. Overhead a large rush paddle waved back and forth, pulled by a string in the hand of a small Indian boy. He crouched in the corner, his skin covered in the lumps that came from eating too much fish. His rhythmic wafts moved the air but could do nothing to dispel the flies that peppered the white walls, that tumbled and buzzed above the table.

The Mayor and two of his councillors were present. As were various officers of the viceregal staff and of the *flota*. All watched the proceedings gravely.

Don Emilio faced Ortega with a list of charges. 'You deliberately acted against my explicit orders, and your precipitate action cost His Majesty ten thousand quintals of cargo, including four hundred quintals of mercury without which the silver mines of Potosi will come to a complete halt. Seven ships are sunk or irreparably damaged. Four hundred of my men are killed. I have written to His Majesty informing him of this. I'm bound to say that if it were up to me I would have your belly opened and your entrails stretched around San Lorenzo Square.' He glanced briefly at Luzon. 'However, your Admiral reminds me that I am obliged to hold you until I receive instructions from Madrid.'

Ortega's stare was flinty. 'I acted wholly in good faith, Excellency.'

'You acted without honour, Captain Ortega. You failed me. You are
a traitor.'

'Before God, I merely followed my profession!'

Ortega lowered his head and stared fixedly at the floor before him.
Luzon could smell fear on his breath.

'So. You have nothing more to say for yourself?'

'Nothing, Excellency.'

'Then, hear my pleasure. I shall not take a traitor to Mexico City.
You will await the King's reply in Vera Cruz. In the *prisión*. Get him
out of my sight.'

The captain of the guard hesitated.

'The *prisión*, Excellency?'

'Did I not say so?'

'I am to confine Captain Ortega *with the Englishmen?*'

'That was my instruction.'

'But – they will tear him apart, Excellency.'

Don Emilio brought his hand crashing down onto the table. 'Do as I
say. Immediately. Or you will go with him.'

Luzon held his silence. Ortega was marched, white-faced, from the
room. As he passed, he looked at his Admiral but said nothing. Only
when the tribunal had been cleared and they were alone did Luzon draw
the Viceroy to the window and speak softly to him.

'The *flota* leaves for Spain the day after tomorrow, Don Emilio. I
must have Captain Ortega with me.'

Don Emilio turned to face him. 'That's impossible.'

'I cannot forget that it is I who am responsible for delivering the
King's bullion safely to Spain. Captain Ortega has assuredly shamed
himself, but he is a most able officer – and, unfortunately, essential to
the security of His Majesty's gold.'

'He stays here.'

'Surely in the interests of expediency –'

The Viceroy's eyebrows jerked up. 'Expediency, Admiral?'

'In the interests of *justice* may I suggest a compromise?'

'There are no compromises where justice or *hidalgo* honour is at
issue.'

'It is to protect your honour and mine, Excellency, that I beg this
favour of you.'

Luzon took a pace back. Don't crowd him, he thought. Give him
every chance to comply with good grace. It was always difficult knowing
precisely how to deal with Don Emilio de Martinez. He was as unpredictable as a left-handed swordsman. 'Otherwise . . . I cannot guarantee
the contents of my own report to His Majesty concerning the losses.'

Don Emilio stiffened. 'Am I to understand that you intend sending
separate dispatches to the Court?'

'That depends, Excellency.'

'On what?'

'On whether you and I can agree on Captain Ortega's future.'

The Viceroy bristled, then nodded shortly. 'Very well. I shall order him loaded with irons and confined aboard the *Santa Teresa* where he will pass into your jurisdiction.'

'Thank you. A very wise decision, Excellency.'

Don Luis Zegri hovered by the door. 'Excellency, may I ask what you intend to do with the English hostages?'

'I shall have them marched to Mexico City where they will be examined and then executed. You have no room for heretics and pirates here.'

'They are contraband traders and smugglers, but perhaps they are not pirates, Excellency,' the Mayor suggested hopefully.

Don Emilio's eyes strayed to Luzon. 'Perhaps Don Luis looks for the return of English ships carrying gold for ransom?'

The Mayor's voice quavered. 'I seek only justice, Excellency.'

'Well, if they are not pirates they are certainly heretics, and don't you burn heretics here in the City of the True Cross?'

Don Luis's jaw flapped, and the Admiral took up his cause.

'Doubtless Father Tomas would condemn them without hesitation, but he is a Dominican – we call them the "Dogs of God" in Valladolid. It strikes me that no matter how unlikely the chance of an English vessel coming this way again perhaps Don Luis may be successful in trading the lives of a few worthless sea rats for gold. I'm sure Vera Cruz has a good use for any extraordinary sums of revenue that come its way.'

The Mayor began to nod, then stopped abruptly.

'You seem remarkably ready to make light of the King's law. I say these men are pirates!' Don Emilio insisted, adding acidly to Luzon, 'Was not your own ship, the *Todos Santos*, blown to hell by them? Did you not see with your own eyes the *San Felipe* burned to a hulk? Yes, they are destructive vermin, and they must be stamped out!'

The Mayor said, distantly, 'Perhaps they will be back.'

Luzon saw the longing in Don Luis's eyes. Gone were the days when an English barque might sail quietly into a Spanish port with a hold full of Guinea Negroes and good, cheap English cloth. Gone too were the commissions amicably arranged in a spirit of mutual gain.

Don Emilio inspected the Mayor, revealing his teeth in an indulgent smile. 'That is why the King in his wisdom sent me here. A new sword cuts clean and His Majesty's orders are quite explicit. He foresees further incursions unless the English and French can be shown that we have the will to protect our empire. All ports are to be fortified and garrisoned in strength. No foreign shipping is to be permitted leave to trade or suffered to use our anchorages. If the previous *corregidors* of the Caribbean had been more scrupulous about His Majesty's laws we would not be in this position now.'

'Fortification is very expensive, Excellency,' Don Luis said, aghast at the Viceroy's words. 'How will His Majesty be able to pay for the work?'

'You will find a way, Don Luis, I'm sure of that. You seem to have a most – enterprising populace.'

'Only when the *feria* comes is Vera Cruz as you see it. Ordinarily, our city is a humble and wretched place.'

The frenzied *ferias* that sprang into being upon the arrival of the plate fleet transformed Vera Cruz and every mean hamlet within fifty miles of the port into a boisterous market packed with traders, freebooters, harlots, ship-jumpers and revellers. As far inland as Jalapa the fairs blistered with soldiers and traffickers dicing and drinking for weeks on end, buying and selling wine, paper, glass, cloth, jewels, anything and everything disgorged by the ships.

'As I see it, the sole reason for these *ferias* is that in Mexico no one is willing to work for a living. You're all too busy digging silver and gold to make things for yourselves. Everything has to be brought in from Spain. Isn't that so, Don Francisco?'

Luzon made an ambiguous gesture. As he watched the Viceroy pick fastidiously at a speck on his braided sleeve, questions came unbidden to his mind. Why were you sent here? Is it, as you claim, to enforce the King's orders and to protect the Indies from English traders? True, these smugglers undercut Spanish goods, but they are hardly threatening the stability of the Empire. Did Philip send you here to deal with them? Or was it for another reason altogether? To remove you from the Court? Perhaps it's easy to understand why the King would want to banish you to faraway Mexico, Don Emilio. You're a zealot, a rash champion of lost causes, and because of that you're a danger to him despite your devotion to the Crown.

The Mayor wafted at a fly. 'Have I permission to ransom the English?'

'Perhaps I need to make my position quite clear to you, Don Luis. I will tolerate no infraction of His Majesty's law while I am Viceroy.'

'Of course, Excellency. May I ask what you plan to do with the English?'

'I have not yet made a decision. Since I intend to remain here for some weeks yet, there is no need.'

Don Luis raised a cheerless smile. 'It's just that with so many extra people in town, so many malefactors and rogues, we have need of prison space.'

'Please don't trouble me with the details of your arrangements, Don Luis. You can't expect me to deal with every minor problem.'

'Of course not, Excellency. But if we could just make a little bit more room –'

'Enough. I will make my decision presently.'

Luzon's thoughts turned once more to the King. Whatever else he may be, Philip is meticulous. He makes no move unless it is thrice considered, laid aside and considered once again. His method is all to him. Don Emilio's impetuousness must therefore affront him. So what better place for the man than slumbering Mexico? Here he can busy himself with trifles while the King directs his Empire through the Commissioners in Seville, the *real* centre of power. So long as gold continues to flow across the ocean as it has done uninterruptedly these past fifty years then you can do as you please. But I'd give a year's pay to know what you did to upset the King, Señor Viceroy! What precisely was it that brought you here?

The Admiral's reverie was disturbed by a commotion at the door; it was the lieutenant Don Emilio had put in charge of the hostages, exquisitely uniformed, immaculate, pleased with his own efforts. He broke through to the Viceroy's presence.

'We have captured another Englishman, Excellency.'

Don Emilio regarded the man coldly. 'Another Englishman?'

'Yes, Excellency. I personally caught him on the south side, trying to creep into the city.'

'What have you done with him?'

'I threw him in with the others, Excellency.'

'Quite correct. Good work, Escovedo.'

'Thank you, Excellency.'

Luzon's eyes followed as the man scurried away loaded with the Viceroy's approval. Why incarcerate this one with the others? he thought. If I were you I'd interrogate him before he infects the rest with lies. Aloud he said, 'I wonder how many more of them came ashore. I shouldn't be surprised if they sailed ten leagues up the coast and landed an armed party. I would have. There could be hundreds of them crouching in the jungle. Personally, I'd double the guard.'

Don Luis paled, but the Viceroy leaned back in his carved seat. 'Let them come. We're a match for any vermin-ridden Englishmen. How many does that make in your gaol, Don Luis?'

'Thirteen, Excellency.'

'Ah, an appropriate number to eat a last supper together, no?'

They roared with delight when he told them.

'We hit her just right. Dropped a burning hot ball right into her powder room and she went to pieces with a couple of hundred men aboard.'

'You're the Devil himself with shot, Gunner!' Thomas Ellis said, grinning broadly so that his big gravestone teeth and red gums showed.

'T'was a true eye God gave you, John Tavistock. No mistake.'

'More luck than judgement, Master Barrett.'

'Verily, 'twas a bang that shook the foundations of Vera Cruz. We thought it the *Jesus* blowed up by their treachery.'

'So the Spaniards said nothing to you?'

'They taunted us with promises beforehand, the proud bastards. But nought since! They daren't admit to nothing now!'

'None of us speaks enough of their gobbling tongue, Gunner.'

'Maybe that accounts for their bad grace in putting you in this mean guesting house.'

Barrett cleared a space in the straw-covered flagging. 'When we were first come unto the town the Governor showed himself right severe to us. These arse-sucking gaolers took our swords and our money and locked us in here.'

'They stole away my louse comb and pocket dial,' Horne, the purser, said sourly.

The cell in which they were confined was cramped, five paces square, with a central stone pillar and a high window in each of the two end walls, one looking into a cobbled courtyard, the other onto the street. The courtyard was sinister, furnished with *picata* and whipping stake so that the prisoners preferred to take the air by the higher front window. The door was bound with steel, and riveted to a thick lock and hinges, while into all four walls, on which had been carved a thousand names and obscenities, iron rings were bolted. Even so, half of them were secured, the rest were chained to one another and had been taking turns to ride shoulders at the windows. Now, most were standing, some sitting with their backs to the wall.

John Emery, an experienced man who had lost an eye on the first Hawkins expedition, spat in disgust. Immediately flies settled on the green phlegm. 'The big feller with the keys at his belt come aboasting of what they planned. He threatened to hang us.'

'If this were Charing Cross a cove like you'd've slit his gizzard as soon as piss, Emery.'

'That's without a doubt.'

Barrett rubbed his stubbled cheeks. 'If but one of us had gotten to the ships. Just one!'

'It wasn't to be.'

Thomas Marks, an able hand, said, 'Aye, locked up here with three halfpenny loaves between us a day, bugger all to drink and not knowing what's happening. 'T'aint right.'

'Think yourself lucky you aren't aboard the *Minion*. She's a starvation ship,' Tavistock said, thinking about his brother. Had he survived so far? Or had Peter Grosse killed him with his doctoring? Could the *Minion* possibly get back to England?

'At least she's going somewhere,' Marks said.

'The General'll get her home.'

'Aye, to piss bile.'

'I saw a crew starve two year ago,' Emery said darkly. 'Frenchies they was, out of La Rochelle, and got the worst end of an argument with some wicked brutes off of the Skeleton Coast. There was one man aboard could feel his backbone through his belly. Weren't above four stone, poor bugger.'

Barrett lowered his voice. 'What's become of the others, Gunner?'

He told him of his escape. He had been suffocated by thick clouds of smoke that came from tar barrels on the fireship's beakhead, and he had caught alight when ropes saturated in burning pitch had trailed across his head and shoulders. With his shirt and hair in flames he had leapt blindly into the sea and thrashed out in hope to carry himself clear. The lasting image of an arm thrust through a hawsehole in the *Jesus*'s stern, and Señor Villanueva's terror-white face imploring him to come back and release him from the smoking cable store had stayed with him for a long time.

'Let all Spaniards roast in hellfire.' Peter Dean, a scrawny sea cook with thinning hair and quick, darting eyes let himself down from the window, his chains rattling. 'Seeing as the Spanish General's thrown his treaty over his left shoulder and pissed off up country, what's likely to become of us?'

Emery stretched himself. 'You can speak their poxy lingo, Gunner. Are they going to kill us?'

Tavistock made no answer.

'Yes!' Marks's voice was thick with scorn. 'I was on the *Lion's Whelp* in 'sixty-five when we went privateering against the Flemings an' all. We never had much mercy for Spanish crews. If'n we caught 'em we used to roll 'em up in their own sails and chuck 'em in the sea.'

'We don't know what they intend,' Tavistock said, hating the way hopelessness turned quickly into easy acquiescence in some of them.

'That's the worst part, Gunner – not knowing!'

'Jesus, I feel as rough as a ragman's strumpet.'

John Bone was despairing. He came out of the corner and stood close to Tavistock and breathed on him. His body was sour and his teeth were so rotted that the stink made Tavistock recoil. Even aboard ship he was watershy. He was a sailmaker's mate and had spent most of his time festering in the sail-loft away from the weather. He had lost a lot of weight. 'They're starving us. We've been stuck here to die. I haven't had a mouthful in two days. Did you bring any water with you, Gunner?'

Tavistock looked at the man then turned quickly away.

'Ignore him, he's raving. He's bleeding at the arse, Gunner. It's the bloody flux.'

'That or the yellow fever.'

Forrest, an able hand, small and ratlike, whose feet were anchored in bilboes, laughed. 'Just our luck to be banged up with a bleeding arsehole like 'im. He drinks all the water and then cries for more, and he stinks the place out with his eruptions.'

Tavistock continued to recount how he had come to land after abandoning the flagship. The *Minion* had been no more than fifty yards away, but was already picking up the wind. He had known that to try to swim after her would have meant exhaustion and death, so he had struck out for the shore, wading through the muddy shallows with the last of his strength. He had lived for two weeks in an abandoned Indian shack made of dried leaves, sleeping in short bursts, ranging the land at night, stealing to eat, trying to get hold of a weapon with which to rescue his compatriots.

Tavistock eyed the rough stone gutter that led from the corner of the cell. It was black with midden-flies and stank worse than Bone's mouth.

'I supposed I'd find you in some such hellhole, but before I could devise a scheme to get you out I was myself taken.'

'Hellhole is right.' Anthony Jacob, one of the *Jesus*'s officers, got up. He untied the lacing of his codpiece and sluiced the sewer with a stream of dark urine, sending the flies up in a cloud. 'We're greatly annoyed by night insects,' he said languidly. 'The Indians call them *tequani*, though the Spanish name is *mosquito*. They're much like a gnat but they have a wonderful appetite for blood. If you kill them while they're sucking, the bite swells up in an itching weal, but if you let them drink their fill they do no damage other than a fleabite –'

Bone screamed and brushed at his lap in a frenzy. There was a chorus of mouth-filling oaths, then raucous laughter.

'Get it off me! Get it off!'

Emery elbowed him viciously. 'Keep still, you little shit-monger!'

A great ginger-coloured spider, the size of a man's hand, had dropped onto Bone from above. At the street window there was the sound of childish laughter and running feet.

'What's the matter? Scared of a spider?'

Emery picked up the spider by its bulbous abdomen and turned it over so that its jointed legs grasped at the air. 'That's the best yet! Bloody brats!' He offered it to Bone who cowered back in horror, his face twisted and flushed pink. 'No! Please! Take it away, Emery. I can't take spiders. I hate 'em, I tell you!'

'Woooo!' Emery held the spider closer and squeezed it so that its legs struggled. 'It's only a little ol' spider, Johnny lad. Listen 'im plead for mercy.'

Jacob came over and examined the creature. 'What say we drop it on the next Spanish lady to pass this way?'

The two went across to the window, leaving Bone panting in his corner.

'Listen!' Tavistock said, turning to Barrett. 'Don't you hear that?'

All eyes turned to stare at him, listening.

'God save us!'

Those who could crowded to the rear of the cell to watch what was happening in the courtyard. The screams grew louder and then a troop of soldiers came in sight with two slaves struggling fearfully in chains. Tavistock pressed up against the bars and watched.

'What they saying, Gunner?'

'I can't tell.'

'It's a whipping!'

'No.'

An officer read sentence – something about running away, as far as Tavistock could tell. Then he barked orders at the soldiers who stripped the slaves and hoisted them to hang side by side, spreadeagled and upside down from the timber whipping frame. Their ankles were tied to the crossbar, their hands were secured behind their backs and their heads dangled a foot off the ground. A priest stood beside them mouthing incantations.

Jesus Christ, they can't be! Tavistock thought, as he realised what he was about to witness. No crime, not even treason, warrants that. They're going to use the axe on them.

He turned his face away, unable to watch. Only Emery remained, gripped by the grotesque horror of it. His face contorted as the screams intensified and they heard the sounds of a butcher's cleaver biting into flesh.

Then one of the voices stopped.

There was a deafening silence. Tavistock felt the sweat pouring from him as the methodical chopping began again. When the screams died altogether Emery shook his head and slid down to the floor.

'They've cut them in two,' he said. 'From arse to Adam's apple. They're dripping there like four sides of beef.'

Not a man spoke for many minutes. The truth of their position was suddenly very real to them. Despite the futility of trying, escape was on all their minds, and when they spoke again, they began to ask Tavistock sober questions.

'The city's packed with people. Yesterday I lay in one of the great buttressed trees that line the road, quietly, to espy the town and look out for an opportunity. I saw a procession. It passed right beneath me – the Viceroy on horseback with five of his guard around him – and I could have dropped on him if I'd had my shark-knife and slit his throat.'

'It's a pity you didn't, Gunner. He'll surely do for us.'

'How were you taken?'

'I made a mistake. A slave-child saw me when I hid in a ditch. She went running from the field to her mother. The mother raised a hue and cry.'

'And?'

'Next I know there's most of the garrison pointing ordnance at my head.'

'Bad luck, Gunner. This place stinks of Satan.'

'The dice are agin us.'

'No doubt on it.'

'My balls are aching. Damn these bilboes!'

Marks shrugged. 'There weren't no chance of getting us out of here anyway, Gunner. When we saw you coming bound at the neck like that we hoped you'd been caught in a skirmish. We had hopes of a landing.'

Emery snorted. 'It ain't like the General to sail off and away without seeing what can be done for his boys.'

'Aye, a hundred lads with cutlass and small arms would see us right.'

'The *Minion* was packed tight with men when she took her leave,' Tavistock told them, quick to squash false hope. 'It was all she could do to shift herself. There are still five hundred booted troops in Vera Cruz, and a good half of them sober.'

William Lincoln held up a hand swaddled tight in his shirt. 'Cruel soldiery as my hurts testify, Gunner. They'd've cut a landing party to bits like these here fingers.'

Spanish regiments were the fear of Christendom, well-drilled, well-equipped and arrogantly certain of their prowess. All had heard the horrible stories that had come out of the Netherlands shortly after the Duke of Alva had descended on the rebellious province with his *tercios*.

'Cheerly, now. We're not forsaken yet, Billy-boy.'

'Did you find out anything that might save us, Gunner?'

There were noises outside. A heavy key in the lock.

'Ingléses perros! Luteranos! Enemigos de Dios!'

The door of the cell swung open, pushing Ellis aside. Then the sergeant gaoler entered. He stood just inside the doorway, a steel-tipped cane in his hand, his bushy black moustaches concealing his mouth as he looked about him. He spoke again, rapidly. It was an order.

'What does he say, Gunner?'

'He wants one of us.'

'Which one?'

A second Spaniard with big iron keys jangling at his belt pointed to Barrett and motioned him back.

'Go to Hell, you idol-worshipping son of a whore!'

Another took hold of Tavistock's wrist-chain but he pulled the man down, over him, looking for his knife. Emery threw himself at the third, tearing at the man's face with his bare hands. Then other soldiers began pouring into the cell, dragging out those who were not chained to the wall, beating down the others with truncheons.

They separated Tavistock and took him out into the courtyard, slamming the cell door shut once again on the others who crowded to the window shouting and reaching out to him helplessly.

One of the guards cracked a thonged whip at the window, laying open Emery's face where it pressed against the bars.

'Satan's blood! I'll have your eye for that, Spaniard!'

'God give me strength!'

'They're going to kill us all!'

Bone's voice quailed from the corner, 'Christ have mercy on our souls!'

Emery turned on him. 'Shut your mouth, I told you!'

'You an' all, Emery!' Barrett roared.

'Jesus God, what are they doing to him?'

More faces pushed the bars to witness the Gunner's fate. The Spanish sergeant had a thick bullwhip coiled in his hand. He ordered Tavistock stripped and shackled to the whipping post.

A Dominican friar in a black habit and crossed chasuble came to stand before him. The cowl was thrown back revealing a man in his forties, a grey-fringed tonsured head, a beak-like nose, face pinched and directed downwards in silent inner contemplation. Under his sandals the flagged yard was sticky with blood and flies buzzed up around them like the Devil's familiars.

He's communing with the Devil, Tavistock thought, his sweat frozen to his flesh. Wasn't it the black brotherhood who ran the Inquisition in Spain? Who tortured their captives into degradation until they abandoned their faith in God? His heart thumped faster and he felt his testicles shrivel. This is it, he thought. This is where I die. An example to the rest. They'll flay me and leave me to dangle. At least I'm first. At least I don't have to watch the others. I hope I can bear the pain without crying out. What if I foul myself? Jesus, let me die well. Oh, God help me to resist the monk's whisperings ... He began to pray furiously, the repetitive lines marching unceasingly through his mind, blotting out the world.

An Indian labourer wearing a shoulder yoke brought two pails of water and the sergeant poured one out over Tavistock's head. Then the Indian began to scrub at his body. The rubbing hands worked over his head and face, down across his neck and shoulders, then his chest and belly. His limbs were sponged right down to his fingers and toes. When he was quite clean the second bucket was dashed over him and the Indian began to towel him down with a rough cloth.

After a minute he was unshackled. He was still too shocked to speak, but when a shirt and a pair of fustian trousers were handed to him he put them on. Then leg irons and manacles were bolted back again on his ankles and wrists.

The friar motioned to the chief gaoler.

'*Marchad! Marchad, Inglés!*'

'Where are you taking me? he asked shakily.

The Dominican replied in heavily inflected English, 'To the Viceroy.'

Tavistock felt the mix of relief and soaring hope in his belly turn to water. 'The Viceroy?'

'He wishes to question you.'

'Me?' Tavistock's mind raced. The shock still gripped him and he felt lightheaded and shivery. 'But why me? What about the rest?'

The friar gazed at him with an unsettlingly earnest expression. 'The rest? *Where are they left by God's righteous judgement save in the mass of perdition where they of Tyre and Sidon were left?*'

Tavistock's flesh crawled at the friar's Latin. Oh, yes, he thought, you're one of the insane monks who speaks the Devil's riddles because plain speech would show your villainy. In my childhood I remember your brothers tightening the halters on the necks of women and children, using torment and fear as your tools until all England ran with blood.

My parents died because of pain-loving filth like you!

'But, why am I –'

'His Excellency has ordered that you be separated from the others, my son.'

'I'm not your son, monk.'

'As you wish.'

They marched him down the street named *La Calle de Los Tres Reyes*, past the long raised veranda where he had seen the Spanish woman, and left into a dusty square. On one side fruit vendors crouched in the shade, wrapped in coloured blankets and wearing straw hats, succulent fare spread out in front of them on rush mats; on the other a squad of thirty soldiers drilled with pikes to the insulting commands of a sergeant while an officer astride a dark bay barb looked on. Behind, the church, brilliantly white under the tropical sun, with angels in niches and a pair of great carved doors, and above, the Virgin Mary with rays blasting from her. Tavistock was led up the steps of the other big building that fronted the square. There was a column on each side of the main entrance, and within, deep pools of darkness that hid from the sun. It was surprisingly cool inside; a breeze channelled from windows on the seaward side played on his damp skin. He ran his hand through his hair, making it squeak as it flowed back over his head.

They made him sit in an ornate chair placed in the middle of the room. Through the large window he could see an iron-railed balcony and the anchorage of San Juan. His eyes went immediately to the *Swallow*, his brother's old command, and he thought again of Richard and knew that whatever happened he had already cheated Satan, swapping a better man for his own skin on the burning deck of the *Jesus*. A death for a death, that's fair. Let them do me in, now. I've already won and I'll go to the scaffold laughing. And I'll laugh in their faces now.

Then he thought of his mates stewing in filth and degradation and he knew that God had appointed him spokesman of them whether he liked it or not. He had a duty to try his best to secure their lives.

The Viceroy was seated at the centre of a table set across the room, a silhouette ten paces away. There were others beside him, armoured men, priests, town functionaries and a woman.

A pack of proud cats! Look at their vanity and disdain. What does he want of me? Tavistock asked himself, trying to impose discipline on his chaotic thoughts. Concentrate! It's hard to imagine, but what would I do in his position? What would I want to know? The ships? Our mission? An account of General Hawkins's mind? What? Perhaps there has been a landing like Emery thought. God help me to think! How do I keep Master Barrett and the others alive?

'What is your name? Do you understand me, Englishman?'

Tavistock stared stupidly at the Viceroy. There was a short, muttered exchange between him and the woman, then she asked in English, 'What is your name, heretic?'

'I am John Tavistock, but it's not I who am the heretic.'
'What did he say, Doña Isabella?'
She translated accurately.
'Perhaps you should warn him to be less proud. Tell him I am the Lord of this place and to mind his manners or I may choose to cut out his tongue.'
There was a pause, then Doña Isabella spoke again. 'He says – he says he could tell you nothing if you did that.'
'Make him understand that it is the Viceroy of New Spain he addresses.'
Tavistock listened without reaction.
'He understands that you are the Viceroy, Don Emilio Martinez, and calls you the King's own man.'
'Ask him where he thinks the two escaped English ships have gone.'
Doña Isabella's voice was staccato and shrill, the prisoner's reply calm and deliberate.
'He knows nothing of the location of the English fleet and adds that he would not tell you if he did.'
'Fleet?'
Beside him, the secretary dipped his quill, scrawled, and dipped again. Don Emilio's eyes roamed over the prisoner. An insolent puppy, he thought. I will drown you in the sea for your hubris. There is not enough time to let you learn deference by rotting in gaol like your fellows. In any case, Doña Isabella says that all English have the manners of animals, perhaps a spell hanging like a bat in the gyves would make you more respectful. To Hell with them all, he decided, suddenly weary of the interview. Don Luis is crying for the return of his prison, I'll simply let Friar Tomas burn them as he wants.
'He says that a fleet of English ships is waiting in twenty-seven degrees to ambush the *flota*. He knows that the silver ships sail round the Gulf to Havana then take advantage of the current of two and a half knots to assist them north through the Florida Strait.'
The Viceroy narrowed his eyes. You answer like a pilot, he thought. You are clearly no ordinary seaman, and by your bearing I judge that you're used to giving commands.
'Who are you, John Tavistock? What's your rank and how came you to be here?'
Tavistock's reply was concise. 'I am – or was – Gunnery Captain on the Queen's Majesty's ship *Jesus*, the same that you did burn with your fireship. Our General told you the truth. We were separated from our fleet by a hurricane two months ago and sought refuge in this place. When your crews turned treacherously on us, I was one of those that took out *Minion*, but after was cast into the ocean and swam for the shore.'
Don Emilio's pulse quickened. A gunnery captain, he thought exult-

antly. One of those that caused so much havoc among Don Francisco's galleons.

He turned once more to his wife, his face deadpan. 'And how came you to be a gunnery captain so young?'

'I have eight years in the casting of guns. It was thought I might test them in battle – to learn the better how to sink Spanish ships!'

When Doña Isabella translated his words the room erupted into indignation. The Viceroy quieted them. This was like a gift from Heaven! Madonna, such a prize!

'He came ashore after the battle. Two weeks ago. Ask what mischief he has caused in the interval.'

Tavistock gave a brief account.

'He claims that he has lived in the forest for two weeks since then.'

'Stealing food, no doubt?'

The Englishman replied, but Doña Isabella shook her head and laughed shortly.

'What does he say?'

'He's lying! A laughable transparency! He knows that you have trapped him. His answer was that he ate by snaring wild animals.'

'Tell him to fear not. I pardon him for the food he has stolen.'

'But, Don Emilio!'

'No, no. Tell him that exactly.'

The Viceroy's eyes watched John Tavistock carefully. He saw that his clemency had been understood the moment he had said it, not as the words were interpreted. So, you understand Spanish too, eh? Of course! Yes, I know you. You were the man Hawkins sent aboard my ship to ask favours. Then you must be a trusted man, in your General's confidence, privy to his strategies. I can certainly use you, John Tavistock.

He spoke directly to the prisoner: 'And the fleet of which you speak?'

Tavistock hesitated but saw he had been recognised. In Spanish he said defiantly, 'I will say nothing of the squadron save that it lies abreast the Bahama Bank in wait for your *flota*.'

'Is that where your General was heading? To a rendezvous at Bahama Bank? A rendezvous with English warships?'

'I'll tell you nothing more.'

Don Emilio sat back in his chair and stroked the tab of hair under his lip. He was disinclined to play cat-and-mouse with this arrogant young man any longer. Apart from anything else, protocol required that such a game must be played out before the local dignitaries; necessity had meant that Doña Isabella was present. It was demeaning for a Viceroy to be resisted in front of his wife and his functionaries. That morning he had read dispatches from the Governor of Cuba, and others from Castillanos in Santo Domingo. None of them had made mention of a fleet of English ships. I understand your reasons but you are a poor liar, Englishman. However, you have your uses. As for the rest, they can tell me nothing I don't already know. I will let the good father burn them on the beach as an entertainment for the townspeople.

'If you are obedient I may spare your life.'

'Obedient?'

'If you do as you are told. If you do not, I will order you burned along with the others.'

'Will you slaughter helpless prisoners of war?'

'War? England and Spain are not at odds. We are ancient allies. You, on the other hand, are merely piratical smugglers.'

'You fired on two of Her Majesty's vessels.'

'No insult to your monarch was intended. I merely wished to rid my coast of a gang of smugglers.'

'We are not smugglers.'

'You are undeniably heretics. In Spain, we always –' Ah, but this is not Spain, Don Emilio reminded himself. I was sent out of Spain by His Majesty. Only the King and I know the real reason I was sent here. Philip was at his wits' end. It was I who acted. It was I who saved his throne. It was I who prevented his crazy son Don Carlos fleeing to become a focus of intrigue against the kingdom. Yes, and it was I, with my own hands, who murdered him.

And how the King has repaid my loyalty! By assigning to me the task of fortifying the viceroyalty of Mexico he has swept me into obscurity. But I will return to Spain one day in triumph and the King will see that I am indispensable to him. For that, guns are required. Not old, obsolete guns, but guns like the English make, that combine power and aim and are accurate at long range.

He knew that the best Continental cannon makers were Flemings. Their foundries, which clustered around the rich cities of Ghent, Bruges and Antwerp, had manufactured most of the big guns on Spanish vessels. But the founders were Calvinists who could not be tempted into Spain at any price for fear of the Inquisition. And since the revolt many had fled to England, taking their guild secrets with them. If I can bring those secrets into Spain, our ships will become as invincible as our armies, he thought with growing excitement. We will be able to conquer the Ottomans in the Mediterranean and obliterate the Protestants in the Channel. Then, finally, we will destroy the French and unify the territories of Spain into a single domain. Any honour will be mine for the asking.

He folded his arms and regarded Tavistock thoughtfully, his decision made. Then he turned to Father Tomas and said, 'You will burn this heretic in thirteen days' time. Tomorrow you will begin burning the rest of them. One each day. For the glory of God.'

Chapter 4

A dark shape melted from the blackness and moved swiftly out from the cover of a rain-drenched oak copse before dissolving into sodden ground ten yards from the crossroads. There it waited in lethal silence for the lamplight to draw closer.

The light was ten yards away when it halted. Three – no, four of them, and an ox cart that wallowed in the mire so that the three men put their backs to freeing it from a rut while the girl led the beast forward, a smoky orange lantern waving in her hand to light the way.

That was the light that had driven Robert Slade to seek the copse of oak trees, tie his horse there and ready himself for murder. He squeezed himself against the earth and drew a concealed dagger smoothly from his boot as he watched the wavering light. With this serrated knife he had many times severed the strings of a horse's leg or cut a man's throat. He held his breath, feeling the hairs on his neck begin to rise like needles.

Reports said that this road had seen strange movements these past six months, unexplained visitors going up to the manor at Foot's Cray, foreigners and jacknasties of all kinds. By their sure-footedness he could see that these men knew the road well, had travelled it many times at night. By the accent of their rough voices, and the way they goaded their animals, he knew they were local Kentish men and acquainted with the sea. There could be only one explanation, Slade thought, not allowing himself to relax. There had been snow all week, turning, in the thaw, to hail and freezing rain. This was the first night in five when prints would not be left in the morning. The villagers of North Cray were bringing contraband ashore, landing it by night and moving it inland along the River Darent. Damn their souls! How they'd jump if they knew they were watched by Sir William Cecil's man, he thought. It's a powerful temptation to send them flying and put their cart into the Cray stream. Summary justice, as scum who bleed the exchequer deserve, but justice must wait. Secrecy drove me off the road and secrecy must drive me on to Foot's Cray.

He watched the cart lumber on until the voices were lost in the wind, the lamp red and distant like Mars on a summer night, then he stood up. He wore black boots and a black cloak. He had chosen a black mare from the stables, smeared her white flash with grease and lampblack before departure. Five years in Sir William's pay had taught him cunning in the art of carrying a message. From London via twelve staging-posts, riding twelve fresh horses, he could ride breakneck to Exeter in two days, or two days to Norwich, England's second city, or four to Newcastle in the far north, arriving lathered and next to dead. The ordinary post took twice that, changing men and horses, but a courier for the President of the Privy Council must carry letters in person, and swiftly. The security of the realm might some day depend on it.

He walked back down the road along the exposed sweep where rain and darkness cowled him. The stream gushed and bubbled, swollen with the melt. England was a hard country, a dangerous land, packed the length and breadth with perils. There were sucking bogs and lethal high moors, wolves, certain inns that preyed on the lone traveller, vagabonds with cudgels and others who stretched cords neck-high on fast straights. Each season brought its peculiar difficulties, now it was the back end of the year: a time of freezing fogs and clogged roads and pitch blackness when a man needed the gift of second sight to be a courier. Robert Slade had that gift. For half a dozen years he had been the best courier in all England, good enough to become what he was now: not simply a deliverer of the government's most secret messages, but an agent for his master, and for his Queen.

Only ten miles as the crow flies from the city of London, but night and November weather had turned the land here as dark and hostile as any in Europe. He unhitched his horse, led her from the rain-spangled spinney; a stand of gaunt birches glowed ghostly where the mare's breath touched them. Once back on the track he sped on, following the stream up from Dartford where the Greenwich road had taken him. A mile and a half further on he saw the sullen glare of lamps. Foot's Cray Manor, an old two-storey thatched house, twisted chimneys, wooden beams, redbrick, a garden of hedges surrounded by a high wall with studded wooden gates locked against the night.

He reined in and dismounted two hundred yards away. There was no sign of activity but he knew that the master of Foot's Cray always posted a man to watch the road. Tonight, foul weather or no, would be no exception.

Grimly he knew that he could afford to take no chances. Slade had never married. A wife and children were baggage he could not afford to carry, they were but hostages to fortune. In the world of politics friendships shifted, alliances were melted down to be poured into new moulds, powerful structures were intrigued against and undermined. Half a century ago, Henry the Seventh, the Queen's grandfather and progenitor of the Tudor dynasty, had maintained his hold on the Crown only by ruthlessly dismantling the power of the aristocracy. His son,

Henry the Eighth, had broken with the even greater power of Rome and then consolidated his success by stripping the Church of its wealth to pay off those he recognised as allies. Under the violent religious volte-faces the country had endured, first under Edward, then Mary and now Elizabeth, constant purgings of its ruling caste had occurred until all England seethed with the dispossessed. The new men who had risen up in their place were insecure, watchful and given to swift realignment in order to save their necks. The man I seek may be Sir William's most confidential associate, Slade thought, a Member of Parliament and a zealous Protestant, but a year ago his name was unknown and a year hence he might be fomenting rebellion. Didn't he angle for my services when we met at Richmond Palace? Didn't he seek to put me in his pay? Subtle questions that don't amount to evidence, but the intention was real enough. He's ever out to catch the unwary. But I'm not weak and I'm not greedy. I know my duty is to my own master, and I render fealty to one man alone. And to one woman.

He swore silently as he stumbled, his foot twisting in a rabbit hole. He searched the darkness but there was nothing. Carefully! It's on nights like this, after a slow ride, twelve miles by a roundabout way, that a man gets sloppy. He begins to think of his comfort and cut corners, but I'm different because I never do. I make it my unbending rule to take elementary precautions. Which is why I'm alive and others are not.

Again he led the mare off the road, patting her flanks to quiet her. He found a fence post and left her there, making his way to the wall where it backed onto the Manor's stables. He stared up at the circular dovecot then pulled his woollen neckscarf up over his mouth and nose to soak up his steaming breath. The wall was ten feet high. At its foot he leapt and caught the top. Silently, with great strength, he pulled himself up the crumbling brick and peered over into the yard. Rain drummed on the shingle roofs of the outbuildings and dripped from the stable eaves. Inside he saw a bay, two brown hakenays and, on its own in a separate stall, a big grey of sixteen hands.

A glow of satisfaction surged through him and he smiled. Discipline, he thought. That's all it takes. Nine times out of ten no result, but every now and then ...

The horse they had tried to hide was an Andalusian. A Spanish military breed. Very costly, and very rare in England. Slade knew it could not belong at Foot's Cray Manor. It raised its head and flared its nostrils, smelling the mare on him despite the rain. A young groom came up off his stool, alerted by the horse's behaviour, and began to look about warily.

Slade ducked out of sight. He lowered himself down, paused, listening, then crept back to his own horse, blowing softly on her muzzle as he arrived to reassure her in the darkness. Then he led her to the causeway, remounted and cantered to the gate.

A small, rectangular aperture opened in it, framing a thin face. 'Who are you?'

'Robert Slade, messenger to Sir William Cecil of the Privy Council, on official business.'

'Where's your papers?'

An envelope was drawn from Slade's glove and passed through. The small shutter closed. After a space the gate began to swing open.

He was admitted by a man in coat and hood. The groom appeared and led his horse away, remarking on what a fine mare she was, and the house servant, Thomas, met him at the door: huge, slow-moving, powerful, drawling, and as stupid as a dumpling.

'Announce me, Thomas.'

'I can't do that, Master Slade ...'

'Do as I say!'

Thomas looked dully past the windows of the vestibule and into the flagged hallway. The dark oaken walls were cast in relief by candlelight that guttered and spilled. The hall contained no tapestries, no carpets; only a long carved table and bench seat, like a pew, set under the candle holders. The servant banged the heavy door shut behind them but seemed to remain unconvinced that he should place Slade's imperative above his master's. A pool of water collected on the floor, where it dripped from the corner of Slade's cape.

'He said no one was to disturb him. On no account.'

'Yes,' Slade said, barely controlling his irritation with the servant. 'But he doesn't know that I am here.'

Thomas turned his moon face away and began to slouch down the hall. Slade followed him. Wooden doors stood to his left, all furnished with stout panels and ornate iron mechanisms that bore the obsolete arms of the undersheriff of London, and to his right small diamond-leaded windows bowed and shivered in their frames as the rain lashed them. Thomas's light knock on the furthest door was rewarded by silence: the hum of conversation beyond had paused. Impatiently, Slade tried the door handle. It was locked and would not move.

'Robert Slade?'

The voice was not entirely composed, a little irritated at the intrusion. Slade spoke up. 'Forgive me, sir. I have an urgent message for you.'

'Just a moment.'

Seconds later, the door swung open revealing a brightly lit interior, warmed by a roaring fire. It was opened by a man of about forty years. He wore a black felt skullcap, an unpretentious doublet with squared linen collar, and he sported a greying beard, clipped short. He was of medium height and light build, but he had piercing, dark brown eyes and a rich, soothing voice that revealed something of the qualities of mind that had carried him in a single year to a position of almost unparalleled influence in the realm. Officially, until last year, Francis Walsingham had been Member of Parliament for Lyme Regis. Now, although he held no official post, he had good cause to lock his doors securely and watch the road with care. He had lately assumed control of England's secret service and was now coordinator of her Continental network of spies.

'Thank you, Thomas, it's all right.' Walsingham closed the door and turned to Slade. 'Please sit down. It's an evil night and you're soaked.'

'That it is. Thank you, sir.'

Slade went over to one of two armchairs that had been pulled up close to the fire. As he sat down, a second door into the room opened, and a grotesque figure entered.

'Good news, I hope?' Groton asked. The cipher expert remained in the draughty doorway, hesitant. He was an old man: bent, rheumy and myopic. Slade shivered inwardly. Groton was malodorously diseased. Where the fleshy parts of his nose had eroded the septum was exposed, but over the deformity he now wore a hollow silver nose that made his voice ring incisively when he spoke. The bandaged, ravaged flesh of his hands was his greatest handicap and by the way he held objects Slade judged there was no feeling at all in the stumps of his fingers where the infection had first attacked.

'I should say not, Master Groton.'

'Ah, bad news travels quickest. Isn't that so?'

'And always on the dirtiest of nights.'

Groton watched as the messenger sat down. Slade was in the flush of his manhood, virile, sturdy, and full of arrogance. Silver-spurred and booted he was a match for any roadside detainer, but Groton did not like him. He seemed always to be sneering. And he feared the taint of leprosy mightily, though he tried not to show it. You crude, untutored lout, Groton thought genially, you're out of the same military mould as Alva's mercenaries. Wild bulls, thrashing around madly, destroying, stamping out civilisation under your cloven hooves. Why does a man like Cecil surround himself with men like you?

Walsingham offered the courier a pewter pot of ale, and Groton watched distastefully as Slade ran a glowing fire iron into it, making it fizz and foam.

What's the matter, Master Roger? he could almost hear Slade thinking. *Don't mulled ale square with your Continental ways? Ain't it Eyetalian enough for you?*

The owner of Foot's Cray on the other hand had sophisticated tastes. He was ever mindful of small courtesies, a fine intellect, though unskilled in the mathematics, a good Protestant, and a powerful accumulator of allies. They had first met in Paris in the years when Bloody Mary sat the throne. Fifteen fifty-three. As prudent men, they had both gone abroad on her accession; Walsingham then a student, fresh from his studies at King's College, Cambridge, and Gray's Inn, Roger Groton, an angry fifty-year-old academic, late of Christ Church, Oxford. They had planned to keep out of England until such time as a Protestant monarch could be found for the tortured realm, and they had done so, travelling and travelling, Groton indulging a newly discovered sexual desire with every woman who would bed with him, Walsingham all the while spinning a delicate web of contacts and acquaintances. Finally they had come home for Queen Elizabeth's coronation ten years ago, and Groton had relied on his friend since then, increasingly so since the disease had come upon him.

Their recent associations with Sir William had filled Groton with hope. Cecil had long been Chancellor of Cambridge University, and how dearly Groton would have loved to be installed in one of the new colleges to study mathematics, to correspond with his young Danish friend, Tycho Brahe, and to debate the theory of projectiles with the students of Senore Tartaglia whom he would bring from Venice. But there had been no professional chair granted him. He had so far hoped in vain, his mathematical genius unrecognised within the gnarled carcass of a leper.

I shall have to wait, he thought. Wait and rot a little more. Soon I'll no longer be able to hold a pencil stub. But still the work these hands can do you'll deem worth a university sinecure soon enough, Mr Secretary. You'll see!

In five years together on the Continent, he and Walsingham had visited France and Italy, Germany and the Low Countries, scores of cities, making hundreds of contacts. When, last year, Cecil had been approached, they had been able to divulge to him the names, whereabouts and current doings of all parties across the whole of Europe who wished Her Majesty ill.

'So, what bad news brings you here so urgently, Master Slade?'

'An evil tiding, sir.' The leather of Slade's boots steamed as he unbuttoned his jerkin. Strapped next to his heart was a kid wallet; inside that, a parchment folded and sealed under Sir William Cecil's signet. Slade's granite face hardened. He turned to Walsingham. 'If I may ask, sir, how called you my name through a closed door? How did you know me?'

Walsingham took the communiqué, examined the seal and lowered himself into the second fireside chair, answering without looking up. 'A man writes his signature in many ways, Slade. You have a certain brusque way with doorhandles.'

The Manor of Foot's Cray had been in the Walsingham family for forty years, and its owner was reluctant to leave it, despite its mounting upkeep and the inconvenience of its remoteness from London. Walsingham had been born here, and knew every corner, every sound of each loose board, each crack in every worn stair. He had remarried a year ago, again to a widow. Ursula was a good wife and like his first had brought from her previous marriage two grown sons and a goodly sum of money, which was fortunate since Walsingham was not himself the owner of a large fortune and the maintenance of a network of foreign contacts was an expensive undertaking.

He turned over the communiqué again, opened it, and saw immediately that the information it contained was of the first order of importance. As he read, he decided that the situation it described was potentially ruinous for England.

Can it be true? Has there really been a disaster? If not, who would want to make me think there has? What vested interests would profit from a tale about a massacre? Which of the Queen's councillors would strengthen his position most as a result? Or could the letter be a forgery?

The fire spat a burning spark onto Slade's lap and he dashed it to the hearth with a quick movement. A significant detail about his appearance caught Walsingham's attention momentarily, and was quickly put to the back of his mind. He had met Slade twice and knew him to be dogged and determined, and above all physically tough. He possessed the best qualities of a sergeant, with just enough of an enquiring nature to make him useful in carrying back answers. If the message was important, Secretary of State Cecil could know that short of death, whatever the circumstance, whatever the bribe, to give it into the care of Robert Slade was to hand it personally to its intended reader.

But Slade was also vainglorious, and thought himself unsurpassed at skulking round the countryside. Which was lately no longer true. Nevertheless, Slade was unswervingly Cecil's man, a loyal servant. The letter was certainly from Cecil.

Then, what about Cecil? Does the Secretary of State stand to gain in any way by lying? On the surface of it, he surely has most to lose. Cecil has invested three thousand pounds in Hawkins's expedition and, much more importantly, more than three years of painstaking foreign policy making – all of which could be plunged into doubt by this letter. True, Cecil has begun to use my network, but it's possible he feels himself becoming overdependent on me. Perhaps he sees my Puritan faith as an obstacle: too firm, too righteous – too extreme? So do I trust Sir William Cecil? Do I judge he trusts me? Do I still hold him to be England's sole hope of deliverance? Yes, yes, and thrice yes! I can do no other. The dispatch has to be taken at face value.

'I may see?' Groton enquired gently.

'You should read it.'

Groton took it and put on his eye-glasses. After a space he spoke again. 'So, Hawkins is dead?'

'If Spinola is to be believed.'

'Cecil clearly believes it, and William Hawkins, in Plymouth – he will believe it too, when he reads the day after tomorrow that his brother is dead, all his ships shattered, and four hundred mariners sent to the bottom. No cheer for him – or us – this Christmas.'

'Premature, Roger.'

'Ah! You mean you don't believe it?'

'I didn't say that.'

Groton cackled. 'How much did you have in the venture?'

'A small sum.'

'Then beware wishful thinking. Do you think Spinola would make up such a tale?'

Walsingham did not answer. Spinola, the Genoese bankers, were represented in London by Bernardino Spinola himself, but the source of this intelligence was their executive Guiseppe Gradenego, a Venetian who had come from the Spanish city of Seville to the Thames port of Deptford, arriving that morning.

'Master Slade? What judgement had you of Gradenego?'

'A foreign person. And probably as damnable a liar as any of them.'

'But capable of the truth – for a consideration?'

'I did pay him well, and I think he spoke the truth to me, and to Sir William.'

'The truth as he knows it?'

'He did say that Seville was afire with the news of Don Emilio Martinez's handiwork. The motherless Papists count it less than treachery. They say that the Indies silver fleet has safely sailed for Spain after Hawkins tried to destroy it in a surprise attack.'

'If the Spanish are accusing Hawkins of piracy –' Groton began.

Slade twisted round. 'If Hawkins is dead and his fleet destroyed no one will be able to gainsay that accusation. It's a perfect pretext and the door to Europe can be slammed in London's face. The Empire of Spain has long counted us heretics and looked for a means to strangle us. If they close their ports to us there will be chaos and panic in London. English merchants will be ruined, English cloth will moulder on the dockside and Antwerp will have lost nothing but a dangerous new competitor.'

Walsingham closed his eyes and leaned back, lacing his fingers tightly. 'I think not. Spinola may be deliberately passing on false information, but if Hawkins does return the bank will be exposed as a spreader of false rumour. They'll lose all credibility.'

Groton answered: 'By that time they might have achieved their aim. A lot may happen in a week.'

Walsingham shook his head. He cursed Groton's rude, doltish logic, and the slow suspicion that was growing in his own mind, and tried to suppress his rising excitement. He said, 'All for a few bales of wool worth perhaps ten thousand pounds? No, Spinola's no fool. He wouldn't risk his position here for ten times ten thousand pounds. If Antwerp were to face civil war again he might need to move a portion of his business to England.'

'Another war in Antwerp? Do you think so?' Groton's voice rose with derision. 'With Alva's murderers sitting on its back? Not a chance! That city's most secure!'

'That Flanders is so heavily garrisoned is a measure of the province's potential for unrest. And remember, Alva's troops are yet to be paid.

Unpaid mercenaries take orders from no one.'

'Perhaps there *has* been a disaster,' Slade said darkly. 'Gradenego's words seemed to be spoken truly. He gave details – the itineraries of Hawkins's ships, the names of captives imprisoned at Vera Cruz – just as if they had been set down by the Viceroy's own hand. The timing's right. Two months and one week is a good crossing, but Spanish dispatch boats can be very fast.'

'I don't believe that.' Walsingham fell silent again, then he stood up and began to pace. What game is Spain playing? he asked himself. And what are the Italians about? They're just as Catholic as the Spaniards, and a hundred times more dangerous. Using leverage gained from loans, Italian finance houses have infiltrated all the royal courts of Europe. They maintain agents in every port, spies on every ship and servants in every significant household, and since the time of the Black Death, merchant bankers like Spinola and Grimaldi have grown fabulously rich by financing the campaigns of kings.

The legendary House of Fugger could defeat any army, they could make invincible any state, protect any monarch. Their gold could hire the most proficient mercenary soldiers and their bribes could unlock the doors of any fortress. It was the Fuggers who had secured the election of two popes and even the accession of Emperor Charles himself, and it was Italian banks that continued to mortgage the wealth of Spain.

Walsingham sat down again, and the courier stirred, warmed now by the decaying fire.

'I shall ask Thomas to bring you a piece of pigeon pie.'

Slade sighed, but roused himself and sat up, scrubbing at his head. 'No. No. I thank you but I must get back. Is there a message of reply to Sir William?'

'Yes.'

Walsingham bade Thomas have Slade's horse saddled, then he told Groton to fetch his pen and began to dictate slowly. Groton's quill scratched rapidly across the paper a sequence of numbers recalled with faultless precision directly from memory. It was sanded, sealed with Walsingham's device and handed over in minutes.

'Deliver your master this, and tell him he must use page sixteen of the red book to resolve it.'

Slade got up and buttoned the pouch back inside his jerkin. Then he took his leave. As the door closed on him, Groton looked to Walsingham.

'So you intend to counsel patience?'

Walsingham nodded. 'Without doubt. There is little to be gained from an incautious move now.'

'But the news will be all over London tomorrow!'

'That's why it's imperative we get to the city merchants first. I want our people to put about an alternative story: that Hawkins landed secretly in Ireland a week ago with a cargo so rich that he's buried a third of it for himself before coming to England to split the rest. The story must be passed along with an embroidered Spanish tale that his ships are sunk, so the Spinola rumour may be dismissed as a jealous lie. That will keep the markets in flux for a week or two.

'Next, we must post to Dover and Rye that all friendly privateers keep watch for Spanish ships attempting the Channel in convoy. Any found must be intercepted immediately. I will offer a good reward.'

Groton's face puckered. 'A convoy?'

'I think so, five or six ships, fast, small, probably out of a Biscayan port and making for Antwerp. That's what we must seek. Under no circumstances must such a convoy be allowed to reach the River Scheldt.'

'I don't follow –'

Walsingham silenced him impatiently and began ticking off the points on his fingers. 'Firstly, the Duke of Alva's *tercios* in the Netherlands thirst for payment. A *tercio* consists of more than three thousand men. Alva's probably got fifty thousand troops under arms in Flanders. How long can they live on promises? And how can Alva keep his iron fist closed if his troops begin to desert?

'Secondly, there are but two ways in which gold may be got to them: either by caravan through France – presently a poor alternative now that France is embroiled in civil war – or by sea through the Straits of Dover. Both routes are perilous enough to explain Philip's reluctance to act before now.

'Thirdly, we know that Philip raises funds with Italian banks on surety of gold arriving from the Indies. Those same bankers are now apprised of the progress of the gold *en route* from Mexico. There is no guarantee that the shipment will reach Seville but the *flota* has left Havana so the most hazardous part of its journey is already complete. The risk is therefore good. Good enough for the banks to extend their best customer any sum he names. Philip has the soul of a notary. I believe I know his mind well enough to predict that he's already borrowed the exact sum required to pay off Alva's troops.'

Groton gasped. 'At one hundred ducats per man, and fifty thousand troops, that's five million ducats. Four or five ships to share the burden of risk. A convoy will be faster and draw less attention than one ponderous galleon. They could arrive in the Channel any time during the next few weeks!'

'It's vital they are found and taken – as a retaliation.'

'So you do think Hawkins has been destroyed!'

We may yet cause Philip the agony he deserves, Walsingham thought. If the ships under Elizabeth's letters of reprise can arrest Alva's gold, and if I can persuade Sir William to take a strong diplomatic line by demanding the release of the hostages held in Vera Cruz, we might seize and retain the initiative for months!

He moved to the mullion and cracked open the heavy curtain. Through the glass he could see the stableyard and Slade's booted figure swinging up onto his steed.

'I fear so,' he said. 'We have good cause to plan hard. If Alva's troops are paid there will be a potential invasion force camped in Flanders. His men are crack professionals. I have no doubt that were they camped in the hopfields of Kent, a mere one hundred miles west of their present billet, they would be saying Mass in St Paul's Cathedral this Sunday.'

A tremor passed over Groton's face. His hand twitched so that he dropped his quill knife. 'Aye, but in that hundred miles there are twenty-two of salt sea.'

'And therein alone may lie our deliverance.'

Walsingham went from window to door, the one from which Groton had appeared. He opened it and passed through into the next room. From there he went to the next again, to where his wife sat reading by the light of a candle.

'He's gone.'

Ursula was a tall woman, angular, approaching forty. She had dismissed both of her maids to bed two hours ago.

She shivered. 'That man is the very Devil incarnate.'

'Perhaps, my dear, but England depends on such as he.'

'Well, then, that is regrettable.'

The room was richly oak panelled to above head height with scroll-work and decorative beading that hid an invisible seam in the second panel from the door. The crafty piece of carpentry opened now under Walsingham's knowledgeable hands. It was one of the secret hiding places that had been built into the house during Mary Tudor's murderous crusade, a bolt hole for the various Protestant clergy that his mother, Joyce, had encouraged. Its interior was a dark space not quite two feet wide, between double walls. Ursula had shown the guest where to hide and had pushed her chair in front of it. It was impossible for the occupant to have overheard anything of the conversation with Slade.

'My lord, the danger is passed. You may come out now.'

The figure who appeared from the darkness was also in his mid thirties, tall, dark-haired with long moustaches which slanted down to his jaw above a wispy beard. His clothing was exceptionally plain, the plainest doublet Walsingham had ever seen him wear, but still of conspicuously fine quality, and to ride here on such a horse had been a vain folly.

Despite his wait, the Earl had maintained his dignity. He bowed and smiled charmingly to the grey-haired woman. 'For the trouble you have taken to safeguard my anonymity I thank you kindly.'

Walsingham found himself regretting again that the Earl had not adopted a more effective disguise. How could a man, reputedly so skilled at courtly deceptions and able to disarm the Queen almost at will, have been so careless?

Ursula curtseyed. 'Milord Leicester honours my husband's humble home by agreeing to overnight here.'

'I fear that before midnight Sir William Cecil will know of your coming here, my lord,' Walsingham said, frowning.

'How so?'

'Your own horse has given you away.'

'You showed him my horse?' the Earl asked, astounded, as he was conducted back to the room where Groton waited.

'I don't doubt that he saw it. Sir William's courier is a careful man. I understand he carries with him a phial of poison should he need to still his tongue, he has another which will drive his horse on like a mad thing until its heart bursts, and at night he wears black against detection.'

'The common people call Robert Slade "the Raven",' Ursula said.

'But black is a poor shade in a parlour, my dear. I saw there were stains of brick on his jerkin. From the wall, which is old and in places crumbling. He can have scaled it for one purpose. He has a sure eye for horseflesh.'

Colour rose visibly in the Earl's face. 'You should have hid the nag. If Cecil knows then we are undone!'

Yes, Walsingham thought. Sir William loathes your innocent manner and resents the way the Queen has showered you with favours. He thinks you are an artful opportunist, and he's tried on at least two occasions to revive the story that you murdered your wife. He'll continue to hound and isolate you until you've followed the rest of your clan to the headsman's block.

'I believe that I have more to fear than you from Cecil's knowledge of our meeting, my lord.'

'How so?'

'You are England's wealthiest man. You're both a baron and an earl and therefore greatly superior to Cecil. I'm but a penniless private individual. Which of us do you think has most to fear?'

'Conversely, I have most to lose. If our meeting is known to Cecil we are each implicated; it bodes ill for us both.'

Walsingham noted the way Leicester's tone had hardened. Had he begun to suspect duplicity? 'Sir William despises you.'

'Whereas you seem to have become his familiar.' Leicester stuck his elbow into the bricks of the fireplace and chewed on his knuckle. 'Cecil is a danger to us all. The Queen is not safe so long as he has a head on his shoulders.'

'Perhaps your plans are well advanced in that regard?'

Leicester adopted a puzzled look. 'What do you mean?'

'You and the Duke of Norfolk have sealed a pact against Cecil.'

'A pact?' The question was echoed with disarming innocence.

Walsingham smiled. 'The admiral who watches a great storm building at sea is a fool if he takes no heed for the safety of his ship.'

Again that incredible blankness. 'You talk in rhymes, Mr Walsingham.'

That's for the safety of my own ship, Walsingham thought. We both know why you're here. The Scottish Queen's arrival in England threatens you just as it does the woman you still hope to marry. If Elizabeth dies childless Mary will succeed her, and you, my proud peacock, will lose your head. Unless ...

'My lord, I must know your purpose if I am to aid you.'

Leicester looked aside at Groton who had retired to a corner and seemed oblivious to them, engrossed in a book.

'I cannot speak with that beggar present.'

Groton sat up. 'He that is in poverty be always suspected of iniquity, milord.'

Ursula smiled at Leicester. 'You came here to discuss the Scottish Queen, did you not?'

Leicester hesitated. 'I did.'

'Then, please do so, and fear not that my husband permits his wife and a humble beggar to listen.'

The Queen of Scotland, Mary the Whore, had been forced to abdicate by her half-brother the Earl of Moray who was outraged by her behaviour. Not only was she a Catholic, but she had married the syphilitic drunkard and sodomite, Lord Darnley, and she had compounded her crimes by pursuing adulterous affairs with first her French secretary, then the Earl of Bothwell. After Bothwell had made her pregnant, she planned with him to pack the cellars of Kirk o' Field, where Darnley was sleeping, with gunpowder. The house was blown to pieces, and when by some miracle Darnley walked from the smoking ruins uninjured, he was set upon and strangled to death. The Protestant Scottish lords reacted. Mary's year-old son, the heir James, was taken from her by Moray who appointed himself Regent. Mary raised support and clashed with Moray at Langside, but her army was destroyed and she was forced into England where she had cast herself at Elizabeth's feet. If she expected mercy of a sister sovereign she found none, Walsingham thought. Elizabeth has wisely had her arrested and imprisoned.

'I fear our good Queen has a wolf by the ears,' he said.

Leicester braced himself and spoke. 'I seek to extract the wolf's teeth. I believe she can be persuaded to marry the Duke of Norfolk. By that marriage she becomes chained to England's peerage, and thus easily controlled. I must know what support I can expect from Parliament.'

Walsingham knew that Parliament's influence over the Queen's authority was slim. Only through the judicious manipulation of pursestrings could they hope to direct the Queen's hand, and it had been Elizabeth's policy to enrich the Crown so that parliamentary subsidies were unnecessary. He said, 'Mary is an obstacle to Elizabeth's security. In the north there are many Catholics who regard her as a bastard, and Mary as the true heir. And if you want evidence of Mary's attitude you need not search far. Her arms impudently incorporate those of the English throne. Parliament regards her as a dangerous pretender.'

'Norfolk is England's only Duke. As such he is our foremost aristocrat.

A marriage to Norfolk would effectively neutralise her.'

As the conversation proceeded, Walsingham considered the alarm he felt as dispassionately as he could. Why was Leicester allowing him, and therefore almost certainly Cecil, to hear his thinking? The pretext that he had come merely to canvass opinions on Parliament's probable reaction was utterly transparent. Perhaps he thinks I'll carry the plan to Cecil and in so doing expose the Secretary to attack. It is no secret that Leicester hates Sir William, but does he have the nerve to go against the Queen? He's her lap dog. He draws his power and prestige from her alone. The moment she's gone, he'll be cut to pieces. Unless . . .

Walsingham felt his palms dampen as he made the connection. The heightening threat of war with Spain. An invasion force camped across the Channel. The arrival of the Scottish Queen. And now Leicester's unscrupulous writhing. It had all suddenly begun to make coherent and terrifying sense.

Chapter 5

'They say the porpoise plays before the storm, Captain.'

Richard Tavistock stirred from his doom-laden thoughts at the Scotsman's words. He had not slept for twenty-four hours, wanting to see the *Minion* through this new crisis despite his cold and hunger. The hours on deck had finally brought him to a decision, but they had done little to improve his foreboding humour.

'The men waste their time with that harpoon, Fleming.'

'It gives them hope of something to fill their bellies, sir.'

'Their best hope is to attend to their duties and save their strength.'

Tavistock steadied himself and watched the deck of the *Minion* pitch once again into the North Atlantic swell. Her staggering, exhausted helmsman held her on the starboard tack, but the wind was sharpening, swinging north-easterly, and deep sea rollers were beginning to ripple and break into white streamers before the blow. In the bows two of the duty watch were in desperation over the dolphin which breached playfully and stayed maddeningly out of range.

'Do you think it's sign of storm, sir?'

Bowen muttered, 'The best sign of storm is the look on the pilot's face.'

'Keep your thoughts to yourself in my hearing, Bowen.'

'Aye, Captain.'

'Put about, and stand on the larboard tack, Fleming.'

'Aye.' Fleming's reply was toothless and indistinct. His mouth was festering with black sores – none of them had eaten at all in six days – nevertheless he got about his business. Tavistock knew that if they were hit by one more gale they would founder and if the wind dropped they would starve. It had become his habit never to lie to himself, whatever the circumstances, and he had known for three days that they could not possibly reach England. That was why he had ordered the change of course.

The weather braces were stretched along, and he saw to it that the lee tacks, weather sheets and lee bowlines were properly hauled through the slack. Then he looked to the pennant fluttering at the mainmast. 'Put her hard over to windward.'

The helmsman heaved weakly on the rudder. Though he used all his force he could not accomplish it, and Tavistock had to lend his weight to the bar.

'Helm's a-lee!'

The *Minion*'s head moved once more into the wind; Fleming's gritty voice shouted over the singing rigging, 'Fore sheets, fore top bowline, jib and staysail sheets let go!'

The power of the sails forward of the ship's centre of gravity slackened. As soon as the sail began to touch, six men hauled on the weather-fore topsail brace, until she came to, and the yard was braced up again.

An empty barrel rolled across the deck.

She's come to nor'east by north, Tavistock told himself, looking into the lodestone compass that rocked on its gimbals. She's within three points of the wind, and dragging her belly as if she's full of lead. He watched the wind blowing on the leeches – extremities of the after sail – making them shake and flap noisily.

'Off tacks and sheets!'

Fleming repeated the order to the ragged remnants of his men and the shaking stopped, but still he was unsatisfied. At the best of times the *Minion* was liable to sternway, and he eased the steering so that water pressing on the starboard side of the rudder pushed her stern back to larboard and her head round due west.

Great bursts of white spray dashed up out of the sea and across the decks, drenching them. The ship's way was falling off rapidly and when the after sails began to fill the word was given 'Let go and haul!'

From his position, high in the stern castle, he surveyed the ship and tried to recalculate the course. The *Minion*'s waist was a dismal sight: desolate and washed by grey swirls of water each time she heeled. The patched and rotting main course billowed and strained, the canvas looking like it must be blown out at the next gust. Cutting the grey sky above their wake in broad arcs, apart from the dolphin their sole companion in this vast ocean: an albatross.

After rounding the Bahamas they had run out of provisions completely. One by one, the parrots had been caught and stewed, the dogs and cats too, then the pangs in their bellies had drive the men into the bilges to hunt down 'millers' – a speciality in times of famine aboard ship. When skinned, topped and tailed and cooked in seawater they ate not unlike hare, but on a starvation ship they were scrawny and stringy and lacking in meat, and a rat was a rat all the same.

'English mariners have stomachs strong enough to eat horseshoes,' Hawkins had told him once in better times. Hunger made anything savour sweet. And when on this passage Tavistock had watched an older man showing a younger how to stew hides and chew goodness from their leather belts he had believed it. The youth, Twide, had spoken of his fantasy with a dripping mouth. 'I'll take my gold here, and I'll have such a day: a huntsman's breakfast, a lawyer's dinner, a merchant's supper and a monk's drink at night, I'll have it all on my first day in Plymouth town!' But he had died a week later and had given the same to the fishes of the deep. Tavistock thanked God for his constitution. He had been overmuscled in the Indies. Too much good living and too much respect for his past not to lend a hand on all physical tasks had given him plenty to spare. He had always been keen to do everything himself, no matter how arduous. If that was his failing as an officer Hawkins had put him right. 'Stay aloof from your men, Richard. Give them a chance to show you what they can do by themselves. Jump in like that when you're commanding ship and your crew won't thank you for it.' It had been like that on the *Swallow*. Days of vigilance and giving orders. He had become the mind of his ship, tightening a sheepshank here, slackening off a lashing there, finely tuning her stays like the strings of a viol so that the wind sounded all the right notes in her timbers.

That was being Captain: a comfortable suit to wear, a suit of responsibility patched with old errors, and it had been experience with the Merchant Adventurers, sailing short cloths across the German Ocean to Emden that had given him those early trials, and later, on his first Indies voyage, when he had first supervised a barque and lost his first seaman to accidental death he had learned again. He could remember it clearly, seared onto his mind like a criminal's brand. There was nothing he could have done, but it had not stopped him blaming himself. The old lessons had come the full circle of experience. He had remembered then the day years before that he had been caught whittling on watch. It was rare and unlooked-for and memorable because of it. Amyas Poole had cuffed him and treated him to a lashing tongue, then he had said something he had never forgotten. Never let boredom get at you, Richard. A good ship's officer is never bored. And if he is then his mind's where a shipowner can't afford it. At the time, he had felt the threat cut into him, then wondered what else Amyas had meant. Then the days had never been long enough, when he was seventeen. In port there was the shipwright's yard, learning proper stowage, hiring and firing, careening, watching the carpenters; at sea shiphandling, gunnery and the rigorous mysteries of navigation to study. On clear nights there were the constellations. He had loved to look at those star patterns like a young girl loves to look at her mother, and he had learned how to hold a steady course by Polaris. He had had to learn how to do every job himself, and he had done so, diligently, until he could do it blindfold and backwards.

The *Jesus* had been a big ship with plenty to occupy a man prepared to seek it out. There had been deck upon deck of her, four in the huge forecastle alone, and he had made it his business to acquaint himself with every inch. Before his day she had been one of the ships in King

Henry's Navy that had repulsed the French off Spithead, when the *Mary Rose* had turned turtle and sunk. It had been the *Jesus* and her sister ship the *Samson* that had tried to raise her up again, but that had been a task beyond her and the King's ship had settled in the mud for ever.

He had learned and learned, assiduously, every day, until he thought he knew everything that made a captain, but it was only when he had put on Amyas Poole's boots aboard *Swallow* that he had discovered command was something beyond learning. He had had cause to remember the hundreds of small lessons an excellent mariner had taught him about that, and he had understood that the rest was down to him.

He shifted his weight, watching the lateen sail flap fitfully and thinking of Hawkins.

The General had fallen into a decline and the sickness lingered in him still. He was still unable to stand. Even though the fever had broken, it had left him weak and covered in sores. In the next few days, Tavistock knew, he would either gain strength or the malady would carry him off. Perhaps that was what Hawkins wanted. He had reached his limit and lost hope, and that ultimately was what invited the Reaper of Men to call on some, and not on others.

Since the Cape of Florida and the passing of the *Minion* beyond the last dangerous shoals and into deep water, he had tried to put hunger out of his mind by keeping himself engrossed in wind and weather. Concentration was a powerful weapon against pain, and only those who could master themselves could hope to master a ship. Though he had eaten no more than any of *Minion*'s crew, he had stayed strong because he had been economical with his movements, had slept in furs that kept out the cold, had rationed his consumption strictly, had refused the pitiful offal that passed among the men, and because he had needed to prove himself their master.

He watched the helm drifting and ordered Bowen up to give the helmsman a hand. Then he went aft to Hawkins's cabin.

The General's eyes were yellowed, his pallor grim.

'Where are we, Richard?'

'West of the mouth of the Tagus.'

'How far west?'

Tavistock breathed deeply and bent over the chart. 'Six or seven days.'

Hawkins struggled to sit up. 'No. You'll not take my ship to Lisbon! The Portugalls won't —'

'Not Lisbon, Pontevedra.'

'Pontevedra?' Hawkins's voice was breathy, as if his mind was still half in trance.

'The wind is against us as it has been all the way from the Indies. We can't run directly home.'

Pontevedra was a port on one of the drowned river valleys of Galicia, that part of the coast of Spain north of Portugal that looks west towards

the Atlantic. There were many English wine traders there, ships like the
Minion that plied the Bay of Biscay. There they might find help.

'Do you know what day it is, General?'

Hawkins slumped back. 'No.'

'It's the day when we celebrate the birth of Our Lord.'

'Christmas Day?'

'Aye,' he replied bleakly. 'Good cheer to you, General.'

He went up on deck and sent Ingram and Rush, the men who had
been taken off the pumps, back to their drudgery, but Ingram returned
with five others and reported that during the day the water in the hold
had risen another foot.

'We're fighting and losing. Her timber's sprung, sir.'

Tavistock listened to the fear in Ingram's voice, saw the unspoken
question on every man's face. *What are you going to do, Captain?* It
was a question that had no ready answer. He had gone below and seen
the swirling, stinking weight that made the *Minion* wallow like a
beached whale, and had felt each tack grow more sluggish and difficult.
Like Hawkins himself, the crew had fallen to a sweating fever. Each day
another marble-grey corpse had been rolled stiff from its sleeping space
and sent into the ocean deep. Some days there were none, others three
or four; last week, with the weather turning wintry, they had begun
dying so fast it was hard to keep count. With barely thirty men left to
handle the ship – men weak from starvation, or whose guts were bleeding
over the side faster than the rain could be collected to give them sup,
Tavistock knew their chances of survival were thin. Half the crew had
already been driven close to madness. They did no work, they did not
sleep, but starved and wasted and stared. There was only one way to
stop it, and that was by fear.

A voice came unbidden into his head.

'Put your crew first. Be good to them,' Amyas Poole told him. His
first sea tutor whispered back across the years as he watched his men
hollow-eyed and staring, demanding his explanation. 'Give them your
respect, always treat them like Christian men. Even the lousiest inland
scum. Save their worthless lives, because they alone stand between you
and a watery grave.'

'It's bad seepage helped by the cold of these northerly waters. I've
looked at it and she'll hold tight.'

He sounded confident, but the deputation remained. Ingram's question was direct. 'Where are we now, Captain? She's shipping water too
fast to bale.'

Rush was in utter despair. 'She'll not last another day.'

'She'll hold. I promise you,' he lied.

'How's that? Because you tell us so? Because it's God's will?'

'I don't presume to know God's will, Ingram.'

'What's *your* will, Captain?'

Tavistock controlled his temper. 'Get about your work, lads. We'll keep *Minion* afloat. A week is all we need.'

'A week? Where are we now?'

'Standing in forty-two degrees of latitude, a hundred and fifty leagues west of the Portuguese coast.'

'Then, we can make for the Azores! With this nor'-easterly blowing we can run –'

Tavistock's voice dropped to a growl. 'You're not piloting the *Minion*. *I am.*'

'She sprung, I tell you! She was rotten with teredo worm before we put into San Juan!'

'Let's make for the Azores, eh, Captain? That's best, eh?' Rush pleaded, his eyes bulging from his head.

'He's right, Captain!'

'Aye! It's that or die!'

'Well, Captain?' Ingram said.

Tavistock flared with anger. For days he had known that the planks of *Minion*'s starboard beam opened up a gap two fingers wide in a heavy sea; it was packed tight with felt and nothing more could be done about it. He also knew that to make Ingram and the rest of the men believe the planks would hold and that they could still sail home was essential. I'll make them believe, he swore inwardly. I'll make them take this shit-bucket home despite themselves. And no filthy sea rat is going to tell me how or where to sail any ship that I command!

'You want to go to the Azores, eh?'

'Aye, we do. We all do!'

'You want to spend the rest of your lives pulling on Portuguese galley oars?'

Mention of the slave galleys where prisoners were chained to their labours and replaced instead of being fed filled them with confusion. The man behind Ingram shrank back visibly.

'Remember that Portuguese carrack we took off Sierra Leone? The Portugalls would call that piracy.'

Ingram shifted his weight. 'Jesus, Captain, anything's better than being starved dead!'

'What waits for you in Hell, Ingram, is ten thousand times worse than anything in this life. Do you want to go to that? The Portugalls are Catholics. They'll burn your legs black at the stake and take your soul before they kill you, and they'll be watching for us. Now get back to the pumps.'

Ingram began to speak but Tavistock took his shirtfront in two fists and sent him crashing into the scuppers. He wheeled on the others.

'We're all in God's hands from the day we're born into this life until the day he calls us to him. Those are the only certainties. But I promise you that *Minion*'s strong enough and, if God allows, we're going home. If any other man wants to dispute that with me I'm ready for him.'

The Puritan, Rush, fell to his knees, his hands laced together and his face raised skyward. He prayed hoarsely, 'Almighty God, I beseech thee! Take us to the Azores –'

Tavistock dragged him to his feet with difficulty, strength draining from him like brine from a bunghole, but he slapped Rush's face back and forth until the man collapsed into sobs.

'Get back to that pump!'

Rush staggered to his feet, raving now. He rose up in a fury of possession. For a split second, Tavistock saw Satan in his eyes, heard him laugh frighteningly. He grinned with a bright, unnatural strength and went for his Captain's throat. Tavistock was rooted by the terror of Rush's madness as it took him. His mind slipped from his control and into panic. Then Rush froze. His arms fell limp; he turned and walked sniggering in triumph to the gunwale. Before anyone could stop him he had climbed up and dived over the side.

The men broke away and saw their shipmate's body, rigid as a crucifix, drift into the wake. His eyes and mouth were wide open and his eerie laugh was drowned as the water swilled over his face.

In silence Ingram took his men and went below, his surly anger utterly shattered. Tavistock knew that neither he nor any of them would be back.

Chapter 6

'What're they going to do with us?'

'Jesus's pity, we're dying here!'

'A hundred and thirty days in this stinking hole!'

Four pale faces crowded the bars of the prison window rattling their chains on the stone sill as he passed by in the street below. It was two months since they had taken the Gunner from them.

'Aye, Gunner, what do they want with you?'

'Take heart, lads –'

'*Silencio!*' The voice commanding him came from the horseman following. It was the same man who had arrived shortly after Tavistock's capture. He had appeared twice since. And twice Tavistock had noticed and disliked his disdainful countenance. Clearly, he was disliked by his soldiers, for whenever he approached they grew tense and cruel.

Tavistock raised his eyes to the prison window defiantly. 'They say the Viceroy's leaving tomorr –'

'*Marchad!*'

A halberd staff crashed down on his neck and he staggered. It was dangerous to ignore this proud young officer of the Viceroy's staff. He wore a smart uniform and everything about him was neatly ordered down to the soles of his polished boots. Arrogant bastard, Tavistock thought. You treat us like dogs just to win the Viceroy's praise, but every bruise you raise hardens me. We have strength because God is with us and against you. What's your name, you bastard? I promise you, one day I'll find out. And then I'll kill you.

Each morning for twelve weeks Gunner Tavistock had been taken under guard to the bellfoundry of Santa Catalina; each afternoon he had returned the two miles, to be billeted alone in a stinking stable. He had watched and listened and recently he had begun to engage in conversation. At first, he had been kept apart from the men who cast the bronze bells for the cathedrals and churches of the New World. They resented the Viceroy's interference in their work and had little desire to admit a hated heretic to their sheds. Lately, though, he had

93

begun to win their friendship and that of Pedro Gomara, the old man who brought him food each night. Gomara had taught him much about the Indies: the *ferias*, the system of the *encomienda* that parcelled out the land and controlled the people, and he had begun to understand a little of what a massive achievement the Spanish had made in subduing so huge a portion of the globe and bringing it under their heel.

When they had first taken him from the others he had been chained in this same stable. He had awoken from nightmare to find great sucking ticks, their abdomens filled and distended like black grapes, clustering on his neck and chest. He had pulled them off and burst them bloodily in disgust, and for the rest of the night he had been unable to find rest. But in the calm warmth of a new dawn he had awoken to find the future stretching out before him like a golden carpet, and he had known that a part of his life had been left behind for ever. The toothless man who had brought him a pail of water and a bowl of starchy gruel had sat by him at the door, nodding amiably as Tavistock washed.

'It is hard to wash in chains, *señor*. May I not be unlocked?' he had asked in Spanish.

The old man's eyes had narrowed. 'You are a soldier?'

'A gunner.'

'A gunner is an honourable profession?'

'I have always thought it so.'

'Ha! An honourable gunner! And have I your word that you will not try to run away?'

'Where can I run?'

'Your word, Gunner? On your life?'

'You have it. On my life.'

'Then you may wash as a free man.'

The old man's hair had been wispy iron-grey but it had seemed to Tavistock that his spirit was still young. As he had washed, Tavistock had talked, wanting to know more about his captors and about the Viceroy. Anything the Spaniard could tell him might be useful. As he had begun to eat, he found that the old man slipped easily into conversation.

'My name is Pedro Gomara. When I was your age, *señor*, I too was an adventurer. A soldier. Then, one year, I joined with my Captain, the famous Francisco de Orellana, on a great enterprise. Ah, what a man he was! I too – young and strong and full of great ideas as a young man should be, and for the glory of God we followed the great river Amazonas all the way down from Peru to the sea. Two thousand miles! Where the savage warriors are women and there are serpents that may swallow a horse whole. That was twenty-five years ago, *señor*, but I remember it as if it was yesterday. Some things a man may never forget. Many of us began but few returned. Is that not always the way of the adventurer? Every man must have his time, eh? He must face death, or how may he know life?'

'The glory of God?' Tavistock had asked in Spanish between ravenous spoonfuls. 'And of your Captain, eh?'

The old man grunted.

'You live here in Vera Cruz?'

'Here, and in Mexico City. It is my good fortune to go for ever betwixt these two great cities with my mules. I have dogs and horses and many mules. I never married, *señor*. They are my children, and my living. Mine alone. He that hath partners hath masters, eh?'

'You came from Mexico City with the silver?'

'I drove my *recuas* all the way from Potosi. It is a place in the heart of Mexico, and in its centre is a mountain veined with silver. From a great plateau seventy-four hundred *pies* above the sea, across the place they call *La Pedregal*, the Plain of Stones, down past the lakes of salt and sweet water and the fuming volcanoes that guard the highlands, the land where the sunsets go. Below them the broad-leaf jungles begin. They grow densely like a Turkeyman's carpet, Señor Gunner, all the way to the sea, dark and dangerous because of savages and the *Cimarons*, the slaves that have escaped from the plantations and make their homes there.'

The big bells hanging in the open *campanario* of the church across the *plaza* had begun to peal, bringing him back to the present. He watched the hooded father peg back a huge bronze door and clap the green stains from his hands.

'I must go.'

'You will go with the Viceroy's train tomorrow?'

'*Si*. Tuesday. And if the Viceroy is not a fool he will take you to Mexico City also, where the English ships cannot find you.'

Tavistock looked up suddenly. 'Do you believe he will?'

Gomara shrugged, picking up the shackles. 'It is possible.'

Tavistock watched as people appeared from side streets, heading for the church across the parade square of red compacted earth. Yesterday, the morning's rain had dappled it with pools of water that had steamed gently in the rising heat of the Sabbath. He had watched the fierce sun of noon bake the horseshoe marks into hard semicircular ridges that would eventually be worn away by the bare feet of Indians and black slaves, the sandals of the friars and the boots of soldiers and what traders remained. By night the *plaza* had been peaceful once more and it had been then that he'd seen her. She'd come from the *Alcalde*'s house alone, her mane of black hair unpinned, dressed in a loose linen gown as if she had stolen from the house unobserved, and he had watched her hurry across the square towards him, oblivious of his presence. He had felt a pang of shame at his wretchedness and had hidden himself among the shadows but he had continued to watch as she came inside the stable door and stood by the horses, patting their necks, speaking softly to them and blowing onto their nostrils.

'*Señorita*, you are so kind to visit us here,' he had whispered in throaty

Spanish, and she had jumped back in surprise, unable to see anyone in the darkness.

'Who's there?'

'Only we horses.'

'Horses?'

'Did you not know, *señorita*? In the Americas we horses may talk.'

She had seen the white of his smile then, and tossed her head.

'And mules too.'

She left, not hurriedly, not scared by him, not embarrassed, but boldly and with a natural dignity. All day he had been unable to put that impression of her out of his mind.

Now he looked at Don Luis's residence until the glare from its walls hurt his eyes. The ornate white house stood over the square in splendid authority. At its door the immaculately groomed officer on the bay horse sat erect, exchanging words with that same graceful woman who had come unannounced into his reverie. She was dressed in a blue dress and filigree veil now, and he saw that she was without doubt the young woman he had bravely bowed to when he had been captured.

He flicked his head towards the horseman. 'Tell me, Pedro, who is that man?'

'He is the officer of the guard, *señor*. An important man in Mexico City. His name is Gonzalo de Escovedo.'

'And the lady he talks with?'

'His sister. She is beautiful, is she not?' Gomara grinned, showing the stump of one canine tooth. 'If I was but a young man again!'

Tavistock smiled wistfully. He felt something – what? He couldn't say. Passion and apprehension coiling and uncoiling in his belly as Gomara bolted home the chains on his wrists and ankles again.

Across the *plaza* the horse shimmied and was still. Gonzalo reined it in tightly. Maria saw the spur marks on the horse's ribs and frowned.

'What do you call him?'

'The horse? His name is Jupiter.'

She snapped her fan shut, nettled by her brother's unyielding poise. Can't he understand it's I, Maria, his sister? she asked herself. Can't he show just a little emotion in his face for me? It's as though he doesn't really want me here. That I'm nothing to him.

She remembered seeing Gonzalo for the first time after coming ashore. He was now a grown man and greeting him had been a shock. She could not have counted the number of times she had thought of him on the journey across the oceans, always thinking of him as the sensitive boy he had been so long ago. Now he is a soldier and in love with honour and ambition. Since coming to Vera Cruz she had longed for him to relax so that she could glimpse the other, former Gonzalo.

'Something troubles you, Maria?'

'It's nothing. I was thinking of the journey ahead. Is it very arduous?'

'You will be well looked after. Don't forget that I'm here to protect you.'

'They say there are dangerous savages in the jungles between here and Mexico City. Is that true?'

'They will not dare trouble us. We are many and they are curs that will not fight a fair and open action. Their bows and arrows are no match even for those of our Indian escort, much less the firearms of my men.'

She looked away, thinking of the sadness that had been in his eyes at their parting. 'May I ask a favour of you?'

He smiled. 'You know you may ask anything of me, Maria.'

'May I ride Jupiter when we leave for the interior?'

'My horse?' His smile disappeared.

'It would make the journey more bearable if I were free to ride alone – within the bounds of the column, of course.'

Gonzalo demurred diplomatically. He rippled his heels over the bay's flanks and reined in, giving contradictory signals. 'Think of your complexion, Maria, and, look, this nag is so skittish. If he were to throw you and you were to hurt yourself, father would never forgive me. I could never forgive myself.'

'Forgive yourself, Escovedo?' The Viceroy's elegant figure appeared at the door. His eye moved over Maria's face, searching her, before meeting his lieutenant's. 'What is there for you to forgive?'

'Excellency.'

Don Emilio's voice was superficially genial. 'I ask myself why you sound so guilty, Escovedo. It was a simple question.'

Gonzalo's shoulders went back and his chin jutted. 'I was merely explaining to my sister, Excellency, that for her to ride to Mexico City would be out of the question.'

'Oh? How so?'

'It would not be fitting, Excellency.'

Maria put her hand to her breast. 'It was only a vain fancy, Don Emilio. Please don't trouble –'

'It's no trouble, my dear. I'm sure your brother will be delighted to loan you his horse. In any case, I have other duties in mind for him.'

Gonzalo fought to keep his face blank. 'Other duties, Excellency?'

'You've shown commendable interest in the English captive. Your notion that bellfounders may be taught to cast cannon also was worthy. He's proved that he's knowledgeable, and so I've decided to bring him with us. He has much to tell us, but he must be persuaded to unburden himself of his own free will. You'll be responsible for his safety. See if you can imagine a way to unlock his secrets.'

As the Viceroy moved out of earshot, Maria turned her eyes to Gonzalo in apology. He dismounted stiffly, handed her the reins and said, 'Here, take the horse. But you'll do well in future to curb your tongue in front of my superiors. And to remember that I have responsibilities now.'

By ten o'clock the next day their journey had begun.

The road that snaked out of Vera Cruz was difficult and there were many delays as wheels stuck in the red mud, but as they reached higher ground the road grew rocky and dry. They passed many small settlements, huts made of woven reed and thatched with banana and *palmito* leaf. Old Indian women squatted at the doors and naked children with globe bellies and broad, running noses stared at them. At each halt there was refreshment, and at night fires were lit and tents rigged for the soldiers who lay down on colourful bed rolls of Gossopine cotton. A guard was diligently posted on the fringes of settlements which had been hacked from the screaming forest. In daytime, at high points of the road, the vistas were of unbroken foliage, an ocean of steamy, tropical *montana* stretching unendingly to the horizons, clothing hills and valleys alike.

Don Emilio rode in the centre of the train. Three other high-ranking horsemen rode with him; one was a priest and two others, the *Adelantado*, or marshal of the military region around Vera Cruz, and the *Maestre del Campo*, his second-in-command. Ahead, there were three platoons of soldiers, marching in formation where possible; behind, the merchants with their carts and wains and mules. In the rear there were more soldiers, a thousand in all, and lines of Guinea Negroes chained three abreast, and the baggage cars.

Maria rode sometimes ahead of them all, or at the tail. She liked to let the horse range as he would up and down the line, but she rarely fell in beside the Viceroy or the wagons that carried the other ladies. She had taken her maid's advice and wore a long, loose-fitting kirtle and a wide-brimmed straw hat tied under her chin with broad white ribbon.

Gonzalo walked a few yards behind the main body, keeping the Englishman in sight. At the halts he would watch with disapproval as old Pedro Gomara came to the Englishman's side and shared a little food with him or shaved his beard. The chains had been taken from the Englishman's legs but still his hands were looped together.

'I see you did find yourself a horse, after all, my lady,' he had called to her in his best Spanish.

Naturally, she had ignored him, but that night, at her lodging in the *adobe* mission of the Franciscans, Gonzalo had warned her not to approach the captive again.

'Gonzalo, I did not –'

'You know he is a heretic,' he had said fiercely. 'And possessed by Satan.'

She had stared in disbelief at the intensity of the warning.

Of course, Gonzalo was right to warn her. But then he had also warned her to ride obediently in one place in the caravan, not to stray and not to go within ten *varas* of any of his soldiers.

'This is a dangerous place, Maria. I have warned you time and again, and still you defy me.'

'Why shouldn't I exercise the horse? He likes to walk the verges and so do I.'

'Wilful girl! Have respect! I've told you: there are savages in the jungle who fire poisoned darts. There are escaped slaves who will carry you away!'

'I'm not afraid. You said they were cowards who wouldn't dare to attack so large a body of soldiers.'

'Do as you are told, Maria! For your own good! And keep away from the Englishman!'

She had slammed the door on him then, and wished her brother a hundred leagues away. And then she had cried, realising that the old Gonzalo was dead and the new one a complete stranger.

Now she looked at the Englishman again. He was tall, more than one *estado*, which was normal for sailors and soldiers, and now that he had choice to wash and comb his hair he seemed almost noble. But he was English, and he was a Protestant. Maria felt a seeping dread deep within her. He had rejected Jesus Christ and the Holy Virgin and so he must be possessed by the Devil and able to do the Devil's bidding. That was what Doña Isabella said. That was what the holy fathers said. It must be true.

Then why did she disbelieve it? And why should disbelieving scare her? Was not the Englishman's soul his own concern?

She nudged her horse into a canter and rode forward to the head of the train.

Praying silently and thinking of the hopes and fears that attended the meeting with her father.

Don Bernard had taken his wife and son to the New World ten years ago. His enemies at the Court in Madrid had gained the upper hand and he had chosen Mexico as the place to rebuild his wealth. His two young daughters, Maria and Angelina, he had left with his sister in Toledo, partly as a sign to his enemies that he intended one day to return, partly that they might be educated and schooled in the ways of Court. Later, as holder of a large *repartimiento* and with growing influence in the viceroyalty, Bernard had begun to dream of a return to Spain but the news of his daughter's violent death at the hands of the *Infante* had thrown his hopes into ruin and he had sent to Madrid for Maria. The act had effectively severed his last links with Madrid, and ended all thoughts of a return to Spain.

Ahead, Maria watched the mountains rising majestically. The road across the *pampa* was ending, leaving the dense, forested region and heading up into the *puna*, a high, treeless savannah. There was a shining, rippling sparkle on the road ahead. It looked like a river. Perhaps there was a ford. She urged Jupiter forward, past the leading body of soldiers who looked up at her passing and began to call out to her to come back.

The horse was thirsty. She would let him drink. And a plague on Gonzalo's men and their shouts. Already they were left behind.

The road narrowed. She saw something black and thick as a tree trunk slung across its ochre surface and the horse shied, pulling up, stamping nervously. The black thing was moving loathsomely from one side of the road to the other, rippling, tumbling like a serpent, but it was no serpent. It was a mass of huge insects, like ants but half a finger in length with long, sharp jaws.

They *were* ants. Jungle ants. Thousands of them. They moved like a military column, carrying leaves and insects and other like booty tirelessly in their flow from the left-hand verge to the right.

She watched them, at once horrified and amazed. And then she saw the bodies. Two human forms, clothed thickly with a prickling mass of black. They had been deliberately staked out in the insects' path and then, with a second spasm of horror, she realised that the perpetrators were not long removed – for both of their victims were *alive*.

They came by midday to a town of two hundred inhabitants surrounded by groves of citrus and pomegranate and built by the great river beside which broad salines had been cut and in which slaves laboured.

Gomara brought a loaf of *clashacali* – maize bread, and parted it, grinning. They talked, seated comfortably in the shade, Tavistock listening to the old man's reminiscences, all the while keeping an eye on Escovedo who was less inclined to brood over him.

'It was the work of the *Cimarons*,' Gomara told him. 'Two in every five of the black slaves in Mexico have deserted their masters. They live in the forests and worship pagan gods, as they did in Africa. Sometimes they attack isolated settlements and steal away slave women to increase their numbers. They hate us because many of the *encomenderos* and *estancieros* are cruel men who think only of profit.'

'And the men they killed?' Tavistock had seen the shocking sight as they cut the victims out. The rescuers had had to prise each ant head from the flesh individually but much of their skin was gone and their eyes had been devoured down to the nerves.

'*Mestizos*. Half-castes. The blacks are no friends of the Indians. The Indians buy salt here and carry it into the interior. They are often robbed. Once I myself used to bring salt down to Vera Cruz and to Tamiago and Tamachos where it is taken by sea to Cuba ...'

Tavistock began to drowse. The noon stops were often of two hours or more and afforded welcome respite from the heat and the chafing of his irons. The sound of his own breathing filled his ears, and as he lay back he caught the faint waft of pig pens on the air and he slit open an eye, looking for the source of the smell. Then he stirred and sat up.

Gomara roused himself suddenly. 'What is it?'

Tavistock shook his head. 'I thought ... it's nothing. For a moment I thought I heard English spoken.'

'You are dreaming of home.'

'Perhaps.'

Tavistock forced himself to relax and Gomara settled once more. Pushing his broad-brimmed straw hat forward over his eyes he was soon breathing regularly.

It came again. This time Tavistock got to his feet, slowly, so that the chains made the minimum of noise. He walked in the direction of the hog sties.

'I must relieve myself,' he said to a nearby soldier who watched him uninterestedly. When he turned the corner of the nearest building he saw the face at the gate. It was pressed against a narrow gap and he recognised the man. It was Hawkins's steward.

'John Chamberlain, can it be you?'

The face stared back at him. 'Gunner!'

'Quietly!'

Through the gaps he could see that there were perhaps twenty of them confined in the sty. They were naked and the smell of ordure rose powerfully from them in a stifling wave.

He went as close as he could.

'The General, is he with you?'

'No.'

'How came you here?'

'We were set ashore at the Panuco River.'

Chamberlain explained how the party had divided into three, twenty-five going north, another thirty south and the remainder striking inland. His group had been set upon by Chichemichi Indians who had stripped them but left their money. They had gone six days without water and had finally come to a settlement where they had been taken by mounted lancers. They were brought here and after the local *Alcalde* had relieved them of what little gold they carried, they were imprisoned.

'They shut us all up in this little cote and threatened to hang us, Gunner. They gave to us sodden grain, which they call maize, and which they feed their pigs withal. Many of us had been grievously wounded by the Indians, and we desired help of the Spanish, but they told us we should have no surgeon but the hangman, which should heal us of all our griefs, and they reviled us as Protestants and as pirates.'

'What of the *Minion*?'

'Gone home, God willing.'

'My brother was alive?'

'He is well – or was when I saw him.'

Tavistock raised his eyes skyward. 'God be thanked for that!'

'He gave me a token –'

Tavistock heard movement behind him and saw the horse. He stood up and pointed angrily to his shipmates' misery. 'They are my countrymen, locked up here in worse squalor than I would permit swine to suffer. Is this the way the noble Spanish treat their prisoners?'

Maria stared down at him and at the sty, then she nodded, turned her horse and left, returning with her brother almost immediately.

A great moaning arose from the captives when they saw the soldiers. They feared death and implored God to help them because Gonzalo de Escovedo's men carried halters.

Tavistock's heart pounded as he listened to their cries helplessly.

'They're going to hang us!'

'God of mercy, take pity on us!'

His heart raced. He looked from Chamberlain to the officer and stepped forward, imploring Escovedo to reconsider. The Spaniard brushed him away.

'No. Please. They don't deserve to die! You can't hang them.'

'Get out of my way.'

'What is their crime?'

'Stand aside, *Inglés!*'

Tavistock's eyes flashed around for a weapon, but there was none. Next, he heard himself scream and felt his bare hands tearing at Escovedo's collar, then he was down on top of him, his grip on that vile neck unbreakable. He wanted no more than to strangle the life from this man. It felt like freedom and like justice but it was madness. The soldiers lifted him bodily and prised his fingers from the flesh and Escovedo came alive again, gasping and choking.

He had changed nothing.

A dozen drawn rapiers pinned Tavistock's chest to the ground, the points digging through his shirt to draw blood. He saw the woman dismount and run to her brother. She held his head and helped him to breathe, and her eyes flashed at Tavistock, full of anger and hatred.

'Devil!'

'He was going to hang them!'

'He should hang all of you!'

Escovedo's sergeant staked the point of his halberd over the Englishman's heart, looking to his superior for a nod of command. When none came from the coughing, gasping officer he asked with relish, 'Shall I kill him now, sir?'

'No!'

The sergeant hesitated, expecting another answer. Then he put up his weapon reluctantly.

'Bring him!'

Tavistock was hauled savagely to his feet and brought before the Viceroy. Escovedo, recovered now, his jerkin torn open, dragged his collar aside and showed the marks where the Englishman's fingernails had clawed into him. He explained angrily that he had tried to kill him and demanded the satisfaction of seeing him dance on the hangman's *picota*.

Don Emilio looked up from his papers icily.

'He tried to kill you?'

Escovedo showed again the weals on his neck.

The Viceroy turned to the accused man. 'Is this true?'

'Your pardon, Excellency,' Tavistock said breathlessly. 'He was going to hang my friends.'

'I ordered him to take these filthy pirates from their hole and bind them.'

'His men had halters –'

'Did you expect them to be marched to Mexico City unbound?'

'I thought –'

'You thought?' Don Emilio motioned to his guards. 'Get him out of here.'

As Tavistock was led away Don Emilio turned to Escovedo, a half-smile on his mouth.

'So, the Englishman saw fit to assault you after all, Escovedo?' he said with mild reproach. 'I thought you said you had tamed him.'

'These English are never tamed. They respect nothing but force.'

Don Emilio regarded Escovedo thoughtfully. 'You're a hasty young man, but you've proved something about the Englishman's temper that you yourself did not suspect.'

When Escovedo had suggested the bellfounders as a test of the Englishman's knowledge he had agreed to postpone the executions. And when the head foundryman at the Santa Catalina forge had made an excellent report of his abilities, he had cancelled the order. The Englishman had obviously worked for many years as a cannon maker's apprentice and knew well the practices and pitfalls of the bronze caster's art. In that, he had not lied, but neither had he offered any important information. He is wary still, and unwilling. If he is to truly render his secrets to us, we who have made him captive and who he hates, he must be persuaded by means other than bare compulsion. But there is time enough, and I am not impatient.

Escovedo began to speak, but Don Emilio overrode him.

'I told you that the Englishman was to be brought to Mexico City alive. That he is valuable.'

'Yes, Excellency.'

'And you can think of no other way to loosen his tongue, other than by force? That's very sad.'

'I think I understand you, Excellency. If a man will not be obedient for the sake of his own skin, often he will be so for his friends. He was willing to die to save his comrades.'

'Quite.'

Escovedo brightened. 'Shall I order them all brought to Mexico City?'

'Do that. And send word to Don Luis in Vera Cruz to deliver the Englishmen in his gaol to me. Next, send these instructions ahead to

Mexico City. Then you will see how the strength of an enemy may be used against him.'

Two days later they arrived at Nohele.

There they rested. The English prisoners were treated well by the White Friars of Santa Maria, given clothing and mutton broth and ointments to heal their wounds. From there, they came to Metztitlan, forty leagues from Mexico City, a town of three hundred Spaniards, where they were lodged in the house of the Black Friars. Their stay at Pachuca, where the silver mines lay, was of two days and nights, and five days later, stopping off at *estancias* and farmsteads along the road, they came to within five leagues of Mexico City, accompanied by a great many Indians.

Don Emilio watched the Englishman carefully throughout all that time, and saw that he was as a brother to his countrymen. He also saw the way that Escovedo's sister attracted his eye. And he began to see another way to wrest the Englishman's secrets from him.

At Quoghiclan they halted at the house of the Grey Friars, and from thence were taken to the church of Our Lady of Guadalcanal where the healing springs eased their hurts. Before they departed each Spaniard of the train, of whatever rank, mounted or on foot, would not suffer to pass by the church until he had first entered it, knelt before the image and prayed to *Nuestra Señora* to deliver him from evil.

At four o'clock on the next day they entered Mexico City by the street called *La Calle Santa Caterina* and were brought into *La Plaça del Marquese*, where the palace of the Viceroy stood. In Don Emilio's mind, a plan concerning the Englishman, and now Escovedo's sister, had begun to form.

Book Two

Chapter 7

'Are we at war?'

'We are not, Captain Hawkins.'

The Cornishman's reply came as he climbed over the *Minion*'s gunwale. He was Walt Tremethick, owner of a south-coast caravel, on his way from the Thames to Penzance. He had happened upon them as they prepared to drop anchor in Mount's Bay. Hawkins questioned him anxiously for news, knowing that all their lives hung on what he had to tell them.

Tremethick was stocky like a wine butt, whiskery, with a round face and cleft chin, and still open-mouthed at coming across Hawkins's ship. He took off his skewed hat and kneaded it in hands as big and red as boiled crabs. The weather was icy and the coast wreathed in mists, but still it was England and indescribably beautiful to every man aboard the *Minion*.

'Then why're the Spaniards seizing English merchantmen in Spanish ports?' Tavistock asked.

Tremethick hawked and spat juicily over the side. 'That's the blockade. It's common to all trade this past month. They say the Spanish are furious over some great seizure of gold made at Southampton — money to pay Spain's blackbeards garrisoned in Flanders, so it's said. They have us embargoed in all the King's dominions. Nothing's going in or out of the Scheldt.'

'Devil sunder us! That's bad. Very bad!' Hawkins's eyes were deep-set in a gaunt and disease-ravaged face. He looked to his fortunes with a bleary eye. 'The Queen can be as sulky as a child after a tantrum. She'll ruin us all and in as high-handed a fashion as Zeus!'

'Not if what they say in the taverns about Deptford be true,' the Cornishman told him, relishing the chance to pass on his thoughts. 'In the matter of seizures the Queen has had the best of it so far. The Spanish forget they can't communicate with the Low Lands except by the Channel, and there's plenty rebel Dutchmen waiting in Kentish ports to harass them. They won't let a single Spanish bottom through the

Narrows if they can help it. Upriver they say Senyor Spez, the Spanish ambassador, is fuming mad, that he's a cove with but one thought in his brain – an embargo of England. And he has gotten his friend the Devil – may God on high protect us! – to set his hand unto his scheme.'

Tavistock asked incredulously, 'Antwerp is closed?'

'Aye. Tight as a duck's arsehole.'

'But that's suicide!'

'For the Flemings, maybe.'

'For London!'

'You been away too long, my friend.'

'We're well enough informed. Since New Year's Day we've been a week in Pontevedra. They told us there had been some seizures and a slackening of trade. But this!'

Hawkins explained how on the point of death they had found the Spanish port and begged men and provisions from the impounded ships of English wine traders, effecting hasty repairs and putting out before the Spanish authorities came to understand what was happening. He and Tavistock had picked up the confused rumours that abounded about an embargo and the incident at San Juan and they had kept their identity secret just long enough to escape to sea again.

'It's a storm that must blow itself out soon,' Tremethick said. 'Any play the Spanish make, short of force, loses them the game.'

'Aye! Short of force,' Hawkins replied. 'But that's always their king card.'

The Cornishman sniffed a dewy drop from his nose and told him how trade was flowing north now, through Hamburg, where the north Germans and Baltic traders were taking all the woollen cloth that English ships could land. As Tremethick spoke it seemed to Tavistock that the situation was not as bleak as Hawkins had supposed. He was fervently loyal to the Queen, but his fevered brain had imagined a traitor's death and no way out of it. But things had changed. Spanish pay ships had been driven into English ports by sea rovers. There they had fallen legally under the Queen's control. So long as the Queen released the Spanish vessels she contravened no law. She could even claim to have acted faithfully by giving them safe haven against Channel pirates. However, there had been no reason to release the ships' *cargoes*. The owners of the gold on board, and those responsible for its safety until it reached Alva, were Genoese financiers. Tavistock saw that their position must have been a sorry one. Faced with Elizabeth's request to transfer the loan to her they had taken the only course possible and done so. And now the bullion was safely lodged in the Tower.

Tavistock considered the position carefully. 'The King of Spain will certainly interpret this action as a piece of diplomacy designed to damage and humiliate him,' he told Hawkins exultantly. 'The Queen may have chosen it as a method of squaring the outrage done to our ships at San Juan!'

'In which case our return may only heighten the quarrel.'

'Will Elizabeth back us or will she bury us? Hard to say, but I'd guess the former.'

Hawkins sacrificed his caution regretfully, but hope was beginning to stir him. 'That's her character from what I know of her: ever ready to play the injured party in order to gain an advantage, ever willing to clench her fist against the Grandees – *if* there's gain in it.'

'If the embargo's hurting the Netherlands that will suit her well. If what we heard in Pontevedra's right, Spanish merchants will soon be crying for a settlement. Perhaps the Duke of Alva's beginning to regret listening to Don Gerau de Spes? And perhaps our return is well timed after all!'

Tavistock's thoughts soared as they anchored.

'I must get quickly up to London,' was all Hawkins would say of his plans. He seemed to Tavistock to have drawn other, darker threads into the pattern of his thoughts, threads he would not hint at. Still his assessment of their prospects and the reception they might yet meet with seemed unduly guarded.

News of their arrival had gone before them from Mount's Bay to Plymouth, carried in Penzance fishing smacks along the coast like a sea wave breaking across all of Cornwall; at market towns like Helston, Truro, St Austell and Liskeard the word was relayed along the main road, then across the River Tamar so that by the time the *Minion* rounded the Point of Penlee she was escorted by scores of small boats. In reply, her flags and pennants made a brave show for the folk who had crowded the headlands to wave. All Plymouth had come to a halt.

A familiar face grinned up at Tavistock from the boat that came alongside as they entered the Cattewater.

'Damn me to hell! Can it be?'

'You got me up from my bed, caterpillar!'

'That's a bloody miracle!'

'By Jesus, it's good to see you, Richard. You're a lucky bastard.'

'You too, Francis. But if it was luck we had aboard, it was all cross-grained.'

'You're looking fine!'

'Healthy enough – for a dead man.'

Drake scrambled aboard and the two men clasped each other's fore-arms in the way of men made brothers by the sea. The almost windless calm had turned the inlet to glass and despite the earliness of the hour the frosty dockside was swelling; half the people in Plymouth had come down to the waterfront to see who had lived and who had died in America.

Drake looked aloft. 'A difficult passage, by the looks of your tops. And you too.'

'Not so bad since Pontevedra. We took on twelve good lads, and the

rest of us have fattened up like sows since then. Those of us left.'
Tavistock's breath steamed as he looked away from the ship's rigging
in disgust. He was in no mood for bantering and could think only of
his Jane and their son now.

'Where you been?'

'We sighted Gwennap Head two days ago. You?'

'I beat your ragged arse home by five days. While you were wishing
yourself here, I've been a-making nests out of a feather bed with Mary
Newman these two days up Hingston Down way. No callers on pain
of death! Call yourself a mariner, you big, no-hope lubbard?'

Tavistock scowled down at the stocky man. 'I may be out of trim,
but I've enough left to sink your fornicating barge, so watch your mouth,
bedbug!'

Drake roared and slapped his thigh. 'Come ashore, it's past time I
stood you a round aplenty with some of that money you owe me.
There's a lot of news you'll be wanting to hear. Me too, I can tell you.'

'Eh – don't spoil a man's privacy. I've some haymaking of my own
to do first.'

'Aye, there's priorities, if I knows Richard Tavistock!' As Drake
looked about him, he saw that those coaxing the *Minion* towards her
mooring were not men of her original company. He became suddenly
serious. 'How many did you fetch back with you?'

'Fifteen.'

'Christ in heaven.' Drake's voice was low.

'You?'

'Sixty-three.'

Tavistock was warmed at the news, but it did not show on his face.
He said. 'We had a marooning.'

Drake's pride guttered. 'Marooning? God's death, that's an evil thing.'

'A hundred set ashore by the Panuco. Make of that what you will.'

Onshore, William Hawkins waited at the quayside where hundreds
of wives and mothers congregated, anxious for their men. The tearful
meetings of the lucky few leavened the sickly disappointment of the
many as they came ashore. He saw Chamberlain's girl, Amy, her face
showing her heart struck hollow as she heard the boatswain read the
list of those who had been left behind on the Main.

He was hardly aware of it. The charge of emotions around him
penetrated his chest, filling him with expectation. Suddenly his reserve
burst and he gave in to the feeling he had kept iron-bound these many
months. He strained his eyes searching the dock for Jane and young
Harry. The bonnets of the womenfolk were of dazzling white. Damn
it! Where was she? It would be like her to hang back in a doorway with
their son and watch him search her out then come to her privately, away
from the rest, to hug wife and son tight in his arms.

His eyes roamed the quayside frontages and then he felt Amy tugging
at him, her tear-stained cheeks pale with shock.

'Master Richard.'

He heard her distantly, not wanting to be caught up in her grief for her man at this thousand times looked-for moment. Where was Jane? *Where was she?*

'Master Richard. Listen to me, I beg of you!'

Again she clutched at his sleeve.

'Later, girl.'

'For God's sake!'

Then he saw the faces of the old women around him and their looks reflected his sudden agony.

'Your Jane is taken away from you.'

The girl's words cut his heart from him.

'*Taken?*'

'She's gone with her baby, Master Richard. Carried off by the small-pox this two month.'

He threw off her grasping fingers and closed his mind. But the words continued to wound him like hot knives. *Taken? Could it be true? Could it?*

'No!'

He bellowed out his anger. Strode off. Threw his fists at the stout wooden door of the warehouse. Then he sank down to his knees wrapped up in himself so tight that no one approached him, nor dared speak to him. Even Drake left him, wishing his tongue cut out for what had passed between them minutes before. He had not known about Jane's death. He went back to the quay where William Hawkins, finely girt and hung in golden chains, embraced his emaciated brother. He led the men of his employ past the warehouse and to the steps of the town hall where payment tables had already been set up. As they walked, their gladness turned to business. Drake saw that William kept his words private, and sought to overhear.

'Some reports had you down as destroyed, others said that you were gone to Ireland.'

John spat. 'Ireland, is it? That's a worthless fancy!'

'There were many in London who believed it, and many who believe it still. The word is that you buried a quarter ton of gold and two hundred thousand pounds of silver there. It will take a hard proof to shake that tale.'

John Hawkins grunted. 'Let them think what they please.'

'It'd be a powerful disappointment to people if we were to shake such a belief too early,' William said.

'Aye, and a sharp pain in the neck for us both if we do not. We were in Pontevedra two weeks ago. All Spain was swarming with lies against us.'

'Were you recognised?' Drake asked.

'They found us out, and a great prize they thought us. Their belief is that we attacked Don Emilio out of greed to steal his treasure. It's vital

I get up to London at once.'

'The Queen and her Council may be disabused of the lie in secret?'

'And timely quick if we're both to keep our heads and bodies joined. We've a chest of pearls and silver, some bits of gold, but precious little else. Thirteen, maybe fourteen thousand pounds, depending on the state of the market. That's all told. *Minion*'s fit only for making into barns. We're not in profit.'

The elder Hawkins nodded gravely. 'So, it seems our Indies ventures are ended. I wish the Queen's mind were better known to me.'

'Will she grant me audience?'

'That's what my lord Leicester is paid for. He is currently in some debt. Which suits us well.'

'Then we may yet save our necks.'

William glanced around and said quietly, 'The Queen, too, is looking about her since the Scottish Queen came hither. I have it that Elizabeth's cornered in her own Court, adversaries ranged to left and right, and assassins pledged against her life. Some think Mary's claim is the better.'

John showed his disbelief. 'Assassins? Fain to kill Elizabeth?'

'Tread with care, John. She may desire your head yet in payment for your endeavours. But she has need of friends at this moment, so be discreet in how you show yourself to her.'

'If any trade is to go forward in the Indies, we must have her approval. Tacitly at least.'

'You must have the Sovereign's, it's true. But who knows who will sit the throne of England a month hence? Who knows if a Catholic Queen would give you right of passage across the treaty line of Tordesillas. When Philip shared Mary's throne all such commerce was strictly forbidden –'

'What of your promise of rescue?' Drake broke in.

John Hawkins eyed him irritably. 'What rescue?'

'The rescue of our hundred men marooned at Panuco River.'

'That will have to wait.'

'Wait?'

Hawkins turned on him. 'Aye! Wait!'

As the counting out began, Drake moved away. His stomach had been knotted by Hawkins's reply. He collected Boaz, the huge black man who had come back stronger than any aboard the *Minion*, and went pushing through the crowds in search of Tavistock. War was coming, and in war it was not enough to think as a merchant thinks. A man had to have the temerity to do what others could not guess at. In war, a certain kind of man was needed. And he knew a way that would bring Tavistock to his cause. Since pulling the *Judith* out of San Juan he had spent many hours constructing an elaborate plan of revenge. For the first time, he had the money and could raise powerful backing, and at last giant affairs of state were swinging the right way. Now was the time to leave Hawkins's employ and put his ideas to the test.

At dusk Drake found Tavistock alone in his empty house. He knew what must be done and led him to the alehouse called the King's Head on the corner of Portlowe Street. The big blond fellow went like a walking dead man, stiffly, with Drake's hand clamped under one arm and the Negro's under the other. The cobbles were icy. Lanterns shone dimly in windows. Since he was last there, King Henry's smiling portrait had been taken down from the walls; now a rough painting of the King of Spain's head impaled on a spike swung on a board above the door.

The night was frosted with rime, but inside it was warm and full of familiar smells. A one-legged fiddler scratched out a tune in the corner. Drake gave him a coin and threw him out. Faces gaped at them until Drake raised his fist to them.

'Begone, insects! What's the matter, never seen a blackamoor before!'

He brought them a hock of beef, some new-baked bread and a quart pot of spirit each and cleared a corner for them. The ruby in Boaz's ear scintillated as he watched the man who had navigated him to this cold land and kept him from starvation.

'Coming down here's the only way,' Drake said, but he got no answer.

He knew Tavistock wanted only to be alone, but he would not let him be. He was a captain and he had his duty. A debt to pay after the stranding. Drake told him to eat, and then to drink the pain out of him amongst his people as was only right. That way no one's sorrow could fester. Within half an hour, as Drake knew it would, the tavern became a smothering hell for Tavistock. The alehouse had filled to bursting. Down its entire length, dead men's relatives were shouting and throwing up their hands, the uncommonly piercing voices of women still looking vainly for their husbands, and children wanting fathers that would never return. Often the names turned to shrieks, and rucks of violence flared up.

It was a family's right. They wanted accounts by those that had seen it happen. Stories that paid in full for the peace of their souls. It was a survivor's obligation and a captain's solemn duty. The agony of the marooning at Panuco River had to be faced squarely, but all the while Tavistock sat mute, frozen inside his own heartbreak. Another jostle broke out at the door. Drake made him drink. And he complied, gulping the burning liquid down mechanically as though he could not taste it. Then a shower of silver coins ricocheted off the table where he sat.

'You bastards! You foul-livered liars! A curse on all your children and your children's children to the fourth generation, you scum!' In a frenzy of words the harridan flew at them. She was a marooned man's wife, held back by Amyas Poole's widow. 'There's your blood money, you brace of godless bastards! I hope you burn in hellfire!'

The woman was grappled and pulled outside. Boaz calmly gathered up what coins he could see into his empty ale pot and handed it to the woman's brother.

'I'm right sorry, Captain. She's high-strung, so she is. Her with seven young 'uns, and all.'

The man left them, seeing suddenly the bloodless grey of Tavistock's face. It was different when a ship went down with all hands lost. Then the grief was shared equally. With a marooning it was as if they had all died but then some had been resurrected, as if the families thought the survivors had cheated the victims out of their homecoming.

'Where's Hawkins?' Tavistock said in a lost whisper.

'It's not his place to be here.'

'Nor mine. This place stinks. I must get out.' Tavistock looked suddenly as if he was about to vomit.

Drake steadied him. 'If you go now they'll never forgive you, Richard. You know that. You've to show them plain that you've no guilt. Before them! Face to face!'

'I'm burning in Hell, Francis!'

'Drink!'

He lifted the tankard to Tavistock's lips again and made him swallow until the amber liquor coursed through his beard.

'I want to die.'

'You will. When God ordains it.'

Tavistock's rigid paralysis gave way to a mighty shaking. He heaved himself to his feet and staggered to the door. Drake stood over him in the alley as he brought up a bellyfull of pungent bile.

'That's the way. Cast it out!'

The cold night air seeped into him. The polar stars above pitiless and white, like needles. And Boaz's hand on his back slapping him until his eyes watered. When he straightened he was sucking in breath and panting.

'I must go to my house.'

'There's things I want to say before we part.'

'It can wait.'

'No. It can't!'

'Get off my arm!'

Drake let go, and Tavistock shrugged his sleeve and began to walk.

'You want to go back for your brother, don't you?'

He stopped, but did not turn.

'My brother's dead. My blood is dead. All I ever loved.'

'Your brother's *alive*, Richard.'

The life drained from Tavistock's body and he sank down against the wall. For a moment the din from the tavern seemed to fade away and the deep wound in his shoulder seeped pain all across his breast.

'Alive?'

'It's my custom to ask questions of my crew. John was seen. By two of his lads who'd been left for dead on the island. They crawled out from the corpses and got off in a small boat. We took them aboard at first light next day.'

Tavistock's mouth hung open, his eyes shot with glistening moonlight. 'Is it true?'

'One of them says he saw your brother jump from the *Jesus* and strike out for shore, and the other swears he watched him wade into a mangrove swamp.'

'He knew it was John?'

'Only one man I know wore a red neckerchief made from a signal flag.'

'They're lying! Hoping to pick up a reward from me!'

'I know when a lad of mine is telling the truth.'

Tavistock's voice was a breath. 'Christ Jesus!'

Drake leaned forward, his eyes wrinkled and his mouth split showing a set of pearl-like teeth in a devil's grin. 'How would you like to come in with me on another venture? A return trip to Vera Cruz? This time with a hold full of round iron to trade?'

The road from Plymouth to London was iron hard in the frost. Their salvaged treasure had been packed across four horses and watched-after overnight by men of the Hawkins company, but the journey was a long and tiring one on January roads.

Jouncing over rutted tracks had made Tavistock sick in the belly and each time he dismounted, the dizzying solidity of the ground under his feet made him stagger. Everything on land stunk of excrement – the roads smelt of horse-dung, the villages of pig-shit and the towns of human middens. On land there was no 'side' for a man to stick his arse over. Everywhere he looked was cluttered with rocks and trees and dwellings and even at midday when a watery sun warmed his aching shoulder and softened the iron-hard road it remained for him the cold night of winter and everything in England was dead to him.

Beyond Exeter the road improved. They travelled the sheep-cropped meadowlands where queer chalk giants showed through the turf, and the plains where bogeymen had built their stone dancing ring, and soon enough they came into the valley of the Thames, thick with skeletal trees and a promise of rest, because from here they could avail themselves of water traffic. On the seventh day, some of the pain in Tavistock's heart melted and he felt his soul begin to thaw.

When Hawkins had asked him to organise the moving of their salvaged treasure to London Tavistock had been silently obedient. He had taken orders mutely and given them to his men in a monotone. He had done as he was told, nothing more nor less, walking, speaking and doing without spirit or commitment. When Hawkins told him he was to accompany him to the capital Tavistock refused. In this he was adamant, clinging to the words Drake had spoken. Only when Hawkins explained that he needed a trusted witness of events, and promised to take Tavistock to the Queen's Court, did he speak to him.

'I intend to lodge a complaint with the Privy Council about the treatment we've received at the hands of the Spanish. And to demand reprisals. Will you come with me?'

'Do you want me to come?'

'I do.'

'Then I will – if you will undertake to get the Queen's permission for a rescue as you promised our men.'

'I cannot ask that.'

'Then I cannot come.'

Hawkins had spoken sternly to him then, and spoken of a scheme that must secure all their futures against a turmoil that would soon sweep across England. Tavistock had acquiesced and, for the week following, the bitterness and pain that had attended his homecoming had been a degree diluted by the work he had been thrown into. The promise that Hawkins had made kept the fire that Drake had ignited within him alight. Without it, he might have let it burn out.

They transferred their load to a river barge at Weybridge, and passed the splendid royal palaces at Hampton and Richmond. Both were of red brick, with soaring towers, leaden domes and castellated turrets. Tavistock was awed by Richmond, which stood hard against the river's edge, flanked by a long court of outbuildings and a royal chapel. It rose up six storeys, full of big, square glass windows, and the chimneys and spires of its roof were new-gilded and decked with metal pennants. There were many river craft here, and a busy towpath on which he saw a swarthy-faced 'Egyptian' leading a horse on which five little Gypsy children dressed in coloured tatters rode. A second led a horse laden with stolen poultry and for some reason unknown to him Tavistock smiled sourly at the thought that even worthless moon-men fared better than he.

The path grew more congested with wains and swagmen as they passed Mortlake, and Tavistock began to smell salt in the tidal river mud. This was where the Queen's wizard, Doctor Dee, lived. Many times, he knew, Hawkins had gone to his big rambling house and there consulted him for astrological readings, and often to check the auspices of a sailing date.

'He's a figure-caster of great power. A man of tremendous intellect, a reader of geography and astronomy. He has the biggest library in England,' Hawkins told him.

'Books of Welsh sorcery and alchemy?' Tavistock asked, frowning at the cawing rooks that nested near by. 'They say he is a man to fear.'

Hawkins nodded. 'He dreams of an empire for England greater than Spain's. And he possesses an obsidian mirror in which he can read the future.'

'Do you believe?'

'The Queen believes, and that's good enough. It's what stops the local people burning his house down and roasting John Dee in the embers for witchcraft. That's what the Queen's Majesty means.'

'And when she dies?'

'There will be a new monarch. The house will burn and Dee with it.'

Tavistock folded his arms, unsure of his own belief. Something told him it was ungodly and against the proper order of heaven and earth, but at the same time he gloried in the notion of there being such a thing as a useful science. Did he not make use of it himself? He daily made calculating figures and dialled himself answers upon complex instruments of navigation; the unlearned would deem star-lore or the use of an astrolabe to be sorcery. And what of the invisible power that influenced the compass needle? Was that Satanic? And if so, what did that imply about a man who lived and found his way by it? Was it a different force to that which permeated the world and deflected men's bodies and souls across the globe to live or die, that power they called the Queen's Majesty? An empire greater than Spain's ... That, for a certainty, was a dainty thought to ponder on.

In the afternoon, Tavistock looked about him at the quiet meadows of Chelsea and Battersea and wondered what it was that had made him English and had motivated him with feeling for a whole country, most of which he had never seen. What was England but an idea? And what was God's purpose in bringing him back to it just to torment his soul? It was a mystery.

The riverbanks slid by quietly. Set upon them were ancient manor houses, rolling estates, tilled fields, everywhere the hand of man had created order and regularity from the rough flesh of the land. Come calm or storm, come war or peace, nothing had varied that harmony in five hundred years. It was the spirit of a dour island tribe. Stolid, cold weather people who looked inward, and who found peace in the routines of earth and sky. Neither prince nor tyrant could disturb that clay, stamped and sifted as it was by the stock of Albion as their own these hundred and fifty generations.

But as he watched, the land seemed to Tavistock suddenly to be filled with a great and gathering force, a puissant spirit, as though Albion was a giant, and the giant was stirring from a sleep of centuries. It was deeply awesome and at the same time fascinating to his mind's eye; he saw the meadows cracked by fissures and the soil riven and everywhere men unbound from their plot, men who in their whole lives had moved not a five-mile from their place of birth, freed as if by war. And across the land fires were struck up that would never be quenched. He knew with a soul-shocking jolt that the constancy of the old order was passing. The minds of men were clearing as if fixed now with a new purpose and a new vision. But was it of heaven? Or was it of hell?

Instantly they came into London he felt the vital force that only this huge city could create. As they left the boat and led the horses up into the city he felt like a ghost, an invisible eye, watching but ignored, and in his detachment he saw the truth of the place. It was astonishing! An exciting, aggressive, intense stew of human endeavour. A city growing

fast, drawing all things and all men to it like a magnet, so that it doubled
in size each thirty years. It was sure to become soon the most populous
city in Christendom, and the most diverse. He saw apprentices and
vagabonds in the streets, tradesmen and servants; there were the great
houses of earls and statesmen, cathedrals and royal palaces, shopfronts
and low shiels and hovels crammed in alleys. Everywhere from Queenhythe up to Cheapside there was a bedlam of noise. Fish pedlars hawked
their dripping wares with loud cries, iron-shod carts rattled down
cobbled streets, whipjacks cried for bread and silver, watched by cat-
chpoles who would take a share, or arrest them. Every minute, it seemed,
each man, woman and child fought the Devil and his brother for profit
in the middle of this most scoffing, most respectless and unthankful city
there ever was.

They spent the night at Hawkins's house in the Strand, where his
staff of servants fussed after them and warmed their beds with copper
pans full of ash, and in the morning they ate a magnificent breakfast
and went once more to the river at noon, taking a waterman's boat to
the city of Westminster, its operator chatting like a philosopher until
they commanded him to be quiet. On the Surrey side they saw the
Archbishop's palace of Lambeth, and on the other the Abbey's ancient
towers and many piers where a clutter of little boats were tied up. At
the stairs of Star Chamber, they were caught by the ebb and rounded
to the river steps at Whitehall where a gallery jutted over the water.

Sickly palliards licensed to beg there held deformed hands out as they
mounted the steps and guards challenged them and took away their
swords. Next, they were conducted within the precinct of this old and
decaying palace to the hall and chamber where the Privy Council met.

It was a maze of lodgings and covered ways. Within, aristocrats and
knights sauntered in chains of gold, brocades and velvets. There were
tapestries and painted murals and carved stones, and below them a
separate estate of chamberlains, almoners, sergeants-at-arms, and
beneath them a bustling underworld of servants, spies, chaundrymen,
sewers, harbingers, buttery maids and dog-keepers.

Hawkins's petitions to the Council had preceded them and they
were met courteously by Queen's officers who brought Hawkins to the
meeting. When Tavistock tried to follow, guards clashed their halberds
together across his path, their stony lack of response leaving him in no
doubt that he had been excluded unnegotiably.

He lingered outside the chamber of the Privy Council for an hour.
Uninvited, he paced the stone-flagged corridor, wondering what was
happening with Hawkins, if he would be called as witness to events, and,
if so, what he must say. Anxiously he imagined the Privy Councillors in
their heavy-mantled robes, grave-faced, pompous, outwardly deploring
Hawkins's actions of piracy, and inwardly soured that he had failed to
bring them the booty he had promised. This was the moment Hawkins
had dreaded in his fevers. The moment of account when credit turned

to deficit. When fairweather men kissed the cheek and called in the soldiery.

Tavistock looked up as a troop of twelve red-and-black uniformed yeoman guards, each carrying a pikestaff, turned into the corridor. They clashed to attention ten paces from him and remained at attention, staring glassily ahead.

Their arrival unsettled Tavistock, who saw no virtue in their presence. When he was approached by a man who might have been a lawyer, he felt an alarm course through him. Dressed in a black fur-trimmed coat and skullcap he seemed to be of some consequence and standing. His face showed him to be a man of intellect and he had a sonorous voice to match the brown liquidity of his eyes.

'Captain Tavistock?'

Tavistock returned the stare. 'Yes.'

'Be kind enough, sir, to follow me.'

Tavistock remained rooted where he stood and the man turned back after three steps.

'I'm waiting for Captain John Hawkins, a merchant of Plymouth. He's currently within the council chamb –'

'Yes, I know. Please come with me.'

Still Tavistock did not move.

'What is it?'

Tavistock's guarded words came slowly. 'I do not know you, sir. And I do not know how you know me. Am I under arrest?'

The man glanced at the guard and shook his head. 'These fine fellows are nothing to do with me, Captain. My name is Francis Walsingham. Your servant.'

'Your servant, sir. And your business with me?'

Walsingham's eyes sparkled. 'You are lately become a man of some reputation and I have need of you. That is enough.'

Tavistock recoiled from the intensity of the man, the presumption of his words, but something in Walsingham's mien held him, and when he asked him to follow a third time, Tavistock did so.

Chapter 8

It was another cold February night, eight o'clock by the chimes of St Martin's, and Ambassador Don Gerau de Spes sat alone, sweating over a piece of paperwork that he had been postponing for days. It was hard to know how best to proceed – in a begging letter to the King of Spain.

'*Sacred Catholic Royal Majesty*,' he wrote, obedient to the formula. '*My obligation to serve your Majesty, and the natural faith and love to your Majesty, induce me, with the greatest submission, to propose that which appears to me fitting . . .*'

Don Gerau was a heavy man, thick-set, with a bullet head. His apparel had a military cut, the same grey as his eyes, and his pink jowls nestled in a pie-dish ruff, undisguised by a goat beard. He ran a hand uncertainly through hair that was combed straight back from his forehead in greased furrows as he searched for words, but his concentration was unfocused and his plucked eyebrows rode querulously as he listened to the sound of a cart rattling through the streets below. Could this be the visitor he was expecting?

The man – a sea captain, or so he said – had written a letter of proposal and that too lay on his desk. It was cautious but at the same time extravagant, and the promise it held out was tantalising, and Don Gerau decided that it was no longer a question of whether, but *when* he must act on it.

The Ambassador applied himself anxiously to the other, vastly more important letter again. All Spain's stars are in the ascendant. We must seize the moment now, he thought. For if we hesitate we'll let fall the finest opportunity there'll ever be to destroy the Jezebel of England.

Don Gerau laboured under no illusions about his position. He knew that he had replaced his well-liked and well-respected predecessor, Don Guzman de Silva, as a reprisal in kind. At the same time, in September of last year, King Philip had expelled the uncouth English Ambassador-resident and ex-academic, Doctor John Man.

He remembered Man with indignation; his vitriolic temper and vile manners had outraged the whole of Madrid. He had picked his teeth, got in his cups and, before hosts of the royal blood, had called His Holiness the Pope 'a canting little monk'. Eventually the Court had been driven to petition the King, who was spending Lent in prayer and penitence in the cloistered gloom of Abrojo, and within six months the King had complied, but Man had refused to surrender the apology Philip had demanded of him, and so he had been thrown out. Surely it must have been a deliberate insult delivered on Elizabeth's behalf, the Count of Feria, a man vastly experienced in the iniquities of the English, had told the King. The fact that she had sent such a low-born, ill-bred creature, a fellow unskilled in all but the most vulgar social graces, can only have been a calculated slight – especially when Philip's Ambassador to England had been so elegant, so punctilious and so refined.

Four months ago I thought the same, Don Gerau decided sadly, but four months in this country has convinced me that such delicacy of understanding is utterly beyond the English. They think themselves a civilised people, but in reality they are as barbarous as the Irish tribesmen they despise.

When we landed at Dover – the Madonna and all the suffering saints, it was so cold and wet! – I couldn't imagine. It rained all the while and our horses were hock-deep in mud bringing us to London. All my fine velvets were rotted by mould before we got halfway here. It's a terrible place. Cold and dark, but no more than they deserve. They are not civilised people. They live in hovels with earthen floors and dried rushes for a roof, and they smell – I still can't believe how bad!

And their Queen is a monster. They say her father's hair was the same bright orange. She had the affrontery to keep me waiting more than an hour before she would receive me. And she had her sword of state marched in procession before her when she came so that I might be in no doubt regarding the esteem in which she holds herself.

Don Gerau shook his head, thinking. Maybe it was God's curse on England that Mary Tudor had died childless and her half sister had usurped the throne. The English deserve their government. To a man they hate us for we lord it over them, and that they cannot stand. I see it in their eyes every day. Hostile, mannerless, brooding like hogs. The common people gawp and must be compelled to take their hats off to us, and when we come to their capital they give our lords neither respect nor civility. But Philip forbids any reaction. I am to bear all insults, whatever the humiliation. My staff are jostled and subjected to contemptuous indignities at every turn until every last shred of honour is stripped from us. As long as I live I will never, never forget it. Nor will I forgive.

Yes, he thought savagely, they're cruel to us, but they'll pay for their sins. Especially their heresy. Just as Our Lord was crucified to save our souls from eternal damnation, so Philip will one day bring this evil land back into the embrace of our Holy Mother Church. They'll pay for their heresy when the Scottish Queen comes to the throne. It's time to show

Elizabeth that she can't affront the King of Spain with impunity. It's time to remind Europe that Philip is verily the son of the great Emperor Charles, and that at any time we can do to England what we have already done to the Low Countries and are presently doing to the Muslims of Granada.

'If harmonious relations are to be preserved between England and my Court,' the King had instructed him coldly just before he had taken ship, 'those relations must be based on mutual respect. Failing that, there must be an embassy of mutual disrespect.'

The shame of that parting burned in Don Gerau still. The King's words had transmuted a golden, crowning moment into a leaden shame. Insult and innuendo had followed. Don Gerau thought hotly of the story he had picked up on board the ship to London that the King's half-brother, Don John, had suggested sending a pig, dressed in ambassadorial velvet and wearing a lace ruff, to Elizabeth's Court. Of course, the story had gone, Philip's unsmiling sobriety had overruled that idea, and instead, he had sent Don Gerau de Spes to teach the English manners!

And teach them he would.

Four months! Four months in this terrible country. Four months spent huddled close over draughty fireplaces, four months of blackness when the sun rises at nine in the morning and sinks at three in the afternoon. But the last four months had seen history at its rawest. Huge upheavals were afflicting the land, and each successive tremor nudged Elizabeth's downfall an inch closer. Yes, he told himself, heartened by the thought, the shame of my appointment is subsiding. I understand well that the ambitious diplomat can only forge himself a successful career in the furnace of conflict, and even if it sinks me in debt I will buy my King the victory he craves. Yea, and at the same time I will buy a victory of mine own, for I long to see the streets of London lit up as bright as day by the funeral pyres of Elizabeth's Protestants, and in this, the sea captain may help me.

The letter he must now write to Philip would be superficially a request for money. Though a man of some status, with a comfortable income from his estates, Don Gerau had found his purse strained after just two months in this freezing hellhole. The extravagant demands of the gathering crisis had bankrupted him. King Philip had to be made to understand. His English embassy must have funds. Now. Immediately!

Should this letter fail to sway the King, Don Gerau knew, all these careful efforts would fall to dust. Starved of funds, the choice would then be to languish impotently, or turn to the detestable Italians whose financial tentacles were everywhere. Anything but that, he thought, turning over the ornate Moorish pistol that lay on his desk. It was inlaid with mother-of-pearl, heavy and well balanced in his grip. The snaphance flint was shaved to a perfect angle, its mechanism oiled and sprung ready. If the Italians were brought in to underwrite a Spanish

King's policies there would be interference and constraint and all secrets would be compromised.

Truly, the moment is coming, he told himself, levelling the weapon. If England were not an island Alva's men would have annihilated this filthy town and cut the throats of every last one of its obstinate inhabitants months ago. But soon enough the English would learn that their insularity was no protection against the might of Spain.

The very air of London is heavy with flammable vapours, and the Court of the bastard Queen is tinder dry, he thought with anticipation. A spark! A single, flint-struck spark at the right instant would set Europe ablaze. The entire Continent would rage with war, and not just war, but a holy Armageddon that would consume, once and for all, the vile Protestant heresy.

He aimed the pistol at the distant steeple of St Martin's and pulled the trigger, sending sparks showering from the frizzen steel into an empty pan. The Lutherans would be eliminated for ever! And I, Don Gerau de Spes, Knight of the Order of Calatrava, Member of the Council of His Majesty, will have touched off their destruction!

He closed his eyes and willed the images that cascaded through his mind to be still. This was no time for flights of fancy, there was still much to be done, he thought, growing suddenly severe with himself. The sea captain talks big, but are not all mariners loose-tongued braggarts? Surely he cannot possibly deliver what he says. Better to write the letter to Philip, and leave dreaming to idle men.

He dipped his goose quill and wrote, couching the letter to his King in flowery, subservient terms, struggling to strike the correct tenor, and appending the standard 'first priority' close:

> 'May our Lord preserve, for many years, the sacred and Catholic person of your Majesty. From the lodgings, this twenty-eighth day of February 1569, of your Majesty's creature and most humble servant, who kisses your royal hands.'

Before the clock struck the third quarter, Don Gerau heard the knock at his door. He hurriedly put his papers and the pistol into the drawer of his writing desk, locked it, then stood up and gave permission to the doorman for his visitor to enter.

He was a tall, blond man dressed in rib-fronted doublet the colour of an ocean wave, fashionable breeches padded out with horsehair and black thigh boots rubbed up to a magnificent polish. His teeth were white, he smelled of bergamot oil, and he carried a massive gold stud, enamelled with a rearing phoenix, in his earlobe. But the most exquisite and the most provocative item of his apparel was a spiral-linked gold chain looped three times around his neck and hanging to his navel. It was clearly of Spanish origin and too expensive to have been got honestly.

Don Gerau was caught momentarily speechless.

'Your Excellency!'

'*You?* You are – Captain Tavistock?'

'The same.'

A broad smile. Don Gerau looked the man up and down in amazement, then he recovered and quickly stifled his incredulity. This man was a full head taller than him, and built in proportion, though he had little fat about him. His hair and neatly trimmed beard were sun bleached and his skin was bronzed; he had the spread stance of a seafarer. And his finery no doubt came of profit he had made in the Indies. The man's hand came off the wrought hilt of his dress-sword to clasp his own in a crushing squeeze.

'You – you will of course take wine?'

'That I will. I thank you.'

He had expected someone very different: one of the bootless waterfront scum that clustered about the Hollander's basin by St Katharine's Church, or a cloaked sneak-thief from the back door of a fat merchant's house on the Strand. But this man was no Londoner spy. By his accent he was of the West, bluff and uncultivated, and there was a fierceness in his eyes, but it was not a fierceness that threatened. Perhaps I can tame this lion, Don Gerau thought, pouring from a silver decanter. In his letter he spoke of a great advantage to me and my cause. He's worth a cup of wine at least.

'Do you have any preference, *Capitán*? I myself will take a wine grown in La Mancha, from a vineyard my family owns.'

The Captain hesitated. 'My taste is for Malmsey or Bual, if you have it.'

Don Gerau smiled delicately. 'Ah, the wines of Madeira. Regrettably I do not keep a single bottle of Portuguese wine. You have sailed there?'

'Indeed I have. And I'm sure I can arrange for a pipe or two of Bual to be delivered to Your Excellency, if you wish it. I can even supply it to you at cost.'

Don Gerau's hand hovered. 'Thank you, but perhaps not, *Capitán*. My position requires that I, more than any other, am seen to remain loyal to the produce of my own country. And loyalty is important, is it not?'

'Loyalty?' Tavistock laughed scornfully. 'You'll pay through the arse if it's loyalty you'd sup.'

Don Gerau replaced the decanter and smiled again. 'I know well the cost of service. Do you know that an ambassador must pay his own expenses?'

'Aye! But his King will underwrite him, if necessary.'

Don Gerau paused. Then he nodded slowly, understanding. Dealing with thieves and liars was an education; they invariably called proceedings down to business with unseemly haste.

'So,' he said genially. 'You have your audience. What is this "great advantage" of which you speak?'

Tavistock leaned forward gloatingly. 'Both a boon to your cause and a profit to me. If you hear me out you may think so too.'

Don Gerau learned first who he was, and then with shock that he had been at Vera Cruz on Hawkins's ship. As he listened he took comfort in the guards that waited at his door and in the sword of Toledo steel fastened at his belt, but he swiftly discovered that he would need neither.

'A hundred men were left in Mexico, Your Excellency. My brother among them. And I would recover them all, or severally, from the King's keeping. My proposal is this: in exchange for their safe release and delivery here, a sum of gold and certain guarantees – I will give you England.'

Don Gerau stared at Tavistock, inwardly unsure whether to throw him out or to hear him further, but the look in his visitor's eye held him and at last he said, 'Go on.'

'Your King has an army of fifty thousand in Flanders. He knows that Antwerp is a loaded pistol pointed at the head of England. Conversely, Dutch sea beggars and vessels under the Queen's royal command swarm in the Channel and paralyse your communications at will, and you are powerless to prevent them.'

'That is a common belief here,' he said, attempting nonchalance.

'And with good reason. As you know well, unless the Duke's troops are paid they will rampage through Flanders and put its prosperity to the torch. The Dutch Calvinists will renew their rebellion and Spanish rule will cease. How long do you think it will be before France recovers her wits and wrests that province from you?'

Acid bubbled in Don Gerau's stomach. This rude sea captain had described the situation accurately. His analysis was perfect, his insights uncommonly well informed, and uncannily, Tavistock's views were identical to his own worst fears. Don Gerau decided to hear the man out.

France was Catholic, but her ruling house of Valois was wrestling with other internal factions for control of the country. Geographically, she occupied the heart of the Continent and her position connecting the Mediterranean and Northern Europe posed a massive potential threat to Spain. Madrid's greatest nightmare was that once France's twelve million people were united again under a strong leader she would rival Spain for mastery of the Catholic world, and a France that had annexed the rich heartlands of Flanders would be a France of unthinkable dominance.

'You need Flanders,' Tavistock insisted, seizing the initiative. 'But Flanders is slipping away from you. And there's nothing you can do to stop it. While Elizabeth sits on the throne of England the Channel will never be Spain's artery and Flanders will never be secure!'

Don Gerau's palms were damp with anxiety. 'The new taxes in

Flanders will soon raise enough money to pay the Duke of Alva's garrison.'

'Wrong! Alva's a fool if he believes that,' Tavistock laughed scornfully. 'The Duke's new taxes are resented. They will be resisted. And in imposing them Spain will make enemies of the men who create and control the province's wealth. If every hundredth penny of property, and every twentieth penny of land sales, and every tenth penny of all other sales is to be clawed from them and spent on oppression, what must the Netherlanders begin to think? You take no account of their liberties, *señor*. The very Papists perceive that the Duke makes slaves of them!'

Don Gerau recoiled from the vision Tavistock had thrown up before his eyes. The words of that archrebel, Louis of Nassau, burned in his mind: 'We have come to drive out the intruding, foreign and shameful tyranny of these cruel ravishers and persecutors of Christian blood, to bring back your old privileges ...' He felt his hands turning cold now and fought to steady them. 'I don't accept what you say,' he began slowly, 'and if I did I could not expect such as you to provide a remedy.'

Tavistock leaned back, a humourless grin on his face. 'You do me an injustice, *señor*. As well you know, conditions here are ripe for change and it is a mistake to think that everyone in England wants this situation to continue.'

'Are you not loyal to your Queen?'

'Merchants are loyal to themselves! Men such as I are sore hurt by any embargo. I have had commerce with many in Spain who think the same.'

'And do they propose rebellion as an answer?'

The fierceness in the Englishman flared up. 'Listen! Princes come and princes go. I mean to prosper whoever wears the crown. I've sailed with the men who stand between the Duke of Alva and London. And I know their minds. Mark you this most carefully: a handful of trusted agents, spending gold in the right places, can keep the English Channel clear of ships long enough for your Duke's men to make the crossing. I can put five ships of two hundred tons burthen at your disposal at any time. Five ships that will guarantee a successful landing.'

Don Gerau made an effort to marshal his thoughts. 'Why would you do that, *Capitán*? You enjoy low rates of interest in England. There are no tenth or twentieth penny taxes here. Why should an English merchant wish to be put in the same bower as his Flemish competitors? You know that could happen if England falls under Spanish dominion.'

'If that happens then some merchants will be more highly favoured than others, eh? Come the day, those that've shown themselves most friendly can expect the choicest cuts in return, isn't that so?'

'Ah! Now we return to questions of loyalty, do we not, *Capitán*?'

The Englishman sucked in his cheeks and placed his hands flat on the table before him. 'I merely offer you the aid you require. The cost is two thousand pounds. Take it or leave it.'

'Two thousand pounds is a lot of money.'

'That depends what you're buying.'

'I will think about it.'

'Don't think about it too long. My offer is limited. And like your wine, it does not keep well.'

Don Gerau watched the man rise massively from his chair to leave him to his thoughts. It was true that the English Queen had never been in a more bellicose mood. It was also true that without safe passage across the Channel intervention in England would be impossible. According to his spies there were hundreds put out of work by the embargo, many of whom were reaching the limit of their patience with Elizabeth. Sooner or later, one of them would stand up and do something. Perhaps this man really had brought him the key that would open the door to England. And, if so, he, Don Gerau, must surely grasp it.

As the echo of Tavistock's boots died away, Don Gerau opened the drawer and brought out his royal letter, feeling a stab of annoyance. If the sum of payment the Englishman had demanded was to be included, the whole letter would have to be redrafted.

Tavistock left the Residency and made his way back across London via lanes and dark wynds that any sane man avoided at night. Feral dogs bayed at him and were sent yelping as he strode down the middle of dark streets between overhanging upper floors that almost met above his head. Kicking aside heaps of filth and swinging his arms for warmth, he was almost willing some jacknasty to jump from the shadows and attempt to take his purse. There was a reason to come this way. No one would dare follow him here, and if they did he would detect them more easily.

'I've put a hook right through your jaw, Spaniard,' he said aloud, flexing his fists. 'I've got you dangling right where I want you.'

Hawkins had disclosed little of what had passed at the meeting with the Privy Council. To Tavistock's dismay all he would say was that he had delivered a statement of facts concerning the events at San Juan and that the meeting had been adjourned to a later date. He had expressed neither hopes nor fears about the outcome, but he had ordered Tavistock to remain at his call and to await further instructions.

Tavistock longed to be released from that pledge now. He desired only to go back to Plymouth, to find Drake and further their plans. What was needed was action! A definite course, plotted with intent and sailed with strength and courage! This ha'penny politicking was a waste of time and its hourly passage served only to cool the iron and blunt the steel.

In a barely suppressed rage he moved across a city that mirrored his mood. London fumed with crisis. The atmosphere was thunderous with revolt and charged with rumours of every kind. He emerged into a main thoroughfare, into streets lit by oil lamps and thronged with night traders, beggars, harlots and drunken packs of men, all blowing hither and thither in a wind of huge fitfulness. He lost himself in the jostling night that no curfew could quiet and then, recognising the dark stump of St Paul's Cathedral, he made for the appointed meeting place. By the sign of the Golden Gun and down Spanish Chare, out by the Standard and into Fleet Street. At the bridge over the River Fleet an evil stink rose up, poisoning the air. Upstream was Fleet Prison, he knew, and this place was the foullest running sore that ever ran tributary into a river. He closed his mouth and tried not to breathe in the fetid mists as he crossed.

Soon he had come to the gate of an impressively large house of stone and new French brick. There was, it seemed to Tavistock, more window than wall to it. As he passed within, he was obliged to leave his sword with the guard. Without it he felt naked but as he was admitted he began to stare around comfortably. The house's great hall was spacious and well heated by a giant fireplace. Liveried servants went about the tables with serving dishes; there were pieces of game and roast meats garnished with rosemary, and other herbs.

There were persons of quality here, many young people dancing in courtly steps, students from the Inns of Court, the owner's offspring, his wards, and numbers of elegantly dressed official post holders. Above them, a high plaster frieze was lit up by a hundred candles and, above that, an ornate white ceiling. The air was filled with exquisite Venetian music, played on lute and pipes.

He picked out Hawkins almost at once.

'How went it?' the shipowner asked, keeping his voice low. He could not disguise his anxiety.

'Good. Why are we here?' Tavistock looked around again at the lavish décor. 'What is this place?'

'Tell me, damn it! Don Gerau took our proposals up?'

'His interest was aroused. Why am I brought here?'

Hawkins pursed his lips. 'Richard, there's one who must speak with you. Tonight there is a great fury brewing, like unto an ulcer ready to burst.'

'Is Mister Walsingham here?' Tavistock asked, surprised at Hawkins's tense restlessness. Immediately he thought of the Privy Council adjournment. Was Hawkins priming him because he had wind of some danger? He had never forgotten that all their lives hung by a slender twine, but then caution and responsibility had supplanted raw faith in Hawkins's soul long ago. Hawkins could never fully abandon himself to his fate as an adventurer must. As a man grows older and richer, Tavistock warned himself, he loses his will to fight and his taste for trying Destiny's hand. But I will! See if I don't. I'll take Destiny outside and brawl with him in the dirt until he submits to my desire. And I'll never surrender.

'Richard, I must speak with you privily!'

'Surely, but will you tell me what place this is?'

Before Hawkins could reply they were approached by a tall, bony woman of middle age and serene expression. She held the hand of a small boy of elfin looks, five or six years of age. Beside her stood a young woman of delicate looks and shy demeanour, her features showing a passing resemblance to her mother. Tavistock was first struck by her willowy beauty, but was then shocked to see in her the ghost of another. He realised who her father was, and whose house this must therefore be.

Hawkins presented him with great deference.

'Lady Mildred, Captain Tavistock.'

'I'm very pleased to meet you, Captain.'

'Likewise, madam.' His bow was crisply formal.

'This is my son, Robert – say "welcome to my father's house", Robert.'

The boy did as he was bid and smiled. Tavistock bowed low and took the boy's small hand briefly.

'May I present my elder daughter, Anne?'

'Charmed.'

The young woman took his bow in silence. She was elegance itself and Tavistock felt the warmth in her smile. He was aware of a finely attired youth watching them intently from a couch some distance away. He seemed mean-tempered and to have taken too liberally of the hospitality. Tavistock saw how Anne looked to him modestly. Her smile disappeared and she stepped back.

Her mother detected the urgency in Hawkins. 'We shall not detain you, Captain. I believe you have some business with my husband.'

As he led the way, Hawkins whispered fierce words that sent a shock through Tavistock's guts. 'This is where the Privy Council's adjournment has brought us. Consider your words with care and understand that tonight we plead for our lives. I have it from my Lord of Leicester that we already stand condemned. Take care, for we go to meet our executioner.'

They drew close to the fireside. Nearby, on an upholstered couch, an austerely garbed man dandled a child on his knee and told another three or four standing about him a fantastic tale that captivated their attention. He was in his mid-fifties, his face was long, his eyes deep-set but alight with a warm humour, and he gently disengaged a tiny hand from his long beard as Hawkins came to him, acknowledging him with a nod. He was Sir William Cecil, Principal Secretary of State of England; though not an aristocrat, still the most powerful of all the Queen's councillors. At length, he stood up tall and straight, and ushered Hawkins and Tavistock to a door and along a dimly lit corridor to a large room stocked with hundreds of books and displaying seven or eight small pieces of Italian sculpture. A profusion of genealogical charts and heraldic devices adorned the walls.

Tavistock scanned the bookshelves with awe. The room was a library, twenty yards by ten, dominated by a ceiling rose from which hung a girandole of fifty pure wax candles which a silent manservant patiently lit for them. Chairs were brought and the fire was blazed up. There were more writings here than Tavistock had imagined could ever be in one place.

The oaken desk at which Sir William sat was huge and neatly arranged. He listened intently, all trace of merriment erased from his face and replaced by a solemnity that was graven deep, as Hawkins explained that Tavistock was the witness of whom he had spoken to the Privy Council.

A charge of power emanated from Cecil, Tavistock saw, but it was not a dead authority born of cold responsibility. It was said that Cecil had the capacity to interlace fifty separate thoughts in his mind simultaneously; that it was impossible to outguess him. When he spoke his voice was distinctively nasal and soft; his words were admirably to the point.

'You have been at the residence of Don Gerau de Spes. What did you say to him?'

Tavistock cleared the burr from his throat. 'I told him that I would give him aid in his enterprise.'

'You told him exactly as Captain Hawkins said?'

'I did, yes sir. And more. The proposal was thus: for a thousand pounds in gold he will have the service of our ships and he will make our people in Mexico free.'

'Your brother is among them.'

'Yes.'

'And Don Gerau accepted?'

'Not straightly. But I believe he will.'

'Good! Now tell me word for word what was said.'

Cecil sat back as Tavistock made his report, listening and judging. As Hawkins had said, this was a man with an impressive presence and a quick, clear mind. The detail in which he laid out the interview with de Spes confirmed that amply. Hawkins had vouched that Tavistock was reliable, describing his loyalty in the highest terms, and praising his political understanding. Above all Hawkins had said that Tavistock's personal loss fitted him for his task exactly. As Cecil watched and listened he saw that Tavistock's feeling for his stranded brother shone through like a ray. He had faith, and that faith, though surely misplaced, gave his manner an earnestness that was impossible to fake. It would be hard to order the execution of a man like this.

Cecil decided with regret that such an order would probably be necessary. The great test is coming, he reminded himself. The least fool can see that the pulse of the city is quickening by the hour. The leviathan of war is stirring from sleep, and it inflames and terrifies the populace.

Slade has brought me intelligence of unease from all quarters of England. It's well that Leicester plans to move against me tomorrow. If he carries the Queen, I will fall. *Therefore, I must decide on Hawkins tonight.*

Cecil's knuckles cracked as he squeezed his left hand with his right. If Philip has decided on invasion, as Hawkins insists, then it's imperative that he be countered and confounded. In that case, Tavistock's desire for his brother's release may serve to convince and mislead de Spes to great effect. So much is plain. *But is Philip's mind made up to invade?* If it's not, then to back Hawkins will enrage Philip and push him into war. That's futile. Appeasement would make much better sense.

Cecil considered the latter course carefully. Perhaps I should cease to oppose Leicester and make my peace with those who seek to heal the rift with Spain. Then I would cease to be their target. Wouldn't it be better to stop this double-dealing now? To square things with de Spes and arrest Hawkins and Tavistock in a grand gesture of friendship? Walsingham's meddling had already made that more difficult – but not yet impossible.

Cecil silently cursed the timing of events for the thousandth time that day. Crushingly, just as the million seeds he had planted during his incumbency as Secretary were coming to fruit, there had sprung up an overwhelming combination of forces and circumstances from which escape seemed impossible.

The toil has been immense, he thought proudly. My plan to cut expenditure and restore the value of the currency has provided a sturdy base for the national economy. Years of peace have prospered the land. For a decade I've sought to build up England's weak defences, her army, her navy and her industry. I've striven to attract foreign artisans and manufacturers to England. Last year I ordered the formation of the Royal Mines Company. That's now bringing in German zinc prospectors to find sources of the metal essential for making cannon brass. Dutch and Flemish Protestant refugees have for years been bringing to England their knowledge of textiles, dyeing and a hundred other crafts. Italian glassmakers are fetching their guild secrets from Venice, Huguenots their shipwrighting skills, Swedes and Danes and even Poles from the far Baltic, are importing a great diversity of useful arts. Ten years of peace, prosperity and stability have created a glory in England. What a tragedy of waste if it's allowed to collapse now!

Cecil toyed with his heavy chain of office as Tavistock finished his report, still unconvinced about Hawkins's game. Of course, the man was looking out for his own interest, but there was a good deal of truth in what he said. However, the growing enmity with Spain was throwing the gains of ten years to the winds. That could not be ignored lightly, even if it meant sending patriotic men to the scaffold.

'We must have a united country, secure and strong,' Cecil told them openly. 'That is paramount. Neither can we afford to contemplate a war with Spain. My foreign policy is on a knife-point. It seems that

Alva's legions must win in the Netherlands and that the Catholics will soon crush the Huguenots in France.'

'Then what?' Hawkins asked tightly.

'A Franco-Spanish alliance against England. It's the only sensible course for our enemies, an opportunity they cannot overlook to destroy us. Already Mister Walsingham has intercepted correspondence between the Cardinal of Guise and Philip. A meeting in two months' time, so he says, to plot our downfall. What can I do? Tell me. How do I save England from the wrath of two Catholic titans?'

Hawkins's words were brave and unswerving. 'You must have a defensive alliance with Protestant Germany, Denmark and Sweden. You must suckle the newborn Calvinist movement in Scotland, shutting the back door against the French, who for years have used Scotland against us. You must stamp out the Popish plots in Ireland, where the Spanish seek to establish bases against us, and you must step up aid to the Huguenots and the Dutch, who, while they live, continue to exhaust and distract our enemies.'

'But time is passing short.'

'Then you must decide to do it now.'

'Alas! What you counsel is not enough. Sweden is too far away, Denmark is weak, and the Germans divided. Our only hope against Spain is to cement an alliance with France, and the only way to do that is for the Queen to agree a marriage with the French royal house. My attempts to secure such a marriage have so far failed.'

Cecil's mind ranged free over the bleak political landscape as he sought a way to save Hawkins. If Walsingham was right, the French civil wars would soon cease. Dowager Queen Catherine, head of the house of Valois, was ambitious to crown the heads of each of her three male offspring. Though attempts to marry Elizabeth to the Archduke Charles had foundered, and his brother, the King, was married, there was another. It was still minutely possible that an alliance with France could be made through the nineteen-year-old Duke of Anjou. If Walsingham was right . . .

Cecil brought his thoughts back to the matter in hand severely, and decided to lay the central aspect of the maze before Hawkins.

'You can't hope to know the answers to this riddle, because the greatest threat comes from within,' he said throatily, his words coming like a confession. 'I am at the centre of a power struggle. A vicious conspiracy to unseat me. Lord Leicester has opposed me consistently, searching out support in the Duke of Norfolk, in Lord Arundel and other branches of the old aristocracy. The Catholic barons of the far North particularly, Northumberland and Westmorland and their allies, detest the Queen's reliance on me. They complain of my influence. Jealousy and resentment are my chief enemies. And if the Queen is prised away from me now, I must answer with my head.'

'So we are all in the same position, Sir William,' Tavistock said suddenly. 'For God's sake let us stand together! Those who would make peace with Spain are the same men who would usher in Spanish rule. They would destroy us. Are we to go that way meekly?'

Cecil's attention fastened on his words like a talon. 'Brave sentiments, Captain. *But I must have a plan.*'

'I have a plan.'

Hawkins's disquiet rose visibly. His eyes flashed a warning, but Tavistock ignored it, seizing his chance. 'The Dutch prince, William of Orange, is a sovereign of royal blood. He is enabled therefore to arm ships. Already he has issued letters of marque to eighteen privateers. Inside a year, he could have eighty ships under arms. The Low Countries are by no means lost yet. These men whom the Spaniards call "Beggars of the Sea" need our succour. Victualled in Kentish ports they can patrol the Narrow Seas and stand between England and Flanders as a wall of oak.'

'Another cause for the Spanish to resent us?'

'Give me command of six ships, Sir William, and if, through de Spes, I can draw Alva into a premature invasion I will fall upon his barges and send them to the bottom. Imagine that! His *tercios* defenceless in mid-Channel when his mercenary escort turns on him with a hundred pieces of ordnance. I would deal the Spanish such a blow that they would never recover in ten years!'

'If only it were that simple, Captain.'

'Which of us is not a pirate at heart?' Tavistock said quietly. He braced himself, clearly aware that his life and the future of England depended on what he was about to say. 'Sir William, I am an Englishman, and I know that if Englishmen are to succeed in this world we must dare to do what no one else dares. We are poor and our nation is small and weak. But our people have the courage of gods. Put your trust in them and they will not fail you.'

A knock at the door prevented Cecil from replying. The man who entered was of middle height, corpulent and with the white curly hair of a sixty-year-old. Sir Nicholas Bacon was Cecil's immensely rich ally in Council. He and Cecil had first met during their student days in Cambridge, and since then Bacon had benefited hugely from Henry the Eighth's distribution of monastic property and had weathered the storms of Mary's reign despite his firm Protestantism. He owned lands in six counties and now occupied the position of Lord Keeper of the Great Seal. It was Bacon who had championed Hawkins at the giving of his depositions before Council and it was he who had protected him by calling for the adjournment.

He greeted Hawkins warmly, nodded amiably at Tavistock, and sank into an armchair, red-faced, sweating and breathless.

'Ill news. I've sounded Pembroke and Sussex. They are with Norfolk and Arundel on the Spanish question. They favour an immediate restoration of relations with Philip.' He turned bulging eyes on Hawkins.

'And your neck girt with a halter, sir!'

Hawkins's pale face was unmoving. Bacon went on, this time to Cecil. 'But there's better. The Queen this afternoon slapped down my Lord of Leicester in a savage fashion for opposing you. It was a wonder to behold, my dear William! Her Majesty, roiled up in a terrible fury, stabbed him with her finger and sent him away broodingly! A remarkable performance! A remarkable wonder it was to see.'

Cecil experienced a tremendous wave of relief. He had been fearing what would happen when Leicester put his poison before the Queen. He had worried that Elizabeth would be swayed sufficiently by her favourite to let events ride their course. Without her explicit protection he was as good as dead. But she had confirmed him in her esteem by pre-empting Leicester's attack.

Cecil turned to Tavistock, knowing that he needed time to consider these new developments. 'We must talk further. Please, Captain, you must enjoy the hospitality of my house. But excuse us, for we have pressing business to discuss.'

Tavistock rose stiffly, and left with a display of unwillingness. When he had gone, Cecil told Bacon of Hawkins's plan and what had passed that evening with Don Gerau de Spes.

'We must move swiftly!'

'What will you do?' Hawkins asked.

'I will follow my instincts – as always. I may yet have a use for your Captain.'

Both men watched Cecil go over to the fireplace. Bacon had been his closest friend for many years now. They had stood godfather to each other's children, they had been through many crises together, planned together, seen their fortunes rise together. In this sea of troubles they would sail together.

Cecil stooped over the hearth and picked up a bundle of twigs. He turned and held up the bundle, flexing it in his hands.

'See! Together I cannot break them. It is beyond my strength. But singly –' He pulled out one twig and snapped it, then another and another. 'One at a time, Nicholas, they are at my command. One at a time.'

When Tavistock returned to the great hall he saw that the younger children had gone to their beds and the dancing had ceased. The evening's amusements were settling to more leisurely matters, turning to cards and tables of backgammon and lovers' conversation. He fell to making polite accounts of his foreign voyages to those that asked.

The Lady Mildred found him drowning in a tide of young gentlemen eager to learn the truth about the New World. She brought him along with her, but examining him so artfully that Tavistock had no doubt that her appraisal of him would reach her husband that night.

They walked the long gallery, Tavistock enduring a string of elaborate introductions, until they came to a knot of spectators; the sight arrested Tavistock's attention. An adjoining room had been cleared of furniture and strung with a net. Two young men in shirtsleeves were playing a game. They appeared to be swiping a feathered missile back and forth with wands shaped like butter pats. After the weighty proceedings in which Tavistock had been engaged it seemed feckless and trivial behaviour.

'My lord the Earl of Oxford, Edward de Vere, and his opponent, Nicholas Breton.'

Tavistock recognised the Earl as the arrogant chancer who had caught his attention on his arrival. So, that's Edward de Vere, he thought. He remembered the rumour he had picked up from one of Hawkins's servants that Oxford had murdered a servant of the Cecil household a couple of years before. Watching his vicious lashings now, Tavistock felt certain his first impressions had been correct.

'The Earl has lived with us here as one of my husband's wards. My husband hopes that one day soon he will become a member of our family by marrying my elder daughter. He is a keen player, is he not?'

'What is the aim of it all, madam?'

'We oftentimes amuse ourselves with games here, Captain. This one you may not know. We call it shuttlecock and battledore.'

'I have never seen it. I doubt whether it may be played adequately aboard a ship.'

Lady Mildred looked askance at him. 'We play others, some more of the brain than of the limbs, pretences with which we pleasantly divert ourselves.'

Mildred Cecil's eyes strayed to her daughter and back. 'Do you play chess?'

Tavistock sighed. 'Poorly, madam.'

'Indeed? Then you shall play against equal opposition, but the best my husband's house can afford. If you will.'

'I would be honoured,' he said, feeling otherwise, but was pleasantly surprised when presently Anne Cecil came to him and set up a chess board on a small carved table between them. They sat quietly in a corner on padded stools, well apart from the noise and hubbub at the centre of the room, but as they played, Tavistock's thoughts were interrupted time and again by stratagems wholly unconnected with the board. Had he acquitted himself well enough with de Spes for Hawkins's plan to be taken up? Had his plain speaking jeopardised the plan with Sir William? What was the import of the news that Bacon had brought?

He tried to shut from his mind the possibility that Sir William would decide to condemn them, and explored instead the damning consequences of success. Suppose the Spanish agreed to surrender John and the other survivors, what then? Would they not murder them all in rage if he betrayed de Spes at the crucial time? What tortures would they not inflict on a man whose brother had destroyed an entire Spanish *tercio*?

Anne's voice came to him again. 'It's your move, Captain Tavistock.'

Absently he picked up his black bishop and began to move it, then saw her frown and corrected his mistake. She played well. Too well. He watched her slender hands as she fingered one of his captured pawns. He had thought her shy at first, but there was an undeniable boldness about her. Strands of brown hair had escaped from her hat and trailed beside her ear and she twisted them as she concentrated. With a pang he realised that it was a gesture that reminded him of Jane. Poor dead Jane.

'Check.'

'I missed that.'

'Your mind is elsewhere, Captain.'

'Yes.'

'Would you rather we didn't play?'

'No, no.' He sat back, looking at her. 'Tell me. Who taught you to play chess?'

'My father.' She looked up at him guilelessly, pleased to have opened conversation with him. 'He has attended closely to the education of his children. And he's truly the font of all knowledge.'

'I noticed that many a Gray's Inn student comes here to drink.'

She smiled at his joke and the smile touched him. 'Some too liberally, I fear. But my father likes to fill his house with young people. He says that makes him feel young himself, though he is now in his fiftieth year.'

'Few men have led a fuller life.'

Her smile withered. 'My father's workload has been doubled of late. A Queen regnant is a hard taskmistress. Her Majesty refuses to marry and that sorely tries his temper. The Queen is without resolve on any matter. She leans on him as he leans on his ebony rod. His health suffers, I think.'

Tavistock knew that for years Cecil had urged upon the Queen a marriage with the Archduke Charles of France. It was an eligible match but two years ago she had brought all negotiations to a halt over trivialities.

He asked, 'Did you think the Frenchman was a good choice?'

'It's hardly my place to say, Captain Tavistock. The succession is a complex matter, only for those of high understanding.'

Tavistock was aware of the risks surrounding the fact of a woman ruler. Since the death a year ago of Lady Catherine Grey and the arrival in England of the Scots Queen, the succession had fallen into doubt.

She asked him, 'Do you think the Queen should marry?'

Tavistock guarded his thoughts with care, wanting to trust her, but not sure if he could. 'I cannot say. Do you have an opinion?'

A frown passed over her face briefly. 'If Her Majesty takes an English husband, like the Earl of Leicester, she will raise one of her subjects to pre-eminence and thereby create in him a focus of jealousy. If she repeats her half-sister's mistake and marries a foreigner she'll bring her realm under the influence of an alien power. If she chooses not to marry at all there'll be no Tudor heir, and the succession will never be settled while she lives.'

Tavistock nodded, impressed with her grasp of the political realities, but he forced himself to remember where he was, and with whom he was speaking. Anne's father had educated her in the elements of state-craft and it passed through Tavistock's mind that he could learn much from her that might be useful. He said, 'There are many who think the Queen is neglecting her duty.'

'Do you think that?' She appeared shocked.

'No, but there are many attracted by Mary Queen of Scots.'

At that, Anne's face betrayed her inner disquiet, and it became clear to him where one of Sir William's great fears lay. If enough support could be marshalled behind the Scottish Queen, Elizabeth might be usurped and England returned to the Catholic fold without any need for a Spanish invasion.

What I wouldn't give, Tavistock thought ruefully, to be privy to a true picture of the inner workings of the Court. It seems a place where treason walks hand in hand with self-preservation and treachery lurks in every dark corner. And at the centre of all things, the Queen. A goddess, radiant with royal splendour, with the power of life and death over ordinary mortals. Yes, he thought, suddenly awed, she is the key to all riches and status in England – the higher the closer, and the closer the higher! And there was no one closer to her than Sir William.

He thanked God that circumstances had brought him here to Cecil House. There could be no better place from which to launch his own schemes of retribution and reprisal against the Spanish once John's rescue was brought off. Two thousand pounds he had demanded of de Spes, but one thousand he had agreed with Hawkins and reported to Cecil. Much could be achieved with the difference. But that was thinking too far into the future. He was forgetting that in ten days he might easily be heading for the gallows on Tower Hill. Nothing was decided yet. He must ready himself for any eventuality. He remembered what the Lady Mildred had said and knew that from now on he must be very careful.

They returned to the game, Tavistock capturing two pieces to his opponent's one. As she took his queen from the board she asked him innocently, 'Are you married, Captain?'

'I was. My wife died recently.'

'Oh! I didn't mean to –'

She fell silent and looked away, but he spoke up. He remembered how painfully exhausting his grief had been, but realised that for the first time he wanted to speak of it.

'It happened while I was in the Indies. A storm and then Spanish treachery delayed our return. When I stepped ashore, I found that my wife and son had been taken by the smallpox. It takes time to understand what something like that means. Why God would take them from me so cruelly. What was their crime? I asked myself over and again, could her sins have been so great? Surely my son was too young to have sinned.' He felt a sudden intolerable constriction in his throat and swallowed to dissolve it. 'Then I stopped asking. To save myself from pain, and perhaps to wash away the guilt.'

'Guilt?'

'I could not be with her in her suffering.'

She put a comforting hand on his sleeve and he looked at her and managed a smile, but a braying laugh distracted him.

He looked up to see the Earl of Oxford, drenched in sweat and quaffing from a foaming jug. He wiped his full lips, his head of dark, curly hair plastered and wet, then his gaze fell on Anne Cecil's hand.

'I see you've found suitable entertainment,' he told her drunkenly, ignoring Tavistock.

Immediately she withdrew inside herself, acutely embarrassed, fearful even, but Oxford seized her wrist and squeezed until she looked him in the eye. 'You told me you were too tired to watch me thrash Nicholas Breton. Why don't you introduce me to this – *chess player?*'

'Edward, this is Captain Tavistock,' she said tightly. 'He's here at my father's request.'

'Ah! The boatman! Tell him who *I* am.'

Anne looked helplessly around for assistance but found none. Moving to contain Oxford's anger, she complied quickly. 'Captain, this is Edward de Vere, Earl of Oxford.'

Tavistock perceived the warning in her voice.

'The *seventeenth* Earl,' Oxford slurred, turning glazed eyes on the still-seated Tavistock. 'We're a most ancient family. I'm the greatest poet in England, the greatest dramatist and the greatest lover. So I like people to stand when they're presented to me. In fact, I demand it.'

Tavistock acknowledged him with a single nod, detesting the rudeness of the intrusion and the swaggering conceit of the Earl. Talk of Jane had drained him of all anger.

'Stand up, I say!'

Tavistock remained seated on the low stool. He watched with ill-concealed disgust as the Earl violently kicked down the chess table, scattering the pieces across the floor and sending a shock through the appalled watchers.

Tavistock steadied himself, knowing that to rise would inflame Oxford's histrionic display to blows. The Earl caught up Anne's wrist again and ordered her cruelly, 'Tell him to stand up!'

She turned her head from him defiantly and Oxford increased his grip until a crease of pain twisted her mouth and she cried out.

Instantly Tavistock was on his feet. He covered the distance to his adversary in two steps and broke Oxford's fingers away from Anne Cecil's wrist with ease.

'Take care! You're hurting her.'

Oxford's enraged voice rose up. 'You *dare* to touch me?' he demanded. With sudden ferocity his fist lashed out, catching Tavistock on the side of the head, then Tavistock felt hands grappling him. Effortlessly, he thrust his assailant back and pulled himself free.

'Richard!'

It was Hawkins's voice, stern and strained. The tall, black figure of Cecil was beside him. Tavistock took a pace back, his ear ringing from the blow. Every nerve in him wanted to snap Oxford in two, but he knew that for Hawkins's sake, and his own, he must exercise supreme restraint.

He forced himself to say slowly, 'I apologise, my lord.'

The music had ceased so that the entire hall was in silence. A hundred eyes were staring at them. Oxford's face had passed from ruddy to a pallor of rage. His lips were tight and he was shaking with the will to fight. 'Get on your knees and say it!'

Anne stepped forward, pleading. 'Edward, please –'

Oxford's eyes jumped from Tavistock to her and back. 'Get out!' He swept her aside and as Tavistock instinctively made a move towards him the Earl darted back and made a grab for the handle of a long carving knife that skewered a hock of beef on the table beside him.

'You get on your knees, I said!'

Oxford's words rang in the rafters, demonic, insane. Something inside Tavistock triggered. He shrugged off the restraint he had been imposing and lunged at the Earl as he would a mutinous swabber.

The knife was thrust forward but Tavistock side-stepped and allowed Oxford's outstretched arm to pass under his own. With a steel grip he seized the knife hand, trapping the forearm under his armpit, and turned with a mariner's balance so that all his weight bore down on Oxford's elbow. The arm snapped straight, from wrist to shoulder, and the fingers splayed convulsively so that the blade rang to the floor.

What happened next was unnecessary, but Tavistock thought Oxford deserved it. Few saw the knee raised sharply in Oxford's groin, they heard only a gasp of pain as England's greatest lover crumpled.

Suddenly, a dozen hands were on Tavistock and he was lifted bodily from the hall.

Hawkins took him from the guards, incensed. He marched him to the exit, spitting oaths.

'God's blood, you're a bone-headed fool! Can't I trust you to mind your temper for five minutes?'

'*My* temper? Sweet Jesus! Mine is not the fault!'

Hawkins squared up to him. 'Fault is it? Fault? Yours *is* the fault, by God!'

'If that whelp were aboard my ship, I'd –'

Hawkins's shout rent the night. 'Silence! Damn your brawling ignorance! He's a lordling and Cecil's pet. And that's enough to make the fault yours whatever he did.'

The night air washed over Tavistock, cooling him. He bent to recover the sword that was thrown out after him, then turned to Hawkins contumaciously as the heavy doors banged shut. 'We may as well be hanged for wolves as for sheep.'

Hawkins shook his head. 'We're not to be hanged at all – and no thanks to you. Sir William has swallowed the bait. Bacon has brought news from Walsingham that the French prince will entertain Elizabeth's suit. You're to have your damned squadron of ships.'

Chapter 9

John Tavistock lay in the straw staring up at the light that seeped in through crevices in the barn roof. Flies buzzed round his head, settling on the dried blood of his face and arms, maddening him. Every bone of his body seemed to ache and it was agony to brush the insects away. He put on the ring that John Chamberlain had given him. His brother's ring that bore the sign of the phoenix rising. It fitted snugly on his middle finger.

The afternoon and evening of the first day had passed tensely for John Tavistock. He had awaited the moment when he would be confronted with his sins, but instead had been brought to the kitchens and served a plate of game bird by a fear-stricken maid who had been told of the devil that inhabited him.

The meat had eaten like chicken, only drier; it was, the watching soldier had told him, *gallopavo*, but he had been reluctant to believe it could be peacock, and had thought it probably the same American fowl that his brother had once recommended as turkey-cock. He had licked his fingers and eaten it anyway, breaking off pieces of the white flesh for the two bloodhounds which came to sit at his elbow.

Beyond the doorway, the cultivated lands were spread out as far as he could see, citrus groves and tilled fields where slaves laboured ceaselessly to break the hard earth of the high plateau. To the west and south, the servants told him, lay the great mineral lakes of Tezcuco and Chalco; to the south-east the serrated horizon where Iztaccihuatl and Popocatépetl, the great volcanoes revered by the Aztec peoples, smouldered threateningly. Don Bernal, they said, was the lord of this place. It was he who had brought order and civilisation here.

The great house was as yellowed parchment in the setting sun, arches sculpted by shadow; the stucco reliefs were of vines and angelic figures at the front, and red tiles, pitched shallowly all around the inner courtyard where a fountain played into a pool of pea-green water.

He watched Gonzalo's men dismount from piebald horses, drinking from leathers of water or rough red wine and getting their gear down.

They had brought with them a troop of Indians, coppery-skinned, with sinister countenances – good trackers and guides, so the grooms said.

'When I came here, there were only savage Indians,' Esteban, their master's chief servant told him. 'Their king devoutly worshipped the statue of a horse. It was fashioned after one that had been in Cortés's party, left behind lame. But now they grow oranges and live in cleanliness. They are taught to repeat the Pater Noster and Ave Maria, the Creed and Commandments, and they are brought to God!'

Tavistock had watched, fascinated by the Indians who had congregated in the far corner of the open court under the feathery crown of a large tree; several of them had been drinking *pulque* from flasks, or pinching their nostrils closed and swallowing fumes from a tortoise-shell pipe, and Tavistock had known then that he was a stranger in a strange land, and that he would never see home again.

A goblet of rough red wine was put before him, but he had not drunk, fearing the loss of his sharpness in the confrontation that must come. Instead he had dabbled a finger in it, and let drops fall to the table. Drops like blood. A plague on your house, Bernal de Escovedo, he thought darkly. Blood and frogs and flies and hail. May your cattle die and the locusts strip your fields. But most of all may the Lord God seize your firstborn and send him to hellfire.

The guilt he felt over the executions of Robert Howell and Jeremiah Walsh had shaped all his actions in Mexico City. He had negotiated terms, promising and praying: favours in exchange for good behaviour, a bloodless solution to the problem of what to do with thirty desperate, costly men. He had seen how the Spaniards in Mexico would not stoop to waiting upon one another, that they had need of chamberlains and men to serve at table and to attend them as they went abroad, and were not the least rough-edged Englishmen meetest for such tasks above Indians and Negroes? The baser sort could watch over the labours of the slaves in the mines. It was to Gonzalo that he had been forced to swear his own oath of bail. Miraculously, he had backed down from his demands for further retribution, but he had asked Don Emilio if he could personally take charge of Tavistock, receiving him into his father's estates at Chalco.

What does the bastard really want with me? he had wondered. Now that my shipmates are sold out into private hands what more chance is there they'll be used to squeeze me? Now I'm alone and I have only myself to answer for before God. Escovedo knows that I'll see us all in Hell before giving him any secrets.

He had dreaded that which awaited him on the *encomienda*. Two hours before midnight he had been brought, hands bound, before the lord and his son, but he had seen in Don Bernal de Escovedo a man of honour, straight and devout. Still, he had had the uneasy conviction that Gonzalo was using him.

'You will work for your living here,' Don Bernal had told him plainly.

'If you work well, you will have sufficient rest and food and shelter, and after a time money to buy possessions. If you do not, these things will be denied you. If you trouble me – cause hurt to any of my people, or damage anything on my estate – I will have you whipped as I would any other man. Do you understand that?'

'Yes.'

'Tell me, Englishman, what sort of work do you know?'

'My first trade is gun casting, and when at sea, discharging the same at Spanish ships.'

Gonzalo had gone rigid with anger at that, his pretence of control over Tavistock shattered now. 'You were attacking defenceless trading vessels!'

'No! Just treacherous warships that interfered with my Captain-General's business, but foresaw not the power of our reply.'

Don Bernal had grunted impassively. 'Well, I have apt work for you. First you'll supervise the building of a shed. You'll choose the site and have command of all aspects of its design and construction. It's to be a cannon forge, equipped exactly as your master's forge in England. There are five men at your disposal, a quantity of cut timber and stone and anything you require of my smithy. You will report daily to Esteban, who reports directly to me. I will personally inspect your progress every third day. Is that clear?'

Tavistock had stared straight ahead and absorbed the orders thoughtfully. Is this so bad? a voice inside him had asked. They could have killed you instead of Howell and Walsh. They could still do so, and as painfully as the cruel Aztecs of which Pedro Gomara spoke. What's there to object to in this? To build a shed? And for a man you could easily respect.

But you have no respect for his son, the harder side of him had answered. I don't trust Gonzalo. And these are his orders, or, more exactly, the orders of Don Emilio. And he's asking me to dig my own grave, and the graves of my comrades. And it's not just a shed he wants, it's a gun foundry! Sweet Jesus, have I no pride?

The persuasive voice came back. What's the harm in it? Build them a foundry. They can't cast English guns without the secret of English gun metal. Waste their time! Spend their money! Deceive them! Then you will have played them for fools.

He had looked at Don Bernal's open, expectant features and shook his head tightly in refusal.

Gonzalo's face had hardened. 'What's the matter? Don't you understand my father's command?'

'I understand. But I refuse it utterly. You're an unscrupulous bastard and your father's a dupe and the Viceroy is a wicked tool of Satan, and I piss on the lot of you!'

Don Bernal had been on his feet instantly. At the intolerable insult, he had drawn one of the brace of long knives that hung at his belt and pointed it at Tavistock's heart, his fist shaking in rage. 'You dare speak to me like that? In my own house?'

Tavistock had stared fixedly at the dagger, filled with the satisfaction of his defiance, glad that he had sealed his course but suffering the agonising seconds before the pain started.

'Then kill me! And if you're all cowards, tell your slaves to do it.'

Don Bernal had brought down his weapon in a slashing arc, severing the rope that held Tavistock's wrists. They had dragged him into the yard and savagely beaten him with wooden *porras*, raining blows on all the places of his body where bone was near skin

'That is for my son's honour! And that is for mine! And that is for His Excellency! I warned you, Englishman! I warned you but you chose not to listen.'

The blood and the bruises had been spectacular, but the beating had been controlled and careful.

'That is for your defiance! That is for your refusal! And that is for your insults! I have broken this land, and I will break you!'

Gonzalo stayed his father's hand. 'Leave him.'

At last the lord had grown breathless and Tavistock had fallen limp, feigning unconsciousness, and he had heard Gonzalo say, 'Don't kill him. Don Emilio wants him alive.'

'No man speaks like that to me!'

They had struggled then. 'No, father! Kill him and you'll forfeit your own life. He's not worth that.'

He had looked up at them from one eye, blood streaming from his nose.

Don Bernal's *porra* fell to the earth. 'What do you mean?'

'Don Emilio's orders. We must use every means to persuade him. *Every* means. If he does not comply you will lose everything.'

And they had gone back to the house, and the Indians had come and dragged him by the ankles, groaning and hideously hurt, to the barn.

The sunrise was two hours old when Tavistock awoke. He raised himself and felt about his body for broken bones, then he turned onto his side painfully, remembering the night. The straw nestled him as if he were a fragile pot and he felt the unimaginable joy of relief from torment.

I've got you, Don Godalmighty, he thought with elation. You're as much in my power now as I am in yours. And now the respect is mutual.

A shadow fell across him, eclipsing the brightness of the morning sun. The blurred silhouette of a woman, carrying a pail of water. She looked at him for a long moment before approaching further.

'You?'

It was Maria.

'You look terrible,' she said haltingly and set down her pail. 'Let me see your face.'

He turned his chin up and she knelt and sponged his neck and shoulders, untying the rope bracelets that still hung on his wrists. The cool water thrilled him, taking the burn away from his wounds, and he flinched.

'Keep still.'

'But why you?' he asked, amazed that she, the lord's daughter, had come to tend him.

'I told you to keep still.' Her voice was hard as obsidian. 'My father asked me to come. I did not refuse his request, for he is a good man and deserves obedience.

'Did he send you here? Or was it your brother?'

She ignored his question and continued to scrub the dried blood from his chest and arms. When she had finished she dried her hands, then she looked up at him and said with sudden deliberateness, 'Please, John Tavistock, for your own sake, forget your old life and do as Gonzalo wishes.'

Her eyes flashed dark fire at him, and he saw how lovely she was. He steeled himself, hardening his feelings as he knew he must. 'You're asking me to betray my country.'

'You don't have to do that. Please, for my father's sake as well as yours, go along with it. You must.'

He propped himself up knowing that he must oppose the temptation she was laying before him. It's just another trick, he told himself, delighting in her soft words nevertheless. She doesn't mean it. She was ordered here to coax me with her attention. Yet she seems genuinely worried. How can I oppose her without hurting her?

'Couldn't you do that? For me?'

'I could. But it would be for the Viceroy and not for you.'

'Please. I saw the executions in Mexico City. I don't want to see them take you too.'

He summoned up all his strength and spoke scathingly, wanting, and yet not wanting, to drive her away. 'I'd heard that Spaniards have a talent for persuasion. But I thought it extended only to hot irons and *porras*.'

'What do you mean by that?'

'You know very well, lady.'

She stood up, he rising with her, then she bunched her fingers as if to beat on him. 'Open your eyes and see what you're doing! I wish you'd never come here. I wish I'd never set eyes on you, *Inglés*! I hate you!'

'That's no way to persuade me,' he told her quietly, the mocking gone from him now. He knew there was one sure course that would send her away.

There was a long pause before she asked, 'Then how?'

'Like this.' He seized her in his arms, taking her off balance, and kissed her full on the lips.

For a moment she seemed paralysed. He pulled back from her and looked into her eyes, unsure what he would see there. Then she hit his face with all the force she could muster.

'Vixen!'

His cheek stung, and he kissed her again, this time forcefully, so that she struggled against his strength in vain. Her pail was kicked over. Then he opened his arms and she fell to the floor. He scissored his hands as if clapping dust from them. The place she had hit him hurt like hell, his vision popped, she had put feeling into the blow, but he was not going to let her see how it troubled him.

She stared up at him, burning with emotion. 'You're a stupid man! A foolish, proud man! Like all men, you must always be right. You're too proud to see anything. You are all blinded by your own pomposity!'

He sat down on the ground slowly and put his hand to his mouth, as a man disgorging a cherry pip. When his hand came away, there was blood in his saliva and an ivory-white lump in his hand. He thoughtfully probed with the tip of his tongue the place where his tooth had been.

Her anger suddenly collapsed. A tooth! She had done that? Oh, Mother of God, but a tooth was irreplaceable. It was a damage that would never heal. Feelings of guilt flushed through her, washing away her self-righteousness.

It was a molar. A big one.

'Let me see,' she said with brisk concern.

He braced his elbows behind him and meekly leaned his head back. Then she knelt beside him, put one hand softly on his forehead and delicately hooked the left side of his open mouth with her little finger and peered inside.

Blood welled in the hole where the tooth had been. It was dark and pulpy, but the tooth had come out cleanly and no splinters were left. She kept her face straight, rocking back on her heels. 'It's all right.'

'Good,' he said, nodding, and handed her the tooth. Then he turned and spat with as much delicacy as he could. She looked at the tooth guiltily. It was a fine, white tooth. And a shame.

'I'm sorry,' she said. 'Truly, I never meant to hurt you.'

'I'm not hurt.'

'Really? No pain?'

'No.'

'I'll bring you some hot water and salt. If you gargle with it the wound will heal quickly.'

He shrugged. It was not one of his English mannerisms, but insouciant and very Latin. You're learning quickly, she thought. Your Spanish is nine times better than it was when you startled me that night in Pedro Gomara's stable in Vera Cruz. You're almost like one of us now.

A voice in the back of her head nagged at her. It was her mother's voice, or perhaps just one of the sisters of St Teresa's order in Avila where she had sought refuge from Don Carlos's cruelty. It told her to beware. Though this man was under his bruises somewhat handsome and cleverer than she had thought and obviously attracted to her, he was still an Englishman and godless.

It was hard to believe he had no soul as she watched him sitting there like a child in sorrow over a broken possession. He seemed like other men, only more deep and somehow more –

She broke off the thought angrily, remaining outwardly calm, and renewed her plea. 'Won't you do a little of what Don Emilio wants?'

He grew stiff again. 'My duty is to my countrymen.'

She sighed in exasperation. 'Duty! The men settled on the *estancias* are your countrymen too. Do you not owe them something?'

'I owe them less than I owe anyone. I've already paid them their due. Tomorrow it will be six months to the day that we were fired upon by Don Emilio. That half year has been my gift to them, they cannot expect more.'

'Just a small compromise. That's all my father asks. Surely that's possible?'

He saw her face and the pleading it held, and he looked past her and saw the sun shining on the distant lake and the orderly fields of red earth and the distant blasted slopes of the *volcans*, and suddenly he felt that England was a hundred thousand leagues away.

'Never,' he whispered in English, but he knew as he said it that there would be no escape from Mexico for himself or for his comrades, now or at any time, and that she was right – the day for compromise had dawned.

Chapter 10

Night had begun to fall when Tavistock left the heavily armed ship that was moored in the river at Deptford. It was a warm spring evening over the salt marshes of the estuary, a westerly breeze rippling the water and the reed beds of the creek. He was reminded of the broad skies of the Indies and that it was now almost nine months since his life had been saved by his brother.

Very soon, he thought. Very soon now. If all went well, he would have the two thousand pounds from de Spes tomorrow. Added to the thousand he had been apportioned from the profits carried home by the *Minion*, and the five hundred Drake had got, there would be enough to mount the expedition he had conceived. Finally he would throw off Hawkins's controlling hand and finish the business Hawkins had set his word to. With Francis Drake at my side there'll be more than a fair chance of ransoming the maroons, and John with them, he thought. That's if they're still alive.

As he rowed his lighter to shore he decided that the man he had just spoken with, and whose signature was on the paper he now carried, could be trusted.

The *Zeeland*, owned and captained by Jan de Groote, would put to sea on the next tide in search of Spanish *naos*, a type of light trader developed by the Portuguese and once favoured by Vasco da Gama. De Groote called them 'quail', and went after them with the fiery enthusiasm of a moorland hunter. But this time he would find none. Would pursue none. Would sink none. Precisely as planned.

De Groote was a fanatical Calvinist, a native of Sluys, as were all his crew, and each had an implacable hatred of Spain born in the massacres of 'sixty-six. With others like him he had fled to the ports of England to menace shipping and to supply the ragged bands of rebels that hid in the waterlogged north of Holland and eluded the armoured battalions of the oppressor. For de Groote, arguments that depended on gold stood a poor second to those wetted by blood. It had taken much to persuade de Groote that a punishing strike against Spain could be delivered in

148

exchange for a little good faith and considerable patience. But at last the Fleming had agreed.

Tavistock walked through the tumbled shacks of Deptford's Skaw, thinking of the three secret trysts he had had with Anne Cecil. In the first, she had told him of her father's increasing doubts over the wisdom of antagonising Spain; in the second she had spoken of the Earl of Leicester's increasingly contrary view, and in the third she had revealed with breathless fear precisely what her father knew of the Duke of Norfolk's scheme to wed Mary of Scotland and usurp Elizabeth's throne.

The information had been priceless. It had sparked a plan to throw Sir William's doubts into confusion and to carry de Spes beyond all suspicion by an act of outrageous piracy.

He had shed his fine apparel in exchange for a shabby coat of fustian, a round hat and the cracked, salt-hardened boots he had last worn aboard *Minion*. Normally, as night closed in, Deptford's hundred stews competed noisily for a mariner's custom, and when, as now, masts in the river were thick as a pine forest, the maze of narrow streets would be packed with men, spending their pay or profits on quick pleasures. Continental money was easy, and the lucre would run through men's fingers like quicksilver, descending always until it reached the gutter, where pimps and thieves and tricksters and cozeners made it their own. But tonight, though there were a hundred skippers in port, the streets were deserted and money, honest or not, was hard to come by.

Tavistock smiled. This he had hoped for.

The blockade of Antwerp had once more pinched off trade to a trickle, and until the Merchant Adventurers sailed again to open the German ports, the only men to be found spending in the alehouses were those who had lifted their profits direct from Spanish ships. Idle mariners must wait, unpaid, until the Merchant Adventurers' convoy gathered. Then the great stores of woollen cloth would find dispatch and England's trade would once more be set moving and her prosperity assured. But now, there was no trade, and idle men grew poor. It was just such men that Tavistock had come to find.

He made his first port of call the sign of the Surrey Cock.

Inside low beams made him stoop. It was hulk-built, decked and lapped like an old ship's innards. The Cock, he knew, was frequented by men hankering after a trip. Immediately, he saw several of his old crew: Browne's burly frame, and young Momfrey, sprouting a thin beard now, with his face in a doxy's cleavage and his codpiece straining at the laces. And in a corner, face sallow and mouth broken out in sores, Ingram staring around him suspiciously.

'Captain!'

It was Bowen. Despite the season's warmth he was bound up in knitted wool and his felt jerkin was still cross-stitched up the front as if it was winter.

'Well met, boatswain.'

'Aye, verily!' Bowen's expression turned from glad surprise to hope. He lowered his voice. 'You're in Deptford, sir? You got work?'

Tavistock made no offer.

'I'm more than willing, sir, if you needs a whole man and a fair able hand.'

'Don't downrate yourself, man. You've a boatswain's berth in any ship I command.'

'Thankee, sir.' Bowen's hope guttered, but he asked, 'You got a ship, then? And a cargo?'

'Neither.'

The light went out of Bowen's eyes, but they slitted as Tavistock told him about Hawkins and London and how he and Francis Drake had a plan to return to the Indies. He said nothing about de Groote or any dealings with the Ambassador.

'Take me with you, Captain!' Bowen whispered imploringly. 'I'd sooner lay hands on the Spaniards than piss in the wind here.'

'I like to hear that. The berth's yours, but first you must do something for me.'

'Anything!'

'It'll not be to your liking.'

Bowen's face creased as a stack of gold coin was pressed into his palm. 'What's this?'

'I want you to put it about quietly that Jan de Groote and myself are readying to fall upon the Merchant Adventurers' fleet. That we have a pact with Alva, and that the Duke of Norfolk's money is behind it.'

Bowen was aghast. He could say nothing.

'Will you do it, Bowen?'

'But, surely it ain't right, sir – to make dirt of your good name?'

'Can I have your word?'

'But the boys hereabouts are waiting to take ship on that fleet. They'll not take kindly to being told of them that wants to jeopardise it.'

The Court's summer progress had brought the Queen here to Guildford, and Tavistock saw that all had been made splendid for her coming. Manorial lawns stretched out in close-scythed green, for despite the dry August these gardens had been nourished by a host of pail carriers. Here, tables and chairs had been brought outside and a blue and white striped tent pitched close by. The Earls Oxford and Leicester fenced elegantly before it on the greensward.

Tavistock followed Sir William Cecil and Anne towards the contestants. He was briefly aware of the warbling note of a distant skylark, then Cecil's nasal voice rang out, shattering the peace.

'My Lord of Leicester, I would speak with you on a matter of importance!'

Leicester circled his opponent warily. 'Can't it wait, Mister Secretary?'

'No, my lord.'

Tavistock saw how Cecil's cadaverous figure, swathed in sombreness and leaning heavily on his staff, distracted Leicester. The sun flashed on the Earl's blade as it stabbed forward, but Oxford, suddenly seeing Tavistock and Anne beside him, swiped it aside and lunged so that Leicester stumbled back and was brought down.

A ripple of comment passed through those who watched and jeers from a knot of Oxford's supporters.

'Damn your eyes, Edward!' Leicester said, plucking at his embroidered sleeve.

'You're too slow. I could have shaved your beard twice.'

Tavistock recognised that for Leicester the match with Oxford had been a dangerous vanity. Though merely a spar-practice, there would be no quarter offered by Oxford now that Anne Cecil was witness. It had taken all of Leicester's strength to maintain his dignity. He got to his feet, recovering himself enough to say, 'You spar well. As for myself, I fear I'm yet stiff from yesterday's hunting.'

Oxford made no reply but looked instead to Cecil with a half-smile, carefully avoiding Tavistock's eye. 'And how's your own back, nuncle? Bowed with brain-work still, I fancy. Though old age must have some compensations, eh milord?'

Leicester bristled at the implied insult to his vigour. He said acidly, 'I trust your elbow is fully healed?' Adding under his breath, 'And your ballocks.'

Tavistock had learned that Oxford's appearance at Court in February with his arm strapped up had spawned much mocking gossip. He had claimed he had fallen whilst hunting, but the story of his drunken brawl with a common sailor had preceded him to the delight of many, not least Leicester, who hated him cordially.

Tavistock stared hard. Standing in the shade and putting the spayard off his stroke seemed a pleasant enough diversion to him. But what about the way Oxford had called Sir William 'nuncle'? Was that barb meant for Anne? He had seen her stiffen with contempt. Does Oxford believe he's as good as Sir William's son-in-law already? he asked himself. I'd believe that. If Hawkins was telling me true, there's no doubt where Sir William's designs lead.

Hawkins had said that the Secretary had spent much time and effort searching the registers for evidence of an aristocratic lineage. But there had been never a hint. He had paid Doctor Dee a fortune, only to be proved a descendant of King Arthur. Beneath his hauteur, Cecil was a commoner; he had been able to find no noble connections whatsoever, nothing with which to elevate himself. So he had done the next best thing in taking Edward de Vere under his wing as a scholar and a ward. In Cecil's house, Oxford's tutors had doubtless tried to educate him in more than Greek and Latin, but Oxford had turned out an ungrateful monster.

You're of high birth, he thought as he watched Oxford's posturings, but you're penniless; you're of arresting presence and you contrive to be fashionable, but you're also spoiled and possessed of an evil temper; you're comely of body and face so that Maids of Honour swoon over you, but you're also a selfish nine-eyed eel that all England is learning to hate.

The fencers touched swords again. Around them, neatly clipped hedges surrounded a grassy bank. The patchwork garden beyond was green with hotbedded plants and the air was tinctured with herbs and garden blooms. Cecil sweltered uncomfortably in his heavy coat, the matter of the Duke of Norfolk's imminent arrival heavy on his mind. He watched Oxford place his opponent *en garde*, inwardly relishing the confrontation. I've long planned to nurture you as a lever against Leicester, he told Oxford silently. Imagine! If you can be brought to Court with your shapely legs done up in silken hose, leaping in the galliard and displaying pretty manners, you'll turn the Queen's head quite away from Leicester. But you're young, inexperienced and wayward, and you overreach yourself. You were made to look foolish by the sea captain. You should have seen that Tavistock was a dangerous man to provoke. Perhaps you're not ready to play the game I've arranged for you. Perhaps you're too hot-headed to succeed. It's just as well I have another thong to lay on Leicester's back. The Queen's favour is a delicate flower, and there's still the small matter of a charge of murder against you.

Cecil's grip tightened on his staff, his eyes never moving from Oxford's own. Naturally, you know that I'll get you off the consequences of that offence, he thought. After all, the dead man was only a servant, killed in a temper tantrum, but it will take time and money to convince a jury that the victim ran onto your sword. Perhaps I should exercise you on a shorter leash.

Cecil saw how Leicester eyed the murderer's blade. He experienced a pang of dissatisfaction. Leicester's no young pastry-cook. He's thirty-seven, a soldier and the honoured victor of St Quentin, also the Queen's favourite. Take care!

Leicester circled his blade and lunged. Oxford was forced to step back once, then again. Leicester skipped to his left and brought the rapier round in a neat parabola. The strike was swift. Surgical. It drew no blood, done with intent to wound Oxford's pride. As they withdrew to the mark, the elder man permitted himself a smile.

Cecil watched the riposte distastefully. You're a fool, he told Oxford under his breath, but unfortunately you're an indispensable fool. Your blood-ties are still crucial to me: you're first cousin to Leicester's great enemy, Thomas Howard, Duke of Norfolk, and on him all manner of treasons presently hang. Fortunately, I have both Leicester and Norfolk in a pretty cage of deceits.

Cecil knew that for Leicester the exquisite prospect of entrapping and then obliterating Norfolk, then perhaps sending Cecil to his reward also had been too much for the man to bear. He had taken the bait and in so doing he had fallen into a trap from which there could be no escape. Now it was time to bring matters to a head and snap Norfolk like a dry twig.

'I thank you for the play, milord,' Leicester said scathingly as his opponent picked himself up. Oxford ignored the gibe and Leicester turned instead to Cecil. 'Come, tell me Mister Secretary, what is there urgent enough to spoil our amusement?'

Cecil's voice was grave. 'We are in crisis, sir.'

'Crisis? What is there to fear?'

'The Duke of Alva's army is fifty thousand strong, and perched like a vulture on our very shore.'

'But the noble Duke has no navy to command.'

'That may be true – at the moment.'

Leicester put up his sword and tossed it to his fencing tutor, then he picked up a small towel and began to soak the sweat from his face and neck. As he sat down he took a long draught of ale, letting Cecil attend until he had drunk his fill, then he said, 'I ask again: what is there to fear?'

Cecil produced his paper. 'My lord, I would bring this to your attention.'

Leicester took the paper and read it, casting it carelessly on the table when he had done with it.

Cecil picked the paper up again and asked flatly, 'Does it provoke no comment from you, my lord?'

Leicester laughed tauntingly. 'I find it – fascinating.'

'Here is *proof* that the Duke of Norfolk and his father-in-law plotted with the Spanish ambassador three months ago against English interests.'

'What it seems to say is that a party of cloth merchants organised a fleet to sail to Hamburg, since they could not go to Antwerp, and that Norfolk, Arundel and de Spes tried to stop it.'

'They asked the Spanish – the Duke of Alva – to halt the Merchant Adventurers' fleet!'

Leicester shrugged at Cecil's anger. 'They enlisted the help of Channel pirates. So? Was the cloth fleet molested?'

Cecil drew himself up. 'You know perfectly that it was not.'

'Then what consequence has it?'

'The fleet went unmolested only because it sailed two days early. Prewarned by an unknown source.'

'Sir William, what of it? The private interests of Norfolk and his cronies are his own affair.'

'By God, my lord, plotting to panic the City is treasonable behaviour! He is plainly seeking to make conditions rife for rebellion!'

Leicester could no longer maintain his careless attitude. 'You infer a good deal, from a mere memorandum, Mister Secretary!'

'And I'll imply more. To the Queen. If you were privy to this game and did not divulge it to me –'

'Yes?'

Cecil decided to stop short of an overt threat. 'I merely bring you a warning.' He bowed shallowly, turned and marched away, gathering his daughter and Tavistock as he went.

That should be enough to spur him into action, he thought with satisfaction. Incredible that Norfolk could have been so foolish! But there it was. And now the trap was sprung.

As they reached the house Cecil recalled the day Robert Slade had brought the first inklings of the plot to him. Until then, he thought, I'd only seen Leicester kiss Norfolk's arse, and I believed they were in league. Now I'm able to direct and control Leicester's passion I feel much better. Whatever happens now, he thought pleasantly, Leicester is mine, and Norfolk is a dead man.

A motion at the gatehouse tower window caught Cecil's eye. His valet signalling with his handkerchief in the manner they had arranged: Norfolk had arrived.

Leicester appeared, hurriedly rounded the outer court and passed the guard before coming to a place where he could see the Duke. Cecil saw Leicester hang back to watch Norfolk dismount. The Duke had been Leicester's special quarry since their rivalry had spilled embarrassingly into public violence before the Queen's person some three years ago. Norfolk, furious at being bested at a game of tennis and inexpressibly jealous of the familiarity Leicester had shown to the Queen, had threatened him. Norfolk had come with his father-in-law, the Earl of Arundel, to intimidate him and call him traitor.

Oh, yes, Cecil thought with delight, Norfolk made you grovel before him then. Claiming to speak for the entire old Catholic nobility, and objecting to your position with the Queen. But you did not damage the Queen's reputation as Norfolk alleged, neither did you stand in the way of her marrying, as I so charged you. As Master of the Queen's Horse you had every right to approach the Queen's Presence Chamber. But you had to defer to Norfolk, make promises to him, and I know that the rage excited in you by that humiliation will live ever so long as you live, my dear Dudley!

It had taken every moment since that time to coax Norfolk into compliance with Leicester and the scheme that would destroy him. The first real victory had been during a secret meeting in the formal garden of Leicester's own magnificent estate at Kenilworth. That had come after treating with Walsingham at his house in Kent – a ruse to ensure no part of the plan seemed to originate with Cecil. It was the culmination of years of delicate web-spinning. Spies had been hidden at each meeting since, Norfolk never suspecting that the man he had trusted with his security arrangements was in Robert Slade's pay.

Leicester had visited Norfolk several times, and each time a verbatim report of the conversation had reached Cecil. Each time Leicester had poured a little more poison in Norfolk's ear about the beautiful Queen of Scots, a woman who as a Queen would make the perfect match with England's only Duke. Without that match Norfolk would remain a Duke, a lesser Privy Councillor, the controller of vast acreages in East Anglia, but forever displaced in the Queen's favour by a mere Earl: Leicester himself.

Norfolk had been vain and hungry for royal power, and he hated Leicester; all jealous weaknesses that Leicester might easily use against him while the question of the succession still hung in doubt. He was a rival with wealth and position, but one who could be obliterated – *must* be obliterated – if Leicester was to have security.

At the same time, there had been another reason to try to use him, which was why Leicester trod his ground with care, testing the way secretly and in consort with no ally. The Queen's health was ever the subject of concern; were she to die all protection would evaporate like Irish dew and he would reap the reward of a thousand bitter jealousies. That was the reason he had chosen to adopt an intricately roundabout approach: First, he had offered Norfolk flattery, then a morsel of hope. Hope of putting behind him the three disastrous marriages the Duke had already made. Each of his wives had died – Mary, daughter of the Duke of Arundel; Margaret, daughter of Lord Audley; and Elizabeth, widow of the Baron Dacre, the inherited lands of whose children he hoped to use to enlarge and consolidate his position. Next, Leicester had played on Norfolk's dormant Catholicism, reminding him of the position of high favour he had held as a young man at the Court of Mary Tudor.

At last the flattery had begun to work its magic. It was no coincidence that when Mary Queen of Scots took ship to England it was to Carlisle that she came, and into the bosom of Norfolk's very sister, the Lady Scrope. There, Norfolk had visited her, gazed on the whore herself. But he had seen only the gorgeous form of his own desire, and with that he had fallen in love.

Norfolk had been put in charge of the tribunal at York responsible for deciding Mary's future, and there Leicester had administered the ultimate aphrodisiac of power. He had come obliquely to the central issue – the fact that in Mary the Crowns of England and Scotland might be legitimately fused. Delicately, he had pointed out that the man who controlled her might control the destiny of Europe. Such a man, if he went about it correctly, could become first King-consort – and then King of Great Britain! Surely, there could be no better way for Norfolk to cement all his interests and ambitions than to listen to the scheme Leicester had drawn up. Surely, there could be no greater prize! As soon as the Duke's mouth had begun to slaver with greed, he had retired, leaving his potent suggestions to ferment in Norfolk's uncomplicated mind. There had been much to do elsewhere.

Immediately, Leicester had sent a secret message via the Bishop of

Ross to Bolton Castle, where Mary was now incarcerated, suggesting that he would use his best efforts to secure the marriage for her if she wanted it. He then decided to cover himself so far as Elizabeth was concerned. He had gone to the Queen to propose openly but gently that a solution to the embarrassment of the Scots whore might be found in a match with Norfolk. If the small matter of Mary's marriage to Bothwell could only be tidied up, what better chance would Elizabeth ever have of neutralising the threat Mary posed than by coupling her to England's foremost peer? He had waited patiently for Elizabeth to show her displeasure, or at least give some sign as to her thoughts, but she had remained utterly silent over the matter. And so, taking the biggest gamble of all, he had visited Walsingham to convince him that a plot was simmering.

When Walsingham had brought the information to Cecil he had been amazed to find Cecil already aware of the facts. And it had touched Cecil's mind that Leicester was leaking the plan to Walsingham in order to create an alibi should the plan disintegrate.

Cecil had waited, holding his breath, then Leicester had offered to talk with Norfolk at Kenilworth. Norfolk had asked about Bothwell. No, Bothwell would be no problem at all, Leicester had assured him. That filthy, dissolute coward had run from the prospect of battle at Carberry Hill, forsaking Mary his wife, and abandoning her to sign away her realm while still abed after miscarrying the twins he had fathered. He had fled to Norway, but had been captured and taken to Copenhagen where King Frederick had buried him alive in a festering hole under the terrifying fortress of Dragsholm. It would be a simple matter to purchase his death, or to bribe the bishops into granting Mary annulment or divorce.

According to Slade's man the cipher reply Leicester received from Mary had come in the dead of night, handed to him from the sleeve of her ambassador to the Court of St James, the double-dealing Bishop of Ross. Cecil had read it: Mary's meandering hand had grown more and more excited as she dwelt on the glittering prospect Norfolk had opened up for her. So the way had been made clear.

Cecil smiled, recalling those closely-written reports of the way Norfolk had gone running once more to Kenilworth, exhibiting the anticipation that he had been unable to hide. Norfolk, gullible, trusting now, and completely disarmed by the glorious vision Leicester had worked so hard to fix in his imagination, had arrived alone and unattended.

'You're a deuce away from winning everything,' Leicester had told his victim. 'But to make certain you must have allies. First, Cecil must be disarmed and then the proposal put to the Queen in a way she'll find hard to refuse. I'm willing to undertake that, but first I must have your solemn promise that you'll go through with it.'

'Isn't that what I've always said?'

Leicester had flattered then, and laid his hand on Norfolk's sleeve. 'Your campaigns against the Scots in 'fifty-nine and 'sixty were masterful. You're the nation's greatest landowner and the only man living who can end forever the threat to England that Scotland poses. You are a shrewd man, and I agree with your misgiving about the way Cecil is driving Elizabeth into war with Spain. You know as well as I that it is a war England cannot hope to win. With your connections in the North you could destroy that threat at a single stroke by raising the Catholic northern Earls against Elizabeth and supplanting her as Queen.'

They had been talking the highest form of treason. Never before had the full consequence of the scheme been so brazenly stated, and Cecil had gasped whilst reading the report of it. It must have hit Norfolk with the force of a battering ram because he had hesitated then.

'I could. But not without your initial help, Leicester.'

'If you depend on me, think how much more I depend on you. My part would be simple, and once done, it would be up to you. And thereafter I would be in your power.'

'And I in your debt.'

'It's a debt that as King you could well afford to pay. You would have England, Wales and Scotland too, united for the first time ever. Submissive to your dictates. Under your heel completely!'

'What price would you have me pay for it?'

'The price that any King pays a kingmaker. You would raise me to Duke, and give me the lands now controlled by Protestants too stubborn or too stupid to see which way the winds blow. We're allies, aren't we? I'll become your most faithful supporter. Think of it! For me a doubling, tripling of my status. For you, the domination of two realms. We both stand to gain enormously.'

'And in the meantime, my lord Leicester? I must make myself the target of the Queen's displeasure? I must trust you?'

The spy had recorded how Leicester had spread his hands in an open gesture at this point. 'In this cardplay, my lord Duke, the stakes are very high. I can quite easily strip the maiden naked but I cannot mount her for you. That is something you must undertake for yourself.'

'Why should Elizabeth agree to my marriage? What persuasion can you possibly offer her against Cecil's counsel? She is not a fool. And with Cecil at her side she has two heads. What if you're trying to entrap me?'

'Hear me well, my lord Duke,' Leicester had insisted. 'I'm thirty-seven; the Queen is thirty-six. I've known her since she was five years old, and I have always been able to get closer to her than any other. I know her mind better than any man alive and my arguments always carry weight with her.'

'Yet in all that time she has not agreed to marry you.'

'Do you think I'm still ambitious for her hand? It's in her mind that she'll never marry, and even if she did there would be only a small hope now of her getting with child, and still less of a healthy male heir. No. There can never be an heir while Elizabeth lives. There can never be any hope for my ambitions, and I will not suffer to wait for scraps at her table while others simper and call me lapdog. I am more than some *vade mecum* about the Queen's person. What I most thirst for is to see Sir William Cecil's heart pour out its black blood on the executioner's block. For that satisfaction I would take almost any risk, and pay any price.'

'That is a gift I would fain give you.'

'Then it is agreed?'

Norfolk's eyes had narrowed, and he had asked, 'When would you put it to her?'

'As soon as we've drawn up the details in a binding way. Naturally, they will remain secret until you're in a position to act upon them.'

'And if I agree to your demands?'

'You'll seal the contract before two witnesses of my household. There will be a copy for each of us. Solemn. Binding. With no going back.'

Norfolk had hesitated once more. 'As I said, you want me to trust you.'

'Trust me, yes! Our aims are congruent. We have nothing to gain from opposing one another now. If we act, we must win; vacillate and our opportunity is lost. But remember: this is where the road forks – you must decide which way to go. Today. Now.'

'What if the Queen refuses your request? What if she explicitly forbids the marriage?'

'She won't.'

'But if she does?'

Leicester had covered his impatience in persuasive exhortations. 'There's no chance of that, my lord, but if she does, what of it? Still you have nothing to fear. You're head of the great family of Howard, a protector of the realm. It's your bounden duty to look out for the best interests of the nation. You would only be seeking the public good, doing what almost everyone else in a position of power and influence in the land has been doing – trying to settle the vexed question of succession for the future good. You may ask her: is it a crime for a widower to want to marry a widow? No! Is it a crime, then, to ask my Queen's permission so to do? No! Especially – you may tell her – when I am sure in my heart that the marriage would at the same time remove a prickle from my Sovereign's side. No, my lord Duke, there is no danger to you that a mouthful of honey may not soothe down.'

'There is black bile in the mouths of some.'

Leicester had shrugged. 'Be ye well assured that frenzy, heresy and jealousy are three sisters that will never die – unless you are a beggar-man.'

'I may tell you that the price you ask is too high. Consider: Mary's claim to the throne stands up very well – much better than Elizabeth's.

Then there are indeed the northern Earls. Northumberland and West-morland are both worthy Catholic gentlemen whose respect for the old style makes them all but mine to command. As you yourself pointed out: together they can raise ten thousand troops.'

Leicester had hissed at him, 'But that's not necessary! A northern rebellion would set England into civil war – north versus south in a piece of bloody butchery that lays the land open to invasion by Spain! Threat of invasion is a weapon in your armoury, surely! But the people would never rally to a man who brought Alva's murderers down upon them.'

Cecil imagined the contempt in Norfolk's wheezing laugh. 'I am impressed by your concern for the good common folk of England, my Lord. I would be more impressed if you offered your intercession with Elizabeth unsullied by talk of secret binding contracts and other unworthy tradesmen's clutter.'

'There you have it,' he had told Norfolk, unmoved. 'As you so eloquently argue, you may go alone and try to shatter the door to England by the bludgeon, or you may take the golden key which I alone possess. You may take the land by rape, or walk in as if to your own bedchamber, loved by the people, bethought their saviour and deliverer. Which is it to be?'

The sands had run out on discussion. This time Norfolk had been unhesitating. 'Give me your pen.'

They had sat down then and argued over the details, a county palatinate here, a lord lieutenantship there, and Leicester had watched Norfolk's convolute signature being scratched to more than he could ever have dared to dream about.

Cecil remembered the reports of that meeting with rare astonishment. All the while reading the transcripts he had sweated, desperately thinking through the alternative policy Norfolk had divulged. What if he really did opt for that route? A rebellion in the northernmost counties of England! An unstoppable ransacking army sweeping south, gathering support as it went. Jesus God! What a terrifying prospect! There had come a vision of Northumberland's mailed cohorts hammering on his door, dragging him to Tower Hill in contempt and there striking his head from him –

There had been a cold, black void in his mind, a trickle of sweat on his temple and then he had doubled his mind to the present, thought the matter through and seen that his own fear was the last enemy of this intrigue. Norfolk was an asthmatic weakling, and no warlord. He could never inspire a *coup d'état*!

When Leicester had added his own noble signature to the document, he had made a bargain that had sealed Norfolk's future, and his own. The rest had been mere puppet play.

Now, as Cecil watched the final meeting from the chaundry house doorway, he saw that Norfolk had come alone. This time there was no Arundel to lean on, nor Oxford to lend him smirking support. Norfolk's face was ruddy with exertion as he got down from his horse. He snapped the reins at the ostler's lad and paced the cobbled yard, glancing ever up at the clock in the gatehouse tower. Leicester watched him a full minute, making him wait until the faerie chimes struck the hour. Norfolk wrung his kid gloves nervously, his hacking cough punctuating the silence, then Norfolk moved out of the sun. The lord's scent brought in a hunting dog in a velvet collar of unsettling bright red. Norfolk patted it until its tail began to wag, then he spurned it.

Bursting with anticipation, Cecil held his breath, willing Leicester to make his appearance and straining to hear. When Leicester stepped out Norfolk took two steps towards him, an agony obviously boiling in his belly. 'Well?'

'My lord?'

'You've come from the Queen? She's appraised of my intention?'

'The Queen is listening to her godchildren play. I've come from her this instant.'

Norfolk searched for a clue, but Leicester's face was a maddening blank put on apurpose.

'But you put it to her? As you said you would?'

'I ... did.'

Norfolk's agitation increased. 'So tell me. Is my marriage now approved? Speak! How did she receive it?'

Leicester's sigh was tremulous. 'Indifferent well, my lord.'

'Indifferent well ...?'

Cecil watched Norfolk's mouth fall open and his eyes flick to left and right and then settle immovably on Leicester's smile. He took an involuntary pace forward, his hand on his hilt, but before the rage of his betrayal could come upon him Leicester's hand was raised. At the signal Cecil was startled to see three boar-faced men in sky-blue livery step out from the arches and come to their master's heel. They carried bruising clubs in their hands.

Norfolk fell back from them like a man who had been stabbed through the heart. Then he turned without a word and walked away.

Cecil saw his thoughts transparently: if Norfolk could rally Northumberland and Westmorland within the week, and if the Channel could be secured and Alva's troops brought in before the equinox, he could still carry off his plan. If! If! If! The word must have hammered inside Norfolk's head, filling it with pain like a rotten tooth as he took leave.

As he came to his horse Norfolk was wracked with a bout of uncontrollable coughing. Leicester's voice carried to him, cool and distant and utterly terrifying. Laughingly, Leicester told him that the reason he could not breathe was because he was already stitched inside his shroud.

Tavistock lay back on the soft grass, sated, drowsing in an ecstasy of peace, Anne's naked body in his arms. Overhead the leaf-laden boughs of this private place shivered, dappling them with Arcadian sunlight. This is what heaven must be like, he thought, hazily. A virgin and a man whose seed is two years matured. Such a release dissolved all problems, all thoughts, in a golden halo.

He rolled his lover onto her back beside him and caressed her gently. Then he looked deep into her eyes and saw that she wanted to hold the moment for ever, but when he laid her down, the spell was broken, and her words, as she covered herself, brought him back to mortal reality, and he remembered that they were both minor players in the drama of a royal Queen's Court, and that this was not paradise but a secluded place in a wood in the county of Surrey.

'You would be in great danger if Edward found out what had happened between us.'

'He's a harmless fool.'

'His mind is seldom motivated by reason, Richard, but he is no fool. He would act first and repent at leisure. He already detests you for the way you stood up to him.'

He saw the sudden regret in her face and sought her hand. 'Don't speak of him.'

'Neither is he harmless. He's rich and he has powerful kin. He could have you followed and set upon at any time.'

'Not while I reside at Cecil House. I'll snap the lamprey in half if he so much as –'

She silenced him with a shake of her head, getting suddenly up on her elbow. 'You don't understand! My father would have you horsewhipped and sent into exile in Ireland if he imagined that you and I –'

'Do you regret that we came here?'

'No. How could I? But there are greater powers than love in our world. To some we have committed a heinous crime.'

He clenched his teeth and felt a ripple of muscle move over his jaw. 'I am a man. You are a woman. Where is the crime in that?'

'I told you that my father wants me to marry Edward. That is sufficient.'

'While I am tangled with the Spanish Ambassador?'

'How long can that save you? What if –'

She stopped, seeing that he looked at her elfin face, and let him put a finger to the faint freckles that spangled the bridge of her nose.

There was real fear for him in her doe-like eyes, and it made him feel unworthy.

'Such talk,' he said, admonishing her kindly. 'You cannot hedge everything in life with "what ifs". A mariner learns that there is in life a current that carries him where it will. And there is a power within us all, which, if we heed it, takes us around shoals and enables us to skirt the storm safely.'

She looked into his eyes. 'Do you believe that, truly?'

'It is proved to me.'

She seemed suddenly perplexed. 'So men and women do not meet by chance?'

He smiled at her earnestness and ran his hand lightly over the firm smoothness of her body, wondering at the way his touch raised the down in gooseflesh. 'This was ordained. And rightly. In those broad spaces between the stars. The same I navigate by.'

'The same that will take you from me soon?'

'That is ordained too.' He fell silent, his mind turning to his brother and the oath he had sworn. The current was straining to carry him to the Indies. He could detect its pull, could feel the rightness of it, and knew that if he faced any danger it was through opposing this tide. *Resist it not*, his soul cried to him at nights, sternly and sometimes in his father's voice. *Thou hast divided thy loyalties in a way thou knowest thou must never do!*

He hated the impure, impatient feeling that came over him in those quiet times. After months of waiting, it was past time to leave. To catch up on his destiny. To recharge the vessel of his soul.

He told Anne of John's capture and of his desire and she took it well, understanding the power and the passion that motivated him, and loving him because he sought to be true to it.

'What is he like, your brother?' she asked softly, laying her head on his chest so that her hair fanned out across it like the down of a dandelion clock.

He sighed. 'Younger and less tall than I, and dark. He was composed much of my mother's traits, whereas I was more of my father.'

'Then he is a gentle man, with a woman's softness of mind?'

Richard smiled. 'He is a man. Let no one doubt it. And if it were questioned in his earshot he would prove as much. But you are right. He has a calmer soul than I, more patience with fools, more skill in intricate things.'

'I think that you love him dearly.'

'I do. He is my only flesh. My mother is dead. My son and my son's mother both. My father was burned for his Protestant beliefs in the Smithfield pyres, before that he had been a soldier and an adventurer, then a Bristol merchant, set up with his gains in war.' Tavistock's voice was reinforced by pride. 'He was the stiffest-necked bastard in all of England. Under Mary he would not be silent. He knew little of humility, he never preached to John and I that we should not look at what we cannot reach, nor that things above us were not for us. And he was sent to his reward because he would not endure the impositions of Rome.'

'He was a martyr to the Christ's true cause?'

'So it was recorded in the work of the good deacon, John Foxe.'

'And you will be a martyr too, if you don't take care with Ambassador de Spes.'

He sat up, feeling the sudden chill of perspiration on his limbs. 'Think you so?'

'My father is using you. He must compass higher things than justice to one man. When set against the affairs of nations, you are of little significance, Richard. I know that he will cast you aside the moment you no longer supply him with the means to further his policies. His aim is to pilot the body politic as you would pilot your ship.' She reached out a hand to his body, gently touching him. 'My father taught me that the anatomy of England is that of a human form: the prince is its head; ministers of the church are its eyes, which never wink nor sleep; judges are ears, to hear complaint; the nobility are the shoulders and arms that bear the burden of the state, to defend the head with might and main force. But men of lower orders are set as inferior parts, legs to fetch and to labour, painfully to travail. You have seen my father's charts and genealogies. To him, all men have an appointed place.'

He smiled at a stray thought that flitted through his mind as he listened, but Anne insisted, 'When my father has done with you he will cast you aside. Be warned – Why do you laugh at me?'

'Not at you. I was wondering who in all this great physician's catalogue is the arsehole. I think, mayhap, that Edward de Vere must be that ignoble organ.'

She dissolved in a laughter born of tension rather than mirth. It decayed quickly. 'What will become of us all, Richard?'

'With faith we will be victorious. With faith there is always hope. Untune that string, and note what discord follows.'

She looked at him calculatingly then. And, as if she had made up her mind on the instant, told him deliberately, 'The discord of change is sounding in England. In a great rage the Queen has summoned the Duke of Norfolk to Windsor. If he obeys he will be lodged in the Tower, tried and then executed. If he does not, but flees to his estates, there will be war by Christmastide.'

As they walked together back to the manor house, high-piled lightning clouds sent great rollers of sound over the fields and big spots of rain pelted the seven-fingered leaves of the horse chestnut trees. Tavistock found himself wishing that the summer could go on and on endlessly, an endless train of golden days, an idyll without worries or cares, but he knew it could not. The word at the house was that Norfolk had pleaded illness. That he would not come before Elizabeth.

Before night fell, Tavistock was told that Sir William had ordered him to repair to London immediately. There was a squadron of ships to be readied.

Robert Slade rode hard to the royal castle of Windsor, arriving at noon. He carried the report directly to his master, suffering no delay from the guard. The Council was in plenary session. The Queen alone was absent.

The chamber was high-vaulted and panelled in oak that resounded in the uproar. Sir Nicholas Bacon, Sir Ralph Sadler and the Earl of Sussex flanked Cecil; opposite them, seated along a vast and ornately carved wooden table, were Sir Walter Mildmay, Chancellor of the Exchequer, Leicester and his supporters.

Cecil hushed the row as he saw the stony look on Slade's face. This news was urgent, he judged. Urgent and of bad tenor.

Slade's bow was curt. 'Sir William, the messenger from York brings grim tidings. The Duke of Northumberland's men are burning the Prayer Book in Durham Cathedral.'

'When?'

'November the fourteenth. Three days ago. At their head is the Sheriff of Yorkshire, Richard Norton, holding aloft the banner of the Five Wounds.'

'Another Pilgrimage of Grace,' Cecil said, stunned.

That other rising of the North, in 1538, had been in protest over Henry the Eighth's break with Rome and his treatment of the monasteries. It had been cruelly smashed by Henry's despotic hand, but that had been over thirty years ago, and Cecil knew that resentment burned in a new generation of northern Catholics. How eager would they be to avenge their fathers' defeats now? How many men would rally to the banner as it moved south?

'The Earls are even now marching on York with five thousand men. All across the Marches the church bells are pealing backwards, calling men to arms. The port of Hartlepool is taken.'

'Mary must be moved south,' Mildmay said urgently. The Queen of Scots had already been removed from Wensleydale to Staffordshire.

'Instruct the Earl of Shrewsbury to give her into the keeping of Huntingdon who will entrain her for Coventry at once.'

'And our own lady sovereign?' Leicester asked.

'Already done!' Cecil took up his pen and began to write swiftly. 'The walls of Windsor are Her Majesty's best protection. Here we hold council behind a curtain of stone.'

'You think the rebellion will reach here?' Sadler asked, aghast.

The Earl of Sussex, President of the Council of the North, enemy of Leicester, advised caution. 'I cannot be sure of my levies. Sixty thousand men came to the summer musters, but this is no census. I judge that they have no taste for civil war. Let us allow winter to cool the ardour of the rebels. Then perhaps the perduellion will nourish quiet.'

Leicester sneered at him. 'As it did for you in Ireland, my lord Thomas?'

'I am a soldier. And a realist!'

Cecil turned on them both. 'My lords! We face ultimate peril. In ten days, London may be invested by a Spanish army. We must not be caught unprepared.'

'Alva's troop are gathering in Flanders,' Slade said.

Cecil spoke to Sussex. 'Where is the Spanish ambassador.'

'At his London house.'

'The Queen must summon him.'

Leicester grinned. 'Let her summon Northumberland and West-morland too. As she did Norfolk.'

It was normal practice at times of peril for the Queen to command any suspected of disloyalty to attend Court. There they could be watched closely and removed from dangerous associates. 'They will not come. De Spes must.' Cecil bent over his papers, writing hasty directives. He looked up with eyes that impaled Leicester. 'There was yet with my lord of Norfolk time for him to repent of the evil into which you had led him. I hold you responsible for manufacturing a traitor of England's only Duke. Aye, and for your own deceitful ends!'

Leicester leapt to his feet in rage. 'God's hooks, you're a filthy liar! It is no fault of mine that he planned treachery. Nor that he came to the Queen lately, whining like a whipped cur, begging her forgiveness. Your head is so stuffed with the shit of your own intrigues that you see them everywhere!'

Cecil was pleased with Leicester's rude outburst. The Earl's resentment at being manipulated had burst forth, showing that he was a worried man. If the Queen showed mercy and Norfolk's head did not roll, how vast would Leicester's chagrin grow? How huge his fear of Norfolk's eventual reprisals? Leicester had staked everything on Norfolk's downfall. And though he had yet to lose, he had not won either.

One at a time! Cecil thought mercilessly, looking to Bacon and then to Leicester. Robert Dudley's twig humbled then bent double! Mary's royal branch pegged to earth! Norfolk almost sawn off! Almost. Next would come the Northern barons of Northumberland and West-morland. These I must snap in twain!

When Cecil spoke, it was calmly to his confederate, Sir Ralph Sadler, Chancellor of the Duchy of Lancaster. 'The Queen's most forgiving Majesty is disposed to see Norfolk's head stay upon his shoulders. What say you?'

Sadler, sixty years old losing some of his flesh, stared out from under shaggy brows. 'Parliament will see it differently. He is a traitor, craven apologies or no.'

Cecil dropped his voice. 'It may yet be diplomatic to permit the Queen her own way in this. Back me and I will see you appointed Paymaster-General – to supervise Sussex in his Generalship in the North.'

Sadler smiled briefly. 'You seem greatly confident of victory.'

'I am. Slade!' When the messenger came near, Cecil spoke privily to him. 'Take the message to my London house immediately that Captain Tavistock is to put Hawkins's plan into effect. He will understand you. Chatham and Deptford are alert. I will order the Queen's Navy to resort to its Channel station with all strength, but stealthily. You must make sure they understand that Hawkins's ships are not to be interfered with, whatever they appear to do.'

Slade bowed and hurried from the chamber with orders, still sandy and unsealed, in his gloved fist.

God, Cecil thought with satisfaction. Perhaps it's time to humble Leicester a little more. He's spent too much time this year strutting the Court like a cockerel, reingratiating himself. Last week he went hunting with Her Majesty on that proud Andalusian warhorse, and told her he had sure knowledge of my plans to kiss the feet of Spain. Now he's called me liar, openly and before the Council. He rises well above himself. He deserves to suffer a reminder that'll demonstrate to him his true status. What better way than to show him the contract?

He thought back to the day of Norfolk's surrender with pleasure. Norfolk must have taken the royal summons from his retainer as if it was a viper. On that fateful summer day when Leicester had snapped the jaws of his trap closed, Norfolk had fled to London and then to his East Anglian estates around England's second city of Norwich.

In a frenzy, Norfolk had begun stitching together the tatters of his plans. At first it must have looked impossible, but as the leaves of his orchards turned first to gold and then to brown there had grown in him a burgeoning hope. Walsingham had intercepted letters written by Northumberland and by Westmorland, showing they were both solid to the Duke's cause. Mary herself, filled with righteous indignation against her imprisonment, had encouraged him also. Alva, though his temper had been sorely tried, had extended his undertaking to send troops. Against the odds, de Spes's repeated intercessions had persuaded him that the hazardous crossing was possible before winter set in – with English help. Even the vile Pope had agreed to draw up a poisonous document to damn Elizabeth and turn her subjects against her.

Just as it must have seemed to Norfolk that he would succeed, Cecil had spoken to Elizabeth. Then he had reworded her letter of summons to Norfolk, drafting it in conciliatory terms, to make her seem eager for *rapprochement*. Norfolk had wavered. In a few more days, everything would have been ready. So he had fled once more, to Kenninghall, pleading illness.

'*Play for time!*' Mary's voice had screamed at him from Tutbury. '*Delay them. Elizabeth must be made to wait.*'

Norfolk had spoken hoarsely to his secretly disloyal scrivener. 'Tell the messenger I am ill. That I will come in three days – no four. Write that I have taken me to bed with the Sweat.'

Then he had asked Arundel, 'I'll be safe at Kenninghall, won't I? I can raise eighteen thousand foot and four thousand horse. If I can hold out for a week I'll be safe. A week! God grant me that!'

Cecil's spy had told him how, three days later, the colour had drained from Norfolk's distraught face, how he had coughed flecks of blood as he broke the seal on Elizabeth's second, this time unaltered, summons.

'*This manner of reply we have not been accustomed to receive from any person,*' she had written in a high passion, demanding that he come. Instantly. In a litter, if necessary, though the journey should kill him.

He had read the terrifying missive twice, seeing the royal messenger's horse stamping impatiently in his yard and the studded jerkins of black leather. Desperation had crawled over his skin, then he had fired off a message to Northumberland to stay the rebellion.

'I will go to Windsor, and throw myself on the Queen's mercy!' he had told Arundel who was at his side.

'You can still go through with it!'

'No!'

'Coward! Betrayer! You'll murder us all!'

Norfolk's retainers had tried to stop him. They had hung on his stirrups, but he had ridden them down in his anxiety to fling himself in abject repentance at Elizabeth's feet.

And when he had come to Windsor how she had screamed at him, sending missiles over her writing desk, launching threats without mercy, one after another, down upon his head. He had been dragged from her, begging forgiveness, pouring out the pathetic sentiments Leicester had fed him about neutralising Mary and guarding the succession, all the while choking for air as the touch of steel on his neck had reminded him of the penalty he must pay.

It had been extraordinary to watch. And after, it had been so simple to extract from the quivering Duke the damning contract he had made with Leicester. Shall I snap Leicester now? Cecil asked himself, feeling utterly in control of all he surveyed. Shall I show him a facsimile of the contract? It would be like showing him his own death warrant, and sure proof against any pompous spite on his part. Perhaps not. Perhaps I'll save it until I need it. A wise man would.

He thought once more of the bundle of firewood he had shown to Nicholas Bacon. One key strand remained. Tavistock. The next letter he would draft would be to the Duke of Alva. A message to be passed on in total secrecy by Guiseppe Gradenego, via Spinola's Bank, warning that the escort Alva had arranged for his troops would turn on him.

Chapter 11

When John Hawkins saw her, the *Antelope* was standing off the low, marshy island of Walcheren; along with four other neat two-hundred tonners, she drew a watchful curtain across the western mouth of the Scheldt estuary. Each of the vessels belonged to Hawkins, all were merchantmen bought after the Merchant Venturers' successful summer convoy to Hamburg, and all were riding low as if laden with cargo. But Hawkins knew that there was no cargo: the burden was shot, and a great weight of ordnance with which to dispatch it.

He had come to talk business and stood in the prow of a supply boat, a small craft of shallow draught out of Chatham. It was mid-afternoon now, cold, but windless, the sea as calm as window glass.

Hawkins saluted the quarterdeck and clasped Tavistock's hand tightly, as usual, but there was something in his grip that put Tavistock on his guard.

'Welcome aboard, General,' he said with shipboard formality.

'I thank you, Richard.'

'What news from England?'

Hawkins faced him, his glance warning off eavesdroppers. 'News that'll not please you. First, I want your report.'

They climbed up to the poop together, Tavistock made uneasy now by Hawkins's reticence. I've nothing at all to report and you know it, he thought. Twelve days plying back and forth fruitlessly. You've come to tell me the reason, and it'd better be good, God damn it. I wish I knew what devilish ideas Walsingham's been planting in your head and what his position is now. Christ! And what of the rebellion? It's a fact that knowledge is power – without knowledge I'm like a hobbled horse. And you know that too.

He said, 'The Spanish know I'm here. Either they'll come to meet me when they're ready, or not at all. I'm damned if I'm sailing into the Honde to fetch them.'

Hawkins grunted and hooked his thumbs into his belt knowingly. 'Think you they fear the treachery you have in store for them? Aye, that'd explain their reluctance.'

Tavistock cast him a sudden, savage glance. Since receiving Sir William's order two weeks ago, he had been relishing the prospect of paying off de Spes in powder and shot. The ambassador had given him gold for himself and letters to pass on to Alva's emissary. Half the gold had gone to Hawkins, the remainder, in Bowen's possession, had been sent down to Plymouth at Drake's lusty request. The letter to Alva was still under lock and key in his cabin.

Tavistock's spirits had been high then. It had been exhilarating to get back aboard ship after so long laid up in London. To move and to see events move. He had discussed the operation to the penultimate detail with de Spes, then he had sailed to his appointed station off the Flanders coast exactly as the Spaniards had desired. As soon as the troop-laden *urcas* appeared he would fall in beside them, his squadron formed up in line astern, and he would take them to within sight of the English coast. Then the real payment would be made, the part he had not told de Spes: a great opening up with twenty-four pounders!

Would that John were here now, he thought. With expert handling, these thirteen-foot-long Samuel Stanton culverins, each weighing four thousand pounds, could blow any hull on the seas to splinters. Such a gun propelled a twenty-four-pound cast-iron ball with enough explosive momentum to penetrate five feet of ship's timber, at a range of a hundred yards. Alva's flimsy troop barges would be blasted to bits, and the stouter *naos* that might act as escort would be burst open like wine puncheons.

But nothing had happened. No ship from the Scheldt, night or day, had ventured to pass him. And those sailing for Antwerp had tried to bear away as soon as they saw him, increasing the confusion in the Narrows, there to face de Groote and shift for themselves as best they could.

'I have it that Francis Drake's bought himself a fast ship and two pinnaces,' Hawkins said.

Tavistock waited for Hawkins to say more, sensing he knew that Tavistock's own opinion was that a war with Spain must ensue and that it was best to try to inflict as much damage as possible upon them before war was declared.

'I have it that he's sailed without leave or passport. Do you know anything of it?'

'I'm a long way from Plymouth here, General.'

Hawkins grunted. 'Aye. But that's no answer to a direct question.'

'I have occupations of my own. Too many to think overmuch on what Francis Drake may be choosing off his own back.'

The secret plans Tavistock had laid with Francis Drake just before the man's wedding in July had been far-ranging. They had sat together in Hawkins's kitchen and without Hawkins's knowledge had drunk to the working lads of Deptford and Plymouth and advanced their ideas to send a ship to the Indies. Since then, Drake had settled matters admirably. With money of his own and later with the golden pesos Tavistock had taken from de Spes, Drake had bought a fast, light ship, and Stanton ordnance, and had immediately started victualling her for a return voyage to Vera Cruz. If Drake could reach the Indies before news of Alva's drowned army did, he would be able to ransom John and the other English mariners and escape without penalty.

'Nothing spectacular,' Drake had said, grinning at the prospect. 'Just a little piece of midnight horse-trading with the fat and amenable Don Luis Zegri. Open and honest and friendly. Then, when the lads are aboard, we'll leave our answer to Don Emilio's double-dealing.'

The thick-accented words of Jan de Groote had come to him then, 'Spanish generosity is boundless! I ask only for their gold but oftentimes they seek to give me their lives!'

Since that time, Richard had dwelt on the succulent notion that it was de Spes's gold that would finance everything. And if Drake was true to himself the ransom money would be but a lure and would return with him multiplied a dozen times over. But something had miscarried. Ten days had passed and no contact had been made with Alva's emissary. Was it possible that the rebellion was swelling with men and arms? What if the traitor Norfolk had succeeded? If London had risen against Elizabeth? A sudden fear reared in Tavistock's mind and his thoughts turned to Anne Cecil's safety.

'You're to turn for home, Richard.'

Tavistock felt the words break in on him like hammers. 'What?'

'Now. Immediately. I have other work for you.'

This was what he had feared the moment he had seen Hawkins standing in the boat. He had known that backhanded politicking in London had robbed him of his chance of action.

'What's been happening?' he demanded.

Hawkins slapped his hands flat on the rail before him. 'The ports are closed, and I'm defying Sir William's order to come here. You know that Northumberland and Westmorland have mustered? They've taken Hartlepool as the port for Alva's troops to land.'

'They'll never reach Hartlepool, by God!'

Hawkins shook his head. 'Perhaps. But it's not your efforts that'll stop them. The Duke of Norfolk's in the Tower. The Queen is ensconced in her fortress at Windsor, and Her Majesty's cousin, Henry Carey, Lord Hunsdon, is sent to command the militia to oppose the rebels. In London rumours are circulating that Alva's sworn to pay his soldiers' arrears in Cheapside and make the Queen hear Mass at St Paul's on Candlemas. The Countess of Northumberland is stirring it from the saddle at the head of her husband's army. Even now they're marching on Tadcaster with seven thousand men.'

Tavistock's stomach tightened. 'Then I can't leave this station! Alva must be contained!'

Hawkins looked up then. All he had come to say was in his mouth.

'You'll do as I tell you. The rumours are foolish prating. Alva will not attempt to embark. And without his help the rebellion will crumble.'

'Not embark? Are we betrayed to de Spes?' Tavistock's mind reeled.

'No. Alva's said in a letter to de Spes that help will now only be dispatched following the release of the Queen of Scots. He considers that the test of English feeling against Elizabeth, and proof that the rebellion is no lost cause. But the rebel army can never release Mary because they can no longer get to her. They don't know where she is. Lord Huntingdon and Sir Ralph Sadler have moved her to Warwickshire, and that's too far south for Northumberland's army to penetrate without Alva's help.'

Tavistock saw at once that the rebels' dilemma was total: no support without Mary, and no Mary without support. Unless the circle was broken the rising was doomed. Such a manoeuvre had the stamp of Sir William Cecil's fertile mind.

'How was Alva persuaded to impose such a condition? By the Secretary, I'll wager!' Tavistock said angrily. The twin-tongued bastard! he thought. Cecil's tipped Alva off. And I have been here all the while for nought!

Hawkins shrugged, saying less than he knew. 'Sir William is not wholly in accord with our ideas, Richard.'

It was enough for Tavistock. 'I'll have you speak straight to me, now, General!'

Hawkins stood back at his subordinate's display of ill temper, but he held his course. 'Consider: Sir William's object is to confound the rising. The rising may be confounded by the preventing of Spanish support. Therefore, Spanish support must be prevented. There was never a desire to destroy a Spanish army. Simply a need to prevent it reaching English soil.'

'And what of my desire? And yours, John?' Tavistock slammed his fist down on the breech of a cannon. 'What are these spitfires for, else?'

'You might just as well have a belly full of quarry stone.'

'It'd be easier to digest than that which sits in my own belly now!'

'That may be,' Hawkins became suddenly conciliatory, 'but, don't you see? Our way was irrevocable. Sir William had a more subtle and flexible game. He's saved Alva from destruction, and signalled to Spain that he's not seeking war. And he's made a fool of de Spes in Alva's eyes.'

'And a fool of me! He's lost us the chance of a decisive blow!' Tavistock slammed his fist into the breech once more so that his knuckles bled. The thought flashed into his mind that Jan de Groote's anger would know no bounds. That he had worked up his men and his associates with false promises of glory. That recompense would have to be made, from that same store of precious gold he had marked for another task, even to the value of a thousand pounds, but that nothing – nothing at all – would restore confidence in his name among those from whom he most sought respect. 'Satan take Mister Secretary Cecil as the slithering serpent he is!'

Hawkins's eyes narrowed. 'Steady, Richard. Sir William's a powerful man. Dangerous as a serpent, true, but it's well that he's not set against us. When the looked-for Catholic rising in the South fails to appear, and when the rebels are cut off and crushed to dust by Sussex and Hunsdon, Cecil will have carried the victory. It'll not be long before Norfolk and Queen Mary are both sent to their reward, and Sir William raised to the peerage, and all accomplished without provoking Spain. Total victory in his eyes. He will think it a rout, indeed, and why not? You, with your unsanctioned adjuncts and your independent follies of action, you who're dangerous, are dangerous no longer.'

Tavistock looked into the ship's waist where his men stood at their posts, wrapped up in thick, felt coats against the cold, listening yet trying to seem not to be. He saw Momfrey and Riveley, Browne and Gonson, all of whom had come back survivors of the Indies. It had been more than a year, now. He knew well how they chafed to settle their old shipmates' scores. Good lads, reliable lads, lads that'd run to Hell and ream the Devil's arse for you. Not lads to leave forlorn, or to dangle as puppets, as Hawkins is dangling you. Don't fail them now.

'What of our position?' he asked Hawkins bitterly. 'Are we not cast back in the mire as pirates?'

'Our piracy is old, now. The Spanish are most like to resort to sweet flattery and to let matters be, for the sake of the gold Elizabeth still holds. Sir William has, by his twisting, bought a measure of Spanish trust.'

'And de Spes? Are we spoiled with him?'

Hawkins drew a deep breath and expelled it slowly, considering the question well asked. 'I doubt that. I judge Sir William's hand was played subtly, as ever. Alva was warned against mutiny within your crews. The most de Spes will suspect will be the loyalty of your men.'

Tavistock nodded tightly and Hawkins folded his arms. 'I think we had best talk with Walsingham from here in. He has a better task for you.'

'What sort of task?'

'One you should perform amply – smuggling.'

'*Smuggling?*' Tavistock's reply was explosive. 'Am I to be misused again?'

'Confound your eyes, man! Will you not take an order cleanly? This is important work. For a trusted servant. It's not bolts of cloth and pipes of wine I have in mind.'

Tavistock looked at Hawkins with a murderous glance. 'Then what?'

'You're to convey an Italian banker into England. And with him comes the best hope of all our futures.'

The cold had cleared the anger from Tavistock's brain. He was thinking clearly and with perspective. There was no point in exposing useful duplicity needlessly, and Cecil would surely wring every last drop of advantage from de Spes's credulity. But this new labour was an extension unagreed and unwelcome.

'I'll not do more of your filthy work,' he told Hawkins. 'I have a task of my own. My brother –'

'You'll go nowhere without a ship and a passport.'

Tavistock flared. 'And who will stop me?'

'I will. And all the forces at the Queen's command. You'll be a dead man inside a week if you defy me, Richard! But bring me this banker and I'll as soon see you obtain a passport to sail for the relief of the maroons.'

'Who is he?'

'His name is Roberto di Ridolfi. His is an errand of great import.'

'Then what comes to me if I agree should be more than some pissy paper of permission.'

'If you are successful, your payment will be a ship of your own.'

'This one.'

Hawkins spat rancorously. 'Bugger you, Richard Tavistock! Did I not succour you at my family's teat? Have I not grown you from a seed? For what? To have you demand – *demand* of me my best?'

Tavistock's hand gripped the hilt of his cutlass. 'I'm a grown oak now. I already have your best ship and four more. If I learned anything from you, John Hawkins, it's that a Captain is master of all at sea. More than Secretaries. More than Princes. Aye, and more than an owner. You're on my ship now, and she's on the high seas and we can go anywhere that I decide. I'll have the *Antelope* for my pains, or the squadron sails for La Rochelle and the aid the Huguenots will gratefully tender me to punish the Spanish.'

Hawkins eyed him silently, then nodded assent.

Tavistock felt a surge of elation that conquered all. Such a prize! In ancient times, the antelope was an heraldic beast that haunted the banks of the River Euphrates, very savage and hard to catch, having dangerous horns with which it impaled its enemies. The *Antelope* was the perfect ship to carry forward his plans: new-built, lean, fast, well-found, and capable, as he had seen, of mounting great fire power.

His mind roamed over the driftwood cast up on the beach of fortune by the latest turns of this political storm. So far, there had been de Spes's gold and there had been Anne Cecil. If the next pretty piece of flotsam turned out to be a ship, he would have that too. He would wait for Drake to return with John and then they would go out upon the tropical oceans together and the Spanish would see there was more to English pride and English vengeance than old men who dissembled and hunted peerages and shrank from justice.

Hawkins's eyes pierced him, reading his thoughts. His warning was delivered softly. 'You stir my blood, Richard. But be careful. Cecil's ruthless and clever. Aye, even more than you think yourself, Richard.

And he's a thousand times more connected to events than you or I will ever be, with hundreds of spies all over Europe feeding him secrets. He's fanatically loyal to Elizabeth. You saw the interest he has in blood lines, the charts and chronologies of heredity. He'll do anything to maintain power and to elevate himself. You called him a serpent. So he is. He turns this way and that as suits him. Just now, he's turning towards Spain and towards the Earl of Oxford. If you want to keep your leaves, oak tree, you'll remember that. And you'll keep away from his daughter.'

Tavistock stiffened, thinking suddenly of the clashing antlers of the stags in the royal deer parks. It was a universal male urge to lock horns with anything that stands between an individual and his desire. The temptation to tangle with Cecil was overpoweringly strong, but Hawkins was right. It was an urge that was lethal, and, for the moment, must be resisted.

But no one would keep him away from Anne. No one.

On the morning of Beltane – May Day, Robert Slade brought his master the document he had been dreading. It shattered Cecil's inner serenity more completely than if his Queen had ordered his head cloven in two.

When Slade came to him, Cecil was hard pressed with work, drawing up a list of show trials and executions that would best illustrate and punish the crimes of the Northern rebels. Until today, events had proceeded to Cecil's satisfaction. Had not Edward de Vere finally agreed to marry his daughter? Had not the realm been pulled back from the very brink of war with Spain? Had not the North been harsh disciplined and all his enemies reduced and diminished?

Apart from a brief flurry of violence by the diehard landowner Leonard Dacre, a flurry soon quieted by Lord Hunsdon's iron mace, the Catholic revolt had been gutted even before Candlemas. By the end of February, it had been utterly smashed. Northumberland's ragged army had been sent flying over the Border into the arms of Mary's few remaining sympathisers in Scotland, and their Earl had been humiliatingly captured by Scottish Protestants and was now in custody in England. Only the weasel, Westmorland, had succeeded in evading capture, bolting to the Duke of Feria's haven for renegade Englishmen in Spain. The two outstanding questions now were how to deal with Mary and what to do with Norfolk.

Cecil had given the matter great thought. It should be simple, he had told himself two days ago. An orchestrated Parliament was howling for Mary's head, and efforts were daily being made to enfever the London mob with a blood lust against her. It was a simple matter of convincing Elizabeth that Mary's execution was inescapable.

But when he had gone to her, Elizabeth had become intractably, resolutely, intransigently set against it.

Cecil recalled how he had gone too far with her, for he had brought her to within a hair's-breadth of hysterical fury. Yes, and deliberately.

She had been Queen a dozen years and she had learned how to demand, and how to get. But he had been a statesman longer, and knew how to make his Queen want what he wanted. A glance had commanded silence. Her two-fisted gestures, though from the body of a woman, had been recognisably her father's. The pure, insistent power of Henry, revived.

Of course, it was all staged and calculated to cow subjects instantly, and so it did. He had bowed low and fed out his arm in obedient flourishes as he had backed from her presence, feeling he had manoeuvred her precisely as he must.

But beneath the mask, in private, he had seen her face wracked by a warring conscience. There had been no further discussion that week about the delicate matter of Mary's head – which was a pity, but could wait, nor of Thomas Howard's – which was a goodly consolation. The foolish Duke of Norfolk was better alive, for there was a clear use for him. And with the Queen roiled in a definite passion over both, Norfolk might survive. He would present that, eventually, as the will of all England. The offer would be clemency for Norfolk and the block for Mary. And Elizabeth would accept, because it was just and it was wise and because she trusted him absolutely.

Slade's unfussy bow was followed by no preliminary explanation. Instead, he laid a large hand-copied sheet on the table. Its italic paragraphs made Cecil gasp.

This nightmare was why he had closed the ports before Christmas and kept them closed throughout the rising and after. This was the high retribution come down on them from Peter's throne, the thunderbolt he had tried to stave off, and it shot him full of fear to find that it had appeared before him without warning.

'Found posted on the door of the Bishop of London's house in St Paul's Churchyard, Sir William.'

'Thank you,' he said, shocked utterly though he had expected it in some small way at the back of his mind. 'Thank you. Was it seen?'

'Gossips are at work and the Guard have found copies in their hundreds. Soon they will be as thick in the streets as rose petals at Her Majesty's midsummer masque.'

'You brought it straightway?'

'I did.'

'Then you did well. Wait for me here, I will be back presently.'

He folded the paper, got up and marched directly to the Queen's Presence Chamber. Leicester was with her and Cecil saw at once that the interruption was enormously inopportune. It made her waspish, and she chose not to look at him, addressing Leicester instead.

'You are become ill at ease, Robert.'

It was not a question.

Leicester rubbed languidly at his forehead. Cecil saw that he had arrived just as Leicester was hatching some scheme to amuse her and enrich himself. To scheme in the presence of Elizabeth was an electrifying experience at any time. Now, with Cecil's arrival, it was too much for Leicester to stand. There were few who could withhold the truth from her for long, and none who could lie to her face.

Cecil waited patiently for Leicester to scuttle away.

'I fear my physician tells me true,' the Earl said, getting up from the cushions. 'It feels much like a summer ague coming on.'

Elizabeth's voice was feline. 'I shall call Doctor Caius to you.'

'Gracious lady! But please, don't trouble him.'

'He's eminent and knows his Galen well. He will tell you if you have the Sweat, and give you a dose of physic.'

'I have not the Sweat. It is nothing.'

She looked penetratingly at Lettice Knollys, her attractive cousin and Leicester's mistress, and then back at him. 'So why trouble with it?'

'May I beg pardon to speak truly?'

'Granted.'

'I must beg leave to lie down. That I may be of my best for the play tonight. I am overcome by Your Majesty's radiance.'

Elizabeth's pout of annoyance was fleeting. He made bold to kiss her hand uninvited but she drew it back, remembering that Cecil watched.

'You have taken all our favours at one bite. There is no more for you here today.'

As he passed Cecil, Leicester strutted like a peacock. He whispered pleasantly, 'I leave Her Majesty in your keeping, Mister Secretary.'

'Her Majesty has no master,' Cecil smiled and bowed with exaggerated politeness, calling after him, louder, 'Nor peer.'

Leicester turned, then turned again and stalked out. A ripple of tittering passed through the younger of the Queen's ladies. Those that were in earshot looked suddenly stunned. The whispering and sniggering began, eyed coldly by Lettice Knollys, but the exchange with Leicester had done nothing to unfreeze the Secretary's baleful demeanour.

Elizabeth gestured peremptorily. Cecil approached, paper in hand, bowed and whispered to her. Immediately she got up and cleared the room with a clap of her hands. Her face had lost all softness; all around her cats and lapdogs and embroidery were gathered up swiftly.

When Elizabeth took the paper to her desk, she pushed a finger through the holes where the Pope's decree, entitled *Regnans in Excelsis*, had been nailed to, and later roughly torn from, the Bishop's door. She studied it carefully, and made no comment until she had finished.

> We do out of the fullness of our Apostolic power declare the aforesaid Elizabeth to be a heretic and a favourer of heretics, and her adherents in the matters aforesaid, to have incurred the sentence of excommunication, and to be cut off from the unity of the Body of Christ. And moreover We do declare her to be deprived of her pretended title to the kingdom aforesaid, and of all dominion, dignity, and

privilege whatsoever; and also the nobility, subjects, and people of the said kingdom, and all others who have in any sort sworn unto her, to be for ever absolved from any such oath, and all manner of duty of dominion, allegiance, and obedience: and We also do by authority of these presents absolve them, and do deprive the said Elizabeth of her pretended title to the kingdom, and all other things before named. And We do command and charge all and every noblemen, subjects, people and others aforesaid that they presume not to obey her or her orders, mandates, and laws; and those which shall do the contrary We do include them in the like sentence of anathema ...

When the Queen looked up, her face was composed but her eyes flickered wildly. She stared penetratingly at her Secretary and let the paper fall in her lap. Her breathing was shallow and fast.

'I am, by this Bull, *excommunicated*. All my Catholic subjects are made either traitors, or damned to Hell with me.'

'Majesty ...'

Cecil could say nothing more. Hell of hells, he thought, the Catholics of England are made, every one, a small hatch of treason! The menace of Mary is today raised to a new and insistent pitch. Now will the Queen sign to condemn her? Will she? She must!

'Hold me.' Her cold hand sought to squeeze his fingers. 'Hold me until I may conquer the cramp that has come upon my heart.'

She trembled, quaked, like a woman in labour. Sweat spangled her high forehead.

'Will Christ desert me? Will He, my Spirit? Tell me!'

'The love of your Saviour is a firm rock, Majesty.'

'And my people? Will they rise up against me?'

'Your subjects love you dearly, Majesty.'

She snapped to her feet and began pacing. All around her black-and-red clad élite guards stood waxen, immobile in their niches, not daring to flinch. Cecil watched her, terrified, knowing that the massive tension that pressured the Queen's breast could kill the heart of a bull.

Her voice cut into him. 'Is there not a toweringly more formidable and immediate threat to consider? From this day, the price of paradise is put upon my head. There will now be assassins by the gross yearning to buy eternal life for themselves in exchange for the life of this heretic Queen. Not least, perhaps, the arch-Pape himself, the self-appointed commander of God's own iron legions, Philip the King!'

'Majesty, please!' Cecil pleaded. She whirled and clapped her hands and like a discharge of lightning it poleaxed him. He took a step back from her then saw her face split and her teeth, yellow against the bone white of her face. She was laughing.

It was two days later, just after sundown, when Cecil received another urgent visit from Slade.

'You have been successful in your errand?'

'Sir William. John Felton, a merchant of Southwark, has admitted his part.'

'It was he who posted the Bull?'

'That is his confession. Master Felton is lodged in the flint bosom of the Tower.'

'You have racked him?'

'So I guessed you would have ordered me, sir.'

'Yes. Well . . . give him a restful night to think on it, but sing him this lullaby: if he does not speak of his accomplices in the matter of the Bull, then he will face the rack again tomorrow. I must have the name of the man who brought it into England.'

Slade's eyes glittered in the candlelight. 'I have already so persuaded him, sir.'

'Then who?'

'One Robert of Ridolfi. An Italian. A mock financier and agent of the Pope. He brought the papers in from a Continental port.'

Cecil's hand gripped Slade's sleeve. 'What port? How came he into England?'

'That we have yet to learn, sir.'

Cecil watched Slade gather up his satchel and prepare to go. Though the man was his most stalwart lieutenant, Slade had been born and raised a Catholic. Fleetingly, he wondered if the man could be still be trusted, then dismissed the thought as a loose-headed fear. There is none more fanatic than the convert. But only the future could reveal the power Pope Pius's venomous order had to poison men against their Sovereign, and by that time, it might be too late.

Who? he asked the empty room. I must know who is behind this. Who? Walsingham? No. He is a Puritan. Then who? Leicester? Yes! Oh, cowardly, ambitious Earl. Bottle-fly about the Queen. Obstacle. Hated enemy. I'll bring you down. I'll show the Queen that ploy which you hatched with Norfolk – aye, and have Norfolk come before you in the flesh to confirm every line of it to your face. Escape from that, perjurer. Shrug that away, liar.

What if I've misjudged, he thought, suddenly doubting his own cleverness. For the sake of my England, Mary must die and Norfolk live. But what if Mary lives and Norfolk dies? Too bad. Too bad! For England, and for me. I cannot impeach Leicester without I first impeach Norfolk. Then I must wait again. Norfolk must be released. That promise I made to young Oxford, and without his cousin's release there will be no marriage to my Anne.

He looked at the vase of withered daffodils that stood on his window sill. Beyond the open panes, the courtyard was in balmy dusk, and above, the sky was cut out by many twisted chimneys and stone creatures of fancy that ornamented the roof. The sky was a rich velvet blue, raked by streamers of high cloud, waves of salmon pink and molten gold, and below there were smaller, dimmer lights in the windows of the royal apartments.

Elizabeth stood silently at her balcony, alone, choosing to take the calm warmth of the night as an omen. She had been thinking of the bindweed arrangements being made around her to marry her off to the nineteen-year-old Frenchman, and regretting that she could not dash the idea immediately. The thought had led her to consider her brother-in-law's latest dynastic move: Anne of Austria, the new bride of King Philip. This fourth wife was the daughter of the Emperor Maximilian. She was in Flanders and would embark soon at Antwerp for the long sea voyage to Spain. The vast escort that would be required, for purposes of protocol as well as necessary discouragement to Channel pirates, was already beginning to assemble there. How simple it would be for Philip to interpret the Pope's Bull as an excuse to mount his longed-for invasion.

According to Walsingham's spies, Westmorland had found a home in Spain among a pack of exiles that daily petitioned Philip with requests for war. An example made of his fellow conspirator, Northumberland, might douse passions in Spain, but it could equally inflame them.

She had received Cecil's report on Northumberland and had signed the document of execution which even now lay drying on her writing desk. Why was it never easy to snuff out a man's life? she asked herself. Why does there seem to be less steel in my veins than in my father's? If he suffered an unquiet conscience he never showed it. Perhaps that was his secret. But, then, he was a man.

She examined her feelings closely. It was never easy to order the death of subjects who held immovable convictions for that reason alone, and it was invariably unwise to try – eventually. Even so, it was not the suffering but the cause that made martyrs.

For her comfort she decided to give Felton's widow a dispensation to hear Mass secretly in her house for life.

Cecil would have me judiciously murder a sovereign Queen, and for what advantage? A dangerous precedent is the murder of a Queen, and one only contemplated by such men as Popes be. Mary plotted against me. Truly! She is my captive and can do no other. She did as I would have done in her place. I have taken her freedom, but I will not take her life.

And Norfolk, sweet, arrogant, foolish Norfolk! The coward's fool, ever the foil to another's wickedness. But he did confess. He repented unto me as I will, come Domesday, of mine own sins. And before Saint Peter's gate I shall not want for a reason to claim God's clemency!

My realm shall endure, and I shall remain its Queen. But what if the maintenance of that princely power alters the realm, debases it, sinks it in misery? What Prince may enjoy a land so cankered by tyranny? I am surrounded by fools and weaklings who barely know right from wrong.

She thought fondly of the darkest of her days. The sallow morning, sixteen years ago in the reign of Mary, when her half-sister had ordered her brought from Hatfield to London. Twenty-one she had been then. And it had taken all the steel in her to hold her head erect as she passed under the fanged portcullis of Traitor's Gate. Accused of treason, of plotting with Thomas Wyatt against the throne, against the Catholic Church and against the marriage of Mary to Philip, she had been put on trial for her life. And for a year inside the Tower, and the following four years of terror spent at Woodstock and Hatfield, she had been held close captive, the shadow of the awesome blade – the same that had severed her mother's head – maintained ever above her.

But Mary Tudor, repeatedly advised and often tempted to move, had always stayed her hand, Elizabeth remembered. Though daughter of Henry, she had never ordered the fatal stroke against another of her father's offspring. And so, on that fateful November day in 1558, when Mary sank into lasting sleep, it was I who rode finally into London to be proclaimed Queen in her stead, the adoring people welcoming me with strewn flowers as saviour and protector and in the same gasp damning my sister's soul to Hell with their joyful cries.

I have known the terror of the block, Elizabeth told herself, seeing the sunset shadows lengthen across her domain now. I have known it too intimately to welcome it back, or to lay it upon another easily. As Mary Tudor did with me, so shall I do with Scots Mary. Neither she nor foolish Thomas Howard deserves the summary sentence; neither shall have it. No matter what the threat to my life, Cecil or no.

She straightened, sighed, eased fingers over the bridge of her nose. From below she became aware of the sound of a lute plucked by a youth of seventeen, Hugh Travers, one of Sussex's nephews. He was apparently unaware of his royal eavesdropper, but she knew him to be a hopeful petitioner for a place at Court, and thus doubted his innocence.

> I am thy lover fair,
> Hath chosen thee to my heir,
> And my name is Merrie England.
> Therefore come away,
> And make no more delay,
> Sweet Bessie give me thy hand!

Elizabeth stepped back inside, smiling at the youth's charming presumption and the way he had eluded the guard. As she reached her writing desk, she felt a sudden giddiness and grasped the arm of her chair, willing the feeling to pass, but it would not and she sat down, the weight of the world on her back. As she breathed deeply the pain left her, and in that moment she saw the world and her place in it with lucid clarity. Her lips broadened in a smile and she whispered to the night:

Here is my hand,
My dear lover England,
I am thine with both mind and heart.
For ever to endure,
Thou mayest be sure,
Until death we two do part.

Ah, foolish Thomas. Dupe and clown and meddler. How swift would my Robert and my dear Spirit Cecil have you in your grave. But you did confess, and even God asks no more than that. She picked up her pen and wrote ordering Thomas Howard, Duke of Norfolk, to be released from the Tower.

'Halt!'

Whoever they were, the looming man in black and the man with the nose of tarnished silver had no business here, the young captain of the guard was certain.

At least the foul, lion-faced Roger Groton was known to him. He was often to be seen in the company of Francis Walsingham, and throughout the long troubles had appeared wherever Her Majesty's Court made stay. He was a mathematician and conjuror, but even so he would gain no admission to the royal apartments without warrant. Not when Hugh Travers stood captain of the guard.

His uncle's orders were definite. Since the scandal of the Popish document, the royal bodyguard had been doubled, then trebled. The Secretary's fears had bred drill after drill in the guardhouses, until every man was alert to the manifold dangers of the assassin.

All gifts, perfumes, powders, medicaments, sweetmeats, jewellery, handkerchiefs, books, blossoms, anything that might touch Elizabeth's person, was to be denied. The kitchens were to be inspected continuously. All waters, spirits, wines, and ales to be supped by their bringer. All prepared foods tasted severally by cook, table servant and guardsman. Be he maniac Papist with a butcher's knife or French antimony poisoner or murderer posing as royal admirer, the Queen was safe from him.

'Admit me!'

Travers's subordinates ranked behind him, barring entry. Their eyes were upon the figure in black, hooded and wearing a long grey beard, forked like two huge tusks, who dominated the space behind Groton. He seemed to swell with sinister power as he stepped forward.

The loathsome Groton shuffled closer, the scrolled order bunched in his ruined hand. 'See! The Secretary's seal!'

The guard examined the proffered document reluctantly until it was snatched back.

'Well?'

'It *looks* like the seal of Sir William Cecil,' he said grudgingly.

'Then let us pass!'

'My orders are that no one shall pass herein this day, or any, without specific –'

Groton drew himself up so that the morning sun caught in his spectacle panes, blotting out his eyes. 'What is your name, puppy?'

The young guard stood perplexed. Taken aback. He seemed to Groton no more than a beardless boy, appointed no doubt through a family connection to his position of minor significance. Such as he were frequently troublesome, boldly looking out for a means to distinguish themselves. But this one seemed gutless. In front of his men he wavered, unsure whether to bluster or order the insult righted. Lamely the youth said, 'Her Majesty is not here.'

'I know that. D'you think she'd have a young lad with half a mind and no ballocks at all to guard anything but an empty room? Let us pass, I say.'

The youth screwed up his courage. 'And I say: get you gone, Cobweb!'

'Give me your name!'

'I will not!'

'You will do as my associate says, boy!' The new voice was deep and resonant and commanding. The rest of the guards shrank back.

'What is my name to you, Welshman?'

Groton's nasal shout made the young man jump. 'I shall lay your name before Sir William Cecil since you dare interfere with the Queen's business. Did you not see the seal? Or are you fishing for bribes?'

Despite his fearful confusion, the captain's chin jutted. 'I cannot be bribed. The Lord Chamberlain must –'

Groton's words cut him off. 'Do you not recognise this venerable Cambrian?'

'I know that he is not the Lord Chamberlain.'

Suddenly the hood was flung back. The grey face that was revealed was that of the notorious Doctor Dee.

It was said that he drew his power from the great stone of Merlin, and could transmute a man's soul into that of a braying ass merely by sending him to sleep. He asked the guards sombrely, 'You would deny me entry on this most significant of days?'

'Why significant? What is your business here?' the boy replied shakily.

Groton's grin glittered. 'Know you not that the Sun is at perihelion and the Moon at apogee? We have come to undo spells laid on the Queen's privy apartments by her enemies. Devils are sent here daily from King Philip's black tower. Doctor Dee is Her Majesty's only protection. He can look inside men's hearts and know all their secrets.'

Dee's voice boomed, 'He speaks the truth, Hugh Travers!'

The guard captain paled. 'You know me?'

'That is his name!' the soldier behind whispered.

'Then let me pass and he shall keep it.'

'I cannot!'

'You cannot do other. For I see you are an honest man who loves his Queen.'

The captain stepped aside involuntarily and the rest of the guard dissolved away as Dee strode down the long oaken corridor, Groton hobbling after him.

'A pretty trick, Doctor.'

Dee snorted scornfully. 'Soldiers are all simpletons. Young ones the more so. And Sussex's nephew is renowned for it.'

They came to the royal bedchamber, and to the great canopied bed from which Elizabeth had risen half an hour before. Its many mattresses were piled deep under a gorgeous brocade cover embroidered with the splendid motif of state. All was still mussed and bore the imprint of the Queen's body.

Groton watched the door anxiously as Dee flung the sheets back and drew from his robe a glass phial, stoppered with a tiny cork. Inside was a dark vermilion liquid. He poured a little into the palm of his hand and smeared it round, murmuring a silent invocation.

They had come this same errand, always on the morning that followed the full moon, always with the same bottle, for seven consecutive months. Sometimes here to Richmond, sometimes to the Palace of Nonsuch, once to Greenwich, where Elizabeth had been born, and at the stopping places of her summer progress.

Groton hung back, aware that his leprosy tainted the air. He opened the window, laying down the forged paper he had used to gain entry.

Delicately, Dee leaned over to the centre of the bed and dabbed his hand on the linen. Then he pressed down until the red stain began to soak in.

'It is done.'

'Ox blood? With the sun out of Taurus?' Groton asked.

'Ox blood is too dark. Better blood of a hog's pudding, but lamb's blood is meetest for this. Where the sun be, in Taurus, in Aries or, as now, in our Queen's own Virgo, matters not a whit! It is the moon's phase that governs and prevails in these cycles.'

Groton snickered and looked about. 'Virgo, virago! Ah! The pleasures of the flesh! Such a monarch to conquer herself for reasons of state. God knows, I could not!'

'Blasphemer!'

'Your pardon, Doctor.' Groton bowed low, grinning. 'I forget me. For you are Doctor John Dee of Mortlake, a man of much reputation: archconjuror of the kingdom, confidant of royalty, adviser of mariners, friend of the great Gerard Mercator, defender of Copernicus, translator of Euclid ...'

Dee raised a finger. 'Psssht!'

In the listening silence, Groton strained his ears. A creaking board, scuffling – rats in the ceiling.

'We must be gone.'

As they left, Groton accosted the young guard captain, shoving him, for all his size, up against the wall. 'You may let in the ladies of the bed chamber now to make the royal bed, Hugh Travers.'

'Aye, sir. Did you find anything amiss?'

'A minor plot by Spanish devils — nothing for your ears — it is vanquished. And you have rats in the roof space. Doctor Dee perceived them through the plaster. He hath an infernal machine that spies where it will.'

'Verily?' The captain and his men were astonished.

'Verily! I have a mind to forget your name,' Dee told him sternly. 'But mark me well. Whosoever asks, we have not been here. Whosoever learns, your cods are cast in wax for it.'

The captain's face was pained as an effigy.

Groton's voice pierced him. 'And I'll hang on thy captain's cremaster until thy ballocks turn black. Count on it, young masturbator!'

As they passed from the palace courtyard, Dee threw up his hood and led Groton to Richmond pier where a waterman's boat awaited them.

The shallow punt which carried the sea captain and the spymaster negotiated the northward bend in the river, past weeping willows and a patchwork of harvest fields the few miles upstream towards Dee's monstrous home. Walsingham pointed out to Tavistock the meadows of Barn Elms and the manor there which he coveted to reflect the increase in his fortunes.

'Foot's Cray is too distant. This is where I shall live.'

'It's a fine place.'

'And close enough to Richmond and Hampton, as well as the City.'

'As the celebrated Doctor Dee has found.'

Walsingham nodded appreciatively. 'You will find our wizard is no fool. You'll see he has wonders to aid your Indies quest.'

Tavistock watched as a flight of wild ducks took off from the waters, trusting Walsingham better than any he had met in London. When the news of Ridolfi's actual mission had been explained to him, Tavistock had wanted to cut the man's throat, but Walsingham's candid logic had stayed him.

'What does it matter that Her Majesty is excommunicated?' he had said. 'All the world knows that the Pope is her enemy. If security is tightened around the Queen's person, so much the better. That is a boon. And listen: anti-Spanish feeling is running warmer, making Sir William's position less cosy. The cursed document is too late to inflame the North, which is already defeated. Our English Catholics are caught in a bind: to suffer silence or come out and be marked. The gauntlet is cast down but they are in no position to take it up. Our foremost need is for a league with France. If arrangements for a marriage between the Queen and the King of France's brother are set in motion, the league betwixt France and Spain is thus weakened. You have done only good by bringing the Italian here and showing the risk we take with the Queen's person. And mark me: If Ridolfi continues to intrigue with Norfolk as he is now doing, to revive the idea of a marriage to Mary, it will not be long before his head is in my noose. He will go to Tower Hill, I promise you.'

Walsingham had brought Tavistock's thoughts to his Anne then. 'If Norfolk is executed, Oxford will lose all reason to marry Cecil's daughter.'

'That is some consolation for me, who may never marry her, though I love her best of all.'

'Alas, you are no lordling. Though the better man for it, I trust.'

Tavistock watched Walsingham's deep brown eyes surveying the land on the Surrey side with interest. 'So,' he said, 'you have your passport and your ship. Where now?'

'To London again to see Anne, and then to Plymouth. The rest is best kept between me and my fellow mariners.'

'Whatever you do, I shall await news of it eagerly.'

'You won't have to wait long.'

Soon they came by the Eyot, turning south from Chiswick to Mortlake, and their destination, where Walsingham bade the waterman wait. Rambling outworks had been attached to Dee's ancient house, extending it to accommodate books and charts, retorts and chemical furnaces and all the paraphernalia of its owner's practices. Outside, a copse shed leaves, its undergrowth overrun by brambles, its blackberries ungleaned by local people who thought the wasps that patrolled here and the rooks above to be Dee's familiars. On the far side a walled garden, full of the scents of decaying medicinal herbs; inside, the odour of rotting paper and the chemical stinks that wafted through a maze of cluttered rooms complemented the cabalistic diagrams and magic inscriptions that hung everywhere.

Tavistock ventured inside uneasily, but his interest was soon absorbed by what he found. The dusty room was split by beams of intense sunlight that pierced the heavy curtains. The glare fell upon a vast yellowed map. Dee was a scholar of exploration, enough to have suggested means by which to encourage seagoing folk and the building of ships. Like Dee's better ideas, it was simple and strange and magnificent: Catholics eat fish on Fridays, Englishmen must therefore have two fish days per week. More fish meant more fishermen, and an increase in the numbers of those acquainted with the sea.

An Irishman, Dee's medium, a sly man of solemn expression and few words, regarded Tavistock and Walsingham suspiciously from a corner thick with books, candle stubs and medallions. He leapt up to admit Groton and his master at the massively barred door.

'We must be careful here,' he explained. 'Puritans do not understand our ways. There are those who would murder the Doctor.'

Tavistock saw the Magus rise then, a bone-faced, saturnine man swaddled in grey, his beard forked and his eyes as riveting as a falcon's. Though he seemed harmless enough, he unsettled Tavistock and made him crawl with nameless fears.

'Have you succeeded?' Walsingham asked Dee impatiently.

'Yes.'

'And you got in without difficulty?'

'I, my good Puritan, could get past the three-headed dog who guards Hades' gate.'

'They are taking bets in London,' Groton said gleefully. 'Royal marriage bets.'

'I would advise against it,' Dee told him solemnly.

Walsingham had considered the situation more fully. Even when he had first travelled in France, the Valois Court had been ruled by Catherine de' Medici, the scheming daughter of a family of Florentine bankers. When eight years old, she had been caught in a revolution and narrowly escaped being chained naked to the walls of that city to be raped by republican soldiers; when fourteen, she had been married off to Henry, Duke of Orleans. By this means the Pope had sought to bring Milan, Parma and Urbino into French hands, but Henry had married ignoble blood for nothing: the territorial dowry had turned out to be mere promises. So Catherine had suffered a marriage of ignominies. Insults were heaped upon her by a husband whose love-bed was filled instead by the voluptuous Diane of Poitiers.

Walsingham recalled the Catherine he had seen. A narrow-shouldered, broad-buttocked woman with bulging eyes, shrew nose and thick lips. Even so, Catherine had brought forth seven children, five of them male.

For ten years, France had been the anvil of Europe surrounded by hammers that beat upon it. For as long there had been talk of marriage between Elizabeth and one of Catherine's sons. The suit of the Archduke Charles had foundered on Elizabeth's fears. She had told Cecil that, since he was a Catholic, the marriage would bring religious turmoil to England once more, and after the example of the disastrous marriages of Mary Queen of Scots, the project had been dismantled. But now, with Spain and France and the Pope poised to form an unholy alliance, marriage was a weapon that could not be ignored. Four weeks ago at St Germain a peace had been declared that had made it imperative that negotiations were reopened.

The Archduke's patience was exhausted and there could be no revival, but his brother, the Duke of Anjou, was next in line.

Walsingham watched Dee, nauseated by his false spookery but unnerved by the man's eccentric brilliance. Catherine de' Medici might have the weird, Nostradamus, to advise her, he thought with satisfaction, but John Dee's suggestions have a core of hard practicality. So much hinges on our assurances that Elizabeth is fertile! So much rests on the possibility of an heir!

When Groton had told Dee of a French spy in the royal laundry, his strange genius had supplied the perfect solution. If the French wanted proof, proof they would have! The Queen's sheets would be tainted monthly.

Dee's copious concoctions of menstrual blood had been fecund indeed. Already they had spawned fifty reports to the French ambassador. All doubts regarding the thirty-eight-year-old Queen's capacity were eradicated.

'Advise against it?' Walsingham echoed.

Dee shook his head sadly. 'The future is not as we would have it.'

Tavistock got up and walked across the room to where a parchment had been varnished upon a board. He inspected it balefully. The map was of the Atlantic Ocean.

Walsingham spoke. 'Well, now, Doctor Subtle. You have had sundry thoughts about Atlantis. What think you of the future in that regard? Doctor Groton tells me of your imaginings. That you see an English Empire?'

Dee stirred. 'By that I mean to foster interest in explorations. There are many in the land that are eager to get at the riches of Cathay, and you cannot deny the country's need of it. We shall find the Strait of Anian whereby those riches may quickly be transported here to our Sovereign's glory.'

Tavistock turned, heady thoughts consuming him. 'Good Roger spoke of scrolls of evidence? I would have you show them to me. I want to see English ships push out beyond the domains of Spain and Portugal to discover our own routes to the Orient. There's no trade the Spanish make that we cannot do twice as well and at half the cost. Don't you see that our nation is brimming with confidence? We're ready to take our true place in the world. I say send out our mariners to give Spain and whomsoever says he owns the world our defiance – then we'll see what can be achieved.'

Dee's falcon eyes blazed with a strange light. 'Elizabeth's descent from King Arthur and her claim to an empire in Atlantis – which land you call North America, and which was found by the Welshman, Owen Madoc, in the twelfth century *anno domini*. I have petitioned Her Majesty for a patent letter to search, find out and view such remote, heathen and barbarous lands, countries and territories not actually possessed by any Christian prince or people, and there to settle colonists under laws agreeable to the form of the laws and policies of England.'

Walsingham grunted, disappointed that Dee's thoughts were as yet hypothetical. He got down to the nub of the matter. 'It is my policy to move against the Spanish. It may be done in three ways. First, we must destroy their capacity to invade us. Second, we must lever them out of the Low Lands. And third, we must carry the fight into the very heart of their overseas empire. All those ambitions call for ships. Better ships than we now possess, better than the Spanish also. And we need men of similar worth, men like my friend, Captain Tavistock, who is now preparing to sail. Bend your thoughts to all of that, Doctor, and you will do us great service.'

'What do you want, Captain?'

'Give me rutters and charts that will help me. In return I will bring you what I can from the New World.'

'Done!' Rare pleasure showed on Dee's face.

Walsingham said, 'And the other, Doctor?'

'I have it here. Edward! Bring me the very article.'

The Irishman brought out a wooden box, four inches square on a side and a yard long, and laid it portentously on the table.

Tavistock eyed it with caution. 'A chartbox?'

'No chartbox, but something more valuable still. A wondrous thing!'

'Mayhap a new magnetic instrument?'

'Chah! It was brought forth by a Venetian glass blower which Sir William Cecil had imported. His work on the oriels of Cecil House brought him to know Hans van Hoorbecke, a Fleming known to Doctor Groton, through his failing eyes, as a maker of spectacles.'

Groton tapped the panes either side of his silver bridge excitedly. 'See!'

Tavistock examined the long box carefully and saw that there was a hinged gate at each end, secured by a hook and eye. He opened the first and saw inside a silver ring with a smooth glassy pebble mounted in it. The other contained a much larger ring, three inches across, and mounted in that was a bulb of glass. Instinctively, Tavistock looked through it, seeing nothing but a hazy patch of light.

As he did so, Dee swept aside the curtains and flung open the window. He held the box up, carefully easing the smaller silver ring out so that it extended, and clamped it to Tavistock's eye.

'The trees yonder. The throstle who sings there. Look *through* it, not *at* it, man! And shut your other eye, as if in a wink.'

Tavistock's eye blurred and adjusted as he did as he was instructed. He saw the halo of the tree, branches moving swiftly and shaking. All seemed strangely darkened and set about with fringes of red and blue – and then he saw the bird. It was huge!

'Aghh!'

He let out a gasp and dropped the box as if it was on fire, dancing back from it. Then he stared out of the window again, his mouth agape. 'Devil take me! It's bewitched!'

'Have a care!' Dee picked up the box and examined it testily.

'Where is it?' Tavistock demanded, peering across the back lawn in agitation.

'Where's what?'

'The giant bird! I saw it clearly!'

Dee pointed. 'There she is still.'

Tavistock looked again and saw the thrush in the swaying branch, as it had been. 'It's not possible,' he said, turning to Walsingham who watched him eagerly.

'Try again.'

He took the instrument once more, but with great reverence this time. He looked through it, astonished, hardly hearing Dee's explanation.

'It is an *optikon*. It fetches things closer.'

Tavistock felt the hairs rise on the back of his neck. He panned the box speechlessly to left and right, seeing foxgloves and the bricks of a wall and even the church steeple, closer, huger, incredibly so! He looked through and then suddenly past the box, hoping with speed to catch the steeple before it retreated once more. '*How can it be?* A solid church that comes forth and departs in an instant, and yet I've seen it.'

A sudden hammering assaulted the door of the house. Instantly Dee snatched the optikon from Tavistock's hands and spirited it away. The Irishman took up a poker and went to the door, shouting out for identification.

'Open up! In the name of the Council!'

'What do you want?' Dee bawled.

The hammering started again. Sword pommels. 'Open! Or we break down the door. Seek not to fly, wizard. I have fifty men surrounding the house.'

Dee slid back the heavy iron bolts and the door was slammed back, flooding the entrance with sunlight. An army of men were outside. A great boar-faced soldier, helmeted and clad in studded red-and-black leather, strode in, his steel war gear glinting. He was one of Elizabeth's élite corps, granite-faced, unyielding. He held up a scrolled document. 'I hold a warrant of arrest.'

Walsingham demanded of the man, 'In whose name?'

'In the name of the Secretary of State.'

'For whom? And on what grounds?'

'For Captain Richard Tavistock. It is alleged that he brought one Robert of Ridolfi into England with a Papal letter written against the Queen.'

Tavistock surged forward. 'I'm Tavistock. You can't arrest me. I have a passport to sail!'

'It is revoked,' the soldier replied, motioning his men to seize Tavistock's arms. 'You are condemned to the Tower until trial can be made.'

Chapter 12

The toothless smile of Pedro Gomara greeted him broadly.

'Hey, Juan! You son of Satan!'

'Pedro, my friend!'

They embraced, slapping backs, and the old man held him off, looking at him with faded eyes. 'You're looking so good! Like a rich man.'

John Tavistock's clothes were simple but of good quality, baize breeches and a white linen shirt that had once belonged to Gonzalo.

'Where are you going?'

'To Vera Cruz – where else? The *flota* is due soon and I must be there. I have some little bits of the white metal for Admiral Luzon.'

Pedro Gomara had passed through Chalco three times, each time arriving with his *burros* and an armed guard of the Viceroy's men. Each time he had sought out Tavistock, sure of a welcome. The first time he had seen the hospitality of the bare little room at the back of the forge. Later, he had visited a back room of the main house itself. Then, he had slept on a mattress outside, on the flat roof. After many years of itinerant living, he had told his host, it was difficult to sleep under a roof. If a man woke up in the middle of the night it was a comfort to see how far the stars of Orion's Belt or the Square of Pegasus had moved and to know how late or how long before the dawn.

'I have travelled many years, Juan Tabisto,' he would say, unwilling still with Tavistock's unpronounceable name, fingering the *chalchihuitl* jade pendant he wore on a leather thong round his neck. The figure was of a sacrificial victim of the stepped pyramids, spreadeagled, of gold and a queer turquoise that was the colour of a blindman's eye. 'You know this was once Montezuma's? You want to swap it for your ring?'

'For a worthless trinket made by Indian children yesterday?'

'You see, *amigo*, old habits die hard!'

'Tell me. I want to know all about this land.'

'Everything? There would not be enough time if we sat here until the Judgement.'

'I envy you, Pedro. You're free to range across it all while I'm trapped here.'

'But, look! You have a place of your own.' He had banged the timber roof support of the forge. 'A place you've built yourself. There's satisfaction in that. It's almost finished, yes?'

'Yes.'

'And soon you will need brass?' Gomara had said, looking out from under his eyebrows shrewdly. 'And sulphur for making powder? I know a mountain that is built entirely of yellow sulphur – the purest in the world!'

'Which you, doubtless, can bring here.'

'Not I! For there is a curse on it. But bell shards, maybe some old condemned bronze cannon. I can bring you these things. I've seen how they're packed with powder and plugged so that the firing tears them to pieces.'

'Better to have pure copper,' he had said. 'So I can make up my own proportions accurately. You see, the secret of strength in a gun barrel is part design, part purity of casting and part the mix of the alloy that –'

He had stopped himself, then. How easy it was to forget. How easy to slip into old enthusiasms. He had thrust the wineskin at Gomara, saying, 'Here, you drink it. Then tell me about some other wonder of the world that I will never see.'

At first during the building of the forge he had assumed a detached and remote attitude, cynically allowing the load-bearing structures to be erected inadequately, and letting the brick makers produce bricks that would crumble at high temperatures. But as the building took shape he had remembered his long apprenticeship at Samuel Stanton's forge and recalled the envious feeling that had flushed through him as a youngster. It was a dream of those days to have a forge of his own. A dream that one day he could experiment with all the small ideas that had come to him. All the tiny improvements, the suggestions he had wanted the foundrymen to listen to, and which they had never once listened to. They had scorned him in the haughty way of guildsmen, cleaving to tradition and form and their own status. And he had grown up and learned to be the same, knowing that he would never have his own forge or foundry, never have total control, or satisfaction from those unanswered questions: what would be the effect of increasing the proportion of zinc at the expense of tin? And could a barrel be more accurately bored vertically? And what was the white waxy substance that accumulated in the piss-boiling vats *and that glowed in the dark*?

And now he had been given it all! Freely! His own foundry!

He had started to find pride in what was his own personal project. Don Bernal had marked the change in him and given him encouragement. Eventually, he had ordered the mistakes torn down and shown them how to really make a foundry, and at nights he told himself that none of it mattered because he would never, never, never give away the most important secrets.

Later, he'd moved into the Escovedo house. 'I envy you the new family you have, Juan,' Pedro had once said. Tavistock thought of the latest time the old man had come by way of Chalco. 'What a shame you're not a Catholic, Juan. I do believe you would make a Spanish girl a fine husband. Of course, you'd have to take a proper Spanish family name first. You can't give her Tabisto. I think I'll christen you Juan de Tordesillas. You remember the treaty line of Tordesillas? You sailed across it to get here! So now you are Juan de Tordesillas to me! How do you like that?'

'I could never countenance such a thing. Anyway, what Spanish mother would want a heretic for a son-in-law? It's an impossible thought.'

'Then why don't you come with me to see the fathers in Chalco mission? They're good men. If they teach you the Creed in Latin you'll feel more at home here. And if they ask you if you believe of the sacrament and whether there remains any bread or wine after the consecration, answer them yea.' He had winked. 'We're both men of the world, Juan. Neither of us would deny there're more important things in life than how many angels may dance on the head of a pin. You and I both know that a smile here and a nod there can bring a man much comfort.'

Tavistock had neither nodded nor smiled, but feeling something stifling closing in around him had pressed the old man to speak instead about his wanderings.

With dreaming eyes, curving his hands in a lewd way, Gomara had spoken. 'This New World is shaped like a woman, Juan, with a narrow waist but spreading to the south and the north into wide continents. And it has a woman's temper! I have been south into the mountain lands of Peru and the jungles of the Great River of Orellana. But I have journeyed north also. Beyond the Tropic of Cancer. I know it is a worthless country, more inhospitable than Extremadura, a land of desert scrub and lizards that can never amount to anything.' He had spat. 'I lost a good friend there, *Inglés*. In Cibola, while fighting in the army of Francisco de Coronado against the feathered wild men. It is rumoured that there is another kingdom to the west of that place – the fabled Californias – which are full of gold, but I do not know.'

Now, they went into the foundry together and he showed Gomara the machinery he had constructed over the casting pit. The furnace was almost fully lined and there was a tall timber frame rigged with blocks of tackle and equipped with great wooden-toothed wheels.

'Where's this sulphur mountain of yours, Pedro?'

'That's easy! You've been looking at it every day. There!'

'Popocatépetl?'

'The "smoking mountain" the Azteca peoples called it. Its crater is a boiling mass of sulphur, a thousand *varas* across. It stinks like the Devil's armpit! And a mile away there are places in the ground that are so hot that you can bury a chicken's egg, come back in five minutes and it is hardboiled!'

'Nay! With snow capping the volcano?'

'I swear it! But that's nothing. There was a great eruption twenty-one years ago. I saw that. A great power. A great power in the earth.' He grew suddenly weary. 'It makes an old man think of life, Juan, and of death and how foolish we are to worry over small things.'

After sundown, they ate a meal of avocados, maize, runner beans, sweet potatoes and tomatoes, all spiced with a mouth-burning red powder, and after, a pipe of the dried weed that Indians always smoked. It had a pleasant aroma and soothed the old man, making him mellow for storytelling. He brought a paper out from his satchel and passed it to Tavistock, whose interest surged. It was from Robert Barrett in Tezcuco.

As Gomara relaxed into his chair, Tavistock read it. It was in English, each letter painstakingly made.

> Johnn, How is it with Youe? I am Well. The goodly Hous-holde I surve is kinde to my Wants. Richrd Williams has founde a Ritch Widoe of Biscaiy with above Four Thousand Pesoes to her naime and a Faire Hous. David Alexsander and Robt Cooke are marryed to Negroe Women in Tezcoco and Paul Horsewell to a *mestiza* of Spanish Father and Indien Mother from Tolocan. Chamberain had leeve and Lysense to go into Spaine. As for the Others I canne not saye. As for Myselfe I cannot settle though many Faire Offers have been made unto me. I workt at the Mynes and did prosper and Gain Greatly being paide threescore Pounds Sterling per Yeare as well as Monies for the Negroes that wrought extra on Sundaye under my Charge which is worth £4 10shilling of our Monie in a Weeke. Do youe Remember Younge Francis Drake who knowes youre Brother? He is presently Lodged in the Villa MARGARITA, marreied to a Negro named Boaz and with sundry others to attend him. He has a jolly idea to make of Himself a Ritch Man from sacking. If Youe canne wryte to me Do. Pedro Gomara is a Frend when he commes here though a Lier an Idolator and a Cheete at Cardes also. Next Yeere I may be gonne from here, Youre Servant, Robt Barrett.

Tavistock guarded his feelings as he laid the paper down, but inside he was turbulent. He had already had to rearrange his thoughts to take account of new circumstances. Can I change again, he asked himself despairingly, on the slim strength of a carefully coded letter?

A year ago, the question of escape had never been far beneath the surface of his thoughts. Hopes of somehow leading his men down to the waterfront at Vera Cruz and stealing a ship home. The vision had always been piecemeal, lacking in details, and with no plan at all, but there was always the glorious vision of the thirty of them pulling away from Vera Cruz in a captured pinnace. Always it was a moonlit night, always Don Luis Zegri was in the boat, shaking with fear and sweating, and the impotent Don Emilio in a rage on the quayside. And then there had been another detail: Maria, sitting in the prow of the boat, wrapped up in a wine-dark cloak.

But the dream had slowly faded like signal flag silk hoisted in the Mexican sun. How stupid it was to think of escape when those same shipmates were scattered all over the valley and making money hand over fist and enjoying life – some even married! And if there was to be no escape what was he doing cleaving to defiance and resistance? Everything had had time to mellow into something deeply personal on the *estancia*. The worst of it was they liked him: the servants, his labouring men, Esteban, Don Bernal, everyone. He had been here so long now, and he knew the people here so well, that defiance would just be bad manners and resistance would seem like nothing more than a lack of gratitude. He couldn't even remember what Don Emilio looked like.

Perhaps it was as Pedro said. Bend like an ear of corn in the wind. Accept the strange destiny God gave you. You were born in England, you have to die somewhere – you may as well live in Mexico.

And now Drake was in the Indies again, God damn him! Perhaps I should write to Barrett, he thought guiltily. Suddenly everything had been raked up and was laid open.

As Pedro took himself away to sleep, Tavistock walked out to find Maria under a sky bright with stars. His head was throbbing with memories and the chirrups of cicadas.

'There was a place we used to trade,' he told her in a lost voice. 'An island called Margarita.'

'Like my mother's name?'

He raised an eyebrow. 'Yes.'

'In Spanish, it means –'

'Yes, I know. Pearl.'

As she sat down on the swing seat that had been hung from a bough of the shade tree, the chirruping stopped. 'Was Margarita a pretty place?'

'It was a very poor island, and the *Gobernador* was very crooked. There was but one business in it: pearl fishing. They would buy all the slaves we could bring. And we sold them, even though our General knew what was happening.'

Maria held the ropes of the swing lightly. 'What was happening?'

'The *Gobernador* had a system. He worked the slaves until they died, sending them deeper and deeper after oysters until they drowned or until their lungs burst.'

He plucked at the swing rope absently. She broke the silence softly. 'Margarita is also our word for a little white flower with many narrow petals and a yellow heart. They are my favourite. Do they grow in England?'

'You mean daisies.' He looked in her eyes. 'Yes, we used to have them in summer.'

She kicked up her feet, letting the swing move. 'Do you miss your old country?'

'Sometimes.' He said it wistfully. 'When the sun is at its highest and the earth is parched, I think of cool, gentle rain falling on green meadows. I'm sure there's no green like it anywhere else on earth, a patchwork of fields that have been the same for at least five hundred years, probably a thousand, tilled, seeded, manured, harvested and fallowed for twenty or thirty generations. And great forests of oak and elm reaching up like the buttresses of a cathedral, full of peace and cool darkness and carpeted with delicate wild flowers.'

'Do you yearn for that?'

He looked away from her suddenly and put his face in his hands. 'No.'

And she laid her hand on his shoulder then, and felt him cry silently, like the cool, gentle rain falling on green meadows.

That Friday, in the almost completed forge, he told the Spaniards precisely how he would make them a cannon.

'You have to understand what I'm going to need. First comes the model. It must be built up from clay.'

'There's a good source by the banks of the Lake of Tezcuco near Iztapalapan,' Esteban said, jutting his chin westward. He was a tall and spare man with superb moustaches and a permanent ten-day stubble except where a complicated scar meandered over his jawline. He had a bald patch on the crown of his head which he took immense pains to hide from the women of the *Encomienda de Escovedo*. From time to time as they spoke he cast a judicious eye over the men that he had appointed to aid Tavistock. They hammered and sawed and shouted at one another, absorbed in their labours.

'We'll have to test that it's not too salty. It's a pity that we're not still in Vera Cruz. A yardarm from a caravel hulk's mainmast would be admirable for a spindle – that is, a basis on which to form the model, and it must be long. Longer than the gun, to leave room for the feeding head. Like so.' He drew his charcoal across the fibrous *agave* paper, representing the spindle resting in grooves on two trestles. He added four levers, projections from the thick end of the spindle, like capstan spokes, to permit the spindle to be turned.

'The next stage is to grease it – against the day when it must be removed – and then we wind it tightly with rope to build up the basic shape. In England we used to make it from twisted straw, but any rope will suffice. It must be fed onto the slowly rotated spindle and hammered tight. A three man job.'

'The clay is applied to that surface?' Don Bernal asked, raising his voice above the din of Tavistock's men.

'Yes. Sanded for evenness, and with horse manure and animal hair mixed in to bind it. Then it's built up layer by layer, each allowed to dry before the next is applied. Meanwhile, the craftsman has been making his template – what we call the strickle board. That's a metal blade cut with the shape of the cannon's profile, so that when the barrel is rotated against it, excess clay is shaved away and a smooth shape is left.'

'But so much clay will take a very long time to dry,' Esteban objected.

'No. The model will be made over this stone bed in which a charcoal fire can be lit. But while the heat is maintained, the model must be rotated constantly to prevent it from cracking. In Samuel Stanton's factory we used a leather belt connected to a shaft driven by water power.'

'Ingenious. But here we have slaves for that,' Gonzalo said with an aloofness that irritated Tavistock. He ignored him and turned to Don Bernal instead. 'When that's done we pour liquid wax over the whole to seal it.'

'What about the trunnions and the dolphin?' Gonzalo asked.

'What are they?' Esteban's face was screwed up in concentration.

Gonzalo rocked his forearm up and down in explanation. 'Trunnions are pivots on the side of the barrel that allow the elevation to be set, and a dolphin is a loop set on top to lift the gun onto its carriage. They are often fashioned in the shape of those fishes.'

Tavistock nodded, silently deploring Gonzalo's pride in understanding a few common terms. 'All decorations and fittings are attached at this stage. In England it's usual to apply the royal arms, the lilies and lions of our Queen, and her initials. They're made of wax in wooden moulds, and fixed onto the surface with iron nails.'

'You're not in England now. Submit your designs to me,' Gonzalo said. 'I'll ask Don Emilio to be good enough to look at them.'

'Perhaps you could obtain drawings of what the Viceroy desires by way of ornament, and bring them to me. But, I suggest that the patterns are kept simple and the decorations to a minimum.'

'Your skill is wanting in this respect?'

'Don Emilio can have cherubim and seraphim and vine leaves encrusting the barrel if he so desires. But tell him that each vanity will prolong the manufacturing time greatly.'

'What do you do after that?' Don Bernal asked impatiently, staring up at the machine above his head.

'Next the mould is begun. White sand – what we call Callis-sand, the same used for blotting letters – this is made up with the clay and applied, thinly at first and with a brush, so that it adheres to the wax. These first applications must dry slowly, out in the sun. Then more and more is coated onto the model until it's of sufficient depth to allow drying over a small fire. Of course, it's essential we don't melt the wax on the model.'

'This is a far more drawn-out process than I had imagined, Juan. How thick must the mould be?' Esteban asked, rubbing his chin. Tavistock had noticed that whenever Esteban was in the presence of Gonzalo he reflected the other's concerns in his behaviour, acting like a weather vane to Gonzalo's moods.

'Two inches thickness – *dos pulgadas* – for a six pounder, up to four *pulgadas* for a twenty-four pounder.'

'How long does it all take?'

Tavistock shrugged. 'That depends on many factors, Don Bernal. But it could be a matter of weeks. Now you know why guns are made in large batches whenever possible. The method's suited to numbers better than the production of a single gun. The next step is to dress the mould in a cage of iron bands and staves.'

'What's that for?' Gonzalo asked, clearly unhappy that so much costly preparation and material must go to make each and every gun.

'Remember that the mould is very fragile and the gun metal is white hot. When the brass is poured in there are huge pressures that would crack an unprotected mould.'

'So, the next step is casting?' Don Bernal asked hopefully.

'Not yet. The model must be removed. First the tapered spindle must be hammered out from the middle. Then the straw rope that originally wound it can be uncoiled and drawn out. Finally, the clay model is cracked away from the wax and brought out piece by piece with long reaching tools.'

He put down his charcoal stick and pointed overhead at the heavy beams and windlasses that would hoist the mould into the vertical, explaining how first a fire would be lit inside the mould to bake it and to destroy all trace of the wax, how a mixture of lye and soot was then to be painted over the inside of the cleaned mould. Don Bernal nodded as he learned that the bulbous projection on the muzzle end of the cannon was the 'pouring head' – a funnel into which the molten metal would flow.

'It's essential that no bubbles are allowed to form in the brass. They would be weak points that could lead to a cannon disintegrating when fired,' he told them. 'I've seen it happen, and it's terrible. On the deck of a ship it's completely devastating.'

Gonzalo nodded knowingly. 'The power of a big culverin is not easy to appreciate until you have seen it yourself at close quarters. If the explosion cannot escape, the breech is torn apart and cuts down the gun crew and anyone standing within ten *varas*.'

Don Bernal motioned Tavistock to go on. He picked up his charcoal and sketched the hollow mould, saying, 'Gentlemen, I expect you've realised that to pour metal into this mould as we have it would be to cast a cannon of which the most important part is missing.'

'Missing?' Gonzalo's eyes studied the drawing; Esteban scratched at his bald place.

'Gentlemen – the gun would be completely solid. There is no bore.' They nodded and tutted and leaned in closer over the drawing. 'That's why we need a core: an iron bar, longer than the bore by a couple of feet, and about half the diameter, made up with clay just like the model was, and smoothed against a strickle board, then wire wound.

'It's suspended inside the mould with an iron crown ring and chaplets that must hold the core in the very centre. The positioning is critical because the trueness of the gun depends on that, and also the strength – if the core is off-centre the metal will vary in thickness, and its tendency to burst asunder is increased.'

'But when you pour the brass in, won't the core and these chaplets become embedded in the metal?' Don Bernal asked.

'The core is removed easily after the pouring – that's the reason why the iron bar's made long enough to protrude. But you're right about the chaplets. You must have seen this, Gonzalo, with your great experience of cannon – the rust spots on the brass surface around the breech?'

'Yes, of course.'

Tavistock grinned. 'You see, Don Bernal, Spanish cannon are like that. Our own are finished to a higher degree. These chaplet arms are drilled out and brass plugs are inserted and filed flat.'

Don Bernal walked a few paces away across the compacted earth floor. He folded his arms and looked around at the machinery appreciatively. 'You have done well, Juan. This is very impressive. When may I expect to see the first of your culverins functioning?'

'A matter of months.'

'Good. Good. And you guarantee that they will be as effective and as powerful as English culverins?'

Tavistock hesitated momentarily, thinking of the many factors that combined to give the Stanton culverin its phenomenal power. He knew that given time and the necessary materials he could equal the Stanton guns' performance, but should he try? His professional pride wrestled with his loyalty to England. He knew that without any objective comparison, he could claim what he liked. Finally, he said, 'Yes, Don Bernal. I can assert as much with confidence.'

Don Bernal's eyes narrowed. 'Then you'll have no objection to my arranging a test.'

Tavistock shook his head blankly. 'Test? Of course, all the guns must be fully proofed ...'

'I mean a trial. Between an English culverin and the guns of your first batch.'

'If only you could do that,' he said, with regret in his voice.

'But we can do that, *Inglés*,' Gonzalo said.

Don Bernal nodded. 'When Pedro Gomara next comes through Chalco he will bring with him an English culverin. Don Emilio has seen fit to send pearl divers onto the wreck at San Juan de Uloa. The remains of the *Jesus* are lying in shallow water, and three of her long guns have been recovered.'

Gonzalo's forehead went back and he looked down his cheeks at Tavistock. 'So, in two months' time we shall have the gun and we shall see if you are as good as you claim, *Inglés*.'

Damn you! he told Gonzalo silently, trying desperately to straighten his thoughts. What can I tell Don Bernal now? Think!

'There is a problem.'

Don Bernal looked at him. The hammering and sawing had died.

'A problem?'

'A gun is but a brazen pipe. There is not one built, nor ever shall be, that can shift round-shot without powder.'

'We have powder!' Gonzalo said.

Tavistock shook his head very deliberately, seeing his chance. 'Spanish powder. No good.'

'What? These English guns must have English powder?'

'They may be charged with Spanish powder but it is poor stuff. Would you compare guns on an inferior charge? That's like racing two stallions to see which is better when neither may break a trot. To see the full power of the culverins you must bring my powder maker here and we must find a store of sulphur and saltpetre and of this.' He held up the charcoal stick.

Don Bernal considered. He consulted with Gonzalo and Esteban quietly but rapidly, breaking off to ask, 'You have adequate supplies of charcoal, have you not?' Tavistock assented and there was more talking and shrugging. 'Where is saltpetre to be found?'

'*Cerdos. Marranos*,' Tavistock said.

The Spaniards were perplexed by the remark. 'Pigs?'

'The best nitre comes from pig piss. Human piss is not so strong. Pig piss is by far the best. In England, they scrape the crystals that form on the walls of sties and byres. It's the finest saltpetre you can find. Failing that, Gonzalo, you can build a wall and order your slaves to piss on that.'

'Saltpetre can be brought from Mexico City.'

'It will have to do.' Tavistock pressed his advantage, knowing he needed to learn more than Robert Barrett's letter had told him. 'I need my powder maker. His name is Job Hortop. And we must get top quality sulphur. Ninety-nine parts pure.'

Don Bernal nodded briefly and the three Spaniards left, unsure whether Tavistock had all along been laughing at them.

The volcano dominated all.

For two days they had striven to conquer its lower slopes, striking temporary bivouacs and marching hour after hour up the steep stony tracks. Only now was the summit in sight, and they left a dozen of the heavier, slower men at the final encampment, and pressed on with half their donkeys.

At this height, twelve thousand feet above sea level, their long ascent reached its final stage. Tavistock could see small, white clouds moving below him. To the north-west was the vista of Mexico's central valley – a hot plain with its salt lakes and roads and farms. It's a strange illusion, he thought. These commanding prospects were immensely more impressive than he had imagined they would be when, three days ago, he had looked up at the volcano from the plain.

An incredible panorama was laid out before him. Tavistock felt it was a privilege to experience this ancient domain, to survey in one long sweep the vast alien territory that had been taken with ferocity by the proud conquerors of Spain. It was a land that stretched beyond the dusty horizon, outward and outward, for hundreds of leagues, connecting the Atlantic Ocean to the Great South Sea, and it had all fallen to the fathers of the men who stood around him. Such a feat! And such a generation of men! What heroic resolve they must have had, he thought wonderingly, to believe that they could tame all this. It seemed an impossible exploit. But they had achieved it, and in doing so had reaped fortunes for themselves and for the lesser men who had come after.

He put aside his admiration and reviewed their own progress with a smaller respect. The fertile land they had travelled through on the lower slopes was forested, but here the trees were becoming smaller and gnarled and were petering out, and above them the volcano rose in sheer walls of banded rock, fabulously coloured in red and gold and purple. Despite the burning sun, there were patches of fossil snow in the shadows, and, he saw, a convenient rocky crest along which they could climb to the crater.

Job Hortop turned and wiped the sweat from his thin face, looking back down the valley. He was glad to be speaking English once more. 'This is a cruel bastard ain't it, Gunner? How far d'ye think we come now?'

'Five, maybe six thousand feet above the valley.'

'And how far to go?'

'As much again is my guess.'

Hortop's glance was sceptical. He was sinew and bone, with gaunt cheeks; his dark-dyed face lined, clawed by life. 'It don't look that far.'

'Deceptive. They say that about mountains,' Tavistock said, detesting the man. Hortop had changed. His stay in Mexico had transformed him from a quiet, even-tempered man into something moody, suspicious and nervy. For the first time on the ascent they moved out of earshot of the

Spaniards and Tavistock faced him. 'God help me, Job Hortop. Tell me what's your bitch with me or I'll swing for you.'

Hortop's words were flinty. 'I wish you'd never brought me here, Gunner. I do, and that's a fact.'

'What's the matter?'

Hortop stabbed a thumb over his shoulder, towards the valley. 'I was digging gold down there. Meaning to hop off when I could. Until you interfered, damn you. It's the luck of a lousy calf that's lived all winter and dies afore the summer.'

'Quietly!'

Ahead, three Spaniards led by Gonzalo were lifting themselves wearily up the slope, digging their toes into the friable rock. Dust rose up around them, acrid and sulphurous. Occasionally they stopped, panting for breath, before they turned and resumed their upward toil. No Indians had been willing to pathfind, he recalled. To a man they had been terrified and had grown rigid when Gonzalo had tried to compel them, clucking and tutting in their strange bird-like language.

He looked back to where Don Bernal and Maria plodded with the rest of their men. Fifty of them followed, leading donkeys loaded with empty sacks. Don Bernal had chosen to come, drawn to visit just once the mountain that watched over his land. Once he had told Gonzalo of his intentions Maria had insisted on coming too. And her brother had shrugged. He watched her now, Tavistock saw, sullenly waiting for her to falter, but she showed no sign of weakening.

He turned back to Hortop. 'Now, tell me what you've heard.'

Drake's ship was prowling the Caribbean. He had taken a dozen small coasters, routinely ordering them to stand, depriving them of all provisions and sinking them with great display. Always he put the crews ashore, making his name known as if his aim was to herald it as widely as he might. Then, each time, he had disappeared as swiftly as he had come.

'He tried to ransom us, Gunner. Drake tried at Vera Cruz. What do you think of that? When the others called us forgotten. I knew he'd come for us. I kept my faith.'

'Is that the truth?' Tavistock felt a pang of excitement.

'That's the very word. From Guadeloupe to Vera Cruz, the watchword's being whispered, "*Guardarse de El Draque!*" Beware the Dragon! – That's what they calls him – our Captain Drake. What do you think of that?'

'You can't get to his ship.'

'I can try.'

'It's madness to think you can rendezvous with him. If you run away they're sure to catch you.'

'No! I want home. And I've got a plan.'

'Make Mexico your home.'

Hortop's hoarse whispers grew strained. 'I tell you I want home,

Gunner! And I'm going home. I hate it here. I hate everything. Everything! I want to take my gold where I can spend it. Only, you've buggered up my plan good and proper!'

Tavistock stayed tight-lipped for a moment, then he said, 'I've got a job for you.'

Hortop spat. 'Bugger you, Gunner. Getting me out here when I had a plan. I've got four unbreeched whelps back home. What of them?'

'He that's at a low ebb at Newgate might soon be afloat at Tyburn,' he warned.

'I'll take my chances!'

When they called a halt, Tavistock joined Don Bernal. He sat on a boulder next to Maria, the cool wind ruffling him, but something colder and more penetrating battered at his conscience. He picked up a handful of stiff, smutted snow and crunched it in his hands, washing the dust from them. The sounds of the men drinking water and shrugging off their gear were all around him. There was tension in them, an uneasiness emanating from the land and from the awesome mass of rock above. But he was lost in his thoughts and he did not listen to their talk, nor participate in Don Bernal's conversation. There was a bleakness in the air. He knew with utter certainty that trouble was coming.

A rolling, deep-throated rumbling began.

Above them the hillside shook. Tiny stones trickled into crevices. No one uttered a sound.

Tavistock felt his chest tighten. The silence was overwhelming. Even the wind had dropped, the birdsong stilled. It was unnatural and deafening, until somebody shouted an obscenity into it and destroyed it.

All eyes were cast up at the mountain and suddenly Don Bernal pointed at the ragged lip of the crater. A thin, almost elegant wisp of smoke coiled from the summit and dispersed into the air.

He stood up, and the soldiers stood also. They began coaxing the donkeys forward hurriedly.

'Jesus, Gunner – what was that?' Hortop asked wide-eyed. Powder making had turned him brittle to shocks. Now he had the look of a horse that might bolt on an instant.

'A little indigestion.' Tavistock pacified him, thinking to himself that it was a judgement on Hortop's malice, or on his own guilt. Perhaps the powder maker was right. Perhaps he should be trying to find some way to escape. But why should he? Wasn't it just a maniac dream? How could he possibly know where to find Drake? And why should he want to? It would be grand to see Richard again, but what else was there to go back for? 'Aye, just belly ache.'

Hortop showed his teeth. 'Just so long as he don't spew his filth over us, eh, Gunner? That'd be a sorry reward for all this climbing you've put on me.'

As the sun climbed towards the zenith, they pressed on, ever upward, onto the shoulder of the volcano. There the ground was flatter and easier, and the walk to the top was across beds of refrozen snow that hurt the eyes with their glare. Tavistock traversed it marvelling at the way it crunched underfoot, aware that heavier snows were common here and that he was fortunate in the season because now the rock strata were revealed and it would be easy to find the sulphur beds.

As they crested the final rise he was breathing heavily, his lungs bursting. Then he saw the pit. The crater was huge, elliptical, half a mile across and five hundred feet deep, and its floor was ruptured and fissured with steaming vents that poured a choking, fuming stink into the air. Fortunately, the wind was carrying the plume of gas eastward, over the opposite lip.

Then the thought struck him. Perhaps the snow's thin because the volcano's hotter than usual. Perhaps Hortop's right. Perhaps it's ready to erupt. God save us from that.

The wounded earth held his eyes. He shivered, reliving the walls of singeing heat that he had felt on the burning *Jesus*. Suddenly the horrifying image of his father's face filled his mind. The nightmare was always the same. A face which he loved puckering in agony as the skin blistered and charred in a sheath of uproaring flame, before the sight had been blotted out in the darkness of his mother's skirts. She had held him so tightly he had been unable to breathe.

He shook himself, looked back at Maria and was able to contain the rising panic in his heart.

Hortop stared into the pit open-mouthed. 'What do you think of that?'

Esteban crossed himself. 'It's the doorway to Hell,' he said, fascinated by the molten mass that surged and spat far below. Hot rocks belched up into the air, higher than the rim, and rained down back into the crater, leaving trails of smoke in the air.

The powder maker twitched. 'It looks primed for to blow to me.'

'I hope you're wrong about that, Job.'

'I don't like it. Don't like it at all. I wish you ain't have brought me here.'

The soldiers lined the rim, their crimson ostrich plumes rippling as they watched the spectacle of raw power bubbling in the guts of the earth.

'You see that?' Esteban said to Hortop. 'That's what it's like in Hell. When you die you'll be chained in there for ever. That's how God hates Protestants.'

'You know, Pape, because you been there with your swinging of stinks and your bidding of beads.'

'I confess my sins each Sabbath and I am absolved. But you –' Esteban shook his head grimly. 'You're going down there, my friend.'

'Sodomite Spaniards think they own the earth and the seas and even the heavens above. They don't need to waste pity on me.'

Tavistock intervened, pointing a little way back from the crater to a

place where a vast wall of yellow, crystalline sulphur had formed. He
led Hortop to it, saying, 'I didn't like the shock we felt earlier. Best get
our chore done and get down.'

When they reached the deposits Hortop gasped. The sulphur was
feathery and pale. The whole wall was crumbly, like sand, and hot,
seeping, gummy, red resin that was another form of raw sulphur. The
powder maker scraped at it, making a mill of his palms to crush the
grains. He sniffed and tasted it, grimacing.

'It's pure!' he said, astonished at the find. 'Godsballocks, Gunner!
There's tons of it! Perfect natural refined sulphur! I ain't never seen it
so pure.'

'Good enough for you?'

'Good enough?' Hortop looked around suddenly, then grabbed Tavistock's jerkin, pulling him close, his breathless voice urgent and fierce.
'I told you. I ain't doing your filthy job. Did you see the black lead?
There's best plumbago below here. You're not wanting me show them
that are you, Gunner? Show them how to waterproof their powder with
plumbago and lubricate their charges so's they don't crust their gun
barrels up? And what about corning? You don't want me to tell them
about that, do you? They don't know how to make their powder burn
even. They don't know to make it up into grains. And you want me to
tell them. That's why you brought me here!'

Tavistock stiffened. 'Stow that! I know how to make powder. Better
than you. I brought you here because I wanted news. News of Drake.
And you could bring it to me.'

'You're lying. What about the guns you're making for them? I seen
the way you suck their arses.' Hate flared into Hortop's eyes. 'How did
they buy you, Gunner? What did they promise you?'

Tavistock shoved him back, but Hortop clung on and he slipped
awkwardly so that they rolled to the ground together.

'You've sold us out, haven't you? *Haven't you?*' Hortop's eyes were
red, stinging from the acid fumes, and the wind blew jaundiced dust
over them as Hortop straddled him.

'I got you out of the pigsty! I kept you alive! All of you.'

'Aye! And yourself! You want news? I'll give you news. We're at war
with Spain now, Gunner, and you're a traitor!'

'Liar!'

Hortop raised his fist. Then the ground under them heaved. A terrifying quaking began, malevolent in its intensity.

Tavistock heard a woman's scream.

With sudden strength he threw Hortop off and pulled free from his
grasp, running towards the rim of the crater fifty paces away. Maria
and Don Bernal struggled on the brink, while the soldiers stood like
statues, transfixed by the inhuman power of the earth as it blasted
hellish gouts of molten rock higher and higher. Then he watched in
horror as the outcrop on which Maria fought to save her father began

to collapse. A black cleft snaked across it, cutting them off. He saw Don Bernal, furthest from him, slide toward the edge, scrabbling in the dust helplessly. The opening yawned and the nearer face of the outcrop disintegrated, taking Don Bernal down.

'Maria!'

He came out of his trance, and leapt forward, grabbing Don Bernal by the legs as he dangled, head down, over the chasm.

Avalanches deep in the crater echoed thunderously from the walls. The ragged break was two paces wide now, threatening to cut off the entire outcrop on which they would ride to their deaths. Each thrust of his body promised to plunge them into the crater, each desperate wrench only kicked away more of the ground from under him. Tavistock strove to reach Don Bernal's belt.

He looked up and saw Gonzalo and the others confounded by the heaving earth. He reached across the split imploringly, knowing that his weight might easily carry the rock against which he was braced away. Then his free hand found Maria's body and grappled her, trying to link them in a human chain.

Another shock assailed them. Pinnacles of red and black rock that lined the crater wall collapsed, spinning dizzyingly into the void. Esteban ran forward, reaching the outcrop. Two of the donkeys had broken free and they pirouetted in terror around him, caught up in each other's guide ropes. Tavistock watched him break free just as they toppled sickeningly over the edge and plummeted down the sheer cliff.

Maria screamed again as her grip on Tavistock's hand slipped. He shouted for her to save herself. Then Esteban's hands were on her, wrestling her away. Rope lines surged across to them. Tavistock grabbed, wrapped the rope over his hand three times and heaved, the soldiers hauling himself and Don Bernal back from the abyss as the ledge crumbled.

'God help me!' Tavistock gasped as his forearms took the strain. The loops of rope tightened on his hand, squeezing it, cutting into his skin. He felt something crack in the centre of his chest. A jagged pain exploded across his ribcage and he felt himself passing out. In the thin air all exertion was a death struggle, but holding onto Don Bernal's leaden weight was ripping him apart. Still, he couldn't let go. A man's life was hanging from his fingertips.

After what seemed like an age, the strain across his chest stopped. The intense pain in his hand stopped. Blood began to pump again in his arms. He was lying on firm ground again.

He raised his arms weakly towards Maria.

'Juan,' she cried. 'Can you hear me?'

Her face and hair were thick with dust. He was unable to answer her.

Don Bernal was lying on the ground also. Tavistock saw him hazily; then Maria bent over him, careless of her own hurts. There was a backdrop of sparks, fireworks, his vision swimming nauseatingly, then someone remarked on the white of Don Bernal's face and his blue-tinged lips.

'Stand back! Give him air!'

'We must get him down to where the air is good.'

'Yes. Right away. We must all try to get down off the mountain before sundown.'

'It's too far,' Gonzalo said.

'We have to try.'

He saw Don Bernal hoisted between two of his men, unconscious. They dragged him away from the crater, stumbling as they went, wanting only to escape the nightmare violence. The hell demon was now hurling up red-hot boulders like a giant mortar. A rain of debris and small stones began to spatter down around them. Esteban caught him up and half-carried him after the others.

'Quickly! I cannot hold you. Find your feet, I beg you!'

They ran for the pathway, following the remaining donkeys and most of the soldiers who had, at no one's bidding, already made for the security of the lower slopes. Tavistock stumbled after them, feeling Maria guiding him and Esteban's strength support him.

The next four hours were a waking dream of horrors. The huge god, Popocatépetl, risen and angry, pursued them and tore their hands and knees and the shirts off their backs as they descended in a desperate effort to escape his fury. It was only after they had scrambled down to the tree-line encampment once more that they paused and saw that the volcano's anger was abating. Behind them a vast plume of dense, ash-laden smoke reared up, filling the sky as the wind changed. Shocks still traversed the land, sending avalanches of rock and cinder and ice down after them, but their frequency and intensity was diminishing.

Tavistock drank greedily. Maria washed his face.

Gonzalo's men were counting the cost of the enterprise.

'Why don't you stop?' Esteban yelled, shaking his fist at the peak.

'Who can say? This mountain is a devil.'

'A devil who does not want to yield up his treasures.'

'That's so.'

'Aye. We're not wanted here.'

Tavistock sat down and when Maria turned her dirt-streaked face to him he saw that her eyes were full of fear. He comforted her, knowing that she wanted to cry but would not. She whispered, 'Thank you. For the life of my father. And for my own. Surely, we would both have been dead if not for you.'

She kissed him. Despite his exhaustion, Tavistock felt a pure shaft of joy spear him. He was still alive. Maria was still alive. For the moment they were beyond the reach of the smoking mountain, and that was all that mattered.

The soldiers, bruised and ragged and with the remaining beasts, were packed up and ready to move out now.

The journey down was arduous. With Don Bernal strapped up in a bier of sacking slung from a hastily cut pine pole, and Tavistock walking unaided, they forced their aching legs to go on until they could no longer see the way ahead. Tavistock was proud that the entire company helped pitch the tents and light the fires. Food was shared and bottles passed around unselfishly. The mountain's driven us away, he thought, but it's also brought us closer together. It's the same brotherhood that bonds a ship's crew after action or disaster. Everything is suddenly so lucid. Why? Maybe it's like warfare. I've been brought close to death and I can suddenly see with all the clarity of a man who should be dead but isn't. All the small weights that oppressed me have turned to thistledown. My conscience is reborn, fresh and unblemished.

The fear of fire was gone.

It was then, under a vast cloud whose underside pulsed yellow, then orange, then vermilion in the darkness, that Tavistock realised their company was incomplete. Job Hortop was no longer among their number.

Chapter 13

'Time for your sup, Captain! Clear the door!'

Keys jangled and then turned in the lock. Tavistock looked up at the familiar sound. Ballard, the portly gaoler, brought in a covered tray and set it down on the table among the wood chippings.

The cell was the best Hawkins's money could buy: thick-walled, set high above the moat and dry; cool in every season, but with a barred window, too narrow to take a man's head, that glimpsed the river and the stout gate that sometimes opened to admit the Raven. There was a straw bed, a chair and a table on which he maintained a candle, a Bible and tiny pieces of whittled oak that were the ribs and wales of a semblance of the *Antelope*. Outside, the corridor was always guarded. Beyond that, a fortress garrisoned with choice soldiers. Escape by sinew was impossible. Escape by wit remained.

'Porter's ale and an eel pie today.'

'Broken up by you again, I see.'

'It's my function to see that you get no more than eels in your pies, Captain!'

'Nor eel meat either, you greasy-chinned villain.'

Ballard guffawed contentedly. 'If I'm the villain, you're the captive. And one enjoying greater comforts than any I've seen in this place, save when the Duke of Norfolk lived with us. You're a rare man, Captain. Rare as an eel's egg.'

Tavistock flipped him a golden piece. 'Have a care, lest I wriggle past your suet belly!'

'That, sir, you'll never do.'

I'll be as fat as you are soon, he thought sourly, watching the even-humoured turnkey leave and lock him in once more. Aye! Fat as a swine brought to slaughter. And how long before I'm tried and condemned? Cecil's men must have a surfeit of evidence against me. What's holding him?

He eyed the open letter that had come by Wat Painter four days ago. The sight of it unsettled him. In it, Hawkins spoke optimistically about the trial, but warned that Walsingham had gone to France as Ambassador. Conveniently out of the way, it seemed to him. What justice when an innocent can't trust to the telling of the truth to deliver him? he thought wryly. The joke is that I knew nothing of what Ridolfi was carrying, or what he planned. Neither did Hawkins, who danced an angry jig when the news came out, and who has been full of amends since. But Walsingham knew. It was his idea. How, if I threaten to tell the true story and implicate him? My word against that of the Ambassador to France? Seemingly a man clutching at any lie that will give him hope. Can I trust Hawkins to side with me against Walsingham? Doubtful. How true that shit percolates downward. And there is no one beneath to pass on my troubles to. No one that has not been suborned already. In any case, I may stand accused of more than Ridolfi. What happens when the true tale of Jan de Groote is found out, as it surely must be?

He took a draught of porter and paced the lime-washed floor. Then he sat down and opened the heavy book that Dee had sent, turning the pages with a dejection he had seldom felt so deeply.

For months, he thought, I've languished here, with but one thought in my head – the harrowing of the Indies. Now it seems that I'll never sail thither. Why do I continually search through these maps and reports? It's foolish to fill my solitary hours with foreign designs – how best to cut out a galleon, which coast of the Main will most meetly serve as a secure port, what is the least number of men that might hope to take Nombre de Dios and how many fathoms lie in her channel. He looked at the model ship, unhappy with the form of the wing transom and the fashion-piece that sprang up and out and aft from it. All his hopes seemed suddenly remote, and he felt a sudden pang of hopelessness, but he recognised it and cut it down instantly, shouting defiantly at the wall, 'By Christ, if I don't live to further these reflections, others shall!'

The echo died away to silence. His mind drifted, rudderless, entangling him in frustration. He stood up again, trying to think, but whenever a plan of escape became clear to him it fell next into a hindrance. Always a hitch, a clog, a trammel!

He beat his hand on the wall. Then an inner discipline seized him and he heard his own crisp voice say, 'When I sailed *Minion* home, I thought myself a lucky survivor. When Hawkins and I came into London, I judged that we would both lodge in the Tower – or some worse place. And when I lay with Anne, I told her how I walked the razor's edge. I should have sailed then. But I missed the tide and so my fortune ebbed away to that place far across the world where I should have been.'

He sat down on his pallet, put his feet up high and drank the last of his quart. This time his voice was consoling to him. 'In truth, my imprisonment is royal, as Ballard daily declares. While I breathe there must be no despair. Now! *What to do?*'

No answer came.

The sight of Hawkins's letter plagued him. He threw his cup at it, denting the pewter with a dull thud.

'Damn you to the deepest hell of all, Lord Oxford!'

That was better said. A devil cast out. A gobbet of bile coughed up at last. The sharpest barb in Hawkins's well-meant letter was not any lament on his condition, nor any false hope regarding the hangman, but the news of a date set on Anne Cecil's wedding.

He had paid Hawkins's servant, who knew how to accomplish such things, to carry an urgent letter, and warned him on his life to deal straightly. It had been a dire threat, backed by another – Bowen, who was commanded to shadow Hawkins's man, and to give his hide to the Bishopsgate beggars if he played false.

The letter had contained another within, one sealed thrice and finely written, that had passed through the scullery window in Cecil House and, so the servant said, going from maid to maid, would come into Anne's own hand.

'Write to me just once, my sweet lady, then I may die a sane man,' he had written, among many other private things that he could never have said to her face.

Now it was the fourth day, and no news. A quiet Sunday. No courtyard dogs barking at the messengers. A matins chant from somewhere, and the noonday gun. Not a sign of ought hereafter but god-damned eel pie.

He closed his eyes; the pale light of an overcast sky fell across his face. Then as he dozed, his arms over his eyes to block out the glare, he fancied he heard a noise in the approaches. He imagined Ballard's flat footfall and another, lighter.

Again the sound of the throwing lock.

Then the door swinging on its huge hinges.

'One hour,' Ballard's strangely hushed voice said. 'No more.'

Tavistock lowered his arm as the door banged shut and saw that it had not been a dream. There was someone else in his room. His lady had come.

As Walsingham entered the Secretary's room, he focused his mind on the several reasons he had come in secret from France.

Cecil admitted him but chose to keep Slade by his side, perhaps imagining that a witness might inhibit discussion. It's a pity Slade's no babbler, Walsingham thought. The more witnesses to this, the better. Since the matter can no longer be buried.

'Congratulations on your elevation, my Lord Burleigh,' he said immediately. He knew the reward Elizabeth had conferred on her Secretary was for his competence in steering the ship of state past the reefs of the last three years. In that, Walsingham thought wryly, Leicester has succeeded: he has indeed buried the name of Sir William Cecil for ever, though he had misliked the alternative risen up in its place.

This was the first time Cecil and Walsingham had met face to face since Sir William's peerage had been conferred last February; Walsingham's embassy in Paris and the delicate negotiations with the Valois Court had kept him busy. Much too busy for trips home on purely ceremonial matters, he thought, prickled now by jealousy.

'Thank you, Mister Walsingham.'

'Yes. It's a reward you deserve justly enough,' Walsingham said, 'and one that I see fills you with joy and, no doubt, even greater adoration for Her Majesty.'

'Indeed? That is a quantity that cannot increase.'

'Quite.'

He left more unsaid and smouldering: You can't deny that you have your eye on the Garter; they say that when the Marquis of Winchester dies you'll be made Lord High Treasurer. I wish you good luck. But what of me? Where's the recognition for my own part in the continuing defence of England? What lord shall I become? None! It's a measure of power I want. A position of influence, and call me what you will. Titles are meaningless unless they give a man control over events. I want to be the linchpin. And you will give it me. And if I must graft more, then so shall I graft, my lord Burleigh. And if you step out of the Secretary's robes to don those of the Lord Treasurer, those robes must be mine.

'How goes it in France?'

'Sir Henry Norris sends you his regards. We are both sanguine of the prospects for the outcome there. Much is agreed already, which is no surprise: if the brother of the King of France may wed the Queen of England, Catherine de' Medici may consider herself and her son well favoured by fortune.'

Would Burleigh have backed this match of his own initiative? Walsingham asked himself. Will he back it now, when I am the main architect? He supports the idea because it might give Elizabeth a child. What if he knows that Elizabeth's bleeding comes of Doctor Dee's work? How deep is he with the Spanish? Worrying letters are coming from Leicester on these points. Letters I cannot afford to ignore.

'I want to know how you'll treat of the Queen's marriage,' he said directly. 'Are you yea, or are you not?'

'You have my word as Secretary of State that I support the marriage implicitly.'

'And your word as William Cecil?'

'That is my own affair.'

'Then there's a problem. One that concerns another marriage. I must have this in the open with you. Now. I think you know what I'm about to say.'

Cecil faced him motionlessly, giving nothing away, nor any sign of dismissal to Slade.

'You betroth your daughter, Anne, to the Earl of Oxford.'

'It's well known that they are to marry.'

'Yes, and with urgency.'

'Let us say rather that young love is impatient.'

'Oh, how true.' Walsingham screwed at his wedding ring. 'But at what price?'

'What do you mean? The dowry?'

'I have it that the traitor Norfolk's head is set in lieu for a dowry. That price is too high for England, and too high for me, my lord.'

Burleigh sat up, unsettled by the directness of Walsingham's charge. 'You have evidence of this – agreement?'

'It's no secret that you're seeking to make aristocratic marriages for each of your children. That's understandable. What is not, is how you can propose to give Norfolk his freedom after what he's done. That he's cousin to a man who will soon be your own son-in-law is perhaps reason enough.'

'A tenuous allegation.'

Walsingham blew out his breath impatiently. 'You signed Norfolk's release from the Tower. Why? On the pretext of removing him from the plague. You've installed him in his own property, under house arrest. Why? To demonstrate his innocence. You've sought to reinstate him as nearly as you might to his former condition. Why? To show the world he is forgiven.'

'The Duke of Norfolk is a repaired man, Francis. He is contrite. And cleansed by his confession.'

'This was all along Oxford's desire. I deem that the deal is this: in return for Norfolk's pardon, Oxford has agreed to marry your daughter – *even though your daughter is with child!*'

Burleigh stared. Then, swiftly, he recovered and tossed his hand languidly. 'All surmise, Mister Walsingham. My lord Norfolk's misdeeds have been dead a long time. He repented of them honestly. And it was our gracious Majesty, the Queen, who preferred him alive, not I. You spoke of evidence. Present it. Or refrain.'

Walsingham drew out a sheaf and laid the leaves on the table one at a time. His voice was smooth and uncoloured. 'Item: Norfolk has reaffirmed his oath of loyalty to Elizabeth, but denied his intent in a private letter to the Bishop of Ross – which original is in my possession. Item: the Duke has been contacted by Roberto di Ridolfi. And here, my lord, is evidence that since Norfolk's release he has been in constant touch with the Italian. Evidence that Ridolfi, in turn, has talked to de Spes, to Alva, and to Philip. Evidence that ultimately he plans to talk to the Pope himself. Evidence, in short, that since his release Norfolk has spent every waking hour trying to secure Catholic help so that the Queen of Scots may try once more to usurp Elizabeth's crown.'

Burleigh gathered up the papers and scanned them, thunderstruck. He had already been shaken by the accuracy of Walsingham's exquisite intelligence. How could he possibly have known of Anne's pregnancy?

Who did he have in the Norfolk household? Was Walsingham now in league with Leicester?

He summoned Slade from the shadows and talked privately to him. Walsingham's eyes followed him as he left.

'You must believe that this is a surprise to me.' Burleigh watched Walsingham shrug amiably. 'It's true that I wanted to give Oxford what he asked. My grandchild must have a father. It's true also that the Queen counted Norfolk a chastened fool. But in truth I saw in Norfolk a counterpoise to Leicester. He hates him most adamantly for the betrayal he perpetrated, and I saw that if Leicester must continually watch Norfolk, then must he also be less bothersome to me.'

Walsingham rose and went to the window. 'This is too important for either of us to misunderstand each other. You're made Lord Burleigh of Stamford Burleigh because you preserved peace with Spain. But you have other ambitions. You want that sacred peace to continue, but you also want Leicester controlled and curbed. You want your daughter to marry Oxford. And you want the father of her bastard killed.'

Burleigh stamped the heel of his rod into the floor. 'And you, Mister Walsingham? What are your ambitions?'

Walsingham turned, carefully hiding his smile. 'I want my Queen to marry the Duke of Anjou – for then French Protestants may be protected and because it holds promise of an Anglo-French pact against Spain, thus protecting the Protestant Netherlands. I want Norfolk executed and de Spes expelled – for justice's sake. And I want Captain Tavistock released – for my own reasons. With care, we may, each of us, have everything we desire.'

Burleigh's eyes hardened. 'Not so! You want the Queen to marry so that Flanders may be crushed by French forces. You want Norfolk's head to be carried on a plate to Leicester. And you want de Spes thrown out to sever relations with Spain. Lastly, you want Tavistock released so that he may fall on Oxford and root out a man you despise at Court and who Leicester despises.'

Walsingham smiled and cocked an eye at the novelty of the idea. 'Neither of us is a fool, William. So let's be level. Take the French marriage. You've already consented to that in principle. You've said you'll not obstruct it. But neither will you facilitate it.' He turned back to the window. 'However, though we are opposed, you and I are nevertheless in some accord. We both see value in the *prospect* of the Queen's marriage. Even the rumour of it is sufficient to deter Spanish arms, and while they are deterred there can be no war betwixt Spain and England. In this wise may your peace be preserved.'

'And Leicester?'

Walsingham's smile was knowing. 'At the present, you bind him with the contract that he so rashly made with Norfolk. You ask yourself: what if Norfolk dies? How then may my lord Leicester be kept from my throat? I answer you thus: the death of Norfolk, your tacit opposition

to the Queen's marriage and the release of Captain Tavistock will be
enough to convince him to drop his efforts to depose you.'

'The man Tavistock must die! For my daughter's sake. And because
he helped publish a malicious lie about Her Majesty.'

'No! Without his release, Leicester will have no guarantee of your
continuing good faith. Your daughter's standing as the Countess of
Oxford is his hostage. If Norfolk is arrested the day after the wedding,
I promise you there will be ample evidence to implicate Oxford also. It
can become yours, and with it you may control him. The price is good:
Captain Tavistock.'

A fleck of spittle showed at the corner of Burleigh's mouth as his
frustration exploded. '*Why?*'

'I have uses for him.'

'What uses?'

Slade reappeared, followed by an armed party. In their compass was
a ragged wretch who Slade threw down in the middle of the room.
'Here's the very man, your lordship.'

The louse-bitten prisoner scratched and shivered. Walsingham saw
that he had been a big man once, muscular and erect, but now he was
shrunk by illness, covered in festers and hunched. His stinking sodden
rags made Walsingham turn his head away.

'Who is he?' he asked disgustedly.

Slade's voice rasped, 'Speak! Tell the gentleman your name!'

'Jack Ingram, your honour.'

Cecil looked at him dispassionately and his eyes locked on
Walsingham. 'This man will testify to several vile crimes designed
by Captain Tavistock. He has informed me that Tavistock made an
unauthorised deal with the privateers led by Jan de Groote to molest
Spanish ships in the Channel.'

Walsingham's voice became wearily disdainful. 'It's a great pity, Lord
Burleigh, that the full force of Tavistock's dealings with Jan de Groote
was never felt. It was to land a force of men to seize the Dutch port of
Brille as soon as Alva's army had put to sea on its invasion of England.'

Burleigh's anger overflowed. 'He had ideas to develop the foreign
policy of England as it pleased him! I could not allow it!'

Ingram began to cough and hawk.

'I suggest you remove this man before he dies.'

'He's detained here for his own protection. His allegations range
further and implicate others. He says that he witnessed Tavistock bring
Roberto de Ridolfi into England with the Papal Bull. That alone is
sufficient to hang, draw and quarter him as an evil traitor.'

'Only a fool fails to arm himself against the future,' Walsingham said
with sudden anger. 'Evil men abound. Some are commoners, some more
evil still become peers of the realm, and the most evil of all win the
thrones of Europe. Especially that of Rome. Tavistock brought Roberto
de Ridolfi into England on my orders. There was no malice against the

Queen in it. Consider: it was not *he* who excommunicated Elizabeth, but the Pope. I wanted security tightened around the Queen. I wanted the Catholics of England warned of their true position. I also wanted the real intent of Spain drawn out for all to see. Ridolfi, with his plotting and scheming, has proved to be the best possible agent for all three aims. Tavistock therefore is no traitor. He must have his freedom.'

Burleigh watched Walsingham's face carefully, knowing this man was his match. Walsingham possessed a strong mind and a powerful talent for deceit, but his temperament was altogether too belligerent. Always he looked for offensive solutions, always he sought an alliance with France against Spain, not to construct a counterpoise to Philip, but to launch a blow that might unseat him. I would have no foreign alliance at all if I could avoid it, he thought grimly, Walsingham seems bent on drawing us unhappily tight with the French. His efforts in Paris had continued unabated for almost a year. Had he not returned to England periodically since Tavistock's arrest? Once claiming ill-health, and later, in January, to attend the opening of Sir Thomas Gresham's English Bourse, or Exchange, in Lombard Street. That was a tangible result of Antwerp's ruin; approved by the Queen and renamed the Royal Exchange. Its grasshopper crest flew over the City, and over Gresham's Bishopsgate mansion like a weather vane of future ambitions. How closely was Walsingham connected with the growing merchant powers in London? Had he not dined with Hawkins many times? Perhaps he's persuaded others of the immediate benefits of an antagonism towards Spain. It would be a sound argument for ten years' time, but surely the time is not yet. England must play the obedient vassal still. Growing and burgeoning in trade and in skill at arms. Building a head of force and majesty and virile puissance to overcome Philip and his empire. To go off now, with the gun at half-cock, would be a disaster.

The wind was changing. Ever so slowly and by degrees, the little state of England was gaining confidence and men in all walks were seeing new opportunities. Prudent men were building up their affairs. But others looked outward. Leicester was fond of foreign wars, Walsingham wanted to champion the Protestant cause, the damnable Doctor Dee filled Her Majesty's head with fanciful notions of distant lands in the west. Then there was Hawkins and his private argument with Spain. And now this meddlesome brigand, Tavistock.

Burleigh bristled as he thought of how he had been abused. He rued the day he had brought the monster into his house. The man's audacity had shocked him. Crime upon crime. He had come to blows with an Earl. Then he had had the face to lie with Anne and get her with child. A grandchild conceived in a prison cell. The shame of it!

Tavistock's crimes were manifold: he had shamelessly purloined a thousand pounds from de Spes and spent it on equipping a ship in which his fellow conspirator Drake had sailed out of Plymouth, without passport or permission, to maraud in the Indies. He had brought in

Ridolfi and plotted an invasion of the Low Countries. What more of
like unruly conduct could be expected if such a man was let loose on
the world?

He said, 'No. I cannot release him. He's too dangerous.'

Walsingham pressed forward. 'You want to be rid of him.'

'I'm rid of him already.'

'And if he may be made to swear that he will not seek to see your
daughter ever again, nor the Earl of Oxford, nor try to harm him, nor
seek to see the child?'

Burleigh wavered. He pinched the bridge of his nose and then looked
up. 'Could he be so persuaded?'

'Certainly.'

'And he will abide by his promises?'

'Yes.'

'Then perchance he will sail far away to die in some waterspout or
be swallowed down by a sea serpent, God damn him!'

'That I cannot promise.'

'Ha!' Burleigh sat a long moment, watching Ingram who shivered and
stared wide-eyed. There was no doubt what Walsingham was really
saying: that he, Burleigh, could no longer hold Tavistock. He would
have to bring him to trial or let him go. If Tavistock was let out he
would fall in with Walsingham's designs. In England he would be a
lurking presence around Anne, promise or no promise. Out of England
he was a menace. Only a saint chooses good over evil every time, he
told himself. Where there are only evils, a wise man chooses the lesser.
Do I trust Walsingham enough? What does he really want with Tavistock? Wasn't it obvious to him that as soon as Tavistock was released
he would sail to Vera Cruz with some half-chewed notion of ransoming
his brother?

Ingram broke into another bout of coughing. He motioned to him,
telling Slade, 'Give the scum five shillings and let him go.'

Slade goaded the pitifully grateful prisoner from the room with barked
oaths. As the door closed, Burleigh offered Walsingham a cup of wine
to seal the business.

He accepted pleasantly.

'Tell me why you're protecting Tavistock. I don't believe he knows
anything about you that you want kept quiet,' Burleigh said, gathering
his sleeves onto the table. 'And I don't believe he's a New Year's present
to my lord Leicester.'

Walsingham sipped, looked up. He said, duelling mildly, 'At least
your line shall be vigorous through your first grandchild. If he's a boy
he'll be Lord Protector one day.'

'It's dangerous to look too far ahead, Francis. But you? What would
you have? Are you thinking of a royal heir by the Frenchman, with
yourself as Regent? Or will the Scots bairn, James Stuart, better fit your
design?'

'I would not be so disloyal as to imagine the Queen's death.'

'Then what? The long future is a hard place to make plans.'

Walsingham said the word distantly, like a seer's revelation. 'Lepanto.'

The battle at Lepanto had been fought three months ago and Walsingham had heard of it three days later. According to the detailed reports he had received, a huge fleet of two hundred and seventy Turkish galleys under Ali Pasha had been met off the Greek coast by a combined force belonging to Spain, Venice and the Papacy. Philip's bastard half-brother, Don John of Austria, had commanded the Holy League's navy: two hundred oared galleys, backed by a hundred transports packed with tens of thousands of soldiers, and spearheaded by six vast galleasses that mounted fifty cannon each.

Don John had carried the Pope's *Agnus Dei* into battle, falling on the fleet of the Sublime Porte with incredible ferocity. He knew that failure would give the entire Mediterranean to the Ottomans and lay open a defenceless Rome to the infidel. It would also destroy Spanish sea power and encourage the Sultan to send his janissary hoards against Granada.

In the titanic struggle the Turkish admiral had become an especial target. The Spanish soldiery had surged on board his galley and Ali Pasha had fallen. When Don John ordered his head raised on a pike at the stern of his galley the sight of it had turned the battle.

Fifteen thousand Christian galley slaves were released. Only fifty Turkish galleys had got away. The rest were destroyed or captured, and Don John's gamble had succeeded.

'Lepanto,' Walsingham repeated. 'With Philip's victory his Mediterranean coast is secured. How long can it be before the full might of Spain is directed against us?'

The sound of horses echoed back from the high fenestras of Richmond Palace.

Tavistock dismounted and Leicester's men led him briskly on and through a fortalice. Here and there, they passed servants with inquisitive eyes, and women who fell to talking of him. He was met there and taken up the stairs by Leicester himself.

'Hurry. This is no matter to be left a-dawdling.'

'But I am yet undressed. I have no sword.'

Leicester shook his head. 'You shall have not even a butter knife in this place.'

At their swift passing halberdiers stamped rigid, their smart officers saluting. Each oaken portal was flung open. The long corridors rang to their shoe leather; the suite of rooms, upon which was mounted a heavy guard, was most gorgeously decorated by carvings and other delicate work. Tavistock saw, glancing to right and to left, that the opulent hangings seemed to extend for ever in every direction. After his confinement it seemed to him a wonderland of comfort. Finally they

came to a door that was not open, nor could it be opened by the Lord
Leicester's arrival. The guardian demanded who had solicited him, and
what business he might have, and when Leicester gave his letter of
summons it was taken by a chamberlain and passed to a page boy with
a tray who went back down the way they had come and turned off into
a second, narrower corridor.

'What now?' Tavistock asked, swaying his weight from one foot to
another and back anxiously.

'We wait.'

'And when we are inside? What then?'

'I am not to come with you.'

Tavistock was struck with a sudden pang that stiffened him. 'But I
have been schooled in no proper forms, my lord! I cannot go alone.'

'You are *commanded* to go alone. And therefore you will go alone.
Don't worry, Her Majesty is well attended within.'

Tavistock scowled. 'At the least, show me the rudiments. I beg you.'

'Relax yourself a little, and be polite. Answer her "Your Majesty"
and venture no opinion unless you are asked for the same. Such is all
that is required. Now can that be too much for a man to bear?'

Tavistock's stomach gurgled. He stamped one foot forward and thrust
out his gloved hand. 'So, firstly, I shall shake her hand civilly. Thus!'

'No, no. No!' Leicester said, appalled. 'You're coming before the
Queen of England, man, not thrusting at some fencing tutor. You do
not touch the Queen's Majesty at all!'

The face of the Presence Chamber guard captain had turned the
colour of a beetroot. Tavistock shot him a venomous glance.

'Ach! I know nothing of such manners.'

'That much is in evidence,' Leicester said. 'You should come forward
like this.'

He performed a low bow, rocking back on his haunches with unnatural adroitness – Tavistock knew that if he did as much he would
overbalance. Then he swept his hand down as if he was reeving up a
length of rope and knelt.

'Do likewise.'

Tavistock put his head down and waved his hand as Leicester had
done.

Then, before he could straighten his back the doors were flung open
and he was urged forward.

He saw the Queen surrounded by her gentlemen, to her left Burleigh,
and to her right Walsingham. Tavistock approached, thirty pairs of
eyes following him, and knelt in deepest humility, overcome by the
magnificence of the Sovereign's bespangled finery and the chalk-white
of her face.

Elizabeth's eyes darted at him from that taut alabaster face, the
pendant pearls in her red hair quivering, and her crimson lips pursed in
hauteur. Under the Queen's naked brows, her pupils, large as saucers,

rimmed with irises that were near black, were turned on him with the full force of her majesty. Thin lips: a painted crimson bud, cruel, clashing garishly with a head of bright spun copper. Her head seemed almost disembodied, now, raised on its deep collar of ruffled filigree; a fearsome mask.

He heard her voice, high and hard and utterly terrifying.

'So! This is he with the reckless plans? Never mind that he's a wicked fellow who's spent the last several months in the Tower's stony embrace, eh, Mister Walsingham?'

Walsingham's face assumed a smile of massive insincerity and Tavistock cringed inside. 'He is a gallant who has been trapped there by circumstance, Your Majesty.'

Elizabeth gazed at him and snorted. 'Caught up in your machinations, I don't wonder. And this wrong you would have me undo?'

'Majesty.'

She continued to stare at Tavistock, her eyes penetrating him. This is the moment, he thought, the tension inside him building unbearably. What should I say? What can I ask? Give me permission to sink the ships and subjects of your brother-in-law? Grant me leave to maraud a foreign empire as I will? Set me beyond the bounds of your jurisdiction, and though I have suffered your Tower, I will remain your faithful servant.

'What will you have of me, Captain? Speak, now.'

His mouth was as dry as sawdust. 'Three boons, Your Majesty.'

'Only three?'

'It would trouble me sorely to choose amongst them,' he mumbled.

'Then count them out for me.'

'First, I would have my ship back.'

Burleigh bent to whisper an explanation in her ear. '*Your* ship?'

'Aye. She was promised to me upon the word of John Hawkins whose name you may know.'

'This is the ship *Antelope*?'

Tavistock swallowed hard, his nerves jangling. 'Captain Hawkins has been minding her for me, as you might say, Your Majesty, while I reflected on my reckless plans inside your Tower.'

The strike of light in Elizabeth's eye was deadly. 'And the second boon?'

'The second is but a piece of paper. I have not seen such a one but I imagine it as big as a mainsail, for without it my ship cannot go.'

The Queen pursed her lips testily. Her shrill voice split the air. 'The ship of your colleague, Captain Francis Drake, has had no such difficulty.'

Tavistock produced his bow again. This time it was even less accomplished. 'Alas. He is, like me, a man who knows what is right, but knows not what is the right way.'

'He is a villain!'

The Queen's fingers grasped her velvet armrests. She got up from her high throne and took Burleigh's hand. The material of her kirtle crackled and soughed as she descended the three steps of her dais. The jewels sewn there sparked brilliantly. She turned on him suddenly, much too close. 'And if I accede to these rude requests, what shall be your third?'

'Only this, Your Majesty –'

'Come, follow me to the window. I wish to look at the river.'

He followed, awkwardly. Until they were almost alone, separated from the anxious lords and ladies of the Presence Chamber, separated from Lord Burleigh and from Walsingham also. He held his peace, remembering Leicester's entreaty that he should wait for her to speak first after any pause, and seeing that she was deep in thought.

Then she said, 'When as a babe my eyes first opened and saw the world it was this river they gazed upon. I have never seen the sea. Tell me of it.'

Tavistock searched his memory frantically to recall the many ocean wonders he had seen, but he could not. There was nothing in his mind connected with the sea but the thought of eel pie. He tried desperately to focus his brain on something – anything – but it was blotted out by an overpowering desire to blurt out the third boon he would ask. How can I ask the Queen's royal protection for Anne against Lord Oxford's vices? he asked himself, stricken with a dread he had never known. Can't she annul the marriage, or order her Archbishop to make it void? He began to sweat and his heart hammered. Sweet Jesus! This is agony.

His voice faltered. 'If it please Your Majesty, there are oftentimes large storms at sea ...'

She tutted at him. 'I have seen storms in Hampshire, Captain. I would know something of the sea. Quickly now.'

From the far side of the room Walsingham watched Tavistock anxiously. The man's awkward embarrassment lit him up like a torch. I represented him to her as a brave and capable man, he thought. A man to command and inspire other men. A hero. He's barely in command of himself God damn him! I wish I could hear what he was saying. This is a disaster!

Then he saw that Tavistock had stopped his stuttering. His hands began to move like ocean waves as he spoke. The Queen put her hands together. And Tavistock spoke again. Then the Queen nodded and Tavistock's tale resumed. Incredibly, Elizabeth's humour warmed. She began to listen closely. Took off her glove. Gave it to him. Then she laughed.

Tavistock talked to her for more than ten minutes, the Queen interrupting at intervals. When he was dismissed, it was fondly.

Walsingham followed him, catching him as he turned the corner.

'What did she say?'

Tavistock rubbed at the back of his neck, where the courtly ruff

bothered him. He regarded Walsingham suspiciously. 'She asked me to
tell her of the sea.'

'What did you say to her?'

'I told her of it.'

'And the third boon?'

He darted another dark glance. 'I asked permission to carry her glove
aboard my ship to remind me of her.'

'And she agreed?'

He held up the slim silken glove.

Walsingham blew out a great breath of relief. He slowed as they came
to the great hall. It was hung with fine Flemish tapestries and the long
trestle tables were being laid for a banquet under them. Tavistock was
heading toward the courtyard under full sail. He called out impatiently
after him, his voice ringing off the silverware, 'How did you charm her?
What did you say to her that made her laugh?'

'That's of no consequence, sir.'

Tavistock strode from the palace and into the courtyard. The reins
of a white horse were handed to him by Leicester's man. It was the
Andalusian he had been given by the Earl to ride to the west country,
before the Queen changed her mind. He breathed deeply. Spring! And
the air was full of promise, and he saw that at last his road was straight
and unencumbered, and open all the way to Plymouth.

'There's nought so good for the inside of a busy man than the outside
of a swift horse,' the ostler said pleasantly.

Walsingham caught him up once more. He reached up to clasp hands.
'Godspeed you, Richard Tavistock.'

'I thank you for that, Mister Walsingham. And for everything.'

'But tell me, what did you say to the Queen?'

Tavistock's cheek reddened and he drew himself up to cover it. 'I told
Her Majesty about eels.'

Walsingham stared at him blankly. 'Eels?'

'I told her of the Sargasso Sea, where they lay their eggs.'

Tavistock walked the horse to the riverside arch; Walsingham
watched him as he passed beyond the iron gates and spurred past the
palace guards who tarried there.

Now, at last, the enterprise he had planned for was under way.

Book Three

Book Three

Chapter 14

'Sail fine on the starboard bow!'

The shout from the mainmast crosstrees galvanised Juan Hernando de Ortega. His stomach began to clench in anticipation and his eyes moved eagerly across the horizon. Seeing nothing, he quickly scanned the scene to larboard, promising to have the lookout flogged if he had made another false call.

The other ships of the outward bound *flota* rolled on a choppy sea. It was a bright, clear day, the ocean running high under a fresh wind, as expected in this season west of the Azores. The ships of the *flota* were disciplined, staying tightly formed up in their convoy to larboard, Admiral Luzon in his flagship, *San Lorenzo*, and twenty-six other ships, big and small, running before these spirited north-easterlies. And then there was the *Concepción*.

The *Concepción* was a ship of five hundred tons, a four-masted galleon deliberately rigged to look twenty years older than she was. Her upper works had been extended with light pine wood that made her high charged, and her waterline was emphasised with bulky wales that ran from stem to stern and gave her a ponderous appearance.

But she was not ponderous. Her balance was superb. Her centre of gravity was set more forward than the placing of her masts indicated. Beneath the water she was smooth and handsomely lined, so that she cut through the waves like a razor.

The seven gun ports that ran along her side were flush, disguised and invisible at even a cable's distance. And behind the ports were powerful pieces of Flemish ordnance. She was Admiral Luzon's brainchild, laid down to his specific design, his answer to the French pirates who were coming increasingly into the Caribbean.

Ortega's thoughts turned to the extraordinary man who was his admiral. Ever since the débâcle at San Juan de Ulua, Luzon had worked hard to erase the stain on his honour, but the indictment of his subordinate had required more than just carefully chosen words. So while Ortega had languished in confinement, Luzon had used his connections in Madrid to petition Don Juan, the King's brother. Unhesitatingly, the Prince had secured a command for Luzon, whom he respected both as an admiral and as a man. Luzon had been placed under the Marquis of Santa Cruz, to lead a squadron of galleys against the Turks, and at Lepanto Luzon had repaid the royal trust that had been invested in him. He had triumphed and had returned sequined in glory, yet even in the midst of his victory, when another might have basked in the praise of his monarch and set his sights on higher things, he had not forgotten the disgraced Ortega.

During his long months awaiting his appearance before the tribunal in Seville, Ortega had been a broken man, his career shattered into a million shards, his life hanging by a hair, but Luzon's evidence had been irrefutable, his support magnificent. Ortega recalled the day he had swept into the court wearing the sash of the Order of Calatrava to speak on his behalf. His bearing had dazzled the bench. They had acquitted him, and Ortega remembered how he had burst euphorically from the courtroom, blemishless once more, uttering a catechism of thanks to St Elmo, who protects all mariners, and pouring out a torrent of gratitude to his Admiral.

But the day after, Ortega had discovered that he was no longer Vice-Admiral of the Ocean Seas. Despite the verdict there was to be no reinstatement, no pension, and not a single word of explanation. He had been discharged from the King's service, without honour and without a future.

He had wandered like a soul in purgatory until the Admiral's agents had come upon him one night in a bordello in Cadiz, insisting that he follow them to the waterfront at Port Royal. He had been astoundingly drunk, spent out on despairing carousals, vulgarly rude and sword-happy in his rejection of them. But they had ducked him in brine until he became reasonable and had taken him red-eyed to a secret meeting.

He had been incredulous when Luzon had shown him the *Concepción*. He had been utterly astonished when Luzon assigned command of her to him. 'You'll master her, Juan Hernando,' he had said with dark humour as they stood under the gilded, holy figure at the beakhead. 'I want a man who's hungry for the task and you're the hungriest man in Andalusia. You'll take her with the next *flota* to the Indies and you'll seek out the pirates. To those Huguenot curs the *Concepción* will seem the perfect victim. To their eyes she'll be a fat merchantman, stuffed with silver and wallowing helplessly, old, hog-backed, without speed and lightly armed. And the scum will be drawn to her like rats to a midden. But look at this!'

Yes, Ortega thought now, remembering how Luzon had kept faith. Don Emilio Martinez's condemnation at Vera Cruz might easily have hanged me had it not been for the Admiral. I owe him my life. He's given me a chance to redeem my honour, to prove that I'm neither incompetent nor a coward. God help me do my utmost to repay the trust of a great Admiral.

Ortega strode across his quarterdeck and leaned out as far as he could, until his line of vision cleared the obstruction of the spritsail. Balanced there, he waited for the rise of the swell.

Still nothing.

Lord God castrate the lookout if he's wrong this time, he thought, angered by the shout.

Ortega was unsettled. The alarm six hours ago had skinned his nerves, and this new disappointment was sharp in his throat as he realised he would have to endure longer in purgatory before a real chance to show his spirit arose.

But the *Concepción* was a remarkable vessel, a unique ship, with extraordinary sailing qualities, new to Ortega, and untried to all. The thought of her powerful concealed armament filled him with impatience. He looked up to the masthead and damned the lookout once more; to the sailing master he muttered, 'If he's wrong again I'll have the skin off his back, Diego.'

'It's a clear day, *Capitán*. Hard to make a mistake now the sun's properly up.'

Diego Ugarte replied soothingly, sensitive to Ortega's brittle temper. He was a bluff man, bald as a bladder, but with heavy moustache and brows, he was also a capable officer, highly experienced at handling a ship and its kippage, which was why Luzon had insisted Ortega buy his services.

'No! He's tired. Bloody-minded about missing his sleep!'

'Marco Gines has keen eyes. I know him. He's a good man.' Ugarte turned suddenly to a loitering hand. He bellowed, 'You there! Lay up to the maintop. Find out what Gines is shouting about. Smartly now!'

Gines had been last of his watch to lay aloft when the *Concepción* had shortened sail. The boatswain had handed him the punishment rope and nodded at him phlegmatically; the hand had gone sullenly to the topmost ledge of the mainmast, seventy feet above the deck, and secured himself to the flagstaff, knowing that he must remain there without sleep for four and twenty hours, straining his eyes on the juncture of sea and sky, and understanding that if he should sight either ship or shore after the bowsprit lookout did he would feel a good Manila lash cut his back. Then, after twelve hours, and in the darkness, Gines had imagined a sail to leeward. His shout had brought men on deck and roused Ortega from his cabin.

'Yes, *Capitán*, Marco Gines is a good man.'

'That good man made fools of the entire watch last night,' Ortega said stiffly. He underlined his point, placing the flat of his hand deliberately on the mizzen fife rail before him. 'I *must* have my ship perform to the utmost limit, Diego. That means a disciplined crew. And a lesson for those who're slow to commands. You know this is no ordinary ship. We cannot afford slackness.'

Ugarte scratched his head. 'Yes, *Capitán*. Of course you're correct. I've never sailed any ship like this before.'

'No one has, Diego.'

Men were swarming on the main deck below. The hand Ugarte had sent aloft was cupping his mouth and shouting oaths in incomprehensible Galician.

Ortega felt his hopes surge. Then he, too, saw it.

At first he could not be sure, then his eye latched onto the grey speck. 'Make a signal to the Almirante,' he shouted. 'Unknown ship bearing north-west by north, two leagues.'

The flags ran up the signal halliards and drew a fast response from the *San Lorenzo*. Ortega exulted at the message: *plan red*.

Here, in mid-Atlantic, the water was a fathomless sapphire blue. Here was the chance to dye its transparent beauty with Protestant blood. This place where the sea was infinitely deep was surely a most fitting place to settle the blasted hulk of a corsair. He would send its arrogance plummeting for ever into the cold blackness that lay under all Neptune's oceans. God grant that she's a foreigner, he prayed. Ortega lifted his unsheathed sword and laid his right hand upon the crossbar of its basket hilt.

'God, the King, and Spain!' he said solemnly, as he pressed his lips to it once for each article of his faith. Down below, his officers did likewise.

Look at her, sniffing at us like a prowling wolf. Come on, *el Lobo*, let's see your teeth! She can't be Spanish – if she was she'd be shy of us because of the fines Seville'd impose as soon as she was identified as sailing without convoy. She can't be Portuguese, not here. Only a Protestant would be beating up towards home this far south, ignorant of the westerlies to be found to the north, unaware of the great three-knot current that carries a ship eastward and home. So my prayers are answered! She is a Protestant ship! Probably loaded with thieves' booty, and no doubt red-handed with the blood of Spanish settlers. Is she French or English? Too far to tell yet. Either way they're pirates. Either way they'll pay for their crimes now with their lives!

'Ready drogue on the larboard side,' he ordered tersely.

As the ship on the horizon steadily resolved itself into a three-masted square-rigger, a long cable was flaked out on the *Concepción*'s main deck, pails and butts and leaden weights were attached to it at intervals and the whole made ready to trail over the side from the cathead. It was an action the crew had practised often, and at which they were smoothly skilled.

Hidden from the enemy by the ship's side and sunk in the wake, the drogue would confuse the pirates. As it was paid out, it would drag, pulling the ship back. Already, Ortega felt the *Concepción*'s way falling off. The mast stays tautened and creaked, complaining at the extra resistance. The sea foamed at the bows and he felt the slight increase in the following wind ruffle the hair about his ears. Moments later he looked to see how much the remainder of the *flota* had pulled away. The *Concepción* was gradually falling back. A wounded animal limping after its herd.

'Let go the forecourse!' he shouted to the men on the sheets.

The clew lines that held the lower corners of the sail down and aft and allowed it to collect the wind were suddenly released. The effect was spectacular. It was as if the sail had blown out. It flapped out furiously, and crewmen were sent edging along the yard to begin reefing it up again.

Ortega watched the prowler carefully for a reaction. She seemed to edge a point or two to leeward. Yes, you God-defiling bastards, come closer. You see our sails straining to give us five knots and you imagine we're bursting our hearts to get away from the wolf!

'Run out stunsail booms and rig stunsails.'

Ugarte passed on the order urgently to the officers of the watch, knowing that the frantic activity aloft as the hands tried desperately to load more canvas onto the extremities of the straining yards would be seen by the stranger as a bid to outrun them. He ordered more drogue paid out to compensate. The other ships of the *flota*, now strung out half a league ahead and to larboard, were also rigging extra sail. Steadily they began to pull away. Escaping. Abandoning their weakest to the predator.

Still the lone ship approached, on an interception course, with no sign of her slackening. Her yards were braced round tightly so that the sails were hardly visible. No sign or device could be made out on them. Nor was there any jack or ensign. That *proved* she was a pirate.

Ortega watched the ship grow larger. As she came closer, her aspect changed, she showed less of her side, and he realised that the pirate planned to cross her bows and force her to broach. Then he'll come round abaft and run with us, stealing up on us with his better turn of speed. That's when the ultimatum'll come, he told himself savagely. And that's when they'll see they've cornered not a lamb, but a lion!

As the marauder came to within two cables' lengths, Ortega began to resolve the men aboard. They were heavily tanned, he saw, and a guncrew was clustered on the forecastle. He expected the forward-firing guns to loose a shot across their bows soon, and to hear the legendary hail of all oceanic highwaymen. Only then would he respond.

He turned to the boatswain. 'Is this end of the drogue weighted?'

'Yes, Captain.'

'Are you ready to cut free?'

'There's a man with an axe at the cathead, Captain.'

'Let go the instant I command.'

Below decks, on the orlop, fourteen demi-cannon were being charged with black powder and iron. All were breech-loaders that did not require to be run in and out after each firing. Their ports were masked by two long strakes of canvas, painted tawny brown like a ship's timbers and pierced by a pattern of small holes through which the gunners could judge their targets. Ortega knew that the numbers of men he had sent up and down the ratlines would have been enough to give the impression that the *Concepción* was commanded by an inexpert captain. The apparent chaos of her decks was carefully rehearsed.

Two shots from the pirate's forward falconets cracked out, pluming the waves on the starboard bow. The accuracy of the shots impressed Ortega and he saw Ugarte look away from him wordlessly. He knew that the man thought him reckless, and his tactics overly flamboyant, but for all his skill in ship handling Ugarte was at heart a shrinker from action. He could scent caution about the man like a bad smell.

The hands in the *Concepción*'s forecastle began to panic as the other vessel bore down on them. It looked like a certain collision. Some men scattered, others shook their fists defiantly. Then, at the last moment Ugarte ordered the rudder put hard over.

'Let go drogue!'

The *Concepción* broached. Wallowed in the swell. The pirate cut across their bows, open gun port after open gun port drawing a bead on their stem, frighteningly close. Every detail of her threatened under a bright sun as she circled. The gleaming muzzles of her armaments were run out and she could easily have loosed off a staggered broadside that would have blasted the bows of the *Concepción* to oblivion.

The sweat stood out on Ugarte's hairless head. He stared at Ortega, disbelief in his eyes.

'Shorten sail!'

'Captain! What are you thinking? Can't you see they have us at their mercy?'

'Shorten sail, damn you! And prepare to heave to.'

'Captain, please! For Christ's sake!'

But Ortega's attention was riveted on the pirate. Slowly she came around so that the ships were abeam separated by no more than a quarter of a cable – fifty paces.

'Closer, you bastard! Closer!'

Ugarte's complaint was doubled. 'Captain! Order the broadside, I beg of you! Before they come astern!'

Ortega's eyes were unseeing. His ears unhearing. The pirate was so close, undoubtedly coming astern – just as he had gambled.

'Captain!' Ugarte's voice was hoarse. He grabbed Ortega's arm, but he threw him off.

'Order the guns to fire before it's too late! Order them. Or I will!'

'No!'

Then the critical moment passed as their target moved out of the arc of fire. He could see the rings glinting on their fingers, in their ears, the enemy's faces burnt dark but originally fair. No Iberians these, but northern peoples. Of the three figures on the poop deck none was dressed in the raiment fit for a captain, but the foremost wore a dark green cross-belted seacoat trimmed with white lace and a broad-brimmed felt hat feathered with pheasant quills that tied under his golden beard. The man's lieutenant hailed from the other ship as she came about; the guttural order was sharp and uncompromising, delivered in dog-Spanish.

'What ship is that?'

Ortega replied immediately, his voice strong despite the tension in his belly. '*Santa Teresa de Avila*,' he lied, 'trader, out of Cadiz. I am Captain Martin Garcia de Onaz, carrying Fernando Torres y Portugal, Conde de Villar, to Mexico under the protection of His Imperial Majesty King Philip of Spain. Who have I the honour to address?'

Two small stern-chasers down near the waterline and a pair of *versos* – swivel guns – mounted high on the poop were all that the *Concepción* could train on the pirate now. In the terrifying silence the swell lapped against the ship and its sound filled the air. The rest of the *flota* had passed beyond sight and there was suddenly the immense oppression of being alone and friendless in the wilderness.

Inch by inch, the other ship moved across their stern and came round to windward so that her beakhead lay a pistol shot off their starboard quarter.

'For Jesus's sake, stand off from them. They'll see the canvas strakes,' Ugarte warned.

'They're not close enough.' Ortega gripped his courage in both fists.

'Look! They suspect something!'

Ortega wheeled on him, hissing. 'That's no man o'war. They're pirates! Greedy bandits who live on what they can catch. They want to take us, not destroy us.'

'What if they open fire and cripple us?'

'They want to take us as prize!' Ortega's voice raged at his subordinate. 'Damn you to hell! Where's your valour?'

Ugarte was suddenly sobered by the insult. He seemed to realise that his care had been seen as cowardice, and his jaw jutted. 'I'm only thinking of the ship, Captain.'

'Don't think. Just do as I tell you.'

Ortega's mind tried to bury the distraction. His heart hammered as he tried to bury the knowledge that the moment he had dreamed about had come upon him. Soon he would know whether he could afford the reckless luxury of point-blank range. And soon he would discover how the *Concepción* and her crew would behave in action.

'Come to me,' he whispered through gritted teeth.

Guns made of wood and hammered copper stood visibly unattended on the main deck, but all along the starboard gunwale, out of sight of the enemy, his men were crouched, rolling back sailcloth covers that had hidden a stock of pikes and primed muskets and heavy-bladed swords. Ortega watched the pirate ship slide inexorably into position.

Her captain would want to put her in the most threatening place he could – abeam and as close as possible, so that all his larboard guns were trained on the victim's waist. A pirate would trust to no code of honour. To him, the Consulate of the Seas would mean nothing; he would want to come alongside and send a boarding party swinging onto the *Concepción*'s decks to disarm all opposition before he came himself. To do so he would have to get into bed beside the *Concepción*.

Ortega heard indistinct orders being shouted aboard the pirate as she worked closer. What language was that? He saw that the chief of the rabble, the great gold-bearded brute, was so sure of himself he had scorned breastplate and helm. When the man put his hands to his mouth the same arrogant gruff hail rang out again in bad Spanish. 'Order your people to put down their weapons and stand back along the scuppers with their hands raised, *Capitán*. We're coming aboard. If you resist we'll blast you from the water.'

Yes! The swagger! The temerity! The unmistakable insouciance of the man. They were *Gabacho* scum, the same that had almost closed up the seaway to Flanders through the English Channel.

Ortega raised his hand. He closed one eye and with his thumb he mentally obliterated the mocking figure as he would a dung fly on a window pane. Down below, at the head of the orlop companionway, the gun captain raised his hand also, and when Ortega brought his arm sharply down the other did the same.

There was just enough time for the pirate to realise that it was not a sign of acknowledgement but an order to fire. Seven head-bursting explosions tore open the air between the ships. The *Concepción* shook under his footing and heeled as the recoils hammered her over. Momentarily, the hull of the pirate was obscured by billows of dense grey smoke over which her masts and yards thrust like the crosses on Calvary hill.

As the choking clouds began to clear, Ortega steeled himself against the reply, but none came. Furious shouts below told him that his own gun crews were reloading. Then his heart leapt as he saw the devastation they had wrought. The pirate's gun deck had been carried away. Instead of seven holes punched through the ship, the whole of her side between channel wale and waterline had been torn out. The upright members of her frame were like the ribcage of a blasted corpse, daylight spilling across the debris from the far side where human fragments and the wrecks of gun carriages lay hideously mingled. Water swirled into the bilges and a shout from his own deck told him that the pirate's mainmast was cracking and splintering, its footing shot away.

Before the echoes of the blast died his crew had begun screaming like berserkers. Transformed, they rushed forward, armed and lusting for the fight. Four-hooked grapnels were flung towards the enemy, some falling short, some lodging in rails all along the stricken ship. Teams of men on forecastle and quarterdeck were hauling their victim to quarters.

Ortega was suddenly filled with the sweet knowledge that whatever happened now he had carried the day. He turned to his men and raised his naked blade, shouting, 'Santiago! For King Philip and for Spain!'

A tremendous wail of answering war cries went up, and the assault began.

Ganging boards were slammed down from waist rail to waist rail and men poured across the narrowing gulf, or swung like jungle beasts from the yards, cutlasses clamped in their teeth. The cracks of arquebuses pocked the air and the pirate rabble were smashed back before they had time to regain their feet. Then the *Concepción*'s soldiers were bursting across the decks hacking and slashing, until the planks were awash with blood and strewn with convulsing bodies.

Some of the pirates bolted for rabbit holes, others found themselves cornered and leapt into the sea, still others swarmed into the tops, prepared to make a stand or crying pitifully for mercy. Ortega himself crossed with the second wave, cutting his way up the enemy's quarterdeck companion, towards a looked-for duel with her captain.

But he was too late. The man was dead, a lifeless mass of grey entrails looped out beside him, his lower jaw blasted off bloodily, and his shaggy blond beard with it, now raised aloft as trophy by a delighted arquebusier.

Ortega saw that battle had become rout; it was, he knew, the point when, if left unchecked, desperate courage soured to fanatical savagery. He cut it short, watching which of his men came down latest to his order. Such men, he knew, were always the cowards, the least obedient, those with the brittlest minds, men who needed most watching, and whom he would be rid of as soon as he might. He sent them off the listing deck, back aboard *Concepción*, sent the rest speedily below, to search out battened-down captives and whatever booty should be discovered before the gutted vessel sank.

In his magnificent cabin aboard the *San Lorenzo*, Don Francisco de Luzon laid aside his log feeling hugely gratified. Ortega had carried out his orders to the letter and demonstrated the power of the *Concepción* to lure sea thieves to their deaths. The single-minded courage of her Captain had been quite superb. Luzon felt certain that had he given the task to any other subordinate the execution would have lacked that particular edge of daring that was Juan Ortega's gift of rebirth. It's true, he thought, congratulating himself. The plucking of Ortega from disgrace had been a master stroke, and of course he had performed his duties with that special eagerness born of his difficult position. In another's hands the *Concepción* might have proved less than worthy, but the unfortunate pirate had met a man for whom there could be no release from torment, except through death or glory. Certainly, the value of such a man was impossible to overestimate.

Luzon was about to open his cabin door when he saw the crimson robe, and immediately his pleasure abated.

'My son,' the priest said, his voice rising questioningly. 'If I might beg a moment of your time.'

He was Don Pietro Moya de Contreres, a man of bird-like frailty whose face was pinched and unsmiling. On deck, in the sun and in sight of the men, he habitually wore the wide-brimmed hat of his Office, but in the gloom below there was only the pious skullcap which rode the back of his sparse grey hair like a monk's shaven pate. Contreres had come aboard with King Philip's blessing, bringing with him a trunk full of indulgences to sell. He had been appointed to carry his mission to the Indies, for the glory of God, to safeguard men's souls in the King's remote lands across the sea. Luzon knew his reputation and hated the cleric with such detestation it was hard for him to reply civilly. He managed to make his voice coolly formal. 'Don Pietro. All is well with you, I trust? Please, come in.'

The Admiral's cabin was luxuriously appointed. All the stern accommodation aboard the twelve-hundred-ton flagship was fit for the highest-ranking officers of the Empire, for their families and their extensive staffs. Every effort had been expended to see that the greatest convenience was provided for. In a voyage that would last two months, and which might be intolerably crude or confining to a landsman, a premium had been placed upon comfort. They dined upon the best silver. Wine was liberal and of good quality. Rich, gilded carvings embellished the quarter galleries and stern lights. And because the *regidors* who ventured westward upon the King's errands and the nuncios of the Holy See were notoriously unused to the pitching and heaving of a ship's decks, the beds were capacious and expensively appointed with mattresses stuffed with down plucked from the breasts of year-old geese. Even so, Don Pietro and his coterie of zealots had strayed from their quarters, accosted the mariners and interfered with the working of the ship.

Luzon went down on one knee, took the gloved hand, kissed the bloodstone in the Papal ring, crossed himself.

Uninvited, Don Pietro settled into the Admiral's chair, raising his fingers to decline a glass of wine. 'The heretics: how many are there?'

'Twenty-one.'

'Why have you had them brought on board your ship?'

Don Francisco politely put his knuckle to his lips and coughed, trying to conceal his resentment at being examined. Contreres was exceptionally skilled at asking questions. He obviously relished the sense of power it gave him. It's the same with all physically weak men, Luzon thought with sudden penetration. Don't they always try to compensate for their lack of stature or girth in other ways? And isn't it the sexually constrained who are the worst? Have you ever in your sixty years had a woman? he asked the old man silently, watching his soulless eyes search everywhere but his own. Never! And if you had, how would you have performed? I can see you as the novice you were forty years ago, white-faced and straining to shoot your seed into the belly of an abbey whore. It was over-zealous offal like you who drove Luther mad with your excesses and started the schism. Filthy-minded monks twisted tight with lust and perversion. Wasn't that the truth of it, for all their piety? Up against the marble pillars, or on a stone-cold tomb, guilty under God's all-seeing eye. Guilty of surrendering to the animal lust He gave you. Ah, I'd give plenty to know which heinous sins you committed when your celibate resolve faltered! Was it the father abbot's slavering mouth? Or the arses of castrati from the cathedral choir? Or perhaps you were the victim – the buggered runt of the seminary? That would explain the serpent of hate which writhes in your breast. There are many ways a man dies inside – what was it that snuffed out your humanity?

'These prisoners are my responsibility,' he said, keeping his voice neutral. 'They are French pirates and the law of the sea requires that I hang them.'

'Ah! But I asked you why they're on board the *San Lorenzo*. Why were they brought from the other ship?'

'Since it is by my authority that they will be executed, it is only proper that they be brought before me. I shall explain to them their crimes so they may repent of them before they die.'

Luzon made a final gesture that should have stopped further enquiry, but Don Pietro seemed suddenly alerted. He tried another tack.

'Of course, they are worthless scum, but they have souls. Is it not your duty to make their deaths sing a hymn of praise to our Lord? Are you not of the Faith?'

'I know my duty, Don Pietro. And my faith is my own affair.' He regretted that as soon as the words had left his lips.

The Inquisitor's eyes travelled slowly to his. 'No, Admiral. Your faith is my concern also.'

Luzon felt the muscles of his stomach knotting. He tried to deny it to himself, but realised that he was experiencing something he had not felt since he was a young man – a spasm of cold-blooded fear.

'The hangings will be witnessed by the men, Don Pietro,' he said guardedly.

'It has, quite naturally, occurred to you to execute them as a warning to others, but – correct me – you will hang them for *piracy*? That's an example to no one. Unless you suspect that there are those among your crew who are liable to turn pirate.'

Anger rose in Luzon. 'The crew of the *San Lorenzo* – all my crews – are loyal to the last man!'

The other smiled insipidly. 'Ah! Your loyalty to them is such a marvellous example. It is good that a soldier has faith in his subordinates. But you miss my point, for there is a much more glorious example to be made, a greater loyalty to be tested – to a principle much higher than obedience to King and country.'

Luzon's fists had bunched and he carefully relaxed them. He had divined the direction in which the priest's octopus words were leading, but he knew he had to oppose Don Pietro, to show him that here, at sea, the Admiral must be absolute master. Still, the strangling tentacles of the Holy Office were many. He must contain his impulses. It was madness, he knew, to gratuitously make an enemy of one of the Inquisition's most exalted and ruthless instruments.

It had been Don Pietro Moya de Contreres who on Trinity Sunday fifteen years ago had persuaded Inquisitor General Valdez to present the great *auto de fe* in Valladolid. There, the proud Francisco Herrero had died unrepentant. That day, Augustin Callaza had publicly forgiven the Holy Office their treatment of him, but he had burned nevertheless, screaming his sins to God and to the King who watched. And later, it had been Don Pietro who had instigated the huge *auto* in Seville in which seventy-six men and women had been paraded. In an act of supreme piety he had burned Leonor Gomez with her three daughters, and the quarrelsome prior of San Isidro who had dared speak out against him. And as his power grew, so his public spectacles had reached new heights of terror. At Malaga an imprisoned Jew had cut off his own penis in hope to deny the hellish priests their proof of circumcision and thereby save his pregnant wife. But they had found him guilty nevertheless and Don Pietro had burned him, then he had burned his wife at the very moment she gave birth so that all the people might see how deeply the Church despised those who had sent Jesus to the cross.

But for the past five years Don Pietro's particular speciality had been his fanatical obliteration of heresy in those foreign sailors who came into Spain. He had seen that this activity more than any other would bring him the reward of a grateful King. Thus, he had been promoted to the post which he craved. Don Pietro was to be the man who would extend and consolidate the policy of racial and spiritual purity. He would be responsible for stamping out the Lutheran curse in Spain's dominions; it was his pious dream to bring the Inquisition first into the Indies.

'Are you not of the Faith?' Don Pietro was asking. 'Do you not hope, as I do, to inculcate the Word of God in all men, however worthless, before they die?'

Luzon bowed his head humbly, feeling nothing but disgust and revulsion inside. 'In Jesus Christ alone do I hope. Him alone do I trust and adore, and placing my unworthy hand in his sacred side, I put my faith in his keeping.'

Don Pietro's words sharpened as he felt the resistance in Luzon. 'I ask you: shall we hang heretics as common criminals?'

'That is the law of the sea.'

'The law of the sea. And what of the law of God? That law says that heretics shall die by fire.'

Don Francisco felt the grip of the octopus tighten about his throat. With an effort he shrugged. 'It is a matter of practicality. We cannot burn men aboard ship, but we can hang them. Unless you would have me carry them into Mexico?'

'You are a commander, Don Francisco. You think like a man of action.' The priest's smile lingered, then suddenly his aspect changed and his tone grew subtle. 'I've heard reports of your gallantry in the great battle against the infidel. Did you not command a squadron under the pennant of the Marquis of Santa Cruz? And was it not your own galley that carried the green banner of Mecca from Ali Pasha's vessel? They say it was riddled with shot until its vile message was made unreadable, but that the azure standard, emblazoned with the figure of our Redeemer suffered no blemish, that not a crucifix in the whole fleet was touched by bolt or bullet, that not a single Muslim set foot upon any Spanish deck. When men do God's work righteously, they are protected and favoured. Are they not?'

Don Francisco stared into the bloody dregs of his wine, despising the priest even more as he remembered the horrifying truth of Lepanto. The Turk had been a fearsome enemy: when they took the island of Cyprus they had skinned the Christian garrison commander alive, stuffed his skin with straw and sent it as a trophy to Constantinople, and when news of the outrage had reached Madrid, Philip had been persuaded to act. The Christian fleet had surprised the Turks off the Gulf of Corinth, surprised them utterly.

With the enemy unprepared and in confusion, the battle had been over by mid-afternoon. The Turkish right and centre were smashed and routed. The remains of the left wing, under the Algerine Viceroy had struggled away – a mere thirty galleys, badly mauled, seeking the coast of Morea. The Ionian dusk had decayed that day over a scene of absolute devastation; the sick sea for miles around had been stained with blood and strewn with the broken bodies of ships, and of men. And through it all the boats of fanatical priests had plied with sword and halberd, chopping down the bobbing heads of the surviving enemy. When night settled, the ghastly flare of fifty burning ships had continued to illuminate the heaving carnage, sending tongues of flame towards heaven so that God's work could go on.

Luzon felt the tensions within him polarise. Maybe the priest's right, he thought with dread. Maybe my belief is failing. He knew suddenly why men clung to their faiths, for without faith the world was too terrible to contemplate, a chaos of evil, a catalogue of inexplicable atrocities. He remembered how his own victorious ships had made for the haven of Petala, where he, along with the other admirals, had received the grateful thanks of Don John. High Mass had been celebrated there by the Inquisitor, Geronimo Manrique, under a magnificent pavilion bedecked by the purple blooms of almond trees and accompanied by the blasts of battle trumpets and the chanting of monks, and at the raising of the Host each ship of the fleet had fired a triple salute. They had lost seven thousand men and more than twice that number

grievously wounded; the Turks had lost twenty-five thousand. Yet all
had believed in the same God.

Don Pietro's voice came to him, insistent and cold. 'The purpose of
the trial and execution of unbelievers is not to save the souls of the
accused, but to put fear into those who are witnesses.'

'I'll have no *auto de fe* on board my ship,' Luzon said, rising to his
feet. His words were hard and final. He had made his decision. The
next move was the priest's.

Don Pietro regarded him silently for a moment, then gathering his
robes he stood up.

'I shall pray that the Lord sees fit to alter your resolve, my son.'

He went to the cabin door and without turning back left the Admiral
alone with his choice.

The next day being Sunday, a compromise was agreed.

And the Inquisitor was allowed to address them, holding out before
him a great scroll with golden stoppers and great tassels flying in the
breeze, and it seemed to the Admiral that Don Pietro's eyes never once
strayed to the parchment, but roamed thirstily over the faces of those
upon whom he broadcast his words.

'Hear me, now ye faithful Christians, men and women, friars and
priests, officers of state and of His Majesty's ships, mariners and soldiers,
men of every condition, quality and degree, whose attention to this will
result in salvation in our Lord Jesus Christ.'

The day was calm, peaceful, with a sky full of mackerel cloud, rent
by silken banners. All the secular splendour of state was displayed
for the occasion, the entire complement of the *San Lorenzo* ranked
on deck. Three hundred lowly men stood in the waist in their tatters,
the *marineros* of the first class, and *grumetes* of the second. Above them
were fifty more in ascending rank, seated on the quarterdeck, and above
them all Don Francisco de Luzon, the *Admirante*. Five *Capitáns* from
the fleet's other ships flanked him, including Ortega and Sancho de
Aldana, the *San Lorenzo*'s Captain. Then came the *Gobernador*, commander of infantry, with his *Sargento Instructor* at his side and a line
of fully kitted soldiers. The ship's lesser officers dressed the forecastle:
the *Piloto*, the *Contramaestre*, or Boatswain, and ranked behind, his
craftsmen – Cooper, Carpenter and Caulker, Constable, Surgeon and
Gunner. Even the merchants and other passengers and the King's treasury officers with whom they dealt were assembled: the *Maestre de
Plata*, or silvermaster; the *Veedor*, or overseer; and the *Contador*, or
accountant.

Don Pietro's voice grew incisive. 'You are hereby warned to declare
and manifest the things you have seen and heard of any person or
persons, alive or dead, who has defamed or acted against the Holy
Catholic Faith; or who has cultivated or observed the filthy laws of
Moses or of the Mohammedan sect; or who has perpetrated any crime

of heresy. Do you know any who say that our Lord Jesus Christ was not the true Messiah promised in Scripture? Or the true God? Or Son of God? Have you heard any man or woman deny that He died to save the human race? Deny the resurrection and his ascension into heaven? Say that Our Lady the Virgin Mary was not the Mother of God? Or a virgin before the nativity and after? Or who say or affirm scandalous libels against the Inquisition or its officers? Or who assert that the Holy Sacrament of the altar is not the true body and blood of Jesus Christ? If you do then I command you to speak now!'

Twenty French prisoners were shackled in a miserable line below the quarterdeck. One had died of his wounds overnight and had been dispatched overboard before news of the death could be communicated to Don Pietro. Facing the Frenchmen now were God's own officers. There could be no denying the visible authority of these men: Don Pietro, their chief with his crimson robes; Felipe de Bovilla, his studious companion who carried the cross. It was he who had at one time controlled the Index of heretical books and had spent years examining the library of the Escorial itself. Luzon knew that Bovilla's obsession with Jewish *conversos* was total; he prayed that neither Ortega, nor any man, would be foolish enough to admit that their blood was tainted. Beside Bovilla sat Juan Sanchez, the Fiscal, and to his left Cristobal de los Rios, the Secretary. Both were cowled and sinister.

Luzon boiled with indignation. He had made a compromise, but he had not given permission for this. Don Pietro had agreed to the hanging, and in return for that concession he had asked to deliver his sermon, to address the men on the evils of heresy. Surely the Admiral could not deny the Holy Office that small thing? Even an Admiral who regarded the law of the sea above the law of God? Luzon had let the insult pass. Don Pietro might be beneath contempt, but he was also above the law.

Luzon watched the proceedings with an immobile face, unwilling still to focus the malign spite of Don Pietro's fanaticism on himself or his officers. That much he knew was expediency. But doubt raged in the private quarters of his mind. One part of him wanted to put an end to the foul priest, the other part was sure he was giving in to evil. Men must be punished for what they do, not for what they are, he told himself, and he replied, equally angrily, that surely what men did *made* them what they were.

No one moved, and Don Pietro lowered his scroll a little, growing more intimate with them, his gaze dwelling in turn on the officers and merchants.

'And if anyone here knows of any person, being children or grand-children of a heretic already condemned by this Inquisition, let him come forward. For those vile offspring are disqualified and may not make use of any office, or bear arms, or wear silk or fine cloth, or ornament themselves with silver or gold, stones or pearls.

'And is there a man here who knows of any once condemned person who now possesses confiscated or forbidden goods? Furniture or apparel, jewels or money? If so, come forward!'

This is outrageous! Luzon thought, suddenly awake to what was happening. The priest was delivering no sermon, he was conducting an exercise in terror. But still he did not move to intervene.

Now Don Pietro leaned back, angry with them. His shrill voice blasted them with threats now, rushing like a torrent.

'If you have knowledge and, after the period of grace, will not speak and still hold your heart obdurately, know that it is greatly to the burden and prejudice of your soul. You shall have incurred the sentence of excommunication, and you shall be proceeded against as an abetter of heresy. You shall be denounced, separated from the holy Mother Church and its sacraments, accursed of Almighty God, and of the glorious Virgin and of the beatified apostles, Saint Peter and Saint Paul. And upon your heads and houses shall be loosed the plagues and maledictions that fell upon Egypt, and upon the loathsome cities of Sodom and Gomorrah who perished in brimstone, and of Athan and Abiron which was swallowed up into the earth.

'Accursed be the man who abjures God! May he be afflicted in living and dying, in eating and drinking, in working and sleeping, and ever may his body suffer pain. May his days be evil and few. May his children be orphaned and his wife and chattels enjoyed by others. May his family ever be in need and may none help them. May they be turned out into the streets and trampled down to die in want. Accursed be they to Judah and to Lucifer and all the devils in hell!'

Don Pietro stared at them, filled with a holy power. He saw the seraphic light emanating from his hands and feet, felt the fear in the devils that capered before him. The Frenchmen were goaded back and forth at his command, dressed only in canvas bibs of bile yellow daubed with the cross and tied around the middle with rope. Their tall, conical hats were taken off and they were made to kneel down, bound, so that their heads might be shaved. Incense burners swung, perfuming the air. Holy water was cast over them as the Edict was read. Bovilla's liturgy rose shrill above the bowed heads before him, terrifying the captives who suffered it uncomprehendingly. Then his hand was thrust out and the crucifix pushed into each face so that each was turned away.

'Kiss the body of Christ!' Sanchez demanded in Latin each time.

The seamen stared at one another unable to understand.

'See how they spurn the Redeemer!'

The thuribles belched and fumed, the long crimson cassocks swirled, as the Inquisitors passed among the crew. Don Pietro raised the cross above the Spanish sailors now, reciting a list of heresies.

'Your Admiral's desire shall bring us into the New World in thirty days. Half that time shall be your period of grace. If you know, or have heard of, any Judaisers, who keep the law of Moses, who use no lights on Friday, who bleed their meat into water, or cut the throats of cattle and cover the blood with earth; or any who eat meat in Lent, or who turn to the wall to die; or any who speak the name of Luther, or who will not admit the changing of the substance of the bread and wine in the Eucharist into the Body and Blood of Christ – come forward! Which among you fall short of God's grace? Come out! Ah, yes! Which of you has evil thoughts? I promise you will not suffer serious penalty if you confess. Step forward! Come to Christ, I say!'

Luzon remained fixed in his chair, mesmerised by the mounting wrath of Don Pietro's oration. He wanted to act but he could not. He knew he must order the priest to stop but something powerful smothered his will, making him listen to the insistent words. Below him, the men's mouths dropped open as they contemplated the rapturous questions. Fear warred within their hearts but their souls were captured. Luzon raged inwardly as he watched his mariners wrestling with the terrible urge to confess. Then he felt his hatred rise up and burst the invisible bonds that held his own mind fast.

'Enough!'

'Confess! Do not wait for your brothers to denounce your crimes against God! Confess! And it will be the better for you!'

'Halt! I command you!'

'Confess! God is waiting!'

Don Pietro was deaf to the world. As he swept down onto the ship's main deck, the sailors fell back from him as if his satin skirts had been reddened by their own blood. He walked, sure of his power now, erect and bigger than he had been, hands joined before him in a pious steeple, until he was beside the longboat. The ecstasy flowed in him unstoppably as he approached the climax of his work. That morning he had convinced a boatswain's mate to do his bidding. He had suggested he must paint the boat's insides with pitch and gunpowder and sulphur and tallow and then replace the canvas rain cover to conceal what he had done.

Ah, yes! Look how they revere the Holy Spirit, the familiar voice said inside Don Pietro's mind. Their respect does them credit, but who can deny that all are lost to Christ? Tell them they are to witness the deaths of heretics.

He told them.

Tell them they have the chance to show God how they glory in the destruction of evil!

He told them.

They are simple men, and simple men are weak, prey to all manner of heresies. They must be helped to salvation, for the sake of their immortal souls, their demons flung out for the love of Christ, their hearts brought to God to reclaim them from Satan. Show them how the holy water burns!

He cast it over the Frenchmen.

'See how they shrink from the holy water! See how it eats their flesh!'

He stalked along the line of kneeling prisoners. They began to wail, imploring him for mercy in French, caught up in the horrifying power of the ritual, and as they showed their fear so the soldiers that held them increased their grip.

Ah! How their spirits cry out to me. How they repent their sins. Don't worry, my children. I will do what I can for you. I know how hard it is for you to fight the Devil without help. But I know suffering. Long have I fasted alone in my cell. I have spent the long years of my manhood in contemplation and self-mortification. Ah! I know how to fight Satan. I will be your guide. I will show you the pathway back to God. I remember each lost lamb whose soul I have saved, each one I have brought back to the fold. Though their bodies were infested by devils, have I purified them. Though their minds were corrupted, have I saved them!

He threw back the longboat covers, revealing the black combustibles within, and the stink of it swirled out, making men groan with understanding.

'Only the inviolate flame can destroy the evil within men,' he shouted. '*Nam verae voces tum demum pectore ab imo eliciuntur, et eripitur persona, manet res!*' – Not till then are the true words drawn up from the depths of the heart, the mask torn off and the truth exposed!

'Swing out the davits! Ready the boat!'

The order rang out from the boatswain's mate who had been induced to prepare the punishment. Three *marineros* ran to obey.

'*No!*' Luzon grabbed the arm of the first man and threw him back, his face contorted. To allow the captives to be cast adrift in the longboat and the noxious mixture flamed as this barbaric priest wanted was monstrous. He had had to stand up. Whatever the cost. Whatever the risk. He had *had* to.

'I will not allow it!'

Don Pietro turned on him. 'You cannot prevent the will of God!'

'This is not what we agreed!' Luzon shouted.

'Stay where you are!' Don Pietro's fingers clawed heaven. 'No man may interfere with God's intent. No man here will allow that!'

Luzon halted, a thousand eyes locked on him. His way was barred by his infantry captain. 'Suarez! Step aside! I order you! Diaz, you will prepare the halters! You there, Sergeant! You will hang the prisoners now! Move!'

No one flinched. The men's eyes flashed to the priest.

'Move I say! This is mutiny!'

'They will obey only the word of God! Take him!'

'No!'

For an interminable moment all was frozen in a terrible stalemate. Luzon saw that he had lost. He went for his sword, then the universe crashed sideways and he was carried off his feet.

The ship's deck had canted hard over, sending men toppling down or scrambling for a handhold. Overhead the sails spilled air and began to flap noisily as the *San Lorenzo*'s head swung crazily to starboard. The huge ship righted, then heeled again, her main deck dipping to the wave crests before she righted. Immediately, Luzon realised what had happened and he thanked God.

In the confusion, Ortega came from the shadows under the quarterdeck arch. He drew his sword and advanced on Suarez. 'Obey the Admiral – or I shall run you through, *señor*! The rest of you, get to your stations! Now!'

Instantly, the confusion of men in the waist threw off their doubts and dispersed, driven by the familiarity of orders and suddenly awakened from the terrifying spell that had been cast over them.

Luzon tried to order his thoughts, but his mind raced feverishly. He damned his own foolishness. Incredible how Don Pietro had spellbound everyone with his sorcery! And thank God that Ortega had had the strength of mind to grab the whipstaff from the helmsman and put the ship hard over. What a mistake I made! I was disobeyed by my own men. It was mutiny until Ortega slapped them back to their senses. The way the priest bent them all to his will was truly amazing. I felt it myself. Luzon's spine chilled at the thought. But how can I oppose him now? I can't placate him – the affront was too much for him to ignore. Jesus Christ, how can I stop him?

He seized his panicking thoughts and savagely bent them to the present. At all cost, the initiative Ortega had gained must not be lost.

'We must carry out the hangings immediately,' he told Ortega. 'The quicker, the better.'

He knew his authority depended on it. Fear spurred him, crept into his voice as he fired his orders to Aldana, the *San Lorenzo*'s Captain.

Hands swarmed up to the tops and out along the yards, their feet shifting like lightning in the stirrups as they brought the ship under control.

Luzon ordered that twenty nooses be slung from the mainyard and rigged through blocks and deadeyes to the larboard cathead where one of the *San Lorenzo*'s big, fluked anchors hung acockbill. The thick, hempen anchor cable was not rigged – there was no time for that – so it must mean the loss of the anchor, but Aldana did not hesitate. He ensured that the weight of the anchor was taken on a thin purchase rope that chafed as it was secured to the forward fife rail. Next, the Frenchmen were hauled to their feet and marshalled quickly into line. As the blindfolds were tied on their eyes some began to pray, others to defaecate.

Luzon searched out Don Pietro. The priest leaned drunkenly against the gunwale, his whole body wracked with a strange passion. His eyes were rolled up white and his lips curled back, flecked with foamy spittle. Luzon struggled to understand. It must be the vacant sickness, the same that afflicts those awakened from sleepwalking, he thought, horrified. Then Luzon saw what he must do.

He sent a man to dip the end of an axe handle in pitch and set it alight. Then he steeled himself, seized Don Pietro and shook him until the pupils of his eyes looked once more on the world.

'If God's law says that heretics shall die by fire, I'll not be the man to break that law!' But they shall hang all the same, he thought. 'Here! Take it! Execute them with your own hand!'

He closed his grip over the priest's fingers, and clamped them to the firebrand, holding it under the straining rope until the flame leapt onto the twisted hemp, charring its fibres black. Then the line parted, cracking like a bullwhip under the huge weight, and the anchor was falling.

Luzon heard it impact the water with a deep, smothered thud, then the pulley wheels were squealing in the blocks, the noose ropes tensing, and the pirates were jerked one after another off their heels and high into the air. They soared up for a sickening moment until their necks hit the blocks and were snapped.

Ortega watched the twisting bodies with disgust, he stared at the vacant eyes of the Inquisitor and knew that the Admiral had done his duty. Don Pietro was shaking, the hollow husk of the man who had addressed them minutes before. The Admiral had been magnificent: what courage it had taken to stand up to the Inquisitor at that moment!

'Have Captain Aldana cut them down,' Luzon told him, his voice infinitely weary now.

'Yes, Admiral.'

'And – thank you, Juan.'

'Suarez, take Don Pietro below and confine him to his cabin.'

'Sir.'

Ortega felt his glow of satisfaction fade. He saw that Luzon had pitted himself against an implacable enemy.

'What have we done?' he asked.

Luzon shook his head hopelessly. 'We have a devil by the tail, Juan.'

'Yes.'

'He's Satan's own henchman. What's to be done with him?'

'You've locked him in his quarters, sir.'

'But I can't keep him confined there for ever.'

'You'll have to, Admiral, at least until we reach Mexico.'

Luzon wiped his mouth, then he took his hand away and nodded. 'Yes, I can do no other. But then what? When we reach Vera Cruz I'll have to release him.'

Ortega swallowed hard. He knew well that the Inquisitor would covet revenge for his humiliation. The thought of the impeachment that could greet them when they returned to Spain turned his bowels to ice. He looked around him at the men who remained on deck; all were intensely occupied, working furiously at whatever tasks they could find. They had been scared by what they had witnessed.

'Did you see his eyes, Juan?'

'Yes. They were – unearthly.'

'He's mad. You know that?'

'Yes.'

The Admiral's voice dropped. 'Do you know what we should do?'

The terrible thought broke over Ortega like an ocean wave, followed by another, more sinister consideration. He blanched. 'Holy Mother, you can't mean that. Unless –'

'What is it?'

'I dare not say.'

'I order you to tell me what you're thinking.'

Ortega clasped his hands together as if in prayer. 'I asked myself what we would do if – if we discovered that Don Pietro was *possessed*.'

Luzon stared at him, unable to believe his ears. '*What?*'

'What if he requires exorcism?'

'Those are dangerous thoughts, Juan Hernando.'

Ortega seized his arm. 'Yes. But thoughts that explain a lot – and perhaps solve much more.'

Luzon's eyes widened as he began to understand the implications of Ortega's words.

'Think of it, Admiral. If the Chief Inquisitor is possessed by Satan.'

'Madonna! That's meddling with unspeakable things. Can you imagine the upheaval that must follow if it were to become known that so exalted a functionary of the Holy Office has been debauched by Lucifer's servants?'

'Precisely.'

'You're suggesting I make that *known*?'

'No! That would certainly destroy you.' Ortega's face was taut with anxious hope as he pressed his plan. 'But as a threat, what better lever can there be to control Don Pietro after he's put ashore? Tell him that if he seeks your downfall the price will be his own exposure. I'll back you. And I'll see to it that other witnesses do likewise. It's the only way to contain him.'

Luzon closed his eyes. When he opened them again he said, 'I agree. I'll put it to him just as you propose. Such a threat might deflect him – it might conceivably save our skins, but it won't contain him. He'll find some other way to slake his thirst for blood. And God help them all in Mexico if I succeed.'

Chapter 15

Maria saw the church and squeezed her father's hand. St Lucar of the Franciscans, she knew, had stood here since the days of Father Olmedo, the priest who had come with brave Cortés himself more than half a century ago. The white stucco walls were uneven where its porphyritic stones had been roughly mortared together, and above, the short tower cast no shadow at all because its walls sloped inward and the sun was almost directly overhead. Trellised blooms hung about it, brilliant climbers garlanded the leathery trees and aromatic shrubs loaded the air with their perfumes. St Lucar, her father had told her, had been built amid the ancient flower meadows where for hundreds of years the Aztec peoples had gathered decorations for their galas.

'Are you nervous, my daughter?' he asked her.

Maria nodded and searched out her father's hand. He was seated beside her in the carriage, watching the countryside pass by. She looked out also and sighed at the beauty of it. Bright sun had baked the road to dust under the horse's hooves but its rays were kept from her by the tasselled canopy which swung rhythmically on its canes. All about them was planted now with the bountiful *maguey*, and square yellow fields of maize stretched to the foothills of the Sierra Madre. She thought it a fitting landscape and knew that she had been right to insist on this place, and on a small gathering in the church, despite the proprieties of her mother.

How her father had been her strength! A quiet ally, persuasive and encouraging. He had swayed her mother and brought her round to see that this must be Maria's choice.

Don Bernal caught her looking at him. His kindly eyes strayed to her face and he grunted amiably.

'You haven't altered your mind, have you, Maria?' he asked with mock severity.

'No. I haven't altered my mind.'

'You have no regrets?'

'None, father.'

She thought of her brother's opposition, but banished it from her mind instantly.

'I hope your mother told you about constancy? I'm sure she did. They are her most precious words, treasured up in her heart for thirty years. She received them from her own mother's mouth – after it was found that a handsome but foolish young *caballero* called Bernal de Escovedo had begun to find her beauty irresistible. She has been a faithful adherent to those high principles ever since, even though the man she married never deserved such devotion.'

Maria protested at her father's modesty, dwelling on the sentiments her mother had passed to her in the quiet of her bedroom the night before.

'My dear little dove,' she had said, tears glinting in the corners of her eyes. 'Our Lord knows that you are our own flesh and blood, and it is my duty to instruct you as my mother earnestly charged me. Who else will tell you what it is becoming for you to do and what to avoid? Neither must you forget the things your father has told you, since they are all wise and most precious, but there are things no man can tell you.' She had drawn closer then, enfolding Maria's hands with her own as if in prayer. 'Listen, my daughter: in this world, it is necessary to live with much prudence and circumspection. You must treat your husband with respect at all times, then he will respect you. Do not cross him in manly matters, or he will secretly despise you, and when the day comes to ask of him that which you desire he will spurn you. Beware that in no wise should you commit the treason against him called adultery.

'My dear daughter, whom I tenderly love, see that you live in the world in peace and tranquillity and contentment all the days of your life. See that you disgrace not yourself, that you stain not your honour, nor pollute the lustre and fame of your ancestors. And though I remember the day when your husband-to-be first came here and I would not have him enter our house, I now bless you both, so that God may prosper you and your marriage.'

The grove of trees parted as the carriage came round the last bend of the road. She felt a fluttering within her as she heard the first notes of her prothalamion being sung, growing louder as she neared the church. What will the Viceroy say when he finds that he has not been consulted? she asked herself. Don Emilio's permission was not sought, even though protocol demanded it. Gonzalo did not take the announcement well, nor after that the oath his father had demanded of him.

A small knot of women were gathered at the door, maids and servants. Beyond them, was a group of labourers, who knelt and bared their heads as they dismounted, staring at the fine lace wedding dress she wore.

Her father led her on his arm to the door. Inside, light filtered sparingly through splinters of coloured glass, staining the stone floor with the blurred images of saints. It was cool and clean, Spartan after the flowers. She looked to her mother and searched her face, saw that Gonzalo was not beside her. Then she was filled with reverence as she gazed upon the great gold cross. She walked the aisle and stood before God and his priest and smelled the incense and tasted the Body of Christ and His Blood in her mouth, and the minutes were strung out like pearls, hardly passing.

'On this Michaelmas Sunday, in this Year of our Redemption, one thousand five hundred and seventy-two, in the church of San Lucar of the Franciscan Order, we receive Maria de Escovedo, daughter of Don Bernal de Escovedo and Margarita, his wife; and Juan de Tordesillas, son of unknown parents.'

Maria repeated the words of devotion with solemnity beside the man who had come into her life and won her and who had taken the Faith for her, so he could be her husband. Lord Jesus know that Juan truly believes now, she prayed. Lord, may you destroy me if I lie, if he lies. And I know he loves me as much as a man ever loved a woman. When my father came to him with thanks for his life after the struggle on the fiery mountain he offered him his pledge. 'What shall I grant you?' he asked. 'You have but to name it.' Lord, I watched him playfully appraise Don Bernal's favourite horse; I saw the smile on his lips as he stole a glance at me. He must have seen the expectation in my face. And then he boldly said, 'I ask only permission to marry, for there is one whom I would wed.' And my father, who is a good man, nodded and drew himself up. 'One life for another? That is fair and just. But will this one that you desire return your love?' Juan looked to me then, Lord, and he said, 'Yes, Don Bernal. I can say that.' He was right, Sweet Jesus. Please hear me! Whatever he may have done in the past, he is not a Protestant now. He truly believes. And I love him.

The church was completely silent as the vows were asked of them. He promised to cherish her and she him, come what may in life and unto death. Juan, her husband. Maria, his wife. The witnesses were hushed, but into the silence the sounds of a hundred horses galloping closer rose, drowning the priest's words as he began to speak again.

'*In nomine patris, et filii, et spiritus sancti.*'

He placed a band of gold on each successive finger of her heart-side hand, removing it each time, then he slid it tenderly on to her third finger.

'I, Juan, give my body unto you, Maria, as your loyal husband.'

'I receive it. I, Maria, give my body unto you, Juan.'

'I receive it.'

The friar placed his hand over theirs, which were entwined, making the sign of the cross. 'I join you in marriage in the name of the Father, the Son and the Holy Ghost.'

She looked at him as if for the first time and saw that his face was filled with adoration. Unveiled, she had taken his ring, the token of a man and a woman joined, and the priest had said, 'God has made thee man and wife, let no man divide thee.'

He kissed her, his eyes full of colours, so that she caught her breath.

The tumult outside the church grew louder. The clangour of war gear and shouted orders and the clattering hooves of horses. She turned, and saw her husband turn also. Then the doors of the church flew open and in the glare the plain aisle flooded with unstained sunlight. Outside, her brother, proud and armoured – Gonzalo at the head of two ranks of armed men. All heads turned; the priest raised his hand and man and wife walked hand in hand toward the light, sure and unafraid, for what God had joined no man could now unjoin.

Don Bernal shaded his eyes, rising from his contemplation, and in the brightness sharp rapiers sang from fifty scabbards and were raised. Then a volley of shots rang out. And they went in procession, followed by their pages, by Don Bernal and his wife, walking the gauntlet of soldiers which Gonzalo had brought from the Viceroy to salute them to their marriage bed.

He warned Esteban to stand back, remembering that terrible day in his first year at Samuel Stanton's foundry in the Weald when the old iron smelting chamber had split open and molten metal had spewed out over Old Ned, the blacksmith's drudge, and killed him.

With so many people gathered here now, Tavistock had roped off a space ten feet around the casting pit but there were few who could bear to stand closer. The furnace was roaring white-hot now, the boys pumping the bellows furiously like black devils working the organ of the Antichrist's cathedral in Hell. The heat was intense, rushing from the open maw of the firebox as its heavy door swung open periodically. And above it the great fire-blackened vessel of molten brass stewed evilly, its surface scum being skimmed away by a long wooden pole, charred at its tip, flaming each time it touched the incandescent mass. Cristobal, the slave who wielded it, wore a thick leather apron that reached below his knees, a leather helmet with flaps that covered his neck and ears, and massive gauntlets.

'Everything is almost ready,' Tavistock announced with satisfaction, walking back towards the assembled dignitaries. It was the same in all the foundries of Christendom when grand ordnance was cast. As the climactic moment arrived, the pace of work heightened, illustrious visitors were invited and the pouring was done with great ceremony. Necessary witnesses were those connected with the factory, the purchasing authority and the state. It was a tradition that Don Bernal insisted must be observed.

Tavistock paused appreciatively, enjoying one of the few moments when his attention was not demanded by some practicality. The aldermen and councillors of the municipality were here in full uniform. The *Alcalde* of Chalco had honoured him, the friars and priests of San Clemente and Santa Barbara flanked the Bishop in his regalia, and the

Adelantando and his captains representing the military, resplendent in their armour. Even the local *Oidor* and the secretaries of his legal bench had come to enjoy the occasion and the lavish entertainment that was to follow. It was an opportunity too good to miss to be seen to be in the company of the Viceroy.

Don Emilio himself stood on the raised gallery that had been built for the most important visitors; Don Bernal and Gonzalo were both at his side. They gazed up at the heavy timber frame that stood idle now above the buried moulds, and down at the furnace. Maria waited proudly with the ladies, the wives and mothers and young children, close to the big barn doorway, away from the filth and the heat and the danger of explosion. He saw Margarita there, engaging the formidable Doña Isabella in conversation and pointing to the Viceroy.

Tavistock was being questioned closely by the military men. He explained how the pit had been dug out, how the six biggest moulds – those of the culverins – had been lowered in one by one from the massive blocks that hung from the frame. They were placed vertically, he said, not too close to one another, muzzles uppermost, and their lower ends bedded in sand. Then they had lowered in moulds for the culverin bastard and three demi-culverins, this time further from the tapping point, then filled the pit higher, and finally they had made up the rest of the space with a variety of lighter pieces, mostly falconets and sakers, so that twenty moulds were buried up to their filler heads. Six men had spent the morning tamping the earth down with stamps, not too tightly, and Tavistock had supervised, dampening the earth with pails of fresh water at intervals, but sparingly, so that not too much moisture was allowed to seep in around the carefully dried moulds.

'Of course, the top of the pit slopes this way,' he told them, sweeping his hand across it and shouting up at the Viceroy's party. 'At its highest it must be lower than the tapping hole so that the liquid metal can be poured off from the reservoir, and lower still as the distance from the tapping hole increases. The brass will come from this gate here, and flow along these clay channels. You can see the way they branch. Each branch leads to its own individual gun barrel.'

'What's that man doing?' the Viceroy asked, indicating the helper who stood on top of the pit. He was delicately chasing fine ash from the channels with a horsehair brush and a small pair of bellows.

'Two hours ago the channels were heated to drive off water, Excellency. His responsibility is to do this by means of small charcoal fires in each section along which the brass will flow. He's simply removing the last traces of that charcoal ash. Remember that molten brass will pick up any dirt it encounters as it runs along. If this is carried into the mould it will weaken the barrel.'

'Ah! And these small gates you've placed in each channel?'

Gonzalo answered, 'If you will permit me, Excellency. As the brass begins to solidify the gates will be closed so that the metal in the mould is not continuous with that which remains in the channel.'

'Of course. Yes. I see that.'

'Excuse me, Excellency,' Tavistock shouted up. 'All is ready. With your permission I'll begin the pour now.'

He climbed the ladder swung up onto the top of the pit, donning his gloves. He was tired. For the past day and night he had been on his feet unceasingly, weighing the metal with which to charge the melt. And his obsession with secrecy in this had driven him to hide his procedures, especially from Esteban.

At first, the mixing of quantities had been a problem, so ingrained had the English weights become in his mind during his own apprenticeship. He had laboriously learned from his men the Spanish equivalents – the *peso*, or sixth of an ounce, which was slightly more than an English ounce. Sixteen *onzas* made a Spanish pound, or *libra*, and twenty-five libras were one *arroba*. A quintal was four *arrobas*.

'The proportions of metal in the mix are fundamentally important,' he had patiently explained to Esteban, who had struggled to calculate the volume of the moulds using the Spanish *azumbre* and *cantara*. 'Above all there is the secret of the alloy. That's essential. We must get it right.'

And Esteban's openness had betrayed him again. His eyes had gleamed and his lips pursed. Someone – Gonzalo, Tavistock guessed – had charged him with learning that key secret especially. But Esteban was a poor spy because he had become a good friend; he had helped him build the foundry, he had been the man who had stood at his shoulder at his marriage, and Tavistock had asked himself, how can I lie to him?

So far he had given Esteban all details freely and without deceit. But these were techniques already well known to Spaniards, and to Flemings, and even to certain Italians. The alloy secret was different. It was what lay at the heart of the cannon's great strength, what permitted a greater charge of powder to be used, what permitted greater accuracy when the bore was reamed, and, ultimately, what lengthened the effective range of the gun.

The problem had kept him turning in his bed, knowing that soon he would have to divulge his secret to the enemy. But then he had realised his error. Where was this enemy? No man who worked for him was his enemy. The household of the *encomienda* were, none of them, his enemy. His new family? How could they be his enemy? Even cold Gonzalo and the haughty Viceroy were simply acting as functionaries of the state. All their moves had been sanctioned and prescribed by circumstance. It had been their duty to imprison him and the others. And afterwards, had they not shown incredible clemency to mere Protestants?

The Viceroy had been right: John Hawkins had been guilty of breaking the laws of the sea. He had deliberately provoked the Spanish who, in truth, were the conquerors of this land and had the right to use it as they pleased. Who did the English think they were to interfere?

'What's the matter, Juan?' Maria had asked him tenderly that night as they lay in their bed. 'Is the heat keeping you awake?'

He had sighed. 'That and an unquiet mind.'

'Perhaps I can help.'

'Perhaps.'

And he had told her and she had listened, and all the while he had remembered Job Hortop's stubborn and suspicious mind and his accusations, and he had asked himself what kind of man could keep himself so stiffly aloof and spurn the hand of friendship as consistently as Hortop had done. Only a barbarous Englishman, a stupid, stolid Saxon peasant with legs rooted like tree trunks in his own Lincolnshire earth. Without refinement, without music in his language, or light in his soul, contemptuously damning all things foreign.

In England there lay a deep and dark and brooding spirit which held on to its people and never, never let go. Left to itself it slept, but once stirred up it awoke and roared forth with ferocity. Yet it was subtle also. And invisible. It cast no sensible shadow. He had only seen it because he had been plucked from England and all things English, and by chance had come to see as an outsider sees. No wonder the Spanish spoke of the English as they did, as men possessed by cold, cunning, single-minded demons.

The insight had chilled his heart. There was something awesome about that knowledge, and he wondered how much of the dark spirit was dormant within him. He watched Maria: the night's blue-blackness fired her hair, the silken surface of her body was dark and magnificently arousing against the white sheet on which she lay. He felt himself harden, as he told her, 'Do you know that if Englishmen see a comely foreigner they will not say, "He is fine of face and handsome", rather they say "Does he not look English?"'

She had laughed at that.

'And are there many handsome men in England? Doña Isabella told me that the English are all ugly, like pigs. But you are English, and you are quite the most beautiful man I have ever seen.'

'I was English. And your eyes are lover's eyes.' He kissed her forehead. 'In England there are many lumpish people, ignorant people, ready to hang a man on an instant. The subjects of Her Majesty are far from pure, far from blameless.'

'It is the same in all countries.'

He placed his hand flat on her stomach, his fingers splayed, his touch infinitely soft. 'Since we married, I have wondered many times how it might have been for a Spanish crew cast upon an English strand. I do not doubt that, had I been a Spaniard and arrested in Plymouth or Dover, I would now be dead.' She placed her hand over his, and he lightened his words. 'Foul stories were common coin in the latter days of my life in England – that Spanish men had forked tails which they kept hidden in their breeches, and Spanish women possessed two cony holes, side by side.'

Maria's teeth showed white in a smile.

'They truly think that?'

'It's hard to believe, but yes they do.'

He held her for a long moment then, watching the fireflies dance in the garland of jasmine flowers that surrounded their window. The air was heavy with fragrance and filled with the high-pitched sound of frogs singing in the ditches. Then they made love, unhurriedly, until the bed was damp with their sweat, and the mosquito shroud tangled.

Afterwards, they had lain together until their hearts stopped hammering, and he had told her what really troubled him.

'Surely you can still make working guns without the ingredients that are so special?' she had asked at last.

'Yes.'

'Then, do so. Give Don Emilio adequate guns, but deny him magnificent guns.'

He had sighed. 'I cannot. Because I love my profession. I have my pride invested there. And I owe it my best.'

'You feel you must live up to that art?'

'Yes, I do. But the masters who trusted it to me – and who therefore saved my life – are Englishmen. It would be a sin to betray them. To give their secrets away would break the oath I swore when first admitted to the guild. I cannot do it.'

She thought for a moment, then said, 'I know a way.'

He lay back, smiling at her words; it was as if she thought there could be a simple solution. 'If you do, then tell me.'

'Your art was learned in another life, an old life. And in that life you were true to it. But now you have a new life, in a new world. You must be true to that also. Tell no one how to make the special metal, *but make it all the same*. Order many ingredients that you do not need as a blind, use sleight of hand. Cover your actions. That way you will make your fine guns, but the secret you will have kept.'

He had made up his mind then, giving in to his vanity. They would be *superb* guns! The best he could make. Nine parts copper to one of tin for the base. Three pounds of lead to the hundred to lower the melting point and to ensure a smooth pour with fewer bubbles in the cast. Latten – an alloy of copper and zinc – to bind and give the metal a better colour: four and a half pounds to the hundred. Lastly, three silver coins: one for himself, one for the gunner, and one for the souls of the men who would die. Only this time he would add a fourth, a golden peso, for Maria. And the guns would bear his name and no one would know but him how it was done, and when asked how, he would lie.

Yes, he was tired, he decided as he stood on the casting pit. Tired, but only through lack of sleep, and this was the great moment he had been waiting for, the one he had anticipated in his dreams for five strange, difficult, rewarding years. A buzz of delighted expectation tingled in him.

The furnace was ready, its top freshly skimmed, its temperature exactly stabilised. The watchers waited as smoke belched up into the rafters and found its way out through the vents at the peak of the roof. Tavistock picked up a long iron rod and burst the taphole open, driving the plug inward. When he withdrew the conical tip, a gush of golden light and heat, liquid metal, radiant like the sun itself, poured into the channel and flowed, splitting at each branch into three, four, then five incandescent streams. He stepped over it as it poured, raising the iron blades that dammed the mouths of the filler heads, and he saw how the smooth flow reached the spue holes and disappeared down into the five big culverin moulds. They drank lustily like babes at suck.

It had been a long time since he had done this, and never had he supervised a pour alone, but his skill had not deserted him. The feelings that steered his actions were sure. He chose the right moment to close off the flow and redirect it by opening more of the channel to the molten brass. More bright rivulets branched off, this time to the medium-sized cannons, then again to the smaller pieces, and finally the excess metal poured away to clay gutters at the end of the feeding channel to solidify and be broken up for use next time the furnace was charged.

As the glowing metal reddened, its vitality spent, he looked up and saw a hundred faces looking on, silent and engrossed, so he held his hands out to them, like a showman might, and there was applause.

The furnace fire was raked out and soused. At the sight of the billowing steam people emptied from the foundry and into the courtyard where tables had been set up.

Gonzalo walked with him. 'His Excellency is anxious to see the guns perform. When may I tell him they will be ready?'

'It's difficult to say until more work has been done.'

'You know that he's losing patience. The fortifications at Vera Cruz and Tampico are nearing completion. Of course, we have salvaged three more of the guns from the English wreck, but a large battery is planned.'

'I hope our new culverins will soon be ready.'

Gonzalo nodded shortly. 'Good. It is Don Emilio's hope that he may have the guns in place at Vera Cruz in time to protect the next *flota* in September.'

'Protect it from whom?'

Gonzalo seemed surprised at the question. 'From pirates, of course. English pirates.'

A week later, Tavistock prepared to meet Don Bernal and the Viceroy at the proving ground. A dozen sturdy gun carriages were lined up along the wall. Before them the newly mounted barrel of the *Jesus*'s culverin recovered from Vera Cruz, tarnished bright green and still with the

marks where undersea growths had formed on it, and the rope marks
where it had been hauled across half a continent. The sight of this piece
of the *Jesus* turned his thoughts again towards his brother. He touched
the boss of the cast Tudor rose with his fingertips, felt the milky green
roughness imparted by the sea to the place he had once polished as
bright as a looking glass. He sensed that Richard was alive. So where
was he now? Could he be one of the pirates prowling the Caribbean of
which Gonzalo had spoken?

He tried to put the painful thought away, but he knew that if Richard
had survived he would surely come back to the Indies. Strange that he
should feel this anxious excitement; there had been a great sense of loss
at their parting, perhaps this was its counterpart at Richard's return.
He considered Gonzalo's words for the fiftieth time, then he examined
his feelings and saw a greater deception.

'It's because I am changed now,' he said aloud, feeling afraid at the
traces of regret that came with the declaration. Anger stiffened him. Go
home, *hermano*, he said silently. For the brother you once had is long
since dead and buried. This is my home now. I am a new man. A married
man. Reborn. And of the other there is no trace remaining.

Beside him, his carpenters worked amid curls of wood planings
and sawdust, making more heavy mounts. They whispered anxiously,
wondering at the illustrious party that had arrived, and laying bets on
the performance of the culverins. The guns had solidified in the hot
earth of the pit, then the filthy work of digging them out had been done.

'José, Diego, Cristobal – you must take off the iron staves and
break the clay moulds open, and take out the cores,' he had told his
foundrymen the day after the pouring. 'Then, if everything is satisfactory
at my inspection, Juan-Baptista, Raul and Salazar – you'll saw off the
feeding heads. For the largest guns that will take a day and a half's
continuous work. You'll work in teams of two until the job is done.'

'Then we'll be ready to ream the barrels?' Esteban had asked.

'Yes! And be careful to collect up the metal you remove. We shall
waste nothing.'

He had checked each gun carefully to see that the cores had remained
straight during casting, and he had supervised the mounting of each one
in the great vertical boring engine. Then he had set the hard steel tools
that would cut out the bore, each barrel descending fraction by fraction,
under its own weight on to the cutting tool. The tool, geared to a
treadmill, was forced round thousands of times until, twelve hours later,
the bore was completely reamed.

'We must remove precisely the right amount of metal to accommodate
the windage,' he had explained, placing calipers across the diameter of
the iron ball. 'A bore one quarter inch greater than the shot is ideal.'

'What is this "inch", *patron*?'

'I'm sorry, Cristobal,' he had corrected himself. 'This much. See.'

Then he had checked again before polishing, with a 'searcher' – a small candle mounted on a rod, a shard of mirror glass on another, pushed down all the way, peering minutely, searching for the tiniest cavities in the metal. He had worked meticulously over the five great culverins, his apprentices following him on the smaller pieces, and he had seen them grow jealous of the size of the guns they were given to work on. He had smiled inwardly at that, for this was how it should be. They had learned that the esteem of the master and his trust in them was thereby expressed, and to them all his praise was of the highest importance.

Next he had shown Miguel de Caravantes how to drill the vent – a hole narrower than his little finger that would connect with the chamber. It was the means by which the charge was ignited on firing. He specified that each be tilted back towards the cascabel at seventy-five degrees, the most convenient angle for the gunner.

Esteban had come to him full of woes. 'We'll never be ready in time!'

'Don't worry.'

'I'm not worrying!'

'We'll soon be finished.'

'But we have yet to prove the guns, Juan!' Esteban shook his head.

'Leave that to me. We can't prove an unfinished gun,' he had replied with satisfaction, polishing the best of his guns on its elegant snout.

'She's perfect now! Perfect! What more can there be? Don Bernal demands that we are ready before the Viceroy comes here again on Friday, the agreed day. He says Don Emilio's patience is at an end.'

'One thing remains.'

'Not a big thing, please God?' Esteban had said, resigned to the fact that the gun making would never end.

'The most important thing of all.'

And that afternoon he had done it, proudly incising the maker's name, *Juan de Tordesillas*, on every base ring.

Now, four of the five big guns were laid out on the patch of ground that had been apportioned to him as his proving butts. Each barrel was a masterpiece of polished brass weighing five and a half thousand pounds, each was canted up on timber sleepers so that their muzzles were just above their breeches. The fourth gun, the best of them, was in its mount, charged and ready, standing beside the culverin from the *Jesus of Lübeck*.

Don Bernal met the Viceroy in the courtyard and they walked towards the butts together with a dozen stern-faced officers of the Viceregal Guard who followed Gonzalo. When Tavistock asked them to inspect the unmounted guns, Don Emilio's irritation overflowed. 'How long before the guns may be fired?'

'In due course, Excellency.'

'Answer my question precisely.'

Tavistock felt an unexpected shaft of anger at the Viceroy's impatience. Yes, he thought darkly. There's much more to gun making

than you first allowed when you brought me here. Much more. But you'll not hurry me, and I'll give you what I promised you and more.
'I beg your pardon, Excellency. I can discharge the guns immediately if you wish.'

Don Bernal intervened. 'Please, Don Emilio, if I may explain –' He raised a placating hand, outlining a timber target that had been erected a mile away. It was in the form of a three-masted ship.

'You intend to fire on those targets?' Don Emilio asked, screwing up his eyes. It seemed to Tavistock that the Viceroy was unable to believe that the guns could reach that far, much less hit the target.

'When first I came here, Don Bernal asked me to demonstrate the power of my best gun and to compare it with the gun from the *Jesus* in a straight contest. In those days he believed he could not trust me to render my best skills to His Majesty's service.'

Don Emilio's sidelong glance was condescending. 'Let us hope his doubts were groundless.'

Gonzalo regarded the mounted culverin appraisingly. 'The weapon seems impressive, Excellency.'

'It is,' Tavistock agreed.

'Perhaps we should proceed.' Don Bernal moved to the Viceroy's side.

He grunted. 'Yes, demonstrate the guns. Show us that your skill is all you claim, Englishman.'

Tavistock smiled briskly, unsettled by the Viceroy's manner. The way he had called him 'Englishman' had been deliberate, and he was clearly preoccupied with some weighty matter. That made him dangerous.

'Before I demonstrate the guns may I ask you all to retire to safety.'

Don Emilio looked about him. 'Safety?'

'It is usually unwise to stand too close to unproven guns, Excellency.'

'Unproven guns? I expected them to be ready. Today. Now.'

'So they are, Excellency. Ready to prove. As you can see, the guns have not yet been fired. I thought it best to –'

'You thought to wait until I arrived?' The Viceroy's manner froze still harder.

'It is customary in England to show proof that the ordnance is fit.'

'I see.'

Tavistock indicated the barrier that had been erected fifty paces away. 'May I request that your distinguished party retires to the rope?'

Gonzalo began to lead his officers to the rear, but stopped when he saw the Viceroy was not moving.

'You will come too.'

'I cannot.' Tavistock made a gesture of apology. 'I made the guns. It is I who must test them.'

The Viceroy laced his arms together. His suspicions were aroused and he watched Tavistock like a falcon watches a rabbit. 'Then we shall stand with you.'

'That will not be practical –'

'I said, we shall stand with you.'

Tavistock blew out a breath. 'As you wish, Excellency.'

Gonzalo and the others began to gather again uncertainly, their hat plumes bobbing as they looked to their chief with sidelong glances, detecting the mistrust in him. Finally Don Emilio said, 'You seem ill at ease, Englishman. Explain to me the real reason why we should not stand here. Why are you so unhappy?'

Tavistock's pride overcame him, but he trod warily, facing the Viceroy with coolness. 'I have faith enough in my own skill. I can assure you that *in service* these guns will perform properly.'

'Then why suggest that we retire? Do you think me afraid?' Don Emilio looked to his officers imperiously.

Tavistock stared at the earth. 'Of course not, Excellency.'

'Tell me: have you made unsound guns? Are they unsafe?'

'It is merely that a gun, any gun, no matter how well wrought, may have vugs in the metal – unrevealed cavities that have not been seen. They may weaken the structure sufficiently so that it explodes when first fired.' Tavistock blew on the smouldering stub of his match. 'And, were it not for one small fact, I would welcome your standing beside me as I touch the match to the vent.'

'One small fact?'

'I've made up good black powder, corned and granulated in the English way. The guns are proof charged with an amount of powder equal in weight to the ball, whereas a normal charge is only two-thirds the weight of the ball. Consequently, if there is any weakness it will show on this first firing.'

Don Emilio looked at the weapon with new respect. His certainty had deserted him, and Tavistock enjoyed the moment. He allowed a slight smile to play over his face as he explained quietly, 'If we stood here, and the gun failed on proof, it would turn us all nicely into butcher's offal, Excellency.'

The Viceroy's response was sharp. He barked an order to Gonzalo, who ran up and came to attention before him, then he turned back to Tavistock. 'I have made it plain to you that your function is to manufacture guns for my batteries. How dare you jeopardise your life unnecessarily? This man will prove the gun.'

'But, Your Excellency, it is my duty –'

'Silence! Your duty is to do as I order!'

Tavistock made a gesture of concession. The blood had drained from Gonzalo's face. He turned and saw the gun crew regarding him with little respect.

'Gonzalo is not a skilled naval gunner.'

The Viceroy rounded on him furiously. 'Guns are guns! Tell him what to do.'

Tavistock's eyes were fixed on the Viceroy's own. Then he shook his head slowly, almost insolently. 'I must apologise humbly, Excellency, but I cannot allow Gonzalo to prove my gun.'

Don Emilio's anger grew. 'You will do as I say.'

'With respect, Excellency, I will not. I must be sure that God intends Spain to have my skills.'

The Viceroy halted, bottled his threat, seeing suddenly that nothing he said could counter Tavistock's logic. 'Very well. Retire.'

Tavistock watched them go, feeling the sweetness of his victory as they trooped behind the rope. His crew buzzed with anxiety but he calmed them, saying nothing about the extra quarter of powder that only he knew had been loaded into the new gun. He motioned his crew away to safety, spitting the dryness from his mouth. All he had told the Viceroy was true, all but one detail. There could be faults. His life was hostage to that, to his skill and his conviction, as was only right. Then why had he lied about the charge? Why had he added an extra quarter of powder, over and above his proof limit? It was a reckless, foolhardy action. Had some part of him secretly wanted to goad the Viceroy to stand here beside him and blow them both to hellfire? No. It would have been very easy to have manipulated the man's dignity to that end.

Then what was it? And why, when the Viceroy had retired, had he felt a sweat come upon him? He knew suddenly that the extra quarter of powder was enough to carry the experiment beyond any reasonable certainty. It made the outcome a true gamble. He had told the Viceroy the whole truth when he had spoken of God's will. That single massive charge would in one firing prove the gun to the gun maker, and the gun maker to *his* Maker.

He sent his crew away a safe distance, then, alone, he knelt and prayed to the gunners' patron saint. He had done so a thousand times before, but this time it was a Catholic prayer, silently mouthed in Spanish. Then he blew on the match for luck and touched it to the vent.

The concussion was terrifying. The explosion flung the gun and its carriage high into the air and ripped him to the ground. As the gun crashed back, clods of dry earth flew around him. For a few seconds he was enveloped in smoke, then he saw his crew running towards him. He stood up ecstatically, deafened by the roar, finding his hat and casting it up through the cloying smoke.

The barrel was intact!

In the distance, flocks of birds leapt from their roosts as the sound thundered out across the fields. Far away the planters straightened and looked up. He looked to where the Viceroy stood, saw Don Bernal raise his hand and wave it in congratulation. He ordered the culverin reloaded immediately, this time with a regular proofing charge. Cristobal threw his chest across the barrel to draw it down on the trunnions. Eduardo brought out the water pail and sponged smouldering wadding and corrosive powder remnants from the bore, sending a blow of blue smoke siphoning up through the vent into a smoke ring. Another charge was loaded, wadded with hay and rammed home forcefully with the long pole. Salazar lifted in the great iron ball, wadded it again and compacted it. Then the crew were dismissed to safety.

Again the gun bellowed and bucked. Another great plume of smoke filled the air and drifted thin in the breeze. All was well. They repeated the reloading, faster this time. And a third angry blast roared forth.

Tavistock began to feel the ringing in his head, the familiar gun drunkenness that stretched time and made everything euphoric and unreal. He felt as though he had been clouted hard on the ear, slightly concussed, but paradoxically able to aim the culverin the better for it. He measured the new charges of powder with infinite care, set the elevation with wedges until the range was correct, tested the wind and laid the gun's azimuth.

The shot threw the gun back violently with another ear-shattering roar. A further gout of acrid smoke spewed out from the muzzle and Tavistock watched the pads of burning wadding arc to the ground leaving smoky trails. He moved to windward so he could follow the ball. The men downrange raised red flags above the earthworks in which they hid, showing that the shot had carried just beyond the target.

He ordered half his crew to reload and led the remainder ten paces away to the *Jesus*'s gun, checking the wind once more. It was already charged and ready to fire, but he levered the carriage fractionally to the left with a long iron spike before touching it off. This time a green flag showed that the ball had fallen short.

He felt the urge to destroy overwhelm him, just as it had that day in the harbour of San Juan. The timber target became real, the ground on which he walked was a deck and the rough earth between grey waters. He urged his men to double their efforts, turned on his crews ferociously, exhorting them in savage language, willing them to work faster against one another, to compete.

With the next two shots the target was bracketed, the range found. Then they scored a hit. It was too easy: a sitting target, no roll of his gun deck to compensate for, little wind and what there was steady. His shots began to batter the landbound ship into pieces, and he saw exultantly that his own sun-bright gun was the deadlier. He had made one of the most precisely destructive weapons in the world.

First the makebelieve forecastle was destroyed, then the stripped tree that formed the mainmast was blasted in two. White flag followed white flag, from the observers downrange, showing that the target had been hit, but Tavistock continued to fire, now with his own gun, now with the gun from the *Jesus*. After a two dozen shots, the barrels were almost too hot to touch. The air tasted of powder. His crew were slicked with sweat. A dozen shots more, delivered as fast as they could fire them. Still he shouted them onward, and they saw how he was touched by the Devil. Angry, yet not angry. Time passed, but its passing did not reach him. Nothing diminished the passion and intensity of the attack. The target that had once shown the silhouette of a ship was reduced by the bombardment to a splintered heap of timbers, but still he urged another reload and another and another, until all fear and all grief and all anger and all hatred were pouring from them, on and on and on and on, until there was no more will and no more breath and no more strength in their arms and legs with which to feed the guns and the terrible flame within their master.

As they fell to their knees, he took up the irons himself, threw off the hands of those that tried to stop him.

'Enough!'

Then the officers of the Guard were hurrying across the field. They saw the glaze in his eyes, the stark rawness that lingered there, and they knew they had witnessed a man who was prepared to push himself to the utmost limit to demonstrate his skill.

Don Emilio looked at the gun with awe and fascination. From the very first shot he had been profoundly impressed by the demonstration, by the rate of fire, the consistent accuracy of the shooting, the power of the shot to destroy. The anxieties of the morning rose up in him again as he faced the Englishman. He had been half expecting, half hoping that the demonstration would prove nothing. After so many delays it was not unreasonable to suppose that the results would not justify the expense, that the experiment would prove a costly and inconclusive failure, but the Englishman had done all that he had promised and more. Such a pity that the prize must soon be lost, he thought. Tavistock is now a real asset and not simply a potential one. How unfortunate it has taken so long to manifest itself. How cruel the turn of events.

'That was magnificent shooting, Englishman. I congratulate you.'

Tavistock's eyes were staring through him blearily. Don Bernal took his arm, wiped the sweat and grime from his face, his own breathing fast and excited. 'Do you hear that, Juan? Such guns! Who now would be our enemy?'

The Viceroy watched his host's delight grimly. If we had a hundred of these guns we might subdue the entire world, he thought. But five is hardly a start. Is there still time? *Is there still time?*

'Don Bernal, you will immediately put your foundry into full production. By this time next year, I want a hundred of these culverins in my possession. No delay is to be tolerated. No expense is to be spared. Do you understand?'

'Yes, Excellency. Thank you. It's a great honour, but perhaps a *hundred* cannon in a single year is too many for our small foundry to produce.'

'Then you must build another. I will pay whatever is necessary. You will start tomorrow. Today. Now.'

'You do us too much honour, Excellency.'

Don Emilio drew the *encomendero* aside. 'Can it be done without the Englishman?'

Don Bernal seemed not to understand the question.

'I ask you: can the foundry operate without the Englishman? Have your men learned enough?'

'I – I don't know, Excellency.'

'Then, find out. You have a year to make those guns, Don Bernal.'

But the Viceroy knew that he did not have a year. That very morning he had learned from his council that Don Pietro Moya de Contreres was preparing to put out his blessed hand in search of heresy. To begin its quest the Holy Office wanted first to examine the captured Englishmen, and the name of John Tavistock was at the head of their list.

Chapter 16

Francis Drake shaded his eyes and looked from the stockade to the *Pasco*, to the *Swan*, then back to the stockade again. This had been his secret anchorage, the place he had named Port Pleasant because of the lagoon and the white sand and the towering, buttressed trees that shaded it. Behind, the land was clothed in luxuriant green, rising steeply – beautiful with the sun sinking low, casting the shadow of peaks across it. A rock stood at the entrance to the cove to shield his ship, three fathoms to anchor in, and not far from this spot a waterfall of pure crystal that he had first washed in almost two years ago.

But the Spaniards had come here and found their stockade and all was destroyed.

Drake stood on the beach and stared at the fire-blackened ruins two hundred paces away, feeling the pain in his leg and tasting the bitterness of yet another disappointment. Behind him, the landing party stirred uneasily, watching the undergrowth and straining to listen for dangers despite the wind and the surf.

'So. The whore's bastards have found us out,' he said.

'We're betrayed!' John Oxenham, his second in command, came to his side. 'They must have learned from those who we left for dead at Nombray. From Gardiner or Taft.'

'Aye, and maybe it was just bad luck!' Frane said. The belligerent Dorset coxswain threw down his hat. He and Taft had been close. 'We're ill-starred, I tell ye!'

'Shut your mouth, Frane. The Captain don't allow of that kind of talk.'

The longboat crew pulled the cutter up, helped by the breakers that crashed onto the steep shelf of the beach, then fanned out. An onshore wind howled in the trees, driving small clouds westward, giving movement to everything in earth and sky.

They followed him warily toward the ruin, pushing through rain-damp leaves, their shirts fluttering. Port Pleasant was to have been their base of operations; a secure port where he could replenish his ships and

263

stockpile the booty they had meant to take from the Spaniards. But now their stores were stolen, their provisions spoiled or carried off; there was only sodden, charred wood and the threat of ambush. Port Pleasant was known to the enemy, and so it was useless.

'Are you a'right, Captain?' his thick-spoken coxswain asked, respectful once more.

God blind ye, Frane! he thought uncharitably, wanting to savour what the Spanish had done, the better to decide on a fit way to chastise them. The deep wound in his calf muscle raged, echoing the disaster that had befallen them at Nombre de Dios. Three months had passed since then and still the leg had not properly healed. He hated it because his men thought him a cripple and because it reminded them of the bloody failure. *His* bloody failure.

'Get the landing party back aboard. Let's piss away out of here.'

'Aye, sir!'

They sat meekly at their sweeps, buffeted by the surf, waiting for him, watching him limping into the water. The brine burned as it seeped into the bindings.

Frane hesitated. 'Captain –'

'Get about your tasks, then,' he shouted, his voice rasping hoarsely.

The new loss infuriated him. The shame of it. *This piss-burning leg!* He'd have the bastard off if it didn't improve in three days. He waded deeper through the water and heaved himself into the boat smartly, knocking away Boaz's helping hand, unwilling to fill their eyes with any more of this goddamned crippled captain sideshow.

He looked at their faces and saw they were all troubled and lined. None would meet his eye. He knew they could not lightly put aside this new setback. He read their thoughts: Betrayal. Fuming anger. Above all, disappointment. Gardiner and Taft again. Stupidity! Gardiner. Wanted to be a hero. Gardiner, the trumpeter, was certainly dead, his brains had been dashed out by a ball, but Taft might have been alive. Drake folded his arms to stop his hands going to his knee. A tourniquet might stop that blood-pounding ache. Oh, no! Suffer and smile you whore's son! Put your mind to something else.

There was another explanation. What if Richard Tavistock was taken and had talked? No, surely not. Not Richard. His men, then? But Richard alone knew the full extent of the plans, he alone knew the place where Port Pleasant had been. Richard would have died before telling any Spaniard. And he wasn't indiscreet in marking up his charts.

So it was Taft. Bumbailiff Taft. Rat-faced runt. Scumbucket. Maybe not ... maybe they cut his cullions off first. Aye, think of that, Francis, and save your bile up for them that might have done it.

When they reached the *Pasco* he swung up the side with gritted teeth, looked for and found the furtive way the rest of the men regarded him. None would hold his gaze and that angered him and the anger showed and made them more evasive still. He cast about him with his jaw tight as a fist and his lips protruding, and went below. Immediately he broke out a bottle of wine but there was no comfort in it and no spirit to light up inside him. He could not put from his mind what he saw in the faces of his crew.

He had promised them riches beyond imagination. So far there had been struggle and toil and death. Twenty-five of them had fallen to the calenture and other fevers, five more to ship accidents and infected wounds, two taken by Carib cannibals whilst rewatering. And the remainder had seen neither gold nor silver with which to prove the virtue of his promises.

That had been the original plan: take enough to redeem the men who had been carried into Mexico, finally discharge that debt that John Hawkins had run up in the marooning. But what to do now? The Englishman they had picked off that Spanish ship had changed everything. The powder maker had given him much to think on.

A promise was a promise, but Peru silver was as soon spent in England as in Vera Cruz, whatever Richard Tavistock thought about it.

He remembered how they had seen it, tons of it, stacked in huge ingots, in the treasure house in Nombre de Dios. But they had carried away none. *He had failed them.*

It had been a sorry débâcle. He had seen storm clouds and intended to land at break of day, but the party under Peter Gilbert's command had made their sally prematurely at three o'clock, in pitch blackness, and they had been forced to follow. Then their four boats had been seen by a caravel and the bells of the town had been rung before they had even scrambled onto the beaches.

It had been chaos! Caution and order had flown away. They had assaulted the breastworks in a screaming fury, pulling down the defences, running and shouting like madmen, careless of life and limb, into the sniper fire that had peppered them randomly from the blackness. Utter indiscipline. Utter, uncoordinated, piss-boiling chaos!

Incredible, but the shooting had died away.

Nombre de Dios, a town the size of Plymouth, had been emptied by the alarm. The townsfolk fled before them, panic-stricken, crying in their terror of the devil horde that had come out of the night, but the three shivering prisoners they laid by the heels had told them of the Governor's house and the fabulous treasure it contained and so they had swarmed through the narrow streets, their mission coursing with undeserved good fortune, riding unhindered on the back of surprise.

Drake smiled bitterly at the memory of it. What a nonsensical miracle. By God's providence, and his own eerie inner certainties, they had come upon the very place where the wealth of the Indies was concentrated. Tons of silver! A bar for each day of the year. Three fortunes for each Englishman. Bars stacked two fathoms high in the cellar, filling the space completely. It had gleamed like moonbeams under their torches, astounding every man who gazed on it, for it was without doubt the greatest single repository of silver in all creation.

But in the queer tension before a tropic storm, when the night air is thick enough to curdle milk, a man's mind can easily slip away from reality, and then silver seems like some other, baser substance, fresh-poured lead, or bright iron.

He had forbidden them to touch any of it. Trusting his own mind, he had been sure that another place was near by that contained the same immense hoard – *but of gold.*

And so it had been! In the King's Treasure House by the quay they found the unattended strong room bursting with bullion. Their glee had been unutterable – Oxenham and Frane and Gilbert and Moor-black Boaz and his own brother, John – all his lieutenants had bathed their hands in it, capered and gawped, seeing the plate and the coin and the heavy-wrought baubles thick-crusted with jewels. They had stared with the eyes of wonder. Next they had turned those gorged eyes on him and he had exulted in the knowledge that he had delivered them here, and that his promises to them were thereby fulfilled.

Then the cracks of musket fire had come to them, and the sounds of Spanish throats. The craven garrison had composed itself and returned, seeing their four boats and understanding how pitifully few they were, and as the Spaniards came on to repossess their town the golden vision had vanished. A pregnant heaven had opened, suddenly, delivering a dousing downpour that rendered their firearms and bows useless, soaking their powder and strings.

It was God's will that they take this stuff away!

He had felt strong and charged with confidence, unbreakable and unstoppable, but how his boys had read the omen differently. Huddled in that queer light, amid an immeasurable wealth flashed blue by tridents of tropical lightning, those old feudal superstitions had flared up in them.

The many awed voices had spoken out in their paralysis, the plough-boy turned deck hand and the orphan signed as carpenter's prentice and the swineherd come along as cook's mate.

'It's a sign! It's a sign!'

'It's God's punishment!'

'It's not for such as we are!'

'It's a dying dream! A man's last sight on earth.'

'Oh, Captain, poor men were never meant to look upon such wealth as this!'

'Remember: thou shalt not steal! We're doomed!'

'Oh, God save us. We're going to die!'

'God gave this to the Spaniards! Not to us! We cannot take it!'

'Help us, Captain!'

And he had risen up in a mighty fury at them. His voice had filled with power and flame. 'Listen to me! I have brought you to the treasure house of the *world*! Follow me, until the job is done! For if you leave without it, you may blame no one but yourselves.'

His rage had shaken them. The spell of fear had abated. They had begun to gather up King Philip's tribute, knowing, because he told them so, that were they to leave this bounty then that black spider of a King – whom no one loved, least of all God in his heaven – would use it to trouble all the world with Catholic arms.

'Do you want them to come into England to pillage your own people? Rape your wives? Smother your babes?' A rope of white-faced pearls had swung in his fist. '*This* is the pay they give their mercenaries.'

Then he had let out a groan and staggered in a sudden faint. And they had seen the gore spilling from the hole in his boot and the flame within him guttering.

Those foolish ploughboys and orphans and swineherds had dropped their armloads of treasure to pick him up. They had carried him to the boat and rowed him away, still their Captain, and still much more precious than any spider king's load of scrap.

'Take the gold and leave the man. Surely I taught them that much?' he said, sick at their misplaced loyalty. 'And tan their hides for it, for our mission is to rob and to plunder, and not to care a damn for anyone, least of all a fool who parries a lead ball with his leg.

'God blind me! *Why do I feel so weak?*'

Drake stared dispiritedly into his looking glass. The man he saw before him was a sorry piece of loot, skin roasted puce and peeling. A mane of rusty hair, elfed up in a headband that was salt stiff and caked with sand. There was a line of chigoe lumps on his neck; where he had scratched at them to get at the burrowing ticks they were skinned raw. He stripped his shirt off and examined his chest, seeing the whiteness of his upper arms and the freckle-tanned forearms where he had toiled by his men with his sleeves rolled up. When his heart moved in his chest each beat sent a pulse of pain down his thigh and into his calf muscle.

Sullenly he looked inside himself, finding a pervasive fatigue there, like the sour dregs of a water barrel swilling in his belly. I did fail them, he said silently. They look to me alone for their future. Mine is the driving force. But there's little remaining within, and nothing I can do to stop the soreness growing in my eyes. And nor do I look the part I ought. That small thing I should do, at the very least.

He took another draught of wine and wondered suddenly in which place his heart would beat its last, how many beats it yet contained; then he was ashamed of the thought. It was the first time in all his life he had asked himself such a question. He stoppered the bottle and vowed never to ask it again.

But listen, he thought, slamming the bottle back in its place in the cupboard, only I, Francis Drake, have borne the burden of hopes and fears for a hundred men these many months, only I have filled them with dreams and harried them onward, never asking any return save obedience and blind faith. And my men have followed me gladly and without quarrel, suffering trustingly, some even unto death, because I am their leader. Their Captain. And it was neither fear nor law that made them do it, but good feeling. Be worthy of them, Francis, you sorry bastard! You hear me?

When a knock came at the door, he was ready for it. John Oxenham, his tall, unsmiling second-in-command, came in, surprised that his Captain was stripped to the waist. Drake was shaving out his cheeks over a pail of water. His hair was combed back wetly and had been trimmed around the ears.

'Well?'

'I thought that –'

'What did you think, John?'

'I – the helmsman would know if you're ready to weigh anchor, sir.'

Drake's reply was distorted by his shaving. 'We must away to find ourselves a new place to lay up, but I'm yet undecided. What would you do, John?'

'Set up another fastness down Margarita way, and thence to Trinidad.'

'Not further north? To Santa Domingo or Hispaniola?'

'Seems to me, sir, preying on the coasters's our only hope of profit now, sir. Unless we each lose a belly we'll sleep hungry tonight. The 'tween decks is like a pauper's plate. We'll have to find victuals somewheres – we have sore need of a new base.'

'Then you'll consult with me over where it shall be.'

'A new place far from the Spaniards. So's we're not displaced again.'

Drake looked up and shook his wet hair so that droplets flew from it. 'No, by God! I want none of that. We're here to do a job of work. We'll keep close by our quarry.'

'If you think so, sir.'

'I think so. In any case, the autumn's fall is coming on in England and I mean to repair to a rendezvous long appointed for November of this year.'

'Aye?'

'Indeed. There's a man, who if he can, will meet us at a pleasant isle between the Leewards and the Windwards in that month. A man we owe plenty.'

Oxenham's face lit up as he fathomed the riddle. 'We're to meet Captain Tavistock in Dominica?'

'If it be God's will.'

'Will you tell him about the powder maker?'

'I'll have to, though it'll break his heart.'

Drake shrugged on a fresh shirt. His breeches were newly laundered, laid out on his cot. He would change into the pair he had sworn not to wear until they had something to celebrate.

'Help me with my boots, John.'

Oxenham took hold like a man shoeing a horse and eased the boot off. The right was easy, the left impossible until Drake sat down on the lip of his cot.

'Shall I fetch the surgeon?' Oxenham asked, too circumspect to make comment over the pus-drenched bandage and the stink that arose from it. Drake flexed his ankle so that the calf was laid open from top to bottom, and the redness all around grew purple.

'Surgeon? No! The clumsy bugger's too ready with his knife. When he took the ball out he nearly killed me. He'll have my leg off and then what'll I say to Captain Tavistock?'

Oxenham was unamused. 'Brandy, then?'

'I'll not waste good liquor on a wound, and that Froggy rotgut burns like sodomy.'

'I meant for to bathe your innards, sir. For to kill the pain.'

Drake straightened instantly. 'Do I seem to you to be in pain?'

Oxenham shook his head. 'No, Captain, but the putrefaction —'

'I need a clear head, and there's a better way. One I learned of Amyas Poole, God rest his bones. Open yonder shutter. You'll find a foreleg of beef there. Bring it to me.'

The joint had been crudely skinned, and still bore the hoof. It had been rotting outside the portal in tropical heat for a week. Drake hefted it and split it open with his knife, flicking out half a dozen pale-coloured grubs with the tip.

Drake grinned. 'A blow for a blow, that's what Amyas used to say, eh, John? Come out of there you little beauties!'

He placed a dozen maggots into Oxenham's palm and then one by one onto the place where the suppuration was worst. They wriggled and quickly dived into the wound.

Oxenham watched with absorbed interest, kneeling at Drake's side.

'Pick the smallest for their appetites. See? When they come out of the air they have a mighty taste for pus and dead flesh. It's their meat and drink and what makes 'em grow fat. They'll clean me up for sure. I can feel them doing good already.'

He clapped a wad of cotton torn from his old shirt over the wound, tied it round and forced on his boot again, feeling hugely pleased with himself. He danced a jig for Oxenham's benefit, ending on a clap and a stamping flourish.

'You see?'

Oxenham's grin swelled and Drake clapped his back with a full-bodied clout. He could feel the spirit rise in the man.

'Well? Shall we away and tell the helm where we're bound?'

'Aye, Captain! Aye!'

Tavistock left his ship, relishing the prospect of a good roast and after it a long talk with Drake about how best they might bring off their plans. The *Antelope* was anchored beside Drake's ship, *Pasco*, in the

place they had named Providence Bay. Their meeting at first light had
been premature by a day, and the crews were lighting great fires on the
shore to make a ritual of it. Tavistock had met briefly with Drake at
noon, but their talk had been so taken up by small practicalities that
they had not had chance to explore any deeper matter.

Tavistock looked around him. It was good to be back under a tropical
sun, good to see it westering red at the ending of each day. But each
night there was a rage in heaven the like of which he had never seen,
and it made him think of his brother, and the real reason he had come
to this rendezvous.

Fires burned around him as he stepped ashore.

'Richard.'

'Francis. So what news?'

'Not good. Come sup with us.'

Tavistock sat down with a roast fowl to learn of Drake's doings. It
had been May when Drake left England with seventy-three men and
boys in the *Pasco* and the *Swan*. Provisioned for a year, they had got
off before anyone could stop them with a countermanding order from
the Privy Council. By June they had reached this spot, and, after
rewatering, had headed for the coasts Drake had surveyed on his
reconnaissance the previous year.

Drake grinned as he recounted how they had sighted the Guatemala
coast. 'We attacked Nombray in July. That's where I got this.'

He pointed to the leg. The bulbous muscle in his calf was knotted
with scar tissue, but seemed not to impede him now.

'You were almost killed, they tell me.'

'That he was, Captain Tavistock,' Boaz growled protectively. The
man's shipboard Devonish seemed strange, and Tavistock remembered
the terrible day Boaz had first seen Plymouth, how he had sat with him
in the tavern after the news of Jane's death. Then, the man had had
barely a dozen words of English. 'I had to carry him out of the King's
strongroom myself, he was so heartset on that treasure.'

'I fainted away,' Drake confessed, disgustedly. 'Filled my boot to
overflowing with blood. But I swear it'll take more than a lucky shot
from a peon to put me down for good. And so it'll prove.'

Tavistock poured more wine into his mouth, and ripped the flesh
from a chicken crate. 'You took away their silver, then?'

Drake shook his head ruefully and told the tale, the bright firelight
flickering across his face. Despite the failures, Tavistock thought he
seemed utterly at peace with creation, except for one thing.

'Bewitched, it was! In my palm and my fingers closing over it, when
psssht! In truth, there might have been too much to shift. And we were
a right lollardly rabble. It won't be the same next time.'

'Next time?'

'I'm resolved on it. Penniless but game. Give me credit for that at
least.'

'Pity about Nombray. Some of it might have made a princely ransom – for the lads.'

'Might have,' Drake stirred uneasily. 'I was meaning to tell you ...' He looked down.

'What?'

'Oh ...'

After a pause Drake stood up and walked barefoot toward the tide line. Tavistock picked up his leather satchel and went after him, knowing that what was to be said was for them alone.

Waves lapped gently there. Out of range of the beach fires the sky was brilliantly dark and spangled with stars. One star in particular, an intense blue-white point, riding at forty degrees elevation in the north, was brighter than Arcturus or Vega or even Sirius himself. Tavistock looked at it unhappily.

'The new star terrified my men,' he told Drake.

'Aye, and I confess it weighs heavy on my own mind.'

'A bad sign, think you?'

'Ain't natural that a star do flare up so.'

Tavistock continued to stare at the sky. Like Drake, his pilot's instincts had been greatly disturbed by the apparition and what it might portend. It blazed like a diamond, riding in the lap of the Princess Cassiopeia, a jewel, bright enough to cast a shadow, and, because it shone in the black of night, it was more impressively luminous than Venus.

Two months ago it had been invisible, then, suddenly in early November, Tavistock had seen it, only as bright as the other stars around it but his eye had been drawn immediately to the oddness of the pattern.

He had said nothing to Thomas Sark, his sailing master, or to Bowen, but the following night it had grown brighter still, and they had come to him to ask what to do.

New stars did not suddenly appear in the sky – all mariners knew that. And Tavistock had had no better answer for his crew. The stellar sphere, as even Copernicus had acknowledged and Doctor Dee's writings confirmed, was immutable, crystal and permanent. Long hours laid aloft as lookout had taught Tavistock that the sun and the moon and the planets were changeable quantities, even the shooting stars in their bright silent showers speckled the sky according to a predictable plan. That much was normal and to be seen at all seasons and in every year, but in times of earthly crisis odd things happened in the sky, for it was a mirror and in it all things were reflected.

There were comets, which appeared like ghosts to terrify the world with their bloody omens of plague and war. They came but once in a generation, emissaries of the archangels, sent as dire warnings. He had never seen one, but in his younger days when he was more inclined towards the rare and strange than the commonplace he had heard tell of them from old sailors. Those men had spoken of fantastic forms, of comet swords and comet skulls, baleful and mystic, hanging over a city for weeks and then fading or wasting away. And always there had followed cataclysm or the death of princes. But never, never in the history of the world, save once at the Redeemer's birth, had there been report of a new fixed star coming into the sky unannounced.

'Doesn't it shiver you?' Drake asked, troubled. 'My people have asked me how we shall navigate if all the stars begin to come and go. How shall we regain England? Though it's but a single star it troubles me. To tell truly I have never seen the like of it. What do you think it portends?'

Tavistock studied the unwavering spark, deeply shocked by the message he knew it carried. 'Ask rather what earthly matter can be of such importance that a new star must herald it. I think I know that already.'

'What?'

Tavistock told him the startling news he had read at Plymouth whilst he provisioned *Antelope*. In that letter Hawkins had told him that the Duke of Norfolk had been beheaded for his crimes, and that de Spes had been ignominiously sent out of England after an attempt to have the Secretary shot down in the street, but there had been another report enclosed, recounted in harrowing and despairing terms. It had come from Walsingham in Paris, and told of an infamously bloody massacre.

The French King had, on the feast of St Bartholomew, ordered the assassination of the Huguenot leader, Admiral Coligny, and the entire Calvinist nobility save Navarre and Condé.

Drake was stunned. 'So the rabid dogs of Paris have fallen on their Protestant neighbours?'

'All, of whatever rank, indiscriminately butchering tens of thousands until the Seine itself ran red. Walsingham admits he was completely unprepared for it. Unto the very day he was continuing royal marriage negotiations with Catherine. He even had to fortify the Embassy against the murder gangs that roamed the streets. It's said he barely escaped with his life.'

The killings had plunged England's position into doubt once more, changing everything. As Drake's oaths against the atrocity subsided, Tavistock took from his satchel the papers he had been waiting to give him. Sweeter news, but needing explanation.

They walked along the lapping water, hearing the boisterous carousing of the men at their fires, shouts and laughter and the strains of 'John Dory' being sung. Drake concentrated on the documents in the flickering glow, finally grunting with livid scorn.

'Iniquitous papers!'

'Better news than we might have hoped for.' The papers were passports, letters of marque and a permit signed by a clerk to the Privy Council; accompanying them were copies of the financial arrangement

Tavistock had bargained out.

'Better news, you say? Then you know not the shape of a stinking deal!'

'You're wrong, Francis.' Tavistock kept his face stern and lowered his voice. 'We're backed by powerful factions now, you and I. Lord Leicester's put money into our voyage – without him I'd not have raised a crew. Capital's come from Walsingham, and there's the money I took from de Spes. Our crusade may not be official, but we're watched for, and our dealings will be close followed at home.'

Drake thrust the papers back at him. 'God's blood, the Queen's sign manual comes at a high price! With so many ways to cut the pudding, we'll be lucky to come out ahead.'

Tavistock felt his anger rise unstoppably. 'Look further than your close horizon, Francis. There's more to this than the weight of our own purses!'

'Is that a fact?'

'Aye. Don't you see? There's no alternative.'

'No?' Drake squared with him. 'We could choose piracy! Then what we do is all to our own advantage!'

'Be ruled! This is a better way. We'll be Elizabeth's instrument. If I've read her intents correctly, we have leave to punish the Spanish as we see fit, so long as we turn a profit, and so long as we turn half of it over to her.'

Drake's face set in a mask of grim mistrust, and Tavistock went on. 'Because we're financed by private subscription we're unaccountable to the Council. That means we by-pass Cecil's – Lord Burleigh's – authority. We may conduct a private war, with riches at its centre, and freedom to take from the Spanish what we might.'

'And if we should fall into Spanish hands?'

'The Queen'll deny all knowledge of us.'

Drake spat. His voice dropped scornfully. 'That's a balanced deal you've got us. You begin to sound like Hawkins. The Queen risks nothing and gains half. What do we get by alliance with her?'

'We keep our heads. And leave to walk about in England.'

'Ha! I can sail to a pretty coast up beyond the Florida cays and found an England of mine own. I'll live of my own and take what I choose from the Dons and be content where I know my head's secure, for I'll be my own king!'

'Never more to see England, or your wife?'

Drake's defiance stood firm. 'She may easily be cut out by a raid on Plymouth and carried off. Aye, and enough of the female kind to satisfy the rest of my lads.'

'And where will you spend your gold and silver north of Florida? Where money is nothing and any proportion of it is still *nothing*?'

Drake grunted, but Tavistock saw that his squall had blown itself out. They sat down and he came again with his plan, more coolly now.

'Our duty is to England. We're all moths ranged round the Queen's flame, and the Council is the window in which we may fly. Those fifteen men of gravity watch after the affairs of England as if it were a lordly household and estate, jealous of all things, mostly of one another. Think! We want riches and revenge, and, after that, status among our own and the knowledge that we kept King Philip's greedy hands off Protestant liberties. That's what the new star tells us. We will carry home enough of Spain's ill-gotten glory to confound her.'

'But a clear half of all we take, Richard! It's a trugging shame!'

Tavistock picked up several small white cockle shells from the sand. 'Do not imagine the Queen's motive is avarice.'

'Then, what?'

'From each casket we bring her, she'll take a choice jewel to adorn her – and justly – to show the people how she prospers, how England's monarch is the equal of any.' He got up and flipped a shell towards the water. 'She will then pluck out another for the maintenance of a fleet at Chatham; and another for the repulse of Spanish plots in Ireland; and yet another to loan the Prince of Orange; and one more to aid the Huguenots.' The last shell he held up significantly. 'D'you see now?'

'You know all this? You who have come lately from her Tower, and almost had your neck stretched at her command?'

'I do. For I spoke with her directly.'

Drake levered himself to his feet, scratched at his head. 'Satan roast me, I cannot see how you did that!'

'John Hawkins is well connected.'

'Aye! John Hawkins is!' Drake's voice was edged with steel. 'But you say you spoke *with the Queen herself*?'

'Do not doubt me.'

'I doubt Hawkins. And I have my own schemes that won't cost me a bloodsucking.' Drake stabbed a savage finger toward the anchorage. 'There's *Antelope* – Hawkins's fine ship. Built to his specifications. I think he uses you, Richard.'

'He has talent in that line. Also the services of the finest shipwrights in England – which means the finest in the world. But *Antelope* is mine.'

Drake took a deep breath. 'To look at her lines, she must have been conceived apurpose for her present use. Can you satisfy me that John Hawkins isn't still working you like a puppet?'

Tavistock's chest swelled up. 'Is this a puppet you see standing before you?'

'I don't know. But I don't believe you. Or you've not told me all. Prithee, Richard! Aren't we confidential with each other any more?'

The pause between them dragged out, tormenting Tavistock until he felt he must break it.

'I was sworn to silence.'

'Aye! And we're sworn to be straight with one another.'

'Then believe that John Hawkins never had a part in this endeavour.

If you would know the main part, then know that I was in love!'

'In love? You?'

Tavistock caught Drake's surprise and the angry part of him called it mockery. He made at Drake dangerously. 'Yes! Me! In love! And I married – in spirit – just as you did in body and soul.'

In the light of the fires, Tavistock's face was as hard as iron. The words spilled from him, telling how he had come to love the Secretary's daughter, how he had pursued her and played a dangerous sport under Cecil's nose. He finished, stilting his words, and sat down again on the powdery ground, his head in his hands.

Drake was shaking his head in wonder. 'You *amaze* me.'

'She married in Westminster Abbey before I departed England. With Her Majesty in attendance, and bishops and lords ranged all about. And my child was in that bride's belly.' He lifted his head, staring at the bright point in the constellation of Cassiopeia. 'Yonder star shines for my son. It is his star. But when he comes into the world there will be a better bed for him than the poor manger this common sailor could provide. Wise men there will be aplenty, travelling to behold his face. And the Queen herself shall be his godmother.'

The waves lapped slowly on the gently curving, shallowly sloping beach. Some of the fires had burned down to embers, some of the men were stretched out, ankles crossed, elbows out from their ears. Others told likely tales, still others laughed at them. Happy crews with all before them and no cares about the morrow.

'I want my brother, Francis.'

'I know you do.'

'Then will you help me, or hinder me? I must know which, for in consort or alone I mean to get him back.'

Drake sighed. 'You cannot now.'

'I can. There's not a man alive that cannot be ransomed out of Mexico,' Tavistock looked up defiantly, 'if the Spaniards are offered enough.'

'Not so.'

'Listen, if –'

'No, Richard. No!' Drake laid hands on him.

'Why no? Explain.'

'Just this: I have news of my own. News you will not find to your liking.'

Drake shouted for Frane, who went on his errand, reporting back with another of Drake's crewmen. Despite the way the man's cheeks had caved in with the loss of his teeth, Tavistock recognised him immediately.

'Tell me, are you not –'

Drake cut in. 'I prayed to God to spare you this, Richard, but you won't be deflected,' he said, then he turned to Job Hortop. 'Tell Captain Tavistock the same tale that you told to me.'

'Aye, sir.'

Tavistock listened silently but with mounting dread as Hortop recounted his story. He spoke about Mexico City and how he had been imprisoned by Don Emilio Martinez. Then he spoke of his toiling in the silver mines, but this was only preamble to a more shocking tale.

Hortop faced him miserably. 'It was like this, Captain Tavistock, your brother he robs me of my chance of bringing away a fortune in gold. A lousy fortune, d'you see, sir? That's what I lost through him, so I did. And all for his love of a Spanish woman who is a Mexican squire's daughter. It makes my heart sick to relate, sir. He tells the Spaniards to bring me to him, to teach them how to make best English powder for their guns. Aye. Guns he's making for them. Great culverins and bastard culverins. Using all his skill on their behalf is he, and of his own free will, and living like a lordling's whelp on it in the bargain. I'll tell you true, he orders a grand party of soldiery to take themselves up to a fire-mountain, like the mouth of Hell it was, but whereat a wonderful pure sulphur is found. He set them for to work it, but the Devil himself came out to greet us and only by my wit and strong running did I escape death in that place.'

Drake questioned the powder maker on several more particulars, then dismissed him. When they were alone again, Drake said, 'We picked Hortop up when we took a trader bound for the Mosquito Coast. He was working his passage, calling himself a Portugall, looking to get first to Cuba, and eventually, so he says, to ship for home. I heard his story some two months back just as you've heard it now.'

'He's lying!'

'No, Richard.'

'He's lying I tell you!'

'Why would he lie? For what reason? Eh?'

Tavistock's mind boiled with impossible explanations. The shame of it! It couldn't be true. Not John. Not his own brother – making cannon for the Spaniards? Making eyes at an *hidalgo* woman? No, it was Drake's lies! All Drake. He'd put the man up to it! Yes.

'You've set this play-acting afoot –'

Drake leaned back, his face showing his compassion. 'It's no play-acting. You know the powder maker. You know he went into Mexico four years ago. He's no reason to lie.'

'No. I don't believe him.'

'But you'll believe this.' Drake pulled out the ring. Its black stone carried the rising phoenix. It was the same Tavistock had once passed to John Chamberlain. 'It went from the steward's hand to your brother, and from him it was taken by Hortop in their struggle on the fire-mountain, and thence to me. You must face it, Richard: your brother's made a fool of you.'

Tavistock twisted the ring over and over in his fingers, burning with humiliation. By God and all His Saints, how could John have done it?

According to Hortop, they had not tortured him. He had given of his priceless skills freely.

'I can't believe it,' he whispered, knowing it was a lie.

'He's made fools of us all –' Tavistock tried to shut out Drake's words but they came to him like relentless daggers '– and he will do so again.' Drake spoke flatly, but he could not keep the reproach out of his voice. 'Once Vera Cruz and Nombray and Cartagena and all the other ports along the Main are fortified with English cannon we can kiss farewell to any more landward jaunts. We'll be reduced to scavenging hides and chickens and butts of wine off'f coasters and sniffing the arse of the *flota* to see what falls away in bad weather –'

'Sweet Jesus, that's enough!'

'I'm right sorry, Richard. But you had to know.'

Drake walked away, went back to his bonfire, and Tavistock let him go. His plans were in ruins, and his soul was in Hell.

Chapter 17

The Viceroy's apartments were in darkness. Don Emilio Martinez lay on his couch, his satisfactions over the work of fortifying the havens of Mexico temporarily driven from his mind.

He lay back, rubbed at his eyes. He was tired, but he had to unknot the problem before he surrendered to sleep. Go over it again, he told himself. Once more to get it clear. From the beginning.

The first ominous sign of trouble had come when the *flota* had docked. News of Don Pietro's arrival had preceded his appearance in Mexico City by two weeks, wild rumours carried upcountry from Vera Cruz that had inflamed the whole valley like a disease. Immediately, a committee of worthies had formed and he had agreed to meet with it, ostensibly to prepare a welcome for the distinguished Inquisitor, but the true function of the meetings had been otherwise.

The coming of the Inquisition had long been dreaded by the *estancieros*, or peasant Spanish, and was being established very much against the minds of many of the *encomienda* owners. In all the years since the Conquest they had never been subject to the cruelties of that Office. In all those years, Madrid had respected the status quo; as a matter of practicality the men who were the source of King Philip's wealth were spared the spiritual policing so necessary in Spain where Jews and *moriscos* abounded. But over the years the Inquisitor General had been able to build up an irresistible pressure on the King. They had used their earthly influence on the Cortez, who in turn had approached the monarch, and so the blessed hand had reached out across the ocean.

Don Emilio recalled with sour regret the way he had recognised the threat the Inquisition posed to his own temporal powers. He had seen a way to accommodate the Office, and to deflect for the moment the fears of his burghers, but the committee had been right about giving the Inquisitors a morsel and expecting them to be content with it.

Don Pietro had settled in the grand house across the *plaza*, next to the White Friars, and decided that it was best to call to question first the Englishmen – especially those that had become rich men through

278

their toils in the mines.

The orders had been read out and the notice posted that the English were suspected of heresies and must come to make account of themselves. They were sent for and sought in all parts of the country, and proclamation made upon pain of confiscation and of excommunication that none should keep secret any Lutheran.

At first, Don Emilio had done nothing. He had taken no steps to protect his investment, deciding that discretion might be a more effective policy. He had sent Gonzalo de Escovedo to speak with his father about the gun maker, and to reassure the family, but nothing more. After all, wasn't he now a true Catholic? Hadn't he taken marriage vows and been doubly confirmed in his spiritual purity? The man had a new name. He applied himself assiduously to his work. Was confined on the *encomienda*. With luck, Don Emilio had thought, it could be years before the Inquisitors came to Chalco.

But Tavistock had been betrayed. By whom, it did not matter. A servant, one of his own men, another of the English who knew where he was, and learned of his work and had chosen to befoul him ... Whatever the means, the Inquisition had found out about him and he had been taken.

At this point Don Emilio had pressed his viceregal privileges. As proconsul to His Majesty he had certain rights, could make certain small demands. He had indulgently explained about the guns. 'A matter of the utmost strategic importance, Don Pietro. I'm sure you understand?'

But the Inquisitor had shaken his head. At their second formal meeting, Don Pietro had been at pains to clarify his position. 'Your Excellency may be assistant to a King, but please remember that our Holy Office is the instrument of God.'

'Of course, and we agreed that Lutherans should be exposed. But this man is not a Lutheran.'

'Agreed?' Don Pietro had echoed, leaning back without any hint of his former amity. 'I was not aware of any agreement between us. The term "Lutheran" implies and includes so-called ex-Lutherans and those who profess to be *conversos*.'

'Come, come!' he had cajoled, pricked by Don Pietro's inflexibility. He had swallowed his pride again. 'How can that be? This man is a convert. I can see that with my own eyes. He's as good a Catholic as I am.'

'Indeed?' Don Pietro had paused significantly until the debating point was both scored and acknowledged. 'I salute Your Excellency's noble efforts on our behalf, but I must point out that accurate measures of depth of belief and sincerity of conviction are impossible, save by application of that great fund of learning and skill in enquiry that *calificadores* of the Holy Office alone possess.'

He had sighed, humbling himself further. 'But surely this one man, who may do His Majesty great service? Surely he could be overlooked?'

Then the Inquisitor had laid the closely written scroll open to his inspection, passing a hand over the names. 'It is God's will that all – *all* – herein proscribed shall be brought captive to the city of Mexico and committed separately to prison to undergo examination.'

'And if you should find him innocent?'

'Ah,' Don Pietro's smile had shocked him with its ugliness. 'If he was found to be innocent, then we should release him.'

'I'm gratified, Don Pietro,' he had said, readying himself to leave. 'Gratified, and so pleased we understand one another.'

Don Emilio's eyes continued to dwell on the Inquisition House whose cellars had become dungeons, one of which held the man who had been the key to glory. It's too bad, he thought. I tried. But the Englishman's survival is probably no longer an issue. He's served his purpose now; his gun-making secrets have almost certainly been learned by his apprentices. I pray God that's so, because I'll lay a silver platter to a pewter jug that he'll never get out of the *Plaça del Marquese* alive.

'Do you believe in the divinity of Christ, John Tavistock?'

The Chief Inquisitor, a small, grey man in red, sat in a tall chair behind the centre of a broad oaken table. To his right sat another, a severe, heavy-browed man in his late forties, in black cassock piped in red, buttoned to the neck and cloaked at the shoulder. He was silent, staring down at his papers. To the left, a younger man in plain black, taking notes with practised ease as they spoke, and in the shadows at the side, seated against the wall, a big man in a black habit. Upon the table, which was spread neatly with a cloth of green baize, stood a small handbell, a halfhourglass, a silver inkwell, quill holder and penknife. Alone in the centre, gilded and tooled in old leather, was a Bible.

'I ask you again: do you believe in the divinity of Christ?'

'Yes.'

'Witnesses say that you do not.'

'What witnesses?'

The man seated to the Chief Inquisitor's right spoke. 'Many good people offer themselves as our *familiares*. A person needs only a clean heredity to help our Holy Office root out evil.'

'Who informed on me?'

'It is our rule never to say.'

'Tell me who alleges I am a heretic now.'

'We do not break rules. We adhere to our methods.'

'What is the specific charge?'

'It is our practice not to divulge that.'

'Then how may I defend myself?'

'It is not for you to prepare defences, only to answer our inquiries with the whole truth.'

'Do you believe in the divinity of Jesus Christ?'

Tavistock's thirst raged, blood pounded in his head and the light from the tall candles pierced him. He had been confined in absolute blackness for a long time. How long? Three months? Six? Nine? It was impossible to say. The scratching of the stripped quill filled his head, plucking his nerves raw, he watched the sand running down through the glass as the questions were repeated endlessly, the same questions put to him time after time until he longed to answer them with other words.

On the second turning of the glass, a new question.

'Tell us about yourself.'

'There is nothing to tell.'

'Every man has one story to tell.'

'Some have more than one,' Bovilla said.

'Can you read?'

'Yes.'

'And write?'

'Yes.'

'You know what this is?'

'Of course. It's a tallow candle.'

'Take it.'

'Why?'

'Take it with you to your cell. Pen and ink will be brought. You will record for us a full confession of your life. Every detail, exactly as you recall it. Not until that is done and we have examined it will you be brought before us again.'

'And if I refuse?'

'You will not refuse.'

He ached all over.

He could not tell if it was night or day. He might have been here a month or six months or a year, but there was no way to tell, no regularity about the appearance of bread or water or the times when that intense, blinding candle was lit for him. No sunlight penetrated to the hot, humid cellar, but still the flies found their way in, attracted by the stench in the corner.

His ears were sharp to the sounds that came from beyond the great iron door, muffled sounds, as if the feet of the guards were wrapped in felt rags to deaden their noise. They had ordered him to make no sound, and they had beaten the soles of his feet to insensation when he had disobeyed. No one spoke outside, though often he could hear them faintly passing by. No human sounds, except a distant coughing, a retching or the screams that trailed away beyond another felt-muffled door.

How long before they came to beat him again? The dread kept him awake interminably until his mind grew leaden and his thoughts stewed into chaos. Am I ill? he asked himself, unable to understand the incredible lassitude that filled him. Am I dying? Have they drugged the water?

Have they wished on me a fever?

He lay back, imagining the room upside-down, that he was falling. He dreamed that he was dreaming fractured dreams on the fetid straw matting and felt the need to relieve himself, but he could not get up, could not will his legs to lift him. He had written the confession after the third beating, filling the papers with every item of his past that he could recall, and after that they had come and collected the papers but left him in his corner. He felt the pressure in his bladder, but he could not move and he could not raise the effort to halt the unmistakable series of relaxations in his belly. He tried to hold his muscles shut, but it was too late, then he felt the hot urine flood his groin and the smell was rich and dark, like rotted malty ale, but he could do nothing save lie there and tell himself that it did not matter because it was not real and that the nightmare was only a nightmare.

When he was called again into that intense light before the Inquisitors they told him kindly that they had read all the papers he had written. They were seated as before, and they told him their names as before, and examined his faith and commanded him to say for them the Pater Noster, the Ave Maria, and the Creed in Latin, which he could have done at one time with ease, but somehow as he recited the words he found his mind wandering and they gave him some water so that he might continue like a man and not bray like a donkey. He thought of Robert Barrett and the rest. A great many, he knew, would be able to recite nothing, other than in English.

Then they demanded in thin, flat voices, 'Does there remain bread or wine after the words of consecration?'

'No.'

'Do you believe that the host of bread that the priest holds above his head is the very Body of Christ? Do you believe the blood in the chalice is His Blood?'

Tavistock said nothing.

'Answer.'

'I believe.'

'You're lying!'

'No.'

The one called Sanchez exploded with anger. 'You're lying, trying to save your life, for you know that if you answered as you truly believed, you would die.'

'I want to die.'

'What were you taught as a child?'

'To believe in the Lord Jesus Christ as my only Saviour.'

'Nothing else?'

'My childhood was poor. Deficient in all kinds of learning. Which was no fault of mine own.'

'But as an adult you paid no heed to those who warned you of your error – until you came to Mexico. Why was that?'

'In all my days in England, no one questioned me as to my faith.'

'There are many Catholics in England.'

'Those there are keep silent.'

'Who commands that?'

'The Queen.'

'An evil woman!'

'Yes.'

'Jezebel of the ages!'

'Yes.'

'But the Queen was not in every place in England.'

'No.'

'Then who compelled silence of Catholics? Who was your shepherd?'

'No one. I don't know.'

He began to shiver, his teeth chattering together like ivory dice.

'You attended church each Sabbath?'

'Yes.'

'A Lutheran church?'

'We called it Anglican.'

'Of your own volition?'

'I think so.'

'Yes or no?'

'Yes.'

'Then, you went willingly into heresy.'

'I went only as everyone around me did.'

'As a sheep goes?'

'Yes.'

'Yet you say there was no shepherd?'

'It was the law in England to compel all men and women to attend church.'

'Then, you did not go of your own free will. Do not lie to us again.'

Another asked him, 'Were there never days when you had doubts? Never days when you preferred not to go inside to endure the heresies of a Protestant ritual?'

'There were some days like that.'

'Were you taught about the images of the Holy Saints?'

'Images were not allowed.'

'You had a word for the practice of keeping images?'

'We called it idolatry.'

'Do you believe in God?'

'Yes.'

'Open your eyes.'

Bovilla consulted the paper, adjusting it to the light. 'I read your history and I ask myself this: what can account for the late changeabout in your convictions?'

De los Rios, the blue-chinned Jesuit, explained. 'We find as the ancients found before us that the mind of man is as a clay vessel, malleable at first throwing upon the potter's wheel, but as a man ages so the vessel is fired. The form is imprinted indelibly and may no longer change.'

'And when pressure is applied,' Bovilla added unsmilingly, 'the vessel shatters.'

'And yet you say you changed, John Tavistock,' Don Pietro said. 'And you did not shatter.'

'My beliefs are as changed as my name, which is Juan de Tordesillas.'

'Ah! It is no matter to change a man's name.'

De los Rios said, 'All criminals maintain aliases.'

'I am no criminal.'

'And alibis.'

'I am no criminal!'

Bovilla slapped the signed paper before him. 'Is this your alibi, John Tavistock?'

'It is the truth, as you asked it of me.'

'Strange, then, that it does not accord with the confessions of certain other Englishmen.'

'How so?'

'They all claim to have been born and bred Catholics.'

'That is fear talking.'

'Do you have no fear?'

This time he did not answer.

A brazier glowed with coals, branding rods thrust among them. He recognised the horrible twisted figure of John Rider hanging unconscious from the strappado, his marked body suspended from wrists tied together behind his back and heavy stones in a net at his ankles.

Peter Goode's naked body was bound down, his head confined in a leather hood, his nostrils plugged with linen, his throat packed, and water was being dripped into his mouth through a funnel.

James Collier's feet were smashed in the bastinado. His face was a hideous yellow. A pail of urine was thrown over him, rousing him to groans. The great wooden frame below was bloodied, and he screamed at the sight of his legs, unable to do other.

A priest knelt at Collier's side, with book and cross.

'Help me! God help me! Oh, God let me die!'

'Confess!'

'Anything!'

'Repent of your sins!'

'I repent!' the victim screamed again, his eyes popping, his breath pumping. 'I repent!'

'But the truth is what God wants, my son.'

'The truth ...'

'He's fainted again, Father.'

'Here's another.'

The cleric got up off his knees, came smilingly to Tavistock. 'Do you like our pretty bed, *señor?*'

Then Don Pietro asked, 'Did you become a *converso* only that you might be allowed to marry Maria de Escovedo?'

He stared at them, his anger suddenly stronger than his fear or his exhaustion, but the mention of his wife's maiden name sent shivers of panic through him.

'If you will only tell us the truth you will be set at liberty.'

'I have told you the truth.'

'Are you sorry for the sins and offences you committed in England against God and our Lady and all the blessed Saints?'

'God's mercy! Yes!'

'Rack him!' Bovilla demanded.

'Must we rack you?'

He knuckled his eyes, his mouth was dry again.

Don Pietro renewed his question, his voice cooing now, redolent with regret that such action was necessary and unavoidable. 'Must we?'

'Yes!' Bovilla shouted.

'If only you would be frank with me and make a sincere confession.'

'I have told you everything.'

'Oh, wicked man. Show him what is coming.'

They had recruited foul butchers and men of dull mind for their shop of terrors, and others who revelled in watching the pain brought up in others.

'May I lie this one face down, Father?'

A foul voice whispered to him, 'We'll bugger you with hot irons before you sleep in this bed, heretic.'

They made him look at the *potro*, tied his ankles and his wrists, but if it was a bed it was fashioned after the one that the monstrous Procrustes owned. They put a stout rope across his mouth, levering his teeth open so that it gagged him like a horse bit, and twisted it tight, then the windlasses were turned at top and bottom, the wooden pawls clicking as they turned like the winder of the well rope outside his forge.

Where are you, Maria? he thought, his brain blinded with terror. Are you thinking of me?

And then the true agony started.

Maria had not hesitated to steal either the heirlooms or the horse. She had finally broken free from the confinement her family had imposed on her at Chalco and come to the city of Mexico to do what she could. Night and day she had lingered outside the Viceroy's residence with her petition, but the guards would not admit her without authority and she had not dared to reveal her identity for fear that her father's searchers would find her.

She had fixed her hopes on Gonzalo. Surely her brother must help her. Surely he would fix her an interview with Don Emilio. But when she asked after him they told her the honourable Captain was far away in Vera Cruz.

Friendless, the city was a changed place. A dark pall of fear had fallen over it. Well-to-do doors were barred against her. Few dared listen to her pleas, and those that did professed themselves as helpless as she, or took the opportunity to remind her of her foolishness in ever consenting to marry a heretic. Some even tried to trap her, to send her back to Chalco. So she had turned away from her high-born acquaintances.

She had sold the horse and got herself mean lodging and dressed in the black weeds of a widow woman. There she endured the whispers of the street. Peasant women thought her mad. They gossiped acidly at her misfortune and speculated on her sins. She bore unflinchingly the stones of children who made faces at her and danced out their parents' superstitious hatred insolently in front of her. And the stinking drunks that encountered her at night pressed themselves on her when they saw her fine looks, making foul suggestions and pawing her until she showed them the razor-edged protector she kept in her skirt.

There had been talk. Her father's people had heard the rumour. Clara, her maid, and two of her mother's servants had laid hands on her to bring her away, but she would not surrender herself, telling them that they should help her rather than hinder her, but they only repeated what her father had said. So she had pulled out her dagger and threatened to spill her own blood if they did not let her run from them.

So she had come at last in utter desperation to the stables of Pedro Gomara.

'Please, you must help me!'

'Come in, Lady. Come in.'

He had dusted a place on his bench for her and offered her bean broth, which she would not eat, apologising for his humble home and smiling toothlessly, but compassionately, until her tears dried.

'What can be done for you now?' he asked, facing her across his rough table top, stroking the long, greying head of his oldest bitch lurcher. The heady stink of *burros* permeated the byre-like house, and harnesses and other gear hung from nails driven into the walls. Just outside the stable doorway she could see a foal delicately stripping a thistle with its mouth.

'You know that Juan is imprisoned,' she said.

'I heard the proclamation, Lady.'

'I must try to save him.'

He patted the dog's head and clasped his hands together. 'Surely you know that to save him now is too much to hope for.'

Her face was white, drawn with anguish and lack of sleep. 'I can't believe that. I must not believe that. They are going to burn him, Pedro. Do you understand? *They are going to burn my husband.*'

'Hush, hush.'

'Pedro Gomara, you are an honourable man. You have been a soldier. You must help me or I shall die by my own hand!'

'Quiet, now, Lady. Listen to yourself! Are you not a daughter of the family Escovedo? I will help you. Take courage. And plan, as your father would plan, to think how you might make the Inquisitors change their decision. But take care also for your own life. Those black monks will see your devotion only as the taint of heresy.'

She nodded rapidly, recognising the wise counsel of an old warrior. 'I must find a way to see Don Pietro, explain to him that Juan is a true Catholic, that his conversion was real. But the guards he has posted on his door will not admit me.'

Gomara put up his hands. 'No, Lady! You must not go to Don Pietro.'

'But if any man can reverse the decision of the tribunal, surely it is he.'

Gomara's eyes clouded. 'There is nothing you can offer him that will change his mind.'

Maria hitched up her skirts and took from them a leather bag. She unlaced it and spilled a glittering assortment of gems across the scarred wood. 'Look! My jewels can be his ransom.'

'I don't think so, Lady.'

She went on, breathlessly in fervent hope. 'But I have been told that Don Pietro's rapacity is boundless. Doesn't the Inquisition finance itself through confiscation? These are not French pastework, they are real, and worth much money!'

'Then, for Jesus's sake, Lady, do not show any of them to Don Pietro.'

'But —'

Gomara was shaking his head. 'I have seen Pietro's like before. And in Vera Cruz the *marineros* told me about the time his zeal was unleashed on board Admiral Luzon's flagship. No, Lady, he is a fanatic. You cannot bargain with him. If once you show him your pretty things he will take them. Then he will be forced to commit you to prison to cover his theft.'

'But, how then?'

'We have few allies in this battle, Lady.'

'Even Gonzalo is in Vera Cruz.' Her mouth twisted with bitterness. 'All of those who I thought my friends have deserted me. I could hardly believe their cowardice.'

'Don't fault them. They are scared. You must see that when the Englishmen are used up the Holy Office will begin looking for others to indict.'

A canyon of silence opened.

'So Juan must die?'

Gomara's head lifted on his shoulders. 'Do not lose hope.'

'Do you think he will escape?'

'He's imprisoned alone and well guarded in a cellar with walls three feet thick. He cannot escape. But —'

'Yes?'

Her eyes were luminous with tears, her whole being hung on what the *muletero* was about to say.

'I know one thing, Lady. Your brother, Gonzalo, is certainly not in Vera Cruz.'

Then he told her what she must do.

The market square was in darkness as she ran through it. The spires and crenellations of the viceregal palace stood out starkly against the star-peppered sky, and the wooden edifice of the Inquisitors' stage was eerie and empty. At the iron gates she was stopped by the guard, who looked at her mean garments and denied her entry.

'Away, woman! You cannot come by here.'

The guard was armoured, a well-thewed soldier with poxed face and tattered beard.

'How dare you speak to me in that manner?'

'Get you gone, before we set the dogs on you,' the other, a man of slighter build and shorter ways, thrust his lantern into her face. 'Go.'

She stood her ground. 'I am the sister of Captain Gonzalo de Escovedo. I must speak with him.'

The first guard shifted his weight and peered at her unconvinced. 'The Captain is not here.'

'Don't lie to me, soldier.'

'He is not here, I tell you.'

She produced a big oval ruby and held it up so that it reflected the lantern light brilliantly. 'This stone says that your Captain is dining with the Viceroy tonight.'

The slighter guard took the stone and examined it, spitting on it and polishing it on his gold-banded sleeve. He looked about him and stepped to a window pane, reaching up to incise a mark on the glass.

'I'll fetch the Captain, *señora*.'

'Quickly.'

He vanished and reappeared moments later with Gonzalo, who was furious at the disturbance. He seized her roughly and brought her inside, out of earshot.

'Maria,' he whispered fiercely, towering close over her. 'Are you mad? What are you doing? Don't you know that our father is here in Mexico combing the city for you? Where have you been?'

'I want to see the Viceroy.'

'Don't be stupid. That's impossible!'

'Gonzalo, I must see him!'

He shook with anger, pinching finger and thumb at her. 'Don't you *understand*? By the Virgin, you are that far – *that far* – from getting us all impeached by the Inquisition. Thank God I've found you. Now your father can put you in hand.'

'You didn't find me! I found you!' Her voice rang out in the vaulted ceiling, then grew intense, pleading. 'You must help me, Gonzalo. If ever there was a time a sister needed her brother's help it's now. Do not deny me, please!'

'Help you? What for? So you may find a way to get the Englishman out of his gaol. You'll get us all killed.'

'He is your brother-in-law. Where is your duty?'

'I warned you at the very first not to look at him, Maria. But you disobeyed me.'

'Hypocrite! Don't give me your lies. You brought him to me in the first place. And now, for fear of the Inquisition you deny all. Bring me to the Viceroy, or I'll denounce you to Don Pietro as a Devil worshipper!'

'For Christ's sake, control yourself!'

She inclined her head and set her words in a deadly threat. 'Take me to Don Emilio, or I will do exactly as I said.'

All around faces appeared at corners. Doors cracked open. He hurried her deeper down the candlelit corridors, to the heart of the palace, a quiet flagged quadrangle with fountain and colonnade, then he stopped again and implored her, his hands curling in the empty air at his breast. 'Think carefully, I beg you. I have been to the Viceroy once already, and I have heard his answer. He'll never back down. And if he did, what could he do? He has no authority over the episcopal prison. Even he is powerless to save your –'

'Take me!' she shrieked, and the sound echoed like murder in a cathedral.

He clapped his hand over her mouth and led her away to a great, intricately worked copper door, guarded by two sentries, who snapped to attention as they saw Gonzalo's uniform. Neither looked at Maria, but gazed ahead, allowing the Viceroy's principal lieutenant to pass. Inside, Luis de Vega, the Viceroy's nunciate, was at his desk.

'Is Don Emilio within?' Gonzalo asked without ceremony.

Vega, a man in his forties with eye-glasses and a shock of sleek black hair, looked up slowly from his reading, appraising the grime-streaked woman who stood beside Gonzalo with interest. 'He is, Captain Escovedo. But you can't go in. The Chief Inquisitor's with him. Who's this?'

'Thank you.' He looked dangerously at his sister, but when he turned for the door she refused to follow.

'Maria –'

'We'll wait.'

'As you wish.' Vega shrugged and sucked a tooth. 'His Excellency may be quite some time. May I enquire the nature of your business?'

'It's confidential.'

'Very well.'

Maria perched on the edge of one of the upholstered benches opposite. Gonzalo stood with his back to the secretary. His intense embarrassment that Vega should see him thus exposed showed in the colour of his face, which was reddening. He seemed to be waiting for Vega to offer some slight, but the secretary merely unfolded the wires of his spectacles and looped them over his ears, allowing disdain to be suggested by his indifference.

Was the donkey man right? she wondered. Was the Inquisitor so terrible? Should she throw herself on Don Pietro's mercy when he appeared? What sort of man was he? Surely a man of God would have compassion. For the sake of her husband she would put herself at his feet, beg him to reconsider, and the Viceroy would add his voice to hers and Juan would be saved.

The Viceroy's door opened. Maria was surprised to see Doña Isabella standing at his side. Don Emilio was subdued, almost reverential before the tiny man in red.

She steeled herself. This was the moment. If she was going to fall at the Inquisitor's feet it must be now.

As she rose, the Viceroy looked up suddenly, seeing them for the first time, but his expression was so full of displeasure that she froze.

'What's she doing here, Escovedo?' he muttered furiously, touching Gonzalo's sleeve, then he swept past with the Inquisitor, his wife conversing banally with him.

As the echoes of Doña Isabella's nasal tones died away, Vega said to Gonzalo, 'I warned you he was rather busy tonight. Would you like to stay a little longer? I'm sure he'll be back presently.'

'We'll leave now.'

He grabbed her arm but she fought him off. 'No! I won't go!'

When Don Emilio returned, he ushered Gonzalo and Maria immediately into his sanctum. 'Explain yourself, Escovedo!'

'Excellency, I'm sorry. My sister —'

The Viceroy turned his anger on her. 'What are you doing here? Don't you know that your family's worried about you? That it's dangerous for you here?'

'I – I *had* to see you, Excellency,' she stammered, terrified to be confronting him this way. 'It's about my husband.'

'What of it? He's under arrest. I can do nothing for him.'

Doña Isabella came in, eyeing her coldly.

'Please, you must save him. For your own sake, Don Emilio.'

'What does she mean, Emilio? Speak up, child.'

'The cannons. It's the cannons. Juan told me that he has kept the secret of how the metal is made in his head. Without that knowledge the foundry cannot make others. If he dies you will not impress His Majesty with your work, and he will not order you back to Spain.'

The Viceroy's eyes flashed to Gonzalo. 'Is this true?'

He made a helpless gesture. 'I don't know, Excellency. It might be.'

Doña Isabella watched her husband sit down heavily. Though she held her peace she seethed with anger inside. You fool, she thought. Why didn't you stand up to Don Pietro like a man? Now we're both trapped here in this vile colony for ever. I'll never see Madrid again.

Never. I hate you, Emilio. I hate your weakness and your pride and the way you treat me. You knew the cannons were our only hope, and yet you let Don Pietro take the Englishman away. And tonight, instead of working for his release, you humbled yourself before the stinking little priest. Don't you care that we're marooned here at the outermost edge of the world?

'Do you know why the Chief Inquisitor was here tonight, *señora?*' Don Emilio was saying. He was calmer now; regret edged his voice. 'Tonight I asked Don Pietro for your husband's release, but he refused me. There is no legal way I can countermand him.'

'Then find some other way. I beg you!'

'Gonzalo, please take her to her father. She must understand that she can do no good here.'

'Yes, Excellency. Come here, Maria!'

Doña Isabella stepped forward. 'Leave her to me, Captain. I know how to calm her. It's a woman's comfort she needs not harsh words.'

The girl was shaking as she allowed herself to be led from the Viceroy's rooms. When they were alone, she said, 'Tell me, child, how do you know that the King would be reluctant to recall his Viceroy from Mexico should my husband desire that?'

Maria looked up at her, suddenly speared by the realisation that she had revealed her knowledge about the Viceroy's past, but she seemed no longer to care. She said, 'I saw long ago that Don Emilio's appointment here was in effect an exile, and that he wanted the guns as a means to recover the King's favour.'

'That's very perceptive of you, Maria.'

'I know also that the King sent him here because he committed a great crime but at the same time a great service to His Majesty.'

'And do you know what that service was?'

'No, Doña Isabella.'

The girl's perfect oval face stared up at her unsettlingly, paining her unbearably. She might have had a daughter like Maria if she had not wed a man unable to impregnate her in twenty years of fruitless marriage. Emilio has ruined my life, she thought as she watched those grief-reddened eyes. It is time he was made to pay.

'I will tell you Don Emilio's crime,' she said. 'But only if you promise to use it to persuade him to help free your husband.'

Chapter 18

Tavistock stood on *Antelope*'s quarterdeck at peace with the world, arms laced together, deep in contemplation. The morning was cool and pleasant: the sun low on the eastern horizon, lost in a great tangerine haze. Sea mists clung to the small islands through which they navigated. The deck was still wet, undried as yet by the sun and gritty under his boots from sand scrubbing. Here and there on the broad rails and gratings, huge patterned moths shivered for warmth – green triangle wings, powdery mantles, feather antlers, thorn legs, and amethyst eyes. So beautiful. Each one the intricate handiwork of God. They had been blown out to sea on the fetid breath that the jungle exhaled nightly, and Tavistock wondered fleetingly how many countless millions of them were scattered as fish bait over the ocean waves. Beautiful but wasted, unseen by any human eye. Wasted like the rain that fell over the ocean. Wasn't it strange that God made it to rain at sea? Unknowable, indeed, was the mind of the Father.

He took another turn about the deck, and his thoughts focused down on practicalities once more. His eyes followed the experimental shrouds. A new shroud-laid rope, four-stranded, twisted right to left, a strange fibre, quite unlike anything he had seen before. The Portuguese trader they had taken it out of had been rigged with it. 'Sisal' the pilot had called it, saying it was made from the agave plant of Mexico. He ran his fingers over one of the mizzen shrouds where it was rove through its deadeye. It had been his intention to renew the standing rigging as necessary with the new rope, but he had decided against it. After so long at sea, a man grew to know rope, how it weathered in cold and under the sun, how much strain it would take, where it would fail and where it would hold. He had learned from Amyas Poole how to bend it, whip it, splice it, seize it, hitch it, weave it, worm it. But this 'sisal' seemed a poor substitute for Manila hemp. It would have to go.

Thoughts of old Amyas turned to thoughts of his brother. Job Hortop's words haunted him now, shamed him with images of John sitting comfortably in Mexico with a wife and his own forge, making weapons for the enemy, *being* one of the enemy. After all the moments he had imagined John's peril, all the nights spent in the Tower worrying the problem of his release like a dog at a bone; the defiance, the risks he had taken – and for what? It had soured him more deeply than anyone among Drake's men, or his own, could know. The Spaniards had taken John bodily, that he could understand – for that he could almost forgive them man to man, could conceive bargaining John's release in civil terms. But they had set a spell on his mind, the foul priests had suborned his spirit, and, by God, for that they must pay.

But slowly, and by degrees, with smooth plans and much aforethought he would descend on the King and take from him due compensation. A brother's ransom it would never be, but he would have a thousand pounds from Spain for each pennyweight of John's body.

Since the time he had gathered his crew about him, Tavistock had worked on them like a hammer upon white-hot metal, forming them to his principles. He had quietly told Thomas Fleming, the Scot, and John Oxenham, his own trusted men, that leadership was an art he would have them learn.

Both men were, like Bowen, capable of being brought on. It was born in a man, but leadership could be encouraged by good policy: 'Make yourself loved by your subordinates, if they will not love you then fear must hold sway, but respect they *must* have for you. In punishments, anger has no place. In all cases seek first to have the misdeed repaired by the wrongdoer. Suffer no disrespect for the Queen's Majesty, and take a blasphemy against her as one against yourself. Pick a chosen few among those you command, so that the others might have examples among their number. Trust them, but expose them to greatest hazard and demand more of them than you think they are capable of delivering. Beware of men with too much mouth. Give them petty secrets and follow those secrets to see who betrays you, for when a great secret is to be trusted you must know where it will go. Always tell your men to act as if an enemy were spying on him, and remember that in battle five men of valour will always destroy ten men of valour and one coward.'

In the days and nights of their passage, his principles had seeped into the flesh of all on board, armouring them more securely than any plate of steel. And though they knew that they were but one hundred and seventeen souls, they had had faith that his plan must succeed – whatever it was.

Between the seasons of the treasure ships the *Antelope* had made excellent progress towards Panama, hugging the Darien coast. They had taken five small coasters on their progress west, provisioning as they went: beef and pork barrels, a hogshead of wine, spirit kegs, barrels of pease and sourcrout, soused and pickled fish, robs of lemon, vinegar, oil, malt and oatmeal, mustard seed, bread in bags, dried vegetables, salt, flour in barrels. Everything they could want. They had arrested the Spaniards with little opposition, each time putting their crews out in boats within sight of land, and burning the pillaged vessels. No blood, but inordinate fear, and fear was a contagion.

The Islas Mulatas had been their destination.

'Boaz, go ashore now, and God speed you, brother.'

'Aye, Captain.'

Boaz's unearthly smile had flashed in the blackness of that awesome night, the whites of his eyes gleeful, though he was embarking on the most dangerous course of all, and alone. And all who watched him depart wondered at the brave mission he was to try, knowing that if the Spanish should catch a black man he would be skinned alive, Englishman or no.

Then, under John Oxenham, they had landed a store of goods in the archipelago: coal, firewood, bales of cloth and gifts to placate Indians. Near a steep beach they had hidden equipment chests: a carpenter's bench, careening tools and timber, collapsible pinnaces, boatswain's stores, hammocks, mariner's chests and bags, mess tables and stools, buckets and tubs, lanterns, blacksmith's forge and bellows; tools – plus spare anchors, and weapons: new and expensive wheel-lock pistols, cutlasses, muskets, pikes, barrels of gunpowder, shot and enough ordnance to blow the Spanish out of the New World.

Then they had sailed on westward, standing out to sea near Nombre de Dios. The Portuguese pilot from Havana had told him much, that the treasure fleet was expected in the isthmus port in a short time, that her commander was Diego Flores de Valdes, and that the treasure would not be waiting in Nombre de Dios.

'The attack made by El Draque has altered the habits of the Spanish, *senhor*,' the pilot had said. 'And they now know that another English pir– ah, ship, is cruising the Caribbean. But there's no danger to them on the South Sea coast of Panama. Perhaps they will hold their bullion there until Valdes brings his ships into port.'

'How can we harry the Spaniards after Captain Drake's visit?' Fleming had asked after they had put the pilot ashore. 'Nombray will be like a hive of wasps.'

'We're not going to Nombray,' Tavistock had said.

'Then where, Captain?'

'In good time, Thomas.'

At length, they came within sight of land exactly at the mouth of the Chagre River, at the very narrowest part of the Americas where the trend of the coast runs south-west by west. Tavistock knew this was called by the Spaniards the Golfo de los Mosquitos. There, in a bay near the island of Escudo de Veragua, they anchored beside Drake's ships and discovered that his party had come close to disaster.

'Twenty-eight've died in all, so far,' Drake reported. 'Mostly of the calenture.'

Tavistock feared that lethal fever in which sailors rave and sweat and fancy the sea to be green fields and desire to walk in them. He saw that concern lay heavy on Drake's heart and probed him. 'Brackish water, you think?'

Drake shook his head, shrugging off the suggestion. 'The affliction's past now, but the fight's gone out of them that remains. Most of them want home. They figure a promise that failed their dead shipmates might just as soon fail them.'

'And you?'

'I'm a human man, Richard.'

'Be careful your people don't catch the wind of that.'

Drake did not smile; he scratched at his arm. 'We're few, and growing fewer. Another blast of fever and we're broken as a raiding force.' Then, seeing Tavistock's eyes upon him, he admitted, 'Two of my brothers died – both John and Joseph. John in an attack I would never have mounted had I been there with him. Joseph of that piss-boiling fever. And the surgeon that cut him up did not over-live him by more than four days through the taking of his own medicines.'

'They're at Heaven's gate now.'

'Amen.'

'And a right good mariner was John.'

'Aye.'

Tavistock studied him again, seeing him bottle his grief, remembering Drake's bluntness when Job Hortop's report had been made. 'Then, we must punish Spain for three lost brothers, eh? And put heart in the men for the job.'

'Aye.'

Three days later, Tavistock received the message he had been hoping for. Smoke smudged the top of a hill near by, and he went secretly a short way along the coast, alone in one of the hide canoes they had taken aboard *Antelope* some weeks before, to receive it. Then he had consulted with Drake urgently.

'We'll rouse the meinie. I'll be the mountebank and you my merry-andrew, if you will.'

'A conjuring trick with their souls?'

'See me do it after you brief them on the particulars.'

'Done.'

That night, under flickering torches, the Captains laid their carefully rehearsed plan before both companies of men. They gathered midway up a mainland beach hedged in secretly with overgrown headlands and backed by forest. Drake smoothed the sand flat at his feet and drew a map of the isthmus with the tip of his poniard.

'The land bridge of Panama runs east–west. This is the north coast; along this we've sailed. Here –' he stabbed a spot on the middle of the coastline ' – is where the Spaniards have planted their port of Nombray. And this is the south coast and the Great South Sea beyond on which no Englishman has yet gazed. This is their port of Panama. Both ports

are strong and well defended. But you may plainly see that to bring
their gold and silver up from Peru and send it into Spain they must first
land it at Panama and bring it overland to Nombray. This they do on
pack mules following the Royal Road, thus.' He scored a line between
the two ports.

Tavistock listened to Drake explain further and watched him finally
stab the middle of the road and leave the dagger there, buried to its
jewelled hilt. This was his cue. He scanned the faces of the mingled
crews, saw them lit variously with greed and the promise of a fight,
willing and unwilling, seeing with pleasure the eagerness in some faces
as they crowded in on him. He noted most those that seemed least
hungry for war, then, just as he and Drake had prearranged, he cracked
his knees and stood up.

'Come, now, Captain Drake,' he said, acting his part with relish. 'It's
a tough request for your weary boys. Shall we pick twenty men and
hope to overcome a thousand? I know which of my men are fit for the
task.'

'So your men are men, and mine are boys, is it?' Drake replied with
mock rebuke. 'You think your own company so loyal, and mine not at
all?'

Tavistock leaned in on him. 'I'll tell you this, Francis. Any man of
mine would cut your throat on an order from me, though they love you
dearly and respect you more.' The eyes of the hundred men who
clustered around them stood out in disbelief at what they were hearing.
The attention of the least of them was nailed to Tavistock as he
continued, 'It's to fight the Spaniard, we've come here. Spanish gold is
our aim. Tons of it, aye, and silver too! And pearls such as this!' He
drew a monstrous orient from his tiny waist pocket and rolled it in his
palm. 'Big as a cow's eye – near enough. And there's more. Huge
emeralds that burn with a green fire that'll captivate any gal who looks
into 'em! Enough to make every man here rich as a lord's bastard.

'Where did the Spaniards come by it? That's a question I'll put to
you! And who does this wealth really belong to? – for they certainly
stole it!'

No answer came.

'To a pagan king in far Peru, whose warriors are women and who
fight with feather cloaks and wooden sticks and bladders of air. Yes!
That's the valiant enemy the Dons have overcome! They talk of their
great Empire but the truth is that they stole it all from sops and
nidderlings with no idea of war. You've all seen Spaniards. Is there a
man here will tell me a report of Spanish valour? No! You've seen
Spaniards handle their ships. Is there a single one of you thinks much
of that? No!'

They stirred and shook their heads.

'And more! What courage these Spaniards once had is gone rancid in
the heat and the blasts of papist priests. The men of Spain are grown

fat and full-bellied on their luxuries. You've seen them! You've spied them staggering drunk and gouty on their wharves.'

Ned Allen, Drake's boatswain's mate, barrelled his arms and blew out his cheeks and made a lolloping pantomime for them. Some grinned and some jeered and poked him, then Tavistock's fists clenched and Allen was himself again.

'We're not Spaniards. We're a different kind of men. Men who know adversity. Isn't that the truth? And though I see there might be one man, or two, among you that wants to roll in self-pity like a three-legged sow, that's not the true feeling of your hearts. You, Job Harper? Are you a coward? A Spaniard?'

'No, sir!'

'Good lad!'

'And you, Daniel Taylor. What of yourself?'

'Not I, sir!'

'Well said, Danny lad! Remember, he who attacks carries the day, and he who thrusts at the enemy's softest place will be the victor. How can we fail when God and all England stand behind us wishing themselves in our place?'

He saw them fill with belief, some shouted out, others whooped and made agreement, and all the while he and Drake were sorting the ardent from the faint, knowing by their outward show which of them were only carried by words and which were at heart fit to take inland, and which again were fit to put in charge of the ships and pinnaces they would depend on for escape.

Tavistock simmered serious now, seeing it was time to draw them that were new-heartened back from the far extreme of encouragement, and put to them instead the opposite view.

'But we are few. Twenty of us can be spared to set upon the Spaniards. Twenty only. Ten shall be of my company, ten of Captain Drake's. And though you are lions, this is a wilder country than Devonshire and fraught with peril. Thank God then, that we're not alone in our mission.'

'God is with us!' a zealot cried out.

'Aye!' they assented all around. 'God hates the Spanish.'

'Amen,' he said. 'But I have another meaning, as you shall see.'

Then Tavistock pushed through them, clearing a way before him, and he cupped his hands to his mouth and brought in the armed, silent men who had been planted in the fringes of the forest as sentries. He brought them in and made them sit all together and called again into the darkness three times with a great voice and they waited and watched until their eyes deceived them with expectation.

After a space they heard movement in the undergrowth. Drake hissed at one of his men who reached for his pistol, and stilled him. In the gloom the palmetto leaves parted and a headless, armless, legless figure appeared, coming upon them like a ghost dressed in a white tattered shirt and duck breeches.

As he approached, the torchlight picked him out and the men began to cry his name and praise heaven for none had thought to see him again.

'Boaz!'

At his back was a host of black warriors who came out one by one and waited, some crouching down, some standing with spears and with bows. Only one came forward and Boaz presented him to Tavistock and Drake with great ceremony.

His name was Pedro Mandinga, chiefest among the Panama Cimaroons, and there was none in all the New World who hated the Spaniards more nor knew their habits in this province better.

The next day, provisions were prepared, new edges were whetted onto weapons, shoes passed out to those that were chosen. Boaz interpreted tirelessly to discover from the Cimaroons what was best to take and how precisely the land would tax them. The first day's march inland was arduous, the second and third more so, and at certain places scouts were dispatched ahead, pathfinding and leaving a trail of subtle signals by ripping leaves and snapping stems. Silence was imposed on the rest as they walked. Stealth was their watchword.

All morning they climbed higher into a land filled with the chattering of monkeys and birds, scaling the mountains that stretched east–west like a spine across the isthmus, Tavistock swearing that they would find no rest until they had broken the back of the land. Some time before noon on the fourth day, Drake called a halt. The Cimaroon chief pointed to a thickly forested hill lying a mile or two off the track. Its peak rose above the general lie perhaps a hundred feet and Tavistock agreed that now they should take the weight off their backs for an hour. Although it was approaching the hottest part of the day and the sun had burned away the morning mists long ago, leaving the day clear and bright, the trees hereabouts were lofty and full of shade and the red earth beneath was moist and cool.

Drake came over, his ebullient face gleaming with sweat.

'I've spoken with Pedro. He says there's value in an excursion. Will you come with us? You'll thank me for it tomorrow.'

Tavistock felt the ache in his thighs. The climb had been steep and growing steeper as the morning wore on and as the climax to the pass neared. He slumped against the bole of a tree and charged his mouth with water, swilling it round his teeth before swallowing. The distraction unsettled him.

'Had we not better rest now? And keep our minds on the business in hand?'

Drake put his chin back, balked. 'I promise you a rare delight and you tell me nay?'

'I've eaten enough of the special game this place affords, and I have no great taste for more roasted otter flesh tonight.'

'It's no hunt I propose, Richard. And I have something to say to you.'
Tavistock sighed and found his feet.

'That's good. Lustily, eh, Richard?'

'I'll swear you were born with the energy of a devil.'

'Energy conquers all. And that's a fact.'

'Aye,' Tavistock admitted, realising that there might be good strategy in the walk. Reinvigorated by the thought, he picked up his sword against mishap, gave charge to his best man and followed. 'What is it? Sight of a Spanish camp?'

'Better.'

'I can think of nothing better at this moment. Except a foot bath.'

Tavistock followed the two Cimaroons who took them along the spur and to the ridge that led to the hill. After a deal of walking Drake thrust out his hand.

'Look you, there?'

'What?'

'Do you not see the tree?'

'Francis – *this is a forest!*'

'Agh! There. There! Look!'

'What of it?' Tavistock followed the line. An especially tall tree, huge in girth and sturdy, stood in a clearing, surrounded by five or six equally impressive stumps. 'Yes, a great tree, but no bigger than a gross of them we've seen this morning. Francis, if you've brought me here to show me a tree –'

'A most special tree.'

' – even one worshipped by our noble allies. I swear I'll –'

He stopped, looking at the steps that had been hewn in the living bark. High among the upper branches was a vast nest. It was big enough for a dozen men to sit in.

Drake clapped a hand on Pedro's shoulder. 'Our hosts are not savage birds, Richard, but *Protestant* birds, converted by myself and taught to say properly the Lord's Prayer, eh, Pedro?'

'*Pratasans, si,*' the Cimaroon chief agreed gravely.

Tavistock raised an eyebrow. 'Misuse by the Catholics converted them to something, but I doubt they're Anglicans yet.'

'Nonsense! Come up to their bower.'

They threw off their boots and climbed, Tavistock without more good humour than resignation, rising up fifty feet into the first branches, seeking handholds and footholds where they could the rest of the way, until they came to the highest part.

Drake was first onto the log platform where the view burst upon them spectacularly.

'Sweet Jesus, Richard! Would you look at it!'

Despite himself, Tavistock absorbed the panorama with an inrush of breath. The quiet moment that followed was heightened by his bodily tiredness, a moment of soft peace and silence, filled with the green smell of the forest tops and the echoing cackles of rude-faced monkeys, and other strange creatures. In the distance, the cordillera stretched away magnificently. To the north they could see the faintly shimmering Atlantic, to the south another sea, blue and infinite. It rent their eyes with its colour, and held promise of bounty enough for any mariner's soul.

'That's her,' Drake said, greatly awed. 'The Great South Sea. A salt ocean so big she girdles half the world and might swallow England and Spain and a dozen other countries and not rise a fathom. Almighty God grant me breath enough to go a-booting upon her in an English ship one day.'

'You will, Francis.'

'I know it.' Drake's manner waxed expansive. 'I've long considered it. And I swear by my design that in so doing I'll smash the Spanish and Portuguese monopoly to the East. I'll open a way through Magellan's channel and break a path for honest shipping to ply to Cathay and Zipangu and the Sultanates of India. And in that way I'll show my countrymen how to make a princely realm of England, for wealth comes of trade, and power of wealth, and so by my acts I'll have at last the most hurtful and lasting revenge on them that killed my brothers.'

They marched south another day until the forests subsided, to be replaced by tall knotgrass, huge tracts of champion land which had been cleared by burning. Pedro insisted on greater care and secrecy, knowing that they approached Panama, and after consulting with him, Drake suggested that they come to a more secluded place along the road. They doubled back, and sought out the protection of a dry riverbed, following it some distance until the luxuriant forest came up about them again. Then, as they were passing along a gravel bank on an eastward bend of the river they heard the noise.

Tavistock ordered silence. What was it? The road was narrow here, and overhung with big trees that followed the watercourse. Instantly the whole company fell unseen into the shadows under the road.

The rhythmic noise came again on the light breeze: diffuse, light pitched, murmuring like children's voices, then the sound grew plainer and Tavistock saw the mule train.

Their bells jangled like a lure in the distance; fifty beasts roped one behind another, each burdened with three hundred pounds weight. The *arrieros* – muleteers – walked beside with switches, at the head a soldier mounted on a horse followed by a column of twenty foot soldiers, at the tail another column of troops. Each carried a quartered arquebus and a bandolier of powder pots about him.

When Tavistock looked down past the bend he saw with amazement that another pack train followed on a short way behind with a further seventy mules, separated by more soldiers, and a third of sixty mules.

He silently calculated that together they must contain more than *thirty tons* of bullion.

A soft blasphemy escaped Ned Allen who hugged the earth beside him.

'Belay that,' Drake answered him grittily.

They walked on unaware of the men that crouched under the river bank ahead of them. He prayed that surprise would be advantage enough to overcome the guard, but there was little time to deploy.

The trains continued to approach. Drake sent a dozen men scampering over a bend in the road with Boaz, a further dozen working back one train length and the rest up ahead with him. Tavistock took the remainder, six Cimaroons, Pedro, Jenkins, Allen and Fleming, with him forward another train length. He pulled Pedro down behind the bole of a plantain tree.

'Tell your men I want no shooting until I make challenge and until the Spanish have replied,' he whispered, his voice a rasp, his hands making explanation. 'Do you understand?'

Pedro nodded. He turned and passed on the command, dispatching his archers to hidden locations on each side of the road, then he drew out his first arrow. This time it was no hunting bolt, but a long and deadly shaft, tipped with cutting iron like a boar spear, a full pound and a half in weight. He nocked it to his bowstring and crept out of sight.

Tavistock's heart thumped and he breathed deeply to calm himself. Somewhere in the distance he heard the sound of rushing water. It mingled with the mule bells, filling his head with music. Methodically he re-primed his pistols, charging them with dry powder from a horn and adjusting the set of the flints minutely. The clicks as he cocked them seemed to echo through the forest.

Twenty paces away, Allen grimly loaded his gun with hailshot and lay low.

The horseman came on at a walk, blithely unaware of the danger ranged about him, his horse's tail flicking. When he had come to within five paces Tavistock stepped out in front of him pistols in hand.

The *caballero* pulled up, sharply.

'*Buenas tardes, señor,*' Tavistock greeted him, his eyes deadly on the man's own.

'*Qué gente?*'

'*Inglés.*'

The Spaniard's face contorted. The effrontery of the challenge had stunned him but he recovered himself immediately. The footsoldiers drew their rapiers but stood back, held by their sergeants who ordered the first mule train to a halt.

'In the name of the King of Spain, whose road this is, lay up your pistols, Englishman!'

'Why should I do that?'

Both barrels pointed directly at the Spaniard's chest. His eyes were wide as his horse broached under him. 'If you do so we shall use you with all courtesy.'

'I must come this way.'

'Surrender, *señor*!'

'In the name of the Queen of England, get you back the way you came!'

The horseman ripped out his sword and dug his rowelled spurs, sending his horse up and forward in a leaping curvet, but before the war cry could escape his mouth an arrow appeared lodged across his throat and he crashed to the road at Tavistock's feet.

'*Emboscada!*' – Ambush!

Once, twice, Tavistock squeezed his triggers, blowing the nearest two soldiers into the arms of their comrades.

Instantly, the reports of other guns came out of the forest. More heavy arrows flew, impaling the infantry and showering the roadway. The mules, panicked by the sudden concussions of shot that assailed them, tried to scatter but their harnesses held them in some order. Even so, the train began to buckle like a huge serpent. It surged across the road and cut off the soldiers at the head from falling back.

Another shower of arrows thudded into them. Two men fell. A third fought on though impeded by shafts embedded in his shoulders and back. When the Spanish got off a volley into the shadows it was random. Tavistock felt himself wheeled round as if by a giant hand slapping his chest and neck.

God's death, he thought, that was too close! He looked down and saw the tiny holes plucked in his jerkin and shirt. The Spanish arquebusiers had loaded up with hail shot. Their weapons could fling a one ounce lead ball with enough force to kill at four hundred paces, but their accuracy was very poor. At close quarters the virtue of hail shot was that it could blind and incapacitate as well as kill when fired into an ill-defined group of men. Tavistock knew that the heart of the spray was deadly. A couple of paces to his right and he would have caught the full force of it.

Blood began to trickle from somewhere on his head and cascade into his beard, but he was careless of it. Three soldiers, swords drawn, were advancing on him, the desperation on their faces grotesque. He threw down the useless pistols and flung out his sword, jumping forward to parry the first blow.

All around now the road was a struggling mass as lithe black bodies came crashing from the undergrowth and into the armoured guards, slashing and stabbing with their new English cutlasses. Through a blur of red, Tavistock saw mules stumbling closer to the edge of the roadway. Their small hooves clawed for purchase on the crumbling earth that overhung the riverbed by two fathoms. Peter Jenkins darted from his cover with his shark knife and plunged into the frightened beasts, rending the lines that held them where he could. Those closest to the drop, big animals more horse than ass and fourteen or fifteen hands, began to topple, crashing over under their burdens and rolling helplessly into the green pools below. Others were drawn down until a dozen were kicking and flailing in the shallow water.

Tavistock flung a hand over his face and brought it away sopped with blood. The gore trickled from him so that it seemed there could be none left within. Then the Spaniards were on him again.

Tavistock's anger hammered in his head. He chopped a huge swathing gash in the first man's ribcage, notching him so that the sword lodged in his side. The trooper clung to it and Tavistock abandoned the struggle and his sword. A rapier lunged at him but he deflected the blade down so that it passed between his thighs. Then he drove his fist into his assailant's face knocking off the man's unlaced helmet. But he was now unbalanced himself and falling to his knees. He staggered back, fingers reaching wildly, and the third soldier, an arquebusier with no breast-plate, came upon him wielding the butt of his firearm like a club. He rolled away from the initial blow as the man tried to dash his head open. His fingers found the chinstrap of the iron morion that had rolled within reach. He swung it up, launching it with desperate strength into the Spaniard's way. The sharp brim bit into the man's fingers where he gripped his weapon and it fell from his hand. It was enough to buy Tavistock the split second he needed. He tore his dagger from his belt, gripped it ready for the upthrust, remembering what his first boatswain's mate had taught him about brawling in his youth: that a man's ribs are shaped like a louvre, that a down stab jags off the bone, but an upthrust slides in.

The man was defenceless before him now. All he needed to do was hug him close and dispatch him, but then he saw the stark fear in the Spaniard's face. He was young, hardly able to grow a beard. In that moment there was a change in the sounds around him, the solid rage of battle resolved itself into a hundred separate noises and fell away from his ears.

Through the blood the man Tavistock gripped seemed suddenly to be so like his brother, John, that at the last instant, instead of the kill, he doubled his fist and knocked the wind from his opponent, then he kicked him down, furious at his own weakness.

When he looked up he found that the remaining guards were fleeing like animals into the forest. The Cimaroons were expending their arrows, crouching in their strange way, their bows held horizontal. He called them back.

Two hundred paces away Drake's party had already triumphed, and the rest of the Spanish were in rout.

Tavistock felt exultant. A wave of intense triumph beat through him as he realised that they had actually won. He felt the blood course down his cheek and drip onto his shoulder; the burning points on his neck and chest where the lead shot had dug into his flesh were a distant discomfort, but he felt no pain. Only numbness and elation.

It had all been so *easy*!

A vast treasure. A staggeringly vast treasure. *They had just taken a bullion train.* Just like that. Here, strapped across a straggle of abandoned mules in the midst of a tropical forest, was more wealth than had been raised in taxes in the whole of England since Elizabeth had come to the throne. It was awesome. Immense. Impossible to comprehend.

'They'll be back soon.'

It was Drake, winding his hand in a strip of shirtcloth.

'Aye. In God's name, Francis –'

Drake grinned evilly. 'It's not ours yet.'

Panama was close by, the garrison there would turn out immediately the first survivors reached it. At worst, there might be a mounted column riding down upon them within the hour and a thousand troops combing the forest before nightfall.

While Ned Allen's men fell to rounding up the mules, Tavistock and Drake took each other's counsel breathlessly.

'How many dead? Tavistock asked.

'A brace. Johnson and Kennedy. Peter Pole's elbow is broken.'

'Spaniards?'

'Some. And a dozen maimed or prisoners.'

'Put those that can't walk across the mules. One man can lead them back towards Panama. The rest we'll tie up out of sight of us.'

'Agreed.'

'We must get off the road.'

'Which means unloading these cuddies.'

'Thirty tons?'

'Jesus's sake! There's more than we can carry.'

'Half the job's to take it; half to keep it.'

'We can keep the best of it, by God!'

'And we'll bury what we can't shift. The choicest part we'll take into the forest. Forty pounds per man. No more. Tell your boys strictly, only gold and stones. Leave the silver.'

'Is there time to sort it and bury it? They'll surely find fresh-dug earth.'

'We'll have to crack on with the job. I've a good place.'

'Where?'

'Down there.' Tavistock pointed to the stagnant pools. 'Bury it under the riverbed.'

'Yes! And we'll stuff the lesser tackle into land crab burrows for them to discover and take back. And sprinkle coins along false trails. That should hold up pursuit.'

Tavistock's fingers searched through the blood-matted hair at his temple.

'Let me see that.' He submitted as Drake satisfied his curiosity. 'Not much: a cut no more'n an inch long. And no depth to it.'

They got to work, dashing out the contents of the panniers across the road, scrambling down the banks with armloads, digging out trenches and sinking masses of silver into the green water. The Cimaroons looked on, at first with cool amazement, preferring to cut their own trophies from the dead Spaniards. To them, neither silver nor gold was of the least account, iron being their prized metal. They menaced the wounded and the captives, declaring that they would take their victory payment in ears and noses and the like until Tavistock told them that this was no way to hurt the Spanish who loved gold better than life itself, and that if the Cimaroons would help in this job they would have all the iron the *Antelope* could land.

It look them five arduous days to recross the mountains and come again, through rain and wild weather, to Rio Francisco, the place where they had arranged to meet with their pinnaces. But there was no sign of them.

Instead, a Spanish frigate cruised off shore, and Tavistock looked upon it, heartsick.

Ned Allen voiced the great fear of them all. 'If the pinnaces are taken then we're lost, Captain. For by torture they'll come to learn where our ships lie, and the *flota* has strength enough in Nombray to lay hold of them!'

'Courage, Ned. This is no time to fear, but rather to hasten to prevent that which we fear.'

Drake railed against the disappointment, then his temper cooled. 'At worst, if our pinnaces are taken the Spanish must have time to search them, time to examine the men, time to mount their counterstroke. If all these times be added, we may yet get to our ships.'

'God has sent the wind against them,' Bowen stated.

'And also our pinnaces,' Tavistock agreed more hopefully. 'Therefore, if they were late coming here and arrived to see that ship they may yet be lying low along the coast. Have you so little faith in your shipmates?'

They wasted no more time in idle speculation, but quickly made up a raft of logs and raised a biscuit sack for a sail. Drake led three others out on it, on the far side of the headland, going west to scout the coast in hope to find the pinnaces. Tavistock stayed to comfort the remainder with encouragements and to guard their loot. He told them they were now sitting on a treasure that amounted to only one tenth of that which they had won, but that was still fifty thousand pounds – a single pound being three months' pay had they been fool enough to sail with the Royal Navy.

Two hours into the dusk Drake returned in the pinnaces and by nightfall of the next day they had regained their ships. As they came aboard the hands enquired fervently how the enterprise had gone.

Tavistock pulled a great quoit of gold from his shirt and cast it casually onto the deck. 'Oh, surpassing well.'

That night they divided the spoils, paying off Pedro in the manner he desired. They ate like King Neptune's courtiers and drank ale from tigs – wooden-lidded jugs, tarred inside. It imparted a flavour never tasted ashore, and made for mirth amongst the men, so that they sang of their conquest, jumping onto the gratings and posturing with fist and sword.

Lockjaw, the sinewy crewman whose tongue had been cut out by Algerine slavers, sawed on his fiddle fearsomely. Tavistock had never seen him without his serrated knife. Half the crew called him a Gypsy, the rest a Jew. No one knew for certain.

Young Harry Hart raised his voice:

> 'All things we have ready and nothing we want,
> To furnish our ship that rideth thereby.
> Victuals and weapons they be nothing scant;
> Like worthy mariners ourselves we will try.'

Boy Jacky joined beside him, then a third, Jenkins, the top man with a voice like a serpentine. Together they raised a dozen verses, and while the crews caroused, Drake and Tavistock consulted together to unburden their minds.

'You know I would take my men home,' Drake told him. 'I've a mind to sail past Cartagena with our flags new trimmed and sails set slanting aloft, to show we fear not the Spaniard in any wise.'

'You know I would stay, to prove as much.'

'Then, our partnership must dissolve.'

'I wish you God's love, Francis. Will you carry my share homeward with you?'

'That I will. And save it as I save my own against your return.'

'So be it.'

Chapter 19

They came forth into the sunlight to the beating of a hundred *atabales* and the blowing of beflagged trumpets, and the mass of people wondered that these Englishmen and heretics were fêted in so royal a fashion when they were only here to die.

Tavistock walked on in procession, sweating under the heavy suit of yellow and the tall hat they had strapped to his head. He felt a sudden faintness; fear daggered him. Where was Maria now? Was she here among the crowd? Was she imprisoned? Was she about to go through the same terror as he had suffered? He had not dared speak of her to Father Tomas, the confessor they had pressed on him, fearing that any questions might precipitate her arrest. Pray for my soul, Maria, he asked silently. Pray for mine as I pray for yours. If only I could see your face. Once. Just once more. But no, an answering voice said. Don't wish her here to see your degradation. You must wish her far from this hell. Imagine her far away and happy and free. You're together in spirit. The thought of her safe deliverance will give you strength to acquit yourself like a man.

He stared ahead towards the market square. The plaza had been transformed. A scaffold that was a hundred feet long and thirty high had been erected in the square, fronted on one side by the towers of the Ecclesia Mayor, and on the other by the Viceregal palace, the balcony of which formed a part of the upper tier. Forty steps led up to the stage on which the Chief Inquisitor's rostrum was placed. Opposite, in a rectangular dock, stood the rows of pews towards which they were being led, and all around the huge timber tiers of the theatre that filled slowly with invited witnesses. Down below, a crowd vast enough to have emptied the city waited.

The stage for their *auto de fe* had taken many weeks to build. The sounds of hammering and hewing and sawing of wood had penetrated even to the dark quarters in which he had been imprisoned in these latter days, since the bodily sufferings had abated.

Tavistock was revolted by the pomp of the grand rite and the way it consumed reason and displaced all that was good in simple souls and made a vile spectacle of the intimacies of death.

When the sessions of interrogation and torture had stopped, and the severity of their confinement relaxed he had thought it a mercy. But his flood of relief had been stemmed by the realisation that this was not mercy, merely a time set aside for reflection, a span in which a man might be tempted to surrender himself utterly.

Through all that time his priest had visited him daily, soothing him at first then urging him as one friend might urge another, to swerve. Father Tomas had been patiently deaf to his protests that he was already converted and could not therefore be brought again to God. Even so, they had allowed him light and food and then a short period each day in the high-walled yard to exercise alone. Lastly, the rule of silence had been withdrawn and he had been permitted to associate together with the others.

'A man can't trust his eyes and ears,' Robert Barrett had said wonderingly on that first day of blessed greeting.

Tavistock had embraced him, but John Bone had searched the blank walls, full of suspicions. 'Aye, they give us this liberty for some great mischief.'

'They're making their judgements now. Depend on it,' John Emery had said ominously.

'It's their rule.' Tavistock had known the way of it. The Holy Office took pains that its victims were watered and well fed, that the ills men had suffered in the torture chambers were sufficiently healed prior to their coming forth for judgement. 'We're soon to go before the people.'

'Wouldn't do to burn a cripple,' Thomas Ellis had grinned sourly. They had taken out each of his gravestone teeth to teach him the love of Christ.

'Aye. This holy hellish house has taken care to keep us alive – else how could they murder us?'

'They may not do us to death, according to their own law,' Tavistock had said, his voice laden with irony.

Thomas Marks had snorted at that. 'Except in a great public ceremony, to show how high their power stands. That's their way.'

'No. *They* will not kill us.'

Tavistock had been assured by Father Tomas that the Inquisition's own rules forbade killing, that the Office was merciful and just. He had debated the matter from his nightmare bed, asking how men of God could justify the weeks of foul torment they had inflicted, the rending of men's bodies, the repeated tortures. Father Tomas had explained earnestly that what they had suffered had not been *repeated* tortures. Unlike other less enlightened authorities the Holy Office's rules allow torture only once, therefore he had suffered only one torture. One torture *continued* over many sessions. That was their way and the measure of their mercy.

Tavistock had told his English brothers the mind of the Office. 'Since they cannot kill us themselves they must hand us over to the civil authorities for execution.'

'A pissy fine distinction!' Peter Dean's thin red hair was all gone now, but the wounds on his face were as livid as the hatred his captors had stored up in him. He had spat. 'Does it matter to you, Gunner?'

Tavistock had bridled at that. 'To me their guilt is plain. They try to wash the blood from their hands with legal niceties.'

'Their Papist consciences plague them. Like yours maybe?'

'What's that?'

'They say you took their religion!'

'And you their silver!'

'Silver? You dare to talk of silver? I *earned* it honestly, Gunner. In the mines. Every day. Moiling and sweating. What was *your* pay?'

Barrett had got between them with his big sailor's fists, and calmed them. 'You're both married men, anxious for your wives. Undo your anger: there'll be fire in your bellies soon enough.'

'Aye. Don't give 'em any satisfaction. They're spying on us,' Emery's single eye roamed the walls. He bit his thumb insolently at the sightless socket of a window.

'See there, they look on us,' John Bone whispered, pointing.

Then Horne spoke softly to him, 'Have you not heard the rage that goes abroad? It was your brother's interference that brought us all to this place, Gunner.'

'My brother? How so?'

'Truly you don't know?'

'No. Tell me.'

'The word is that Richard joined with Francis Drake to bring off a famous theft and that now all of Peru's bullion is taken away from Panama in their ships. They have annoyed the Spanish sorely, brought rich men to ruin and spread panic throughout the Empire. It's even said that the King's surety is undermined, that he must go scratching for Italian loans at twice the rate he once enjoyed. Mark me, Gunner, the Spanish are well angered.'

Tavistock had let out a hanging breath, stunned by the news. 'Which is why we are taken by the Holy Office?'

'Some of the men believe so.'

'And you?'

Horne had shrugged. 'As for me, I think not. For the supreme and untouchable Inquisition does what it will. It takes no heed of King, Pope or of God Himself, much less your brother's doings.'

Then Tavistock had sunk back against the wall and there had been silence until William Lincoln's light singing voice had floated up, sweet as a boatswain's whistle. 'King Philip has us in his grip –'

Answering voices had given the refrain. '*Fie, men. Fie.*'

'King Philip has us in his grip –'

'*Who's a fool now?*'

'King Philip has us in his grip, but through his fingers we shall slip.'

'*Thou art a well-drunken man. Who's a fool now?*'

Tavistock had watched the song cheer them, whilst above shuttered windows had opened and hooded acolytes had looked out on them, mystified that there could be a semblance of mirth in such a place. The song had made them think of ale and women, made an English crew of them again, but despite the first smiles to light their pale faces in a year, they had all known, deep in their hearts, that none of them would slip from the King's fist; each had understood that those that were deemed fully repentant would be flayed through the streets and then sent into Spain to be chained in the galleys; those that were deemed unrepentant would burn. Tavistock had known then with great certainty what his own sentence would be.

A month later, Father Tomas had brought him news that a proclamation had gone out, warning the citizens of Mexico City that the judgement was to be served in the marketplace, and that all people must lay aside their toils or their leisures and attend to hear the sentences solemnly announced. Those of the populace who attended would be granted indulgences, Father Tomas had said in his fervent way, adding at Tavistock's asking that those who failed to attend would be roughly chastised.

Last night they had all gone without sleep, soldiers incessantly marshalling and drilling them in the prison yard so that they were set in order and given instructions where they might walk and which man should follow which. Then, in the waning hours of night, Juan de Bovilla had arrived with a squad of men. They brought out the sanbenitos, the sleeveless fools' coats of sulphur yellow, all cleaned and made straight. Bovilla had passed them out to the penitents personally and with great reverence, telling each man that his suit should hang one day in the rafters of the great Ecclesia, as immortal reminder of their correction. All bore the red cross of Saint Andrew in front and back. The *corazos*, or tall hats, were painted with fireballs and devils, the more to demean and to humble the wearers.

At six o'clock they had been breakfasted on bread fried in honey and a cup of wine. A shower of rain had quenched the dry earth and gone away again, and, at eight o'clock, the great procession was begun, marching a crooked mile through streets packed with people, headed by a column of soldiers carrying long pikes and leading two hundred Indians with great baskets of cut wood strapped to their backs. Next came a cadre of Dominican friars, attired in black, with white crosses on their surplices. Following them a dozen pages carried the standard of the Inquisition, and after a green cross decked with black crêpe, all flanked by guards in black and white.

Tavistock moved forward at the solemn pace the cruel ceremony dictated. Now he saw the Grandees take their places in the procession, headed by Don Emilio, a distant, upright figure, clad in his suit of midnight blue, beruffed and hung with the medallions of his temporal power. Along the far side of the *plaza* Tavistock saw the ladies of the nobility ranged at balconies and windows overlooking the scaffold, bright in their finery and fanning themselves under multicoloured parasols. Today had been proclaimed a great public holiday, but the buzz of gaiety and expectation was fuelled by a dark and seething fear that he saw keenly in their faces. Every spectator, no matter what his rank or station, knew that though this day they watched the procession from afar, tomorrow they might be walking in it themselves.

Tavistock walked as if in a dream, flanked by Father Tomas and another, younger monk who watched and prayed continuously in rote Latin. Around him were raised the horrific effigies, as big as life, of those of his shipmates who had perished when they had first come ashore, or who had died since, and whose names the diligent enquiries of Juan de Bovilla had brought to light. Job Hortop's straw image was there as were those of the men who had been murdered by the Chichemichi Indians. They were raised up on poles, dressed in the same sanbenitos and *corazos*. Also, there were chests painted with flames containing the remains of John Rider and James Collier and Silas Hooke whose obstinacy had killed them in the Inquisitor's cellars, though publicly it was said that they had died of fever.

Each Englishman was accompanied by two familiars – monks who like his own Father Tomas prepared them for death as they walked. Each prisoner wore a rope about his neck and carried a tall green wax candle. John Emery had been manacled and gagged to stop up his blasphemies. Behind him, Peter Dean mouthed the Lord's Prayer, his eyes burning red as coals. Those that had wives and children that they cared for went meekest, knowing that their families were hostage to fortune, hoping with good behaviour to save them.

Tavistock suddenly saw the fallacy of his hopes. My skills will save me again, he had thought. Surely, Maria has told Don Bernal that I retained the secret of the alloy. Surely Don Bernal must have passed that on to the Viceroy. Surely, the Viceroy has struck a bargain. He must have. Yes, he must have. He's not the sort of man to give in so easily. But what if he hasn't? And what if the Spaniards want revenge for Panama more than they want English guns. I'm trapped, he thought, looking around. Trapped. It's insane. I'm letting them lead me to my death. Without complaint. Without a fight. Is that what a sane man does?

Panic rose in him. His eyes searched to left and right for a way to escape, but there was none. To the rear the procession snaked on with the representatives of each Holy Order walking two by two in their distinctive habits, followed up by a column of brightly armoured horsemen. On each side double ranks of pikemen stood shoulder to shoulder along the way, holding back a pressing mass of people. Every window was full, every gallery likewise. People fringed the rooftops and clung to any high vantage point they could find in every building save the viceregal palace itself.

The rumour swept before him that this was the brother of the pirate that had stolen the Panama silver, heads turned as he came into the square. At the first sight of them a huge shout went up. He saw the purple plumes of mounted officers riding ahead, making a way through the jeering crowd, the sun glinting on a drawn sword as it was waved.

As he breasted an alley he smelled the tang of woodsmoke from a vendor's fire. Dread boiled up in his belly. He remembered the fireship. The face of Villanueva the Spaniard imploring him. Then the deep memories of the fire that had consumed his father came upon him. They had played in his mind in that dark cell, haunting his unguarded moments. And he had confessed it. They had written it down. *The Englishman, John Tavistock: witnessed his father burned for obstinate heresy in the time of King Philip's reign in that Godless land*. He had signed that declaration, but they had smiled, delighting in the special terror he had for the flames.

He stumbled then, but his familiars took his elbows and helped him up. He stiffened, but they pulled him on until they reached the timberwork. There the prisoners were urged forward to climb the steps and take their seats for the celebration of the Mass, and he suddenly saw himself as others must have seen him, cringing and being carried forward as a coward. Something unbearable squeezed his heart. Will you stand up, or will you be led like a beast, John Tavistock? Choose! But look how John Emery battles them every step of the way; he gets nought but bruises and only rouses the crowd further with his wrestling. So is that courage, or cow stupidity? Isn't courage nine parts stupidity? Isn't that what Richard used to say? And the last part was what? *Defiance!* He heard Richard say it clearly. Show the world you defy it and it runs like a kicked dog. Dare to do as you please. Rise up! Go boldly, and be proud!

He felt the tight fist in his breast loosen. He shrugged off the hands that held him, climbed unaided. His shoulders went back. His head lifted. And courage did fill him, driving back the terror as he mounted with the others into the prisoners' dock.

An 'oyez' rang out. Silence was called. The great banner of the Inquisition, as big as a mainsail, was broken out on a tall mast, rippling across the façade of the most impressive church in Mexico. Green, with a crucifix, flanked by the sword of justice and the olive branch of clemency, wreathed by the inscription, EXURGE DOMINE ET JUDICA CAUSAM TUAM. Then a tiny form in vermeil red silk mounted his high podium under that immense flag and soon the goggling crowd was silent, hushing children and straining all to hear the piercing words ring out.

'By the authority of the Grand Inquisitor and of the Council of the

Supreme and General Inquisition of Seville, according to the precepts contained in the Instructions of Toledo, I do hereby declare this judgement made.'

Don Pietro began to read out the sentences. He came first to those that were dead or escaped, dealing with them at length, and discussing the baseness of their crimes. As the man spoke Tavistock watched the mood of the people change; a great stirring in the crowd began, swirls of ill temper rose up like a squall passing in the wide mid-ocean, ruffling the sea of heads as their feet shifted and shuffled. He could feel their indignation grow into hatred; their voices raised in ritualistic answer responded louder each time. One by one, the vile effigies were taken up and imprisoned in cages, each to be absurdly lectured at and shown in ridicule to the baying crowd.

Then a gate in the dock opened and Roger Tradescant the *Jesus*'s chief armourer was hauled up.

'Gunner, can you hear?' Barrett growled suspiciously. 'What's the Inquisitor saying about him?'

'That he secretly spits on the cross, and that the crucifix weeps and sheds blood for shame at it.'

'The devils,' Barrett said. His shaggy brows set close over his eyes. 'I was at Tenerife in 'sixty when the Inquisition took Thomas Nicholas on the evidence of whores and thieves, and the year after when John Frampton was took in Cadiz when he went a-trading for wine at Malaga. They banged him up in the Castle of Triana, the Inquisition's great fortress in Seville. They racked him like they racked us, and made him wear the sanbenito for all his life, charging him never to quit Spain. And do you know why?'

'Their poxy religion,' young Miles Philips mumbled. At fifteen, his voice was not fully broken and it grated as he spoke.

'No, lad. They took him for his ship, and all her cargo and above two thousands ducats in gold. That was how Don Pietro de Contreres got his first fortune – by plain robbery.'

'And they dare to call us pirates!' John Chamberlain said.

Horne scratched at his chin. 'The money I had stashed up! God's light, it makes me sore with weeping.'

Paul Horsewell grinned tightly, full of false bravery. 'That brother of yours'll punish 'em, now, eh, Gunner? They got no answer to men that's aboard stout ships. Free Protestant men curdle their blood!'

'No man'll save us now,' John Bone told him balefully. 'We'll be locked up till we die.'

'You think that's what'll happen to us, Gunner?' Jacob the sailmaker asked hopefully, not daring to face the other possibility. 'That we'll have to wear these stinking yellow suits for ever and all?'

'We'll know that soon enough.'

Horne pointed to the street that led from the square and toward the *braseros* of the execution ground. It passed under an arch on which was built an old guard tower at the northernmost corner of the viceregal palace. It now served as a store, and many times he had seen millers' carts standing and sacks of flour being hoisted up, and he had passed the time of day with the drovers. But now the arch was dressed with soldiers of the Viceroy's personal guard.

'Look at those ugly bastards in black jackets. Trust the Viceroy's men to get the best view of the stakes.'

'They'll be severe on us,' John Bone said. 'Don't doubt it. They all fear what Richard Tavistock can do, and they want us for examples!'

Philips's voice quavered. 'What became of them, Mister Barrett?'

'Who, lad?'

'John Frampton and the other one?'

'They got away, don't you fret now, boy. And they both got home and wrote great books of words for the Queen's astrologer, Doctor Dee, and other discourses which I know for a certainty our own John Hawkins read. Just like you will in a year or two.'

'D'ye think so, sir?'

'An idea is a powerful thing, Miles. If it catches fast in a man's mind. I swear that quill of yourn'll bring our plight to Englishmen not yet born.'

'Aye, and if Frampton hadn't escaped with his quill, we might not be getting burned now,' Dean whispered fiercely.

Young Philips swallowed hard, staring at the crowds.

Barrett leaned across. 'They'll not burn you, lad. You're too young. It's lardy buggers like me they want for candles. Men set in their ways. They know there's no hope for the world but for to keep the English down, lad. We're all bad bastards, that we are. Now get your chin up.'

'Aye, sir.'

A hush swept across the *plaza* as sentence was made on the armourer: to receive three hundred stripes on horseback and condemned to serve in the galleys for ten years as slave. He was led out of sight by another way. John Emery was next to be dragged out. He fought like a wild thing, mouth still gagged, nostrils flaring, his single eye vicious. His fool's cap came off again and he knocked down a guard, but his hands were bound to the yoke about his neck and his struggles soon subsided.

'What's he say, Gunner?'

'A burning to ashes.'

'God help him.'

Paul Horsewell's 'Amen' was echoed a dozen times among the remaining prisoners.

Next, Miles Philips was brought out and given to serve in a monastery for five years. He also was led away. Tavistock strained to watch the way he went, disappearing behind the staging and reappearing briefly before being clapped astride a donkey and conducted under the arch towards the prison. It was at this place at the corner of the viceregal palace that he had lost sight of John Emery a second time. He had passed under the guardtower arch and had been taken right instead of left, towards the execution ground instead of the prison. Already part of the crowd was breaking away from the main body and trying to get through the bottleneck to congregate in the spots that gave the best view of the *braseros*, but the soldiers forced them back. On the far side partly obscured by the church, the stakes were visible. Men were busy at their bases. Faggots of brushwood were being heaped around them.

Another was led up before the Inquisitor, then another and another in strict order. One by one the rows of benches in front that had been packed with his comrades were emptied. Nausea rose in him at the sight of those vacant seats. Then the next man was called, the first of his own row. John Collier and Mathias Roberts went up, then Davy Wingrove and soon Henry Smith. Beside him Robert Barrett was pulled to his feet. He turned and offered his hand in a final gesture and Tavistock took it. For the first time he saw fear sparkle in Barrett's eyes.

'God love you, Robert.'

'And you, Gunner.'

Then the gate was opened and Barrett went out to receive his sentence of death.

Pedro Gomara climbed into his cart and stood up to get a better view, but what he saw dismayed him. Things had come to a pretty pass. It wouldn't have happened like this in the days of the Emperor, he thought. Not in those days, when this land was a truly new world and the only Spaniards in it were heroes. Nunez de Guzman; Panfilo de Narvaez; Francisco Vasquez de Coronado; the great Cortés himself! And those that followed them – real men, soldiers and pioneers and iron priests that blazed the path of righteousness, not bureaucrats, nor milkpap administrators, nor soulless rakehells like Don Pietro.

'Get down, old man!'

The shout made him turn in anger and brandish his fists at a bear of a man. 'Beware, cobbler!'

'Hoh, what's this, old man?'

The cobbler's wife slapped his apron. 'Leave him be, he's crazy.'

'But I can't see.'

'Get on! Yah!' Gomara turned away furiously, pushed two urchins off the high, latticed sides of his cart and lashed the oxen. One groaned languorously, both moved forward. People parted before the pair as they stumped toward the cleared roadway. The big solid wheels creaked and turned, ploughed a furrow through the crowd. Necks craned forward to hear the latest sentence, those he displaced looked on him with annoyance and offered insults, others tried to hush them.

'Where are you going?' the moustachioed sergeant demanded, flourishing his iron-tipped partisan.

Anxiety swept through Gomara's belly. What if they stopped him? Or held him up? Had he moved too soon, or too late? 'I am to go to the *brasero*, sergeant.'

'You can't go that way.'

'How else can I get there?' He shrugged.

'I said, you can't go that way!'

'But I cannot disobey orders!'

'What orders? By who's command?'

'A mighty captain,' Gomara said defiantly.

'Which captain?'

He looked around and pointed across the square. 'The one in the fine coat, with feathers graven on his armour. Him. There, you see? His name is Captain de Escovedo, and he said that if I had any trouble with —'

'All right, you old snake. Come with me.'

The sergeant laid hold of the ring in the nearest animal's nose and tugged. Once again the beasts lumbered forward, into the lane down which fifty condemned heretics had already been led to their reward.

Another orchestrated roar swelled out from the multitude, but this time it was louder. It echoed under the high arch of the disused guard tower at the corner of the *plaza*, and round the dark chamber within which Maria had hidden herself. The room was dark but shafts of dusty sunlight speared the gaps in the tiled roof, piercing the gloom. The sounds of the *auto de fe* filled the space around her.

Oh, God help me. Please help me. I beg you, sweet Jesus, let him be saved. Her heart hammered under her sweat-soaked partlet. She tried to still the shaking in her fingers as she knotted the frayed end of a rope that ran up over the roof beam and down in a coil; she had tied it to the beam and knotted it at two foot intervals, but it would be useless unless she could shift the sacks and open the hatch which they covered. She sank down, braced her back against the wall and kicked out at them but she could not shift them.

'God give me strength!'

The hatred of the people had blazed up each time sentence was passed, then each Englishman had been put on a donkey and led beneath her to be pelted and abused. Each time she had seen it and had gone over the plan in her mind, growing more and more certain that it could never work, but knowing she had to try.

Both of the sacks were of milled flour. Each alone was too heavy for her to move, and the terrified miller who had let her into the store had fled, taking her jewels in payment for aiding her so far. He had refused to help her further, no matter what else she pledged him. The block and tackle hung above her head on its steel eye as if mocking her stupidity. She had unthreaded the rope from the pulleys and knotted it and there was no time to repair her mistake. She kicked out again at the sacks in fury as the roar of the crowd rose to a new menace.

This time the Inquisitor's denunciation attained a terrible pitch. His acid speech dwelt upon the treacherous robbery in Panama and the murdering pirates that swarmed in the Caribbean.

'*How shall you deal with this Lutheran devil?*' he demanded of the crowd. '*Tell me!*'

The answering cry was poisonous with hatred: '*Burn him! Burn him!*'

Were they leading him down so soon? The thought filled her with panic. She stumbled in her haste to get to the window. Fell. Lifted herself up. Pressed her eye closer to the broken slat of the louvre and stared out into the brightness.

There, standing upright and alone in the centre of the great stage in his suit of yellow, was her husband. She had no time to think. He would be under the arch in seconds.

'*This son of Satan was treated with all courtesy by the King and his Viceroy, and by the people of Mexico, but how has he repaid you? Even now his evil brethren lie in wait to destroy all who venture forth! How shall we deal with him?*'

'*Burn him!*'

Maria cast around in desperation then fed her trembling fingers through the shutter and broke away the dry, jagged wood, turning it over in her hand like a dagger. One of the Englishmen was clattering below on a donkey. She could see his craggy face set in a frightful mask. Then she saw Pedro's oxen appear to the right, led by a sergeant of the guard.

It's too soon, she thought desperately. Go back. Go back! Holy Mother, we're lost! Lost!

She watched Pedro's eyes stray up to the small shuttered window and then dart away. He nodded very slowly. As the cart rumbled twenty feet below her she saw that its steep woven sides were bedded with hay and that it carried two great earthenware wine jugs; between them was a long-handled scythe. She saw the old man reach for it, sun flashed on the newly honed curve of steel, and then the cart passed out of sight under the arch.

She looked at the sliver of wood in her hand and then at the sacks, cursed herself for a fool for not thinking of it sooner and set to work on the sacking.

Tavistock watched the storm of malevolence surge around him and abate. Silence suddenly filled the yawning space. Ten paces away Don Pietro's head was a shining skull. His sunken face was turned skyward, his hands stretched out in a piteous gesture of appeal.

'Lord God receive this wicked and unrepentant heretic whose sins are so grievous in Your sight and whose crimes are too evil to be heard. We, Your humble servants, deliver his body unto You.'

Bovilla put his mouth to Tavistock's ear, whispering hideously, 'Repent and you will receive clemency, even now!'

'Do as he says. Please!' Father Tomas begged him. 'For pity's sake!'

Terror swarmed in him again, but he shook his head.

'You may be spared the suffering. Consider the flames, John Tavi-stock! Think of them consuming your flesh, burning you to ashes even as you watch! Show the people you repent, and the executioner will strangle you! Repent! Or you'll burn for all eternity in the everlasting fires of Hell!'

'There is nothing to repent.'

He heard himself say it, coolly, defiantly.

Then they were leading him from the stage and down the steps, his hands bound numbingly tight, and they put him on a small donkey so that his toes almost touched the ground. The animal trotted stiff-legged under his weight, stepping through the dung of the others that had come this way. His deadening fingers felt the rough of its neck hair, bunched the bristled mane in his bound hands; his thighs felt the bulbous abdomen of the beast; the ridge of its spine knuckled his testicles as it walked. He looked straight ahead, unseeing, and as the street closed in he felt the dream falling from him. The killing ground beckoned.

Feculence rained down on him, strewed his way, spattered the street with stinking swill, spattered the robes of the priest that led him. The pungent smell of filth and corruption filled his nostrils. Suddenly he saw with great clarity. This was the circumstance of his own death march. It was real. Sharp. Actual.

I must ready myself for death, he thought, confronting the inevitability of it for the first time. He looked about him. The details of faces impressed themselves upon him. They were no longer a crowd. The sound of every throat was distinct. He saw each watcher: young and old, man and woman, Spaniard, Indian and half-blood, as an individual vessel, each the receptacle of an individual human spirit. He saw that some wanted to see him burn, others to excuse him. He saw hate raw in the eyes of some, and in some there was horror. Souls dull, souls radiant, hysterical souls, souls pleasured by the prospect, others ashamed, how some were twisted with guilt, how some had pity and some mere curiosity and others yet a saintly compassion.

The crowd thinned as the lane narrowed. In the square the ranks of soldiers on each side had stood shoulder to shoulder with overlapped halberds held horizontally across their corslets like a barrier against the press of the multitude, here they stood singly, backs to the wall of the *palacio*. Several had left their stations, and as the shadow of the guard tower passed over him as cold as death he saw why.

An ox cart blocked the street in the bright sun pool beyond. Soldiers struggled to unhitch the team and clear the way, but one of the oxen lay heavily in the middle of the road, lowing fearsomely. He saw oozing red on its hocks and hindquarters where it had been untidily hamstrung.

'Clear a way, there!'

Orders rang out. Troopers tugged helplessly at the deadweight, dragged on the horns, holding their morions back out of their eyes as they tried to unfasten the yoke. The cart shaft lifted, bucked suddenly upward, the cart tipped back throwing out its bed of straw and a big brick-red *cantaro* was dashed to shards on the ground splashing gallons of wine across the ground. Another rolled out, guttering its contents forth.

A sergeant jabbed the air with his partisan. 'Watch him!'

'You there! Get back to your prisoner! And you! Get that old idiot away from the cart!'

The cart driver scrabbled in the ruts bathing his hands in his lost wine and the straw that was scattered all around, bemoaning pitifully. Then Tavistock suddenly saw the man's face. It was Pedro Gomara.

This can't be happening, he thought, his mind knocked sideways by the confusion. It can't be!

He almost shouted the name of the *muletero*, but saw the intent in the old man's face. Gomara's eyes met his disbelieving gaze as a brawny, rock-faced soldier grabbed his waist.

'Get out of here!' he shouted directly at Tavistock, then he twisted away and began to wriggle out of the soldier's grip, raising as much noise as he could.

'Hold him!'

Tavistock heard a scraping sound above his head, then movement drew his eye upward, but he looked away again instantly, certain that the tilt of his *corazo* would make others lift their eyes. White powder began to sift down from a hatch that was hingeing open in the planking high above his head. It's a miracle, he thought. Either that, or I'm already dead. What's that falling? God's eyes, it's flour! Then a heavy coil of rope dropped on him from above and he grabbed for its knotted end instinctively, at the same time kicking out at the man who held his donkey, sending him sprawling and the beast skittering away.

'Juan!'

The shout made him gasp. 'Maria!'

'Quickly!'

The square above his head filled with her hair and face and great billows of fine white dust. All around the arch, clouds swirled out. He locked the rope under his wrist bindings. It jerked tight wrenching his elbows half out of their sockets and he was climbing for his life, his bloodless hands as weak as a baby's. He lifted himself up to the next knot, clenched his thighs on the rope, got purchase with his feet and thrust. Below the soldiers came to their senses. A hand closed over his ankle but he stabbed furiously with his heel and shook it off. He pulled himself up another knot.

'Look out!'

A barrel toppled, pushed over the edge of the hatch and fell past him to burst on the ground in a mass of staves and hoops. Another knot. Then the sergeant was under him, thrusting up with his partisan. The evil axe-headed spear jabbed, lanced through the yellow fustian of his leggings. He felt the back fluke strake his shin as it ripped away. He was nearly halfway up but the strength was dying in his arms.

'Climb, Juan! Climb!' Maria was screaming at him, showering the torn sacking and its load of flour into the eyes of those below. Her hand groped for his wildly and then his foot slipped off the knot and he almost fell back. He was blinded. Blinking. Rubbing his eyes on his shoulder. Coughing, choking on the flour – each breath caught in his throat. The world was spinning sickeningly. And his hands! They were insensible to his commands, all feeling gone from them.

'Help me!'

'Get up after him!'

'Madre de Dios, he's falling!'

He felt the rope tighten under his instep. One of the troopers was climbing, but the man's weight only served to hold the rope straighter and stop its wild twisting. Then he felt Maria's fingernails graze his arm. Her grip closed over his elbow with manic strength. His head butted the lip of the hatch as he burst through, panting, rolling on the floor as she dragged him inside.

'The rope! Cut the rope!' His voice was hoarse.

She stared about her, looking for the slat of broken wood she had used to rip open the sacks in order to move them. It was buried under the flour or gone through the hole. There was no time to find it. The rope was creaking, twisting. A trooper's steel helm appeared in the space.

Tavistock got to his feet as she swung the heavy trapdoor over on its hinges and slammed it down. It failed to close flush because of the rope, but the falling cry of the soldier told them he had dropped. Maria untied the slack rope and let it fall, then they were out and running, through the maze-like passage of the Viceroy's palace.

Chapter 20

Richard Tavistock's ship followed the Tropic of Cancer eastward, her longitude some eighty-two degrees west of her home port of London. By dead reckoning she was a dozen leagues off the northernmost arch of the coast of Cuba; to the south lay the port of Havana where *Antelope*'s sudden appearance a week ago had thrown the town into confusion, but she had sailed on, ignoring the bristling hubris of the enemy. Her timbers creaked and her stays squeaked drily now, making Tavistock think of the many schemes of running maintenance he had been obliged to put in hand of late.

On deck, burners boiled up the full-bodied aroma of molten pitch and caulkers applied it to the seams. The methodical chunking of an adze sounded as a yard was shaped up. Caged sheep bleated. Above, the sky was leaden and troubled by an unrefreshing wind that was both humid and close, a day of restless peace and short comfort for a captain and his crew. A day that seemed to presage violent rain and looked for action in a man.

He sat in his sea chair on the poop in the waning forenoon, riffle-edged papers spread across his knees. He was planning the last piece of daring of his campaign and needed to think over the matter, but the warm breeze would not clear his head. For a while he allowed his mind to steer where it would, but ever his thoughts returned to that fine *hacienda* constructed in his imagination where his brother enjoyed gains more ill-gotten than his own. It was a picture upon which his mind's eye often dwelt, and one which distressed him greatly.

The chant of the boy as he turned the sandglass reminded him that they had three alone left of the twelve timepieces they had first sailed with. They were made by Venetians exiled in London, and very accurate, but prone to breakage and once gone the *Antelope* would have to find an ocean-going Spaniard and relieve her of inferior wares. Seventh turn: half an hour to noon and change of watch. It would be useless to try to shoot the sun with this soggy overcast and soft shadows. He stretched, called for a cup of water, downed it and sent the lad away for one of

the small, sweet oranges that ripened in his cabin. When he closed his
eyes there was a bright moorland, fresh with snow, glorious cold on his
cheeks and frost numbing his toes. Oh, for an English winter, he thought.
A wind that bites and blows through a man, skeleton trees, iced ponds
and those subtle greys that hold more hidden colours than any garish
Caribbean scene. How I long to see Polaris fifty degrees high in the
night, and the Bear overhead, ah, so much John has lost ...

The boatswain's whistle sounded and Tavistock opened his eyes. The
black ring-stone of reproof glinted at him from his finger, reminding
him again. Though John was long-since disowned, he was not forgotten.
The shame of him could never be completely stamped out, nor could a
man stop himself from wanting to see his brother again – if only to put
unanswered questions to him directly.

This was the fourth day since they had last sighted land, and his
meticulous sketches of the last three anchorages they had visited were
by now fully notated with bearings and sailing instructions and
reminders of shoals and landmarks and notes taken from the leadsman's
slate. These were the real treasures he would bring back to England
because they would enable others to follow in his wake and significantly
improve their chances of success. He looked upon them with great
pleasure, but there was a worm in his satisfactions, for there were lately
new problems to overcome, problems born not of failure, but of success.

Each month, *Antelope* had ploughed virgin waters, sailing eastward
as far as the solitary Isle of Barbados, grazing the riches of the Windwards and of the Leewards, before disappearing for a time to recuperate.
In June, without warning, they had surfaced at Pine Island near the
westernmost tip of Cuba, taking some useful small game – shallops and
a bigger ship – among the Canary Isles. Then again at Santo Domingo,
flying long bunting and the cross of St George from *Antelope*'s tops to
infuriate the Spaniards as Drake had done. In October, they had taken
a great bucket of a ship, full of presents meant for the King and sent by
the Emperor of China, in which he found a casket of superb emeralds
belonging to the Master. He had levelled a pistol at Tavistock's breast
to protect them, but his powder had been damp, or his flint worn, and
without doubt the Lord had stoppered up the Spaniard's barrel to
protect His own.

Tavistock had had the man thrashed round the ship to roars of
laughter. Then he had 'bought' the emeralds for a bottle of water and
a straw hat when the villain was about to be sent off in his longboat
fifty leagues from land – close enough to save himself, far enough to
give him a raging thirst and shivers from the sun and to make him think
ruefully of his rashness.

'Tell your countrymen these green flints are a present for my Queen,'
he had shouted down at the man. 'Who, if you be in doubt, is Elizabeth
of England, and is right royal, so have no fear for your stones' pedigree,
for she will wear them prettily.'

In the year that had followed, Tavistock had sailed the *Antelope* by all the main ports of the enemy and found that no big ship could catch her. Those handier craft that could overhaul him were too light to hit him, and he knew that while he kept his crew well fettled he might care neither for pursuit nor ambush, for in the matter of espying ships from afar he could certainly have no equal.

In December of last year they had harried the Honduras coast from a temporary base in Grand Cayman, and in spring they had come upon Maracaibo and took a frigate there, relieving it of forty thousand gold ducats. Tavistock's confidence had grown with each success, and he found his fame had spread among the seafaring men on whom he preyed so that now few dared to resist when he closed with them. In all the Indies no Spaniard could explain his ability to find and assess enemy ships or how he was able to distinguish which were ripe and which to be avoided. He had not told Drake of his clever trick, and he never divulged his method to any other man, no matter how trusted.

Bowen was the worst for curiosity, and after him, Fleming. Thomas Sark, the grey-bearded sailing master, thought it devilish queer but knew better than to ask questions. From the corner of his eye, Tavistock had many times seen Bowen and Fleming standing together; trying too hard to be surreptitious during each spell he had taken himself up to the maintop to use the spying-glass. And he had toyed with them to a fault.

'There's no sorcery to it,' he had told Bowen blankly when his best boatswain had brought the subject up for the fifth time. 'Good sailing and a handy crew is the root of it. See all. Hear all. No more to it than that.'

'Yes, sir,' Bowen had replied, unhappily scrubbing at his head. 'But how do you *know* when a ship's worth the taking when she's no bigger than a grain of sand out there?'

'Like any man might.'

'But, why *do* you lay up into the maintop yourself? There's not another captain I know does that.'

'My mother's mother was an eagle, and I have her eyes. Away with your questions, now.'

'Please, Captain, won't you tell us what's that long box you draws out from its sack each time we sight a ship?' Fleming had asked.

He had stood up then. 'Come, Mister Bowen, Mister Fleming, look at my pictures. They're a fine record, are they not? And a great aid to our comings and goings?'

'Aye, Captain,' Bowen had said, as mournful as a bloodhound.

'Look you – every place we've ever been, marked down in a canny likeness.'

'Aye, sir.'

Bowen and Fleming had listened politely and gone away unsatisfied, and Tavistock had known that one or both would be back, a week hence, two weeks, two months – whenever the next ship was found and his inexplicable feat repeated.

Tavistock settled deeper in his sea chair now and, smiling to himself, watched Bowen. The problem was worried ragged now, but still unsolved. He had told no lies. The secret of taking Spaniards was indeed mostly discipline and the correct keeping of his ship and crew. And there were other factors: his policy was always to promise his intended victims that they would be accorded clemency if they surrendered, but that on the first shedding of English blood no quarter would follow. And he had abided by that, landing prisoners within sight of habitation and playing host to their captains, generally with lavish grace, and by this means he was able to plant the seeds of rumour in his guests and in return learn news of the world and draw off intelligence and thus come to some understanding of how intensely his operations pained the King's officers and how those operations might be made more troublesome.

Tavistock eyed the sky again with disapproval. There would be no noon reading today. Another day lost in the quest to correct his sectional charts for compass variation, and in arriving at a better estimate for the distance of a degree of longitude at the Tropic. The man who has the most accurate charts is the man who lives longest, he thought.

So far, their blend of good information and good luck had held them above water. There were enough uncharted islands in the Americas to plant a dozen bases, and enough slaves to free to provide each with a permanent garrison. They had discovered fine anchorages for use in time of hurricane or sore need. Ashore, the men made good use of their time and relieved themselves of the wants a mariner must endure. Bowen had gotten three women with child at least, and in three separate countries. He had sworn to each that she was his only wife, though none were that in any Christian sense as Nowell, the Puritan gunner, had scolded him. Despite Nowell's frowning disapproval many of the men had done likewise, and he himself had eventually yielded to the carnal temptations that fate delivered his way.

A happy crew, then, he mused, and a contented captain. But there were times when he was alone and quiet when he was reminded that there was more to his life's quest than enjoyment and the arresting of King Philip's lesser traffic. The strange star under which his son had been born had long since faded into the blackness of the sky, and with its waning he had progressively forgotten the shape of Anne's face, the timbre of her voice. How was she faring? As a mother? As a woman? How was she faring as another man's wife? And there was that bottomless question he had had to ask himself in solitary and soulless moments: is she even alive?

Lately he had begun to think about the real aim of his labours – to return home replete with the means to take what was rightfully his. As for his crew, they were already richer than they had ever dreamed they would be. He alone had need of a wealth so great it would buy the heart of the Queen of England. But that remained a ransom greater than any he had yet won. As season passed into season, and year into year, Tavistock had seen the boldness of his crew increase in step with their competence. It gave him cause to consider, for he found that to keep his men sharp he must give them greater and greater challenges. They began to spurn the small coasters that had once been their staple, looking instead solely to the bigger ships. Each arrested vessel outstripped the last in bounty and the richness of its pillage, and he understood that soon they must meet their match when their power to intimidate by reputation alone would fail. It was the fate of many a privateer who had grown too greedy. Eventually, a pitched battle would be joined on adverse terms, good men would be lost, they would not prevail. It was something Tavistock knew they must avoid at all costs, for the people of his crew were no longer poor sailors with nothing to lose. They were all of them rich men with gold in great store and there were many who wanted to spend it.

At first he had put them off easily, a fob here, a petty threat there, but their unrest had become a canker. He had told Robert Butcher, the sailmaker who never could keep his mouth closed, that the gold that had gone back to England with Drake was in trust, and that Drake was commanded to deliver shares only if Tavistock returned. The rumour had persuaded some to give up their agitation, but eventually a deputation had asked him straight: 'When can we go home, Captain?'

He had roughly reminded them of their oath to him on Drake's departure when the choice had been put before them which Captain they would follow.

'Traitors to our mission, and to me! You laid your words to it, gave your promises to me, every one of you!'

Stubbes, their ringleader, had spoken up. 'Captain, a man may live in but one house, and take to him but one wife. What more must we get to satisfy you? How many years and months more? We want to go home.'

'We sail home when I decide. Not before.'

'Captain, our fortunes're made. We have no more appetite.'

He had ramped at them, brought to blows by that. 'Shall I suffer it said of me that I was defeated by my own? That my crew were grown craven like the Spanish as soon as their hunger abated? God damn you all! And may He take you out of my sight before I lose my good temper!'

So their opposition had subsided into muttering, and to teach them to count their blessings he had taken them up into the Bahamas, along the Tongue of the Ocean, and planted the choicest of their booty in deep holes and gone quite secretly about it in case some among his boys entertained other ideas. Then he had ordered Dunne, the carpenter, to take the hinges off the *Antelope*'s treasure store so that all might see the empty space inside.

'How hungry are you now?' he had asked when they were ranked up before him on the following Sabbath day. 'The Queen herself charged me to take Englishmen into this Spanish lake and do what harm I might. And so I shall do. And–we–will–not–sail–away–until–I–say–so.'

After that, there had been more digging, this time back in the wilderness of Panama, but the iron-loving Cimaroons whom they met with again told them that most of their silver had been got out and the rains had washed away the bars which they had sunk under the riverbed, so they had contented themselves with what little they could find and repaired to the Cabezas leaving three bridges in ruins and more than half of Venta Cruces in flames. He had seen that both Panama and Nombre de Dios were bristling with new ordnance and Tavistock knew then that there was no alternative: he would have to find a big ship and take it, or go home unfulfilled.

The first likely ship they came upon got away under cover of night. The second scudded for a secure port and so also escaped. The third was no easier prey. They followed her for forty leagues across the Caicos Bank and into the Hog-sty, and she was fleet, almost taking them for fools in the maze of small islets, but when she saw she was cornered she made to fight, struck her Spanish ensign and ran up a black rag set with white antlers, which enraged them because that was *Antelope's* own private mark and it looked like mockery. Tavistock had cursed aloud, though his profanity was shot through with disappointment because the jest made the quarry's Captain a man known to Tavistock.

'She's a captured hull,' he told Bowen angrily. 'That's Jan de Groote's trick. He's a powerful rash man, and he has but one thought in his head and much of the Beggar way about him. He'll steal anything, even a man's good repute!'

'Shall we punish him, then?'

'Punish Mad Jan? No! I would know where he's been and where he's going and what he's doing here without leave.'

Bowen had grinned. 'You speak like he's a trespasser across your own garden.'

'He is. Though a welcome one now he's declared of our company.'

De Groote had come roaringly aboard and Tavistock had received him with wines and good meat, but that night the Beggar had said much to unsettle them all.

He had taken out his knife and cut a paring from his thumbnail in the pause. Black curls were tight about his head like a bonnet of sheepskin, and his blue eyes were half-lidded as he scraped the filth from under his fingers in turn. His English was heavily accented. 'You may ask why I am come out here, but the answer I shall give will not please you, for we Dutch are rudely expelled from your Queen's country. She turned against us to appease the King of Spain, eh?'

Alarm had run through Tavistock, and he had stared hard at his officers to quell them. Another turnabout in English policy was precisely what he had most feared and he wanted to open de Groote out. Doubts for Drake's safety and the safety of their profits seized him. 'Go slowly, Dutchman, for I have been away a long time.'

'We were sent out of Kentish ports to fend for ourselves, eh? The proclamation was that no manner of sustenance should be carried to the sea for the victualling or relief of the fleet serving the Prince of Orange. That was no way to treat allies, eh? And then what could we do, but go back to the Meuse? Do you remember the idea we hatched together about taking Brille from the Spanish?'

Tavistock had nodded. That plan had been to land a force in the port and to resupply its wants from England. 'Yes. I remember.'

'I made it real, eh? Without our allies we were thrown back on our own resources. Still, we held Brille and a week later we took Flushing also.'

'Desperation makes men good fighters,' Tavistock said, seeing de Groote's resentment and fearing his tidings more than ever now. How far can I trust the Dutchman's account, he had asked himself, knowing that there was little chance he could now predict the reception he would find on his return to England, or learn that which Drake had received. If Burghley's counsel had held sway, the Queen would have been persuaded to open negotiations with Philip, perhaps even to offer to mediate between Spain and William of Orange, power broking in order to get English Catholic rebels repatriated out of Spanish territory, and to set the seal on a partitioned Netherlands. A mantle of pleasantries would have descended over Anglo-Spanish relations, and Drake's head might have been an appropriate token for Burghley to lay at Philip's feet. That, and the expulsion of the Beggars might just have bought the conditions Elizabeth so wanted to secure.

'So the pistol of Flanders has back-fired on Philip?'

'Oh, ya. That's very true,' de Groote went on, 'we found many ways to impede them. When Alva came with an army to squash us, we cut the dykes at Alkmaar. When Haarlem was besieged the Spanish lost twelve thousand men, and at Leyden we sent shallow barges across the floods to relieve the city.' De Groote's thick lips swallowed up another chicken leg but his eyes were tempered by hard memories. His hand waved and banged extravagantly as he explained. 'Because Alva couldn't crush us he was recalled like a whipped cur. Don Luis de Requesens replaced him because Philip thought him better fitted to parley, but we kept our bases and shut the Channel tight and starved him of money until God struck Requesens down with a fever. No money and no leader, eh? – the scum mutinied, my friend, they rioted through the south, burning and looting everything. Antwerp was completely ruined and ten thousand citizens killed. But in the north it was different, eh? William's Stadholder now. He's taken all of Zeeland and all of Holland, and it's too late to talk because the Spaniard's fury has united the entire Fatherland!'

'You say Requesens is dead?'

De Groote bolted his mouthful and swilled ale after it with a gasp of satisfaction. 'Last year. Of the typhus.'

'Who is his successor?'

'Who do you think, eh? He's named as Don John of Austria, but I sailed before he came to Luxemburg. The terms of the Pacification confirmed freedom of worship for our Calvinist church, so my work there is finished, eh?' De Groote nodded shortly. 'But I still aim to get rich by killing Spaniards, which I can no longer do in the Netherlands.'

Tavistock had sucked in his cheeks. Don John, Spain's new General, in Antwerp? Could it be true? What could that mean? If the terms of peace really included Calvinist freedoms as de Groote said, then Burghley's policy had triumphed. The many factions of the Low Countries united against Spanish tyranny? The army of occupation to be disbanded? Philip still nominal King but all liberties secured? No, he thought. It's more likely that de Groote's adventure in the Indies has been prompted by another, more personal, cause. I'll lay that you've been run off by the traders for some reason, de Groote. You must have many enemies among the Flanders merchant community after the way you've gorged yourself upon their wares, and you're by no means a diplomatist. But what if you're telling me the truth? If Don John's really about to take over in the Netherlands it can only mean that Philip wants to bring the province totally under his control once more. Under the bastard prince's personal command forces can be raised and gathered for a strike, and hasn't Walsingham always said that Don John's hawkish ambitions are a danger to England? Don John believes that Spain can never consolidate her power in the Netherlands until England is returned to the status of Philip's vassal.

'I see by your ship that you've had success,' he had said to de Groote, switching the subject sharply.

'Some. You're not the first rover we've met with, eh? There are many Huguenots to the north. They say they've suffered great loss of late. More privateers sunk this three years than in sum total before that.'

'The King's Viceroys are under orders to reinforce their demesnes.'

'That's not the reason.'

'Then what?'

De Groote's scowl had revealed an engrossing fear. 'I don't know. But have a care, something evil's cruising this sea, taking men and ships wherever they strike at the Spanish. It's maybe new ordnance the Spanish have. The French say that too many of their number have disappeared off Florida. They say there's a monster loose in this sea, and I believe it. That's why I took the *Trinidad* and scuttled my own *Vrede*, which was a better ship, to sail warily under Spanish colours.'

'And then mine?'

'Oh, ya. But that's a joke, eh? Between friends.'

'You showed my flag, Jan. You stole it.'

De Groote dropped his knuckle of mutton into his plate, splattering himself with gravy. Slowly he said, 'Truth is, I heard the Spanish hate your arse so much it saves a man a quantity of powder to hoist that rag.'

Tavistock had grinned at that, knowing that his own poles seldom bore any readily recognised device until he judged good reason to emblazon them with his antlers. He said, 'I have heard some men think it possible to paint a ewe grey and call it a wolf. But not you, Jan. So no more antlers. Understand?'

'If you want that, Richard.'

'I want that.'

He had bidden de Groote good luck then, and given him copies of his lesser sketches of Jamaica and the coasts of the Windward Passage to aid him in his work, then they had parted to trust God in their separate ways, knowing that once out of sight the Dutchman would continue to fly the antlers as it pleased him.

That had been a month ago, and Tavistock roused himself from his thoughts; the wind was getting up and the noonday bell sounded, bringing up the starboard watch, so he laid below to bait. He spooned down a meal of *tasajo* – salt beef, with onions and a mop of some green herb not unlike cabbage, then he kicked off his brodkins and read a while, drowsing in his cot until his mind was triggered by a commotion. By the time Daniel Peters, his steward, had rapped and brought him the hail he had his boots back on.

'Lookout reports sail, Captain.'

'I heard him, Daniel. Give me my belt.'

Peters's hands were red with buck-washing filthy linen in lye. He hovered anxiously. 'You'll be wanting your sword and buffcoat?'

'I'll call for you if there's any likelihood of fighting. And I'll endeavour to keep your darning work light. Now leave me.'

'Thank you, sir.'

Peters took himself away sharply. His concern for his master's safety was commendable, but Tavistock wished he would restrain the urge to swaddle him in gear whenever battle came in prospect.

As soon as Peters was gone, he took the cupboard key from his neck, flung out his belongings onto the floor and unlocked the secret compartment, sliding out the sack-bound box from inside. Then he took himself on deck, clamped his precious cargo under his arm and began to climb the ratlines of the starboard lower main shrouds. When he reached the maintop he glanced down at Fleming who was shouting a wanion on the larboard watch for being slow back on deck. He sent the lookout to the forecastle before unwrapping the spying-glass and putting its end to his eye. What he saw made his heart beat the faster.

'Yes, by God! Look at her!'

Through the windowhole in John Dee's wondrous gift the ship showed slate blue against the paler sky. She stood among a rainbow of spurious colours that boiled like a summer's heat haze with that odd foreshortening the instrument gave to distant objects. She was a big ship: four masts and the tip of her bowsprit showed above the horizon, two billowing topsails, a spritsail and two lateen sails were rigged around her main and forecourses – a full press of canvas cut in Spanish mode. Five hundred tons, if she's fifty, he told himself with unholy joy. His blood began to flame at the prospect. She's doing five knots, or I'm a Portugall. What a beauty to behold.

'Steer for her, Master Sark!' he shouted. 'Boatswain, rouse the men to arms!'

The answering cries barked up at him.

This was what he had been hoping for. With luck, she would be as heavy-laden as she looked. He watched her hull rise slowly above the waters then, some minutes later, she began to sheer off to the south-east.

He met Fleming on the poop with his astounding conclusion. 'She's a Spaniard, and she's seen us,' he told him, unnerving the man mightily. 'She's out of Havana, heading, I trust, for Florida and the way home to Spain, but it's my belief she'll try to hide in the Sabanas if she can.'

'If you say so, sir.'

'Do you doubt it, Boatswain?' Tavistock turned to Sark, smiling. 'Follow her, keep to windward and close as soon as you can.'

As the sand fell in its glass the galleon grew, fulfilling the predictions Tavistock had made. The reefs and small islands of the Sabanas archipelago were strung out to starboard, slipping by as the afternoon wore on. The Spaniard was making for them like a cony bolting for its burrow. It's her only chance of shaking us off, Tavistock thought, as he watched the manoeuvre. In a straight stern chase she would be relentlessly overhauled by *Antelope*'s better speed, but the deep draught of the galleon was a powerful reason not to stray too far into the dangerous channels of the island chain. She must have a knowledgeable pilot aboard to try here. One who knows this coast well. And a handy leadsman to try the bottom as she threads her way. It's what I'd do, if I were in her Captain's position. Perhaps this one's got spirit and is willing to make a fight of it. She's a pregnant beast, heavy, and crossing to Spain she'll have more than a hold full of hides. Maybe she's rich. Maybe she'll be our last prize and our passport home. Light fails here in five hours. With God's justice we'll catch her before then, and we'll find out.

Captain Carlos Solano sweated as he waited for the pirate to close on him. He was a fleshy man, of broad beam and bristling with body hair, tufts of which showed at the cleavage of his buckram shirt. His good ship, the *Nuestra Señora de la Popa*, belonged to Garcia de Jerez, a rich merchant of Cartagena. Her holds were full of silver and her sternquarters carried twenty-five passengers, from the exalted brother of Francisco de Toledo, Viceroy of Peru, who had embarked on the day of Quasimodo, or Low Sunday, the first after Easter, down to the taffeta weaver and his pregnant wife who had come aboard three days ago in Havana, and whose waters had broken the moment they had sighted the pirate.

'Why does God trouble me so,' he asked the sky. A shout of *seis brazas* – six fathoms, came from the leadsman. The channel was narrowing as the ship bore along the blue shallows between Sheet Island and its rocky neighbour. 'I knew I should have denied that woman.'

The cries of labour came from below, upsetting the men and making them mutter about bad luck as they worked. I knew there was something suspicious about them, Solano decided, watching the weaver standing anxiously at the quarterdeck rail. And yet I allowed them to come aboard. The woman is beautiful, far too beautiful to be a weaver's wife. And she has the bearing of nobility about her. It was she who had done all the talking, and the weaver had said little. His accent's strangely unplaceable, that alone should have warned me. The men are right: nothing has gone right since they came aboard.

But there had been the fine gem which she had paid for passage. It had been too much for a man to resist. In Havana he had thought the stone was stolen and she the miscreant, wanting to escape to Spain, but there had been no evidence of that, and since the ship was to sail on the next tide with one corner of her accommodation yet to be filled, he had decided not to deny her. Even though the woman was perilously close to her confinement and he had explained to her that the voyage would last at least five weeks, she had implored him.

'You understand that there are no special facilities aboard my ship for a woman who must give birth?' he had told her kindly on the Havana dockside, turning the jewel over so that it caught the sun.

'I have been on board a ship before, *señor Capitán*, and so long as I may have privacy and clean linen I shall be content.'

'Your need to leave Cuba must be urgent to adventure yourself so.'

She had taken the stone back angrily then. 'With the *calentura* killing hundreds in Havana, *Capitán*? Which course would you try? I must think of what is best for my baby.'

So he had shrugged and allowed her to come aboard, even after she had produced her idiot husband – it was truly a very fine gem – but he had begun to watch the man closely, and he had seen the way his apparent imbecility fell away from him when he thought himself unobserved.

Look at the way he regards my guns to distract himself, Solano thought. Is that not an *examination*? He says nothing, but sits alone watching my men come to quarters, but is he not itching to tell them their errors when they run in and run out? And errors are not difficult to find, for this crew has been gleaned from every low waterfront hole in Cuba and Mexico and is the scum of the Indies. They are without the basest elements of gunnery. But, by the Madonna, there's no doubt – that's a look of appraisal if ever there was. This man propped against the demi-culverin so innocently is no taffeta weaver.

Solano looked out over the stern rail once more, eyeing the pirate solemnly. Because the con was with his Havana pilot, he felt redundant and extraneous. Stern chases were apt to be long chases, but this whore's whelp was fast and would be upon them within the hour. He had gambled that they might shake her off amongst the islands where the local knowledge of his pilot should prevail. Without sufficient occupation, Solano's brain fretted for the safety of the Peruvian Viceroy's brother who was *hidalgo* to the core and would rather die than allow himself to be ignominiously ransomed. If the pirate was of a certain kind he would think nothing of destroying them all for having dared to attempt escape. Pirate gun crews knew the business they lived by, but *Nuestra Señora* was a big ship and her guns were adequate and pirates feared the loss of their means of escape. A trinity of well-placed shots might send her off after other carrion. And there was still a slim chance that she would ground on the treacherous reefs of the Sabanas.

He descended the quarterdeck companionway, passed hurriedly by the nearest starboard side gun and by the weaver who leaned against it, then he turned as if in sudden absence and commanded him to hand him the quoin.

The weaver bent to it immediately and his fingers closed over the handle of the wedge used to adjust the elevation of the gun. Then he froze, realising his mistake.

'So, weaver, you know something of cannon and the parts thereof?'

'No, sir. That is – I don't know, sir.'

'Don't lie to me, dumb fellow, or I'll feed you to the sharks.'

John Tavistock stood under the Captain's eye, thinking furiously and damning himself for his foolishness. The privateer, which was almost certainly English from the shape of her hull and the cut of her sails, would be upon them before the next bell sounded. That meant a running battle or surrender, and judging by Solano's actions so far and the stories he had heard of what choice suckets lay in the vessel's strongroom there would be no surrender. He heard Maria cry out in pain from the babe in her belly, and icy sweat broke out over his face. The frights of battle or a stray ball through the sternlights could easily carry the child away if they made a stand of it, but if he refused to aid Solano and the privateer overcame them, what then? How might a pregnant woman be used aboard a pirate, English or not? He itched to punch Solano's mouth for his rudeness, or to show him what he might do with a gun, but he maintained his humble stance.

A shout rang out from the bows. '*Cinco brazas, con arena blanquecina!*' – Five fathoms, with white sand.

'Please let me go to my wife. The birth is starting. Please, Captain, sir, I only know the words your sailors speak.'

'Liar!'

'No, sir. Please, sir. I'm a weaver of taffetas and grograms, prenticed to a silk weaver of Cuba these past two years.'

'I don't believe you.'

'It's the truth, sir. I swear.'

It was no lie. The escape from the viceregal palace had been miraculous. Almost the entire guard had been in attendance on the *auto de fe*, and Maria had led him to the courtyard where two fast horses were tethered. They went unchallenged as they fled, following totally deserted streets until they had run out onto the eastern highway and the open country. There, Maria had proposed that they turn north and head away from Chalco to the place Gonzalo had designated as a rendezvous, but he had overruled her on a powerful certainty that the escape had been too easy and that the Viceroy's hand was deeply in the matter.

'Did you tell Don Emilio that I alone possessed the secret of the alloy?' he had demanded of her at that crossroads.

'I had to, Juan. To secure his help.'

'Then we ride east!'

'But Gonzalo is waiting for us.'

'Yes! He's waiting all right. With a troop of soldiers and torture rods. Don't you see? It's not me they want to preserve from the Inquisition's fire, but my secret. Gonzalo'd have it from me and serve me back to Don Pietro like a spitted hog!'

They had ridden wild for two days and two nights towards Vera Cruz where the *ferias* would be packed with strangers, and then they had gone down to San Juan de Ulua and taken ship for Havana where the Inquisition had not yet spread. After another day they had shipped to Cuba and hidden themselves in a small town there. He had bribed a silk weaver to take him on as apprentice so that their identities might remain hidden, and for two years he had drudged at the man's command, until Cuba too began to come under the basilisk stare of the Holy Office. He was recognised by a soldier in the marketplace in Havana where he had gone to sell hens, and immediately he had known they would have to leave, despite Maria's condition.

Solano's impatience flared up. 'I warn you, foolish man, don't try my mood. I give you a choice: if you will be a gunner and will help us fight, then you may stay here. But if you will be a weaver, you'll be a weaver below, and in chains. Now, answer me.'

'Captain, am I not a paying passenger?' he wailed, feeling himself tighten inside. 'You cannot do this. Let me go to my wife!'

'*Cuatro brazas y media!*'

Solano let out a gasp of frustration. Four and a half fathoms! The channel was growing dangerously shallow, but no matter how shallow it became the raider would always be able to follow. 'Take him away!'

Two *marineros* seized him and pulled him below. Then the muffled boom of a cannon sounded and a plume of water fountained half a cable's length to larboard. It was the pirate's bow-chaser – a warning rather than a meant shot. Solano wheeled and went up onto the poop, forgetting about the weaver.

The pirate had come within range and it was time to make a decision.

Ahead the channel was beginning to widen. Solano saw that now there would be no chance of shaking off the pursuit and he determined to make his stand if God gave him the hint of a chance. He asked the helm to take a wide line about Sheet Island and then head for the open ocean where he might at least have sea room to bring his larboard guns to bear. The pirate followed, understanding his decision and waiting for the moment menacingly. It began to dawn on Solano that there could be little hope of outthinking his predator. He ordered a shot fired off from a stern falconet, for the purpose of exaggerating his report, then he gave his ship to heave to, the words bitter as gall in his mouth.

The hail rang faintly across the intervening stretch of water, but the words were distinct and in Spanish.

'Speak with us, for we are Englishmen and therefore well disposed to all if there be no cause to the contrary. Those who will not, or those that run from us, then his be the blame! Know also that if there be cause for warfare, we will be devils rather than men.'

As he was guided below through the fusty darkness, Tavistock could hear the soft moans of his wife's efforts. He was banned from attendance at the birth by the customs of the peasant Spanish, which he claimed to be. But a *peon* would have belonged to a village and that village would have had women experienced in childbirth and a bevy of midwives to assist instead of one loaned maid who knew nothing.

'Do not chain me, I pray you,' he begged the mariner. 'She is helpless.'

'Captain's orders,' the man said woodenly, then he relented. 'I have children of mine own. Go to her and help her if you can.'

'I promise I shall not leave my wife's side,' he said gratefully.

'See you do, or I'll lose the flesh from my back.'

A makeshift bed filled the narrow box that was their accommodation. The great timber knees that supported the deck above thrust out across the space only a couple of feet above Maria's head, and she had braced her hands against them to fight the contractions. At her side a terrified young girl, the servant of a merchant's wife dabbed sweat from her face with a rag. They were the only other women on board.

'You can't come in,' she cried when he appeared. 'The baby's coming.'

'Calm yourself,' Tavistock said, wishing he could do the same. 'I'll help.'

The stifling heat was almost unendurable, the bed was soaked. Maria looked up at him and her exhausted eyes broke his heart. I wish I could help you, he thought, but how can I? He held her hand then, squeezing, willing his strength into her. Her pains ebbed and she breathed pantingly, so tired and waiting for the next surge. When the falconet fired the maid jumped, but Maria merely rolled her big eyes up, oblivious to anything beyond the confines of the room, then the sweat began to stand out on her face again and she gathered herself to fight a fresh wave of agony.

Tavistock looked up past the tiny deadlight and glanced across at the sea. A small boat was approaching, packed with armed men. He could see from the boat and the way they moved that they were without doubt English, even though they were too far away to hear. That's something at least, he thought. At least if they come here I have the tongue to parley. With luck they'll loot us and leave and there'll be no firing. God forbid that there's any firing.

Maria's hand tightened and he held her as she grunted. The young maid knelt between her splayed legs. She looked up over the great swollen belly with a look of awe on her face. 'I can see the baby's head. Push, *señora*. Push harder!'

The wonder of the moment possessed him as he looked on. He heard the sounds of a boarding party, of feet on the deck above, then the oaths and gruff shouts in English of a body of men systematically combing through the ship for loot. But John Tavistock had only ears for his wife's grunts, and eyes only for the wrinkled head that was emerging from her. He stared, mesmerised by it. Wisps of dark hair and incredibly a small bloodstained face screwed tight against the shock of the world, then a narrow shoulder, slick inside its mucous coat, and a perfect tiny hand. He reached out to deliver the arm and the torso and the purple trail of cord which he cut with his fish knife as soon as the legs came free.

Maria lifted her head to see.

'It's a boy, Maria. A son!'

He wiped the face and saw the toothless gums as the mouth opened, and some instinct told him to clear the slime from it with the tip of his finger to allow the first intake of breath. And there was a shuddering angry wail, like that of a small animal. Maria received the baby in her arms immediately and cradled him, and Tavistock saw the joy and adoration shining from her and he knew that he had witnessed the mystery of a profound miracle.

Slowly he became aware of a deathly silence pervading the ship. The Englishmen had gutted the *Nuestra Señora* and gone and he pictured Solano's men dourly watching the boat struggle away with their wealth. Then a torrent of cries rang out from above, and he turned and put his eye to the port. There, sliding out into the channel from behind the concealment of the island that lay two cable-lengths away, was a ship. And at her staff was King Philip's arms.

On his quarterdeck Richard Tavistock watched the boarding party returning, and he tried to assess the value of the haul they had brought off. It looked good. Very good. Bowen was signalling, elatedly waving his arms from the sternsheets of a boat that was sunk to its rubbing strakes by the weight of four great chests. He had told Bowen particularly: 'No greedy diversions, no time-wasting. You'll take only what's in the strong room and we'll be away again swiftly. Don't even bother to spike her guns, she'll not catch us.'

The *Antelope*'s own fearsome ordnance was conspicuously run out and trained on the Spaniard's waist, guaranteeing there would be no rash change of heart by her Captain, but as Tavistock watched he saw that there was activity on the other's decks, more than there should have been. On each previous occasion they had lifted spoils from a victim and let her proceed, Tavistock had almost been able to taste the burning humiliation of the other master. It had manifested itself as a sullen paralysis. No shouted insults, no bravado, just the shame of defeat and a skulking resentment. But this was different.

'Look you, Captain! She's running out again!' Fleming warned.

She can't be, Tavistock told himself incredulously as he too saw the Spaniard's gunports begin to lift. Can't her Captain see this is no bluff? We've position and enough fire power to tear her to pieces. And she's already lost her treasures. God's blood, what's he doing? At this range she'd cripple us if she could work round enough to give us a broadside, but we'd blow her to Hell before she moved.

'Keep us on her quarter, Master Sark!' he shouted forward.

'Aye, sir!'

A vision of horror came into Tavistock's brain. They're unpredictable, these Spanish, hot-headed, aye, and as proud as cats. What if he's weighed his losses and decided he can't take responsibility for it? What if we've brought so much off him that he can't show his face ashore? Ever? He'd risk plenty to counter that, but he must see there's nothing he can do. He's raging! That's it. The mad belswagger's lost his reason!

Tavistock swept up his spying-glass and searched the other ship. He saw two men at the swivel gun on her poop, lining up on the boat as it smashed through the waves towards *Antelope*. Then he saw the scene dissolve in smoke and the sound of the discharge reached him a second later. It was closely aimed, fountaining the water around Bowen and throwing down the oarsmen's heads. Then Hell's hounds broke free among his men.

'Sail astern! Sail astern!'

'Captain!'

Tavistock turned, taken totally by surprise. The prow of a galleon was cutting into view from a channel on the far side of Sheet Island. He saw at a glance that she was a big, old merchantman, with few guns and what there were probably old and weak, but she was making fast way towards them. He realised immediately that the *Nuestra Señora*'s Captain had seen her approaching and it had fired his courage.

'We can take them both without trouble,' he told Fleming, training his glass on the newcomer. 'Starboard ordnance, prepare to fire.'

'Pieces ready,' Nowell, the gun captain, shouted back, his Puritan black coat and brim hat making him a stout brimstone preacher.

'Teach them your gospel as you will, Zeal-for-God!'

'That I will, sir.'

A second shot seared from the *Nuestra Señora*, skipping dangerously across the waves and amongst the small boat's oars, sending them up like skittles. It was from a demi-culverin, and the ball plunged under the water just short of *Antelope*. Had the Spanish gunner not been shooting for the boat it would have taken her rudder off. Tavistock reflected on the acuteness of their situation. Bowen's shouts of 'Puuull! Puuull!' were anxious. They had fifty yards to stroke the boat; at least three oars were shattered.

'Fire!' Nowell's brassy voice bellowed. *Antelope*'s full broadside went off in a ragged line along the deck, flinging taut the gun breechings, the crews dancing aside to reload immediately as the gunners watched their shots impact on the *Nuestra Señora*. Shards of timber were flung up from her sides, shuddering her. Tavistock turned to the new ship, something eating at him about the speed she was making. He lifted his glass once more and studied her magnified image. At once the unease grew within him. Nothing squared. She was closing with all speed, manoeuvring as if to come deliberately athwart his larboard guns. Either her Captain's a fool or he's the bravest man alive, he thought. She can't trade iron with *Antelope*. Surely he can see that? Surely he can see what we're doing to the other ship! He can't be trying to bracket us. Then his eye ran along the smoothness of her sheer. She was handsome in profile, and under the beakhead the joggle planks were neatly tapered into the bluff bowed stem. He followed their line back across the bloated image and as she rolled he clearly saw it: the planks of her maindeck strake were *rippling*.

'It can't be!' he roared.

He banged the spyglass with the heel of his hand in exasperation, polished its bottle end with his sleeve, looking to Bowen's boat and willing its rowers to come on faster before fitting the glass once again to his eye. The strange rippling was still there, and there were scallops in the line too! Almost as if the planking joints were ... *painted on canvas*?

It was crazy. Canvas aprons, painted up to look like timbers! To conceal what? *My God!*

The *Nuestra Señora*'s reply roared out. One after another, three balls stabbed toward the *Antelope*. One crashed into the sea, another moaned through the space between fore and main masts, but the third was aimed at the poop and slammed into the quarterlog beneath his feet. A section of poop rail was carried away and he was thrown sprawling. When he regained his feet he was momentarily dazed.

Fleming ran to him. 'Captain, you're hit!'

'Get about your work, God damn you!'

He searched the deck for his glass. It was gone. When he reached the rail he saw that it had carried over the side, but there was no time to mourn. *Antelope*'s second broadside rent the air, punishing the Spaniard's masts and spars.

'Look to the other!' he shouted, marshalling his people to get the
Antelope under way. 'The fight we came here for is upon us. Whatever
betide, we have come to our last trial. Show them Albion's glory!'

Sails broke out above him. Down in the waist and across the quarterdeck his gun crews struggled to line up on their new quarry. A running
fight this cunning Spaniard wanted, and a running fight he would have.
He looked upon the bronze muscles of his men and knew there was no
force on God's earth that could match them when their spirit was in
flow. Suddenly his oppressions left his shoulders. His lungs filled with
good air and his soul flamed. All the injustices of San Juan de Ulua were
serried before him and he felt the omnipotent power of the great Satan
of the Escorial falter and fade. Nobody could face down the sons of
England's soil when they were free upon the ocean. Nobody. This was
the beginning of the end for Philip's foul godless empire and the Lord's
warriors would not be denied.

Bowen watched the sails billow with slitted eyes. The space between
his boat's prow and the *Antelope*'s side that his rowers had valiantly
fought to narrow began to widen – thirty yards, forty, fifty again as the
wind took her main course. No matter how hard they rowed they could
not catch her now, but that would not stop him trying to the limit of
his ability. His men were exhausted. They looked over their shoulders
at the galleon and he saw their agony. A couple more shots from the
Nuestra Señora's guns or this new danger would do for them, and every
man knew it.

'We're forsaken!' the youngest cried.

'Yare! Puuuull you, stoop nappers!'

He saw Stubbes ramming a cannon sponge down the quarter swivel
gun and turn it on them. Then he fired, and the six foot pole flew at
them like a salmon leister. A line snaked out behind, coiling in the air
and lashing across them. A dozen hands fell on it, hauling greedily, and
on *Antelope* a dozen more as the boat cut through the foam of her
curving wake.

A cannonade blasted out from Nowell's culverins, shattering the
cheeks of the great galleon that stole upon them. Tavistock saw the
seven great guns that were suddenly revealed on her. All pretence had
been dropped, and he praised God that he should have had the fortune
to see the threat soon enough to escape it.

'That's the monster de Groote spoke of,' he told Fleming.

'Aye! I'll wager she's worked that pretty trick on many a ship. She
nearly worked it on us – and she might yet have us in her jaws.'

'Not this side of Hell's gates!'

'Fire!'

Zeal-for-God Nowell's second broadside flung down the decoy's
bowsprit. His chains cut her raked foremast just below the top. Barshot
somersaulted among her yards, ripping her sails to tats and ribbons.

'We'll see her fret her guts before we go from this place!'

Without her fore press, the Spaniard's stern came about, spilling air from her driving sails, and her helmsman was forced to go hard with his rudder to compensate. The sea foamed at her stern, braking her headlong rush, and halting the manoeuvre that was bringing her guns' muzzles across them. English fists punched the air. Cheers rang out. Lockjaw flung Nowell's hat high for lack of voice.

As the sun settled in the west, *Antelope*'s guns slowly reduced the Spanish vessel to a hulk. Hot shot set her upper works alight and a searing cannonade pierced her bows so that she began to list and then to sink. Tavistock watched the *Nuestra Señora* creep away, to save herself in the dark of night, and he allowed her to go, seeing her stern quarters smashed to a ragged pulp. In that condition she would not make Spain, and he was not surprised to see her Captain take advantage of a shift in the wind to repair for Havana once more back the way she had come.

The rejoicing that night was prodigious. Bowen had succeeded in bringing aboard a great quantity of minted gold, and after the accounting Tavistock told them all on his life that he was satisfied, that they were done with roving and that they would return home by way of their buried hoard for lack of any more space to fill in *Antelope*'s hold.

There was a gawping silence, followed by a trickle of cheers.

'Are we then to say farewell to our women and children here?' one man somewhat crestfallen at the news asked him.

'What? I say you shall go home and you answer me thus?'

He left them, shaking his head, and found his own quarters then, to muse on the mighty awkward nature of men and what they professed to want.

Chapter 21

Marsh mists hung low over the Thames Estuary. The tide was flowing, but the royal barge sliced over the grey waters like a knife cutting Cathay silk, bringing Elizabeth's guest to Greenwich Palace. The orange disc of the sun was scarcely above the eastern horizon at his back. It was half-past seven by landsman's reckoning, a week short of the winter solstice and he had been away exactly two thousand days.

The velvet hats and surplices of the ten oarsmen glittered with embroidered silver like the dew that gathers on autumn spiders' webs as they dipped their red-bladed sweeps into the river, propelling the sharp-prowed royal barge upstream. At the stem the gilded, crowned lion of England stood rampant. The thickly embroidered banner of Elizabeth draped the sternpost. Amidships the rowers and abaft them the canopied seat in which Richard Tavistock sat like Great Harry himself. His muscular calves were knotted under fine hose, a bearskin cloak hung about his shoulders, making them massive; in his lap lay a casket of huge Peruvian emeralds, the report of which he had sent on ahead.

At the pier the rowers put up their oars, yeomen used their staffs to keep back the curious and the idle who were gathering. Despite the earliness of the hour an honour guard had been got out. A fanfare blown on silver announced him as he stepped on England's shore.

'Well met, Richard.'

'Mister Walsingham, it's good to see you.'

'You will remember my lord Leicester?'

'Your servant, my lord.' Tavistock bowed low and Leicester shook his hand. The strains of court life had marked his sallow face, but his wit was intact.

'I see you've forgotten your lesson on how to bow with elegance.'

'Captain Tavistock has had little occasion to show respect for noblemen these five years,' Walsingham said pointedly, and Tavistock felt the turn of his words like a razor slash. He had forgotten the keen edge politics and the pursuit of power put on a man's tongue, and felt momentarily disadvantaged. Perhaps there was some intrigue between

340

them at present. He decided to tread with care until he had learned more, thinking fondly of the judicious preparations he had made against things falling out badly on his return. He said jocularly, 'Too few I've met with of late have been English, and those that were Spanish were better served by an arrow than by a bow, my lord.'

'Indeed!'

'And you, Mister Walsingham? I see that you wear the chain of office that did once hang about Sir William's shoulders.'

Leicester jumped to the explanation: 'He's our whip in an unruly Parliament. He took Charles Howard's Surrey seat after Howard's father died and left him Baron of Effingham.'

'Are you then, *Sir* Francis Walsingham?'

The spymaster avoided a direct answer. 'Oh, but I care little for honours.'

'Cry shame on falsehood!' Leicester grunted and gestured undiplomatically. 'Her Majesty's policy has ever been wise regarding recognition. You understand that our Queen is not a gratuitous sovereign. The rarer she makes knighthood, the more prized it becomes. However Sir Francis might not wish it, this is his second week a knight.'

'A deserved honour!'

'I thank you, Captain, but it is not good to praise a ford till a man be over it.'

'Then, the winds do not blow to your liking?'

'At Court, our faction is in some standing at present.'

Tavistock glanced around and stopped. He had expected Hawkins to be here, and his absence had put him further on his guard. 'Tell me: how was Francis Drake received?'

There was silence then Walsingham pulled on the tab of hair under his lip and walked on. He said evasively, 'I'll say that his return was somewhat – inopportune.'

'How so?'

'We were obliged to act three ways round on his behalf.'

A shock of concern speared Tavistock's belly. 'Where is he now?'

'You would that he were here to greet you?'

'Why, yes.'

'Ah, me! But to find Francis Drake elsewhere is no snub to you. Do not think your unfinished business with him postponed, I have your monies safe and will show you the same presently.'

Tavistock's frown deepened to anger. 'Hang the monies! What of the man? Does he live yet?'

'He's alive,' Leicester said gently. 'But we do not speak of him, except in hushed voices.'

'Sorrow makes silence her best aid and her best orator!'

'Calm yourself, Captain. My lord Leicester means only that Drake is not with us. Ask in Deptford and you'll hear that he's voyaging to Alexandria. Lend an ear to the Spanish merchants in the city and you'll find talk of a sailing to Scotland to kidnap the boy King out of Edinburgh.'

'But you know better,' Tavistock said, his fears multiplying.

'What if I tell you that his recent voyages have been to the west?'

'The west? What, am I to have riddles from you?'

Walsingham whispered genially, 'To the house of delights in Mortlake.'

'Yah! Stoat!' Tavistock grinned, and punched Walsingham with unseemly enthusiasm. If Drake had been to Dee's house it must mean there was some far expedition approved by Her Majesty. Doubtless some grandiose undertaking. 'Where? The Moluccas? Goa? Macao? Zipangu? They say there's a fortune in silver comes out of there each year. This is your doing, Mister Walsingham!'

'Partly.'

'Walsingham's pennies back the voyage.' Leicester said. 'Sir Christopher Hatton is the principal. I also am part of his venture. My nephew too. None of us have any particular quarrel with the Portuguese.'

Tavistock wracked his brains thinking of the charts he had seen in Dee's house and visualising the company that must have assembled there during the long, light evenings of the summer: men of daring and men of imagination. What destination would they have chosen? What would they attempt?

Nova Albion? Martin Frobisher's dreams lay there, and those of Humphrey Gilbert and his apprentice Walter Ralegh. Then there was Richard Grenville, whose project was to discover the Land of Beach, the semi-mythical land mass that supposedly lay beyond the Spice Islands. But Walsingham and Leicester would certainly have been most interested in where Drake could most effectively damage Spain . . .

That was it!

Tavistock caught his breath as he suddenly remembered another time, another place, swaying high in the topmost branches a forest tree. Years ago but clean in his mind, bright and vivid still as it would ever be while breath sustained him: that jewelled sapphire sea, that wondrous expanse, bedazzling them with its brightness and its promise. An unknown ocean, beyond the furthest shore. That was it, whether Walsingham had suggested it or no. Drake had gone into the Great South Sea!

The extravagance of the plan captivated him.

The South Sea coasts of Peru and of Mexico were wide open to attack. The South Sea was an exclusive preserve, only Spanish and Portuguese ships had ever found their way through the Straits of Magellan and round the five-thousand-league north–south barrier of the New World. Spanish transports plied those coasts, filled to the scuppers with silver, utterly fearless of attack because no one had ever come upon them there. Unarmed ships carrying Philip's wealth would be at Drake's mercy – if he could find a way there.

Reluctantly, he put down his speculations. There was immediate business to put in hand. It was important to learn where he stood, and what changes had overtaken England in his long absence. He probed Leicester on the main elements, saying nothing of his chance meeting with de Groote.

So, Tavistock thought as he listened, Walsingham has found his promotion. He's been joint Principal Secretary since the Christmastide of 'seventy-three, and Burleigh has so far resisted the pressures of Leicester and Walsingham to intervene in force in the Low Countries. The Queen has kept her hand on the reins of Flanders by spending ten thousand pounds here, and sending fifteen hundred volunteers there. De Groote had spoken the broad truth about affairs across the Narrow Seas.

As Leicester's font ran dry, Walsingham schooled him in further details, warning him that he must be acquainted with much before he met Burghleigh. It was no easy task to appreciate the intricate web that had been spun by the Queen's ministers, but in essence it was simple: the disquiet in Europe remained England's greatest guarantee. The expulsion of the Dutch from English ports had been a master stroke conceived by Walsingham's fertile mind; the notion had been transplanted whole into the mind of Burghleigh where it had taken root and begun to flourish.

Walsingham watched Tavistock's rolling gait as he walked beside him through the sprawling palace ways. The years had changed the big man, coarsened his manner and filled him with a confidence fit to bust empires. He had thrived on his crusade and put behind him the consuming distraction that had once driven him, that of his captive brother. It was just as well. For in coming time England would have need of all her heroes.

Walsingham recalled the day he had advanced the idea.

'Convince Her Majesty to throw out the Dutch?' Roger Groton had asked from his deathbed, mystified by the suggestion. And at supper that night Ursula had looked at him queerly. 'You bend credulity to its limit, Francis. Beware lest one day soon your policies snap in twain and you return to a humble condition. Though if that happens I'll not complain, for it will cost less in sundry expenses.'

But he had comforted her, understanding that his continual payments to spies and European correspondents had tried their household purse, more than he had ever tried her credulity. Most of the finance had come from Ursula's father's will, and she was sorry – sorrier even than any Puritan woman might have expected to grow from the spending of any Puritan man.

'Faith, wife! You will see that rewards are hidden at this rainbow's end.'

'Such a husband! Your talk of rainbows no longer holds lustre for me, Francis. Too many years have I heard it.'

When they had lain abed that night he had offered her a small observation. 'Poor Roger believes that there are human traits which leap the even generations as they pass down the bloodline. The royal line is no exception, and Elizabeth's parsimony is certainly come out of her grandfather. As you complain, my increase in standing is as yet unmatched by a like increase in fortune. But mark me, I shall be Principal Secretary within the year, and you shall have the fine house on the river that I have long promised you.'

'By throwing honest Calvinist Dutchmen to their doom?'

'I think so.'

'I'll grow hare's ears before Her Majesty will do that. I hope I prick your conceit, Francis. Aye, and your conscience.'

'Hush, woman!'

'I will not hush.'

'Burghleigh wants a settlement with the Spanish over the seizures. He's talking to Alva through Antonio de Gauras. He'll see the idea as an appropriate overture.'

And so the Queen had ordered the Dutch raiders out of Kent and Essex, just as Philip had wanted. But the Dutch that departed England's shore were not the pathetic refugees that had landed under the shadow of Dover Castle years before. They, like de Groote, had grown strong and dangerous, nourished as they were by the killings they had made in the Channel.

'Yes, Richard, they were well armed and provisioned, and of desperate habits. I thought that if Philip wanted these Sea Beggars sent out of England's compass, he might as well be obliged, eh?'

'You think Lord Burghleigh saw your design for what it was?'

Walsingham smiled. 'Certainly he thought that Alva – and Philip – would be well pleased by Elizabeth's new accommodation.'

They came to a courtyard containing a great lead tank filled by rainwater channelled from the roofs and raised up on stilts in the form of angels. Under it, four engraved faces pointed in the cardinal directions, attached to a crafty engine of rods and levers and toothed wheels. A can filled patiently from a slow drip-feed and tripped the clock mechanism as they watched.

Walsingham told Tavistock elaborately of how the royal command had expelled the Count de la Marck's ships from their safe havens, sending him into the Narrow Seas. 'Burghley sent John Hawkins to read the proclamation, they went straightway – all of them, de Groote's ferocious men too,' Walsingham examined the back of his hand, 'sweetly and without complaint to Brille.'

Tavistock gave a broad smile that recognised the genesis of the plan. 'To take up old business.'

'The Count and I thought that Brille might be meetest: a small town of South Holland, no garrison, a serviceable harbour. The inhabitants all ran away. We sent unadvertised presents of powder and suchlike, the better to organise the Count's defences, and I seem to recall that there were some few Netherlanders who took the call for volunteers. A call that was somehow posted in most every tavern in England.'

'Netherlanders who spoke no Dutch, I'll warrant!'

'Many of them. But they must have been in some wise Dutchmen for they found their way to Flushing without delay – and took it.'

Tavistock laughed, seeing how the tactic had been to strangle Antwerp and seize the greater part of Zeeland and Holland.

'There was a happy coincidence,' Walsingham went on innocently. 'William of Orange, across the German border with twenty-five thousand mercenaries, and Louis of Nassau marshalling ten thousand Huguenots in France.'

'A three-pronged attack.'

'Philip called it Satan's trident.'

Walsingham had known that it was more than enough to keep any thoughts of offence out of Alva's mind. Attack was but a superior form of defence, but the impecunious William of Orange had been held up on the Rhine and Burghleigh had come alive to the extent of the plan, and his meddling had turned the trident thrust into a stand-off between France and Spain, with English aid to the Beggars regulated meanly only to simmer the pot.

'Burghleigh was convinced that once Alva was destroyed, the French would pour into the Low Countries and seize it, with all the consequences which that must bring for French policy in Scotland, and ultimately England.'

'There can never be victory without a decisive blow,' Tavistock said watching the water clock's artful operation with interest.

'If only I'd succeeded in marrying Her Majesty to the Frenchman,' Walsingham shrugged his shoulders in fossil regret. 'Then we might have joined Charles the Ninth in obliterating Alva. But the Queen was turned. She became opposed to a policy that would completely evict Alva from the Netherlands. We were commanded to engineer the most level balance in that province, Spain counterpoise to France – that was her ideal. But I feared for the liberties of good Protestant souls there. I didn't believe that our promise to aid Alva against the French would guarantee the ancient freedoms of the people, or free them from Alva's tyranny, or expel the Inquisition. But –' Walsingham threw up his hands in a gesture of loss. 'The Paris massacre changed everything. Without the French, William of Orange's brave gamble failed. He retreated to his amphibious strongholds in the north.'

The way France had disintegrated into chaos had been staggering. In the Embassy on St Bartholomew's Day he had sheltered young Philip Sidney, brilliant eldest son of his Privy Council ally, Sir Henry Sidney, and Leicester's nephew and protégé. He had newly left Christ Church to tour Europe, but had been trapped in Paris and had narrowly escaped the slaughter. Later Leicester's gratitude had showed itself in an impressive way when he had backed Drake's case in person before the Queen.

The precipitous evil of St Bartholomew's Day had echoed throughout

Europe. King Philip had said that the massacre had given him one of the greatest pleasures of his life, and Rome burned bright for three nights as the bonfires of celebration were lit, but in England the Queen had donned black velvet to receive the excuses of the French Ambassador. Beneath her public outrage, she had been secretly delighted. Catherine's huge error had provided an impeccable excuse for calling off the French marriage, but it had also driven France back into the mire of civil war, and at the cost of French blood, not English. And there was better: Catherine's son, France's King Charles the Ninth, had died within two years, his young man's body wasted to a consumptive corpse by God's slow, sure justice for the massacre, just as John Dee had said the new star foretold. His successor, Henry the Third, was a diseased and perverted degenerate, given to making up and dressing like a whore and debauching the Court with his excesses.

On Henry's accession, his brother Francis, the Duke of Alençon, whom Walsingham had worked so hard to bring to Elizabeth's bed, was created Duke of Anjou. So deep was his disgust at the King's behaviour that he joined with the Huguenot cause, and so strong was his instinct to power that he had gone to war in the Low Countries, to carve himself a kingdom there.

Walsingham remembered the way that Elizabeth's looked-for balance had almost been achieved through Burghleigh's patient diplomacy. Walsingham told Tavistock, 'As a gesture of amity, Alva was taken out of his post, and replaced by the less martial Don Luis Requesens. But in March last year Don Luis was struck dead, poisoned by a fever, and Philip chose to send Don John in his stead. It was a costly decision.'

Tavistock nodded as if the information was news to him. 'The victor of Lepanto? But his reputation is for war.'

Leicester said, 'He's had a setback. Before he could take up the reins of his army, they mutinied and sacked Antwerp which did not please the free Dutch. The demands made of Don John were uncompromising: they wanted the Spanish soldiery sent out of their lands altogether.'

Tavistock listened unmoved as Leicester explained, then said sceptically, 'Do you suppose the Low Countries are soon to be free from Spanish domination? A self-governing country, with Protestant liberties?'

'No. Even if the south continues to recognise nominal sovereignty, Spain will not allow that.'

Walsingham redoubled his efforts, seeing from the face of the water clock that there was little time. 'Listen! I know much better than Burleigh that all balances are unstable; without constant care they are easily disturbed. Burleigh is an intelligent man, but he is a bureaucrat to his marrow. He thinks the country may be managed by quiet tinkerings and fine tunings and in his scheme there is no place for men of fire and imagination. What he does not comprehend is that without the latter any country must slowly slide into complacent decline. The worst of it is that without imagination, Burghleigh's supposes others to think as he does, but with somewhat less power. I tell you that is a mistake. Don John is no weakling, he'll never concede to Holland and Zeeland their freedom of worship. Their Stayholder knows that and will never accept his governorship. But I cannot believe Don John will crawl away with his tail betwixt his legs.'

Walsingham knew that although Don John's outward design was to pacify the Low Countries, he held another, less ostensible ambition. Now he had his proof: Don John had long fostered links with English Catholics exiled abroad, with the renegades' seminary at Douai and with archtraitor Cardinal Allen. Through his spies there, he found that Don John planned to embark his troops for Spain, but land them in England. He had boasted that he would marry Scots Mary himself.

'That's where the Queen's money will go, Richard. Of the riches that lie in your ship, one hundred thousand pounds is already earmarked as loan to the Marquis de Havre, five thousand infantry and a thousand horse to go out under Leicester's command. We shall make a deal with Philip that the States General accept William of Orange as their leader, and the Spaniards are sent off to Italy, overland. If the Queen will listen to reason.'

'Do we go to the Queen now?'

'No, to Burghleigh. He has news you will mislike, for I fear you have been outmanoeuvred by a consummate businessman, as he'll tell you himself.'

'Our contract is made, Captain. You understand the terms as well as I do. One half of the total belongs to Her Majesty.'

'As it has done since it was taken from the Spanish.'

'A further quarter of the – cargo, is to be divided between the following investors.' Burghleigh read out their names – twenty-five of the richest and most powerful men in the realm – along with the proportions they would receive. Burghleigh's own name was not among them. 'That leaves you the remainder.'

Tavistock tried to appear outwardly gracious, but saw that the Lord Treasurer was feeling for his true opinions. 'The remainder for myself *and* my crew. My own share is a little less than one half of that which you show. Also, you may exclude from these tottings the most exquisite item. I shall make that a personal gift to Her Majesty – let's say a premature New Year's gift – a quantity of emeralds, a debt of thanks to her faith. So, rightly, that is, one eighth part for all the men who won the treasure with their blood and sweat, or for their bereaved kin, and one tenth part for their Captain who imagined it in the first place.'

'You wish it were more?'

Tavistock shrugged. 'Had I thought so, I would have gotten more.'

'A pity you did not, then.' Burghleigh's eyes narrowed in a shrewd look. He rose from his seat and touched his hand to the fireplace. 'Because the investors I named did, to a man, sell their shares to me. Two years ago, when news came that you were dead.'

'Then I thank you also for your faith,' Tavistock said sourly, concealing his shock and anger as best he could. 'I hope the shares did not cost you too dearly?'

'Contrariwise. The price was cheap. They cost me half what I might have paid on your departure, plus the going rate for a well-made rumour. I wish to build a house in Northamptonshire, and my mansion of Theobalds is a costly enough place to run as it stands. However – I can afford to make some of my gain over to you and your crew. Enough to make them all blissfully wealthy men, and yourself a magnate, with enough to buy half a dozen ships.'

Tavistock's voice betrayed him. 'So? Therefore I can be a magnate with what is mine already! This is a proper marvel!'

'I can make you a gentleman of considerable means.'

'A gentleman, you say?'

'Why, yes.'

Tavistock's voice sank low, but his eyes never faltered as he stared at Burghleigh's own. 'Strange to think that you believe I might be transformed into a *gentleman* by money. I had it that you were of a different mind; that a man's quality lies in his blood stock.'

Burghleigh's confidence was undented. He said mildly, 'Men have been knighted for serving their nation's interests before.'

'Knighthoods are not yours to give.'

'Nevertheless, I may confidently promise you one.'

'Your promises are other men's bonds, my lord.'

Burghleigh delighted in the danger into which the exchange was hotly plunging. 'Let us think instead of –'

'No, my lord! Let us think of what makes a man noble and what does not. It seems to me a matter of achievement and reward, as in your own case.'

'What do you want?'

Tavistock's gaze remained steady. 'You know fine well what I want.'

Burghleigh sighed and put up his hands. 'My daughter is a married woman.'

'In name.'

'In *fact*, sir!'

'Not according to my understanding.'

'Damn your understanding. And damn your eyes! You forget yourself.'

'I forget nothing, Lord Burghleigh. I have refreshed my mind daily with the thought of my Anne and of the son I have never yet seen. I will see her, and you will not interfere!'

Burghleigh felt anger prickle him, whipped by the coarse tongue of a man who had no humility, who had issued only commands to others for five long years. He turned, tight-lipped and furious, and began to stalk away, then he halted, and he knew precisely why he had done so.

Lie to whomsoever you must, William, his conscience told him. But never lie to yourself. It had to be admitted. The last five years had been years of continual torment to his daughter. No sooner had Tavistock gone to the Indies but that Oxford had begged the Queen for permission to furnish him a ship also, so that he might follow. She had, of course, refused him, liking his presence at her Court for the sake of his dancing and tilting and perhaps for his quarrelling spirit, which she admired in young men and enjoyed observing.

Oxford had thought the prohibition Burghleigh's own doing, and there had been some truth in that, for he had given the Queen honest counsel on the matter. 'He will kill himself,' Burghleigh had predicted balefully, part of him wishing as much could be arranged. 'A ship sent to the Indies with my Lord Oxford its master will be thrice charged with mischance.'

Oh yes, he had thought, a triple measure indeed, and of volatile powder: one, in that Oxford would surely have caught pink-eye, or sunk in a storm, or had himself blown to fragments in an engagement; two, in that he must bring the Queen to grief at this – and she hardly to be controlled already; and three, in that he must provoke a Spaniard sooner or later, if he did not die, and in so inexpert a manner as to result in his capture and expensive ransom, or, conceivably, the rupturing of that delicate membrane that kept Spain and England out of war with one another.

Oxford had sworn to revenge himself on Anne.

'I'll see her weep each of her days away,' he had warned poisonously. 'I'll damage her. See me do it!'

Burghleigh had humbled himself to plead: 'You know the Queen herself says that you will not take ship. Will you be disobedient to her over a petty jealousy?'

'*Jealousy?* I am jealous of no man, Father William! I shall go fight in Flanders, and find honour there!'

And he had gone, without Elizabeth's consent, relieving Anne, who had grown to detest the tread of his foot on the stair. 'May he be shot through the hare brain,' he heard her pray nightly. 'Swift and clean, but final. Sweet Jesus, I want him away from me and my child.'

It was then that Burghleigh had known the depth of Anne's anger and despair and the enormity of the error he had made, and how right Mildred had been in the matter of her daughter's wedding. But he had set his face and like everyone else part of him had assumed Tavistock dead. A year and a half without word had been a long time, but still he had traded those shares in Tavistock, just in case, swapping them one-for-one for shares in Drake. Then Drake had come back with his booty and his happy tales and many had sniggered in private because he had sold out on a winner and bought in on a dead man.

But they were not laughing now. Not now. And Burghleigh felt no pleasure, nor even gratification, only a cold dread at Tavistock's return that outweighed the money. *Why?* And in any case, what was done was done. And though Anne might wilt as a flower wilts in a climate that does not suit it, she had married and her vows had been made in the Abbey, before God and the Queen. But that was not accounting for her wilfulness.

After the Flanders episode, in 'seventy-four, Burghleigh had had Oxford fetched home, induced him to apologise to the Queen, which he did genuinely. Having seen war in some wise, Oxford renounced it as barbarous and unworthy. His pretensions to an adventurer's life had already been reduced, diverted from sea to land by the news of Panama and Drake's fabulous reception. A marvel how that had turned every other young gentleman into one ardent mass ready to sail west, but Oxford had shunned all celebration, calling it a youthful fad of which he had already wearied. And so he had returned instead to his youthful posture as a poet of genius for in that pursuit there was no hard standard to be set against him, only opinions and critiques which might be easily twisted to his self-satisfaction.

Burghleigh cringed inwardly as he thought of the burbling hexameters that Oxford had offered up for praise, and – God–save–us–all – the tight band of dissolute hangers-on whose whole game was to wait upon Oxford like a new messiah. The following year Burghleigh had disbursed him a sum sufficient to take him off on a tour of Italy, to Milan and to Venice, but he had returned home within a year, crammed with new poses, conceited in all points, overspent and sporting sweet bags and perfumed clothes and finely worked gloves. He had presented a pair to the Queen, but there had been nothing for his wife, and thereafter he had been a stranger to her, and she almost banished to the mean house of Low Houghton.

Walsingham had been disgusted, and Leicester delighted, until he was brought to the brink of choking. 'My lord Oxford's a mirror to Tuscany,' he had said, laughing scornfully, but out of Oxford's earshot. 'God's hounds! A little foppish hat, like an oyster. Worn with French cambric ruffs! Ha! A quaint array! A passing singular oddity!'

It was Philip Sidney who had caught the bile that should have been vomited over Leicester, for poet or not, fashion maker or not, Oxford's violent temper was intact, and he had made war on Leicester's nephew with offers to duel and even an extravagant murder plot.

Burghleigh looked at the iron-hard man who stood swaying before him, tempered in war and toughened by adversity. Here was a man who knew exactly what he was, exactly what he wanted and would brook no opposition to that. Small wonder Anne contrasted him so readily against the man to whom she had been matched in wedlock.

Burghleigh faced Tavistock stubbornly, sure in the state power at his disposal. The time had come to employ it. 'Your oath was sworn never more to speak of my daughter.'

'That oath was made under duress. It is *revoked*.' Tavistock's fingers snapped, recalling the day the soldiers had taken him blood-drained and amazed from John Dee's house.

'Shameless man!'

'No, my lord! It is *you* who is shameless. Did you not force your firstborn into a foul marriage against her wishes for your own ambition? Did you not deny your grandchild his birthright? *Did you not*, my lord?'

'I warn you, Tavistock –'

'And I warn you! Not a groat of the bullion I've won will pass to your treasury until you oblige me.'

Burghleigh straightened, weasel sly. 'It is unwise to threaten me, Tavistock. I have your ship in the Thames under armed escort. This time, you cannot flee. Guards!'

Six pikemen sprang from the dark recesses of the room, their halberd blades cut down towards him. Tavistock fell quiet, stared at his feet, inwardly delighting that his foresight had put him in this position. Even so, he remained carefully self-possessed.

'I had no mind to flee, my lord. Though I guess I am looked for in the city.'

'Your arrival is presently somewhat secret.'

'It cannot remain so long.'

Burghleigh, recollected now to his cool and reasonable self, called his scrivener, who brought the papers. 'The people would fête your return, and I shall not interfere with that, because the people's wants are our care and our responsibility. But heed me, Captain, if you seek to cause me pains, I'll take the people's hero away from them.'

'You did so once before, I remember,' Tavistock said.

'You dare to smirk at me?'

'I don't smile at you, my lord.'

'Then, what?'

'Simply at your bribery. I perceive that you're about to make a new offer.'

Burghleigh's gall showed but he locked it away. 'Hear this: keep your word and you shall be a knight. You shall have a warrant to war in Ireland. A new ship and a new mission. What say you?'

Tavistock's thoughts leapt again to Francis Drake, to how England had gratefully received his hundred thousand gold pesos from the Panama jaunt, and paid him off with little thanks and a wearying time in Ireland.

As the conflict with Spain had cooled, Drake's embarrassing presence in England had had to be dealt with; he was sent to Ireland to persecute the Redshanks.

Those Gaelic warriors had come from the Hebrides and from Argyll, Scots that roamed and marauded in Ulster, a totally wild breed of men who loved to prey on the Irish, dangerously destabilising the land. Walsingham had said that Drake commanded the escort of Black John

Norris, but that he never spoke the name of Rathlin Island out of shame for what the Queen's forces had done there. Yes. Good Francis had little stomach for the massacre of innocents. 'A fair fight at best, something to get my teeth into, that's what I like,' Tavistock had heard him roar after Panama, though in truth, Captain Francis Drake preferred huge odds against, believing like an ardent English Protestant must do, that he was God's chosen and could only prove as much to the satisfaction of all by overthrowing a great burden of infidels. That he had gone off on his extravagant expedition now, was a mark that he had lost none of that firmness of belief. A man *complete*, sure, full of his own self. A *man*.

Tavistock felt suddenly careless of the circle of men who surrounded him. He brushed one halberd aside, ignoring the way the remainder made at him threateningly. Seeing the intimidation fail, Burghleigh signalled them impatiently to put up their arms.

So, Burghleigh thought it convenient to let Drake leave, Tavistock told himself. He could have vetoed Walsingham and Leicester and the lot of them had he thought it best. Yet Walsingham said that Spanish irritation with England was boiling up once more. Tavistock felt the change in the wind, and steered accordingly. For what reason did Burghleigh want a valuable sea commander to kick the heads of clansmen in barbarous Erin? It's a diversion – shelve me, keep me from the Spanish, keep me from Anne also. Stand me in the middle ground, neither at home nor away.

'What say you?'

'I say, no.'

'The offer is good.'

'To beat up and down the Irish Sea? To fight in a bog? No.'

'You *will* oblige me in this.'

'No.'

Burghleigh shook his head and looked down at the contract, striping a line through it matter-of-factly. 'Your ship is confiscated, and all it contains. You are under arrest.'

'A shame.'

'You will soon think so, respectless devil!'

As the guards closed in around him, once more, Tavistock thrust up his hands as if addressing the heavens. 'Lord God take me from this old fellow before I split my sides!'

And the peals of his laughter rang out as Robert Slade escorted him away.

Tavistock got down from his horse; thoughts of Christmas goose and claret were far from his mind now as he hitched the bridle. The ground was white and deeply covered, the east wind had blown everything dry and hoary and crisp. He was alone and strung so tight inside that he felt he must snap.

The house of Low Houghton seemed to him drear and quiet under
its laden thatch. There were flakes in the air, and no echoes because of
the white blanket. The lime walls were made creamy against the virgin
burden of the roof. A snowman stood on the lawn; pebble eyes, twig
nose, fearsome shards of plantpot for teeth. It wore a cloak and wide-
brimmed hat and held a broom, but it might have been an eel-brog for
that it struck him with shivers.

His mouth was dry. At his back the steamy-flanked jennet stamped,
jangling his gear.

The day Burghleigh had imprisoned him he had marked the afternoon
with a nap and the tuneless whistling that often accompanied his most
strategic thoughts. He had counted the chimes until enough had passed
for a customs barge to row to the *Antelope* and back, then he had
listened out for returning footsteps. Slade appeared within the hour to
fetch him before Burghleigh, who was white-faced with rage. He had
shaken his staff in Tavistock's face and demanded, '*Where is it?*'

'Where you can't get it.'

'I'll rack you, Tavistock.'

Tavistock said nothing.

'I'll rack your men!'

'They know nothing.'

'That won't stop me.'

'How will the Queen take it when she hears that you make victims
of her mariners? Her mood will deepen if she may no longer prosecute
her policy in Holland for lack of gold.'

Burghleigh spat at him, enraged. 'England has enough gold for that.'

'And the monies she would have to rebuild her Navy?'

He pushed open the garden gate, sweeping a sector of snow up behind
it, trying to savour the moment he had imagined so differently so often.

As he did so, he grinned, thanking God that he had remembered the
rumours that had surrounded his and Hawkins's return so long ago,
rumours of how they had buried their profits in Ireland.

All that had passed since his landing proved the wisdom of his
prudence: he had told Burghleigh that the treasure was buried in Ireland.

'*Ireland?*'

'A desolate cove. Fifty feet down a hole where no man can spend it
until I'm satisfied.'

In actuality, he had had it committed to a Spaniard's belly, a store
hulk taken at the Canaries and brought up to Plymouth Sound. The
whole treasure lay there now, packed around with kegs of black powder
and guarded by Bowen with a lighted taper at the ready and all the
jealousy of a dragon atop his hoard.

Tavistock took off his riding gloves and walked slowly up the path,
his boots crushing the snow with a sound like grinding teeth. He was
hot and he loosened his collar and threw open his bearskin stole. A
small brown bird fled from him, shaking down fine snow from a twig,

and the rhyme of his youth came unbidden into his head: 'The robin and the wren, God's cock and hen, The martin and the sparrow, God's mate and marrow.'

Then he caught a flash of fair hair and a twitch of curtain at the window. The light, high voice pierced him and he steeled himself to lift the heavy knock-ring, but as he reached for it the barking of big dogs began within and the sound of them rushing to the door made him step back.

When the chained door cracked open it revealed their dripping muzzles and their anxiety to be at him, but a woman servant with fleshy arms and an apron shouted for her husband to restrain them, and Tavistock was roughly asked his name and his business, despite his fine attire.

'I am Captain Richard Tavistock, and I would have the Countess of Oxford to know I'm here.'

'The Countess does not receive callers.'

A small voice squealed. The blonde-haired girl he had glimpsed at the window galloped into the flagged hallway. She wore a tidy velvet dress and straddled a wooden horsehead on a stick. She stopped when she saw him looking at her and twisted about with incredible coyness. Then she slapped the nearest dog's eye and told it to hush, which it did resentfully.

'Is this the Countess's only child?'

The woman nodded. 'She is, sir. But you can't –'

'How old is she?'

'Five years, but I must ask –'

Tavistock knelt to the girl, 'What's your name, child?'

'Lizbeth.'

'Elizabeth,' he echoed back tenderly, taking her hand. Then he drew a large pink conch from his jacket and gave it to her. 'Put it to your ear and you shall hear the sea.'

And as he turned he saw the woman in sombre green standing at the head of the stair. It was his Anne.

Book Four

Chapter 22

To Nicolau Almeida the knowledge of the King's death was like a knife constantly twisting in a wound.

He dismounted heavily, swabbed the sweat from his face, and riffled the mare's hogged mane affectionately with a broad hand. 'We're in a big hurry now. Still, a horse must drink, eh, *formoso*? You see how I take care of you?'

The low morning sun played on his horse's dusty quarters as she lowered her head delicately to the trough. Then, as she finished, he remounted and scanned the road that he had travelled a hundred times before with his pigeons, knowing that never in his life had he felt such urgency.

He had ridden hard for almost an hour and was midway on the journey from his house in Lisbon, on his way to the village near Saint' Ubes where the rumour had originated. He had known that, given the faintest hope that the story was true, he must go himself, and quickly. As the mare pulled around he brushed his heels across its sides, sending it cantering down the rocky decline towards the village, and towards the 'ghost ship' of which the fisherman had spoken.

A dismasted ship, badly treated by the weather and deserted, that's what they'd said, so he had left, immediately and as unobtrusively as possible. Like so much valuable news, it had started with the sardine fishermen. He'd always taken pains to maintain a cordial relationship with them, as with all who lived betweeen Saint' Ubes and the Cape of Saint' Vincent on southern Portugal's Atlantic coast. It was important – after all, they were his eyes and ears, and had he not grown rich keeping his eyes open and his ear to the ground? What business was better than selling information? he thought. You've got a commodity. You sell it, but you've still got it. What could be better than that? Unlike wine, however, information rarely improved in the keeping, and the information Nicolau Almeida dealt in was volatile and, now that King Sebastian was dead, immensely dangerous.

Almeida encouraged his horse again and slapped its withers. He was well liked by fellow merchants and farmers, famed for his garrulous good nature and as the father of five grown sons. His family made a good living from all the small ports of the south, buying from foreign traders, sending bolts of cloth inland as far as the Guadiana and the border and handling wine for what remained of the English trade. He could afford to be a generous man, a man who kept a big open household, mostly out of choice, but also to show everyone that he had nothing at all to hide and that no one need fear anything from him.

But difficult times were coming, and in difficult times a man needed a staff on which to lean.

'Yes,' he told the horse, 'that's the Nicolau Almeida everyone knows: a man who spends his time listening to local gossips and quietly building his prosperity. The townspeople, my fellow traders, Captain da Silva at the garrison – even the filthy Jesuits – they all know that I'm a good and generous man who'll help anyone and harm nobody.'

And yet I'm sure there are those who wonder at my luck, and there are certainly some who draw their livings from the ports of the Alentejo who're jealous of the inexplicable way I've grown richer than they have. They're the dangerous ones.

He saw the ship the moment he arrived at the quiet line of grey and white fishermen's houses that made up the village of São Paolo. She was lying in shallows a quarter of a mile down the inlet. Many times he had seen ships limping into the refuge of the Baia after being caught in storms, but this ship was exceptional; she was almost a hulk. Trails of rust red streaked her timbers from the ironwork, and any gilding she might once have had was gone. What remained of her masts were jury rigged and there was a canvas cradle strapped under her bows, showing that she had been holed below the water line. She sat low in the water as if she was overladen or sinking and there was no sign of life aboard her.

By her lines she might easily be Spanish, he thought, but what made Almeida view the battered hull with greater interest was that she had been in a sea fight – and she had been severely beaten.

Almeida's spirits rose. So! Inacio Ribeira had been right! There *was* a 'ghost ship' – and she had come into his arms. There was good money to be made in salvage. This was not an opportunity to pass up lightly. Already there were too many villagers on the beach, scratching their chins and wondering how the ship had come to be in the middle of the estuary. But the women were chiding their children and sending them indoors and the men had pulled their fishing boats high up on the beach. No other outsiders had yet come to the village, and Almeida realised that time was critical.

João Ribeira, his young local agent, hitched his bridle and helped him down. João's grandfather, Inacio, a man twenty years Almeida's senior, white-haired and leathery, was by his side.

'Senhor Ribeira, may I beg a favour of you?' he asked, extending his hand to touch the old man's arm. 'May I borrow your boat for just a little while?'

'I'll not go out there, Senhor Almeida. Not for any money you might offer me.'

'Grandfather!'

'That's not necessary. I'm sure that João is willing to row me to the ghost ship.'

The old man shuffled uncertainly. 'You say there may be gold out there? *Gold?*' he asked. A flicker of interest lit his dim eyes.

Almeida took the old man's arm and nodded towards the other fishermen. 'I want you to persuade them to keep back. Tell them I have a cross blessed by the holy fathers against sea wraiths. Ask them if they have any such protection.'

Inacio cackled, screwing his face into a grin. 'Oh, *senhor*, you are a wise man.'

João watched his kinsman wander away.

Almeida laughed. 'Which is his boat?'

'There, the blue and green one. Please.'

They crunched down a gravel beach that smelled of crusted salt and sunbleached fish heads. João laid his hands on the stem and slid the boat out clear of the pebbles so that it rocked in the water, then Almeida waded knee-deep and heaved himself in, steadying the oars.

It was a pull of five minutes. Almeida put his back against the sternpost and studied the ship carefully as they approached. When they came to within thirty *varas* he told João to row them no closer. He cupped his hands and shouted. The greeting echoed back eerily, but there was no answer.

At a word from the merchant João sculled slowly in, meeting the ship on the beam. The timber walls rose up six feet above them and Almeida could see beards of deep green weed pulsing below the water line. Could she have been abandoned? he wondered, his fingers tingling with hope. He had heard tales of ships being caught in terrible storms and left for dead by their crews. Perhaps a sea serpent attacked them. Perhaps the crew are eaten. It's a mystery!

'A-hoi!'

He shouted again. Still no reply. The young man was searching the empty gun ports, fear contending visibly with avarice on his face. 'A-hey, there!'

'Maybe there really is no one on board.'

'If that's true, then she's ours. We found her, didn't we, *patrão?*'

Almeida swallowed, wishing despite himself that he had the fictional cross to brandish. 'We have only to board her to claim her.'

João licked his lips. 'Maybe we should go back for weapons – for the others?'

Almeida turned towards the beach. Three upright figures in black had arrived there; they sent a shiver through him.

'And share the prize? Are you mad as well as frightened?'

Impulsively, the younger man stood up and leapt for the rail. He heaved himself over and froze there, listening and looking. The gun deck was empty, there was no sign of life. Almeida watched the youth's caution as he surveyed the decks. Truly, it was as if the crew had been lured overboard by the Queen of the Mermaids. She was a big craft, no warship but a trading galleon, lightly armed to allow heavier cargoes, like most of the ships that plied the silver routes, but the cannon were gone. João went as far as the quarterdeck and looked down the companionway into the darkness.

'There's no one here at all,' he shouted, and returned to help Almeida aboard.

With fervent hopes that the derelict was filled with valuable stores, the merchant went first to the hatches and found them battened tight. Then he went aft. It smelled foul and dense below, like fermenting brewers' mash. The Captain's cabin would be the place to start if he wanted to unravel the mystery. She's Spanish, he decided, glancing up at the carved woodwork of the stern castle. Yes, Spanish-built, and Spanish-worked. He had seen many different ships in his time and had learned to distinguish the small signs that showed nationality. The longboat was certainly made in Seville, and the shipwright's arrowhead marks cut into the joints proved that the frame of the ship had been constructed there also. Could it be? Was she really from one of the Spaniards' New World fleets, the *silver* fleets? Almeida's hope soared, but he steadied himself. Men did not simply abandon fortunes in silver, even at the cost of their own lives. What horror had evacuated the ship?

He went further aft, passing out of the harsh sunlight. The smell of salt and tar gave way to a cloying stuffiness. The creak of wood and taut rope came on each gentle motion of the tide. How much simpler if she had been Portuguese or French, or even English, he thought. But Jehovah has seen fit to send a Spanish ship, and that could only mean officials and bureaucratic investigations and endless delay. Ultimately, it must mean confiscation, for this was Portugal, and Portugal's independence was now a poor and threadbare thing.

If only our young King had seen sense, he thought. Why, in God's name, did he go adventuring? What stupidity! What madness to jeopardise the succession! Ai! Fighting the Moors in Morocco was an expensive and ludicrous diversion, no doubt an idea put there by an advisor whose pockets were a-jangle with Spanish gold. That Sebastian should die without an heir to succeed him! There's only the Cardinal now, the King's aged uncle, and beyond him Philip the Accursed, who waits like a crocodile to devour our land. It's their Satanic design to destroy four and a half centuries of cherished independence. They know Cardinal Henry is not long for this world, that he will leave no one but Dom Antonio, the bastard son of his brother Luiz, with whom to contest ownership of our country.

A more uneven contest was difficult to imagine. The vision of proud Portugal subdued like Flanders by Spanish infantry burgeoned garishly in Almeida's imagination. Already Philip had men stationed along the border. He could now lean so heavily on Portugal that her state policies, both internal and external, would be distorted out of recognition. Philip itched to absorb his neighbour and snuff out the ancient identity of Lusitania. The strategic and material benefits of a bloodless conquest of Portugal would be overpowering when set beside Philip's greed. And Sebastian has given him the perfect excuse! Two years, maybe three, as senile Henry sinks into an arsenical stupor – then what? Butchery and terror – or the meek acceptance of Spanish domination. And then it will be the death of all good things.

Almeida damned the watching fishermen on the beach. They had brought him the news, but they had also brought the churchmen, and they would bring official witnesses to the fact that a Spanish ship had come into the Baia. He damned King Philip to hell. To the deepest, hottest, cruellest circuit of it. Then he damned all things Spanish.

Spanish embargoes on English ships and English goods, the Inquisition's terror, Spain's meddling in Portugal, these things have slashed my profits by half, Almeida thought, staring into the gloomy depths of the Spanish ship. But, by God, they'll repay me!

Is it not an invariable rule that the war horse of a prince tramples the poor merchant underfoot? There's no justice in this world, only a God who enjoys irony. Still, He comforts His suffering people in their great loss, and I know He stands by those who seek to stand up for themselves.

Almeida gritted his teeth at his secret thoughts. He detested the Spanish fulsomely, hated the idea that they could seize Portugal. Yes, a Spanish ship! Maybe she became detached from a silver fleet in a storm. It often happens. Pray God that pirates have not attacked and stripped her. Or maybe she's a lone milk-cow that attempted the crossing in secret to avoid Philip's shit-eating taxes! That would be justice!

The way the wheel has come full circle! Aiee! If I lose money this year I'll have only myself to blame. My monthly accounts will certainly show small returns on wine, but the sale of information is much more lucrative. The facts concerning the sailing of ships must be worth more than all the wine in Setúbal, though the payment I receive is comparatively meagre. Perhaps this ghost ship is sent by God as a reward!

He pushed open the door that led to the Captain's cabin and entered it, filled with a growing confidence. Then the confidence left him as he felt the touch of steel between his shoulders and whirled to see a ghastly face and two pistols cocked and pointing at his belly.

The apparition was fierce: yellow eyes with pinpoint pupils, a clenched jaw, menace in every fibre of him. The man was shaking as if from a terrible fury, raving as if in fever, and his voice was like a demon's.

'Put your hands up, dog!'

The order was sudden and savage, but Almeida understood. Involuntarily he took a step back and raised his palms above his ears. Then he watched with incredulity as the man's unearthly eyes rolled up, one of his pistols almost trembled from his grip and his knees gave way under him so that he crashed to the deck.

Then Almeida's shock was penetrated by a familiar noise. It took him a moment to identify it because it was the last sound he could possibly have expected to hear in this place. It was the wailing of a baby.

John Tavistock staggered, overcome by another wave of agony. Desperately his mind clung to the sounds he was hearing and he fought back to consciousness and tried to muster his faculties once more. He got to his knees and his pistol wavered in an opaque blur. Stand up! Find your feet, or you're a dead man. This is Spain! Spain, don't you see? Lord God how could you betray me like this? We've landed while Solano's still alive. Didn't I promise you I'd glorify your name for the rest of my days, Lord, if only you'd smother that worthless bag of rotting shit before we reached Spain? Wasn't that the bargain? How many times did I tell you that the Captain's going to betray us to the Inquisition. Maria and the babe, who you love as I do, who we've both fought so hard for, *they're going to die*! Don't you understand? The Hellish Office will have the victory. Who's more important, Solano who lives stewing in his own black vomit? Or your previous beloved? Shall I murder Solano? Shall I cut his throat as he writhes, Lord? Wouldn't that just be a mercy to him as he suffers now?

Tavistock's eyes popped. The sound of screams in the dim distance, the music of rage ringing peals in his head. It was as if a giant hand had slapped him. Listen to your son cry, John! Listen to him cry! You must stop gawping and seize the initiative now! Do what is right!

He saw, penetrating through veils of mist, as the frightened Spaniard raised his hands. The man was well dressed, an expensive doublet and breeches, his girth supported by a wide, sagging belt, a bright cambric shirt, taped and edged, and above it a forty-year-old's face, nut brown, high forehead, badger-streaked beard and eyes full of surprise. Why don't you rush me? Why don't you try to shoot me with my own guns? Can't you see I'm next to helpless?

'Please, don't –'

'Get you back!' Tavistock growled, fighting back the dizziness that threatened to engulf him. 'Try me and I'll blow Your Honour's throat out!'

'Don't shoot, *señor*. I mean you no harm. I am not armed.'

'I told you to put your hands up! Up! Higher!'

'Are you the Captain? What ship is this? I only want to help you.'

'Back, now! Stir yourself! In there!'

The man fell back before him into the cabin, Tavistock keeping him on the end of his pistol; he did not take his eyes off him until they were safely inside.

Solano groaned from his bed. Suddenly, Tavistock's mind became lucid as the wave of nausea passed from him. He forced himself to remember how he had come to be locked into this dangerous strategy. However he looked at it, there seemed no better way. Didn't Solano have me chained and swear to me he'd tell the authorities at the *Casa para la Contratación* as soon as we came in sight of San Lucar? But on the crossing he lost so many men he could hardly work his ship and he freed me for the sake of my labour. It was then he promised to forgo his reward and keep his discovery to himself even after we landed. But I don't trust him. He's a pragmatic man, who cuts his oaths to suit his situation. And he's in need of money and dignity now, and the fear of the Holy Office has too powerful a grip on his mind. He'll recant his promise for silver and they'll arrest us and deliver us to torture and the stake. I should have blown his brains out last night. But I couldn't then, and I can't now. Not a pitiful starving wretch with the hogo of a stink coming off him. Not in cold blood. Even when Maria's life and my son's life and my own life all depend on it. Maybe he'll die yet. Maybe. Maybe . . .

The shaking was starting again.

'You'll be my hostage,' he told the man through chattering teeth, grimly hanging onto his pistol. 'That's a fair bargain. A rich merchant in exchange for passage to England. I want nothing more than that. The means to get my wife and son out of this hell. A bargain, Spaniard. Just like the one at San Juan. Only this time there'll be no payment, no trusting to treaty, and no mistakes.'

'How many are you?' the man asked. Despite the order to keep his hands up, he pulled the sudary from his belt and clamped it over his nose and mouth, then he leaned over Solano. 'This man is close to death.'

'Yesterday we were ten. All fatal sick. All laid up down below. Today I don't know. The fever . . .'

'Please, *señor*, put up your gun. I desire only to help you.'

'Get back from me!'

Tavistock felt the crest of the feverish tremor pass over him. Each day the lassitude of starvation had made it more and more difficult to concentrate his mind, to climb from deck to deck, to roll from his hammock at change of watch, but he was still well enough to pull a trigger. He looked at the hostage then down at the unconscious Solano. Die, you son of a pox-riddled whore! he told the Spaniard silently. Die and let my secret die with you!

'For the love of God, you must let me help these men, *señor*. They are dying. Where are the rest?'

Solano opened his eyes. He would not give up his life easily. He was a fighter, and though his struggles had brought himself and his crew to death's house he had done as he had sworn to do. He had brought his ship home. After the pirate had disabled the *Nuestra Señora* he had tried to make Havana, but a storm had caught them and tossed them into the straits where the contrary three-knot current had seized them. For two days and two nights they had fought it, but the power of the sea had left them rudderless and they had drifted helplessly until fate had grounded them on a Bahamas reef. The coral spines might have ripped the ship's belly out, but the keel had held and they had refloated her after lightening the ship by shucking the cannon and what was left of their cargo, but still without properly rigged sails she had had no chance of opposing tide and wind and regaining any Spanish port.

Solano had sent out all but one of the ship's boats, hoping to get a message to Cuba or the Florida settlement, but no one had returned, and for months they had languished on the miserable island, running short of water and provender and dying from the flux like flies, until in desperation he had realised that they must attempt a crossing or they would all perish.

'Can you hear me? My name is Nicolau Almeida. Where are the others?'

'I hear you,' Solano said weakly but coherently. 'My crew are lying below, streaming blood like me, what's left of them. I am the Captain of this ship –'

'Hold your mouth, Spaniard!'

Almeida's eyes narrowed at Tavistock. 'Then you are not a Spaniard, *señor*? What are you?'

As Tavistock's feral alertness returned, he jabbed the pistol forward. 'I'm English. I want food and water and passage aboard an English ship,' he told the man, his voice rasping now. 'I demand –'

Almeida stroked his chin warily. 'You're in no position to make demands, *señor*.'

'I'll shoot you before I'll rot in any Spanish prison. Do you hear?'

Then, incredibly, the tenor of the man's voice came back at him in puzzled amusement.

'But, *señor*, you are not in *Spain*.'

'Not Spain? Then, where?'

'This is Lisbon. *You are in Portugal*.'

Tavistock felt the resolve drain from him. If this was Portugal there was no need to hide. If this was truly Portugal they were safe ...

Then a young man's arms came around him from behind, enclosing him like barrel hoops, and the pistol was wrested from him.

Maria was sitting in the adjoining room with Nicolau Almeida's wife and the sound of their laughing came to him. The tuna fish dinner had been exquisite, and after the fine red wines of Colares and Bucellas, as rich and heady as claret, Tavistock felt relaxed and receptive.

The mouth of the Tagus was dappled with sunlight in the narrows that sheltered its harbour. From the window he could see the water chopping up as it became the open sea, the Western Ocean that stretched away a thousand leagues along a parallel of latitude to some wild and Godforsaken spot on the coast of the New World that seemed to him now farther than the farthest strand.

'Look at the fishing boats, Martin. See that one with the red sail?'

He stroked the two-year-old's hair gently, but failed to capture the attention of his son, who began to cry. Almeida swept the infant up and stood him on the sill, careless of the precipitous drop below.

'Be obedient to your father, Martin,' he said, pointing. 'That's where you were born. Out there on the waters. Some day you'll sail upon them as your father did and win glory for Portugal.'

The sight of the ocean's calm soothed the child. Tavistock, too, felt the restless draw of it. Memories of past rigours no longer had the power to hurt him. He was healed. How different was this untroubled blue from the mountains of furious water that had once dwarfed and almost overwhelmed their ship; how different this pleasant house and the soft comforts it afforded to the horrors of the *Nuestra Señora de la Popa*; how delightful the hospitality of his good and generous friend, Nicolau Almeida.

'You know,' he told him wistfully. 'When first I set out across that sea my comrades did call me a Portugall, owing to my darkish looks – as a jest, you see, for they dared not call me Spaniard.'

Almeida smiled. 'Then you are come home?'

'I thank you for that. It is so.'

'But do you not yearn for your own country still?'

'I have no country, now.' Tavistock drew a lingering breath. 'At one time I was an Englishman but was called a Portugall, next I was a stateless slave, and then a Mexican Spaniard. Now I am in Portugal but a foreigner. In truth, I know not what I am.'

'You might go into England when the wine ships return. Many are out of Bristol as you know, and I have the friendship of many an English master.'

Tavistock shook his head soberly at his friend's probings. 'I cannot be a Catholic man and have a Catholic wife in England, Nicolau. The Faith is disregarded there, and I have heard there is no toleration. I fear for my family.'

'Is there more for you here?'

'Thanks to your providence.' He smiled. 'I have a living casting bells. And I have friends, and peace at last.'

'But for how much longer? Go to England, *amigo*.'

'Why should you say that?'

Almeida lowered his voice, and as he spoke his words grew bitter. 'King Henry is dying and peace is crumbling. Though Dom Antonio is Portugal's choice, Philip is the son of Henry's sister. His claim is undeniable, and he has massed his legions on our border so he may impose his will. Each week, more and more Jesuits are flooding into Portugal. They are the shock troops, sent in advance with their bribery and casuistry.' He checked himself, remembering that he must keep his loathing for the Jesuits concealed. For all that he hated them, he had to admire their efficiency. The way they had persuaded the authorities to impound the *Nuestra Señora* within hours of its discovery, and afterwards, how their tireless diplomacy had arranged her repair and speedy dispatch to Cadiz, robbing him of his windfall.

But he had robbed them of a far greater thing. He had struck a blow that had been waiting to be thrown for twenty-five years.

The priests had seen João Ribeira waving at intervals from the deck, beckoning them, and so it was that half an hour later they had come out in a second fisherman's boat, three of them, with three well-armed soldiers and Captain da Silva in the bows. Poor da Silva, with the imperiousness of the minor nobility, impractical and hot-tempered, and utterly under the Jesuits' sway.

Their chief had been a tall, thin man, in his early forties wearing an immaculate plain habit, with that look of complete, single-minded self-possession that only those schooled in Rome's *Il Gesu* church could attain. He had been so obviously a disciple of the Black Pope, transformed during his two-year novitiate from a wilful man into the vacant property and willing instrument of the Society of Jesus, that Almeida's flesh had crawled at the sight of him.

Inacio's empty boat had been drifting aimlessly fifty *varas* away and so he had waved his kerchief and shouted down to them. 'I thank God you've come at last, Father! And you too, Captain.'

Da Silva had ignored him, cupping his hands to his mouth and hailing the ship. But the Jesuit had looked up enquiringly. 'What is it that agitates you, my son?'

'Our boat drifted. That good-for-nothing João Ribeira can't even tie his father's boat up properly. We were stranded here, Father. If you hadn't come I can't imagine what would have happened to us.'

Then he had clamped his kerchief tightly over his nose and mouth again while João Ribeira had stood beside him, mutely under orders.

When the frightened fisherman had shipped his blades and brought his fishing boat alongside, da Silva had asked, 'Is there no one aboard? We thought you must have been ambushed.'

Then the Jesuit had tasted the air suspiciously. 'Why do you hold a sudary to your face, Senhor Almeida?'

He had given a hacking cough. 'Can't you smell the stink? This ship is full of dead men, Father. And others alive still, but covered in red sores.'

'Red sores? How many?'

'Yes, ten, I think. Maybe a dozen. It's hard to tell. I've seen nothing like it in all my life. It's horrible. Here, help me down into the boat.'

'Get back!'

The Jesuit had seized an oar and pushed the boat back from the side. His upturned face graven now with fear and anger.

'Please, Father! What are you doing?'

'It's the plague!'

The soldiers had looked from one to another in panic.

'No, no – please. Don't think that. Come now. You must let me get off this stinking wreck.'

'Pull for the shore!' da Silva had ordered. 'It's a plague ship!'

Instantly the oars had been seated in the tholepins and the boat set in motion.

'Captain!' His helpless plea had rung out and he had begun to hoist himself over the gunwale, secretly delighted at the success of his ploy.

'Stay there, Almeida. I command it. This ship is quarantined. For forty days, do you hear me?'

'*Forty days?* But there's no food aboard. I shall starve! And these poor men –'

'Food will be sent.'

'But they need a surgeon!'

'Do what you can for them.'

'No! Captain da Silva, I beg you! Come back!'

The boat had stroked rapidly away, and under cover of night João Ribeira had swum to his father's boat and recovered it and they had crept to shore with the Englishman and his wife and the baby.

But there had been a good deal of substance to the ruse. Almeida recalled the scene that he had witnessed below, men wasted with disease, ragged and feverish, dead or dying. None except Solano able to stand and he a yellow skeleton. He had had a Catalan's tenacity that drove him on when other men gave up. Perhaps he had survived, for the Jesuits had found the courage to board the ship the following day. In any case, they had found him gone, and because of the delicacy of the negotiations surrounding the *Nuestra Señora*'s release, and because the imposition of a quarantine order would have hampered them, his name had appeared in no official reports, and within a week the ship had gone, doubtless to Cadiz, to stack up good credit for their filthy Society with the Spanish King.

'Do you think there will be resistance?' Tavistock asked him, bringing him back to the present.

Almeida put his hands together thoughtfully. 'It's said that Philip's appointed the Duke of Alva to head his invasion. If he's opposed, Spanish troops will destroy our pitiful army and then they will trample Lisbon. They could raze all of Portugal as they choose. We are already in their power. Get out now, while you can.'

Tavistock glanced at his friend, reminding himself that Almeida knew only that he had escaped the Inquisition's stake. He had never told him his true profession, nor the reason Solano had valued his discovery. So far as Almeida was concerned he was nothing more than a bellfounder who had been victimised by the Holy Office, and in that, somewhere, had been the bond between them.

'You're a wise man, *senhor*.'

'If you permit me to write a letter to my son, Ferdinand, he will arrange passage on an English barque.'

'No.'

'But you don't know if Captain Solano survived. If he did, and spoke of you to the Holy Office, you will already be marked.'

'I doubted the Lord's providence once, and I was wrong. I shall trust in God that Solano died, or that he's forgotten me.'

'Reconsider, please.'

'I thank you, but no.'

Almeida put out his hands in appeal. 'I beg of you. For Martin's sake. For Maria's. Listen to me.'

His son began to cry again, wanting to get down from the sill, and Tavistock lifted him to the floor. Nicolau's wise, he thought, beginning to feel the weight of his friend's words. In a Portugal ruled by Spain a single indiscretion could uncover us and unleash the terror again. But there's no place on earth that's any safer for us than here. At least in Lisbon we are among friends. In England we know no one, we have nothing. Twelve years is a long time to be away, and they say that in England there's no peace for Catholics.

'We shall stay here.'

Almeida sighed, his tact failing. 'Dom Antonio has support in the Azores. Perhaps that will remain truly Portuguese. Perhaps if you –'

'No. I'm tired of running, Nicolau. We shall take our chances in Lisbon. For good or ill we'll make our stand here.'

'Is that to be your final decision?'

Below, a cart rumbled by loaded with crates of chickens and fresh vegetables, gutted fish, great stoppered jugs of wine, water, pails of shellfish and big hocks of meat for tomorrow's *festa*. He remembered the first day of his deliverance in Portugal in this same house. He had wanted to eat ravenously but had known that the shock of food on a starving body was like swallowing red hot coals. He had drunk a little and he had fed Maria very sparingly and tried to make sure she did not gorge herself. Then, doubts had speared him. His mind had tried to unknot the problem. Almeida was a rich merchant. Surely he only wanted to ransom them to the Spanish – yet he had insisted that he did not. All along, Almeida had been at pains to comfort him, and to provide for his family. He had jeopardised himself to become the willing helper of an Englishman. That doesn't make sense, he had reasoned, no one in Almeida's position would want to clash with the Jesuits. I can't understand why he's working so hard to preserve us. Would either of the Hawkins brothers have reacted that way if they'd come aboard a Spanish ship half-wrecked in Falmouth's Carrick Roads? No! Then what was it that had made a serene man like Nicolau Almeida hate the Spanish so? And what was it that made him hate Jesuits most particularly?

'Why are you doing this for us?' he had asked him directly.

Almeida had given his patient smile and pointed to English ships on the far side of the harbour. 'I told you. The owners of those barques are my friends. England and Portugal have traded for years as allies and our friendship has prospered both nations.'

Tavistock had been unconvinced by Almeida's easy reply. 'You're asking me to believe that you'd risk your life to save us. Why?'

'In Portugal as in Spain, *senhor*, the merchant has little status. Princes make promises and the common man keeps them. We must protect our own interests. For the merchant, taking risks is our daily bread.'

Tavistock had felt deep guilt at the way he had doubted God, how he had turned against Him when it seemed that his family were cheated of sanctuary. Then he had looked at Almeida's dark eyes and he had thought he recognised the mark of an honest man.

'I ask you again, *amigo*, is that your final decision?'

'Yes. I will not go from here of my own will.'

The broad, kindly face of Nicolau Almeida clouded then. He became grave and stern. 'Well, then, come with me to the coolness of the shade garden. We must talk, you and I. For all is not what it seems here in my house, and if you will stay in Lisbon you must know the truth.'

They went down past banks of tamarisk and gorse under which lizards darted. Among the green blades and purple dragon-headed blooms of flowers-de-luce they walked side by side, Almeida speaking and John Tavistock listening, until the Portuguese had told of the other trade in which he dealt, the trade in secrets and sealed reports, and the places into which he sent them.

The Englishman felt himself sober despite the fermented juice of Ramisco grapes that ran in his veins. He judged himself fully admitted to his friend's confidence, and so he likewise unburdened himself, telling of the skills he possessed, to which Almeida nodded sagely as a man who receives a great responsibility.

In trust he listened to Nicolau Almeida then, and heard him speak with difficulty of the first family he had had, the one of his youth, a quarter century ago, when he had been a Spaniard and the Jesuits had discovered his true beliefs. And as he listened he discovered the answer to a question that no one else knew enough even to ask – what a man born a Spanish Jew was really doing living in so grand a house in Lisbon.

Chapter 23

'Master! Master! There's a gentleman to see you!'

Richard Tavistock looked to shore impatiently. Anne, sitting quietly in the boat's prow, turned the page of her book. The servant was breathless; his shoes, thick with meadow clarts, thumped the earth bank, sending rings rippling over the glassy surface. Vibration at the lake side always disturbed the fish, and this would ruin them for the rest of the afternoon.

'You can see I'm stalking fish, Matthew,' he called back gruffly as he picked another roach out of his pail. It was four inches long, and its gills heaved as he threaded the barbed hook into its back. When it touched the lake it fled, red fins blurring as it towed the cork float on a line of greased horsehair twine.

'He says it's urgent, sir.'

'God save you, man. Can anything be more urgent than a twelve-pound pike?'

'I didn't think to ask him that, sir.'

'Did you think to ask his name?'

'Oh, yes, sir, but he won't tell it. He's a fine gentleman though.'

Tavistock roused himself from his study of the reeds. 'Then tell the fine gentleman from me to take his insolence off my property.'

He had been brooding over the Puritans of the parish who had recently somehow conceived the idea that the master of Low Houghton was living sinfully. If one of them had had the temerity to make representations –

The shallop swayed as Anne laid aside her book and sat up. He spread his legs to steady the boat.

'Perhaps you should attend to it, Richard.'

'If he has not the manners to give his name, he cannot expect civility.'

'I should like to think that any visitor to our home might expect that.'

Tavistock looked at her calm determination and knew he had been justly corrected. Of course she was right. But for all her composure she must have had some small suspicion, as he did. Was this nameless visitor the one that he knew must eventually come to disturb their idyll?

In the time they had lived here, Anne had borne him a second daughter, Katherine, and a third, Amy. And there had been inevitable unvoiced questions among all stations of folk, seeing as the Earl of Oxford *never* came to his wife's house, and that the sea captain appeared to lord it in his place. But Tavistock was no longer a sea captain. For the sake of his family he had forsworn the sea and all it had once meant to him. Except for business visits to London and frequent sojourns in the ports of the south coast he had renounced all but sight of both wave and sail, telling himself that he had fulfilled all promises and realised all potentialities. This lake was his ocean now, and the pike his only adversary.

It seemed only yesterday that he had pushed open the garden gate and come inside to reclaim his Anne, but it had been almost seven years. That first spring he had secretly acquired Low Houghton through an intermediary, relishing the power of his freehold. He had demolished the evil-smelling mediaeval barn to make way for stone brought from a local abbey ruined by King Henry, and then he had built two new wings in the form of a T, to literally stamp himself upon the place, but perhaps more to erase all trace of the previous owner.

He had had no doubts then that the swell of Surrey's green hills were his proper surroundings, or that the meetest occupation of a wealthy man was philanthropy and the management of monies and materials through signatures. For seven years he had played the mercantile game and consigned his roving past to a locked chest somewhere in the back of his memory. But it was undeniable that the spirit of the times was altering, and that events were moving swiftly towards the day when he must open that dusty chest and look again upon its treasure.

He regarded Anne with love and with respect. Her power to surprise him had never waned, and her intellect was an awesome thing that made her counsel indispensable, especially when he retreated into the sullen angers that once might have been slaked by action.

'The weather's changing,' he said stiffly.

'Yes.'

'I suppose we'll see little more of the pike.'

'If you say so.'

'Yes.'

Cloud blighted the sky above the slate planes of the house. A rain of golden leaves shimmered from the trees beside it. He closed his eyes. Aye, there was more than the weather changing. More than the season too. He could feel it in the air, just as he had felt it back in 'seventy-two. Throughout the uneasy peace, England had steadily built up her defences and her economy, seeking ports in Germany and the Baltic for her woollen cloth, bringing timber and rope from Tsar Ivan's Muscovy, and pushing boldly into the Mediterranean to do trade with the Turk. Tavistock had made astute investments, growing richer still, putting his money into the Eastlands Company and the Merchant Adventurers, and helping to set up a new venture – the Levant Company. But the weeping sore of the Low Countries had continued to fester, and Philip's annexation of Portugal had given Spain a much greater power to strangle and control any who dared oppose her. The Straits of Gibraltar had grown as perilous for the English as the Narrow Seas were to Spanish shipping, and the immense riches of the Indies, Orient as well as Occident, were as much a Catholic preserve as ever. In London, too, many things were in need of setting to rights. Too many conversations there had verged on treason and brought him to overturn tables that he no longer gained any pleasure from the city. Elizabeth's Court itself seethed with factions that wanted to see a détente with Spain bought on any terms, and too many of those that remained were cowards who could not see the inevitable.

He grunted. 'Who would come here and refuse to give his name?'

'Go and see!'

'Yes. I will.'

He drew the line back and stowed his pole, giving the last captive roach in his pail its freedom. As he propelled the boat deftly forward, a cloud passed over the sun, there was a sudden chill and the water's surface lost its silver. The English summer, a maid of fickle mood, had grown capricious, and before they had reached the house a heavy, dousing rain had begun to fall.

Tavistock's muddied boots crunched across the path, skittering gravel. He strode around the corner of the house trailing Matthew in his wake. Anger lay like a coiled serpent in his breast and he wished he had his sword at his side. Then he saw the horse.

How if I break the head of Lord Oxford's emissary and send him away roughly? he asked himself. It was not a course open to a country gentleman. How, then, if I treat with him nicely and get me a meeting with that drunken sot, and then break heads?

He turned the buttressed corner of his entrance way, and sensed a figure step out through the rain behind him.

'Put up your hands, you lazy bear!'

He whirled.

'Francis!'

'*Sir* Francis – speak it respectfully, now, brother.'

He advanced on Drake and they gripped forearms, hugely pleased to meet each other again. Rain dripped from the brim of Drake's hat, spangled his russet beard with diamonds. The scar that had been put between nose and eye by an Indian arrow during his voyage around the world wrinkled as he smiled broadly.

'Ah, let me see you, now!'

'You look like Lord Harry Shitfire!'

'And you his brother Tom.'

'Is that any way to address a Knight of the Realm?'

'On my ground, yes. But this knight is welcome. What brings you here?'

Drake's voice went descant. 'Just passing through.'

'Come inside. Will you take a pipe with me?'

'Gladly. Gladly! And you may tell me of your retirement.'

'Retirement? I don't think of it as such.'

They passed under the arch side by side. It was good to see Drake buoyant again, buoyant enough to nettle his friend over his quiet style of life.

Their last meeting had been unhappy; the one before that, glorious. That had been the triumph of Drake's return, when he had sailed the *Golden Hinde* back to England, after three years, laden with half a million pounds of Spanish money. Then Drake had received the highest accolade the nation could bestow. The Queen had thrown off all objections and come herself to Deptford, to the very deck of his ship, to knight him. And how Tavistock had basked in the glory of it, knowing, as his monarch gave her sword to the French Ambassador to dub Drake's shoulders, that by her act the French nation also was included in the snub to Spain. Supping with Tavistock afterwards Drake had delighted that the report must reach King Philip's cell and would there cause the villain acute wounds, and both had pledged themselves to firing up their wild pasts at some future time when the nation's need arose.

Those had been great days. This little Englishman had fought his way full around the globe against the might of Spain and had put such heart into the nation for his pains. But last year Drake's wife, Mary, had died and he had grieved her deeply. They had spoken together again then, and Tavistock had aided his friend as he had once himself been aided, and both had been uplifted. Still, as if by mutual consent, neither had renewed their ideas of going out again upon the sea.

This year the winds of fortune had veered again for Drake. According to his letters he had found employment working on the Navy Commission. He had been elevated from Mayor of Plymouth to Member of Parliament for Bossiney and he had found the love of an heiress in Sir George Sydenham's daughter, Elizabeth. It seemed to Tavistock that the prospects of making a good marriage had brought Drake to fine condition.

They sat down in armchairs, surrounded by mounted ship models – *Antelope* and *Artegall* and *Primrose* – and indulgently reminisced, Tavistock speaking of his investments and Drake telling tales of Court, both sucking on clay pipes until the room filled with blue haze.

Drake regarded the polished wood and tall windows with approval. 'So, you're enjoying your leisure?'

'I am.' Tavistock nodded. 'And you? How went your time with the Navy Commission?'

He watched Drake for a reaction. In the time since Hawkins had been appointed Navy Treasurer Drake had mentioned his Navy work only once, and that dismissively.

'There's a great difficulty with the beacons. At night, or in poor visibility, the whole country might be brought to arms by any casual fire in a hayfield. Twelve times already there have been false alarms and these days we cannot afford to cry wolf.'

Drake said it so lightly that Tavistock took a special note of his guest's manner, of his gestures. Yes, he thought, there's definitely something amiss with him, and it's not connected with beacons. He roped in his curiosity and, equally lightly, said, 'I might think on a solution for that.'

'Do! Yes. And you must bring it to us formally.'

'I'm content to leave Navy matters to Navy men.'

'Yes, but good ideas are rare enough. I'd welcome your suggestions.'

'Maybe, maybe.' Tavistock deflected him, probing subtly. 'Did you know that when Dom Antonio was come to England for aid I spoke to him?'

'Aye?'

'It was just after the change of the Continentals' calendar, when they made their October fifth into October fifteenth.'

'Oh?'

'I found Dom Antonio a witty and inscrutable creature, for a Portugall. I asked him why did he, a Catholic, come over to our shore, and he twines his beard, so, and says: "The King of Spain is a powerful sovereign, and His Holiness the Pope Gregory, a wise and venerable man, but by Heaven, no man shall annul ten days out from my life and have my loyalty."'

Drake chuckled. 'I hope you did tell him that Sunday is still Sunday in Rome as in England.'

'I should have.'

Grinning, Drake turned the conversation again and vied to cap the tale. 'I tell you I heard this plainly, Richard. Walter Ralegh is an excellent charmer who has the wherewithal to try it on in order to get him his way. The Queen does like him well, and he comes to her dressed in a suit as green as a pea swad; says he: "Your Majesty is the bright sunbeam that lights all England through the darkness and gives her subjects succour." And she says to him laughingly like a girl: "Ah, me! Give me that pruning knife, my Lord Burghleigh. God's eyes, if that vegetable does not remind me of Thomas Seymour!" And says Lord Burghleigh – who now attends the Queen's elbow at all times – but in a dry aside that I caught hold of: "Wasn't he the Admiral whose head was cut off?"'

Tavistock grinned at Drake's gesticulations. 'What, there's more?'

'Aye. And then, later, Ralegh comes beside Lord Leicester and says snottily of the enterprise he has all the time been trying to work, "Of course, my lord, I shall call it 'Virginia', in honour of her." But Leicester is full of bouse, and all acid, and tells him back: "Hear me, Walter –

and I speak whereof I know – 'Virginia' is a misnomer. And Thomas Seymour the villain!'"

Tavistock laughed, then he shook his head and sucked in a sharp breath. 'Ralegh and Leicester are rogues both.'

'Ralegh will go far.'

'Or *too* far.'

'Perhaps.'

'Aye. Though sometimes England needs audacious men. As now.'

There was a space pregnant with silence, then Tavistock said, 'So, Francis, Court partics sit well with you. You've a taste for gossip you never had.'

'I've a taste for getting what I want. And I perceive that my old straight way is too blunt for a palace table. Your advice in that regard was better than any I got from you at sea.'

'Well, a gentleman must be amusing, and an ambitious gentleman somewhat an intriguer. So tell me, what really brings you here?'

Drake's face shed its smile, growing suddenly serious and intense. 'Strong matters.'

'Indeed? Then they're too strong for a gentleman of leisure. One who has – *retired.*'

'I want your help, Richard.'

A curl of smoke spiralled up from the bowl of Drake's pipe. The tip of its long, bowed stem was clamped in his teeth, and his eye was steady on Tavistock's face.

'Do you?'

'Aye – call it ambition and intrigue if you will, but do you remember in 'eighty-one how I planned to sail for the Azores and wrest it from the Spanish? How Her Majesty gave her word, then withdrew it?'

'I do.'

'I'd put to sea anew on a fresh game, if you'd come.'

'My seagoing days're over, Francis. There's no call for the like of me while the peace holds.'

'You're wrong.' Drake leaned forward, fired now with his old passion. His eyes smouldered; his hands gripped the arms of his chair. 'Since Philip took Portugal everything's in ferment. England must prepare for war. Now. Quickly. Before it's too late.'

Anne stood in the doorway, a posy of garden flowers in her hand. Her face had lost its warmth.

'It's always been the policy of the Habsburgs to extend their power throughout Europe,' she told Drake coldly. 'But they annex by marriage, rather than war, conquering through Venus, rather than Mars. When Spanish arms overran Portugal the Cortés in Lisbon recognised Philip as King through his mother's line.'

'That's true, my lady, but they also exiled Dom Antonio, who has the stronger claim and who the Portuguese people want, to live among whatever Protestants would aid him.'

'Then we should be glad he found little help here. When he and Filippo Strozzi went after the Azores with a French fleet it was crushed to talwood by the Marquis of Santa Cruz. Had it not been for the Queen's change of heart they might have been your ships, Sir Francis.'

'I beg your pardon, Lady, but Santa Cruz's victory was a boarding action. In that game the Spaniards have no peer, but would I, would Richard, have allowed Santa Cruz to come to grips with our fleet like Filippo Strozzi did?'

Tavistock's dismay mounted as he heard Drake out, fearing his infectious words and the way they must wound Anne. 'Let's speak no more of it –'

But Anne was insistent. 'Please, let Sir Francis have his say.'

Drake's fist balled. 'We must. Because I've been. And I've seen. And I tell you, for the first time, East has met West. Now the whole world beyond the seas is the demesne of Spain. To their empires of the Americas and the Philippines they've added a thousand Portuguese conquests: mighty Brazil, a great chain of bases along the coast of Africa, fabulously wealthy factories and trade centres in India, the Isle of Ceylon, and the Spice Islands of Java and the Malaccas – aye, and the Azores, that most strategic of staging posts in mid-Atlantic. But the biggest prize of all is Lisbon herself. The Tagus is a jewel. A magnificent natural harbour, a place where a thousand galleons might be assembled in safety. You're blind if you fail to see its purpose. They seek to overwhelm us, Richard. To sweep us away in one massive blow. Don't lie to yourself that it's otherwise.'

Anne cast her flowers down onto the table and left the room. Tavistock checked himself from following or calling to her. She was only thinking of him, of the children. But Drake was right, and right to speak. After the battle of Lepanto, Spanish fears over the Ottoman threat had been obliterated. Granada was secured, and when the Portuguese throne fell under Philip's claim two world-spanning empires were put under his sole direction. The moment the Duke of Alva's troops had marched into Lisbon, Spain had become an Atlantic power with an oceanic littoral stretching unbroken for two hundred leagues, and in the centre of it, the greatest natural harbour in Europe. Overnight, Spain had taken possession of Portugal's *Marinha Real* – a dozen huge battle galleons and their men and arms, their naval dockyards and arsenals and storehouses. Then there were the extensive private trading fleets that plied the eastern spice routes that Philip, as King of Portugal, could commandeer at any time. The title had given him mastery over the ocean in the same way that his destruction of the Turkish galleys had given him mastery over the Mediterranean. The focus of his attention was shifting north and his fascinated stare was now alighting upon the heretics of England without distraction.

As if from a great distance Drake's voice urged him, 'We must speak with Mister Secretary Walsingham, Richard. Will you come now to back me?'

Tavistock said nothing, only turned away.

'Not even to hear me speak to him of the iniquities of John Hawkins?'

'Hawkins?' he heard himself say.

As Drake spoke Tavistock looked beyond the great leaded panes of the oriel, watching the rain slash down across his mown lawns, watching the ragged line of labourers coming in from his fields. This was his earthly peace. His home. His haven. Two of his daughters were next door in the library with their tutor, the third lay upstairs sleeping with her wet nurse beside her. At the back of the house Anne would be in the kitchen, ordering the dinner the family would eat tonight: wild duck that Tavistock had shot himself, and hare and carrots, and strawberries and cheeses for later. Must he go to her and ask her to put it all away and tell Matthew to ready his horse instead?

He bowed his head, put his face in his hand, ploughing the fingers through his hair. Drake, his closest friend, had brought him a bigger impediment to his life's tranquillity than any snivelling filth sent by the Earl of Oxford. But there *was* change in the air, and he knew that what Drake had told him was of immense importance.

Tavistock saw with clarity that Albion was stirring, girding herself for battle against an overwhelming foe, and all Albion's sons must do likewise. No one could ignore the beating of war drums that filled the air, the survival of England was at stake, the survival of every hard-won liberty, to speak, to trade, to worship. No one could in conscience set his own freedoms above those of the nation, for ultimately they were one and the same. No one should. No one could. No one.

He turned to Drake. God damn this man, he thought, this brother who has replaced in my heart the one I lost so long ago. Must I leave everything? Must I forgo the twelve-pound pike for another season?

Then he thought of the proverb that spoke of blood being thicker than water.

John Dee's house in Mortlake had lain deserted for a long season, sealed by the Queen's order. The physic garden that was walled and locked was full of dead things, its herbs poisoned, its grass bleached or burnt. At the fringes all was still overgrown with brambles, but in the centre there was only brown, desiccated wood, fungi and moulds and the foul suppurations of decay. Rain beat against the stone sundial which stood beside a pool of green and slimy water. Once fish had sported here, and toads had laid their strings of spawn, but no longer. It was a sobering place to talk of treason.

Walsingham pulled the chain from the iron gate and pushed against complaining hinges. Tavistock shut one eye against the shafting rain, following Walsingham and Drake off the landing stage. The Secretary's men, he noted, made no move to follow from the boat but looked to one another superstitiously, which pleased Tavistock because he wanted secrecy.

He regarded Walsingham closely. Trust your first impression of him as you stepped ashore at Greenwich, he told himself. Sharp-toothed? Yes. A stoat, full of ambition and subterfuges? Twice yes. A villain? Thrice yes. Oh, you're a less righteous man than I once thought. And you're not a friend, for I know you maintain me only as an ally. You have little faith, for you once sold your stake in me to Burleigh. And you're hard of soul, for your business is knowing all through the buying and twisting of other men's souls. All these things damn you, Mister Secretary, but, by God, there's one side of you that saves all. You're not a traitor and so I can trust you.

'Come, then. Tell me what you hope to find here.'

'In good time, Mister Secretary.'

Tavistock looked about him at the devastation, eerily appalled. 'This is a rare place. Did it die when the Doctor departed on his European wanderings?'

'Before. It was made so by noxious clouds released from one of Dee's alchemical experiments. The life of the soil is quite destroyed.'

'It's clear to me why the Queen's Magus has been decreed a wizard and a black magician by the Pope, and why he seeks now to interrogate him in Rome.'

'One devil-master jealous of the powers of another,' Drake said. 'So, Mister Secretary, how fares the good Doctor? Where is he now?'

'It seems the great illuminatus knew enough to prophesy the arrival of the papal nuncio in Prague three weeks beforehand. I can report that he escaped beyond the grasp of the Emperor Rudolph who would surely have served his head to the Pope like that of John the Baptist had he caught him. But he is not infallible, he made a grave miscalculation flying into the castle of Trebona, and the gilded cage of Count Rosenberg of Bohemia.'

'A gilded cage, you say?' Tavistock said.

Walsingham rattled the ring of huge keys. 'Yes. So completely did Dee convince the Count of his greatness that hospitality was extended to him indefinitely. He's to stay at Trebona until he's turned all Rosenberg's suits of armour into gold.'

Drake grunted, and took the iron key from Walsingham. 'If Count Rosenberg wants gold he'd better catch himself a sturdy English sea captain and go search out Spanish bullion.'

'An altogether more difficult prospect than detaining an aged alchemist,' Walsingham agreed drily, adding, 'but I fear that the state of Bohemia is landlocked.'

'Ah, for good sense and a sound policy there must needs be a lady monarch to pinch the purse strings and no borders to her nation. We should take Scotland and abolish it formally.'

'The heir, James, will accomplish that soon enough.'

Drake unlocked the door and went inside. Tavistock, following, drew out flint and steel and struck up candles for them. All was musty and dank: rain had got in, bringing down ceiling plaster; birds had found entrance through broken panes, liming the furniture; insects had wintered and summered in the rooms and vermin had made nesting of the books of knowledge. As they moved throughout the sprawling warren Tavistock realised how little prospect there was of finding that for which he had come.

'Genius, it seems,' Walsingham said portentously, examining a carved gargoyle face to face, 'may be in inverse proportion to orderliness.'

Drake eyed him coolly. 'It stinks highly of cat's piss.'

'You were wrong to let the Doctor leave England, Mister Walsingham,' Tavistock said. 'Why did you?'

Walsingham took the accusation smoothly. 'Dee was growing meddlesome in government and holding too close a station to Her Majesty. I was happy to have him travel elsewhere.'

'A mistake. Men like Dee are rare. A resource more precious than gold. I thought you, better than anyone, understood that.' He pulled a wooden box from under a stack of mouldering papers, opened it and looked inside, then he discarded it carelessly into a gloomy corner.

'What are you looking for, Captain Tavistock?'

'A copy, or a plan.'

'Of what?'

'Many things, but foremost of the *optic* machine. It was a meet and excellent instrument for use at sea, and it might save your watchers a deal of kindling on the beacon hills if we find its secret – and then one who can construct for us its like.'

'You've brought me across the river for toys and trifles?' Walsingham's impatience erupted. He stiffened angrily, as a man pushed too far.

Tavistock ceased his ransacking and levelled a finger at Walsingham's eye. 'I brought you here to talk. There's no more silent place in all England, and no more important matter to disturb it with.'

Walsingham's shoulders sagged and he acquiesced. Drake planted three chairs around the table and they sat down, each with his candle fixed before him in the gloom as Tavistock began.

'Mister Secretary, our country is heading for war. And when war comes she must be properly ready. Say what you will, our Navy's arks are still all that stand between Parma and the snuffing out of the world's liberties, but there's a traitor among them.' He thrust a leather satchel onto the table. 'I have it here.'

Walsingham brought out the papers and examined them, listening simultaneously to Drake's catalogue of treachery. Tavistock already knew the history of it: Hawkins had profited greatly from the dealings they had had with de Spes. The success of that intrigue had brought Hawkins position and power. He had first succeeded to the post of Treasurer of the Navy, inherited, with Burghleigh's connivance, from his own father-in-law, Ben Gonson. Later, he had been raised once more, this time to Comptroller of the Navy, a post that gave him ultimate say over the Naval dockyards. Since then, his avarice had been unbounded.

Tavistock boiled with anger as he listened to the corruptions that Drake reported. Hawkins had gone into partnership with the private yards of his friends, with yard owner Richard Chapman and the Master Shipwright Peter Pett, and latterly with the Storekeeper, Matthew Baker. Between them they had defrauded the Navy, building their own ships in Chapman's yard of the Queen's timber, provisioning them, through Baker, with the Queen's stores.

'It makes me burn to think that this low man can send Her Majesty's mariners to sea in ships diminished by his greed. And in such a time of crisis.'

Walsingham stared back at Drake. The two men were so utterly different. They had never liked one another, which was why Drake had asked for Tavistock's intercession. 'Leave the matter with me,' he said softly.

'Act!' Drake's fist slammed the table, guttering the candles. 'Make it known! Tomorrow! Unseat Hawkins! And unseat Burghleigh!'

'No! There is a better way.' Rain drummed in the silence, then Walsingham smiled for the first time. 'On the high seas, it may be your method to fight fire with fire. Here on dry land we have another way. We fight fire with a pail of water.'

Drake's anger stalled, his face stood in perplexity a moment, and then he too smiled.

In the Secretary's fine house at Barn Elms the three men gathered together again. Walsingham paced anxiously, seeing no way out. England's peril ran far deeper than either of his guests could know. The spies of the Papacy were secretly pouring into the country. Jesuits, the agents of Satan, manufactured by the fanatical Cardinal Allen in Douai and the monstrous factory at Rheims, were infiltrating the nation under cover of giving spiritual succour to the remnants of their Catholic flocks. These Jesuits were paving the way for invasion, striking at the vitals, sapping strength by their devious plots and reporting everything faithfully to Rome.

It required a huge investment in time and money to track such men, and Walsingham's resolve quailed as he considered his task. Admittedly, there had been successes. Had he not infiltrated a swarming nest of traitors in Oxford? Had he not penetrated the Papal network through William Parry? Had he not arrested the seditious Edmund Campion, and disposed of him? As he had lain bleeding on the rack Campion had yielded much, but too late to get hold of Robert Parsons, Campion's controller. Even now, that wretch was running back and forth between Rome and Paris, Flanders and Madrid, designing revolution and the Queen's very death. Had that not been specifically ordered by Cardinal

Como? And had not Pope Gregory absolved and released English Catholics from the anathema imposed by his predecessor, Pius? Why, if not as precursor to a huge and vile effort? To rally waverers and deep-run cowards and those who lay quiet to the cause? But what cause?

Walsingham saw it clearly now, shuddering at the force of the idea. After news of William of Orange's assassination and the overrunning of Brabant and Flanders had reached him, his spies had said that the Prince of Parma, Spain's foremost soldier, had wanted to muster thirty thousand foot and five thousand horse in Nieuport and Dunkirk and then ferry them across in eight hundred barges. With England's Navy in the Narrows that idea was as foredoomed as it had ever been, but then Santa Cruz had returned from his victories bursting with confidence and laid before his King another, more ambitious enterprise.

Yes, he thought despairingly, it was the only answer! Philip must have sanctioned the massive seaborne invasion that his Admiral wanted launched from Lisbon: five hundred ships, fully one hundred fifty of which were great ships. Thirty thousand mariners. Sixty-five thousand troops. The greatest fleet ever assembled. An unopposable, invincible armada.

This time there would be no expensive but limited irritations like the rebellions of Ireland which had been shut down by Lord Grey, no abortive attempt like the one Don John had almost mounted before he was replaced as Philip's commander in the Netherlands by Parma. No, this time, the entire might of Spain would be focused on England. Directly. Like a burning glass on kindling. And *still* Burleigh imagined that war could be avoided!

A tremendous weight of responsibility pressed down on Walsingham as he thought of the terrifying news he had received from the Continent. Months ago, plans for an attack via Scotland had been thwarted. On the rack, the double-dealing Francis Throckmorton had confessed to his complicity. He had run a conspiracy between the Spanish Ambassador, Bernardino de Mendoza, and the imprisoned Scottish Queen. He had succeeded in sending Mendoza the same way as de Spes had gone, but what of the archconspirator herself? What of Mary? To have the least hope of warding off the threat, Mary must die. And Elizabeth must be persuaded to execute her.

Walsingham closed his eyes, feeling the stares of the two men at his back and the sweat beading the peak of his hairline. He wiped it away and examined his hand, imagining blood.

His spies had picked up a thousand terrifying clues, all pointing in the same direction. The darkest days of 'seventy-one were but a pale shade compared to the evil gloom that presently mounted against England. She was besieged on every side. Now, Spain was twice as rich, her navy twice as powerful. All over Europe, in greater Austria, in the Kingdom of Naples, in Sicily and Milan and the lands over which Habsburg arms held sway, a groundswell was beginning. And the hub of it all was the tiny cell in the airless fortress-monastery-palace of the Escorial. Spain's finest men were being recalled to her, assembling in ranks to the beat of war drums, bringing with them arms and levies and the implacable martial spirit that had conquered all the earth, gathering for a decisive blow.

Now Drake's and Tavistock's revelations about Hawkins had shaken to the foundations the one pillar on which England's survival depended. And Hawkins was Burleigh's man.

He tried to drag his thoughts back to the present. Tavistock was right, England needed her able men now, more than ever before. The maritime shires of the south and west were drawing together, trained bands were being mobilised, but it was being done with painful sloth. Under Burleigh and his Lords Lieutenant, the companies raised were small and ill-disciplined, and certainly no match for Parma's war-hardened veterans. If Parma's troops landed there would be slaughter on a massive scale, they would brush aside any army England could scrape together as a prelude to a greater slaughter. Walsingham's blood chilled as he considered it. The Navy was England's only defence, her only hope of survival.

Tavistock told him: 'We must have ocean-going pinnaces to ply the Narrow Seas, fleet vessels capable of outrunning any Spaniard sent against us, to free our battleships for work other than coastal defence. And those battleships must be of the new kind, like unto the *Revenge*, well-armed with guns that outshoot the Spanish at long range. This must be our strategy. Only that can spare us.'

Drake nodded his assent. 'Aye, and we must pinch out the ticks which latterly inhabit the Navy Board, who suck the lifeblood out.'

Walsingham protested, 'But the size of our fleet –'

'If numbers were the crux,' Tavistock told him, 'we would already be dead men. Numbers are not critical. Quality is the key. King Henry's Navy was twice the size of the one Her Majesty now commands. Two dozen ships – that's all I ask. But two dozen like unto the *Revenge!*'

The meticulous designs that Tavistock had worked on spilled across the table. They dated back to his confinement in the Tower and had been augmented by a thousand incredible ideas patiently collected by Dee and the Scots mathematician, John Napier. Years of careful thought, refinements drawn from experience, details culled from Drake and from Martin Frobisher, from brave Richard Grenville and poor, drowned Humphrey Gilbert. It was the alchemy of change, designs that would make an unparalleled fighting force of the Queen's Navy: lower castles fore and aft, a ratio of length to beam of greater than three-to-one, sheathed hulls cod-headed and herring-tailed, lithe ships, manoeuvrable and responsive to the helm, with boarding netting and chain pumps for baling out bilges and a fast method of striking topmasts and a marvellous array of new weaponry.

'Though England depends on it, I cannot get these measures accepted while Hawkins rules the Navy and while Lord Burleigh maintains him there.'

Every nerve in Walsingham's body itched to tell them it would be so, but he knew that he could never present Elizabeth with such an expense. Flanders had been a bottomless pit. Her Majesty had given Anjou thirty thousand pounds to finance the taking of Cambrai, and sent him away with a further ten thousand and then sent Leicester to him with the promise of fifty thousand more, all to convince Philip of Anglo-French solidarity. And still Parma had triumphed. On the day before Anjou's death, the Queen had told him that in war and peace three things alone mattered: money, money, and once again money.

He explained haltingly, all the while searching for a way out of the problem, but as he finished Tavistock served Drake with a significant look. Incredibly, both men seemed oddly satisfied to hear the objections wrung painfully from him.

'What I offer you, sir,' Tavistock said slowly, 'is no expense. But a saving.'

The airless room closed in around them.

'A saving?' Walsingham said with incredulity, sure only that if any contending argument might sway Elizabeth the one least ambitious to drain her coffers must carry the day. 'You say a *saving*?'

Tavistock planted his elbow on the table. 'Implement these plans and the cost of the Navy will be cut from ten thousand pounds annually to half that. See, there's not a captain or master afloat who'd not prefer two hundred and fifty able men to three hundred of rag and tag.'

Drake backed him, leaning in on Walsingham fiercely. 'It's not skill we lack, but the *will* to organise.'

Tavistock nodded tautly. 'If we're wise we'll plough back the corn. Reinvest the saving.'

'In our men,' Drake insisted. 'Ships are hulks without willing lads to work them. To make them willing we must pay them well. As with the *Lion* the charge of wages and victuals for three hundred men at twenty-three shillings and fourpence per man is two hundred and fifty pounds. The same ship furnished with a complement of two hundred and fifty but costed at twenty-eight shillings per man will amount even as before to two hundred and fifty pounds. Make no mistake, the basest man will overprice his heart's blood on a wage of seven shillings a month. Make it ten and he will know for whom he fights.'

Walsingham wiped at his brow once more, utterly weary, but feeling the grim capability of the men beside him. 'Yes,' he said. 'By God, yes! We'll try Burleigh. He may be persuaded. If he is not, I shall go to the Queen.'

Burleigh received them in his office in the river precinct of Whitehall Palace. He was courteous and listened to Walsingham with thoughtful silence. At last he raised his head and said pleasantly, 'Let me take your evidence, gentlemen. I promise I will think on it with all speed. And I thank you for your concern.'

'I want your signature upon a warrant of arrest for John Hawkins,' Walsingham demanded less than respectfully.

'Oh, but that I must consider at length.'

'If you do not reach a decision by noon tomorrow we shall be forced to approach Her Majesty.'

'Her Majesty is still in mourning for the loss of her suitor, the Duke of Anjou. By her request she may not be disturbed.'

'I *will* see her. That is my right.'

'As you wish.'

'And John Hawkins *will* answer these charges.'

Burleigh sighed inwardly and thought again of the tremendous economies his patient work had brought. A tight rein had been held for twenty-five years, despite the monies spent in the Low Countries. Though rebellious Ireland had swallowed up all the taxes granted by Parliament in that time, still the Queen's foreign debts were paid, and the obligations left by Bloody Mary also, making Elizabeth's interest rates half of those Philip was forced to pay. For twenty-five years England had prospered, a quarter century of peace nurtured by his careful guidance, which had brought with it a glorious bounty that other, more impulsive men might have squandered on needless war.

In those years, Burleigh calculated, there had been a tripling of wealth in the land, but it had come only by hard work and diligent effort. The small additions that Tavistock and Drake and the rest of the Queen's sea adventurers had waylaid were as nothing beside that.

He smiled inwardly. It had been a wise policy. Wise to keep at arm's-length a Parliament that would grant the Crown money, but at the same time buy the privilege of tinkering in affairs of state. Although he had first conceived the policy as a way of avoiding political control, it had paid immense and unlooked-for dividends in another way. What Parliament was not called upon to give to the Crown, Parliament did not need to raise by taxing the people. Low rates of interest and low taxes had fostered the merchants and the manufacturers. Successful trade and successful commerce were the key. For the first time all the wants of civilised life could be supplied by English hands at English looms, in English potteries and from English forges. No longer did the realm depend upon expensive imports. Nor did it need Antwerp. Cloth went out through Zeeland, Denmark and Sweden, trade flourished with Muscovy and the Levant. The Duke of Tuscany was taking grain and Atlantic fish, salt and timber. Even Constantinople had been among the new customers, opening in Morocco, on Spain's flank, a pore through which Philip might be obliquely antagonised.

Obliquely, Walsingham, can't you understand that subtlety? Little and by little. In military matters half the battle's concerned with hiding true weaknesses from the enemy. The other half's concerned with hiding true strengths.

'Hawkins will answer these charges before the Queen. Confirm that to me, my lord.'

Burleigh turned on them admonishingly. 'I warn you, Sir Francis. I warn you all. These matters are best left to me alone.'

'In all sincerity I doubt that, my lord. Our country's plunging into a furnace *and you will not see it*,' Walsingham insisted.

'I see that some would have us plunge with unseemly haste.'

'Hawkins is a traitor!' Drake burst out. 'And you, my lord, are his shield! There! It is said!'

'God save me from these foolish accusations,' Burleigh told him mildly, shaking his head. Walsingham's bellicose prating is still dangerous, he thought. He's never learned flexibility. I was right to clip his wings in 'seventy-eight. That's the reason I sent him on a diplomatic mission of pacification to the Low Countries, a mission contrary to his own stance and doomed to failure, and located in the furthest part of Aethiopia, politically speaking. I wasted three months, but I prised him away from the management of the country at a vital time. That's also why I let him waste his energies on attempting to arrange the French marriage. I let him embroil himself in a pretty mess. And now that he's come alive to the backwater he inhabits, and of his impotence, his temper's grown irascible. He must bear the brunt of Elizabeth's menopausal vacillations, but that frustration has done nothing to break him of his readiness to meddle in affairs best left to me. Were it not for the growing menace on the Continent and his sources of information there, I would have side-footed Francis Walsingham into the gutter long ago. But I have my own sources, sources of which he knows nothing, and I am not as ignorant as he believes.

He approached Tavistock who had remained silent throughout the interview. The man's magnificent, but he's a continual embarrassment to me, an ache in my side. Why do I tolerate him? Because Anne loves him? Because while he's with her Oxford dare not go near her? Because while he's in Low Houghton he's not on the high seas? Perhaps. But perhaps because he's the Devil's own culverin. It's not yet time to fire him, but the moment's arrived when he must be primed. He's precipitated it before I thought he would, but what does that matter now? He shall strike the spark that lights the match that fires the gun that projects the ball that breaks the fleet that Philip is building ...

He stood before Tavistock smilingly. 'Can you really believe that I am a traitor, Captain?'

Tavistock drew himself up straight. 'Sir, I believe you are mistaken in your attitude towards Spain. I believe you are reluctant to admit that war with Spain is inevitable, though the evidence for that is clear enough.'

'Your impudence is astonishing. Can you imagine you know more of

King Philip's mind than I?'

'Sir Francis Walsingham knows more than either of us, and his opinion is congruent with mine own. Regarding the complaint we have laid before you today I cannot think other than that you have been deceived, my lord.'

'By whom?'

'By John Hawkins, amongst others.'

'Then you believe John Hawkins is the archtraitor?'

'What else can I call it? Ever there are two edges to his work, ever he cuts two ways. Here have I evidence that he has been awarded a Spanish knighthood by King Philip himself. That is more than plain villainy, more than greed. It threatens the security of the Realm.'

Burleigh sighed, went to his desk and drew out a closely written sheet of vellum. 'This came into my possession some time ago. You may be interested to read it, Captain. It was dictated by a man, one Miles Philips, who knew your brother in Mexico, and who subsequently found his way back into England.'

Tavistock was thrown for a moment, then he took the paper and read it. As he scanned the lines his eyes clouded but the rest of his face betrayed nothing. The paper was an affidavit describing the fate of John, how he had been imprisoned, sentenced and then burned by the Inquisition.

'Your brother was making guns for the Mexican Viceroy. Great guns. Guns whose only purpose was to kill Protestants. Guns that might have even have been used against you yourself!'

'Yes.'

'Then you know he was a traitor. To you, to his country and to his religion.'

Tavistock's jaw clenched. The blood had drained from his face and he found difficulty in speaking. 'Yes.'

'Yet still this deputation dares to accuse me of harbouring traitors? Of shielding traitors? Of *using* traitors?'

The silence that enveloped them was punctuated by the sounds of the city that drifted up through the open window. Vigorous shouts of commerce and of daily trade. To judge from the way Tavistock's stiffness left him they must have seemed to him deafening.

'I disowned my brother long ago, my lord. It's a relief that he's dead. I would have killed him myself if I could have done so.'

Burleigh's demand was suddenly loud and sharp as a rapier. 'You swear to me that that is the truth?'

'Yes.'

'Swear!'

'I swear!'

'Good. Good. There may come a time when I shall ask you to remember that oath.' Burleigh recovered the vellum and put it back into the drawer. Yes, he thought. Primed, but not yet aimed or fired.

He took up his pen. 'Captain Drake, here is a warrant ordering your presence at the meeting of the Privy Council in three weeks' time. There we shall discuss your plans to sail pre-emptively and in force against Spain.' He turned to Walsingham. 'Give me one month. In return I'll immediately put Captain Tavistock's suggestions before the Navy Board and insist they're discussed. I'll even require that the best of them is adopted.'

Walsingham considered. 'And when the month is up? What of John Hawkins then?'

'When one month is up you may hang John Hawkins by the neck if it is your pleasure so to do.'

Chapter 24

Maria met her husband on the Tagus quays as she did every Saturday at this time. It was early evening, before dusk, and the sky was full of golden streamers behind a black forest of masts. King Philip's *empresa* – his enterprise – was gathering for the final blow.

Ships lined the quays, sometimes tied up six deep. More rode at anchor in the harbour; vessels of all sizes, from the small *zabras* and *patajes* to the lumbering, barrel-round *urcas* and the high-built splendour of Portugal's great galleons.

Along the foreshore a great quantity of ships' stores had been stockpiled and all manner of trades had erected open-air shops among the chaos. Throughout the day, a vast array of human endeavour, shipwrights and chandlers, coopers and smiths, carters and labourers, had worked together, but this was the peaceful hour when the toils of the day paused and the builders of the *empresa* looked to their bellies instead of their work.

Maria took her husband's hand and sensed again the unbearable tension in him. He had put the forge in abeyance for the Sabbath after a busy week; with Nicolau Almeida away in Lagos in the far south and sundry extra work coming in every day from the Port Authorities, he was ready to rest, but it was not simple tiredness she felt in him. There was something else, something worrying him and making him unquiet. She squeezed his hand and asked, 'Why did Nicolau go to Lagos?'

He did not look at her. 'Why does Nicolau go anywhere?'

'To trade or to talk – sometimes to see and remember what he sees.'

'Then you know already what Nicolau is doing in Lagos.'

'Juan, why does he take with him birdcages?'

'Birdcages?'

He volunteered no more, and she chose not to pursue it, seeing his nerves raw in any conversation. Perhaps he was regretting his decision to stay in Portugal, realising that the tide of events could no longer be turned, that the juggernaut was now unstoppable. It seemed capable of tearing down any man who stood in its way.

I know you understand that truth, my love, she told him silently, feeling nothing but love for him. You watch the soldiers coming and the ships arriving and the *empresa* growing stronger every week and you feel helpless and Nicolau feels helpless and, though you yearn to act, there's nothing you can do.

They walked together in silence along the huge coping stones that edged the river, threading their way past crates and barrels and bales that were being unloaded from ox drays and handcarts and transferred by great wooden derricks into the smaller ships tied up alongside the quays. And all the time as they strolled they secretly noted and memorised each detail of the preparations to be recalled later verbatim to Nicolau Almeida.

It had been like this for at least a year now. From the shipyards and slipways of the Tagus and from all the ports in Spain great ship after great ship had come here to be rigged and outfitted. Hundreds of carpenters and sailmakers laboured at their work, talking to one another in six different languages. Ship's notaries and provosts and quartermasters supervised from sun up to sun down, overseeing the lading of supplies and the payrolling of crews. Each ship had been designated its own assembly point, *urcas* to their channel stations, big galleons to their deep-water anchorages. Between them, a thousand craft of all sizes plied the fifteen-mile by five-mile stomach of the Tagus, weaving back and forth endlessly with men and materials.

Maria saw the helplessness in his face as he watched the preparations and asked him gently, 'What is it, Juan? Tell me what troubles you.'

He stirred. 'What?'

'You seem so full of cares tonight.'

'No more than usual. I'm just thinking.'

'What is it that weighs on your mind?'

He stifled a sigh and looked out again across the estuary. 'The fleet seems much greater than it did only a week ago.'

'You think the time approaches? That it will sail soon?'

'No,' he said. 'I think this is only the start. It's much bigger than I imagined. The King is bending every resource to this single end. It's staggering.'

Philip's minions seemed prepared to spend all, apply all, risk all, on their King's fanatical desire. For months Lisbon had been drinking in men: soldiers brought across Europe, sailors from Genoa, Ragusa, Naples, every Mediterranean port not hostile to Spain, and nobles of every kind from all parts of the Empire. Even so, the fleet was far from completed. Nicolau had said that it was so far only a quarter, a third, of what it must eventually become. Yet already it was an awesome sight, the greatest assembly of ships ever undertaken.

Not all the contributions had been willingly given. Tavistock's eyes dwelt on the place where the huge *Florencia* rode at anchor. The massive galleon had arrived weeks ago to collect a cargo of spices. She had been called the *San Francisco* then and had belonged to the Duke of Tuscany, but Admiral Santa Cruz had commandeered her to sail as flagship of his Levantine squadron, and he had put his soldiery aboard to make sure his plans were not overthrown.

As they continued to stroll, the outer walls of the castle loomed near by, rough sandstone the colour of lion skin, high and impregnable. The gates were guarded by a dozen men, and only soldiers and specially summoned persons able to show the seal were permitted inside. Tavistock thought again of the great ammunition store and cannon foundry that lay within and his palms began to itch. Since Nicolau told him of the armoury he had been unable to put it out of his mind. Inside these walls were the guns that would be used to subdue England. But to gain entry was like trying to get inside the Tower of London. It was impossible.

They began to return the way they had come when a voice called to them fiercely.

'You!'

They stopped and Tavistock noticed for the first time a soldier ten paces away leaning heavily against a huge anchor fluke among the shadows. He picked at his teeth with the tip of an evil-looking dagger, a jug of wine by his feet.

'Yes, you! Come here!'

Tavistock complied, Maria following.

'I saw you looking at the castle.' The soldier's voice dropped to a growl. 'What business do you have here?'

Tavistock considered, almost denied it, then decided to gamble. 'I must fill an order for iron billets, *senhor*,' he lied.

'Let me see your paper.'

Wordlessly, Tavistock took a written paper from his pouch and handed it over. It was a page from his accounts, showing wages paid to his employees.

The soldier appeared to check it, then broke wind noisily. He stank of wine. 'So – you're a blacksmith?'

'A foundry master, *senhor*. As the paper says.' He leaned forwards, but the soldier pulled the paper back broodily.

'Yes, I saw that. So what's your business here, foundry master?'

'I have a contract to supply iron billets,' Tavistock repeated. 'As it says at the bottom. Is there a problem, *senhor*?'

The soldier held it up once more, inclining it to the light. It was upside down.

'It's all in order. But you can't come this way.' He handed the paper back grudgingly and gestured over his shoulder at sixty or seventy kegs stacked under a tarpaulin. 'Do you know what that is? It's gunpowder. It's my responsibility to check everyone who comes near. You have no seal on your paper.'

Tavistock nodded at the man, mirroring his grim humour. 'No

tobacco smoking here, then, eh? Where's the powder going to?'

'Who wants to know?' The soldier vaguely indicated the harbour; he leered crookedly at Maria, wiping the flats of his knife on his sleeve. 'It's a shame your man's in a reserved occupation. I could've made a dollar on his head. And then I could've spent it on you, eh?'

'Is your regiment short of men?' she asked, forcing herself to smile back at him.

'Short of *real* men.' He reached out and grasped her arm.

Tavistock broke in. 'Maybe I could find you some sturdy farm boys who've hidden themselves away. Maybe we could split the dollars. How many do you need? What's your name?'

The soldier's grin died slowly, then a sickly anger overcame him and he brushed at Tavistock, letting go of Maria. 'Get on your way, Portuguese shit-eater! You ask too many questions!'

They retreated, the soldier still calling after them. Tavistock carefully stored away his thoughts as he and Maria merged with the crowd. Here, along the dusty road, a row of stalls had been set up under canvas, selling religious medallions, leather work, clothing, clay pipes and cured tobacco leaves besides a hundred other wares. A knot of well-dressed gentlemen haggled in Italian over wine, another loitered as his twin whores looked over a garish display of braids and laces. Next to them blue smoke drifted up where barbecued meats basted and spat on a makeshift boucan, filling the air with a mouthwatering aroma.

Tavistock steered Maria through the press of men, amazed at the increase in trade that had occurred in only a single week. It was as if every nobleman in Christendom had suddenly descended on Lisbon in a vast deluge to seek honour and arms in the great crusade. Every day religious orders and private companies of troops arrived, entering the city in great phalanxes and processions, sometimes after forced marches lasting weeks. Every last guesting house and spare room had been turned over to accommodate officers, and acres on the outskirts of the city were now under canvas. Thousands more men made their bivouac under the stars.

An incredible expense, he thought, trying to calculate the scale of it. How can King Philip continue to bear it all? There's almost too many men here for the countryside to support, and even with the crews confined to their vessels, each passing month is a month's fouling of the ships, a month's supplies consumed and a month's wages owing. Philip's purse is not bottomless, he must be mortgaged to every bank in Italy. God alone knows what rate of interest he must be forced to pay.

As they reached the far side of the quay the last rays of sunset deserted the sky across the darkening Tagus. These were the drilling grounds and all around them, weaponed troops dressed-off in columns to be marched to camp behind mounted officers, their places quickly filled by ragged lines of pressed men. Others burdened with full kit formed queues to receive plates of stewed meat, then wandered away to sit in groups.

But the lethargy of the hour was stirring, pierced by shouted orders and sergeants striding among their charges. Tavistock saw the multitude of men begin to rise to their feet. Rumours passed through them like a breeze rippling a cornfield, and they were alert and craning to see, suddenly expectant, as if a saint had appeared above the gothic towers of St Jerome de Belem.

Maria gripped his arm and pointed to sea. 'Look!'

He saw it in magnificent silhouette: a great oared craft, low and slender, triple masted with lateen sails furled tight to three sweeping diagonal spars, stroking swiftly shoreward. She was a galleass, one of the fastest ships ever built, knifing through the calm waters of the Tagus, her sharp iron ram seeming certain to punch into the quayside. Then the drumbeats sounded louder from her deck and the rhythmic splash of her sweeps carried her round like a scorpion as she manoeuvred under the efforts of hundreds of slaves.

Tavistock remembered the sentences served on his shipmates many years ago when Don Pietro had ordered them into bondage on such vessels. He had to stop himself from searching the rows of naked wretches chained at the benches that struggled now to brake the galleass's onward rush. What if one of them recognises you? he asked himself with sudden alarm. Then he realised that recognition was impossible: galley slaves did not survive that long.

The drumming beat changed and changed again and the long shallow craft began to turn with impressive skill in her own length and to back, stern first, into the quay.

Her castle was stepped high and pavilioned in red and yellow stripes, and a great copper lamp threw its beams onto the embroidered threads of a snow white ensign. It was the pennant of Don Alvaro de Bazan, the Marquis of Santa Cruz, Commander of the Ocean Seas.

Tavistock caught his breath, his heart pounding now. This was the man in whom King Philip had vested his total trust. The *empresa* was his responsibility alone, all matters were in his charge, everything was under his personal control. Tavistock felt the anguish rise in him unstoppably. Soon he would glimpse the man who had begged to be permitted to destroy England. Suddenly John saw how much of England lay in his heart. He had spent more years out of his native land than he had spent in it, but he knew that wherever he lived he would always be an Englishman. The patient work he had done for Nicolau Almeida had brought home to him the threat that England faced, and he shook his head with surprise at the cold anger that welled up in him.

Ropes were flung to shore and secured around bollards, a banistered gangway was run out to one side of the scrolled sternpost. To left and right of it an honour guard in corslet and morion assembled, arms clashing, flaming torches raised high.

Tavistock thought, awed by the savagery he had found inside himself, If I had a knife. Yes, I'd kill him! – *No! That's madness! Think of Maria, of Martin.* But look! There's an opportunity to do something at last! To burst forward and kill Spain's greatest Admiral! – *They would inflict terrible torment on you before you died!* – But their Admiral would be dead, and all the strategies in his head would be gone for ever.

A terrible passion possessed him as he and Maria were swept up in the rush of men. It was made starker by the waves of respect and awe emanating from the thousand men who now rallied to the Marquis's arrival. Santa Cruz's standard bearers came ashore, upholding his chequerboard arms surmounted by the dragon crown, and a line of draped and velveted dignitaries followed them. Then a knot of men appeared on the galleass's deck, tall, and long-faced and solemn. A short, solid figure suddenly emerged from among them. He was sixty years of age, with a white beard, and wearing magnificently enamelled white and gilt half-armour. Tavistock saw that under his fine white hose, his legs were bandaged to the knee. From beneath his ruff a thick gold chain hung and from it a pendant in the shape of a scallop shell with a cross incised on it in crimson. It clanked against the centre seam of the Admiral's breastplate as he advanced, emphasising the difficulty he was having walking. His nose was long and his face masklike, deeply lined as if he was in constant pain – not at all the figure Tavistock had imagined.

As he mounted the head of the gangway, ranked troops punched the air shouting their terse regimental huzzahs in unison. He walked down, then paused, nodding his approval of the martial reception, standing no more than five paces from Tavistock. *Five paces.* He held Maria tightly. A knife, a skewer, any blade at all – a sudden thrust at the jugular and it could have been over in a moment. But he had nothing. Only his bare hands. And then the Marquis's officers came close about him again, and the moment had passed.

Maria's hand closed tightly on Tavistock's arm.

She turned, jostling, and turned him also, forcing him to push slowly out through the press of awestruck soldiers, and as they broke free of the crowding men she guided him across the trampled earth away from the torchlight. For a moment Tavistock resisted. He turned her, then he saw the fear in her eyes as she tried to hide her face.

'What is it?' he asked, dumbfounded, after fifty paces. 'For God's sake, what's the matter?'

'Didn't you see him?' she whispered with astonishing urgency. 'Didn't you see who that was?'

'The Admiral?'

She shook her head wildly. 'No! The man following!'

'Who? Tell me who?'

'*I swear it was Gonzalo.*'

'*What?*' He stared at her in disbelief, a spasm of panic clutching at his bowels. 'Are you certain?'

'I swear by the Madonna it was my brother – he looked straight at me.'

He glanced involuntarily back towards the Admiral's party, but was unable to distinguish anyone in the distant flickering light. Then he held Maria tight to him and out at arm's-length once more. 'Did he see you?'

'I don't know.'

'Maria! Did he recognise you? Did he? Think!'

'I don't know!'

Gonzalo de Escovedo looked toward the citadel, following a single pace behind Don Emilio. His mind was in turmoil, and anger gripped him. The pride of all Spain had been wounded and an answer had to be found.

The news from Galicia was incredible. The English corsair, Drake, had actually dared to land a pirate rabble on the sacred soil of Spain. His filth had looted the city of Vigo and desecrated its cathedral. Now he had set to sea again, and was sailing this way. If only he knew what a force of ships lies here, Gonzalo thought gleefully. The Marquis will soon snap you up!

Gonzalo followed Don Emilio dutifully. The climb to the citadel was long and twisting, as tortuous as the strange path that had brought him here to the brink of this most ambitious of enterprises.

It had begun years ago, in the middle of an airless and sultry night in the viceregal palace in Mexico. Don Emilio had summoned him late to his private apartment and there he had spoken strangely, with a queer light in his eye, as if testing him, as if about to single him out for some immensely dangerous task. At last, sweating and dressed in nothing but his nightshirt, Don Emilio had delivered the stunning news: 'The King's brother is dead.'

Don John? Dead? The Governor of the Netherlands, dead? Calamity!

Gonzalo had swept off his hat and knelt respectfully, but he had felt immediately foolish under the Viceroy's harsh laugh. 'Get up, Gonzalo, unless you would mourn the death of a syphilitic blackmailer.'

He had stared back at his superior, utterly stunned, certain that his ears had deceived him in the thick air.

'I beg your pardon, Excellency?'

'I have placed Don John's death at the head of my prayers every day and every night for ten years, and now at last the Lord God has seen fit to answer me.'

'Excellency? – but I don't understand.'

Don Emilio had turned to his window then, regarding the visible token of his domain with total abhorrence. 'Momentous changes are emanating from Madrid, and this wretched, fever-ridden possession is to have a new Viceroy.'

That had stunned him, but he had thought quickly. 'May I conclude that His Majesty has recognised your magnificent work here in the Indies, Excellency?'

He had said it with trembling voice, hoping and praying that this was some kind of reward the King had offered in recognition of the fortification of the Main. God in heaven and all the Saints, please promise me this is not a mark of the King's displeasure, he had begged silently in the streaming humidity of that Mexican night. Grant me that this doesn't mean Manila. Anything but Manila! I couldn't stand being sent there!

Don Emilio's deep-set eyes had locked on him, as black and expressionless as olives. The dark stubble of his cheeks had underlined his weariness, but his voice had cut suddenly formal. 'Captain Escovedo, I ask you now: wherever I am sent, will you follow me as my principal staff officer?'

His hesitation had betrayed him. 'Follow you? But *where*, Lord?'

And Don Emilio's obsidian eyes had fallen, and his voice had become a whisper. 'What a terrible thing it is for a man to be truly alone in this life. My dear Gonzalo ... I see that not even you can bring yourself to trust me. If I tell you it's not Manila, then will you pledge your service to me?'

He had showed eagerness, then. 'Where? Don Emilio, please tell me. I would be honoured to serve you wherever you were, ah, appointed governor.'

The strangeness in the Viceroy's face had been made clear to him then. It was the face of rapture. *Could it be that the King was to entrust Don Emilio with the Netherlands?*

'Where?'

'Oh, how I've waited for this, Gonzalo. I thank Christ Jesus the Antwerp plague took Don John before it was too late.'

'Where, Excellency?'

'Ah, I feel magnificent. Magnificent!'

'*Where?*'

Don Emilio had smiled then, as if answering from within a state of grace. 'Oh, unless I'm quite mistaken, Gonzalo, we're going to Madrid.'

'Madrid?'

Of all the cards Don Emilio might have turned up, this was the ace of spades, the most high, the pinnacle. Madrid was the fulcrum of power. Madrid was a dream come true.

It had taken a year for the royal summons to appear, and the best part of another to hand Mexico over to Philip's new nominee, but Don Emilio had reached Spain in time to see Portugal fall and in time to be appointed to the military council specially convened to assist the King in an examination of the ways and means of subjugating England.

Gonzalo swelled his plated breast, and checked he was in step with his superior as they mounted higher towards the Old Tower. Apart from the *empresa*, the power of this foreign city to impress him was slight. Proudly, he could say that the passages of the Escorial itself – the place of ashes – had rung to his boots. He had worked there for five magnificent years, helping Don Emilio to advise the King. Five years inside the very beating heart of the Empire, before being appointed here as chief security officer. He thought again of the Portuguese spy he had apprehended, relishing the cracking of his ring. Yes, there is much for me to do here, though Madrid was more to my taste. Much more to my taste.

In truth, the granite monument cut out of the Sierra de Guadarrama had been no living heart. It was more like a sepulchre. A vast gridiron of grey stone, with cowled towers at each corner rising to needle spires. Each wall was pierced by hundreds of tiny, slitted windows that watched all who approached. Within were miles of passages, thousands of rooms stuffed with royal impedimenta, a Hieronymite monastery, the Habsburg family mausoleum, and, in the inner sanctum, the hermit-like dwelling where the King lived and worked in earshot of the calling of the Hours. It was said that His Majesty had sworn to build the palace to the memory of San Lorenzo – whose martyrdom had been one of roasting alive upon a gridiron – and that the saint's bones were contained in the King's personal reliquary. It was said also that Philip possessed in his most private and sequestered retreat the head of another saint, a skull crowned by an iron tiara, which he consulted over the most important matters of state.

Whatever the truth of it, the counsel the King had taken had led him, in these latter years, to the greatest triumphs the world had ever known. Year by year His Majesty had increased his prestige. Portugal and all its retinue were taken. Alexander Farnese, Prince of Parma and Spain's most able general, had almost completed his reconquest of the Netherlands; his patient diplomacy had set Catholic and Calvinist to tearing at one another's throats once more. Parma had dissolved the unity of the rebels, and his military skills had begun to push back the last fastnesses of the North. William of Orange was dead, Antwerp recaptured. Yes, the King had chosen Don John's successor well. The laurels had mounted higher and higher. Even France had been humbled. Santa Cruz, the greatest Admiral alive, had destroyed their fleet of sixty sail, and Henry the Third had finally been isolated and brought to sign a secret accord with Spain. One national objective remained. One alone. How could they fail now to bring the Jezebel to her knees? Soon it would be time to mount the assault on the ultimate bastion of heresy, England.

'What are we going to do about Drake?' Santa Cruz asked suddenly. He stopped, and his officers stopped also.

'The latest news is that he's put to sea again, Admiral,' Don Emilio said.

'I know. I asked what we should do about him.'

'When did he sail, Captain Escovedo?'

'Two days ago, Excellency,' Gonzalo supplied respectfully. 'He's heading south.'

Santa Cruz grunted. 'Of course he's heading south.'

'Oh, but that's bad. Very bad!' Don Emilio said. 'We must take steps.'

'Steps!' Santa Cruz snorted, and resumed his climb towards the donjon.

The news has been consistently bad for weeks, Gonzalo reflected, disliking Santa Cruz's manners greatly. Drake's fleet had appeared in force, anchoring eighty leagues to the north, in the Ria de Vigo on Spain's north-western seaboard. There, with diabolic perfidy, he had demanded water and victuals of the local Governor while setting his frigates to prey on defenceless coastal craft. Then, when he had got what he wanted, he had dropped all pretences and allowed his pirate bands to ransack the entire region, stealing thirty thousand ducats' worth of valuables, stripping Vigo Cathedral of its plate and breaking English prisoners out of the city's gaols.

'How does this low pirate imagine he can get away with it?' Don Hugo de Moncada, one of Santa Cruz's most experienced soldiers, asked.

'Because he's got a fast fleet and two thousand men aboard, and because he knows we can't move our own troops fast enough to catch him,' Santa Cruz said, adding drily, 'He's not brave or foolish enough to attempt a pitched battle against a Spanish *tercio*, and quite right.'

'We should put to sea and punish his insolence,' Don Emilio suggested.

'No!' The Duke of Paliano, tall and thin, Santa Cruz's elderly second in command, waved him to silence. 'That's just what El Draque wants. To draw us out of the Tagus, unprepared and half-cocked, so he can eat us up! El Draque is –'

'Gentlemen, I'm tired of hearing Drake's name!' Santa Cruz growled, stopping and turning. He was short of breath from the climb, and equally short of temper. Here the paved way opened out into a punishment ground where several gibbets had been erected. An assortment of chained prisoners awaited whippings for theft or blasphemy, guarded by their gaoler. They got down on their knees as the Admiral approached.

'Get up off the ground!' Santa Cruz shouted. They struggled to obey. 'You're men, not animals. Remember that,' he said, and marched on.

'I agree with Don Emilio,' Moncada said, hardly noticing the line of wretches. 'We should confront the Englishman. Show him he can't insult us. I long for the day when I shall see his head set on a spike.'

The Duke shrugged his bony shoulders. 'But why interrupt our preparations just to oblige him? Why else is he heading for Lisbon if not to tempt us out?'

Santa Cruz's low growl cut across the argument. 'He's not heading here.'

'Not heading here?'

'Lisbon's impregnable. With these shore batteries he'll never get in, and he knows it. He's sailing south because he wants the *flota*.'

No one but Santa Cruz had dared voice that possibility.

'Obviously, he'll try for the *flota*. Drake's no fool – and it's what I'd do in his place. He certainly has strength enough for an interception. That's why I've already taken steps, Don Emilio.' Santa Cruz braced his back, his eyes flickering now over his subordinates, clearly enjoying this demonstration of his strategic prowess. 'Think about this, gentlemen: imagine what would happen to our preparations here if Drake were to succeed. His Majesty's tied down with loans that all hang on the arrival of the silver. Without it we'd all be as bankrupt as beggars on the cathedral steps.'

'Then he could halt our endeavour whether we leave port or not?' Don Antonio de Mendoza said, appalled.

Santa Cruz resumed his climb. Behind the party the flogging was taken up again and hats went back on heads. 'Cheer yourself, Don Antonio. We cannot ignore any possibility, but Admiral Luzon and Diego Flores de Valdes are both experienced men. Both know what they're doing, and they have explicit orders to keep to as southerly a course as the winds will allow. I have faith they'll make San Lucar unmolested, but I'll tell you this, it's a mistake to underestimate Drake and his like.'

As they came to the doors of the great hall, Gonzalo tried to digest what he had heard. He was greatly disturbed at the way Spain's foremost Admiral was prepared to accord a filthy corsair such respect. Though he was indisputably a Marquis, Santa Cruz sometimes exhibited the bluntness of a peasant and the manners of the gutter. Such a pity that Don Emilio has not been appointed commander-in-chief, he thought. Then, his mood brightening, he turned to his own recent splendid success. My position has been strengthened enormously, he told himself. What a stroke of good fortune that within days of arriving the Jesuits should bring the fat merchant to my attention. They say that he's an important spy, perhaps even the ringleader. I wonder how he'll stand up to a second session on the rack. Tonight I'll visit Almeida's cell. By tomorrow there will undoubtedly be a dozen more names on my list.

'Go indoors and play, Martin.'

'But father. I only wanted you to mend my kite –'

'I said, go indoors!'

John Tavistock felt the warm sunshine on his back but inside he was as cold as ice. He watched his son leave him and his stomach tightened. Above him a dozen or so plump pigeons, puffed up and strutting, displayed on the red-tiled roofs. Overhead, the sky was a deep and featureless blue. He watched Almeida's wife search it distractedly as if looking to heaven for deliverance. Her face was pale and anxious, her eyes tired as if unable to rid herself of a bottomless fear that had opened up inside her.

An hour ago, she had told him the news: Almeida had been taken by the soldiers, the house ransacked and warrants issued for the arrest of their sons.

'I escaped by the slimmest chance,' she had told him. 'By climbing onto the roof. I was so scared. And then I saw down in the street as they took him away. I came here as quickly as I could.'

Tavistock too was distracted with worry, his voice barely controlled. 'You came to warn us?'

'Yes . . .' Her face creased as she nodded. 'Help him, Juan. Please help him.'

Tavistock took her hands in his and looked up at the familiar high walls of his house. The walls of a fort, or a prison they seemed to him now. Since the day Maria had seen Gonzalo, he had slept hardly two hours together, worry wracking his nerves tauter and tauter until his head ached.

He had sent a message of explanation to Nicolau and another to the forge that he would be away on business, and for his men to take over. They were capable men. Trustworthy. But now this. It was worse than his darkest fear. What if Nicolau talks? he thought, thinking of Maria and Martin. He could easily send us all to the gallows.

'What will they do to him?' Almeida's wife asked, afraid of the answer.

A maid slipped quietly from the kitchen door and cut across the yard, carrying a big woven basket of laundry. Tavistock felt dread eat at him, dread in case Martin stole away to fly his kite, dread that they would be given away by a maid, dread that there would be a knock at the door.

None of the servants in his household were party to their master's secrets, none knew of his spying, and none were yet aware that the master's friend was in prison.

But how long could it stay that way? The nature of his life was very open and the house was frequently visited so they could not hope to keep anyone here in secret long, least of all Nicolau's wife. Tavistock thought of the friend to whom he owed so much and felt an iron collar tighten around his throat.

Maria came out and sought his eye. 'How long do you think we have before they come for us?'

'I don't know. Maybe a day, maybe –' He broke off suddenly. Three days ago, Almeida had returned to Lisbon with the incredible news of Drake's attack on Vigo. 'Listen, Nicolau,' he had said. 'Do you think there'll be an attack here too? A landing?'

'At Lisbon?'

Tavistock had nodded.

'I do fear for my city,' Almeida had admitted. 'The whole of Galicia has been sunk in mortal terror of Senhor Drake. He's teaching the Spanish a lesson they don't like. But no, I don't fear for Lisbon because of any attack Senhor Drake might launch on her. The city is being ruined without him. I don't know how much longer it can go on.'

'Until the Spanish are ready to leave.'

'God grant that that's soon. Oh, my poor Lisbon! In all quarters trade is booming but it's sick trade. Unreal commerce. The influx of so many mouths is draining the whole country dry. Grain, wine, meat – everything. Demand for commodities of all kinds has outstripped our capacity to supply it. Prices are rising every day, doubling and trebling. The poor are going hungry. But it's no trouble to the Spanish. It makes more cheap labour for them.'

Tavistock had shaken his head. 'No, the Spanish already have more men standing idle than they can use or occupy. It's an impossible job keeping them all fed and orderly. Trouble is setting in. Desertions have begun. They've started confining whole crews and entire companies aboard their ships. The fleet's like a powder keg. *They'll have to sail soon.*'

Almeida had shrugged. 'The enterprise is too big. It will never be ready to sail.'

'Is that what you're telling them in England?'

'That's just my opinion. In my reports I confine myself to the facts.'

Tavistock had watched Almeida's face closely; he had seen anxiety there, buried and suppressed, but it had been massive. And there was the smell of deceit in what he had said.

'Nicolau, where did you go to last week?' he had asked.

'I told you. To Lagos.'

'That can't be.'

Almeida had flashed a glance at him. 'It's the truth. I have a contact there.'

'Then how can you know so much about Galicia when it's three hundred miles in the other direction?'

Almeida had stared at him for a long moment then finally he had gestured towards his dovecot. 'They're the reason I went to Lagos. And also the reason I can know so much about Vigo.'

Tavistock had been mystified. 'Pigeons?'

'Yes, pigeons.'

'But – I don't understand.'

'God gave them a wonderful instinct to return to their home. It doesn't matter where you take them so long as it's not more than a few dozen miles. It was something discovered by the ancients; the legions of Rome used them, but the Romans' art died with them and was forgotten by all except the Muslim.'

'But how –'

Almeida had taken one of his pigeons in his hands, turned it over and revealed a small goose quill case bound to its leg with a thread of waxed silk. He had removed it with great care. 'Pigeons are by far the fleetest messengers in the world, faster than one of Spain's galleys, faster than a galloping horse, and they cross land or water without distinction. Release them and they will circle once, twice, then away they go to the place where they first broke from the egg. I've timed one of my birds, and can you believe that she covered ten miles in only a quarter of an hour?'

'That's incredible!'

Almeida had nodded. 'Oh, yes, incredible. But true. And very useful. Of course they don't fly at night and they're brought down by rain, and sometimes hawks, but even so ... There's a network of watchers along the entire coast. I cannot tell you their names or where they live, but I'm their paymaster, and whenever anything happens it's relayed to me with great speed. That's how I heard about the arrival of the *Nuestra Señora* before the Jesuits did. It's also how I know what goes with Senhor Drake.'

Tavistock had been amazed. 'Who will you report the success at Vigo to?'

'An Englishman. In Spanish, they call him Juan Achines.' Almeida had fallen silent, then he had said, 'Perhaps it's time I told you. Almost twenty years ago, I, myself, lived in Galicia, close to Vigo in the small port of Pontevedra. There I made the mistake of giving succour to an English ship. She was trying to find her way back from the Indies, and I didn't know she had been in battle against Spanish ships. Like the *Nuestra Sēnora* I found her battered and broken and I offered my help as any man might.'

'What ship was she?' Tavistock had asked.

'Her name was *Minion*. And her owner was called John Hawkins.'

The shock had almost paralysed Tavistock, and he had listened in amazement as Almeida had continued. 'I remember Hawkins was in a high fever. Most of his crew had died. They were in a terrible condition and needed help, and so I helped. I brought water and food and I alerted another English ship in the port. But then the Jesuits discovered what I had done. They accused me of aiding heresy, and I was arrested. When they discovered I was a Jew they made me pay with my wife and my children.' A shudder had run through him as he had gently cast the pigeon up so that it clattered free into the air. 'Afterwards I escaped to Portugal, I made contact with Hawkins through English wine shippers and he sent money to me. All this –' Almeida had waved a hand towards his house '– comes from him. In exchange for information.'

'John Hawkins,' Tavistock had said the name again. 'But I sailed with his expedition to the Indies.'

'I know. And I also know that your real name is John Tavistock and that your brother is Richard Tavistock, the famous privateer. Two years after you came to me, when it became clear the Spanish would take Portugal, I wrote to Hawkins about you. He said I should persuade you to go aboard an English ship, but you would not.'

'You should have told me about Hawkins.'

Almeida had spread his hands. 'How could I? I didn't dare expose him as my source. He's twisted himself in many double deals with Spain on Lord Burleigh's behalf. The Spanish are convinced he's their man, so much so that Philip has awarded him a secret knighthood. I couldn't risk it. If you were to be taken and tortured so that you revealed him, his webs would collapse and even in England he would be in mortal danger.'

Then they had gone into Almeida's private business room, the windowless place where he kept accounts and locked away his gold. Spices had once been stored here, it had been cool and quiet and smelled of cinnamon and camphor and candle-grease.

As soon as they were alone, Almeida had put on his eye-glasses and opened the tiny capsule he had taken from the pigeon's claw. He found a hooked pin in his hatband and removed a tightly rolled slip of paper, opening it out delicately. He had read it then touched it to the flame of the candle of his letter seal, pinching it between finger and thumb until it was completely consumed.

'Where's it from?' Tavistock had asked.

'The south. Bad news, I'm afraid.'

'What does it say?'

Almeida had tried to put it aside, but Tavistock had pressed him. The blow had been a hard one. 'This year's *flota* has reached San Lucar in safety. Senhor Drake has missed it.'

Tavistock felt an intense blade of fear slash at him now. He knew! Oh, yes, I see it now. He knew they were closing in on him, even then. Perhaps the Jesuits he hated finally caught one of his pigeons. Perhaps he had been betrayed by one of his 'watchers'. It didn't matter now.

Almeida's words echoed over and again in Tavistock's mind: 'if you were to be taken and tortured ...' and suddenly he was back inside his deepest terror, vividly, seeing the irons and the ropes and the flames of the Inquisitors, and he knew that he could not face that a second time. It was not the fear of death, but the fear of pain. Terrible agony, piously-justified, repeatedly-applied, deliberately-inflicted, to his body and to the bodies of his wife and son, just as it was being inflicted on Nicolau even now. He felt the iron collar tighten on him further, choking him, and the panic began to rise up inside him more intensely than he had ever known. The sweat on his face turned icy. *How can I get out?* his brain screamed. *What can I do?* But no answer came, and he saw that he was trapped beyond hope, and falling, and falling ...

Then Maria was staring at him, looking in his eyes with horror. 'Juan!'

Shame crashed over him like an ocean wave, humbling him as he realised that Almeida's wife must be seeing his bloodless cheeks and thinking him a craven coward. Then he suddenly felt a clarity of mind he had not known for weeks. The flush of fear had settled him like a thunderstorm settles the air. In its passing he had seen the way.

'It's just a matter of time. We're all trapped here,' he said, not knowing how else to put it to the women. 'And Nicolau's a dead man, unless I act now.'

'Act? What do you mean?' Maria asked, her eyes drilling into him. '*Juan, what do you mean?*'

He matched her stare. 'They need my skills more than they need Nicolau dead. I'll give myself to them. In exchange for him.'

'No!' she screamed. 'No! You can't. I won't allow it!'

He could see the deal clearly. Gonzalo's ambition would force him to agree to it; Don Emilio's authority would overrule him if he did not. He would ransom Almeida and have both families sent out of Portugal on a ship bound for England. Hawkins would surely protect them and settle a living on them. His mind was absolutely made up but he needed to convince her. He took his wife's shoulders roughly. 'Listen to me! Without Nicolau we'd all be dead. Long ago. Don't you see? We owe him this! I owe him this!'

'No, no, no! It's crazy! I won't let you do it!' Maria shook her head helplessly. Beside her, Almeida's wife's hands were clenched together as if in grateful prayer, her face a battleground of hope and fear, then her hands parted and she put them out to him, saying, 'You can't do this, Juan. Nicolau would never ask it of you.'

Tavistock stepped away from her, his voice rising. 'You don't understand. It's my sacrifice.'

'Juan! It would be suicide!'

'I'm a dead man already!'

'But you're *not* dead!'

'I'm sorry, Maria, I've seen the future. I know what I must do.'

And before she could stop him, he was halfway across the courtyard and heading for the gate.

Chapter 25

The Thames's muscular waters were restless under a grey and troubled sky.

'The river's up higher than I've ever seen it, Richard,' Hawkins said. They stood five paces apart in a narrow sloping street that ran down to the bank, Tavistock loathing him utterly. 'King Lud's in a mighty rage today.'

He regarded Hawkins as a man might his mortal enemy, having no stomach for pretty talk. Hawkins had twice asked for this meeting, and he had twice turned him down, believing that nothing Hawkins said could possibly assuage the despicable crimes he had committed, nothing he did would restore the respect Tavistock had once had for him.

'It's just a wet month and the spring tide.'

'No, it's a rage,' Hawkins insisted, his eyes hard on Tavistock. 'I can smell it in the air. Can't you?'

'The only smell hereabouts is the reek of treason.'

He had agreed to meet after Hawkins's third time of asking, but only after Anne had whispered that he must. But he had not gone alone; he was dressed down like a middle merchant, wearing his most obvious belt, the one stuffed with two pistols which he liked to sport to deter mischief while jetting around the city. Even so, the first sight of Hawkins had raked up a mix of powerful resentments that put him immediately on guard.

'Say what you have to say,' he told Hawkins abruptly, planting his feet. 'And we'll have done.'

'Not here on a street corner, Richard. I have plenty to say to you, all of it privy.'

'This is as anonymous a place as any.'

'Criminals seek anonymity. I want security. I have words that can only be said in confidence. I'll only speak them aboard the *Roebuck*.'

Alarms rang in him. 'Oh, no.'

'It would profit you. And I'll not speak freely except aboard my ship.'

'I'd be a fool to follow you there.'

'Why do you think that?' Hawkins's smile showed narrowly. 'What do you fear? That I'd murder you? Has your trust fallen that far? In any case, I can see those pistols at your belt are no ornament.'

Tavistock put his fingers to his lips and blew a shrill blast. Hawkins stepped back suspiciously, his hand on his sword hilt. 'What's this?' he demanded.

'Who should talk of trust now?'

Instantly two men appeared from nowhere and ran to present themselves to Tavistock. He turned his back on Hawkins, and whispered to the taller, then dismissed them.

'Who are they? What did you say to them?'

'They're my insurance. I told them that if I'm not on Star Chamber steps by seven o'clock they're to raise a hue and cry on you. Now where's your boat?'

'I have no boat here.'

Tavistock knew his surprise at that must have showed. He remembered well the incident years ago when Hawkins had been viciously stabbed by one of his enemies whilst riding along the Strand. The attack had been in broad daylight, in London's widest, most populous thoroughfare, and Hawkins had almost died of his wounds. Since then he had maintained discreet precautions at every level. To trust himself on the river alone with an armed man who was now all but sworn against him was almost unthinkable.

'You've no boat here?'

'How may I have your trust if I don't show that I trust you?'

'*Trust?*' Tavistock's laugh was short and bitter. 'Your stocks are well bankrupt there.'

Hawkins turned away, tight-faced. 'I'll hire a boat.'

Perhaps it is a trap, Tavistock thought, but some of the tension fell from him as the skinny young boatman who had won the haggle steered them away from Blackfriars' Wharf. All the while the lad chattered at them in high spirits, spinning a rude philosophy and offering fifty services for sale, until Hawkins told him roughly to hold his tongue.

No, the lad's no slit-throat, he thought, nor in anyone's pay but his own. And Hawkins seems to want me aboard *Roebuck* badly. It's no plan to detain me or kill me, so what can he want? What can he be wanting to say? He faced his old master warily as they pushed out from the cluster of small craft waiting beside the tall, round-towered, river-blackened building known as Baynarde's Castle. The ebb tide was now taking the boat downstream. Watch John Hawkins, he's as slippery as an eel, still massively involved in intrigues, deeply scheming at all points. He's slid off the hook that Walsingham threatened to hang him on well before Burghleigh's month expired. And it was done with such smooth grace and skill that a man had to respect it – but not admire it.

Of course, it's Burghleigh who's protecting you, he said silently as he watched Hawkins's eyes scanning the shore. He's paid off Drake and

Walsingham handsomely to maintain you. A miraculous pretext arises
for privateering, one that in less crucial times must have been quietly
swept under the table, but which instead was whipped up and made
much of. Yes, quite the only coin that could have bought Francis, and
you knew that, didn't you? And Burghleigh's style of management
shouts from it: the inconsequential arrest of some small English grain ships
in Bilbao mushrooming into a national cause. How? Like this: gold spent;
the word put about; the City's printers getting out lurid songsheets and
illustrated catalogues of Spanish atrocities; the Mob brought out to
congregate; then flint-hard Puritan preachers demanding retribution in
God's name – that's how Drake had got his mission.

Yes, Tavistock reflected sourly. Drake had dutifully sailed to punish
Vigo and then off to the Caribbean with a fleet of twenty ships to give
the Indies havoc as he really wanted.

Walsingham had also fallen silent. Some deal had been struck there,
but it had been too deep and too secret in all its convolutions for
even Anne to have fathomed it out. The most obvious bribe was that
Walsingham's stepson, Christopher Carleill, had been put in command
of two thousand troops and made Drake's Lieutenant-General in the
Caribbean operation, but there were other ingredients that were as yet
hardly rumours.

So, Drake sent out and Walsingham appeased; it was obvious that
Tavistock too must have his price. Paid off. Bought off. Put off. But
they'll not buy me like that. The moment Hawkins suggests it I'll blow
his guts out.

'Was this Lord Burleigh's suggestion?'

Hawkins shook his head. 'No.'

'I don't believe that.'

'I'd like to shake the pride out of you, Richard,' Hawkins said in the
tones of a man who firmly occupied the moral ground. 'I'd do that for
the Lord Treasurer willingly. I'd have done it years ago, but he forbade
me.'

Tavistock watched London slide by to larboard. At Queenhythe the
quays with their barges and heavy lifting cranes. Behind, the soaring,
spireless tower of St Paul's, a buttressed stump dominating an endless
clutter of thatched dwellings that tumbled down to the waterfront.
Ahead a hundred parish towers held up the sky above the mass of the
city: St Martin's, St John in Walbrooke, St Mary Botolph, the spire of
St Laurence on the Hill. On the south bank the place of pleasures
innocent and savage: Paris Garden and the riverside walk where true
lovers came to stroll, and the oval arenas of bear- and bull-baiting for
the lovers of blood.

'It'll be a ha'penny extra for passing the bridge on the ebb, your
honour,' the boatman reminded him.

Hawkins nodded his assent.

Tavistock settled himself against the backrest, his hands unconsciously poised to grip his pistols. A sharp fetid tang lay on the wind, and the sound of rushing water from the rapids. Up ahead London Bridge spanned the river. Brick and timber buildings precariously erected on its twenty narrow arches seemed about to topple into the water. It had been a very wet week and the ebb was at its height; the great boat-shaped piers on which the bridge stood forced the river six feet higher on this side and the press of water churned and foamed in each tunnel-like gap.

Tavistock saw qualms grip the youthful boatman as he steered the prow of his boat for the nearest span. Clearly, he lacked experience and did not want to risk his livelihood shooting the bridge at full ebb, but he had got the fare against stiff competition only by agreeing to take them direct to the *Roebuck*'s mooring.

As the bridge loomed up he aligned the boat as best he could in spite of his fears. Tavistock felt the suction take them. Where the sharp piers clove the river, swirling vortices of churning brown water were shed; roaring water breaking up and echoing under the arches. Then it was as if the bottom of the boat had fallen out. The front end pitched down and a gout of water sluiced up over Hawkins's knees. Then the roar was behind them and only the marbling foam of water all around the boat spoke of the dangers.

The boatman reseated his oars; he looked at the *Roebuck* visible now up ahead and as he turned his dirty face was smiling.

Hawkins purpled at him, his best breeches drenched. 'Laugh at me, will you, slubberdegullion? You'll lose your ha'penny for that!'

'Leave him be. It was you told him to try the bridge.'

'Aye, and he took the task on!'

The youngster's eyes slitted and his mouth set. 'You'll pay me in full, your honour, as agreed. Or you'll walk from here.'

'You young runt! I'll put your eyes out!'

'You might try it!'

The lad coiled like wire ready to spring should Hawkins try for his sword. In the lad's hand an ugly truncheon had appeared. For a moment, Tavistock considered pulling his pistol, but decided against it; instead he asked mildly and with raised eyebrows, 'Do you know that you're threatening a famous Captain, laddie? One that's sailed to the Americas and back three times?'

The youth was plainly unimpressed. He stood his ground stubbornly. 'It's him that's threatening *me*. And I don't give a sack of dirt who he is. This is England, not Flanders! I'll tell you something, my name's Harry Derbyshire, riverboat Guildsman, and I'm the Captain of *this* boat, so what I say goes, else I'll land and whistle up the Guild to you.'

Hawkins continued to look darkly at him, but Tavistock grinned and held out a coin forward. 'Here's your ha'penny, lad.'

The young boatman made no move. 'That's a penny. And I ain't no thief.'

'Take it, Master Derbyshire – for your spirit. You shot that span like a veteran.'

Hesitantly, the boatman reached forward, his truncheon still gripped in his hand and a feral light in his eye as he tried to see the trick. Then he quickly took the penny and put it away, watching both his passengers mistrustfully as he recovered his oars and steered them past the Tower and the half-submerged portcullis of Traitor's Gate.

'Thank you, sir,' he said grudgingly a moment later. 'And anyway, how do you know I ain't a veteran at it?'

Tavistock winked at him. 'You might say I was a boatman myself, once over. Next time, take the widest span and don't sit so far forward.'

'Yes, sir. Thank you, sir.'

The *Roebuck* was moored a cable's length beyond St Katharine's Stairs. Tavistock climbed aboard her after Hawkins, admiring the sleek, race-built lines of the ship despite himself. The caretaker crew seemed orderly and well-disciplined. Their boatswain welcomed Hawkins with due dignity and answered the owner's questions promptly until he was dismissed. Then they went below to chairs set in the stern gallery. Tavistock expected some surprise every step of the way but there was none.

'Will you share a bottle of Jerez with me?'

'I wouldn't crack a bottle with you if it was the last on earth.'

'Richard, Richard! Sometimes you're a difficult man to deal with.'

'We're on your vessel. I'm ready to hear you. Say what you want to say quickly. Then I'll be away before your corruption makes me spew.'

Hawkins drew himself up then. 'You've wronged me, Richard. Verily. I hate to see a man whispering behind my back.'

'You're a swindler and a thief, John Hawkins. Aye, and a traitor. How's it to your face?'

Hawkins showed no anger at the insult. He dashed sherry into two goblets and set them down, pushed one towards Tavistock and lifted the other.

'Richard, you're a stiff-necked bastard. And blind. But unless you're stupid also, you'll listen to me. There have been developments since you took your slanders to Burleigh's office.' He held up his hand and ticked off the fingers. 'Firstly, Francis Drake raids Vigo and the Caribbean. Secondly, Walter Ralegh's patent to colonise Virginia is confirmed by Parliament. Thirdly, Bernard Drake takes six hundred Spanish fishermen off the New Found Land cod banks. Fourthly, Richard Grenville sails to set up a base from which to harry the Indies. Fifthly, your improvements go to the Navy Board for consideration. Lastly, there's a plan up before the Queen to send ships to intercept the Spanish silver fleet before it reaches Spain. Now, do you think it's all coincidence?'

Tavistock's stare was leaden. Everything Hawkins had said was true but irrelevant. 'Have you finished?' he said levelly.

Hawkins's anger exploded. 'No! I have not finished! It's Burghleigh's work, Richard. All of it. Everything's happening with Lord Burghleigh's knowledge and consent. You're not the sole prophet of Spain's intentions.'

'I never said –'

Hawkins cut him down. 'You have embarrassed me! You have *accused* me unjustly! And when I could make no public answer. Had it not been for Lord Burleigh's patient handiwork I might have been set upon by the Mob, or arraigned for –' Hawkins pressed his thin lips together, stemming the outburst. His face was pale with anger, but still he seemed able to find the resources to control himself as he stood up and paced. 'I'm a broad-minded man, Richard, and I can understand why you did what you did, but I'll never forgive you for swallowing Francis Drake's allegations whole and setting yourself so hard against me. Couldn't you see that most of this has come from Holstocke and Wynter and Borough? I *made* you, Richard. I grew you from a seed! And yet you turn on me. I credited you with more intelligence. Aye, and more loyalty.'

'Loyalty?' Tavistock struck back angrily. He knew well that the expense of keeping warships in commission was great, and although the Navy Board was controlled by Hawkins as Treasurer, the posts of Surveyor of Ships, Surveyor of Victuals, Master of Ordnance and Clerk of Ships were occupied by his political enemies, men who Hawkins had himself accused of gleaning fat incomes from corrupt practices. Now he was trying to shift blame to them once more.

'It won't work. Francis brought me evidence. Written evidence. What was I to do? Ignore it because you were once my paymaster? No, John Hawkins. No man will I place before my Queen.'

'Francis is a great mariner, greater than I ever was. He's bold and he's an admirably honest man, but he's also a hot-head. He always has been. All fire and fury. And because his honesty is so complete he has no skill whatsoever at secret manoeuvrings. No understanding of them. But you, Richard! You should have seen through it all.'

The scorn in Tavistock's voice was bitter. 'Get you down low on your belly, viper!'

'*Don't you yet see?*' Hawkins's face was contorted as he struggled to unseat Tavistock's view. 'My God, and it was I who taught *you* to hand a rumour to a subordinate and see where it would go to test him. Do you forget that? This rumour went to Francis and in consequence to you also. And though Burleigh warned you, you wouldn't leave it alone. Like pit bull terriers at a baiting the pair of you, jaws locked, slavering for blood, and Walsingham whipcracking like a meddling ringmaster ...' Hawkins's hooded eyes dropped then fixed on him like shards of sapphire. 'When first I came into the Navy's affairs I found them in shocking disarray. In the first bargain I struck with the Queen I promised to clear out the filth and end the decline that had dragged our nation's wall so low. And so I did! But I made enemies, Richard, enemies of the selfsame men whose bubble I pricked, and as soon as they could they came back at me in the same way, saying that I had usurped them and abolished their sinecures expressly to benefit myself. I had to have them out.'

Tavistock shook his head slowly, mockingly. 'So it was lies, then? All lies? Served against you by maggots?'

'Yes, lies! Secret, premeditated opposition. A campaign against me. Deliberate. Wilful. They wanted to tear me down! William Wynter – wanted to push me out. William Borough – wanted to see me humbled. Do you see, Richard? Do you see now?'

'And that's the truth?'

'I swear it is so.'

Tavistock's face remained immobile. His eyes met Hawkins's own, staring him down. 'You're a bastard liar. When first you came to the Board, in 'seventy-nine, Her Majesty's Navy had twenty-two ships. Now, after six years of your misrule, she has twenty-three. Do you call that preparation for war? I saw signed orders. Requisitions in your own hand. Papers transferring the Queen's oakwood and the Queen's stores and the Queen's money to you and your accomplices to build your own ships, your own merchantmen! Aye, serpent, ships like this one, to line your own private coffers and to sell out to Santa Cruz the moment his legions touch God's earth!'

Hawkins's fist pounded out his words. 'What–you–saw–was–false–accounting.'

Tavistock stood up, suddenly enraged by Hawkins's bare-facedness. The feet of his chair scraped back across the boards with an ugly sound. '*False accounting?* Do you think I cannot detect a forgery? Can you really take me for so complete a simpleton?'

'They were not forgeries! I wrote them! I wrote them all! Every log of wood, every fathom of rope, every mite of payment –'

'Then you *admit* it! You are a villain!'

'No!' Hawkins stood up also, also angry and stabbing with his finger, Tavistock's pistols totally disregarded. 'I admit nothing. You, who were so quick to accuse, you, who can see only infamy in my doings – *you are a blind man.* And Francis Drake, who collected the evidence against me so diligently, he also is a blind man. Together you were the danger! Unwitting – yes! From the highest motives – surely! But you were more dangerous to England's Navy than any Spanish flotilla.' Hawkins broke away, leaned heavily on the balustrade. 'Of course war is coming! I've known that since the day we dined with Señor Villanueva and you saved my skin by your sharp action – Oh, I haven't forgotten that day: I remembered it when I chose to sell you *Antelope*; I remembered it again when you were locked in the Tower and I walked Whitehall's corridors at liberty, scheming for your release; and I remembered it another time when I argued on your behalf before the Queen that she require Lord Oxford to sell to you the house of Low Houghton.'

'*You did that?*' Tavistock hissed, astonished at the discovery. He sought more words but could find none. His amazement was so complete that he sank back into his seat. 'You *dared* interfere in that?'

'Aye, I did. And more,' Hawkins said, aggrieved bitterness building in his voice. 'Many things have passed betwixt us. Most of them were unknown to you, and all of them were kept from the world at large. Because they were done a-secret does that make them the less constructive? That has always been my way in business. It is the foundation of my fortunes. What conceit is it that would make my dealings common knowledge from the Privy Council to the bousing houses of St Katharine's? No, sir! I don't allow it! Secrecy. Stealth. Discretion. These are what beat an enemy in the end. And so it is with the Navy, *Mister Walsingham*!'

'But ...' Tavistock felt his anger draining away as the cabin door opened and the Secretary appeared. Then he sagged inside. Suddenly everything was starting to become clear and the enormity of his error was dawning.

'But what?'

Walsingham nodded. 'Everything Hawkins says is true. Are we so witless a nation that we must tell all and sundry our private business? Only a fool tells the opposition what weapons he has. The city swarms with Italian financiers, our ports are covered by secret Jesuits; each of them daily reports the strength of our musters and the readiness of our vessels to the Pope and to Mendoza in Paris. So shall we advertise the exact measure of our fleet to the King's Admirals? Lord Burleigh asked that of me when he told me the true nature of this "treason". Sir John and Lord Burleigh have been in consort in this matter for years, as you thought. But there was only good at the bottom of it.'

It was as if Tavistock had been hit with a boat axe.

'This ship,' Hawkins said, jerking his thumb up at the quarterdeck beams. 'Is she warship, or is she merchantman?'

He said nothing, understanding perfectly what Hawkins was saying, and accepting the humiliation as he knew he must.

'You don't know! You can't tell by looking at her! If she's laden with cargo then she's a merchantman; if she's tooled up with ordnance then she's a fighter. Her purpose is not implicit in her design. You can't tell what she is. And if you can't tell,' Walsingham added 'neither can Mendoza's spies.'

Tavistock bowed his head. The lessons being read back to him were the same he himself had first set down in the Tower thirteen years ago for John Dee.

'You ... you were taking the Magus's counsel, even then?'

'I was taking *your* counsel,' Hawkins said. 'I intercepted your every letter. It made good sense. "Seamanship and gunnery, not soldiery and grapple hooks, shall one day win fleet engagements." You wrote that. And you were right. The Spanish are living in the past. They still believe sea warfare can be a matter of closing and boarding with soldiers.

Santa Cruz proved as much against the French. Without conscientious maintenance, ships fall into ruin faster than any other work of man.'

Walsingham said, 'Philip's spies will count the twenty-three great ships of our fleet and think them the same rotted hulks that Queen Mary left us with. But they're not the same. They're totally rebuilt. Philip will hear reported the flush decks and the lack of high-charged castles and he'll call them transports and freight carriers. But by God, he'll not have reckoned with the guns those humble ships shall be carrying!'

The hour was called on deck. Tavistock felt a tremor pass through him, hollowly, as if his guts had been torn out for burning. He had made a cardinal mistake, one for which he would have berated any boatswain's mate: he had allowed his personal dislike of a man to stand across his judgement. Shame for the way he had hounded and insulted Hawkins rushed over him, followed by intense relief that his accusations were unfounded.

'I owe you my apologies,' he told Hawkins throatily. 'I was wrong. Very wrong. Completely wrong.'

Hawkins's pale eyebrows lifted, then his expression softened almost imperceptibly. 'Yes. You were. But know this: I would have done the same in your place, which is perhaps a testament to our similarity of mind.'

'Then you'll accept my apologies?'

'I'll accept with three provisions. Firstly, should I ever ask it of you, you must put your seven ships freely at Her Majesty's disposal, your crews likewise.'

Tavistock nodded, deeply chastened. 'Agreed.'

'Secondly, when Francis returns from the Indies with the gold to finance it, I want you both to help me build this Navy into something that can stop anything Spain sends against us.'

'Agreed.'

'And the third condition?'

'That you and the Secretary drink up this Jerez with me now.'

'Agreed!'

Tavistock stood up and lifted the goblet, thinking ashamedly of the time and how he had set a limit on his return. 'Aye, I'll drink with you, Sir John. I'll drink a toast to the master, who grew me from a seed.'

'And I to a faithless prentice, who became an oak.'

Within a week of Drake's return from the Indies, Tavistock met him in Hawkins's company on the battlements of Upnor Castle. The fort stood guard over the inner reaches of the Medway and the dockyards at Chatham where the silver waters of this most strategic of Thames Estuary inlets shone under an August sun. Drake had been away ten months, and during that time Tavistock had laboured ceaselessly to put Her Majesty's ships into fighting order. An ominous pall was hanging over all of southern England with new rumours every week increasing the nervousness of London. At Court, it was said, the Queen was like a mad thing, half-crazed by anxiety. All fell back from her coming – servants fled, courtiers curbed their tongues and their manners, none dared ask for favour or reward, nor even offer her service. Burleigh himself had twice been banished, cursed from her side by venomous rages; inkpots and slippers had been launched at his head. Although Drake's return had muted some of the more doom-faced oracles at Hampton and Richmond, Elizabeth's mood continued to feed off the unease of her subjects, and the mood of the nation took its key from her.

But above Upnor's grassy ravelin the talking was straight.

Drake, on his way up from Portsmouth, had already received Hawkins's full account of the current state of naval preparation and had been told of Tavistock's work. In return, he had given a report of his actions in the Caribbean, a report he was most reluctant to repeat.

Drake counted his voyage a failure; it had achieved nothing in terms of monetary return or strategic dividend and, though he had done much to lift English morale, he was accustomed to far greater achievement. Tavistock quickly learned that Lord Leicester, the Hawkins brothers, and the Queen had been chief among the syndicate which had backed the voyage. Walter Ralegh, Sir Christopher Hatton and Martin Frobisher had been prominent parties also, and Tavistock began to wonder if he had been deliberately excluded from the syndicate.

He watched Hawkins's dog, a big, gangling, foolish hound with a liver-and-velvet coat, turd-brown nose and eyes and whip tail, zigzagging restlessly, sniffing at everything and piddling on every cannon and pillar. Hawkins had given it a studded collar on which was written, 'Sr. John Hawkyns own propertie'. Tavistock wondered again what the real reason was for the truth being kept from him concerning the allegations he had made against Hawkins. There had never been anything tangible, but he had sensed that Hawkins was keeping something from him. It had played on his mind for several months now, ever since the day he had stepped ashore from the *Roebuck*.

'Her Majesty blew hot and cold over my departure,' Drake was explaining unhappily. 'She is still much swayed by poor counsel from meek and deluded souls who believe it possible to avoid war with Spain. She was convinced that England's ships should stay close about her skirts and I looked daily for some alteration in her that would prohibit my sailing. Then there blew up trouble with a pack of the Queen's soft-handed courtiers who bothered me for permission to embark as if the mission was some pleasure excursion I had in mind. I eventually left on September the fourteenth in *Elizabeth Bonaventure* with twenty other ships and eight pinnaces, most only half prepared and half watered, again through fear the Queen's countermanding order must stay me. We needed for much but I felt sure we might find water just as potable in Vigo and so it proved, and we remained there long enough to prove to King Philip that Englishmen care nothing for his grandness.'

Tavistock listened as Drake related how he had missed the 'eighty-five silver fleet by a single day, and how he had sailed instead to the Cape Verde Isles to antagonise the King's subjects further. There his crews had picked up a virulent fever and it had killed hundreds but he had stormed and taken Santo Domingo; at Cartagena he had done the same. As he returned he had attacked the Spanish in Florida and touched Virginia to bring away survivors of the ill-fated Roanoke colony, but there was little joy in Drake's mind about any of it.

'I brought back a dividend of only fifteen shillings on the pound to my investors. My chiefest failure was that I missed the plate fleet. I was commanding so the cause lies with me. I expect it to cost us dear.'

'The cause is best known to God,' Hawkins said stiffly, his eyes searching for his errant dog. 'But you're right about the cost. Two years' silver is enough to finance their invasion.'

'Touching Borough and Wynter – have you had more trouble from them?' Drake asked, determined not to dwell on his failure. 'It was a wise move to sign Wynter's son aboard my expedition, though Borough is a creature I heartily mislike.' He turned to Tavistock, brightening. 'Your Anne's nephew, William, did acquit himself manfully in the fighting.'

'Thank you.'

'I've already commended Richard Hawkins's handling of the *Swallow* to his father.'

'Aye.' Hawkins took the compliment condescendingly. 'My son knows what the world is about. He seeks one day to sail in your own wake, Francis. To Peru and then to Asia. God grant that he gets the chance. As for Borough and Wynter, they're old men with old minds and neither has it in him to adjust his views. The Queen did very well to appoint me above grey bureaucrats. It's good policy to make a businessman the head of any Board.'

They walked on, Tavistock feeling the tension in the men around him who manned the fort's summer-drenched walls. It was as if each one of them saw a bleak winter approaching – a winter that would have no following spring. He told Drake, 'For every ship officially listed to the fleet, there's a private vessel of equal manoeuvrability and fire power in the hands of a private shipowner. That means we maintain crews and operational ships at nil cost to the Crown.' He pointed to the harbour with pride. 'Ralegh's *Ark* is a good example, a fine ship of six hundred tons burthen, available for Navy charter with minimal notice. It's expensive to keep ships in commission, as King Philip must have discovered. And with the money we've saved and funds the Queen has so graciously allotted we shall in the next year build eight ocean-going pinnaces, two good warships like the *Revenge* and one further ship of middle size . . .'

They debated for more than an hour, Drake still moodily ashamed his half-failure, Hawkins lecturingly, striding along the walls, throwing a stick of wood for his idiot animal to retrieve, all the while saying that time was short and that they must look to the future instead of the past. To revive Drake, Tavistock showed him the real strengths that lay beneath the superficial appearance of neglect. He went through the foremost points with enthusiasm, detailing especially the proposed change of manning from one man per one and a half tons of shipping, to the leaner and more sanitary one man per two tons.

All the while, Tavistock was thinking of the question he had wanted to ask Hawkins. He had perhaps been waiting for Drake's return before putting it. He felt bound to Hawkins now by promise, oath and duty, obliged to atone in full for his past misjudgements. He was working hard for the man, trying to make it up, and so he was controlled and dominated. But it's an unnatural state, he thought, knowing that Hawkins alone in the world had the trick of mastering him. Oh, how I desire to stand again on a swaying deck, free and unfettered, living of my own, looking to stand into a fight. Here I'm a dog on a leash. And I would be off it! Secretly he thought of the pig's ear Francis had made of his chance to annoy Spain. I'd have done the job properly, he thought with some shame for his hubris. No, no, before God it's not right to damn Francis for his singular failure. I don't know the particular circumstances. And God knows how success and failure stand on particular circumstances. And indeed, hasn't Francis demonstrated his capabilities? He's a great mariner. A great captain. Brought his ship around the globe and home again with a hold full of Spain's gold ... Tavistock sighed. Still the doggish, uncharitable thought would not leave him. I'm buggered if I'd have set sail for the Cape Verdes, they're famous for disease. And I'd have roughly taken the *flota* instead of making love overlong to the city of Vigo. Next time will be my chance. My chance.

Apropos of nothing he asked Hawkins, 'Why weren't Francis and I told the truth when first we put our accusations before Lord Burghleigh?'

'A secret is best kept by fewest people,' Hawkins answered carefully, stepping from between them. 'Lord Burghleigh wanted the scandal to break out long enough for the Spanish to get wind of it so they were well advertised of the deficiencies of English strength.'

'We could have play-acted that part well enough,' Tavistock said.

'There's no play-acting realler than life, Richard.'

Drake held his tongue, watching as Tavistock pressed the point. 'We were deliberately kept in the dark, and for an unnecessary period. Why did you not seek to deal straightly with us? It's as if neither of us was thought trustworthy.'

Hawkins laughed. 'Hardly so. Francis was trusted with twenty ships and a mission against Spain!'

'Some might see that as Francis being got out of the way. I remained, but still I was not taken into your confidence.'

The false mirth fell away from Hawkins. 'I asked to see you twice and was turned down.'

'You could have written to me.'

'I never commit secrets to paper.' Hawkins waxed jovial once more, his dog bounding up to him with the chewed stick. 'Richard, what is it you're saying to me?'

Tavistock let it go, knowing that this was not the time to pursue the matter, then Drake asked Hawkins about the thrust of current policy, leaving him to ponder on the soundness of the answer he had received.

'I know you want to put up a blockade around the Spanish coast. But Her Majesty will not countenance any direct and unprovoked show of war lest posterity considers her the cause of it. I told her – and Burghleigh told her – that we must prevent the Spanish from equipping their fleet at all costs.'

'An expedition might be got up,' Drake said, warming to the idea. 'Protestants might be gathered under Dom Antonio's banner. It could be an international effort if we brought in Scots and Dutchmen and Portuguese refugees and –'

'I've thought of that,' Hawkins told him. 'And I've put as much to the Privy Council, but that too was vetoed as overly expensive. What my lords will not realise is that Spanish ships cost three times as much as ours to set to sea. Already Santa Cruz has assembled a fleet of forty great ships and twelve thousand men at Lisbon and there's a second force almost as large concentrating in Cadiz. He will not desire to tarry long.'

Tavistock rubbed at his chin as he listened to Hawkins relating the precise strength of the Spanish. He stared into the mast dock where great oaken members soaked and seasoned, wondering suddenly how Hawkins could have such detailed information at his fingers. He said, 'I'll allow that a blockade is untried, but it's worth the attempt. Our biggest ships can stand off the coast for three months at a time before needing to return to England to revictual. If the meetest three months is chosen we might hamper them sorely. At least we could delay them until the close of the campaigning season, and every day we succeed is a day costing Spain three times what it costs England.'

'Even so, the Queen will not allow it. Too many voices close to her doubt whether a blockade of Spain can work,' Hawkins said cautiously. 'The argument used against us in Council is that of a Spanish fleet getting to sea despite the blockade. If they broke out and our ships were evaded, England would be dangerously exposed.'

'So are we constrained to our own coasts?' Tavistock asked, aware that his disappointment was showing.

'You heard Francis speak of the Queen's mind. It took all my lord Burleigh's wiles and entreaties to make her agree to the reprisals on Vigo, and even then she was only finally swayed by the demonstrations of her subjects.'

'We must wait now like lambs in the slaughterman's yard,' Drake said grimly, walking away along the castle ramparts.

Hawkins looked to him sharply, shouting after him, 'No one wants to be at the Dons more fervently than I. It might have been possible if you'd returned deep-laden with gold.' He turned to Tavistock. 'The truth is, his failure's queered it for us all.'

Tavistock's fist balled with sudden fierceness and his eyes met Hawkins's own. 'It's by decisive action that men come by true honour. Give me a strike force of twenty ships and I'll do the work. A massive pre-emptive blow. I'll sail into the Tagus and blast Santa Cruz's enterprise to bits.'

'I've told you,' Hawkins hissed back with unexpected violence. He looked around as if checking that they were not being overheard. 'Don't even think that way.'

'Sanction it, John! Imagine! In early spring, just as the hive is stirring –'

'Quietly.' Hawkins's voice sank to a whisper. 'As I said, I don't have the power to sanction that.'

A series of yelping barks rang out. Hawkins's dog had found a hedgehog and was trying to turn it over, but the quarry was tucked in a ball and at every nudge the dog flinched back, its nose bloodied by spines.

'Get away from it, then, you stupid animal!' Hawkins roared at the dog, striding across to slap its flanks with the leash.

Tavistock followed and grabbed Hawkins's arm. 'Try Burleigh, then. Prevail on him!'

Hawkins looked slowly down at Tavistock's hand until he was released. 'Not even Burleigh. The Queen is dead set against stripping England's defences for the sake of an adventure.' He paused. 'Besides the Tagus is sealed up tighter than a duck's arsehole. You'd never get in past the guns, and if you did you'd never get out again.'

The fire in Tavistock's belly burned up higher. 'What does that matter so long as I get among them? And I know I can. I can get into any harbour, and I've thought long and hard about the Tagus and its so-called impregnability. See Burleigh. Persuade him.'

Hawkins shook his head. 'Burleigh is busy with Walsingham.'

'What do you mean?'

'Just that. Lord Burleigh is involved in difficult matters. Matters of the utmost importance.'

'What? What can be more important than this?'

Hawkins watched him a moment, considering. Then he said, 'It's confidential. My duty to him prevents me from speaking of it. Even to you, Richard.'

'But you know what it is?'

Hawkins nodded slowly.

'Tell me.'

'Our spy-ring in Lisbon has been broken.'

Tavistock watched after Hawkins, watched the dog bound after him as he followed Drake. Inside his head alarm bells were ringing loud now. From his tone Hawkins was certainly hiding something, but what was it? And what was it that had happened in Lisbon?

'Please, sit down gentlemen.'

Tavistock placed himself in one of the wooden armchairs in the Lord Treasurer's study. Apart from Tavistock, only Burghleigh, Hawkins, Walsingham and Drake had been called here. The meeting had been convened at Burghley's house, *in camera*, and under conditions of great secrecy. Guards had been stationed at both ends of the corridor to prevent eavesdroppers and the cold courtyard below the bolted window was empty except for a pair of men standing at attention by the gatehouse. A roaring fire blazed in the grate, filling the room with radiant heat.

Burghleigh had grown grey in the guardianship of the nation. His long face was pale and mournful as the high winter moon, accentuated by his white beard and the velvet cap which was set askew and back from his high forehead. He put forth his power in measured words. 'I have called you here to tell you how it shall befall. Tomorrow we shall begin the first moves in a chain of events that will save our Sovereign's crown, yes, save it for her – *despite her own best judgements.*'

Every man in the room stiffened at that. Burghleigh's words sounded unwholesomely close to mutineers' talk. Only this time it was not the overthrow of a ship's captain that was at issue but the captain of the state and that crime was called high treason.

'I can see what you're thinking,' Burghleigh went on. 'And you're right to think it. But hear Walsingham out and you will understand the reasons. I hope we can reach accord, for if we cannot we're all of us dead men, and our country is lost.'

Walsingham sat on Burghleigh's right, strained, tired, swathed in black save for a Puritan's collar of laceless cambric that enclosed his throat. Grave-faced, he said, 'The invasion of England has always been built upon three columns: an army to threaten us, a navy to convey that army unto us, and a rising of English Catholics to aid and applaud it as it comes ashore. This last pillar has as its pediment the Scots Queen. For above a year, since William Parry's attempt upon Elizabeth's life, Mary Stuart has been kept incommunicado to disable any Catholic betrayal of England. However, I opened up a channel by which letters secreted in beer barrels might reach her. In June, four months ago, this deception paid me back in full measure. I intercepted a missive from one Anthony Babington. He is latterly the instrument of a conspiracy to bring Jesuits into England. Babington's letter sought Mary's approval for a rebellion, her full compliance in a Spanish invasion and her explicit agreement to the assassination of Her Majesty. In her reply, Mary Stuart laid her hand to all of these treasons.'

Tavistock sucked in his breath at that. Drake was half out of his seat. Both looked to Hawkins who nodded grimly as Walsingham continued. 'By these free actions the Scots Queen did transgress the Act of 'eighty-five in that she did as a claimant to the succession wilfully involve herself with a plot against Her Majesty's life. In consequence Mary has laid herself open to the death penalty.'

'But she's a sovereign Queen.' Tavistock said, astonished at Walsingham's intentions. 'How can she be tried?'

'Oh, she'll be tried. Before a commission of judges, Privy Councillors and peers. And once she's found guilty she'll be speedily dispatched to the block. Once she's brought to trial no power on Earth can save her, except Elizabeth herself.

As Walsingham flashed a glance at the Treasurer Tavistock's mind thundered with the revelation. Now he saw the reasons for the incredible storms that had swept the Court, for Elizabeth's refusal to sanction a foray against Spain, and why when Hawkins had personally put the idea to her she had spat bile at him and allowed him only to take the fleet to its Channel stations. With Mary Stuart dead everything would be plunged into turmoil.

'Mary is foremost a French princess,' Tavistock said to Burleigh. 'If she's executed surely the storm in France will be so great that their King will be driven to back the efforts of Spain and the Popish League all the more, thus multiplying the danger to us.'

'No!' Walsingham cut in. 'Naturally, when Mary is executed there will be howls of indignation from the Guises but her death will prise France away from Spain and the League. The last thing France wants to see is the English Crown on Philip's head.'

'But you have a point, Captain,' Burleigh said, nodding towards Tavistock so that his fine white beard shook among the dazzling threads of his lace ruff. 'French wrath will be echoed throughout Christendom. The Queen fears that she will lose every last stitch of credibility – as well as the peace that follows this life. It's my belief that unless we are able to armour her against accusations of murdering a fellow Queen, Elizabeth will not permit Mary's death.'

Tavistock shrugged tautly. 'Then how can you proceed?'

'That is no concern of yours,' Burleigh told him sharply. 'Understand that this matter is disclosed to you on pain of death, and only that you might be properly briefed in another matter. Sir John?'

Hawkins leaned forward propping one fist on his hip, the other on his knee. The gravity of the matter clearly paining him. 'As soon as Mary is dead, the last hope of English Catholics is dashed. Without her Elizabeth's unseating means their accepting as King either the arch-Calvinist, James of Scotland, whom they detest, or Philip himself. They want neither, therefore Parma's armies will find no enthusiastic reception.'

Drake spoke up, seeing a flaw. 'But conversely, wouldn't Mary's death remove the last obstacle between Philip and the throne?'

'Yes,' Hawkins agreed. 'Which is why we shall move against him.'

Tavistock stirred in his seat. By forcing the issue Burleigh and Walsingham were making a pre-emptive strike against Santa Cruz's forces not only permissible but *essential*. Suddenly the undertaking he had been perfecting and pressing on Hawkins and pleading for over the months was more than a possibility, it was a likelihood.

'The assault on Lisbon!'

'Yes,' Burghleigh said. 'Assault, if you will. I shall call it a naval action, carefully designed and planned.' He turned to Drake. 'I shall inform the Lord High Admiral, Charles Howard, who is apprised and firmly with us in all points, that you, Sir Francis, shall command the expedition. I shall further inform him that you will appoint Sir William Borough as your Vice-Admiral – as protocol demands.'

Tavistock felt utter disappointment descend on him, then his jealous suspicions ballooned. He saw clearly that in Burghleigh's upright mind he had always been a low pirate, a lucky corsair, a criminal sea robber to be despised and ignored. The distinctions conferred by knighthood had never been his, had never lifted him above the lowest station as they had with Drake. That excluded him completely from commanding the expedition that he had studied and planned.

Tavistock's nostrils filled with the stink of Burghleigh's hypocrisy. I am the architect of this undertaking! he raged at Burghley silently. Yet what part shall I play in it? You know how much this operation means to England and to me. And still you work to keep me from my right and due!

Icily he said, 'Am I to have *any* part in this, my lord?'

Burleigh ignored him. 'The precise form of the mission shall be in your care, Sir Francis, but if all goes as I hope, you shall have a number of Queen's ships at your disposal. It will be your last chance to intercept the Armada before Santa Cruz is ready to set sail. Now, go and think on the particulars with care. England and all the future freedoms are in your hands.'

Burghleigh looked hard at Tavistock before signalling that Drake might leave and that Walsingham should accompany him. Drake laid a consoling hand briefly on Tavistock's shoulder as he passed. Then Burghleigh tugged on a bell pull and within seconds one of the guards was at his side. He gave quiet instructions, his fingers playing about his lips, and the guard departed.

'I ask again, my lord. Am I to have any part in this?'

Burghleigh regarded him for a long moment, then he said, 'Do you remember when last we met, how different were the circumstances?'

'I have apologised to Sir John, and he has accepted my apology,' Tavistock said, his spine rigid now.

'Good. That was well done. But relax yourself. I have no wish to

carry forward any part of that unfortunate and *unnecessary* debate.'
Burghleigh adjusted the sleeve of his garment fractionally. 'You may
also recall swearing to me an oath on that occasion? One concerning
your brother?'

'Yes ... but I don't see ...'

Burleigh moved on, deliberately switching away from the source of
Tavistock's unease. 'This meeting was called for your benefit, Captain.
You're a cunning man and I think you must have understood that the
intentions expressed in the last few minutes are a complete volte-face
of the policy I've always promoted. Also, you must have guessed that I
was driven to agree to it.' Burleigh paused again as Tavistock nodded.
'I regret the extraordinary solution we have proposed, but I believe that
Sir Francis Walsingham and I have arrived at the only accommodation
that will give us any hope of preventing a disaster. You see, it has
become apparent to us that if our Navy was to wait for the Armada to
arrive in home waters we would be totally overwhelmed.'

That's not true, Tavistock wanted to say. Even at the last resort, we
stand a better than even chance. We have the ships to contain them, to
herd them into a defensive formation, then to stand off and pour shot
into them hour upon hour, at long range, until they are destroyed or
seriously reduced. But something stopped him; Burghleigh had closed
his eyes as if shutting out a terrifying vision of the future. Hawkins
began to speak, his own eyes never once meeting Tavistock's.

'I had hoped to avoid this, Richard, but events have caught us in a
fist. Your brother is alive –'

The room closed in around him.

'– John's in Lisbon. He's making culverins for Santa Cruz.'

'No! God, no!' Tavistock was paralysed by shock. He felt his face
drain, and he buried it in his hands, the throes of anguish rushing
through him. Despite the cool draughts drawn across the room by the
fire the atmosphere was suddenly too cloying to breathe. His mind filled
with a hundred knotted questions, but none became clear enough to
ask.

'I didn't know the whole truth before,' Hawkins's words were hurried,
as he fell over himself to get them out. 'I knew that John was alive.
That he had escaped the Inquisition. That he had somehow come to
Lisbon. He married, has a son. He's been working for my Lisbon
contact, the man who was the centre of our intelligence network in
Portugal. You remember Nicolau Almeida, Richard? The same who
helped us when we put in to Pontevedra aboard *Minion*. He was
persecuted and escaped to Lisbon. He became my business contact in
the Portuguese wine trade, and when the Spanish began to threaten he
became an admirable spy and crucial to our efforts. He was such a key
man, I dared risk his life to no one. John's life depended on that. You
understand me, Richard? I dared risk him to no one. Not even to you.'

Tavistock's mind swam in the welter of words as he struggled to comprehend. 'Then John's no traitor ... If he's working for you, he's no traitor. Yet ... yet you say he's making guns for the Spanish? I don't understand.'

'John was caught. Or gave himself up to save Almeida's life. But Almeida's dead now and we have only half the testimony of events. Even so we know John's in Santa Cruz's possession and that the Spaniards are using him.'

Tavistock gasped. Then Burghleigh was right! With English culverins the Armada would be impossible to stop in the Channel. Suddenly the image of Hawkins's dog nosing the curled hedgehog came to him. The coat of quills had meant there was no way in ...

He heard the sound of footsteps in the corridor. Burghleigh bade the guard enter; he led two women in. One was of middle age and greying, shrewd-eyed but puffy-faced with crying. She was dressed in a long, dark cloak that completely enclosed her. The other who followed was tall and some fifteeen years younger. A black haired woman in her prime, beautiful, with high cheeks and olive skin, and Spanish pride shining in her face.

Tavistock swallowed involuntarily as he rose from his seat to honour her.

'Richard, this is your brother's wife.'

They walked like trespassers through the banqueting hall, where the walls were covered in rich tapestries in bright, gorgeous colours of gold and crimson and verdant green. The tapestries were seven in number, each near two fathoms tall and ten or fifteen paces long, big enough to clothe an entire room.

'Wait here, Captain,' Walsingham told him. Tavistock thought of the complex web that had brought him here to Hampton, and the irony of his position. Since Mary Stuart's head had rolled Burghleigh had been banished from the Queen's presence. Elizabeth's public fury had been like Hell's deepest furnaces. So totally had she disassociated herself from those who had 'tricked' her into signing Mary's death warrant that she would see neither Burghleigh nor her Principal Secretary. At least Walsingham had had the presence of mind to temporarily install the eminently expendable William Davison as Secretary in his place, and a diplomatic ailment had meant that it was Davison and not he who had brought the warrant from the Queen. Davison had gone to the Tower.

'She approaches,' Walsingham whispered, seizing his arm, and turning his back to the guards. 'Remember, she's read the letter, but your meeting is not arranged; it must seem coincidental. Now I must go.'

He hurried away, leaving Tavistock bare seconds to compose himself. This is the crux, Tavistock told himself, steeling his nerve. That the future could depend so completely on this chance-yet-so-carefully-arranged meeting appalled him.

'Why me?' he had asked Walsingham.

'Why? Because it's your plan. You must plead for it, and eloquently.'

'But what of Hawkins? Drake? Admiral Howard?'

Walsingham had shaken his head. 'The Admiral is too closely tied in with Burghleigh, Hawkins likewise. And Sir Francis's brusque charm has little appeal to her after his financial failure, even less to the ambassadors who know his reputation.'

'But I'm no statesman,' he had said. 'She won't recognise me.'

'Oh, you underestimate her, Richard. She certainly remembers you. You never once failed her and she has an ear for the common man.'

The approaching commotion in the corridor grew louder, then all at once the hairs stood up on Tavistock's neck as yeomen warders readied their arms and courtiers began spilling into the hall.

The Queen appeared. Her incredible presence seemed to fill the entire place with light. Then she paused, and her retinue stepped back, parting so as not to crowd her.

She had seen him.

Immediately he swept off his hat and knelt, sweat trickling down his back, staring fixedly at the floor until a great acreage of silken skirts blotted out the boards.

'Get up, get up, man.'

He stood but was unable to look on her face.

'Who is it impedes my progress?'

'I ...' he stammered, 'I'm ... my name is Richard Tavistock, your humble servant, Majesty.'

'Richard Tavistock?' She aimed a long finger at him. 'I have it. Are you not the man who went in search of the distant place where the eels do spawn!'

A ripple of laughter passed through the assembly.

'Then tell me, Richard Tavistock, what are you doing in my hall? We have no eels here.' Her voice was a stiletto.

His heart raced, hating the sport she made of him. He looked to the wall and back, knowing he was lost. 'I was ... I was inspecting – admiring – the fineness of your Flemish tapestries, Majesty.'

'Indeed?' Then she enquired of him sharply, 'And how do you like my Flemish tapestries, Captain Tavistock?'

'I like them very well, Majesty.'

She turned suddenly, her eyes searching his face for a hint of falsehood, Ralegh was at her elbow, mischievously watching him. 'Oh? And which is to be your favourite?'

Tavistock cleared his throat and looked quickly at the two that hung closest, entitled *Music* and *Dancing*, subjects dear to the Queen's heart. He rejected them. You must have permission to sail, a voice told him in Ralegh's tones. Flatter her now and the order to sail could be in your fist tonight. But take care! She's a difficult bitch to steer. A wrong move could cost you your command, and the chance you've been aching to take.

'Let me see ...'

'Stand away there! Give Captain Tavistock light!' Ralegh said.

Elizabeth noticed his eyes dwell briefly on the hanging of *The Deadly Sins*. He seemed not to approve of it, still less of *The Triumph of Time over Fame The Triumph of Fame over Death* and *Hannibal* were quickly glanced over.

'Do you not think this the finest, Captain?'

She opened her hand at *The Triumph of Death over Chastity*. The significance of it, as of them all, was clear to him. She watched his forehead furrow, his shaggy blond brows knit over the choice.

'To my rough eye, Your Majesty, the subject has but small appeal.'

'Is it a rough eye that imagines the shape of my Navy? And fantasies the future of England on my behalf?'

She noticed his hands flex as Burghleigh's did when he was in combat with any problem. He was simmering now under the eyes of the dozen courtiers, men and women experienced in the ways and games of Court. They knew how suddenly a pleasant stroll through the palace in the company of their Sovereign might turn into a penetrating cross-examination of political motive and loyalty. Tavistock was obliged to answer.

'Your Majesty does me great honour if she means that her fighting ships are now the envy of the world, for I have imagined them to please her. As for finer arts, I understand little and profess much less, but I would say that there are two tapestries here that greatly please my poor sailor's eye.'

She heard Ralegh whisper to her, his piercing blue eyes glittered and she took his suggestion.

'Let me guess your choice.'

Tavistock watched stricken with adoration and fear as the Queen walked the length of the room, her jewelled heels echoing on the polished oak floor, filling the beamed and vaulted ceiling with their sound. She paused and paused again, then returned, facing him with ice-green eyes that stabbed through to his soul. The russet fire of her hair blazed in tight curls about her head and her slim hand fingered a great emerald pendant that hung from her neck on a chain of worked gold. He saw that it was the finest of those he had given to Walsingham to present to her as a New Year's Day gift so long ago. Then it had seemed he and his mariners must perish or give some great token of thanks for their lives. He had made a pact with a she-devil. The cold fire in the massive jewel exactly matched the flame in her royal eyes.

'I cannot guess.'

The courtiers were frozen like statuary, they saw the way she looked at him and recognised the ominous tone in the Queen's suddenly coy perplexity.

'Captain Tavistock, I cannot see what you have in mind. That troubles me greatly. Tell me, do you make *this* your favourite?'

She stretched a bony finger at the tapestry entitled *Dancing*.

Holding himself tall he said politely, 'No, Your Majesty, I do not.'

She drew back her hand, suddenly irritable. 'Then which?'

Tavistock took a pace back and turned. He strode boldly to stand before *The Triumph of Fame over Death*. Deliberately he turned his back on it, then pointed across the hall to the tapestry depicting Hannibal bringing the spoils of Cannae to Carthage.

'With your permission, Your Majesty, I shall speak plainly. That is truly my favourite.'

The courtiers drew breath as one, then there was silence. The arras depicted the legendary general of antiquity in the glory of his victory over the Roman legions. Everyone present knew that at Cannae Hannibal had destroyed the power of the greatest empire of the classical world, annihilating an army of fifty thousand men and laying bare the defenceless heart of Rome. The meaning was clear.

The Queen standing back by her stony retinue threw wide her arms and tossed her head. The stridor of her laugh rent the hall.

'Captain Tavistock! You do well to speak plainly. You shall have my blessing for it – and you shall have your ships. Godspeed to you!'

The regal party swept on, following the Queen from the hall, leaving Tavistock to stand alone, watched balefully by a pair of ramrod-straight yeoman warders. They held their halberds stiffly at quarters.

As soon as the great doors banged shut he punched the air and praised God that his monarch had been born a woman.

Chapter 26

As he watched the élite of Spain's military hierarchy enter the citadel and make their way up the steep steps toward the Council chamber, Gonzalo thought of the culverin maker and felt a powerful frisson of anticipation run through him. Tonight, a glorious war would be made in the blaze of a thousand candles. Here, inside the closed and heavily guarded fortress that protected Portugal's ancient capital, a holy crusade would be formally launched at the brazen head of England. It was good to be alive now that the pact was sealed. He felt the strength that only warriors know, the intoxicating taste of a heady wine, and he knew that his own future, Don Emilio's future, all of Christendom's future, depended upon a decision as unknowable as the turn of a card.

Whichever way the hand was dealt, he knew, the trump would be Tavistock, coupled with the solemn and murderous agreement he had made with Don Emilio only twenty-four hours ago. War was opportunity and war was glory, that's what Don Emilio had said. In war ambitious men were noticed – especially those fortunate enough to be distinguished within sight of their commanders. And those so distinguished became, in time, commanders themselves. That was the way it was; that was the way it had always been.

That's why tonight is the real beginning, he thought. Tonight, the game will be dealt out, and I, Gonzalo de Escovedo, will be privileged to see the cards. I am no longer a young man. This is my last chance for true recognition. And if the cards Don Emilio takes do not turn out well, then I shall, as agreed, scatter the deck and stand the game on its head.

Gonzalo followed as they took their appointed places along the giant, map-covered table, Santa Cruz at the head, his commanders, accompanied by their aides, ranked to right and left. Around this board was gathered the greatest concentration of Spanish chivalry since Lepanto: the Duke of Paliano, Santa Cruz's second in command, was paired with Don Francisco de Luzon. The two Valdes Admirals, Diego and Pedro, cousins who hated each other, were discreetly placed at opposite ends of the seating plan, separated by Juan Gomez de Medina and Don Antonio de Mendoza. Miguel de Oquendo and Martin de Bentendona faced them. Don Emilio sat in the middle, facing Don Alonso de Leyva.

All were distinguished men, men of proud accomplishment and prouder bearing. All wore the badges of their rank and the honours of past victories about them, and the sign of their high station burned as much in their faces as on their tunics and armour. These were the custodians of armies and navies that had fought victoriously for God and King for a hundred years and who now ruled, at God's command, virtually the whole of the known world.

The stone hall echoed into silence as they settled to business. The Admiral astonished them by drawing out his rapier, an incredibly fine needle of Toledo spring steel. It was said that God allowed the swordsmiths to make only one sword in a thousand thousand as perfect as this, a sword that never lost its suppleness or its cut and never rusted. The intricate engraving that covered the hilt testified that this was Philip's personal gift to the Admiral.

'This meeting is long overdue,' Santa Cruz told them, his voice a low growl. 'His Majesty is growing tired of delay. He will bear no more excuses. And now there is another reason why we must decide finally on the battle order of the *empresa*. It has been communicated to me tonight that His Majesty's agents in London have reported a great crime. The English usurper has struck off the head of the rightful heir, Mary Stuart.'

The whole assembly sat in stunned silence while Santa Cruz went on, 'Therefore, before I close proceedings tonight you shall know my decision regarding the ordering of the fleet. First, though, hear me out on the generalities of the matter.'

Despite his shock at the news of Mary's death, Don Emilio smiled inwardly, knowing that his appointment as generalissimo of the sea-borne invasion troops was virtually assured. The order was as good as signed by the King himself. The Stuart woman's death changes nothing, he thought. Elizabeth has merely set a useful precedent for her own execution.

'Each of you will have the opportunity to contribute your thoughts in due course.' Santa Cruz looked from face to face as he spoke, his pained eyes and the way his hand gripped his leg just above the knee the only evidence of his unremitting physical discomfort. He bent over the unscrolled campaign map, touching it with the tip of his sword.

'My intention is to assemble all nine squadrons of ships here at Lisbon. As soon as Atlantic storms permit we shall venture north, keeping at all times within sight of the coast, until we sight Cape Finisterre. Then we shall strike out across the Bay of Biscay, taking advantage of seasonal south-westerlies, on a course that will take us to the Isles of Scilly, here, ten leagues from the English coast. This means we will enter the Channel as far west as possible and then track eastward along that coast. The purpose, of course, is to terrorise the land. Every hamlet, every town, every port and every fishing village along the entire southern coast of England shall see what a mass of arms is thrown against them. Every man, woman and child will know intimately the strength of Spanish resolve, and how useless it would be to contemplate opposition.'

The assembly began to nod, relishing Santa Cruz's plan. All without exception were absorbed by the Admiral's words and felt privileged to hear so accomplished a master strategist expound his thoughts. 'It is my intention to catch the western squadron of the English fleet in its bolthole of Plymouth Sound. If it is there we shall enter and destroy it. Then we shall sail immediately to the Isle of Wight, here, midway along England's south coast. There I shall land a force of six thousand troops to establish a beachhead, occupy the island and obliterate all resistance. With the Solent ports in our hands the main landing will be made. Our army will be able to disembark with little opposition and begin their thrust across the Hampshire Downs towards London.' He paused, looking around the table appraisingly. 'As soon as this force is landed the fleet will put to sea again and continue east to the coast of Flanders where a second force under the command of the Prince of Parma will be embarked. There our task will be to screen his barges as they cross the Narrows, and run escort from Dunkirk to the Medway. Thus, by the time Parma lands in the Thames Estuary, we will have London between hammer and anvil, ready for the crushing. Then and only then will our fleet engage the remains of the English navy.'

Santa Cruz watched their enthusiasm rise. He quieted them, then added, 'I call upon Don Alonso de Leyva to explain in detail how his army will approach the Thames and lure the English land forces into direct confrontation.'

Don Emilio stared, totally unable to believe what he had just heard. Don Alonso's army? Don Alonso, that oily-haired young upstart? But *I'm* to command the landing force in Hampshire. The King himself has said so! Beside him Gonzalo paled. The card had been turned. And the ace had proved a deuce. Never mind, he told himself. We still have the trump. We still have Tavistock.

Don Alonso, young and dashing and supremely self-confident, rose to his feet. His voice was steely. 'Gentlemen, we would do well to remember that the English have suffered no real external threat since William of Normandy attacked and overcame them five hundred years ago. And whereas our troops have yearly hardened themselves against the Lowland rebels, there has been little action to exercise the English for better than half a century. Even now they possess no standing army; just a rabble of untrained levies who hardly know one end of a pikestaff from the other. Our infantry will easily push them aside as I approach London from the south-west.' He spread a detailed map of southern

England before them. 'My first objectives will be to seize and destroy the royal palaces of Hampton, Richmond and Nonsuch, and to raze the den of the Antichrist at Lambeth Palace, here. As you can see, all these targets are conveniently south of the river and should pose no problem to a force approaching from the south-west. At the same time our horse will cross the river here, at this narrow point, and drive east to descend upon the heretic heart of Westminster. When that abbey's ancient stones are restored to God, our main infantry force will straddle the western roads. If it is found that the usurper has fled to Windsor, this will have driven a wedge between her and London, if not, she will be prevented from finding refuge there. Simultaneously, a second force of shot and pike will march east to cut off the northern paths of retreat from the city before turning south to close on it. It is said that much of London has overflowed its old walls and the manner in which our troops acquit themselves among the hovels and heretic temples there will continue my Lord the Marquis's example in Plymouth. Elizabeth must be pinned down in the south-east, for then all resistance will collapse. At all costs, she must be prevented from flying abroad.'

Don Hugo de Moncada, a highly experienced galley commander who had served in the Netherlands, had been listening coolly. He now offered his objection. 'What if the English fleet is at sea when we come upon Plymouth?'

'What of it?' Santa Cruz asked.

'Shouldn't we bring them to battle as soon as possible, Admiral?'

'No. In that case we shall sail immediately for the Isle of Wight.'

'Surely we would have better strength to overwhelm them if we engaged them *before* disembarking our troops?'

Suddenly everyone was speaking and Santa Cruz slammed his sword flat across the map to halt the discussion. 'You forget that this is a joint operation with the Prince of Parma's army. If we are able to land a single force of thirty thousand men, England is ours. Nothing there can withstand one Spanish army of that strength, let alone two. The disembarkation *must* remain our priority.'

The Duke of Paliano nodded in agreement. 'It makes sense. Why attack the English fleet when we can bypass it? They will not dare approach us so long as we maintain order and keep together. I say we follow Don Alvaro's plan to the letter.'

The young Don Martin de Bertendona spoke up cautiously. 'We must not underestimate the power of English naval guns, Admiral. It was my father who brought His Majesty to England thirty or more years ago, and he was impressed by their fleet even then.'

Don Miguel de Oquendo, in his thirties and as dashing as de Leyva – it was he who had captured the French flagship at Terceira – spoke next, his tone scathing, dismissive. 'Their fleet has long since mouldered away. And the present one has been wasted by the miserly policies of the Whore of Babylon – it's only half the strength it was then! They're a nation of pirates. What do they know about the proper maintenance of a fleet?'

More nods of agreement were exchanged, then Juan Gomez de Medina put in keenly, 'I agree. A landing along the Solent is repeating history. That's the place our King went ashore when he married Queen Mary. Our troops will think that a good omen for success. Not that we need depend upon omens.'

'May we consider what happens if the English fleet launches an all-out assault on us?' Don Martin asked Santa Cruz.

Santa Cruz smiled, pleased to deal with the question. He understood the apprehension that moved like a dark current just beneath the surface in all of them. It was the unspoken horror of El Draque and his fellow privateers that now permeated the whole of Spain. Santa Cruz knew that their terrifying reputation was justly deserved. The damage they had inflicted on Spanish pride during their assaults on Vigo and the Indies had been out of all proportion to the actual destruction they had wrought. The Admiral saw his chance to allay his subordinates' fears, he had conceived a strategy that would cope with any attacker.

'If that happens,' he said, his hands moving up and apart in a sweeping curve, 'we shall adopt this formation. It's a shape I saw on the Muslim standards at Lepanto – a crescent moon. When held tight, it works like the head and horns of a bull, an impregnable defensive formation, our *urcas* and transports in the middle, protected by an impenetrable wall of warships at the cusps.'

Don Emilio boiled as he watched Santa Cruz explain the tactics. The flush of pride he had felt at the prospect of being appointed Philip's generalissimo had been obliterated at a word from the Admiral. Over the months he had come to understand that Santa Cruz's position was absolutely central. The Marquis dares to overrule the King on strategic matters and to direct the *empresa* as his own, he thought angrily. All major decisions are being taken by him alone, and how these naval men defer to him! De Leyva too – doubtless because he knows he's going to get his own way. But that's going to change. Oh, yes, that's certainly going to change.

His eyes strayed to Gonzalo, suspecting his aide could almost read his mind.

'I sympathise, of course, sir,' Gonzalo had said the night the culverin maker had fallen into their hands. 'But surely it's Santa Cruz's prerogative to shape the enterprise as he sees fit.'

'Unfortunately, yes. But with Tavistock in our possession we can arm the *empresa* as it should be armed. Think about it. You've seen how tired and drawn Santa Cruz looks. It's clear his leg is turning putrid, poisoning his blood. He overexerts himself. Naturally, I've mentioned it to the King in my dispatches.'

Gonzalo's reply had lacked conviction. 'But the King will not tolerate any postponement. I understand he's writing to Santa Cruz daily urging him to put to sea.'

'Perhaps the Admiral can be persuaded to exert himself even more. After all, he's not long for this world. Suppose Santa Cruz does die before the attack can be launched. Have you considered that?'

Gonzalo had pondered. 'The King will have to appoint someone else. Someone in favour and in full health, someone capable of becoming commander-in-chief.'

He had smiled then. 'So who do you imagine he'll promote?'

'Obviously, the Duke of Paliano. He's second-in-command.'

'No, no. That won't happen, Gonzalo. He's old, and he's too much Santa Cruz's man. With the Marquis dead he'd be like a headless chicken. And I know that the King doesn't approve of him.'

'Then the choice will be between Admiral Luzon and Juan Martinez de Recalde – and, of course, yourself, Excellency.'

'Quite so. *Quite so*. Therefore we must take care to demonstrate our loyalty and our capability. What do you suggest, Gonzalo?'

Gonzalo had grimaced. 'Of course, we have Tavistock. Perhaps it's time to use him.'

'Yes. How many culverins could he make for us between now and our departure?'

As Gonzalo made his calculations Don Emilio's thoughts had dwelt on Luzon. What of Luzon? What Gonzalo said is true. The man's a formidable sailor, renowned for his service to the Crown. He's from much the same mould as Santa Cruz himself. I don't fully know how the King regards him, but whatever his standing I can undermine him. Philip won't want his *empresa* commanded by a man whose religious faith is in doubt, a man who once stooped to blackmailing the Chief Inquisitor of Mexico. He accused Don Pietro of satanic possession, isn't that what his enemies always maintained and were prepared to swear to? No, Luzon should be no obstacle at all to me.

'At least fifty, Excellency. Though that will mean purchasing more powder to fire them.'

'Then I'll ask for a hundred. Prepare a budget for that. The expense has already amounted to four years' contributions of American silver. A little more won't hurt the King. He's resolved on his *empresa* whatever the cost.'

'Couldn't you write to him and beg him to come to Lisbon himself?'

'Why should I do that?' Don Emilio had asked, surprised at Gonzalo's naivety. While the King remained in Madrid, writing letters to his nephew in the Low Countries, to Mendoza in Paris and to Santa Cruz, all was safe. 'No, Gonzalo, that the King never leaves the Escorial is our greatest strength. He's a recluse, and that's good, because the last thing we want is his meddling here. This way, I describe everything that happens in Lisbon and he believes what I say. That's power.' He had sipped at his glass of Monzon then, pleased at the way events were leading. 'You may be right about our culverin maker. Perhaps now is the time right to use him.'

That had been months ago and since then, Tavistock had been confined in secret until the right time to produce him arrived. To have produced him sooner would have given him to Santa Cruz. Don Emilio was sure of that. Stirring, he said, 'Haven't I always forgiven you your sins, Gonzalo? I didn't punish you as some might after you mislaid him in Mexico. You see how God rewards his own?'

Gonzalo's silence had made him think of the night they had put the muleteer to death. There had always been a cruel streak in Gonzalo. Though Pedro Gomara had been the mainstay of his plan to allow Tavistock to escape burning, he had turned viciously on the old man when the plan went wrong. He had taken him to the rendezvous outside Mexico City, but when the wait had turned out to be fruitless Gonzalo had driven a sword into him, thereby satisfying, he had said later, the old man's wish to die as a soldier. After that, despite intense searches by both the secular authorities and the Church, they had never discovered any trace of Gonzalo's bitch of a sister, or of the Englishman. Of course, reports had been twenty to the dozen: Peru, Cuba, Cartagena, even tales of shipwreck and one of escape to England, but there had never been any hard evidence.

'Yes, you must treat Tavistock with care,' Don Emilio said, pushing back his chair. 'Are you still loyal to me, Gonzalo?'

Unhesitatingly, 'Yes, Excellency.'

'And to the King?'

This time Gonzalo had paused, evaluating the trap. 'Without reservation, sir.'

'I wonder.' Don Emilio had stood up, recklessly abandoning himself to the idea in his mind. 'Yes, I wonder. What would you do if I told you the King's patience with Santa Cruz is at an end? That he wants him dead? And that I had offered your name as a mark of your fealty to him?'

What indeed, he thought, relishing again the way Gonzalo's jaw had fallen at that. He rubbed his palms together unobtrusively, his mind suddenly alerted to Santa Cruz and to the present by the striking of the castle's great tower clock.

Don Emilio looked around the assembled Council of War then studied the Admiral closely. Yes, I'm still not sure about you. Your blood's poisoned and you'll be a dead man soon, but will you be a dead man soon enough? On the other hand I've always been able to rely on Gonzalo. He won't take my word alone, but he's stupid enough to have no qualms about disposing of you once I show him the correspondence I've received from the King.

Philip's last letter was the most urgent yet complaining of Santa Cruz's sloth. In it the King had asked to be advised minutely of the state of readiness of the fleet, to have a detailed evaluation of the Marquis's intentions and a list of proposals for how Santa Cruz's difficulties might be eliminated. The tone of the letter had been quite ambiguous, and Philip's letters had always been capable of two or more quite separate readings.

Yes, he thought, stirring from his smouldering reverie, just as I was used by Don John to murder Philip's lunatic son, so I will use Gonzalo to murder Santa Cruz.

The invasion of his thoughts was sudden and unexpected. 'What have you to say, Don Emilio?'

'I'm sorry?'

Santa Cruz fixed him with the stare for which he was famed. 'You seem to be anxious to say something.'

Languidly, Don Emilio sat up. 'Only that I should like to underline the need for proper armament. It's my belief that we should wait until we are able to ship more culverins. Half the churches of the peninsula have donated their bells, it would be an insult to God to sail before we had the means to –'

Santa Cruz's eyes sheered away arrogantly. 'Yes, I was forgetting. You're an expert on how ships may be properly armed to oppose the English.'

Alonso de Leyva saw his opportunity and spoke. 'Surely, more important than that is a quick and decisive infantry campaign. Naturally, that will depend on good summer weather. What date can we now expect to put to sea?'

'Patience, Don Alonso, you'll be at them soon enough,' Santa Cruz assured him, still ruffled by Don Emilio's debonair attitude. 'Your men will fight this summer. We sail in May, June at the latest. Six weeks after we cross the Tagus bar you'll be standing on the ramparts of Portsmouth's fortifications. I can promise you that.'

'Is that possible?' Luzon asked, knowing also that Philip was growing increasingly irate at the delay. 'Are we really able to ready the fleet by mid-May? That's only five, six weeks away.'

The Admiral drew himself up. 'We could sail now if I chose to order it.' Luzon bit his tongue, and Santa Cruz continued. 'I'm only waiting for the squadron now assembling at Cadiz. As soon as that arrives we'll get under way.'

'But we're still short of heavy guns,' Pedro de Valdes said bluntly. 'Don Emilio's quite right. It's something which needs to be rectified.'

Santa Cruz's voice rose, something of the pent-up anger that had made him a legend among Spanish mariners showing itself. 'I can't agree. So long as we have sufficient fire power to keep the English at a distance we'll sail.'

'So you're prepared to gamble the whole *empresa*?' Don Emilio pressed. Immediately all eyes locked on him and he cloaked his following question in a mantle of lukewarm indifference. 'With respect, Admiral, aren't you in your anxiety to sail jeopardising the entire operation?

Don't you think it would be better to wait another month? We could still take London before winter closes in, but our ships would sail with armament heavy enough and accurate enough to destroy any ship they sent against us.'

Luzon said, 'Yes, Admiral. But what difference will another month make? Why must we sail by June?'

'Because the King says we must!' Santa Cruz rapped out furiously. 'And if we lose a few ships, so what? That's to be expected. We are men! Men with pride! Soldiers! Knights! We know war means risk, but we are not cowards, we glory in it! Isn't that so?'

Some showed their approval, others bowed their heads wordlessly.

Santa Cruz looked hard at Don Emilio, imposing his will. 'Isn't that so?'

'Of course, Admiral, it's just that –'

'That's right! There *are* no objections! And who says otherwise? We are Spain's sons! We know our duty! No man may tell us our business! No man may beat us down! No man. If the King says we shall sail for England – then–we–shall–sail–for–England!'

No one moved to Don Emilio's defence. Santa Cruz's eyes bulged with anger and the vein in his forehead stood out. His gaze dwelt upon them all in turn, finally falling on the man to his left. 'Admiral Luzon?'

Luzon hesitated, then said with cool courage, 'There may be some wisdom in what Don Emilio says, Admiral. Several times the Indian Guard has experienced the effect of English guns. Even at long range they can be devastating. However, I agree there's little to be gained by waiting. We may supply the whole fleet with culverins in three months' time, but by then the weather will be against us and we would have to wait another year –'

'That's not true,' Don Emilio interrupted, wracking Santa Cruz with yet another reason to delay. 'I tell you that the cannon foundry here in Lisbon can be producing guns as good as English culverins in little more than a month from now.'

'Impossible!' Juan Gomez de Medina retorted.

'*Caray!* Is this true?'

'What are you talking about, Don Emilio?'

'Silence!' Santa Cruz's order stilled them. 'In little more than a month from now we shall be on the high seas sailing against England. His Majesty has ordered it, and so it shall be. Now, Luzon, I want the battle order announced.'

'Yes, Admiral.' Luzon stood, reading from Santa Cruz's notes. 'The Marquis shall personally command the Flag Squadron of fifteen ships, ten of which shall be the Portuguese galleons, supported by five *zabras*. The flagship shall be the Admiral's own *Trinidad*, of twelve hundred tons, presently at Cadiz.

'The Biscayan Squadron shall be commanded by the Duke of Paliano; ten galleons and four *patajes*.

'The Squadron of Castile: Don Diego Flores de Valdes. Fourteen galleons, two *patajes*.

'The Andalusian, ten galleons and one *fregata*, to be commanded by Don Pedro de Valdes.

'The Guipuzcoan Squadron of eleven galleons, two *fregatas*: Don Miguel de Oquendo.

'And finally in the first battle line, the Levantine, the ten galleons of Don Martin de Bertendona, who shall sail in *La Regazona*. Don Emilio will sail aboard the *Rata Encoronada* with Alonso de Leyva.'

There was a stirring as Santa Cruz examined each man for his reaction. Some had yet to be named, others would not be named at all. But the compromise had been the best he could work out, and though no one seemed to be fully satisfied, still none were resentful to the point of a public demonstration, not even that loathsome practitioner of dumb insolence, Don Emilio Martinez.

'Are there any questions?'

'Do I have your permission to go ahead with my efforts to give your ships the guns they need in case there should be any delay?' Don Emilio asked humbly, inwardly delighting at the way he was tearing Santa Cruz away from his best instincts and forcing him to publicly announce his intention to sail within the King's ludicrously tight schedule.

'Don Emilio, as Inspector-General, you must try to restrain yourself from tinkering with matters that do not concern you. Your task is to make certain Don Alonso's troops are properly equipped and embarked on the appropriate transports at the right time. Nothing more.' Santa Cruz regarded him briefly, as if drinking in his response, then he turned to Luzon. 'Read out the rest.'

'Yes, Admiral. The second battle line is to be as follows: Don Antonio shall command a squadron of twenty-five *zabras* and *patajes*. The four galleasses shall be the charge of Don Hugo, commanding from the *San Lorenzo*. Lastly, twenty-five ships of between three hundred and eight hundred tons to carry the remainder of the Lieutenant-General's troops. Juan Gomez to command.'

As Luzon spoke, Don Emilio's eyes glowed like coals. He watched Santa Cruz's imperious gaze ripple across his subordinates.

'Does anyone have anything more to say? No? Good. I have one thing and one only.' Santa Cruz paused for breath. 'I have commanded many expeditions and fought in numberless campaigns, and each battle has taught me that success in warfare is absolutely dependent on the correct functioning of the chain of command. Those beneath must be made to take orders from those above. Immediately. Willingly. Without question. I have chosen you all after careful consideration. Some of you may not be happy with the gifts I have bestowed, but whether you are or whether you are not, I solemnly ask each one of you to put your personal feelings aside and to pledge loyalty to me and to your King.'

Alonso de Leyva offered himself first. Then each in turn showed his humility and Santa Cruz went from man to man, to shake his hand and receive his promise, face to face. Finally, Don Emilio gave his word, seeing that the absurdly mawkish little ceremony was giving the Admiral considerable satisfaction. 'You'll have all the support I can give you,' he promised as they engaged hands, 'so long as you shall live.'

Santa Cruz took his hand away and embraced Don Emilio stiffly. 'That is well. Now I call upon the holy father to bless our enterprise.'

They genuflected before the prior, to dedicate their mission to the glory of God. Don Emilio's eyes dwelt on the agony of Santa Cruz as he suffered his full weight on his bandaged knees.

The churchman's voice began to intone a droning litany, but he had been speaking only moments when he was drowned out by shouting beyond the door. The remonstrations grew louder. Heads turned from the father prior. Then the Admiral demanded to be helped to his feet.

'What's this?' he raged, appalled at the intolerable intrusion. 'Who dares disturb our prayers?'

The door burst in and a messenger, quaking with fear and white-faced from his tussle with the guards, ran to the Admiral. He crashed down before him, offering up his communiqué in both hands.

'What is it?' Santa Cruz demanded.

'A terrible calamity, Lord!'

'Calamity?'

'It's El Draque! El Draque and a great fleet of ships! He's been sighted off the Galician coast! He's sailing here, to Lisbon, to destroy us!'

In his old cabin aboard the *Antelope*, Richard Tavistock tuned his ears to the familiar creaks of his ship. She was just as she had ever been, kept trim by Jack Lowe, her Master, and James Bolton, her Captain. It was magnificent to feel the living deck under his feet again, her sails close hauled, and her beakhead diving in the salt spray. The oath he had sworn to Anne was undone. Never more to roam, he'd told her, but this was no recantation. She had released him from his vow. This once. As she'd known she must.

He lay back, drifting, as he tried to unravel the reasons why Hawkins had kept John's existence in Lisbon secret from him for so long, only to reveal it once the mission to impeach the King's shipping in Spanish harbours looked certain.

With foreboding he took the packet of sealed orders from his chart drawer and weighed them as if trying to divine their significance. Today was the day appointed for the seal breaking. The day they came athwart the thirty-ninth parallel, the latitude of Lisbon. But the opening was an Admiral's duty. And Francis was Admiral.

He looked down at the chart the Spanish woman had given to Burghleigh. She had said it was in John's own hand, that he had made this detailed survey of the mouth of Lisbon harbour himself. Could this really have been penned by John?

There were two channels, the main northern channel that ran under the Castle of St Julian, and the southern channel which was shifting and treacherous. The pinch-point was patrolled by a squadron of fast, shallow-draught galleys, and from Belem there were shore fortresses and batteries that made the Tagus impassable to any enemy. But what was the plan? And what of the promise he had made to Burghleigh? The news that John was known to be arming the Spanish fleet weighed heavily on him. He knew that with the right weaponry an invasion could succeed.

With his peace blighted he scrolled the chart and laid up on deck, where his coxswain waited. The boat was swift, his oarsmen strong of limb and the seas slight, and within the quarter hour he was climbing the side of Drake's *Elizabeth Bonaventure*.

Drake had been appointed Admiral and Sir William Borough his Vice-Admiral, just as Burleigh had wanted. Hawkins had explained that Borough was there conveniently to remove him from England and so part him from the mischief he was planning against him. He had said that the sealed orders would explain the rest.

'So you persuaded the Queen that her brother-in-law was pissing in the fire?' Drake had roared gleefully upon Tavistock's arrival in Plymouth after gaining the Queen's consent. 'I hope you told her we'll singe off his royal short and curly hairs?'

Tavistock had grinned back. 'I promised we would impeach his shipping.'

'We'd give him a fat lip if the vile Habsburg did not have two such already.'

Outside Drake's house, Looe Street was heaving with men who had waited for this day. Since getting down from his horse he had met countless ghosts from his past: Cornelius the Irishman had come hatless with Captain Bowen and the canny Scot, Fleming, whose own ship he had renamed the *Golden Hinde*. Zeal-for-God, the Puritan gunner was there, and he saw another whose face was black as ebony wood: Boaz, a cloth merchant and shipowner these ten years, but come from Portsmouth in his barque to see what might befall. There had been other men who had suffered with him at San Juan de Ulua, and many more who had shared the riches of the happy homecoming ten years on. Drake too had attracted his old adherents. There had been no shortage of experienced seamen to set against Spain.

Then Drake had taken the signed warrant, and read from it to the assembled crowd: 'Whereas it hath pleased Her Most Excellent Majesty to grant unto Sir Francis Drake, knight, her Commission bearing date the fifteenth day of March in the nine and twentieth year of Her Majesty's Reign, for a service to be done by me with four of Her Majesty's ships and two pinnaces ...' And they had cheered, until his voice was drowned out.

The promise of the Queen's four ships had triggered the cautious city. Elizabeth's seal had been enough to demonstrate her approval. He had pointed out where it had been signed by a crew of fishmongers, grocers, mercers, haberdashers and drapers – Thomas Cordell, John Watts, Paul Banning, Simon Boreman, Hugh Lee, Robert Flick – all his mercantile acquaintances willing to venture a penny in hope of a pound. They had fitted up a fleet loaned from the Turkey Company: ten merchantmen and pinnaces.

To loud acclaim he had offered them their hearts' desires: 'We're ordered to impeach the provisions of Spain, to distress His Majesty's ships within their havens.'

And during the cheers, privately, Drake had listened as Tavistock had told him, 'It's a free hand, Francis. A free hand at last. Much more than Burghley would have gotten us.'

'It's precisely what we needed.'

'Walsingham warns there's a snag to it.'

'What?'

'Within the week Elizabeth will tell Burghleigh that she has repented of her foolishness, and he will send Robert Slade here with a message to stop us.'

Drake had turned at that. '*What?*'

'If we provoke a war, hers shall be the blame. She must prevent us – *officially*. You see?'

The fullness of the plan dawned on Drake and he cackled, then he thundered, 'I need me two days more to be right. I'll send John Harris and Fenner's cousin onto the Exeter road. They'll detain Mister Slade.'

Tavistock had nodded approvingly. 'Added to which is this: the pinnace that the Queen shall dispatch with the orders to recall us is the *Aid*. Her master is John Hawkins's son.'

'Oh, you're a clever man, Richard! A right clever man!'

So they had left Plymouth on April Fool's Day, streaming flags and pennants down to the water, bristling with arms and men, sixteen ships and seven pinnaces, all raring to do war against Spain.

Great crowds had gathered, all the men of the West hoping to sign on at the last minute, and the wives and families of those lucky enough to have a berth waving madly. He had seen Anne come to the quays with their daughters and he had waved to them, hoping they would pick out his red jerkin on the *Antelope*'s quarterdeck. He waved back once before setting his back to the task of getting the ship under way. Then the anchor flukes had come dripping to the cathead and the mainsail had filled and the *Antelope*'s head had turned towards mid-channel. An hour later they had slipped out beyond the Sound and an hour after that they had lost sight of England altogether.

Drake met them as they came aboard the *Bonaventure*. Though all thought Lisbon their target, none but Tavistock knew their actual destination.

William Borough, corpulent, unhappy at the indignity of having a privateer seven years his junior to command him, coming from the *Golden Lion*; Thomas Fenner, Drake's man, a good mariner and one who had sailed in the attack on Cartagena; Harry Bellingham, discreet, honest and efficient; and Tavistock, his sealed orders hot in his hand.

As usual, Drake let them have their say, listening quietly, then Borough gave his reasons why Lisbon was an impossible objective.

At length Drake broke his silence. 'I agree,' he said simply. 'Which is why we shall not try it.'

'Not try it?' Borough said, shocked to his boots.

'You heard me well. We'll hunt down Santa Cruz's flagship, the *Trinidad*. I'll fall upon his second force at Cadiz.'

At three o'clock, on Wednesday, the nineteenth day of April, they came upon the ancient port that basked in the sun midway between the Cape of Trafalgar and the Portuguese border. Cadiz itself stood on a rocky island connected by a bridge to a long spit sweeping out from the mainland. The town overlooked the northern Outer Harbour, but there was a second, Inner Harbour, almost completely landlocked, containing Port Royal and the more sheltered anchorages within. It was from here that a vessel of Don Pedro de Acuna's galley squadron advanced to meet the leading ship of this unknown and unexpected flotilla.

That ship was the *Antelope* and Tavistock strode her quarterdeck, exultant that God had given them so good a sailing wind with which to do the job. As he watched the galley come on, he tried to put out of his mind the terrifying instructions that had been contained in the sealed orders. At the breaking up of the Captains' conference aboard the *Bonaventure* Drake had opened the pouch and let him read the contents. They were no orders, but a personal letter from Hawkins, reminding him of his oath aboard the *Roebuck* and of his promise to Burghleigh. It had explained that John's work in Lisbon was now confirmed and that he must be stopped. Hawkins had had the letter sealed for two reasons, firstly its secret nature, and secondly because he had wanted Tavistock to consider it only when he was standing off Lisbon. The request was that he bring John out, or if he could not, to honour his promise in full.

'What will you do?' Drake had asked him when they were alone.

'What can I do?'

'Hawkins is right. He must be stopped.'

He had groped for the answers. 'But why me? Why his brother?'

'Because Hawkins would rather you brought him away. And if any man can do that, you can.'

'And if I can't?'

'You will.'

But he had chosen to disregard the request. He had sensed some adroitness in Hawkins's hand, but he had known that he could not decide in a matter like this without immense forethought. So, for the first time in his life, he had thrown the burden up to heaven. This time, the Lord would choose, and at Cadiz, Tavistock knew, he would receive his answer.

'Fire a warning over her,' he told his gunner as the galley's spiked prow drew dangerously close. Two saker shots plumed the water on either side of her and he watched her sheer off. No doubt that she had been expecting to hail her challenge to some harmless fleet of Hanseatic merchantmen and he imagined the panic that would ensue when she recovered the port. As in the past, panic, and Francis's fearsome reputation, would be their best allies.

Behind, the English ships sailed on, closing on the Outer Harbour, and Tavistock knew that the tactic of surprise must now give way to extravagant boldness. Almost as one the red-on-white crosses of St George broke out from the trucks of twenty-three mainmasts, and, as Tavistock turned his eye once more on the harbour, he saw with disbelief that the squadron of ten galleys was coming out to meet them.

Their commander's mad to bring them out here, he thought, unable to understand what was going through Acuna's mind. Doesn't he realise that his only advantage is speed? He can't win while this wind keeps up and we've beaten him once he gets into rough water. Tavistock knew that had he been in charge of the galleys he would have used them to block the Puntal Passage and keep the Inner Harbour secure, but Acuna seemed determined to prove his valour.

As Tavistock watched, the galleys emerged and began to manoeuvre into line abreast, the classic formation that protected the flanks of the rowers and made a threat of the bow rams and forward-firing armament. Inside the harbour they could be lethal; their swift swimming and independence of the wind made them a match for any square-rigged ship, but here their show of strength was wasted.

'Signal from the *Bonaventure*, sir!'

It was terse. The four Queen's ships, having greatest broadsides, were to engage the galleys in line astern, Tavistock was to penetrate the harbour and lead the armed merchantmen in among the shipping.

Tavistock thanked Acuna for his chance to lead the charge and thundered into the Outer Harbour, under the battery of Matagorda, steering his followers between two shoals. Then his eyes lit at the sight that greeted them. Inside were thirty-two ships of great burden intended against England and thirty other ships, most tied up head to quay and in the middle of loading ordnance, or riding at anchor.

'They're cutting their cables,' Jack Lowe, his sailing master, shouted. 'What shall we do?'

'What would you do?'

'*Steer for them*,' twenty voices told him.

'Then do so.'

'*Aye, sir!*'

At their backs Drake had blasted the galleys out of his way, sinking one and chasing the others into the shallows. Then the warships bent their heads south, cutting off the panicking Spanish from the safety of the guns on Cadiz Island. There, naked to their assault, stood rank upon rank of great ships, moored and helpless, without sails or yards or guns to return fire.

For the next three hours the entire Outer Harbour was ransacked. Pinnaces loaded with implacable prize-hungry Englishmen scoured the bay, going from vessel to vessel in search of booty. Deserted by their crews, the Spanish ships were systematically looted and fired until twelve thousand tons of shipping had been overcome. Only one ship defied them, a great eight-hundred-ton merchantman, and they closed in on her like wolves, their guns tearing her to pieces while the very gunners who hacked her down bemoaned the loss of her as prize.

When night fell they anchored in the middle of the Outer Harbour, out of range of the shore batteries and impervious to the massed land forces that were pouring to the defence of Cadiz to prevent a landing. The bay was lit by the burning hulks that now littered the seaway and sporadic gunfire cracked from the forts and towers that dotted the coast. Drake called his Captains about him to consult their opinion. Many of them had just doubled their personal fortunes and were willing to follow Drake into Hell itself. But there was one dissenter.

'We've done enough here, and I say we get out while we may,' Borough insisted.

Tavistock, disliking the false gravity of Borough's demeanour, said nothing.

Drake's eyes narrowed, smelling fear and mutiny in Borough's words. He said, 'But our job here is only half finished.'

'If the wind should drop, we'll be trapped. Then the galleys may come out and have us as standing targets,' Borough said, speaking now in some trembling sort.

Drake's considered words cut at him. 'There must be a beginning to any great enterprise, but it is the continuing of it unto the end, until it be thoroughly finished, that yields the true glory.'

'You don't understand my objection.'

Quietly: 'Oh?'

Borough stirred himself. 'Captain Drake, this day God has granted us a great victory. We have bloodied Spain's nose. We must not ask for more.'

Tavistock saw the dangerous light in Drake's eye, knowing well his unwavering rule never to brook opposition from men he did not respect. Thomas Doughty had mutinied during the circumnavigation, and Drake had had Thomas Doughty beheaded.

'Why should we not cast this day aside, since it is passed?' Drake asked with deceptive calm. 'And in this hour let us think out our plans for the morrow mindless of what has gone before. Fortune has no memory, as the meanest dicer may tell.'

Borough blustered, sucked in by Drake's lull. 'Will you dice with us, then? I'd rather away. Quickly. Now. To retire victorious as we now stand. It's the only sane action –'

'Hold your tongue, sir!' Drake shouted. No one dared a word. 'You will hold your tongue.'

'I protest!'

'Protest? *Protest?*'

Borough's mouth tightened. 'You're flouting my right to voice an opinion, and I shall report your disregard for the courtesies of war.'

'This is not war, Sir William, this is a private quarrel between myself and the King of Spain, and you had best go carefully if you would come away from it alive.'

Borough puffed and blew at that. The exchange had bred such a corrosive in his heart that he backed away.

As they were rowed from the *Bonaventure*, Tavistock warned Borough against his course coldly.

'That was foolish, Sir William.'

'But we must get out. All the treatises of naval warfare say –'

'Hang the treatises. You should not anger him or Francis will hang *you* – for a coward and a mutineer. He is the Admiral here, and you would do well to remember that.'

Memories of the summary way Drake had dealt with the quarrelsome Thomas Doughty must have run through Sir William's mind.

'Captain Tavistock, I seek only the good. If the wind drops –'

'Then do as you are bid.'

'You forget that I am Vice-Admiral!'

'Do as you are bid,' Tavistock said, his words hard as iron now. 'You're a faint heart. Francis will have no opposition from a man who misled us, *and who turned us against John Hawkins as you did with your lies.*'

At that, Borough fled into silence until he regained his ship. Tavistock saw the fear dance on his face. Aye, and piss blood, gutter rat, he cursed silently. It's justice that you've been brought to book. You deserve the hanging Francis would give you if he could. Your Navy career is at an end. But it's a shame that you're completely right about what we should do. I agree that the Inner Harbour is a dangerous trap and no place for us. Francis has lost touch with his inner feeling this time, aye, and with his reason.

Tavistock knew that the lure had been irresistible. Santa Cruz's own galleon, the *Trinidad*, a great twelve-hundred tonner, was at anchor beyond the Puntal Passage. He knew how the reports must have inflamed Drake's imagination, and now the argument with Borough had driven him to a poor decision. As he climbed once more aboard the *Antelope* Tavistock wondered if that was God's way of answering him.

When the next day dawned they went in against Santa Cruz's ship. A swarm of pinnaces approached her, blasting their way aboard, storming the hapless galleon until she was taken. They overran her, stripped her and then burned her, then they did the same to six other ships carrying holds packed with millions of barrel staves. His own eager lads lifted a quantity of material from the last of their victims, and as they landed four big chests in the *Antelope*'s waist they prevailed on him to shoot off the locks with his pistols so they might have the sight of two expensive wheel locks being discharged.

He agreed readily and broke the poor iron of the first two locks to fragments, but as the first lid was thrown back they found nothing but twenty neatly folded white monks' habits.

'God bugger me sideways, that's no prize!'

'It's all shave-head trappings!'

'Worth nothing! Torch it!'

'Hie it over the side!'

Their disappointment was acute. Some tried the other chests with the same result and some went off to find other booty and a few fell to rending the garments for the sake of destruction, but Tavistock stayed them. An idea had germinated, and he began to imagine its manifold possibilities. This was indeed a strange answer from God.

The wind began to die at noon, at the finishing of their work, and the men on England's warships looked up to find themselves suddenly prey to the same galleys and the shore batteries they had scorned for a day and a night. Borough had sullenly hung at the harbour mouth and had got into difficulties with the galleys. A pinnace was taken and Drake grudgingly ordered them to make sail.

'We shall make some pastime with them as we go,' Tavistock told his men as they struggled to catch the last breaths of wind in their sails. The exodus was close run, the big guns of Cadiz thundered at them, but the galleys had no wish to taste their broadsides again and they made open water without further loss. Behind them, the pearl of Spain had been left in total ruin. Twenty-four of the thirty galleons they had found were smashed beyond repair. Santa Cruz's own was smashed beyond recognition.

They met together at sea some way south of Lisbon and there Tavistock announced his intention to try for John. Drake departed north, dragging Borough behind him to an uncertain future. He said he would stretch his neck for cowardice and that, until then, Borough would do as he was told as a Vice-Admiral must.

Dawn came in bloody rags over the Castle of St Julian. John Tavistock wiped the sleep from his eyes and looked down over the castle walls to see what the disturbance was. He had watched the comings and goings of messengers and high-ranking officers all yesterday. Something enormous, something unexpected and immensely important had happened. The report pouches were being galloped straight to the citadel without interference. Tremendous activity was suddenly necessary. What had happened? It smelled like a disaster.

Tavistock brought his gaze back within the compass of the walls. He had been imprisoned here since his insane surrender to Gonzalo. Maria had screamed at him that he was killing himself, growing hysterical as she realised he could not be persuaded away from his obsession.

'But for Nicolau we'd be dead!' he had shouted at her. 'Dead! Don't you understand? We owe him our lives. I must try to help him.'

Gonzalo had finally agreed to put Maria and Martin and the entire Almeida family aboard a Baltic ship that would visit London *en route* for her home port. Tavistock felt the void inside him shift as he remembered the parting. Maria's last words to him had been that she loved him and would always love him, but that she knew in her soul she would never see him again.

That had broken his heart, and he had had enough time to dwell on it. After his arrest he had been confined under Don Emilio's orders instead of being sent inside the castle as he had expected. Then Gonzalo told him that Nicolau had tried to sneak back off the ship and he had had to kill him.

Why doesn't Don Emilio use me? Tavistock had asked himself, unable to understand, then, suddenly, when it was almost too late to hope, Don Emilio had produced him and set him to work.

During his captivity Tavistock's hatred for Gonzalo had solidified into a hard mass. He knew now he could afford to mark time and await his chance. Though the castle foundry was working night and day to arm the ships, their efforts would not now affect the fundamental strength of the fleet. The *empresa* was within three weeks of sailing, and they had made only twenty culverins after the new pattern. In a fleet of two hundred, that was negligible – enough to arm only one big ship properly. The months wasted by Don Emilio had cost the King dear. If God granted the opportunity, Tavistock had vowed to make him pay an even greater price.

Only one thing mattered now. To kill Santa Cruz. Without him the *empresa* would lose its impetus and its guiding intelligence. Without him, it would fail. *If only the opportunity would arise.*

Tavistock looked down across the red-tile roofs again and into the street to identify the disturbance. This time it was not a messenger or a provost marshal, but a religious parade. The holy fathers approached, walking solemnly. Their heads were bowed under voluminous hoods, their hands thrust inside loose white vestments that hung down to their feet. At each waist a rosewood crucifix swung. The narrow road cleared respectfully before them, early morning carts moving into side streets, people crossing themselves and pressing back against the whitewashed walls so that the procession could come on without breaking formation.

At the head a monk waved a fuming thurible so that perfumed smoke billowed out to left and right as he walked. Beside him another held aloft the staff and pennant of the Order, a white triangle on which was depicted a crimson heart with golden rays radiating out. Behind came a cadre of twenty-four monks, four abreast, behind them eight pallbearers carrying the gilded coffin over which was spread a white velvet mantle. The bearers were flanked on each side by a single column of eight, and a second block of twenty-four brought up the rear.

One of the monks was chanting, a sad tremulous wail that the others took up in answer.

'Wheyeeee-ee-ee-ee ... Whoaoh-oh-oh-oh ...'

The sound made Tavistock stare. He had never heard any religious chant like it before, but the rhythmic power of it sounded strangely familiar. They must be Flemings, he thought. Flemings or Walloons. Then he saw the hands of the coffin bearers raised high in the flare of a torch, and he saw a sleeve fall away to reveal a tattooed forearm.

Suddenly he knew what the chant was: a work rhythm, sung aboard English ships to accompany the hauling in of heavy cable. *Sweet Jesus, it can't be*, he thought. *It can't be!*

He watched wildly as they came on, passing the castle guard, who admitted the entire procession, respectfully and without question, then they passed out of sight behind the landward battlements. He ran to follow them and found they were coming straight toward the foundry.

Instinct pressed him back against a wall. Then he saw the huge coffin drop down and the monks begin to tear off their vestments. Loaded arms were broken out, hidden swords and axes appeared as if from nowhere. One of the castle guards stumbled round a corner, unprepared, and was hacked down, a hand over his mouth. Then several assailants lit up firebrands. Almost silently, and with great discipline the force split into four separate units and dispersed.

Tavistock mouthed a prayer. Whoever they were they knew the castle well enough to find what they wanted. Already the lead unit was among the foundry buildings, laying fire to the tarred timbers. Someone began to yell. Gunfire cracked out and three of the foundry workers turned and ran back inside, pursued by attackers. Flames began to lick up the outside of the casting shed. Then a huge explosion took off the roof and threw it into the still dark sky, throwing him to the ground. Dazed, he saw a great orange pall mushroom up over him, felt the heat sear his face.

Debris rained all around. When his vision cleared he saw the gates of the citadel slamming shut high above. Troops began pouring from the guardhouse below, their leaders falling as a volley of shot ripped into them. Tavistock watched, shock draining him as the assailants converged on the armoury. They were coming this way. *What about Santa Cruz? What about Gonzalo?* his brain screamed, then something snapped inside his mind. *You can't get at him now the citadel's locked tight! But he must die! He must die!*

He bolted out from his cover, his obsession possessing him completely now. A hail of sniper fire was slicing down among the chaos from the citadel walls, small shot ringing off the walls and cobbles. The foundry had become a roaring furnace, throwing running forms into silhouette against it, and huge, distorted shadows across the yard. Then one of the destroyers saw him and charged after him, a broad cutlass in his hand.

He saw he was trapped.

'No!' he raged at them in his native tongue. 'Stop! You're ruining everything! It's Santa Cruz who must die! Santa Cruz. Don't you see?'

The attacker crashed to a halt, paces from him, his face grimed black and full of fury, his red-leather jerkin stuffed with two wheel lock pistols, the massive silver buckle on his sword strap reflecting the inferno from his chest like a burning heart.

John tensed for the cutlass slash, but there was none. Instead, the sword rang to the ground and he felt his arms seized in a demonic grip.

'John! John! Don't you know me!'

He was paralysed. '*Richard?*'

'I've come for you, John! I've come for you!'

'No! It can't be!' This was madness.

Again the impossible apparition raised its hand to strike, but again the blow failed to come. Instead the demon with Richard's face was blasted back from him, a sniper's ball dead in his heart. He stared at it, then staggered back, slammed down by a heavy blow, and as his eyes found the body again he saw a dozen hell-wraiths descend on it and carry it, fleeing away over the walls that dropped down to the Tagus.

Chapter 27

Richard Tavistock pushed through the rain-soaked crowd and scraped the filth from his boots before following the Secretary's man under the vaulted arch of Whitehall Palace. He was glad that the freezing weather had abated, but the rain had blackened his mood and made his chest twinge where his ribs had been cracked last June in the Lisbon assault.

The sniper's ball had hit him above the heart, but the shot had struck him square on the buckle of his sword strap and the force had spread, breaking ribs and knocking the wind from his sails. His lads had carried him down grapple ropes to the Tagus shore where two captured barques had worked under the walls. It had been a superbly orderly escape with only three men killed and he knew he should feel grateful to be alive, but he had not taken John, nor had he killed him, and at that he felt only shame and huge apprehension.

The new spring was upon them now, and, as if imitating human industry, every stick of living wood in the city had come alive with greening buds. All the signs were for a hot summer, but the pine cones and flocking birds had so far lied: London had never seen such dousings of rain, and the traffic in men and arms had churned her streets into trenches of oozing slime.

'You had a pleasant journey, Captain?' the young man enquired politely.

'Thank you, kindly, but I had a foul journey. The city's awash, with filth and beasts and rainwater and bumpkins gawping at the buildings.'

'Ah, that'll be the Norfolk trained band come here this day from the Brecklands. Few of them have seen two floors in a house in their lives, let alone a royal property.'

'Most have not seen a house at all to look at them, and live in sties by the smell of them. What can my lords be thinking of, to pit such against a Spanish *tercio*?'

'England must as England can, it seems.'

'Aye, so it seems.'

He wiped away the last of the mud from his hands and followed the other up the steps. He had come at Walsingham's urgent request, hoping for news to equal that which had greeted him upon his return from Lisbon in July. Then, he had visited Walsingham to be told how triumphant the rest of Drake's mission had been, and it had gladdened him. Though the folk on his way to town had reported rapturous tales, the truth had not been far short of it. According to Walsingham, Drake had returned four days past Midsummer's Day to an ecstatic reception not wholly in celebration of their handiwork at Cadiz, for after their parting Drake had sailed back towards Cape St Vincent where Portugal's coast turned abruptly east, and there he had led forces ashore to capture the castles of Sagres and Valliera. These commanded the sea lanes from Cadiz to Lisbon and he had waited there a month for Recalde's Biscayan galleons, eager to take them on, until the mean-spirited Borough had panicked and fled home. Left with a depleted fleet, Drake had had no choice but to think of following, but even as he tacked north with that in mind he had miraculously happened upon a great swan: the carrack *San Felipe*, returning from Goa, and laden with East Indian riches.

It was inexplicable, beyond all reason, beyond naming even, save to call it pure chance. But it was not pure chance. Francis's sure sense, he knew, had felt the tide and breathed the salt air and tasted gold. He had *known* of the ivory, the ebony, the silk and calico. Four thousand hundredweight of pepper, twenty thousand pounds' worth of annelle, four hundred fardels of cinnamon, twenty pipes of cloves, a profusion of ambergris, sarcenet, indigo blue, plates of silver and chains of gold . . .

As he was conducted to the Secretary's Whitehall office, Tavistock shook his head in wonder, reflecting again on the divers ways their bold operation had profited the land. Those eighty-seven days had saved a nation – Spanish preparations had been thrown into confusion for three months; all England had taken heart at the news that a fifth part of the Armada was destroyed at Cadiz; and because of the carrack the spoils had been enough to repay the investors handsomely, *and* to swell Her Majesty's coffers by forty thousand pounds. But the year's grace they had bought had been more precious than all the rest heaped together, for though they had obliterated a fifth, still four fifths of the monstrous enterprise remained, and, like a wounded boar, was now the more dangerous for its injuries.

His mood deepened further as he considered again the failure of his brother's rescue. The shock of that moment when he and John had faced each other still haunted him.

He waited outside the Secretary's guarded door, noticing how security had tightened since his last visit. They took away his sword, then he was thoroughly searched for concealed weapons. Even so, the guards missed the curved knife hidden in the top fold of his right thigh boot, and he surrendered it angrily to the sergeant, the better to underscore the lesson.

On his return eight months ago, Anne had met him, and that night they had whispered together in the semi-darkness. She had seen the black bruising across his chest and touched her finger to the twisted silver buckle where the musket ball had been, and he had felt the shiver run through her.

'I hated to see you leave,' she told him, dewy-eyed in the feather bed. 'I looked at the flags and the streamers flying about your *Antelope*, and the sails billowing and your men hauling on ropes and I was sure your ship must sink and you'd be killed and we'd never be together again like this.'

'Ah, but there's a tide only a mariner knows,' he had told her, putting his hand to his chest. 'A tide in here. To know what to do. When to do. How to do. If a man feels it as I feel it, as Francis feels it, and he takes good heed, then he can do no wrong.'

'Reckless man! They nearly shot you through!'

'Yet am I shot through?'

'Silly ocean superstitions!'

'I tell you, Anne, it's no hap that all mariners believe alike. On the ocean the way is clear. When a man lives true to his inner tide, then he actions Fate instead of being at its whim.'

'I know you believe that, Richard, and I have not loved you so long without feeling somewhat a tide within you, but still your going away frightens me. I can't help it.'

'There,' he said tenderly, taking the buckle from her. This is the proof of what I believe, he thought. The belief that has sustained me. He told her, 'Anything but a ricochet would have had the power to penetrate through, and the buckle in any other place would have exposed me. So that the shot hit me at all is a mystery to me. Perhaps it was never intended that I remove John from Lisbon.'

She buried her face in the pillow. 'Promise me you'll never sail away again. Restore your vow to me. *Please*.'

'I cannot.'

'I love you.' Her voice was suddenly lost.

'And I you.'

'Then promise me. You've done enough. Stay ashore.'

'That's not my fate.'

'Make it so, Richard. I beg you.'

He had put his head back, studying the shades of moonlight on rippling water that dappled the ceiling, feeling also the old wound in his shoulder, the one he had taken away from San Juan de Ulua. 'There's a battle coming to make all others that have gone before seem but small play. It's the Armageddon your father foresaw twenty years ago. I must to sea just once more, my love. Once more, then I'll be yours.'

But he had waited out the winter ashore while his cracked ribs healed. The season had seen tremendous mobilisation, and by spring almost the entire eligible population of the south had been put under arms. Huge companies of men and boys drilling with reaping hooks and sticks of wood had been marshalled together. Units of troops, uniformed and trained but only marginally better equipped, had been brought to all the strategic places where a landing was suspected. And throughout that time Tavistock had had frequent cause to wonder at the result if a landing were made.

He knew with a turmoiled heart that that prospect had been heightened by the dereliction he had shown at Lisbon.

'I could not have killed him,' he had confessed to Anne in torment at his failure. 'I stood as close as we stand now, my blade in my hand and still I know I could not have done it.'

'You are the purer man for that.'

'Do you think so?'

'No man could kill his only brother and come away unstained.'

'But if he wouldn't follow? If he had *chosen* not to come away? My promise was to kill him.'

'Yet your hand would have been stayed.'

'Aye, but how many others shall die because of it?'

'That's John's fate, perhaps. And yours.'

Now he had come at the summons from Walsingham's busy pen. He had come straightway to Whitehall and as the door opened he saw the weary face of the Secretary lighten.

'The finest news, Richard! The finest news yet!'

Tavistock's spirits leapt. 'How so?'

Walsingham fixed him with a wonder-filled gaze. 'It was no work of mine. Ah, God be praised for reaching down His finger and plucking him from Lisbon at this time.'

The pealing of bells in the distance and the sounds of marching men in the streets below filled the room.

Tavistock's voice rose. 'Plucking who, Mister Secretary? *Plucking who from Lisbon?*'

'The one who we have most feared, Richard. The white shark. Oh, the ruination at Cadiz must have broken his heart like a potter's vessel! Their Admiral, the great danger to us – Santa Cruz is dead.'

'Don Emilio is very pleased with what you've done, Juan,' Gonzalo said, examining the ruby light within a glass of port.

John Tavistock faced him, hating him more completely than he had hated anyone in his life. To have killed him now would have given his heart the same rest that the murder of Santa Cruz might have given his mind. He remembered the day he had thrown Gonzalo down in a Mexican village, his hands around his throat, choking the life from him. How sweet that would be now, he thought. How sweet and how just. You're filth.

'Yes, he's very pleased. A hundred culverins, and more to come before we sail. Enough to destroy the English fleet, don't you think?'

'Perhaps, Excellency.'

He longed to fall upon the man. With Santa Cruz dead what did his own life matter? Now there was no reason to live. No reason to carry on making guns for Spain.

He forced himself to make Gonzalo the offer. 'Excellency, might I ask a favour of Don Emilio?'

'A favour?' Gonzalo's surprise and amusement were rich. 'I don't think he owes you any favours.'

'Still, I should like to ask him.'

'Ask him what?'

'I should like ... I should like to sail with you to England.'

Throughout the long winter, Tavistock had suffered the agony of knowing he had made a fatal mistake. Ever he had watched for his chance to gain entry to the citadel, but there had been no way to get close to Santa Cruz. One day he had glimpsed the Admiral coming into the castle, another time standing on the battlements high above, but he was not permitted to leave the area of the foundry and Santa Cruz never visited it, except once in great company to see what damage the English had wrought in their impudent raid.

The fires of that harrowing night had burned long and bright in Tavistock's memory. He had hidden his head, pressed into a star niche of the citadel wall, as the massive series of explosions had shaken the entire fortress to its roots. It had been thunderous enough to waken all of Portugal.

By noon the soldiers had damped the embers, and he had staggered among the smoking ruins, seeing the timbers of the boring machine, the trestles, the moulds, everything consumed and reduced to charcoal. The explosions had been the wrecking of the culverins, fifteen of them blown to murdering shards by a triple charge of powder and an oversized ball hammered tight into the muzzle. The English had fled long before the inferno had touched them off.

It had been a brave jaunt, and a hero's gesture, but it had cost his brother his life, and for what? Tavistock knew now the loss of fifteen culverins was less than an incidental damage to the Spanish effort. They would sail with a thousand guns now, for the news had escaped that very afternoon that Cadiz had been wrecked by El Draque and another year must elapse before they might sail.

A year to rebuild the foundry and the machines. A year to use his techniques in a dozen other foundries. A year to make a thousand culverins. With a thousand culverins the *empresa* must succeed, and there was no way to stop it. He could have thrown himself head first off the castle wall at low tide, but it would have achieved nothing. The culverins would still be made. He had lived to kill Santa Cruz. Only that. And now Santa Cruz was dead.

'England?' Gonzalo said. 'Why should Don Emilio agree to that?'

'It is the land of my birth, Excellency. I would see it again before I die. I would ... help to liberate it. I am a gunner and no man knows better than I how to lay a culverin. Do you remember the day on your father's estate when I demonstrated my skill?'

'Yes.' Gonzalo's smile disappeared. 'Yes. But you're English. And I don't trust you.' I hate you, he thought. Because you defiled my sister, and because you stole her.

'Don't I deserve some trust? I offered my services to you. I did not go with the English raiders when I had the opportunity.'

'We have enough adequate gunners,' Gonzalo said, toying with him. Privately he was trying to hide his bitter disappointment. The news from Madrid had been a total calamity and his temper was close to breaking point. It had been made even more fragile by Don Emilio's rage at the King's perfidy, and Tavistock's asking for favours was the last straw. Don Emilio might want the scum preserved, he thought, but I don't. I want to see him pay for his crimes. Perhaps it's time I began to distance myself from Don Emilio. After all the favours I've done him ... Holy Virgin, there's no justice! I didn't poison Santa Cruz in order to see a nobody appointed commander-in-chief! Medina-Sidonia? *Who is he?* A Guzman and a seventh Duke, yes, but what else? A sheep! And hardly qualified to lead the *empresa*! Philip's gone completely insane at last.

He turned to Tavistock, visibly angry now. 'You gave yourself up in the hope of protecting Maria and the Almeida man. And you were not taken by the English because they did not know you were here.'

Tavistock swallowed down the hard knot of bile in his throat and bowed his head humbly. He knew from Gonzalo's reactions that as soon as the last cascabel of the last culverin was polished he would have him tortured, just as he had had Nicolau tortured, unless he found a reason to stop him. Gonzalo's very presence inflamed and disgusted him, but he knew he had to try once more to get himself aboard the *San Salvador*.

'Excellency, you're wrong about the raiders. They came for me particularly. They knew exactly where I was because Maria told them.'

'*She told them?*'

'She's in England. And only I can tell you where.'

All morning the signallers had struggled to keep the beacon's tinder dry but the rain lashed the hilltop with a fury that sapped their strength and rattled the tarpaulins they had thrown over it. From here the party of soldiers and high-ranking men could see the compass's four quarters round, all of it indistinct under grey rags of cloud: to the south was the open Channel, dotted with sail, a curtain of English lookouts flying before the gale; to westward the pale arc of Lyme Bay, Chesil Bank and, seventy miles beyond, Plymouth; to eastward St Aldhelm's Head, and seventy miles beyond, Portsmouth; to landward there was only

England's green and moody sweep, sparse-populated, naked to the enemy.

All present felt that nakedness keenly. News had come today that, at last, and at full strength, the Armada had put to sea.

Tavistock listened as the Puritan preacher, John Law, saturnine, long-faced and all in black, thrust out his Bible, the wind tearing at its leaves. 'O Lord God, heavenly Father, The Lord of Hosts, without whose providence nothing proceedeth, bless Thou our Queen and all her forces by land and sea. Grant all her people one heart, one mind and one strength, to defend her person, her kingdom and Thy true religion. Give unto all her Council and Captains Thy wisdom, wariness and courage, that they may speedily prevent the devices and valiantly withstand the forces of the enemy. We crave this in Thy mercy, O heavenly Father, for the precious death of Thy dear son, Jesus Christ. Amen.'

Lord Charles Howard, Lord High Admiral of England, white-bearded and in his fifty-third year, huddled tighter under the sodden canopy. For almost half a year he had held supreme command for both naval and military preparations. Now the decision was his how to best dispose the fleet. He turned to Tavistock.

'I think the second plan the better. We must have two squadrons, Lord Seymour's at Dover to dissuade the opportunism of Parma, but our main force must lie at Portsmouth to protect our most obvious weakness, the Isle of Wight.'

'Let Isle of Wight fend for itself, my lord!' Drake said, mindless of the assembled soldiery. 'Let us go down to Spain as we did before. On the open sea we'll massacre them, and turn them around before ever they set eyes upon our shore!'

'And if you miss them? What then? No, Sir Francis, I can't risk that.'

'Did we miss them last time?'

'Then they were defenceless, tied up in harbour!'

'The Spaniards can come but one way!'

'If we should lose them in the Bay of Biscay – I cannot risk it!'

'God save us,' Drake barked bitterly towards the preacherman. 'For our ships will not.'

Tavistock felt the worry that was eating at them all. According to Walsingham's spies, the fleet the Spanish had finally put to sea was vast, and with John's aid its armament was likely to be considerable. He repented his failure once again as he took the Lord Admiral's elbow. 'Good my lord, at least have this from me. Three squadrons: Drake's at Plymouth, yourself at Portsmouth and, as you rightly say, leave Lord Seymour to guard the Narrows. A compromise, eh?'

'I'll think on it.'

'Better think fast, my lord,' Drake said from a distance, but the wind carried the words away.

Tavistock could see his own breath steaming in what should have been high summer. Another blast bit into them.

'June, and will you look at it!' Howard said bleakly.

'This is fine weather, my lord!'

'Fine weather for ducks!'

'Aye, and Drakes too, I'd say.'

Howard looked up miserably. 'I don't see why. It's equally wet on the deck of the *Revenge* as it is here on this Godforsaken hilltop.'

'God has not forsaken us.'

Howard turned away, his responsibilities acid-etching his face. Tavistock slapped his back heavily. Water trickled down his own leathery face and spangled his beard like garden cobwebs. He knew that a Channel storm to scatter the Spanish fleet in hostile waters was their only real hope. 'Aye, Lord Howard,' he said, 'if God be an Englishman, then it will rain and rain this summer and we shall all be most glad of it.'

The drumming to quarters began late Friday afternoon of the twenty-ninth day of July, by Spanish reckoning. Aboard the *San Martin* the Duke unfurled the standard of the crucifix, the same the Pope had blessed, and signalled to his fleet. At once, the *San Salvador*'s sailors began flying to their stations, soldiers packed the waist and took positions along the high castles fore and aft. John Tavistock ran to the gunwale, his pulse beating. Ahead he saw what could only be the Lizard. The *empresa* had come upon England.

The fleet had departed Lisbon on the last evening tide in May. That was eight weeks past, and Tavistock had watched the priests prepare their way with bread and wine each Sunday, and he had eaten of it with them, knowing each time he ate that a greater burden of guilt was upon him.

On the first day of their voyage, Don Emilio, with Gonzalo at his side, had delivered them the diatribe. 'Noble soldiers, we sail to glory. We sail to overthrow a most vile Englishwoman. We sail to release from her bondage those in England who still hold to the Faith. And we sail to establish once again the rule of a worthy Prince. Have no fear, then, but hold in your hearts the expectation of victory. For we are God's sword and we shall not be denied. Glory to God who has kept his Grace from the heretics! Glory to His Holy Church, which the heretics have failed to stamp out! Glory to the Holy Saints, who ride with us! Take heart, for you are the blessed soldiers of the Lord, and your reward in heaven shall be a thousand-fold. Brave soldiers, Spain shall have the victory. God is with us, and therefore we cannot fail.'

Tavistock had observed the *San Salvador*'s mariners throughout the harangue. He saw the way they resented Don Emilio for addressing only the soldiers, and looked to the quarrelsome German and Italian mercenaries who had barely understood the speech. There had been not a single word to encourage the poor Spanish sailor.

The *San Salvador* was a great ship of nine hundred and sixty tons,

Almirante, or vice-flagship, of the Guipuzcoan Squadron. Great blue-and -gold painted towers rose up from her; eight turrets, like those of a Castilian fortress, overhung her flanks; a capacious after-gallery occupied the three sides of her stern. On her poop and quarterdeck Don Emilio and his lieutenants strutted proudly in their burnished armour, and aloft she flew huge rippling flags, stripes and St Andrew's crosses in yellow and in red. Across vast, painted sails, sunbursts, eagles and shields proclaimed the Faith and the nobility of the Empire; brilliant gildings and carvings crusted her stern and her beakhead and when the wind blew, coloured streamers a hundred feet long writhed out to leeward. But her outward finery belied the truth.

The *San Salvador*'s complement was sixty-four mariners and three hundred and twenty soldiers. For most of the voyage her cargo of troops had suffered between decks. They had wallowed in their own filth, swapping lice and contagions, suffering intense and unending sea-sickness and paying bodily for the fierce Candia and Condado wines they had drunk on their departure.

Tavistock had staked his claim to a space between the fourth and fifth larboard culverins in the ship's waist. Though open to the weather, the gunwale had protected him from the wind and a canvas awning rigged at night had kept the rain off. He knew, as did the rest of the crew, that summer nights under the open sky would be preferable to the hell below.

By the time they reached the forty-second parallel the stench issuing from the ship's bowels had been stomach-turning.

'Better a place on the weather side, freshened by the prevailing westerlies than diseased air, eh, Juan?' Garcia, chief gunner, had got up onto the upturned shot tray beside him. He picked a wad of pork fat off his dish and scooped up a mass of rice with it before putting it into his mouth.

'That's right enough, Señor Garcia.'

'Want some?' Garcia had asked, a rank goat smell enveloping him. 'Courtesy of Luis de Vega and Diego the quartermaster.'

Tavistock showed his surprise. Rations were strictly limited, and he had seen Garcia eat once already today.

'Here. Take it.'

'Whose is it?'

'*Cabron!* It's mine, of course!' He shoved another lump of salt pork into his mouth. 'Why not? Luis de Vega won't be needing this, or anything else, where he's gone.'

'Gone?'

'He's dead.' Garcia shrugged. 'Yesterday. He never woke from the flogging.'

'Flogging? No one told me.'

'No one may discuss punishments. General Orders, eh?'

'It's General Orders to report a death.'

'You report it if you like, but I don't recommend it. De Vega was flogged for spitting at a nobleman's boots.'

'Flogged for that?'

'It's true. I saw it myself. He was just clearing his throat, but Don Emilio's man took it the wrong way.'

'Which one?'

Garcia swallowed another mouthful and inclined his head toward the poop. 'That bastard de Escovedo, of course. Come on, eat. And don't worry about Diego, the quartermaster's in on it. Joachim!'

The hatred Tavistock nursed for his wife's brother had bubbled up uncontrollably as the surly German gun captain came across and took a pork rib.

'What's the matter? You don't eat also?' Joachim said.

'Yes. Take a rib, Juan,' Garcia told him again, thrusting out the dish. 'Those bastard soldiers steal what they like. Why not us, eh? Gunners need to eat, without us they'll get nowhere.'

'No one knows how long it will be before we get ashore again,' Joachim said darkly. 'Not even our Generals.'

Tavistock recalled the look on Don Emilio's face after his last meeting with Medina-Sidonia. The Duke had invited his commanders aboard the flagship *San Martin* and sent them away tight-lipped and furious. Tavistock had speculated about the meeting but it had been difficult to imagine what had been said. The following day, the crewmen had been even less willing to get in Gonzalo's way; clearly, whatever had been decided, Don Emilio had not agreed with it.

Rumours had run riot through the ship: an Isle of Wight landing had been intended, and it was that which had been cancelled. Medina-Sidonia had ordered a surprise attack on Plymouth by the Biscay Squadron to pay El Draque back for Cadiz. Even that the whole enterprise was a gigantic ruse and they were going to land secretly on the Normandy coast before marching on Paris. The German was right, he thought, no one knew where they were going.

Since leaving Lisbon rough weather had battered them. Strong northwesterlies had forced them south the moment the galleys had towed them beyond the safety of the Tagus. One of the *urcas*, the *David Chico*, was dismasted and returned to port. By mid June the storms had blown themselves out and the winds had backed southerly. Arevalo, the Pilot, told him they were still standing in less than forty degrees, scarcely further north than when they had begun. Don Emilio's temper had flashed white at their lack of progress, while at his back the mariners he despised began to make jokes about the speech he had delivered to them about God's will being done.

'If it's God's will that we sail to England, why doesn't He give us southerlies?' Arevalo had grumbled, but under his breath so that none of the military men heard him.

At sea the ports were sealed tight, and the between decks grew even

more noisome. What light and air there had been was now excluded
and those quartered below were packed tighter than pork junk in a
barrel. The mariners, though daily abused, were now able to make good
their dignity at the expense of the haughty men which high seas had
turned into groaning, green-faced beggars.

After two weeks they had begun to run before the wind, passing Cape
Finisterre. Orders had emanated from the *San Martin* that the Duke
wanted the ships to clear for action, and so they had, jettisoning almost
everything that was not strictly necessary aboard a fighting ship. The
sailors complained, none able to understand why the Duke had made
this order.

'We shall sail from here as if we were in the presence of the enemy,'
Arevalo had repeated, spitting out his scorn. 'What does he think this
is? A castle siege?'

And Tavistock had nodded in agreement. 'You think he's worried
about the English intercepting us so far south?'

'If he does he's a fool.'

'Why doesn't Don Emilio come out?'

'He's sick as a puppy-dog, like all the rest of them,' Arevalo grunted.
'I can't wait to get at the English. They're the real cause of this war. I
hate them and I want to see them burn.'

Then, as soon as the weather had turned noticeably cooler, Tavistock
had gone down to inspect the lower holds with Diego de Mallara, the
quartermaster.

'Those bastard Portuguese! Sorry Garcia, but that's the last of the
extra rations. Look at these water casks! Half of them are leaking at the
seams. We're down to a pint a day for each man already. And if the
water casks are leaking what's the food going to be like? If air gets in
it'll rot.'

'Those bastard merchants in Lisbon have shafted us.'

They smelled the stench as a barrel of salt pork was broached.

'That's tainted flesh, all right!'

'Yes! Look, I've seen that before. Rot gas bubbles out of the meat
and the pressure bursts the wood. The Portuguese must have pickled it
all in piss.'

'What if it's like this aboard the other ships?' Tavistock had said as
they frantically unearthed more and more spoiled provisions.

'Madonna! The smell! The Duke'll have to put in at Corunna, now,
whatever the King orders.'

'You think he'll disobey the King?' another had asked.

A group of mariners had begun to crowd at the hatch, curiosity at
the reek overcoming them.

'He'll have to!'

'He'll see us starve first.'

'I hope they all fester in Hell! Especially Gonzalo de Escovedo.'

'God damn those Portuguese.'

'It wasn't the Portuguese who said it was God's will that we invade England,' a topman said.

'What do you mean by that, scum?' Garcia said.

'Just that I pity the English when we come upon them. They'll keel over at the stink.'

'Get aloft, the lot of you! Or I'll have your backs in tatters!' Garcia had slapped down the leaking barrel angrily and left them, and Tavistock had stared in disgust at the rotted food. Though half the losses were due to the poor quality of the barrels, the rest, he liked to believe, was the vengeance of Nicolau Almeida's friends and fellow merchants.

So, three weeks out from Lisbon and they had had to revictual at Corunna, losing a whole month. The *Gobernador* of Galicia, the Marquis de Cerralvo, had been contacted and the fleet had gathered, half in the shelter of the harbour, half remaining outside. But that night a violent storm had hit the town and the ships outside had been carried away to the west. The *San Salvador* herself had made port, and remained there another month until the ships that had been scattered were recovered and replenished.

Now, Tavistock watched the Cornish coast rise steadily from the sea, recalling the panic that had flooded Corunna the night before their departure. Biscay fishermen had come ashore with the absurd story that El Draque was bearing down on them with fifty sail a mere twenty leagues to the north. Perhaps it had been that which had decided the Duke to stand out from port, Tavistock thought, perhaps he had been encouraged by the sudden southerly that had sprung up, perhaps he had been frighted by the King's urgent letters. It was then that Arevalo the Pilot had told him that the rumour about the cancellation of the Isle of Wight landing had been correct.

When the noon bell sounded, Tavistock was still gazing at the massed fleet ranged around him, watching them form into their defensive disposition. Close by stood the *Espíritu Santo*, named after the ship that had brought Philip to England, the huge galleon *Florencia*, and the galleasses *Gerona* and *San Lorenzo*. To the east, stood Don Alonso de Leyva's *La Rata Encoronada* and beyond her the flag of the Levantines, *La Regazona*. On the far side the *Nuestra Señora del Rosario*, Pedro de Valdes's flagship, mightiest and newest of the Andalusian galleons, and the *Santa Catalina* beside her.

Tavistock saw that the powerful warships were manoeuvring into two groups, following what must have been Santa Cruz's original battle plan, tipping the cusps of the fleet with steel. The *Santa Ana* of Miguel de Oquendo's Guipuzcoans, the Portuguese, *San Luis*, and the four vast battleships of the Duke's van, the *San Marcos, San Mateo, San Felipe* and his own *San Martin*. Despite all the setbacks and all the delays, all the shortcomings, the sabotage and the holocaust of Cadiz, the Armada was still the most magnificent force; the greatest that had ever to put to sea. Tavistock knew there was nothing in England that could hope to stop it so long as the great ships clung together.

Above, on the quarterdeck, Gonzalo, shining in immaculate war gear, watched the gathering host with a half-smile. Don Emilio was a distant figure, austere and solitary on the high poop. Both, in their way, were paragons of *hidalgo* virtue, haughty, proud, inflexible, completely indifferent to the suffering of their men and totally convinced of Spain's coming victory. Tavistock forced himself to look away, hating with an ice cold anger the men who had shaped his life. I've waited to repay you for so very long, he thought grimly, turning his broaching spike over in his palm. I pray to God that hour will come soon.

At the break of the same day, in English reckoning the nineteenth day of July, Captain Thomas Fleming, in a ship bought from the spoils of five years' marauding in the Caribbean under Richard Tavistock, emerged from a thinning fogbank a hundred miles off the Lizard to discover a forest of masts ranged in a loose crescent, surrounding him.

Momentarily paralysed by terror, the Scotsman rubbed at his eyes and then told his helmsman to run swiftly for port. By four of the clock that afternoon he was plunging across Plymouth Hoe with a tale that the Spanish invasion force was no more than ten leagues away.

Behind him the town was in uproar. Fleming found the city dignitaries in a gala sporting party arranged by the Mayor of Plymouth for his naval guests: Ralegh, Grenville, Frobisher, the Hawkins family, all were present. Tavistock and Drake peak-bearded and befrilled stood out on the bowling green, in the middle of a doubles match with Lord Howard and the tough Yorkshireman, Martin Frobisher.

'It's the Dons! The Dons are upon us with a thousand sail! I swear it!'

Tavistock prepared to send his bowl across the lawn, but the Lord Admiral stepped across his line in hot anxiety.

He called after him, 'My lord – the match?'

'God's blood! The Spaniards are upon us! They're seeking to bottle us up in the Sound and they have the guns to do it!'

The aghast silence became a storm of tongues, but it was Drake's voice that rose above them all when the umpire tried to pick up the Vice-Admiral's best placed wood of the day.

He ran his steel halfway out of its scabbard and hissed, 'Touch that ball and I'll take your hand off!' Turning to Tavistock, nonplussed at Howard's agitation, he said, 'The tide doesn't turn for two hours yet. Even if Fleming's right there's still time to play out the match.' But the Admiral was already hurrying away.

Tavistock's anxiety at the prospect of an Armada as heavily armed with culverins as the English fleet had reached its peak. He had persuaded Howard to concentrate his own and Drake's squadrons together at Plymouth, and in the weeks following the Admiral had looked daily for the Spanish, his temper quietly fraying. Then news had come of the

Armada's halt at Corunna. Instantly both Tavistock and Drake had pressed their case to the Council. Burleigh, now readmitted to the Queen's confidence and freed from all pretences, had obtained from her an order to permit the fleet to follow the attack plan, and through most of July they had been beating about in the Bay of Biscay, hoping desperately to catch the great fleet unprepared once again. As he watched Howard making way for the town, Tavistock recalled ruefully how the English fleet had got to within twenty leagues of the Spanish coast before a contrary wind had thrown them back.

'We'll call it a draw, then,' Frobisher said drily, mindful of the wager that rode on the game.

'A draw?' Drake said. 'There isn't such a thing.'

By a quarter after four the Hoe was deserted. The south-westerly wind favoured the attack, and England's trim ships had to be warped out of harbour. Tavistock went aboard the *Antelope* at the height of the flood tide and came athwart St Nicholas's Island before sundown. All around the Cattewater vessels were sliding slowly toward the open sea. Howard's *Ark*, renamed the *Ark Royal* after Her Majesty had used some of the profits from the Cadiz mission to purchase her, cruised forth, followed by the *Elizabeth Jonas*, the *Leicester* and the *Swallow*. Then came George Beeston's *Dreadnought*, in company with the three other Queen's ships, the ones that had blasted their way into and out of Cadiz: *Elizabeth Bonaventure*, the *Golden Lion* and the *Rainbow*. Hawkins's *Victory*, eight hundred tons and bristling with sixty-four guns, was coming out to meet Drake in his *Revenge*. Tom Fenner's *Nonpareil* and Robert Crosse's *Hope* both accompanied *Antelope*. Never had such a salt-bitten and sea-wary crew of men been brought together, and Tavistock felt the tide in his heart surge at the sight of them.

As night fell, the company of English ships escaped Plymouth Sound, reaching open water unseen by Spanish eyes, and during the night Richard Tavistock's squadron stole silently to windward, to begin tentatively snapping at the heels of the giant.

When the next day dawned, Lord Howard's pinnace, the *Disdain*, approached the Spanish flag and gave the Duke defiance as the chivalric code required. Then Howard led his line into battle against de Leyva's squadron. The fighting was reserved and cautious, Howard's line never daring to close with the Spanish. At one point, by chance, they managed to isolate the *San Juan de Portugal*, and like a great bear surrounded by vicious pit dogs, they sent themselves against her, putting two shots through her mainmast, and it gave Tavistock leave to hope.

By end of the second day it became clear to him that they were in great jeopardy. If they sailed to leeward they would be destroyed, and if they remained to windward and westward, the Armada's stately progress up Channel would continue virtually unhindered. He thought of the *San Juan de Portugal* and decided he must press his attack more forcefully, risking himself within range of the heavy, but short-range periers and ship-smasher cannons. One English ship, he reasoned, sailing alone and unattached, might drive into the enemy and detach a galleon for the others to fall upon. It was desperate, and it was suicidally dangerous, but something had to be tried.

He thought darkly of his promise to Anne as the third day began to dawn. Do or die, he had said, this would be his last voyage. And today was the day they would find out whose forebodings had been correct.

John Tavistock had seen the small black-and-white flag at the English ship's sternpost and it had filled him with a tremendous urgency. As the ship closed he ordered the reload and looked desperately for Joachim's return. He was sure at last that his chance had come.

The German had gone below to the *San Salvador*'s aft powder store. He held the keys, while Garcia was fully occupied supervising the forward magazine, and Garcia had ordered him below to augment the powder on deck. He knew that if the coming attack was as sharp as those of the last two days, they would certainly need it.

The same ferocious vessel that had attacked the *San Juan de Portugal* was closing on them now, and Tavistock looked again at her black flag, confirming the flaming hope that the first sight of it had raised up in him. Yes! There was no doubt. It surely was a black field upon which stood out a pure white device in perfect symmetry – antlers. But Richard's ship was heading straight down the barrels of the most dangerous culverins in the fleet.

Joachim returned with a keg of powder. Tavistock took it and set it down. He turned his back to cover his actions as he did so. In his hand was a sponge that had been soaking in the vinegar pail.

He slipped it under the keg. Then, as he set about broaching the powder he took the first sample on his fingertips and tasted it. His brows knit and he tilted the keg up, at the same time flicking the sponge out through the gun port.

'This powder's damp,' he said, standing.

'Damp?' Joachim asked, his Spanish struggling under a thick south German accent.

'Yes, damp! *Fusht! Nass!* You can't smell it?' He thrust a pinch of the first-grade nitrous powder under the man's nose. 'And look here – there's water coming out of the keg. It stinks of piss!'

'But – it can't be!' The humourless surprise on the German's face showed him at a loss to explain the facts.

Praying that the German would defer to his expert knowledge, Tavistock ventured himself angrily, 'Can't be? But it is! *Good God*, if you've been pissing in the magazine, Garcia will have you flayed!'

'Keep down your voice! You think I'm a fool? I don't piss on the powder.'

'Somebody has. And there's only you and Garcia been in there since we left Corunna.'

'I . . . Maybe sea water getting in.'

'You'd better find out. If Garcia finds out –' He pursed his lips at the consequences.

Joachim was aghast. He cast about him secretively, turning the stares of the others away, then examined the wet ring on the deck and the underside of the keg. He looked up, watching the onrushing English ship, shivered by the broadside that crashed out at her. Finally he said, 'Come with me.'

Tavistock felt a spear of exhilaration. He picked up a caulking hammer and followed, but when they were only halfway across the deck a groaning began in the rigging and the despairing yells of the mariners, like witnesses to a calamity, rose to a crescendo. Joachim ran back, following the line of their eyes, and saw that the Englishman had sheered away, forcing Pedro de Valdes's flagship, the *Nuestra Señora del Rosario*, to take sudden evasive action, but she had crossed the bows of another Andalusian, carrying away her bowsprit in the collision. Meanwhile, Richard's ship was tacking round to press home his attack. He darted an anxious glance toward Garcia who was striding along his guns, urging his crews to greater speed, then to Gonzalo and Don Emilio who had been brought out onto the poop by Don Pedro's accident.

'Joachim!'

'I'm coming.'

They went below, Joachim carrying the dampened keg close to his chest. The guard admitted them both to the aftercastle on sight, and they rattled down the two steep flights to the gloom of the powder store. The German twisted his keys in the big iron door. No tallow glim was allowed here, not even a cased lantern, and the only light was the square of overcast at the top of the companionways. It would make looking for a nonexistent leak all the more difficult.

The magazine sill was built up a foot or so and the door edge sealed with waxed canvas to prevent the water that found its way down here from getting in. Its walls were of solid oak, two feet thick. The German stepped inside and bent to put the keg down. 'Show me where you think –'

Tavistock's hammer crashed down across the back of his neck. He hit him again with dispassionate force, this time on the crown of his head as he staggered, and then he lay still, bleeding from ear and nose. Immediately, Tavistock took up the keg and began to calculate the time he would need to get up the steps. Ten seconds to be on deck and three more to be over the side. No room for error.

He split open two more of the kegs and emptied their contents in a heap over the heart of the store. To ignite it he needed time. A trail of powder half an inch wide burned at anywhere between three and ten feet per second, depending on its moisture content. Less than half an inch and the risk of failure due to damp or inert grains increased unacceptably. There wasn't space to zig-zag a safe hundred-foot trail. His mind raced as he tried to accommodate the problem.

Another powerful broadside blasted from the starboard culverins. Soon they would be taking hits from the English ship. What can I do? Any moment now they'll miss me. They'll certainly miss Joachim. It's a hanging offence to desert battle stations so they'll be looking out for him.

He crouched low, hugging the keg tight, stared up the companionway. The guard was still standing, arms folded, back to him. Please God, tell me what to do. Concentrate. Think. Think! What's possible? Ten to fifteen seconds is a minimum. The only sure way's to use a length of match, but I've only got six inches of it here. It burns too slow and it'll risk discovery, unless . . .

Jesus, yes! You've got Joachim's keys!

He examined the beam just above his head. It was smooth and offered no means of attachment. How can I hang the match so it falls right? What if it bounces and rolls away? It must be foolproof. I've got to be certain.

He looked at the motionless German and a hair-raising solution bloomed. Quickly, he propped the bloodied body upright and arranged the contents of the open keg beside him. Then he stripped off the German's belt and hammered the buckle pin into the low rafter so that it hung down. He took his length of match and threaded it through the last hole, and rubbed a little powder from the broached keg on the end of it, then he took out flint and iron and, with grim curses on his tongue, sparked it in his cupped hand, carefully kindling it up, blowing lightly and regularly on it. Then he touched the smouldering end to a point three inches up the match until it began to glow red also.

His neck hackled with a deep-seated fear. Everything he was doing flew in the face of the safe habits and prohibitions of a lifetime. He tried desperately to calm himself, knowing that ten tons of kegged powder stood all around him. He let the burning match hang for a while, studying the extent of its pendulum movement. He watched until he was satisfied that the burned-through end must fall into the powder however the ship heeled.

A sudden pang of terror overcame him and he began to tremble. My knees are going, he thought. What if my knees go? Joachim's inert body lolled horribly as he watched, then the universe blinked out. A bang had torn him away from the mesmeric sight. The door had been swinging ahead of him as the ship rolled and pitched. It had slammed noisily. He twisted round in utter blackness. Only the smouldering match was visible now; only those two swaying red points existed in the whole universe. Where was the door? Where was it? As his hands groped out blindly they touched cold iron. He began to claw furiously at its edge

in the pitch blackness, but his nails could make no purchase. The door
was stuck fast.

'Jesus Christ! Help me!' he shouted, giving way to panic. He pulled
the hammer from his belt and then he realised that the door opened
outwards. He heaved his shoulder blindly forward and burst out into
the cold grey light. Gripping the rope handholds he pulled himself up
the companionway, but it was as if his body was made of lead and his
feet were held fast on the treads. He forced himself up, painfully, one
step at a time, and when he got to the gun deck men were peering down
at him anxiously. He tried to make a reassuring face at them, but he
was shaking and he was aware of how ghastly his smile must be.

The guard turned. 'You! Where's the other one? Two of you went
down.'

Another deafening broadside crashed out from the larboard guns.

'He's there, look.'

Tavistock looked up at where Don Emilio and Gonzalo stood together
on the poop. He took a deep breath and, when the guard bent to peer
below after Joachim, he took two steps towards him and brought the
hammer down on his head. The guard's body pitched into the gloom
soundlessly until he hit bottom.

Three men saw him do it. They broke away from their stations
instantly, yelling as they came at him. He leapt for the rail, hauled
himself onto the upper gun deck and began to make for the side.

'Stop him!'

'Madonna, somebody take him!'

'He's gone mad!'

His own gun crews were before him, barring his way. Garcia's face
was angry and uncomprehending, and he threw himself at the man with
all the force he could manage.

Richard Tavistock pressed home the attack furiously against the *San
Salvador*. She was vice-flagship of the Guipuzcoan Squadron, and almost
three times the tonnage of his own ship. Her armament was heavy and
accurate and the *Antelope* had taken grievous wounds from her in her
attempt to close.

Tavistock gritted his teeth and held his course, heartsick that
Howard's formal strategy had not worked. His impatience had burst
out yesterday. Twice Tavistock's sailing master had warned him of the
folly of sailing within range of the *San Salvador*'s culverin shots.

'She's a sharp one, sir, and no mistake. And though we're handy we'll
not live long if you bring us once more under those roarers.'

'Hold your helm steady, Master,' he had shouted back, knowing that
they had no choice.

As the vast bulk of the thousand tonner grew ahead, he ordered the
antlers broken out at the stern. Doubtless there were enough Spanish
veterans aboard to understand and respect it. Then he had seen the

Andalusian, *Rosario*, eleven or twelve hundred tons of her, standing in, and he had tied the Spaniard's wake in a reef knot and thrown her into collision with two ships so that she lost her bowsprit and forestay.

And so they ran on, the decks jumping with the shocks of their broadsides. *Five hundred paces.* This adversary's the equal of any in the Armada. *Four hundred paces.* I'll blow her to bits and show Lord Charles Howard the way. *Three hundred paces.* And if we die, we'll have died with honour ...

Suddenly, at two hundred and fifty paces' range and just as they were about to come under the lethal broadsides of the *San Salvador*'s fifty pounders, the watching English sailors saw the fist of God appear over the stern of the enemy and hammer her to pieces. A second later the sound of a massive explosion, visible as a ring expanding across the water, shook them and the watchers saw that what had seemed to be a titanic fist was a huge billow of dense grey smoke.

Tavistock looked to his gunner incredulously. There had not been a broadside for three minutes.

'Gunner?' he shouted in the stunned silence, but the gunner held up his hands disclaimingly over his still-loaded weapons.

The whooping and cheering began as the smoke cleared. They watched timbers rain to the waters all around them in burning smoke-trailing embers. Some pieces fell on the *Antelope*'s deck where they were gathered up and brandished triumphantly. The entire stern of the *San Salvador* had been blown away and everyone who had been on her poop was dead. The rest of the crew were trying desperately to recover and turn her head to windward so that the flames licking out from her stern did not overwhelm the rest of their ship.

Tavistock barked his orders, sending the boatswains round with sharp discipline. The Spanish had seen the *San Salvador* explode, and several ships were putting about to help. There were too many for the *Antelope* to fight and Tavistock put her head about too, suddenly iron-certain that it was the right thing to do. The crack of an arquebus by the mizzen ratlines made him turn.

'What's that?'

'There's a man in the water, Captain,' a voice shouted below him. 'He's alive.'

'Put that up!' he called at the sniper, angered at the cowardice of it. 'I'll not have you shooting down survivors. Get a line to him. He may have something to tell us.'

They hauled the exhausted swimmer inboard, and moments later, with the *Antelope* flying northward, the draggled man was hauled up before the Captain.

Those who watched were amazed at the way they fell into each other's arms. It was as if they had been trying to hug the breath from their lungs, and for the rest of that dizzying afternoon brother had looked at brother again and again.

Richard found himself drawn to look at his brother's face and listen to the accent of his voice that was at once dearly familiar and yet completely foreign. And often as he looked, he found John was looking back through the powder smoke, as if trying to fathom the changes wrought by so many years. There was so much to talk about, but a battle was being fought, and John lent himself to the guns.

They shared the *Antelope*'s quarterdeck as England's defenders broke off the pursuit of the massive fleet. Watching Drake in *Revenge* and Hawkins in his *Victory*, both remembered the evil that had been done to them at San Juan de Ulua. John told him that Santa Cruz had been his reason to stay in Lisbon and that the Mexican Viceroy had been blown off the *San Salvador*'s poop. Richard, for his part, told John how his son and wife were safe in England, and when John described the circumstance of Martin's birth, Richard shook his head in wonder before admitting how it had been this very ship – *this very ship* – that had held up the *Nuestra Señora*.

It would have been so easy to have destroyed Solano's ship in revenge for the deception the Spanish had practised, Richard thought. Yet he had not. And again, at Lisbon, when they had met face to face only to be ripped apart by a stroke of chance. How many times had he wondered about that? Why? What unimaginable reason? And when, after Lisbon, he had woken aboard the *Antelope* and had thought his brother lost to the enemy, and there had been agonies . . .

His mind heaved with a strangeness that prickled his flesh and the tide swelled in his breast. He had never believed in blind chance, and it was as if a golden aura, rooted in his life but born of God on high, enveloped them both.

That night their joy at meeting was unconfined, but Richard took his brother aboard the *Ark Royal* to join in counsel with England's Admirals, for he had not lost sight of the menace that still towered over them.

'The Duke has orders from the King,' John said, passing on what the Pilot, Arevalo, had told him. 'Orders he was intending to follow, that there must be no attempt at a landing until his fleet and the army under Parma were united. Tell your army that the Isle of Wight at least is safe.'

There was a flurry of activity as the Admiral ordered an immediate communiqué to Richmond sent out, then Lord Howard said urgently, 'You say you know intimately their guns and their disposition? Our fleet mounts in total five hundred culverins and demi-culverins, but of the big short-range guns designed to fire heavy shot we have less than a hundred. Tell me, how is it with them?'

'The Spanish are mounting three hundred culverins, one hundred and ten of which are of the English kind. In addition, they have five hundred of the big ship-smashers and stone-firing periers.' He turned to Richard. 'Though I do respect my brother's bravery it's my belief that his ship would have been sunk had the *San Salvador* not lost her tail. To come within three hundred yards of the Spanish is but self-slaughter.'

'Then we cannot prevail!' Frobisher said, rising. 'For we must break them before they reach the Narrows.'

'Aye,' Drake whispered to Richard as Frobisher put forth his thoughts. 'We *must* close with them, or we are surely lost! I'll have no man command me but shall sail as I've always sailed according to my best choices, and if the Lord Howard takes issue with me for that, then so be it.'

'And if you're hanged for your disobedience?'

'They wouldn't hang Borough, and his crime was lack of zeal.'

'You are not Borough.'

'It takes a court to hang a man, and a court must have evidence. What I see at night and the reason my sternlight goes out is something I might have fifty sworn witnesses to.'

Lord Howard spoke. 'So, because of their cannon, if we draw closer than three hundred paces we'll be destroyed, but they're shooting at random beyond that mark. And as we've seen, our own armament is not enough to overwhelm so many ships in so little time.'

John said, 'It's their hope to keep that tight new moon made up, a formation which takes a light sea and well-skilled sailing to hold, but if they can hold it they cannot be taken.'

'It's not enough to keep wild dogs out,' Drake said.

Hawkins shook his head. 'It's not enough to follow them like wild dogs follow a herd, for though we be dogs and they a docile breed, still we shall not bring them to a fight in time to prevent their design.'

Howard said, 'He's telling us that if the guns of our ships cannot break a way through their defences, and the weather won't disturb their composure, we're helpless.'

'Helpless?' Frobisher echoed, and Drake told them all, 'I'll burn in Hell before I'll let any man of them ashore. When they're well herded into my lord Seymour's embrace by Dover, we'll go in blazing as we have this day but at point-blank. Aye, a bowshot's distance, where a seventeen pounder will bite them sore!'

'There is a way,' John said. All present turned to look at him. His voice was soft, almost distant. He was remembering the deck of John Hawkins's old flagship, the *Jesus of Lübeck*, and the way fear had engulfed him as he saw the flaming galleon approaching. Though it was almost twenty years ago, he was reliving the hell that had played about him on that deck, the same satanic tongues that had burned his father to death before his eyes. 'Yes,' he said again. 'There is a way.'

Epilogue

On Sunday, July the twenty-eighth, the seventh of August in the Spaniards' reckoning, Spain's Invincible Armada finally ended its long eastward run. It had been successful, running the fearsome gauntlet of the English Channel and achieving its objective of Calais, where it anchored almost completely intact.

As his ships lay in Calais Roads that night, the Duke and his Council met again. Never had the prospect of landing Parma's and de Leyva's troops been so bright; never had the success of God's obvious design been so clearly assured. Then the lookouts began to shout.

Eight foolhardy English ships in line abreast came stealthily out of the night. Every Spanish officer knew that so suicidal an attack mounted at night could only be a measure of the Englishmen's desperation. They started to train their guns on the approaching ships, then lights flared on those moonlit decks and small boats were seen pulling away. Soon all eight vessels had become towering torches of fire, flames raging, wind and tide carrying them into the heart of the anchorage.

By dawn the reluctant Duke's ships were scattered and in confusion. The defensive formation that had protected them was now utterly irrecoverable. The English attack was pressed home. Drake and Tavistock, Frobisher and Fenner, Hawkins and Howard, went in without mercy, each lesser Captain following whichsoever Admiral he pleased. And all day the lumbering gilded giants of Spain, hidebound monsters, their defensive crescent shattered, their Captains chained down with tight orders and the fear of the Provost Marshal's hangmen, were relentlessly searched out, smashed, sunk, sent ashore, annihilated.

The next day, St Lawrence's Day, the day Philip had appointed for glory, the pathetic remains of the Armada found itself driven steadily onto the lethal reefs of the Zeeland Bank. Finally, Don Alonso Perez de Guzman el Bueno, Duke of Medina-Sidonia, came out of his paralysis. The vision of future disaster that had held him in its grip was no longer a mesmeric premonition; with dawning horror he began to understand that it was now a nightmare from which there would be no waking.

As his remaining Captains put away the last shreds of hope for a landing the Duke's fervent prayers were answered. The wind shifted, but it was not the looked-for divine deliverance.

In the ports of Dunkirk and Nieuport, Parma's troops melted away by moonlight; at sea the King's proud invaders found themselves being blown north into the German Ocean by fierce gales. Suddenly there was before them nothing but death and destruction on the ragged coasts of Scotland and Ireland. No Mass would now be celebrated in St Paul's Cathedral. The King's enterprise had failed.

Ten days later, a terror-stricken messenger entered the Escorial, and burst in on the King's presence.

His Most Catholic Majesty was at his writing desk attending to state papers. He did not look at the man who grovelled at his feet, but with inhuman self-control listened to the news without pausing his pen.

When the messenger had gone, Philip rose and stood alone before the wall niche where a gold-crowned saint's skull grinned hollowly at his utter humiliation. It seemed to the King that he was staring in a mirror.

Icily, he told his most constant companion, 'I give thanks to God that I can put to sea another fleet greater than this I have lost whenever I choose.'

On the rainsoaked hill overlooking the Palace of Greenwich a giant straw effigy of King Philip had been erected. Under it, with great perseverance because of the downpour, a huge bonfire was being lit. Sir Francis Walsingham watched its ruddy flare balefully through the leaded panes of the Secretary's apartment. He knew that this was no time for rejoicing – a war had just begun.

Across the courtyard, in the Lord Treasurer's apartments, Lord Burghleigh of Stamford Burghleigh turned away from the window and received his prodigal daughter. He told her the news that the father of her children had been shot through the helmet by a Spanish musketeer during his close attack upon the Spanish flagship *San Martin*, but that the ball had only parted his hair and against the orders of his Lord Admiral he was presently giving his assailant lone chase off the mouth of the Tyne. The incident, Anne was told, had been reported to the Queen by Lord Howard. Captain Tavistock's disobedience, she had said, was to be deplored. He must have the sword on his neck.

But that touch would be from her own hand, and for his gallantry.

Outside, Maria pulled her cloak about her and stepped down from carriage into the damp night air. She had come at the Lord Treasurer's command and was met at the steps of the lantern tower by the dour Robert Slade. Incredibly, the mood of the night had got to him and he was smiling. He informed her that her husband had been picked up from the Spanish galleon *San Salvador* and was presently aboard the armed merchantman *Antelope* which had been most recently reported off the Firth of Forth.

Beyond the Palace gates, the Queen's deer park was filled with thousands of filthy, dancing, rain-drenched revellers. They raised jugs of liquor and torches and a bewildering assortment of agricultural tools they had been carrying about for six months in case the Spanish came on them a-sudden. They chanted and chanted and would not shut up until their Queen came to give them thanks for their loyalty.

Alone on her balcony Elizabeth watched them with love. Such a people as the world had never seen. This was her nation, her England. The histories would call her childless but they would be wrong. She was mother to more children than any woman could ever be. Philip had tried to take them from her, and certainly he would try again, but in her heart she knew it would never be. The pride of Spain's martial chivalry had been shattered; the gleam of her golden Empire dulled for ever. England's rise to glory was about to begin.